PENGUIN CAN

INSPECTOR BANKS INVESTIGATES

Peter Robinson grew up in Leeds, Yorkshire. He emigrated to Canada in 1974 and attended York University and the University of Windsor, where he was later Writer in Residence. He received the Arthur Ellis Award in 1992 for *Past Reason Hated*, in 1997 for *Innocent Graves*, and in 2001 for *Cold Is the Grave*. *Past Reason Hated* also won the 1994 TORGI Talking Book of the Year Award, and in 2001, Robinson won the Edgar Award for best short story. Ten additional Inspector Banks novels have all been published to critical acclaim. He lives in Toronto.

Other Inspector Banks mysteries:

Also by Peter Robinson:

PETER ROBINSON

Inspector Banks Investigates

PENGUIN
CANADA

PENGUIN CANADA
Published by the Penguin Group
Penguin Books, a division of Pearson Canada, 10 Alcorn Avenue, Toronto, Ontario, Canada M4V 3B2
Penguin Books Ltd, 80 Strand, London WC2R 0RL, England
Penguin Putnam Inc., 375 Hudson Street, New York, New York 10014, U.S.A.
Penguin Books Australia Ltd, 250 Camberwell Road, Camberwell, Victoria 3124, Australia
Penguin Books India (P) Ltd, 11, Community Centre, Panchsheel Park, New Delhi – 110 017, India
Penguin Books (NZ) Ltd, cnr Rosedale and Airborne Roads, Albany, Auckland 1310, New Zealand
Penguin Books (South Africa) (Pty) Ltd, 24 Sturdee Avenue, Rosebank 2196, South Africa

Penguin Books Ltd, Registered Offices: 80 Strand, London WC2R 0RL, England

The Hanging Valley first published in Viking by Penguin Books Canada Limited, 1989.
Published in Penguin Books, 1990.

Past Reason Hated first published in Viking by Penguin Books Canada Limited, 1991.
Published in Penguin Books, 1992.

Wednesday's Child first published in Viking by Penguin Books Canada Limited, 1992.
Published in Penguin Books, 1993.

This edition published in Penguin Canada by Penguin Books, a division of Pearson Canada, 2003

1 3 5 7 9 10 8 6 4 2

Manufactured in Canada

NATIONAL LIBRARY OF CANADA CATALOGUING IN PUBLICATION

Robinson, Peter, 1950–
Inspector Banks investigates / Peter Robinson.

Contents: The hanging valley — Past reason hated —
Wednesday's child.

ISBN 0-14-301498-6

I. Title. II. Title: Wednesday's child. III. Title: Past reason hated.
IV. Title: The hanging valley.

PS8585.O35176I57 2003   C813'.54   C2003-900547-X
PR9199.3.R5349I57 2003

Visit Penguin Books' website at **www.penguin.ca**

CONTENTS

THE
HANGING VALLEY

For Jan

PART ONE:

MOTION IN CORRUPTION

ONE

I

It was the most exhilarating feeling in the world. His thighs ached, his calves throbbed and his breath came in short, sharp gasps. But he had made it. Neil Fellowes, humble wages clerk from Pontefract, stood at the summit of Swainshead Fell.

Not that it was an achievement comparable to Sir Edmund Hillary's; after all, the fell was only 1631 feet high. But Neil was not getting any younger, and the crowd at Baxwell's Machine Tools, where he worked, had taken the mickey something cruel when he told them he was going on a fell-walking holiday in the Yorkshire Dales.

"Fell?" taunted Dick Blatchley, one of the mail-room wags, "Tha'll a fell before tha's got started, Neil." And they had all laughed.

But now, as he stood there in the thin air, his heart beating deep in his chest like the steam-driven pistons in the factory, he was the one to laugh. He pushed his wire-rimmed glasses back up to the bridge of his nose and wiped off the sweat over which they had slid. Next he adjusted the straps of his rucksack, which were biting into his shoulders.

He had been climbing for well over an hour: nothing too dangerous—no sheer heights, nothing that required special equipment. Fell-walking was a democratic recreation: just plain hard work. And it was an ideal day for walking. The sun danced in and out between plump white clouds, and a cool breeze kept the temperature down. Perfect late May weather.

He stood in the rough grass and heather with nothing but a few sheep for company—and they had already turned their backs on him and scuttled a safe distance away. Lord of the whole scene, he sat on a weathered limestone boulder to savour the feeling.

Back down the fell he could just make out the northern tip of Swainshead village, from where he had come. He could easily pick out the whitewashed front of the White Rose across the beck, and the lichen-covered flagstone roof of the Greenock Guest House, where he had spent a comfortable night after the previous day's walking in Wharfedale. He had also enjoyed there a breakfast of sausage, bacon, black pudding, fried bread, grilled mushrooms, tomato, two fried eggs, tea, toast and marmalade before setting off that morning.

He stood up to take in the panorama, starting with the west, where the fells descended and rolled like frozen waves to the sea. To the north-west ranged the old, rounded hills of the Lake District. Neil fancied he could see the Striding Edge along Helvellyn and the occasional glint of sun on Windermere or Ullswater. Next he looked south, where the landscape hardened into the Pennines, the "backbone" of England. The rock was darker there, with outcrops of millstone grit ousting the glinting white limestone. Miles of wild, forbidding moorland stretched down as far as Derbyshire. South-east lay Swainsdale itself, its valley bottom hidden from view.

But what astonished Neil most of all was a small wooded valley down the eastern slope just below where he stood. The guide books hadn't mentioned anything of particular interest on the route he had chosen; indeed, one of his reasons for taking it was that nobody was likely to spoil his solitude. Most people, it seemed to Neil, would be off in search of stone circles, old lead mines and historic buildings.

In addition to its location and seclusion, the dale also had unusual foliage. It must have been a trick of the light, Neil thought, but when the trees everywhere else were fresh and green with spring, the ash, alders and sycamores below him seemed tinged with russet, orange and earth-brown. It seemed to him like a valley out of Tolkien's *Lord of the Rings*.

It would mean an extra mile or two and an unplanned climb back out again, but the sides didn't appear too steep, and Neil thought he might find some interesting wild flowers along the shaded banks of the beck. Balancing his pack, he struck out for the enchanted valley.

Soon, the rough tussocks underfoot gave way to springier grass. When Neil entered the woods, the leaves seemed much greener now the sunlight filtered through them. The smell of wild garlic filled his nostrils and made him feel light-headed. Bluebells swayed in the breeze.

He heard the beck before he saw it between the trees; it made a light, bubbling sound—joyful and carefree. From the inside, too, the valley clearly had a magical quality. It was more luxuriant than the surrounding area, its ferns and shrubs more lush and abundant, as if, Neil thought, God had blessed it with a special grace.

He eased off his rucksack and laid it down on the thick grass by the waterside. Taking off his glasses, he thought he would stay a while and relax, perhaps drink some coffee from his flask before carrying on. He rested his head on the pack and closed his eyes. His mind emptied of everything but the heady scent of the garlic, the song of the beck, the cool fingers of the wind that rustled through wild roses and honeysuckle, and the warbling of skylarks as they aimed themselves up at the sun and floated down like feathers, singing.

Refreshed—indeed, feeling as if he had been born anew—Neil wiped his eyes and put on his glasses again. Looking around, he noticed a wild flower in the woods across the water. It seemed, from where he was, to be about a foot high, with red-brown sepals and pale yellow petals. Thinking it might be a rare lady's slipper orchis, he decided to cross over and have a closer look. The beck wasn't very wide, and there were plenty of fortuitously placed stepping-stones.

As he neared the flower, he became aware of another smell, much more harsh and cloying than the garlic or loam. It clogged his nose and stuck to his bronchial passages. Wondering what it could be, he looked around, but could see nothing unusual. Near the flower, which was definitely a lady's slipper, some branches fallen from a tree lay on the ground and blocked his way. He started to pull them aside to get a better view.

But he didn't get very far. There, under a makeshift cover, lay the source of the smell: a human body. In the instant before he turned to vomit into the shrubs, Neil noticed two things: that it had no face, and that it seemed to be moving—its flesh was literally crawling.

Pausing only to wash his face and rinse out his mouth in the beck, Neil left his rucksack where it was and hurried as fast as he could back to Swainshead.

II

Disgusting, thought Katie Greenock, turning up her nose as she emptied the waste-bin of room three. You'd think people would be ashamed to leave such things lying around for anyone to see. Thank God they'd left that morning. There always had seemed something unwholesome about them anyway: the way they kissed and canoodled at the breakfast table, how it was always so long before they set off for the day and so early when they returned to their room. She didn't even believe they were married.

Sighing, Katie brushed back a strand of ash-blonde hair and emptied the bin into the black plastic bag she carried with her on her rounds. Already she was tired out. Her day began at six o'clock, and there were no easy rustic mornings of bird-song and dew for her, just sheer hard work.

First she had to cook the breakfasts and co-ordinate everything so that the eggs weren't cold when the bacon was ready and the tea was fresh for the guests as soon as they decided to come down. They could help themselves to juice and cereal, which she had put out earlier—though not too early, for the milk had to be chilled. The toast could get as cold as it liked—cold toast seemed to be a part of the tradition of an English breakfast—but Katie was pleased when, as sometimes happened, she succeeded in serving it warm at exactly the right time. Not that anyone ever said thank you.

Then, of course, she had to serve the meals and manage a smile for all the guests, whatever their comments about the quality of the food, and no matter what their sweet little children saw fit to drop on the floor or throw at the walls. She was also often asked for advice about where to go for the day, but sometimes Sam would help with that part, breaking off from his usual morning monologue on current events, with which he entertained the visitors daily whether they liked it or not.

Next, she had to clear the tables and wash the dishes. The machine Sam had finally bought her helped a lot. Indeed, it saved her so much time that she could hurry down to Thetford's Grocery on the Helmthorpe Road and take her pick of the morning's fresh produce. Sam used to do that before he had installed the machine, but now he had more time for the sundry business matters that always seemed to be pressing.

When Katie had planned the menu for the evening meal and bought all the ingredients, it was time to change the sheets and clean the rooms. It was hardly surprising, then, that by noon she was almost always tired. If she was lucky, she could sometimes find a little time for gardening around mid-afternoon.

Putting off the moment when she would have to move on to the next room, Katie walked over to the window and rested her elbows on the sill. It was a fine day in a beautiful part of the world, but to her the landscape felt like an enormous trap; the fells were boulders that shut her in, the stretches of moorland like deserts impossible to cross. A chance of freedom had offered itself recently, but there was nothing she could do about it yet. She could only wait patiently and see what developed.

She looked down on the grassy banks at each side of the fledgling River Swain, at the children sitting patiently with their home-made fishing-nets, a visiting couple having a picnic, the old men gossiping as usual on the small stone bridge. She could see it all, but not feel the beauty of any of it.

And there, almost dead opposite, was the White Rose, founded in 1605, as its sign proudly proclaimed, where Sam would no doubt be hob-nobbing with his upper-class chums. The fool, Katie thought. He thinks he's well in, but they'll never really accept him, even after all these years and all he's done for them. Their kind never does. She was sure they laughed at him behind his back. And had he noticed the way Nicholas Collier kept looking at her? Did Sam know about the times Nicholas had tried to touch her?

Katie shuddered at the thought. Outside, a sudden movement caught her eye and she saw the old men part like the Red Sea and stare open-mouthed as a slight figure hurried across the bridge.

It was that man who'd set off just a few hours ago, Katie realized, the mild-mannered clerk from Castleford, or Featherstone, or somewhere like that. Surely he'd said he was heading for the Pennine Way? And he was as white as the pub front. He turned left at the end of the bridge, hurried the last few yards and went running into the White Rose.

Katie felt her chest tighten. What was it that had brought him back in such a state? What was wrong? Surely nothing terrible had happened in Swainshead? Not again.

III

"Well," Sam Greenock was saying about the racial mix in England, "they have their ways, I suppose, but—"

Then Neil Fellowes burst through the door and looked desperately around the pub for a familiar face.

Seeing Sam at his usual table with the Collier brothers and John Fletcher, Neil hurried over and pulled up a chair.

"We must do something," he said, gasping for breath and pointing outside. "There's a body up on the fell. Dead."

"Calm down, mate," Sam said. "Get your breath, then tell us what's happened." He called over to the barman. "A brandy for Mr Fellowes, Freddie, if you please. A large one." Seeing Freddie hesitate, he added, "Don't worry, you bloody old skinflint, I'll pay. And get a move on."

Conversation at the table stopped while Freddie Metcalfe carried the drink over. Neil gulped the brandy and it brought on a coughing fit.

"At least that's put a bit of colour back in your cheeks," Sam said, slapping Neil on the back.

"It was terrible," Neil said, wiping off the brandy where it had dribbled down his chin. He wasn't used to strong drink, but he did approve of it in emergencies such as this.

"His face was all gone, all eaten away, and the whole thing was moving, like waves." He put the glass to his thin lips again and drained it. "We must do something. The police." He got up and strode over to Freddie Metcalfe. "Where's the police station in Swainshead?"

Metcalfe scratched his shiny red scalp and answered slowly. "Let me see . . . There aren't no bobbies in T'Head itself. Nearest's Helmthorpe, I reckon. Sergeant Mullins and young Weaver. That's nigh on ten miles off."

Neil bought himself another double brandy while Metcalfe screwed up his weather-beaten face and thought.

"They'll be no bloody use, Freddie," Sam called over. "Not for something like this. It's CID business, this is."

"Aye," Metcalfe agreed, "I reckon tha's right, Sam. In that case, young feller mi'lad," he said to Neil, "it'll be that chap in Eastvale tha'll be after. T'one who were out 'ere last time we 'ad a bit o'bother. Gristhorpe, Chief Inspector Gristhorpe. Years back it was, though. Probably dead now. Come on, lad, you can use this phone, seeing as it's an emergency."

IV

"Chief Inspector" Gristhorpe, now Superintendent, was far from dead. When the call came through, he was on another line talking to Redshaw's Quarries about a delivery for the dry-stone wall he was building. Despite all the care he put into the endeavour, a section had collapsed during an April frost, and rebuilding seemed a suitable spring project.

The telephone call found its way, instead, to the office of Detective Chief Inspector Alan Banks, who sat browsing through the *Guardian* arts page, counting his blessings that crime had been so slack in Eastvale recently. After all, he had transferred from London almost two years ago for a bit of peace and quiet. He liked detective work and couldn't imagine doing anything else, but the sheer pressure of the job—unpleasant, most of it—and the growing sense of confrontation between police and citizens in the capital had got him down. For his own and his family's sake, he had made the move. Eastvale hadn't been quite as peaceful as he'd expected, but at the moment all he had to deal with were a couple of minor break-ins and the aftermath of a tremendous punch-up in The Oak. It had started when five soldiers from Catterick camp had taunted a group of unemployed miners from Durham. Three people ended up in hospital with injuries ranging from bruised and swollen testicles to a bitten-off earlobe, and the others were cooling off in the cells waiting to appear before the magistrate.

"Someone asking for the super, sir," said Sergeant Rowe, when Banks picked up the phone. "His line's busy."

"It's all right," Banks said, "I'll take it."

A breathless, slightly slurred voice came on the line. "Hello, is that Inspector Gristhorpe?"

Banks introduced himself and encouraged the caller, who gave his name as Neil Fellowes, to continue.

"There's a body," Fellowes said. "Up on the fells. I found it."

"Where are you now?"

"A pub. The White Rose."

"Whereabouts?"

"What? Oh, I see. In Swainshead."

Banks wrote the details down on his scrap pad.

"Are you sure it's a human body?" he asked. There had been mistakes made in the past, and the police had more than once been dragged out to examine piles of old sacks, dead sheep or rotten tree trunks.

"Yes. Yes, I'm sure."

"Male or female?"

"I . . . I didn't look. It was—"

The next few words were muffled.

"All right, Mr Fellowes," Banks said. "Just stay where you are and we'll be along as soon as possible."

Gristhorpe had finished his call when Banks tapped on the door and entered his office. With its overflowing bookcases and dim lighting, it looked more like a study than part of a police station.

"Ah, Alan," Gristhorpe said, rubbing his hands together. "They said they'll deliver before the weekend, so we can make a start on the repairs Sunday, if you'd care to come?"

Working on the dry-stone wall, which fenced in nothing and was going nowhere, had become something of a ritual for the superintendent and his chief inspector. Banks had come to look forward to those Sunday afternoons on the north daleside above Lyndgarth, where Gristhorpe lived alone in his farmhouse. Mostly they worked in silence, and the job created a bond between them, a bond that Banks, still an incomer to the Yorkshire Dales, valued greatly.

"Yes," he answered. "Very much. Look, I've just had a rather garbled phonecall from a chap by the name of Neil Fellowes. Says he's found a body on the fell near Swainshead."

Gristhorpe leaned back in his chair, linked his hands behind his head and frowned. "Any details?"

"No. He's still a bit shook up, by the sound of it. Shall I go?"

"We'll both go." Gristhorpe stood up decisively. "It's not the first time a body has turned up in The Head."

"The Head?"

"That's what the locals call it, the whole area around Swainshead village. It's the source of the River Swain, the head of the dale." He looked at his watch. "It's about twenty-five miles, but I'm sure we'll make it before closing time if I remember Freddie Metcalfe."

Banks was puzzled. It was unusual for Gristhorpe to involve himself so much in an actual field investigation. As head of Eastvale CID, the superintendent could use his discretion as regards his role in a case. Theoretically, he could, if he wanted to, take part in searches and house-to-house enquiries, but of course he never did. In part, his job was administrative. He tended to delegate casework and monitor developments from his office. This was not due to laziness, Banks realized, but because his talent was for thinking and planning, not for action or inter-rogation. He trusted his subordinates and allowed them far greater leeway with their cases than many superintendents did. But this time he wanted to come along.

They made an incongruous couple as they walked to the car-park out back: the tall, bulky Gristhorpe with his unruly thatch of grey hair, bristly moustache, pock-marked face and bushy eyebrows; and Banks, lean, slight, with angular features and short, almost cropped, black hair.

"I can't see why you keep on using your own car, Alan," Gristhorpe said as he eased into the passenger seat of the white Cortina and grappled with the safety belt. "You could save a lot of wear and tear if you took a department vehicle."

"Have they got tape-decks?" Banks asked.

"Cassettes? You know damn well they haven't."

"Well, then."

"Well, what?"

"I like to listen to music while I'm driving. You know I do. It helps me think."

"I suppose you're going to inflict some on me, too?"

It had always surprised Banks that so well-read and cultured a person as Gristhorpe had absolutely no ear for music at all. The superintendent was tone deaf, and even the most ethereal Mozart aria was painful to his ears.

"Not if you don't want," Banks said, smiling to himself. He knew he wouldn't be able to smoke on the way, either. Gristhorpe was a non-smoker of the most rabid kind—reformed after a twenty-year, pack-a-day habit.

Banks pulled into the cobbled market square, turned left onto North Market Street, and headed for the main Swainsdale road, which ran by the river along the valley bottom.

Gristhorpe grunted and tapped the apparatus next to the dash-board. "At least you've had a police radio fitted."

"What was it you said before?" Banks asked. "About this not being the first body in Swainshead."

"It was before your time."

"Most things were." Banks made the sharp westward turn, and soon they were out of the town, driving by the river meadows.

Gristhorpe opened his window and gulped in the fresh air. "A man had his skull fractured," he said. "It was murder, no doubt about that. And we never solved it."

"What happened?"

"Some Boy Scouts found the body dumped in an old mine shaft on the fell-side a couple of miles north of the village. The doc said it had been there about a week."

"When?"

"Just over five years ago."

"Was it a local?"

"No. The victim was a private-enquiry agent from London."

"A private investigator?"

"That's right. Name of Raymond Addison. A solo operator. One of the last of the breed, I should imagine."

"Did you find out what he was doing up here?"

"No. We had his office searched, of course, but none of his files had any connection with Swainsdale. The Yard asked around among his friends and acquaintances—not that he had very many—but they turned up nothing. We thought he might have been on holiday, but why choose Yorkshire in February?"

"How long had he been in the village?"

"He'd arrived fairly late in the day and managed to get a room in a guest house run by a chap named Sam Greenock, who told us that Addison said nothing except for some remarks about the cold. He wrapped up well and went out for a walk after the evening meal, and that was the last anyone saw of him. We made enquiries, but nobody had seen or heard him. It was dark when he went out, of course, and even the old men who usually hang about chatting on the bridge come rain or shine had gone in by then."

"And as far as you could find out he had no connection with the area at all?"

"None. And, believe me, we dug and dug. Either nobody knew or, more likely, someone wasn't talking. He was an ex-serviceman, so we checked up on old army pals, that kind of thing. We ended up doing a house-to-house of the entire village. Nothing. It's still unsolved."

Banks slowed down as he drove through Helmthorpe, one of the dale's largest villages. Beyond there, the landscape was unfamiliar to him. Though still broader than most of the dales, thanks to a glacier of particularly titanic proportions, the valley seemed to narrow slightly as they got closer to The Head, and the commons sloped more steeply up the fell-sides. There were none of the long limestone scars that characterized the eastern part of Swainsdale, but the hills rose to high, rounded summits of moorland.

"And that's not all," Gristhorpe added after a few moments of silence. "A week before Addison's body was found—the day after he was killed, as far as the doc could make out—a local woman disappeared. Name of Anne Ralston. Never been seen since."

"And you think there must have been a connection?"

"Not necessarily. At the time she went, of course, the body hadn't been discovered. The whole thing could have been a coincidence. And the doc admitted he could have been wrong about the exact day of death, too. It's hard to be accurate after a body's been buried that long. But we've no idea what happened to her. And you've got to admit it's damned odd to get a missing person and a murder in the same village within a week of each other. She could have been killed and buried, or maybe she simply ran off with a fellow somewhere. We'd hardly cause to block all the ports and airports. Besides, she could have been anywhere in the world by the time the body was found. At best we'd have liked her to answer a few questions, just to put our minds at rest. As it was, we did a bit more poking around the landscape but found no traces of another body."

"Do you think she might have murdered Addison and run off?"

"It's possible. But it didn't look like a woman's job to me. Too much muscle-work involved, and Anne Ralston wasn't one of those female body-builders. We questioned her boyfriend pretty closely. He's Stephen Collier, managing director of the company she worked for. Comes from a very prominent local family."

"Yes," Banks said. "I've heard of the Colliers. Did he cause any problems?"

"No. He was co-operative. Said they hadn't been getting on all that well lately, but he'd no idea where she'd gone, or why. In the end we'd no reason to think anything had happened to her, so we had to assume she'd just taken off. People do sometimes. And Anne Ralston seemed to be a particularly flighty lass, by all accounts."

"Still . . ."

"Yes, I know." Gristhorpe sighed. "It's not at all satisfactory, is it? We reached nothing but dead ends whichever direction we turned."

Banks drove on in silence. Obviously failure was hard for Gristhorpe to swallow, as it was for most detectives. But this murder, if that's what it really turned out to be, was a different case, five years old. He wasn't going to let the past clutter up his think-ing if he could help it. Still, it would be well to keep Raymond Addison and Anne Ralston in mind.

"This is it," Gristhorpe said a few minutes later, pointing to the row of houses ahead. "This is Lower Head, as the locals call it."

"It hardly seems a big enough place to be split into two parts," Banks observed.

"It's not a matter of size, Alan. Lower Head is the newest part of the village, the part that's grown since the road's become more widely used. People just stop off there to admire the view over a quick cup of tea or a pint and a pub lunch. Upper Head's older and quieter. A bit more genteel. It's a little north-south dale in itself, wedged between two fells. There's a road goes north up there, too, but when it gets past the village and the school it gets pretty bad. You can get to the Lake District if you're willing to ride it out, but most people go from the Lancashire side. Turn right here."

Banks turned. The base of a triangular village green ran beside the main road, allowing easy access to Swainshead from both direc-tions. The first buildings he passed were a small stone church and a village hall.

Following the minor road north beside the narrow River Swain, Banks could see what Gristhorpe meant. There were two rows of cottages facing each other, set back quite a bit from the river and its grassy banks. Most of them were either semis or terrace blocks, and some had been converted into shops. They were plain, sturdy houses built mostly of limestone, discoloured here and there with moss and lichen. Many had individualizing touches, such as mullions or white borders painted around doors and windows. Behind the houses on both sides, the commons sloped up, criss-crossed here and there by dry-stone walls, and gave way to steep moorland fells.

Banks parked the car outside the whitewashed pub, and Gristhorpe pointed to a large house farther up the road.

"That's the Collier place," he said. "The old man was one of the richest farmers and landowners around these parts. He also had the sense to invest his money in a food-processing plant just west of here. He's dead now, but young Stephen runs the factory and he shares the house with his brother. They've split it into two halves. Ugly pile of stone, isn't it?"

Banks didn't say so, but he rather admired the Victorian extravagance of the place, so at odds with the utilitarian austerity of most Dales architecture. Certainly it was ugly: oriels and turrets cluttered the upper half, making the whole building look top-heavy, and there was a stone porch at each front entrance. They probably had a gazebo and a folly in the back garden, too, he thought.

"And that's where Raymond Addison stayed," Gristhorpe said, pointing across the beck. The house, made of two knocked-together semis, was separated from the smaller terrace blocks on either side by only a few feet. A sign, Greenock Guest House, hung in the colourful, well-tended garden.

"'Ey up, lads," Freddie Metcalfe said as they entered, "t'Sweeney's 'ere."

"Hello again, Freddie," Gristhorpe said, leading Banks over to the bar. "Still serving drinks after hours?"

"Only to the select few, Mr Gristhorpe," Metcalfe replied proudly. "What'll you gents be 'aving?" He looked at Banks suspiciously. "Is 'ee over eighteen?"

"Just," Gristhorpe answered.

Freddie burst into a rasping, smoker's laugh.

"What's this about a body?" Gristhorpe asked.

Metcalfe pursed his fleshy lips and nodded towards the only occupied table. "Bloke there says he found one on t'fell. 'Ee's not going anywhere, so I might as well pull you gents a pint before you get down to business."

The superintendent asked for a pint of bitter and Banks, having noticed that the White Rose was a Marston's house, asked for a pint of Pedigree.

"'Ee's got good taste, I'll say that for 'im," Metcalfe said. "Is 'ee 'ouse-trained an' all?"

Banks observed a prudent silence throughout the exchange and took stock of his surroundings. The walls of the lounge-bar were panelled in dark wood up to waist height and above that papered an inoffensive dun colour. Most of the tables were the old round kind with cast-iron knee-capper legs, but a few modern square ones stood in the corner near the dartboard and the silent juke-box.

Banks lit a Silk Cut and sipped his pint. He'd refrained from smoking in the car in deference to Gristhorpe's feelings, but now that he was in a public place he was going to take advantage of it and puff away to his heart's, and lungs', content.

Carrying their drinks, they walked over to the table.

"Someone reported a death?" Gristhorpe asked, his innocent baby-blue eyes ranging over the five men who sat there.

Fellowes hiccuped and put his hand in the air. "I did," he said, and slid off his chair onto the stone floor.

"Christ, he's pissed as a newt," Banks said, glaring at Sam Greenock. "Couldn't you have kept him sober till we got here?"

"Don't blame me," Sam said. "He's only had enough to put some colour back in his cheeks. It's not my fault he can't take his drink."

Two of the others helped Fellowes back into his chair and Freddie Metcalfe rushed over with some smelling salts he kept behind the bar for this and similar exigencies.

Fellowes moaned and waved away the salts, then slumped back and squinted at Gristhorpe. He was clearly in no shape to guide them to the scene of the crime.

"It's all right, Inshpector," he said. "Bit of a shock to the syshtem, thass all."

"Can you tell us where you found this body?" Gristhorpe spoke slowly, as if to a child.

"Over Shwainshead Fell, there's a beautiful valley. All autumn colours. Can't mish it, just down from where the footpath reaches the top. Go shtraight down till you get to the beck, then cross it . . . easy. Near the lady's slipper."

"Lady's slipper?"

"Yes. The orchish, not the bird's-foot trefoil. Very rare. Body's near the lady's shlipper."

Then he half-twisted in his chair and stretched his arm up his back.

"I left my rucksack," he said. "Thought I did. Just over from my rucksack, then. Ruckshack marks the spot." Then he hiccuped again and his eyes closed.

"Does anyone know where's he staying?" Banks asked the group.

"He was staying at my guest house," Sam said. "But he left this morning."

"Better get him back there, if there's room. He's in no condition to go anywhere and we'll want to talk to him again later."

Sam nodded. "I think we've still got number five empty, unless someone's arrived while I've been out. Stephen?" He looked over to the man next to him, who helped him get Fellowes to his feet.

"It's Stephen Collier, isn't it?" Gristhorpe asked, then turned to the person opposite Greenock. "And you're Nicholas. Remember, I talked to you both a few years ago about Anne Ralston and that mysterious death?"

"We remember," Nicholas answered. "You knew Father too, if I recall rightly?"

"Not well, but yes, we bent elbows together once or twice. Quite a man."

"He was indeed," Nicholas said.

Outside, Banks and Gristhorpe watched Sam and Stephen help Neil Fellowes over the bridge. The old men stood by and stared in silence.

Gristhorpe looked up at the fell-side. "We've got a problem," he said.

"Yes?"

"It's a long climb up there. How the bloody hell are we going to get Glendenning and the scene-of-crime team up if we need them? Come to that, how am I going to get up? I'm not as young as I used to be. And you smoke like a bloody chimney. You'll never get ten yards."

Banks followed Gristhorpe's gaze and scratched his head. "Well," he said, "I suppose we could give it a try."

Gristhorpe pulled a face. "Aye," he said. "I was afraid you'd say that."

TWO

I

"Problem, gentlemen?" Nicholas Collier asked when he walked out of the White Rose and saw Banks and Gristhorpe staring up dejectedly at Swainshead Fell.

"Not at all," Gristhorpe replied. "Simply admiring the view."

"Might I suggest a way you can save yourselves some shoe-leather?"

"Certainly."

"Do you see that narrow line that crosses the fell diagonally?" Nicholas pointed towards the slope and traced the direction of the line with a long finger.

"Yes," said Gristhorpe. "It looks like an old track of some kind."

"That's exactly what it is. There used to be a farmhouse way up on the fell-side there. It belonged to Father, but he used to let it to Archie Allen. The place has fallen to ruin now, but the road that leads up is still there. It's not in good repair, of course, and you might find it a bit overgrown, but you should be able to get a car well above half-way up, if that's any help."

"Thank you very much, Mr Collier," Gristhorpe said. "For a man of my shape any effort saved is a blessing."

"You'll have to drive two miles up the road here to the next bridge to get on the track, but you'll see your way easily enough," said Nicholas, and with a smile he set off for home.

"Odd-looking sort of fellow, isn't he?" Banks remarked. "Not a bit like his brother."

Whereas Stephen had the elegant, world-weary look of a *fin-de-siècle* decadent, Nicholas's sallow complexion, long nose and prominent front teeth made him appear a bit horsy. The only resemblance was in their unusually bright blue eyes.

"Takes after his father, does Nicholas," Gristhorpe said. "And Stephen takes after his mother—as handsome a woman as I've seen around these parts. There's many a man drowned his sorrows in drink when Ella Dinsdale married Walter Collier. Didn't last long, though, poor lass."

"What happened?"

"Polio. Before inoculations came in. Come on, let's go and have a look at this body before it gets up and walks away."

Banks found the bridge and track easily enough, and though the old road was bumpy, they managed to get as far as the ruined farmhouse without any serious damage to the car.

A little to the left, they saw the footpath Neil Fellowes had taken and began to follow it up the fell-side. Even though they had been able to drive most of the way, the path was steep and Banks soon found himself gasping for air and wishing he didn't smoke. Gristhorpe, for all his weight, seemed to stride up much more easily, though his face turned scarlet with the effort. Banks guessed he was more used to the landscape. After all, his own cottage was half-way up a daleside, too.

Finally, they stood at the top, where Fellowes had surveyed the scene a few hours earlier. Both were puffing and sweating by then, and after they'd got their breath back Gristhorpe pointed out the autumnal valley below.

"It looks enchanted, doesn't it," he said as they walked down the slope towards the woods. "Look, there's the rucksack."

They crossed the beck as directed and headed for the lady's slipper orchis by the fallen branches. When they smelled the corpse, they exchanged glances. Both had known that stench before; it was unmistakable.

"No wonder Fellowes was in such a state," Banks said. He took out a handkerchief and held it to his nose. Cautiously, Gristhorpe pulled more branches aside.

"By Christ, Glendenning's going to love this one," he said, then stood back. "By the look of that mess below the ribs there, we've got a murder case on our hands. Probably a knife wound. Male, I'd say."

Banks agreed. Though small animals had been at parts of the body, and maggots had made it their breeding ground, the dark stain just below the left rib-cage stood out clearly enough against the white shirt the man was wearing. Fellowes had been right about the movement. The way the maggots were wriggling under his clothes made it look as if the body were rippling like water in the breeze.

"'Motion in corruption,'" Gristhorpe muttered under his breath. "I wonder where the rest of his gear is. By the look of those boots he was a walker sure enough."

Banks peered as closely as he could at the cleated rubber Vibram treads. "They look new as well," he said. "Hardly worn at all."

"He must have had more stuff," Gristhorpe said, rubbing his whiskery chin. "Most walkers carry at least a rucksack with a few dried dates, compass, maps, torch, changes of clothing and what-have-you. Somebody must have taken it."

"Or buried it."

"Aye."

"He's not wearing waterproofs, either," Banks observed.

"That could mean he knew what he was doing. Only amateurs wear waterproofs all the time. Experienced walkers put their clothes on and off in layers according to the weather. If this is all he was wearing when he was killed, we might be able to get some idea of the date of death by checking weather records."

"It's been fairly constant these past few weeks," Banks pointed out. "We had a late spring, but now it looks like an early summer."

"True enough. Still, forensic might be able to come up with something. Better get the team up, Alan."

"The way we came? It's not going to be easy."

Gristhorpe thought for a moment. "There might be a better way," he said at last. "If my geography's correct."

"Yes?"

"Well, if I'm right, this'll be the beck that ends in Rawley Force on the Helmthorpe road about a mile east of Swainshead village. It's a hanging valley."

"Come again?"

"A hanging valley," Gristhorpe repeated. "It's a tributary valley running into Swainsdale at a right angle. The glacier here was too small to deepen it as much as the larger one that carved out the dale itself, so it's left hanging above the main valley floor like a cross-section. The water usually reaches the main river over a waterfall, like Rawley Force. I thought you'd been reading up on local geology, Alan."

"Haven't got that far yet," Banks mumbled. In fact, he'd put aside the geology book, after reading only two chapters, in favour of a new history of Yorkshire that his daughter, Tracy, had recommended. The trouble was that he wanted to know so much but had so little time for learning that he tended to skitter from one subject to another without fully absorbing anything.

"Anyway," Gristhorpe went on, "Rawley Force is only about ninety feet high. If we can get in touch with the Mountain Rescue Post at Helmthorpe and they're willing to rig up a winch, we'll be able to get the team up and down without much trouble. I can hardly see Glendenning, for one, walking the way we did. There'll be a lot of coming and going. And we'll have to get the body down somehow, too. A winch just might be the answer. It should be easy enough. The Craven and Bradford pot-hole clubs put one up at Gaping Gill for a few days each year to give the tourists a look— and that's a hell of a lot deeper."

"It sounds good," Banks said dubiously. He remembered swinging the three hundred feet down Gaping Gill, which opened into a cavern as huge as the inside of York Minster. It was an experience he had no wish to repeat. "We'd better get cracking, though, or it'll be dark before they all get here. Should we get Sergeant Hatchley in on this, too?"

Gristhorpe nodded.

"DC Richmond?"

"Not just yet. Let's see exactly what we've got on our hands before we bring in all our manpower. Richmond can hold the fort back at the station. I'll stay here while you go back to the car and radio in. You'd better let the doc know what state the body's in. He might need some special equipment."

Banks glanced towards the corpse, then back at Gristhorpe.

"Are you sure you want to stay here?"

"It's not a matter of wanting," Gristhorpe said. "Somebody should stay."

"It's been here alone long enough. I doubt that another half-hour will make any difference."

"Somebody should stay," Gristhorpe repeated.

Banks knew when to give up. Leaving the superintendent sitting like Buddha under an ash tree by the beck, he set off back through the woods to the car.

II

"What's wrong?" Katie Greenock asked as Sam and Stephen staggered in with Fellowes between them.

"He's had a bit too much to drink, that's all," Sam said. "Out of the way, woman. Is number five still vacant?"

"Yes, but—"

"Don't worry, he's not going to puke on your precious sheets. He just needs sleep."

"All right," Katie said, biting her lip. "Better take him up."

Stephen smiled apologetically at her as they passed by and struggled up the stairs. Finally, they dumped their burden on the bedspread and left Katie in the room with him. At first she didn't move. She just stood by the window looking at Fellowes in horror. Surely Sam knew how much she hated and feared drunks, how much they disgusted her. And Mr Fellowes had seemed such a nice, sober man.

She couldn't really picture her father clearly, for he had died along with her mother in a fire when Katie was only four, but he had certainly been a drunk, and she was sure that he was at the root of her feelings. The only vague image she retained was of a big, vulgar man who frightened her with his loud voice, his whiskers and his roughness.

Once, when they hadn't known she was watching, she saw him hurting her mother in the bedroom, making her groan and squirm in a way that sent shivers up Katie's spine. Of course, when she got older, she realized what they must have been doing, but the early memory was as firmly established and as deeply rooted as cancer. She also remembered once when her father fell down and she was afraid that he'd hurt himself. When she went to help him, though, he knocked her over and cursed her. She was terrified that he would do the same thing to her as he had done to her mother, but she couldn't remember any more about the incident, no matter how hard she tried.

The fire was a memory she had blocked out, too, though strange tongue-like flames sometimes roared and crackled in her nightmares. According to her grandmother, Katie had been in the house at the time, but the firemen had arrived before the blaze reached her room. Katie had been saved by the grace of God, so her granny said, whereas her parents, the sinners, had been consumed by the flames of hell.

The fire had been caused by smoking in bed, and her grand-mother had seemed especially satisfied by that, as if the irony somehow marked it as God's special work, an answer to her prayers. It had all been God's will, His justice, and Katie was obliged to spend her life in gratitude and devoted service.

Katie took a deep breath, rolled Fellowes over carefully, and pulled back the sheets—they could be washed easily, but not the quilted spread. Then she unlaced his walking-boots and put them on some newspaper by the bed. They weren't muddy, but frag-ments of earth had lodged in the ribbed treads.

"Cleanliness is next to Godliness," her grandmother had drilled into her. And a lot easier to achieve, Katie might have added if she had dared. Apart from an unusually long list of its attributes—mostly "thou shalt nots," which seemed to include everything most normal people enjoyed—Godliness was an elusive quality as far as Katie was concerned. Lately, she had found herself thinking about it a lot, recalling her grandmother's harsh words and "necessary" punishments: her mouth washed out with soap for lying; a spell in the coal-hole for "swaying wantonly" to a fragment of music that had drifted in from next door's radio. These had all been preceded by the words, "This is going to hurt me more than it will hurt you."

Fellowes stirred and snapped Katie out of her reverie. For a second, his grey eyes opened wide and he grasped her hand. She could feel the fear and confusion flow from his bony fingers through her wrist.

"Moving," he mumbled, falling back into a drunken sleep again. "Moving . . ."

Spittle gathered at the edges of his lips and dribbled down his chin. Katie shuddered. Leaving him, she hurried back downstairs. There was still the evening meal to prepare, and the garden needed weeding.

III

Banks leaned over the edge of Rawley Force and watched Glendenning coming up in the winch. It was an amusing sight. The tall, white-haired doctor sat erect trying to retain as much dignity as he could. A cigarette dangled from the left corner of his mouth, as usual, and he clutched his brown bag tightly against his stomach.

Luckily, there had been hardly any rain over the past two weeks, so the waterfall to the doctor's right was reduced to a trickle. The staff at the Mountain Rescue Post had been only too willing to help and had come out and set up the winch in no time. Now, the police team were ready to come up slowly, one at a time, and Glendenning, as befit his status, was first in line.

Puffing as he struggled out of the harness, the doctor nodded curtly at Banks and straightened the crease in his suit trousers. Banks led him half a mile along the wooded valley to the scene, where Gristhorpe still sat alone.

"Thanks for coming so quickly," the superintendent said to Glendenning, getting up and dusting off his seat. Everyone in Eastvale Regional CID Headquarters had found it paid to be polite, even deferential, to the doctor. Although he was a crusty old bugger, he was one of the best pathologists in the country, and they were lucky he had chosen Eastvale as his home.

Glendenning lit another cigarette from the stub of his old one and asked, "Where is it, then?"

Gristhorpe pointed towards the pile of branches. The doctor cursed under his breath as he tackled the stepping-stones, and Gristhorpe turned to Banks and winked. "Everyone here, Alan?"

"Looks like it."

Next the young photographer, Peter Darby, came hurrying towards them, trying to head off Glendenning before the doctor could get to work. To Banks he always looked far too fresh-faced and innocent for his line of work, but he had never been known to bat an eyelid, no matter what they asked him to photograph.

After him came Sergeant Hatchley, red-faced after his short walk from Rawley Force along the hanging valley. The fair-haired sergeant was a big man, like Gristhorpe, and although he was twenty years younger, his muscle was turning quickly to fat. He resembled a rugby prop-forward, a position he had indeed played on the local team until cigarettes and beer took their toll on his stamina.

Banks filled him in on the details while Gristhorpe busied himself with the scene-of-crime team.

Glendenning, kneeling by the corpse, kept shooing the others away like flies. At last, he packed his bag and struggled back over the beck, stretching out his arms for balance like a tightrope-walker. With one hand he clung onto his brown bag, and in the other he held a test-tube.

"Bloody awkward place to go finding a corpse," he grumbled, as if the superintendent were personally responsible.

"Aye, well," Gristhorpe replied, "we don't get to pick and choose in our business. I don't suppose you can tell us much till after the post-mortem?"

Glendenning screwed up his face against the smoke that rose from his cigarette. "Not much," he said. "Looks like a stab wound to me. Probably pierced the heart from under the rib-cage."

"Then someone got very close to him indeed," Gristhorpe said. "It must have been someone he knew and trusted."

Glendenning sniffed. "I'll leave that kind of speculation to you boys, if you don't mind. There are lacerations and blows to the face, too. Can't say what did it at the moment, or when it was done. Been dead about ten days. Not more than twelve."

"How can you be certain?" Banks asked, startled by the information.

"I can't be certain, laddie," Glendenning said, "that's the problem. Between ten and twelve days doesn't count as accurate with me. I might be able to be more precise after the PM, but no promises. Those chappies over there have got a bag to put him in. He'll need to soak in a Lysol bath for a day or two." Glendenning smiled and held up his test-tube. "Maggots," he said. "*Calliphora erythrocephalus,* if I'm not mistaken."

The three detectives looked at the white, slow-moving blobs and exchanged puzzled glances.

Glendenning sighed and spoke as he would to a group of backward children. "Simple really. Bluebottle larvae. The bluebottle lays its eggs in daylight, usually when the sun's shining. If the weather's warm, as it has been lately, they hatch on the first day. Then you get what's called the 'first instar' maggot. That wee beauty sheds its skin like a snake after eight to fourteen hours, and then the second instar takes over and sheds after two to three days. The third instar, the one you use for fishing"—and here he glanced at Gristhorpe, a keen angler—"that one eats like a pig for five or six days before going into its pupa case. Look at these, gentlemen." He held up the test-tube again. "These, as you can see, are fat maggots. Lazy. Mature. And they're not in their pupa cases yet. Therefore, they must have been laid nine or ten days ago. Add on a day or so for the bluebottles to find the body and lay, and you've got twelve days at the outside."

It was the most eloquent and lengthy speech Banks had ever heard Glendenning deliver. There was obviously a potential teacher in the brusque chain-smoking Scot with the trail of ash like the milky way down his waistcoat.

The doctor smiled at his audience. "Simpson," he said.

"Pardon?" Banks asked.

"Simpson. Keith Simpson. I studied under him. Our equivalent of Sherlock Holmes, only Simpson's real."

"I see," said Banks, who had learned to tease after so long in Yorkshire. "A kind of real-life Quincy, you mean?" He felt Gristhorpe nudge him in the ribs.

Glendenning scowled and a half-inch of ash fell off the end of his cigarette. "Quite," he said, and put the test-tube in his bag. "I hope that glorified truss over there can get me back down safely."

"Don't worry," Gristhorpe assured him. "It will. And thank you very much."

"Aye. Now I have first-hand knowledge what it feels like to have my arse in a sling," Glendenning said as he walked away.

Banks laughed and turned back to watch the experts at work. The photographs had been taken, and the team were busy searching the ground around the body.

"We'll need a more thorough search of the area," Gristhorpe said to Hatchley. "Can you get that organized, Sergeant?"

"Yes, sir." Hatchley took out his notebook and pen. "I'll get some men in from Helmthorpe and Eastvale."

"Tell them to look particularly for evidence of anything recently buried or burned. He must have been carrying a rucksack. We're also looking for the weapon, a knife of some kind. And I think, Sergeant," Gristhorpe went on, "we'd better bring DC Richmond in on this after all. Get him to check on missing persons with the Police National Computer."

Vic Manson, the fingerprint expert, approached them, shaking his head. "It'll not be easy," he complained. "There might be prints left on three or four fingers, but I can't promise anything. I'll try wax injections to unwrinkle the skin, and if they don't work, it'll have to be formaldehyde and alum."

"It'll be a devil of a job finding out who he was," Banks said. "Even if we can get prints, there's no guaranteeing they'll be on record. And someone's gone to great lengths to make sure we can't recognize him by his face."

"There's always the clothes," Gristhorpe said. "Or teeth. Though I can't say I've ever had much luck with them myself."

"Me neither," Banks agreed. He always thought it amusing when he watched television detectives identify bodies from dental charts. If they really knew how long it would take every dentist in the country to search through every chart in his files. . . . Only if the police already had some idea who the body was could dental charts confirm or deny the identity.

"He might even be German," Hatchley added. "Or an American. You get a lot of foreigners walking the fells these days."

Across the beck, two men wearing face-masks slid the body into the large zip-up bag they had brought. Banks grimaced as he watched them brush off the maggots, shed in all directions, before they were finally able to secure the zip. They then started to carry their burden along the valley towards the winch.

"Let's go," Gristhorpe said. "It's getting late. There's nothing more to be done here till we can start a search. We'd better post a couple of men here for the night, though. If the killer knows we've discovered the body and if he's buried important evidence nearby, he might come back after dark."

Hatchley nodded.

"We'll arrange to send someone up," Gristhorpe went on. "You'd better stick around till they get here, Sergeant. See if you can persuade the rescue people to wait for them with the winch. If not, they'll just have to come the long way, like we did."

Banks saw Hatchley glance towards where the corpse had lain and shiver. He didn't envy anyone stuck with the job of staying in this enchanted valley after dark.

IV

Sam took Katie as roughly as usual in bed that night. And as usual she lay there and gave the illusion of enjoying herself. At least it didn't hurt any more like it had at first. There were some things you had to do, some sins you had to commit because men were just made that way and you needed a man to take care of you in the world. The important thing, Katie had learned from her grandmother, was that you must not enjoy it. Grit your teeth and give them what they want, yes, even cheat a little and make them think you like it—especially if they treat you badly when you don't seem enthusiastic—but under no circumstances should you find pleasure in it.

It never lasted long. That was one consolation. Soon Sam started breathing quickly, and she clung to him tighter and mouthed the sounds he liked to hear, told him the things he liked to know. At last he grunted and made her all wet. Then he rolled over on his side and quickly began snoring.

But sleep didn't come so easily for Katie that night. She thought about the body on the fell and pulled the sheets up tighter around her chin. Last time, it had been awful: all those questions, all the trouble there'd been—especially when the police tried to connect the dead man with the missing girl, Anne Ralston. They'd acted as if Stephen or one of his friends might have killed both of them. And what had they found out? Nothing. Raymond Addison seemed to have come from nowhere.

Katie had hardly known Anne, for she and Sam hadn't been in Swainshead long when all the trouble started five years ago. The only reason they had met her at all was because Sam wanted to seek out the "best people" in the village. He latched onto the Colliers, and Anne Ralston had been going out with Stephen at the time.

She hadn't been Katie's type, though, and they'd never have become good friends. Anne, she remembered, had seemed far too footloose and fancy-free for her taste. She had probably just run off with another man; it would have been typical of her to take off without a word and leave everyone to worry about her.

Katie turned on her side to reach for some Kleenex from the bedside table, dragging the sheets with her. Sam stirred and yanked back his half. Gently, she wiped herself. She hated that warm wetness between her legs. More and more every time she hated it, just as she had come to loathe her life with Sam in Swainshead.

And things had been getting worse lately. She had been under a black depression for a month or more. She knew it was a woman's place to obey her husband, to stay with him for better, for worse, to submit to his demands in bed and slave for him all day in the house. But surely, she thought, life shouldn't be so bleak. If there was any chance of escape from the drudgery that her life had become and from the beatings, would it really be such a sin to take it?

Things hadn't always been so bad. When they had met, Katie had been working as a chambermaid at the Queen's Hotel in Leeds, and Sam, an apprentice electrician, had turned up one day to check the wiring. It had hardly been love at first sight; for Katie, love was what happened in the romantic paperbacks she read, the ones that made her blush and look over her shoulder in case her granny could see her reading them. But Sam had been presentable enough—a cocky young bantam with curly chestnut hair and a warm, boyish smile. A real charmer.

He had asked her out for a drink three times, and three times she had said no. She had never set foot in a pub. Her granny had taught her that they were all dens of iniquity, and Katie herself held alcohol responsible for her father's wickedness and for the misery of her mother's life. Katie didn't realize at the time that her refusal of a drink was taken as a rejection of Sam himself. If only he would ask her to go for a walk, she had thought, or perhaps to the Kardomah for a coffee and a bite to eat after work.

Finally, in exasperation, he had suggested a Saturday afternoon trip to Otley. Even though Katie was over eighteen, she still had a difficult time persuading her grandmother to let her go, especially as she was to ride pillion on Sam's motorbike. But in the end the old woman had given in, muttering warnings about the Serpent in Eden and wolves in sheep's clothing.

In Otley they had, inevitably, gone for a drink. Sam had practically dragged her into the Red Lion, where she had finally broken down and blurted out why she had refused to go for a drink before. He laughed and touched her shoulder gently. She drank bitter lemon and nothing terrible happened to either of them. After that, she went to pubs with him more often, though she always refused alcohol and never felt entirely comfortable.

But now, she thought, turning over again, life had become unbearable. The early days, just after their marriage, had been full of hope after Katie had learned how to tolerate Sam's sexual demands. They had lived with his parents in a little back-to-back in Armley and saved every penny they earned. Sam had a dream, a guest house in the Dales, and together they had brought it about. Those had been happy times, despite the hours of overtime, the cramped living-quarters and the lack of privacy, for they had had something to aim towards. Now it was theirs, Katie hated it. Sam had changed; he had become snobbish, callous and cruel.

Like every other night for the past few months, she cried quietly to herself as she tried to shut out Sam's snoring and listen to the breeze hiss through the willows by the nameless stream out back. She would wait and keep silent. If nothing happened, if nothing came of her only hope of escape, then one night she would sneak out of the house as quiet as a thief and never come back.

V

In room five, Neil Fellowes knelt by the side of the bed and said his prayers.

He had woken from his drunken stupor in time to be sick in the wash-basin, and after that he had felt much better. So much so, in fact, that he had gone down and eaten the lamb chops with mint sauce that Mrs Greenock had cooked so well. Then he spent the rest of the evening in his room reading.

And now, as he tried to match the words to his thoughts and feelings, as he always did in prayer, he found he couldn't. The picture of the body kept coming back, tearing aside the image of God that he had retained from childhood: an old man with a long white beard sitting on a cloud with a ledger book on his lap. Suddenly, the smell was in his nostrils again; it was like trying to breathe at the bottom of a warm sewer. And he saw again the bloody, maggot-infested pulp that had once been a face, the white shirt rippling with corruption, the whole thing rising and falling in an obscene parody of breathing.

He tried to force his mind back to the prayer but couldn't. Hoping the Lord would understand and give him the comfort he needed, he gave up, put his glasses on the table, and got into bed.

On the edge of sleep, he was able to reconstruct the sequence of events in his mind. At the time, he had been too distraught, too confused to notice anything. And very soon his head had been spinning with the drink. But he remembered bursting into the pub and asking for help. He remembered how Sam Greenock and the others at the table had calmed him down and suggested what he should do. But there was something else, something wrong. It was just a vague feeling. He couldn't quite bring it to consciousness before sleep took him.

THREE

I

"What is it?" Banks asked, examining the faded slip of paper that Sergeant Hatchley had dropped on the desk in front of him.

"Forensic said it's some kind of receipt from a till," Hatchley explained. "You know, one of those bits of paper they give you when you buy something. People usually just drop them on the floor or shove them in their pockets and forget about them. They found it in his right trouser pocket. It'd been there long enough to go through the washer once or twice, but you know what bloody wizards they are in the lab."

Banks knew. He had little faith in forensic work as a means of catching criminals, but the boffins knew their stuff when it came to identification and gathering evidence. Their lab was just outside Wetherby, and Gristhorpe must have put a "rush" on this job to get the results back to Eastvale so quickly. The body had been discovered only the previous afternoon, and it was still soaking in a Lysol bath.

Banks looked closely again at the slip, then turned to its accompanying transcription. The original had been too faint to read, but forensic had treated it with chemicals and copied out the message exactly:

CHOOSE FRESH
CHOOSE WENDY'S
***************Store 006308***************
SNGL / CHZ
WITH . .

```
              TOMATO
              BACON                    2.69
        FRIES                           .89
        SMAL COKE                       .85
   Tax                                  .35
              Inside                   4.78
                      05.26PM  04/25
```

"Wendy's," Banks said. "That's a burger chain. There's a few branches in London. Look at those prices, though."

Hatchley shrugged. "If it was in London . . ."

"Come on! Even in London you don't pay two pounds sixty-nine pee just for a bloody hamburger. At least not at Wendy's you don't. You don't pay eighty-five pee for a Coke, either. What does that tax work out at?"

Hatchley took out his pocket calculator and struggled with the figures. "Eight percent," he announced finally.

"Hmm. That's an odd amount. You don't pay eight percent tax on food in England."

"I suppose it's an American company," Hatchley suggested, "if they sell hamburgers?"

"You mean our man's an American?"

"Or he could have just come back from a trip there."

"He could have. But that'd make it a bit soon for another holiday, wouldn't it? Unless he was a businessman. What about the labels on his clothes?"

"Torn off," Hatchley said. "Trousers and underpants seem to be ordinary Marks and Sparks cotton-polyester. Same with the shirt. The boots were Army and Navy Surplus. They could have been bought at any of their branches."

Banks tapped his ball-pen on the edge of the desk. "Why is it that somebody doesn't want us to know who he is or where he's from?"

"Maybe because if we knew that we'd have a good idea who the killer was."

"So the quicker we identify the body, the better our chances. Whoever did it was obviously counting on no-one finding it for months, then being unable to identify it." Banks sipped some lukewarm coffee and pulled a face. "But we've got a lead." He tapped the receipt. "I want to know where this Wendy's is located. It shouldn't take you long. There's a store code to go on."

"Where do I go for that kind of information?" Hatchley asked.

"Bloody hell!" Banks said. "You're a detective. At least I hope you are. Start detecting. First, I'd suggest you call Wendy's UK office. It's going to be a couple of days before we get anything from Glendenning and Vic Manson, so let's use every break we get. Did Richmond come up with anything from missing persons?"

"No, sir."

"I suppose our corpse is still supposed to be on holiday then, if no-one's reported him missing. And if he's not English it could be ages before he gets into the files. Check the hotels and guest houses in the area and see if any Americans have registered there lately. If they have, try and track them down."

Dismissed, Hatchley went to find Richmond, to whom, Banks knew, he would pass on as much of the load as possible. Still, he reasoned, the sergeant's work was solid enough once he built up a bit of momentum, and the pressure would serve as a test of Richmond's mettle.

Since passing his computer course with flying colours, the young detective constable looked all set for promotion. That would cause problems with Hatchley, though. There was no way, Banks reflected, that the sergeant could be expected to work with Richmond at equal rank. Things had been bad enough when Banks came from the Metropolitan force to fill the position Hatchley had set his own sights on. And Hatchley was destined to stay a sergeant; he didn't have the extra edge needed to make inspector, as Richmond did.

Grateful that promotion was not his decision, Banks glanced at his watch and headed for the car. Neil Fellowes was waiting in Swainshead, and the poor sod had already had to arrange for one extra day off work.

II

As he drove along the dale, Banks marvelled at how familiar some of its landmarks had become: the small drumlin with its four sick elms all leaning to the right like an image in one of those Chinese water-colours that Sandra, his wife, liked so much; the quiet village of Fortford with the foundations of a Roman fort laid bare on a hillock by the green; the busy main street of Helmthorpe, Swainsdale's largest village; and above Helmthorpe, the long lime-stone edge of Crow Scar gleaming in the sun.

The Kinks sang "Lola," and Banks tapped his fingers on the steer-ing-wheel in time with the music as he drove. Though he swore to Sandra that he still loved opera, much to her delight he hadn't played any lately. She had approved of his recent flirtation with the blues, and now he seemed to be going through a nostalgic phase for the music he had listened to during his last days at school and first year at London Polytechnic: that idyllic, halcyon period when he hadn't known what to do with his life, and hadn't much cared.

It was also the year he had met Sandra, and the music brought it all back: winter evenings drinking cheap wine and making love in his draughty Notting Hill bed-sit listening to John Martyn or Nick Drake; summer boat-trips for picnics in Greenwich Park, lying in the sun below Wren's Observatory looking down on the gleaming palace, the Thames and London spread out to the west, the Beatles, Donovan, Bob Dylan and the Rolling Stones on the transistor radio. . . . All gone now, or almost all. He had lost interest in pop music shortly after the Beatles split up and the glitter boys took over the scene in the early seventies, but the old songs still worked their magic on him.

He lit a cigarette and rolled down the window. It felt good to be on his own in his own car again. Much as he loved the superin-tendent, Banks was glad that Gristhorpe had reverted to his usual role of planner and co-ordinator. Now he could smoke and listen to music as he drove.

More important still, he liked working alone, without the feeling that someone was always looking over his shoulder. It was easy enough to deal with Hatchley and Richmond, but with a superior heading the field investigation, it was difficult to avoid the sensation of being under constant scrutiny. That had been another reason for leaving London—too many chiefs—and for pinning his hopes on the Eastvale job after a preliminary chat with Superintendent Gristhorpe about the way he liked to run things.

Banks turned right at the Swainshead junction and parked his car in one of the spaces outside the White Rose. As he crossed the bridge, the old men stopped talking and he felt their eyes boring holes into his back as he walked down to the Greenock Guest House.

Though the door was open, he rang the bell. A young woman came rushing to answer it. She had a slender, dancer's body, but Banks also noticed an endearing awkwardness, a lack of self-consciousness about her movements that made her seem even more attractive. She stood before him drying her hands on her pinafore and blushed.

"Sorry," she said in a soft voice, "I was just doing some hand-washing. Please come in."

Though her accent was clearly Yorkshire, it didn't sound like the Swainsdale variety. Banks couldn't immediately place it.

Her eyes were brown—the kind of brown one sees in sunlight filtered through a pint of bitter, thought Banks, amused at just how much of a Yorkshireman he must have become to yoke beer and beauty so audaciously. But her hair was blonde. She wore it tied up at the back of her neck, and it fell in stray wisps around her pale throat and ears. She wore no make-up, and her light complexion was completely smooth, her lips full and strawberry red without any lipstick. Between her lower lip and the curve of her chin was a deep indentation, giving her mouth a look somewhere between a pout and an incipient smile. She reminded him of someone, but he couldn't think whom.

Katie, as she introduced herself, led him into a hallway that smelled of lemon air-freshener and furniture polish, as clean and fresh as a good guest house should be. Neil Fellowes was waiting for him in room five, she said, and disappeared, head bowed, into the back of the house, where Banks guessed the Greenocks made their own living-quarters.

He walked up the thick-pile burgundy carpet, found the room and knocked.

Fellowes answered immediately, as if he had been holding the doorknob on the other side. He looked in much better shape than the previous day. His few remaining strands of colourless hair were combed sideways across his bald head, and thick-lensed wire-rimmed glasses perched on the bump near the bridge of his nose.

"Come in, please er . . ."

Banks introduced himself.

"Yes, come in, Chief Inspector."

Fellowes was obviously a man who respected rank and title. Most people automatically called Banks "Inspector," some preferred plain "Mister," and others called him a lot worse.

Banks glanced out of the window at the wide strips of grass on both sides of the Swain. Beyond the cottages and pub rose the overbearing bulk of a fell. It looked like a sleeping elephant, he thought, remembering a passage from Wainwright, the fell-walking expert. Or was it whale? "Nice view," he said, sitting down in the wicker chair by the window.

"Yes," Fellowes agreed. "It doesn't really matter which side of the house you stay in. Out back you can see Swainshead Fell, and over there it's Adam's Fell, of course."

"Adam's Fell?"

Fellowes adjusted his glasses and cleared his throat. "Yes. After Adam and Eve. The locals do have a sense of humour—of a sort."

"Do you visit the area often, Mr Fellowes?"

"No, not at all. I just like to research the terrain, so to speak, before I embark. By the way, Chief Inspector, I do apologize sincerely about yesterday. Finding that . . . that corpse was a great shock, and I never take liquor as a rule—or tobacco, I might add. The brandy just seemed, well, appropriate at the time. I wouldn't have thought of it myself, but Mr Greenock was kind enough . . ." He slowed and stopped like an old gramophone winding down.

Banks, who had taken note of Fellowes's declaration of abstemiousness and let go of the cigarette package he'd been toying with in his pocket, smiled and offered a cliché of consolation. Inwardly, he sighed. The world was becoming too full of non-smokers for his comfort, and he hadn't yet succeeded in swelling their ranks. Perhaps it was time to switch brands again. He was getting tired of Silk Cut, anyway. He took out his notebook and went on.

"What made you visit that spot in the first place?" he asked.

"It just looked so inviting," Fellowes answered. "So different."

"Had you ever been there before?"

"No."

"Did you know of its existence?"

"No. It's certainly not mentioned in my guide book."

Fellowes shrugged. "Locals would, I suppose. I really can't say. Anyone could wander into it. It's on the maps, of course, but it doesn't show up as anything special."

"But you do have to make quite a diversion from the footpath to get there."

"Well, yes. Though I'd hardly say it's that much of a haul."

"Depends on what shape you're in," Banks said, smiling. "But you reckoned it would be worthwhile?"

"I'm interested in wild flowers, Chief Inspector. I thought I might discover something interesting."

"When did you arrive in Swainshead?"

"Three days ago. It was only a short break. I'm saving most of my holidays for a bicycle tour of Provence in autumn."

"I hope you have a less grim time of it there," Banks said. "Is there anything else you can remember about the scene, about what happened?"

"It was all such a blur. First there was the orchis, then that awful smell, and . . . No. I turned away and headed back as soon as I'd . . . as soon as I refreshed myself in the beck."

"There was nobody else in the valley?"

"Not that I was aware of."

"You didn't get a feeling of being followed, observed?"

"No."

"And you didn't find anything close to the body? Something you might have thought insignificant, picked up and forgotten about?"

"Nothing, Chief Inspector. Believe me, the feeling of revulsion was sudden and quite overwhelming."

"Of course. Had you noticed anything else before you found the body?"

"What do you mean?"

"The victim's rucksack was missing. We think he must have been carrying his belongings with him but we can't find them. Did you notice any signs of something being buried, burned, destroyed?"

"I'm sorry, Chief Inspector, but no, I didn't."

"Any idea who the victim was?"

Fellowes opened his eyes wide. "How could I have? You must have seen for yourself how . . . how . . ."

"I know what state he was in. I was simply wondering if you'd heard anything about someone missing in the area."

Fellowes shook his head.

Banks closed his notebook and put it back in the inside pocket of his pale blue sports jacket.

"There is one thing," Fellowes said hesitantly.

"Yes?"

"I don't like to cast aspersions. It's only a very vague impression."

"Go on."

"And I wasn't in full control of my faculties. It was just a feeling."

"Policemen have feelings like that, too, Mr Fellowes. We call them hunches and they're often very valuable. What was this feeling you had?"

Fellowes leaned forward from the edge of the bed and lowered his voice. "Well, Chief Inspector, I only really thought about it in bed last night, and it was just a kind of niggling sensation, an itch. It was in the pub, just after I arrived and, you know, told them what I'd seen. I sat at the table, quite out of breath and emotionally distraught. . . ."

"And what happened?"

"Nothing happened. It was just a feeling, as I said. I wasn't even looking, but I got the impression that someone there wasn't really surprised."

"That you'd found a body?"

"Yes."

"Was that all?"

Fellowes took off his glasses and rubbed the bridge of his nose. Banks noticed how small his eyes looked without the magnifying lenses. "More than that," Fellowes went on. "I was looking away at the time, but I felt an odd sort of silence, the kind of silence in which glances are exchanged. It was very uncomfortable for a moment, though I was too preoccupied to really notice it at the time. I've thought about it a lot since last night, and that's the only way I can put it, as if a kind of understanding look passed between some of the people at the table."

"Who was there?"

"The same people as when you arrived. There was the landlord, over at the bar, then Sam Greenock, Stephen and Nicholas Collier and John Fletcher. I'd met them the previous day when I was enquiring about the best places to search for wild flowers."

"Did it seem to you as if they were all in on some kind of conspiracy?"

"I'm not a paranoid, if that's what you're getting at, Chief Inspector."

"But you were upset. Sometimes our senses can over-react."

"Believe what you wish. I simply thought you ought to know. And in answer to your question, no, I didn't sense any gigantic conspiracy, just that someone at the table knew something."

"But you said you thought a glance was exchanged."

"That's what it felt like."

"So more than one person knew?"

"I suppose so. I can't say how many or how I received the impression. It just happened."

Banks took his notebook out again and wrote down the names.

"I don't want to get anybody into trouble," Fellowes said. "I could be wrong. It could have happened just as you said, an over-reaction."

"Let *us* worry about that, Mr Fellowes. We don't usually ask people to stand up in a court of law and swear to their feelings. Is that all you can tell me?"

"Yes. Will I be able to go home now? There'll be trouble at work if I'm not back tomorrow."

"Better give me your address and phone number in case we need to talk to you again," Banks said.

Banks made a note of Fellowes's address and left, thinking what a celebrity the man would be at work for a while. He went out of the open door without seeing Katie Greenock and breathed in the fresh air by the beck. A young man dangled his legs over the bank, eating a sandwich from grease-proof paper and reading a thick paperback; the old men still huddled around the eastern end of the stone bridge; and there were three cars parked outside the White Rose. Banks looked at his watch: twenty past one. With a bit of luck the same crowd as yesterday would be there. He read over the names Fellowes had given him again and decided to make a start.

III

First things first, Banks thought, and headed for the bar. He ordered Cumberland sausage, beans and chips, then paid, took his numbered receipt, and waited while Freddie Metcalfe poured him a pint of Pedigree.

"Is tha getting anywhere?" Metcalfe asked, his biceps bulging as he pulled down on the pump.

"Early days yet," Banks answered.

"Aye, an' it got to late days an' all last time, and still tha didn't find owt."

"That's how it goes sometimes. I wasn't here then."

"Thinks tha's better than old Gristhorpe, does tha, eh?"

"That's not what I meant."

"From down sahth, aren't tha?"

"Yes. London."

"London." Metcalfe placed the foaming brew on the cloth in front of Banks and scratched his hairy ear. "Bin there once. Full o' foreigners, London. All them A-rabs."

"It's a busy place," Banks said, picking up his beer.

"Don't get many o' them arahnd 'ere. Foreigners, that is. That why tha came up 'ere, to get shut on t'A-rabs, eh? Tha'll find plenty o' Pakis in Bradford, like, but I don't reckon as I've ever seed a darkie in Swainshead. Saw one in Eastvale, once."

Banks, growing quickly tired of Metcalfe's racist inanities, made to turn away, but the landlord grabbed his elbow.

"Don't tha want to ask me any questions then, lad?" he said, his eyes glittering.

Holding back his temper, Banks lit a cigarette and propped himself up against the bar. He had noticed that the three men he recognized from the previous day were only into the upper thirds of their pints, so he had enough time to banter with Metcalfe. He might just pick up some interesting titbit.

"What do you want me to ask you?" he opened.

"Nay, tha's t'bobby. Tha should know."

"Do you get many walkers in here?"

"Aye. We don't fuss 'em abaht rucksacks and boo-its and what-not like that stuck-up pillock on t'main road."

"But I understand this is the 'select' part of town?"

"Aye." Metcalfe laughed. "Tha could say that. It's t'oldest, anyroads. And t'Colliers drink 'ere, as did their father before them. Select, if tha likes, but dahn to earth, not stuck up." He shook his head slowly. "A right lad, were Walter Collier." Then he leaned forward and whispered, "Not like 'is sons, if tha knows what I mean. Wouldn't know a cratch from a gripe, neither on 'em. And they was brought up by a farmer, too."

Banks, who didn't know a cratch from a gripe either, asked why.

"Eddication," Metcalfe said, intoning the word as if it were responsible for most of the world's ills. "Fancy bloody Oxford eddi-cation. Wanted 'em to 'ave a better chance than 'ee'd 'ad, did old Walter. Farming don't pay much, tha knows, an' Walter were sharp enough to get out 'imself." Metcalfe turned up his nose. "Well, tha can see what eddication does."

"What are they like, Stephen and Nicholas?" Banks asked.

Metcalfe sniffed and lowered his voice. He was clearly enjoying his role as dispenser of local opinion. "Right bloody useless pair, if y'ask me. At least yon Nicholas is. Mr Stephen's not so bad. Teks after old Walter, 'ee does. Bit of a ladies' man. Not that t'other's queer, or owt." Metcalfe laughed. "There were a bit o' trouble wi' a servant lass a few years back, when 'ee were still a young lad, living at 'ome, like. Got 'er up t'spout, Master Nicholas did. Old Walter 'ad to see 'er right, o' course, and I've no doubt 'ee gave t'lad a right good thrashing. But it's Mr Stephen that's t'ladies' man. One after t'other."

"What's the difference in their ages?"

"Nobbut a couple o' years. Stephen's t'eldest."

"What happened to the farm land?"

"Old Walter sold some on it," Metcalfe said, "and leased t'rest. T'Colliers are still t'biggest landowners in t'dale, mind thee. John Fletcher over there bought a goodly chunk on it." He wagged his chin in the direction of the table. The drinkers were now into the last thirds of their drinks, and Banks decided it would be a good time to approach them.

"Tha still an't asked me no real questions," Metcalfe protested.

"Later," Banks said, turning. "I'd like to talk to these gentlemen here before they leave." Of the gentlemen in question, he recognized Nicholas Collier and Sam Greenock from the previous day; therefore, the third had to be John Fletcher.

"Wait on a minute," Metcalfe said. "Dun't tha want tha sausage and chips?"

And as if on cue, a freckled little girl in a red dress, her hair in pigtails, appeared from the kitchens and called out, "Number seventy-five! Sausage, beans and chips."

Banks gave her his receipt and took the plate, then he helped himself to condiments from the bar.

When he walked over to the table, the three men shifted around, scraping their chair-legs on the flagged floor, and made room for him.

"Do you mind if I eat at your table?" he asked.

"Not at all. Freddie been giving you a rough time, Inspector?" Nicholas Collier asked. His smile showed his prominent teeth to great disadvantage; they were discoloured with nicotine and crooked as a badly built dry-stone wall. His speech, Banks noticed, bore traces of the local accent under its assumed veneer of public-school English.

"No," he said, returning the smile. "Just entertaining me. Quite a fellow."

"You can say that again. He's been behind that bar as long as I can remember." Nicholas leaned forward and lowered his voice, "Between you and me, I don't think he quite approves of Stephen and myself. Anyway, have you met John, here?"

The squat man with the five-o'clock shadow was indeed John Fletcher, gentleman farmer. Stephen Collier, his brother said, was away dealing with some factory business.

"Is this just a social visit or do you have some questions for us?" Sam asked.

"Just one, really," Banks said, spearing a mouthful of sausage. "Have you any idea who it was we found up there?"

After a short silence, Nicholas said, "We get quite a lot of visitors in the area, Inspector. Especially when we're blessed with such a fine start to the year. There's nobody local missing, as far as I know, so it must be a stranger. Can't you check?"

"Yes," Banks said. "Of course we can. We can go through every name in every hotel and guest-house registration book and make sure everyone's accounted for. But, like you, I'm sure, we're all for anything that saves extra effort."

Collier laughed. "Naturally. But no, I can't think of anyone it might be."

"Your victim hadn't necessarily come through Swainshead, you know," Sam pointed out. "He could have been heading south from Swaledale or beyond. Even from the Lake District. He could have set off from Helmthorpe, too, or any number of other villages in the dale. Most of them have at least one or two bed-and-breakfast places these days."

"I know," Banks said. "Believe me, we're checking." He turned to Fletcher. "I hear that you own quite a bit of land?"

"Yes," Fletcher said, his dark eyes narrowing suspiciously. "Walter sold it me when he gave up farming and went into the food business." He glanced at Nicholas, who nodded. "Neither Nick here, nor his brother Stephen wanted to take over—in fact Walter hadn't wanted them to, he'd been preparing to sell for quite a while—so I thought I'd give it a go."

"How is it working out?"

"Well enough. I don't know if you understand much about Dales farming, Mr Banks, but it's a hard life. Old Walter himself had had enough, and he was one of those men—rare around these parts—with enough vision to get out and put what he'd got to better use. I'd never blame a farmer for wanting a different life for his sons. I've got no family myself," he said, and a hard look came into his eyes. "I'm not complaining, though. I make a living—the EEC and the National Parks Commission notwithstanding."

Banks turned to Nicholas. "What do you do?"

"I teach English at Braughtmore, just up the road here. It's only a small public school, of course, but it's a start."

"But you don't actually live there?"

"No. Hardly necessary, really. The house is so close. The pupils live in. They have to do; it's so damn far from civilization. And we have housemasters. Some of the teachers live in the grounds, but a couple of others have chosen to settle here in the village. The school's only five miles north, quite isolated. It's a good school, though I say so myself. Do you have any children, Inspector?"

"Yes. A boy and a girl."

"What school do they attend?"

"Eastvale Comprehensive."

"Hmm." The corner of Collier's lip twitched, giving just a fleeting hint of a sneer.

Banks shifted uneasily in his chair. "Your brother runs the family business, I gather."

"Yes. Managing Director of Collier Food Enterprises. It's over the Lancashire border, about ten miles west, just off the main road. The arrangement suits us both perfectly. Stephen never had a great deal of academic ambition, despite the excellent education he received, but he's bright and he's put his mind to good enough use—making money. It was one of father's wisest moves, buying up that old mill and setting up the food-processing operation. And as for me, I'm happy with my books and a few pliant young minds to work on." Again he bared his teeth in a smile.

They had all finished their drinks and Banks was wondering how to edge them gently towards the murder again, when Fletcher stood up and excused himself. Immediately, the others looked at their watches and decided they ought to leave and take care of various tasks.

"There's nothing else, is there, Inspector?" Nicholas asked.

"No," Banks said. "Not yet."

Freddie Metcalfe ambled over to the table to pick up the plate and the empty glasses as Banks was stubbing out his cigarette.

"Find owt aht yet?" he asked.

"No," Banks said, standing up. "Nothing."

"Early days, eh?"

And the deep, chortling laughter followed Banks out into the street.

IV

Back at Eastvale station things were quiet. Grabbing a cup of coffee from the filter-machine on the way, Banks walked upstairs to his office, a plain room furnished with nothing but filing cabinets, metal desk and a calendar of local scenes. The illustration for May showed the River Wharfe as it flowed among the limestone boulders of Langstrothdale. More recently, Banks had added, next to it, one more decoration: a broken pipe, which he had just rediscovered at the back of his drawer. It represented a vain attempt to project a rural image and wean himself from cigarettes at the same time, but he had cursed it constantly and finally thrown it at that very same wall in frustration over the Steadman case almost a year ago. It hung there like a piece of conceptual art to remind him of the folly of trying to be what one is not.

There were quite a few cars parked in the cobbled market square outside, and visitors walked in and out of the small Norman church and the shops that seemed to be built into its frontage. The gold hands of the clock stood at three-thirty against its blue face. Banks looked down on the scene, as he often did, smoking a cigarette and sipping his coffee. The police station itself was a Tudor-fronted building on narrow Market Street across from the Queen's Arms, which curved around the corner so that one of its entrances stood on the side of the square opposite the church. Looking to his right, Banks could see along the street, with its coffee-houses, boutiques and specialty shops, and out front was the busy square itself, with the NatWest bank, the El Toro coffee-bar and Joplin's newsagent's at the opposite side.

A knock at the door interrupted him. Sergeant Hatchley came in looking very pleased with himself. When he was excited about something he moved much faster than usual and seemed unable to stand still. Banks had come to recognize the signs.

"I've tracked it down, sir," Hatchley said. "That bit of paper he had in his pocket."

The two of them sat down and Banks told the sergeant to carry on.

"Like you said, I tried the London office. They said they'd check and get back to me. Anyway, they found out that that particular branch is in Canada."

"So our man's a Canadian?"

"Looks that way, sir. Unless, like I said before, he'd just been on holiday there. Anyway, at least we know there's a close connection."

"Anything else?"

"Yes. Once he'd discovered the outlet was in Canada, the bloke from Wendy's became very helpful."

Such helpfulness was a common enough occurrence, Banks knew from experience. He'd even invented a term for it: the Amateur Sleuth Syndrome.

"That particular branch is in Toronto, on Yonge Street, near Dundas Street, if that means anything."

Banks shook his head. "Never been over the Atlantic. You?"

Hatchley grunted. "Me? I've never been further west than Blackpool. Anyway, that narrows things down quite a bit, I'd say."

"It does," Banks agreed. "But it still doesn't tell us who he was."

"I got onto the Canadian High Commission and asked a bloke there to check if anyone from Toronto had been reported missing over here lately, but nobody has."

"Too early yet, I suppose. If he *is* from Toronto, obviously every-one back there still thinks he's on holiday."

"Aye, but that won't last forever."

"We haven't got forever. Who knows, he might have been a student and come over for the whole bloody summer. How's Richmond doing?"

"He's covered quite a few places already—Lyndgarth, Relton, Helmthorpe, Gratly."

"Well, his task ought to be a bit easier now we know it's a Canadian we're after."

"There's been quite a few Canadians staying locally," Hatchley said. "It's easy enough to call the B and Bs and make a list from their records, but it's damned hard to trace people's movements after they've left. They don't usually leave forwarding addresses, and it's only once in a while a landlady has been able to tell us where they said they were going next."

"There can't be that many men from Toronto travelling alone," Banks said. "I'm sure if he was a member of a group or a family somebody would have reported him missing by now. Better stick at it. At least you've narrowed the field considerably. Heard anything from Dr Glendenning?"

"The super called him a while ago. Still killing off those bloody maggots in disinfectant. Says he won't be able to make a start till tomorrow morning at the earliest."

Banks sighed. "All right. You'd better go help Richmond now. And thanks, Sergeant, you did a good job."

Hatchley nodded and left the office. They'd been working together for almost two years now, Banks realized, and he still couldn't bring himself to call the sergeant Jim. Maybe one day he would, when it came naturally to his lips. He lit another cigarette and went back to the window, where he watched the people wander about in the square, and drummed a tattoo on the sill.

V

"Sam's not in," Katie said that evening when she opened the back door to find Stephen Collier standing there. "He's having a night out with his old mates in Leeds."

"Can't I come in, anyway?" Stephen asked. "Just for a cup of tea?"

"All right," Katie said, and led him through to the spotless kitchen. "Just five minutes, mind you. I've work to be doing." She turned away from him and busied herself with the kettle and teapot. She felt her face burning. It wasn't right being alone in the house with a man other than her husband, even if it was someone as pleasant as Stephen. He had a reputation as a womanizer. Everybody knew that. Someone might even have seen him coming in.

"Nick tells me the police were around today," Stephen said.

Katie glanced at him over her shoulder. "It's to be expected, isn't it? One of our guests did find a dead body."

"He still here?"

"No. He left this afternoon."

"Well," Stephen said, "I just thought I'd drop by to see if you were all right. I mean, it can be a bit of a shock to the system, something like that happening right on your doorstep, so to speak. Did the police ask a lot of questions?"

"Not to me, no. Why should they?"

"Just wondering," Stephen said. "How are things, anyway?"

"All right, I suppose," Katie answered. Though she had known him for over five years, and she certainly preferred him to his brother, Katie hadn't really spent much time alone with Stephen Collier before. Mostly, they had met socially at summer garden parties the Colliers liked to throw, in the pub and at occasional dinners. She liked Stephen. He seemed kind and thoughtful. Often at social functions she had caught him looking at her in an odd way. Not *that* way, not like Nicholas. It was a look she didn't quite understand, and she had never been able to return his gaze for long without lowering her eyes. Now she was alone with him she felt shy and awkward; she didn't really know how to behave. She brought the tea to the table and opened a box of Fox's Custard Creams.

"Come on, Katie," Stephen said. "You're not very convincing. You don't sound all right to me."

"I don't know what you mean."

"Yes, you do. I can tell. I've felt some sort of bond with you right from the start. I've been worried about you these past few months."

"Worried? Why?"

"Because you're not happy."

"Of course I'm happy. That's silly."

Stephen sighed. "I can't make you open up, can I? But you *can* talk to me if you want, if you need to. Everybody needs somebody to talk to now and then."

Katie bit her lower lip and said nothing. She couldn't talk to him. She couldn't tell anyone the things that went on in her mind, the sins she dreamed of, the desperation she felt. She couldn't tell him about her one chance of escaping from her miserable life, and what it had already cost her.

"Anyway," Stephen went on, taking a biscuit, "I might not be around here for much longer."

"What do you mean?"

"I've had enough of it, Katie. The plant, the house, the village. Lord, I'm nearly thirty. It's about time I got out and about, saw a bit of the world before I get too old."

"B-but you can't," Katie said, shocked. "Surely you can't just up and go like that? What about—"

Stephen slapped the table. "Oh, responsibilities be hanged," he said. "There's plenty of others willing and able to run Collier Foods. I'll take a long holiday then maybe try something else."

"Why are you telling me all this?" Katie asked.

Stephen looked at her, and she noticed that he suddenly looked old, much older than his twenty-eight years.

He ran his hand through his short brown hair. "I don't know," he said. "I told you, we're kindred spirits. You're the only person I've told. There's nobody else, really."

"But your brother . . ."

"Nicky? He wouldn't understand. He's too wrapped up in his own world. And don't think I haven't noticed the way he looks at you, Katie, even if Sam hasn't. I'd stay away from him if I were you."

"Of course I will," Katie said, blushing. "Why shouldn't I?"

"Oh, he can be very persuasive, Nicky can."

"What about John?" Katie asked. "Or Sam? Can't you talk to them?"

Stephen laughed. "Look, Katie," he said. "Nicky, Sam and the rest, they're all good drinking friends, but there are things I can't talk to them about."

"But why me?"

"Because I think it's the same for you. I think you're unhappy with your life and you've nobody to talk to about it. Why are you so afraid of talking to me? You've got all your problems bottled up inside you. Don't you like me?"

Katie traced rings on the table with her forefinger. "It's not that," she said. "I'm fine, really I am."

Stephen leaned forward. "Why don't you open up, show some feeling?" he urged her.

"I do."

"Not for me."

"It's not right."

"Oh, Katie, you're such a moralist." Stephen stood up to leave. "Would that I had your moral fibre. No, it's all right, there's no need to show me out."

Katie wanted to call after him, but she couldn't. Deep inside, she felt a thick darkness swirling and building in power, trying to force its way out. But it was evil and she had to keep it locked in. She had to accept her lot, her place in life. She was Sam's wife. That was her duty. There was no point talking about problems. What could she say to Stephen Collier? Or he to her? Why had he come? What did he want from her? "The thing that all men want," said a strong, harsh voice inside her. "The same thing his brother wants. Don't be fooled by talk of companionship. Satan has a sweet tongue."

"But he was reaching out to you," another, quieter voice said, "reaching out in friendship, and you turned him away."

Katie's chest tightened and her hands shook as she tried to bring the teacup to her mouth. "I'm lost," she thought. "I don't know what to do. I don't know what's right any more. Help me, someone, please help me!" And the cup rolled to the floor and smashed as Katie lay her head on the table and wept.

FOUR

I

Two days later, on May 31, forensic information started trickling in. During that time, Richmond and Hatchley had tracked down all but two wandering Canadians who had left local hotels or guest houses between ten and thirteen days ago.

Events were moving too slowly for Banks. Most leads appear during the first twenty-four hours after a murder has taken place, but this body was about two hundred and forty hours old by the time it was found. Still they had very little to go on.

Therefore, when the first report from the forensic lab landed on his desk at ten-thirty that morning, Banks drank in the information like a man stranded in a desert without water for three days.

Dr Glendenning had established that death was due to a stab wound from a single-edged blade, probably a sheath-knife about six inches long. One upward thrust had penetrated the heart from beneath the ribs. After that, the face had been slashed and then beaten with a rock until it was unrecognizable. The victim was white, in his early thirties, five feet eleven inches tall, ten and a half stone in weight, and in good physical condition. That last part always irritated Banks: how could a corpse ever be in good physical condition? This one, certainly, had been about as far from it as one could get.

Vic Manson had finally managed, through peeling the skin off and treating it with glycerine, to get three clear prints. He had already checked these against the Police National Computer and discovered that they weren't on record. So far no good, Banks thought. The forensic odontologist, a note said, was still working on his reconstruction of the dental chart.

Calling for Sergeant Hatchley on his way out, Banks decided it was time for a discussion over elevenses in the Golden Grill. The two men weaved their way through the local shoppers and parties of tourists that straggled along both pavement and the narrow street, and found a table near the window. Banks gave the order for coffee and toasted teacakes to Peggy, a plump girl with a bright smile, and looked across at the whitewashed front of the police station with its black timber beams. Black and white, he thought. If only life was as simple as that.

As they drank their coffee, Banks and Hatchley tried to add up what they had got so far. It wasn't much: a ten-day-old corpse of a white male, probably Canadian, found stabbed in an isolated hanging valley. At least cause of death had been established, and the coroner's inquest would order a thorough investigation.

"Perhaps he wasn't travelling alone," Banks said. "Maybe he was with someone who killed him. That would explain the need to disfigure him—to give the killer plenty of time to get back home."

"If that's the case," Hatchley said, "it'll be for the Canadian police to handle, won't it?"

"The murder happened on our turf. It's still our problem till the man at the top says different."

"Maybe he stumbled into a coven of witches," Hatchley suggested.

Banks laughed. "They're mostly bored accountants and house-wives in it for the orgies. I doubt they'd go as far as to kill someone who walked in on them. And Glendenning didn't mention anything about ritual slaughter. How's the search for the elusive Canadians going?"

Hatchley reached slyly for another cigarette to prolong the break. "I'm beginning to feel like that bloke who had to roll a rock up a hill over and over again."

"Sisyphus? Sometimes I feel more like the poor sod who had his liver pecked out day after day."

Hatchley lit his cigarette.

"Come on, then," Banks said, standing up to leave. "Better get back."

Hatchley cursed under his breath and followed Banks across the street.

"Chief Inspector Banks!" Sergeant Rowe called out as they passed the front desk. "Telephone message. You're to call a Dr Passmore at the lab. He's the odonto . . . the odotol . . . Oh, the bloody tooth fairy, or whatever they call themselves."

Banks smiled and thanked him. Back in his office, he picked up the phone and dialled.

"Ah, Chief Inspector Banks," said Passmore. "We've never met, but Dr Glendenning brought me in on this one. Interesting."

"You've got something for us?" Banks asked eagerly.

"It's a bit complicated. Would it be a great inconvenience for you to drop by the lab?"

"No, not at all." Banks looked at his watch. "If I leave now I can be there in about an hour. Can you give me some idea over the phone?"

"I think we'll be able to trace the identity of your corpse before too long, if I'm not mistaken. I don't think his dentist is too far away."

"With all due respect, I don't see how that can be, doctor. We're pretty sure he was a Canadian."

"That's as may be," Passmore replied. "But his dental work's as English as yours or mine."

"I'm on my way."

Still puzzled, Banks slipped a cassette into the deck and eased the Cortina out of the lot at the back of the station. At least something was happening. He drove slowly, dodging the tourists and shoppers who seemed to think Market Street was for pedestrians only. The breathy opening of Donovan's "Hurdy Gurdy Man" started on the tape.

He passed the new estate under construction on the town's southern edge, then he put his foot down once he got out of the built-up area. Leaving the Dales for the plain, he drove through a patchwork landscape of green pasture and fields of bright yellow rape, divided by hawthorn hedgerows. Bluebells and buttercups, about the only wild flowers Banks could put a name to, were in bloom among the long grass by the roadside. A frightened white-throat darted out in front of the car and almost ended up, like so many unfortunate rabbits and hedgehogs, splattered all over the tarmac.

The forensic lab was a square three-storey red-brick building just north of Wetherby. Banks identified himself at reception and climbed up to Passmore's second-floor office.

Dr Passmore gave new meaning to the term "egghead." The Lilliputians and the Blefuscudians could have had a fine war indeed over which end to open his egg-shaped skull. His bare, shiny dome, combined with circumflex eyebrows, a putty nose, and a tiny rosebud of a mouth, made him look more like an android than a human being. His mouth was so small that Banks wondered how there could be room for teeth in it. Perhaps he had chosen his profession out of tooth-envy.

Banks sat down as directed. The office was cluttered with professional journals and its one glassed-in bookcase was full to overflowing. The filing cabinets, also, bulged too much to close properly. On Passmore's desk, among the papers and pencil stubs, stood a toothless skull and several sets of dentures.

"Glad you could make it, Chief Inspector," Passmore said, his voice surprisingly rich and deep coming from such a tiny mouth. "I'm sorry to drag you all the way down here, but it might save time in the long run, and I think you'll find it worth the journey."

Banks nodded and crossed his legs. He looked around for an ashtray, but couldn't see one; nor could he smell any traces of smoke when he surreptitiously sniffed the air. Bloody hell, another non-smoker, he cursed to himself.

"The victim's teeth were very badly damaged," Passmore went on. "Dr Glendenning said that he was hit about the face with a rock of some kind, and I concur."

"He was found close to a stream," Banks said. "There were plenty of rocks in the area."

"Hmm." Passmore nodded sagely and made a steeple of his fingers on the desk. "Anyway, I've managed to make a rudimentary reconstruction for you." He pushed a brown envelope towards Banks. "Not that it'll do you much good. You can hardly have every dentist in the country check this against every chart he or she has, can you?"

Banks was beginning to wonder why he'd come when Passmore stood up with surprising energy and walked over to a cabinet by the door. "But," he said, pausing dramatically to remove something and bring it back to the table, "I think I might be able to help you with that." And he dropped what looked like a fragment of tooth and pink plastic on the desk in front of Banks. "A denture," he announced. "Upper right bicuspid, to be exact."

Banks stared at the object. "You got this from the body?"

Passmore nodded. "It was badly shattered, of course, but I've managed to reassemble most of it. Rather like putting together a broken teacup, really."

"How does this help us?"

"Well, in the first place," Passmore said, "it tells us that the deceased was more likely to be British than Canadian."

"How?"

Passmore frowned, as if Banks was being purposely obtuse. "Contrary to what some people believe," he began, "British dentists aren't very far behind their North American cousins. Oh, they might instigate new procedures over there before we do, but that's mostly because they have more money. Dentistry's private over there, you know, and it can be very expensive for the patient. But there are differences. Now, if your victim had come from Russia, for example, I could have told you immediately. They use stainless steel for fillings there. But in this case, it's merely an educated guess, or would be if it weren't for something else, which I'll get to in a moment."

Come on, Banks thought, fidgeting with the cigarette pack in his jacket pocket, get to the bloody point. Putting up with rambling explanations—full of pauses for dramatic effect—seemed to be the price he so often had to pay for information from specialists like Passmore.

"The mere fact that your corpse has denture work leads me to conclude that he's European rather than North American," the doctor continued. "The Americans go in for saving teeth rather than replacing them. In fact, they hardly do denture work at all."

"Very impressive," Banks said. "You mentioned something else— something important."

Passmore nodded. "This," he went on, holding up the false tooth, "is no ordinary denture. Well, it is, but there's one big difference. This is a coded denture."

"What do you mean?"

"A number of dentists and technicians have taken to signing their work, so to speak, like painters and sculptors. Look here."

Passmore prodded the denture with a pointed dental instrument, the one that always gave Banks the willies when he was in the chair. He looked closely at the pink plastic and saw a number of dark letters, which he couldn't quite make out.

"The code," Passmore said. "It's formed by typing the letters in a small print face on a piece of nylon, which you put between the mould and the plastic. During the manufacturing process, the nylon becomes incorporated into the denture and the numbers are clearly visible, as you can see."

"Why do they go to such trouble?" Banks asked.

Passmore shrugged. "For identification purposes in case of loss, or fire."

"And what does the code tell us?"

Passmore puckered his mouth into a self-satisfied smile. "Everything we need to know, Chief Inspector. Everything we need to know. Have a closer look."

Banks used a pair of tweezers to pick up the denture and looked at the code: 5493BKJLS.

"The last two letters give us the city code, the ones before that are the dentist's initials, and the rest is for identification of the owner."

"Amazing." Banks put the false tooth down. "So this will lead us to the identity of the victim?"

"Eventually. First, it'll lead us to his dentist."

"How can I find out?"

"You'd consult the directory in the library. But, luckily, I have a copy here and I've done it for you."

"And?"

Passmore smiled smugly again and held up a schoolteacherly finger. "Patience, Chief Inspector Banks, patience. First, the city. Do you recognize that post-code?"

"Yes. LS is Leeds."

"Right. So the first thing we discover is that our man's dentist practises in Leeds. Next we look up the initials: BKJ. I found two possibilities there: Brian K. Jarrett and B.K. James."

"We'll have to check them both," Banks said. "Can I use your phone?"

Passmore rubbed his upper lip. "I, er, I already took the liberty. B.K. James doesn't do denture codes, according to his assistant, so I called Brian K. Jarrett."

"And?"

Passmore grinned. "The patient's name is Bernard Allen."

"Certain?"

"He's the one who was fitted with the denture. It was about four years ago. I'll be sending down the charts for official confirmation, of course, but from what we were able to compare over the phone, I'd say you can be certain, yes."

"Did you get an address?"

Passmore shook his head. "Apparently Allen didn't live in Leeds. Dr Jarrett did give me the sister's address, though. Her name's Esther Haines. Is that of any use?"

"It certainly is." Banks made a note of the first real lead so far. "You've done a great job, Dr Passmore." He stood up and shook hands.

Passmore inclined his head modestly. "If ever you need my help again . . ."

II

Katie walked down to the shops in Lower Head later than usual that day. There was no road on her side of the beck, just a narrow pathway between the houses and the grassy bank. At the junction with the main Helmthorpe road, where the River Swain veered left into the dale proper, a small wooden bridge, painted white, led over to the village green with its trees and benches, and the path continued to the row of shops around the corner from the church.

As she neared the road, a grey Jaguar passed by with Stephen Collier behind the wheel. He slowed down at the intersection, and

Katie became flustered. She half raised her hand to wave, but dropped it quickly. Stephen didn't acknowledge her presence at all; he seemed to be looking right through her. At first she told herself he hadn't seen her, but she knew he had. Perhaps he was thinking of something else and hadn't noticed his surroundings. She often walked around in a daze like that herself. The blood ran to her face as she crossed the road and hurried on to the shops.

"Afternoon, Katie love," Mrs Thetford greeted her. "A bit late today, aren't you? Still, I've saved you some nice Brussels sprouts."

Katie thanked her and paid, her mind still on Stephen Collier. Why had he called last night when he knew Sam was out? Katie couldn't understand his desire to talk to her about his problems, or his apparent concern for her.

"Your change, dearie!" Mrs Thetford called after her.

Katie walked back to the counter and held out her hand, smiling. "I'd forget my head if it was loose."

She called at the butcher's and bought some pork loin chops, the best he had left, then turned back towards home. Stephen really had sounded as if he needed a friend. He had been tired, burdened. Katie regretted letting him down, but what else could she have done? She couldn't be his friend; she didn't know how. Besides, it wasn't right.

She noticed the speeding Mini just in time to dodge it and crossed the green again. A few people, mostly old women, sat on the benches nattering, and a light breeze rustled the new, pale green leaves on the trees. What Stephen had said about her being unhappy was true. Was it so obvious to everyone, or did he really sense a bond between them? Surely with all his money and success he couldn't be unhappy too.

Katie tried to remember when she had last been happy, and thought of the first weeks in Swainshead. It had been hard work, fixing up the house, but they had done it. And what's more, they had done it together. After that, though, when everything was ready, Sam left the running of it all to her. It was as if he'd finished his life's work and settled into early retirement.

"Ideas above his station," her granny had always said of Sam. And sure enough, no sooner were they in residence than he was off to the White Rose ingratiating himself with the locals. As soon as he found out that the Colliers, who owned the big house over the road, were the dale's wealthiest and most powerful family, there was no stopping him. But give him his due, Katie thought, he never fawned or lowered himself; he just seemed to act as if he'd found his natural place in the order at last. Why they accepted him, if indeed they did, she had no idea.

When she wasn't busy running the guest house, Katie became an adornment, something for Sam to hang on his arm at the summer garden parties. She was a kind of Cinderella for whom the ball was always ending. But unlike the fairy-tale character, Katie hated both her roles. She had no love for gowns and glass slippers. Finery, however stylish and expensive, made her feel cheap and sinful. Once, a workmate fortunate enough to go on holiday to Paris had brought her back a pretty green silk scarf. Her granny had snipped it into pieces and scattered them like spring leaves into the fire.

Perhaps, though Katie hated to admit it, she had last been truly happy when her grandmother died. She and Sam hadn't seen much of the old woman after they went to live with his parents in Armley. They visited her in hospital, though, where she lay dying of cancer of the colon, bearing all the pain and humiliation with the same hard courage as she had suffered life. She lay there, silver head against the white pillow, and would accept no comfort for what "God's Will" was gracing her with. It was almost, Katie thought, as if she had found true joy in the final mutiny of the flesh, of its very cells, as if dying was proof to her that life on earth really was nothing but a Vale of Tears. But that couldn't be true, Katie realized, for her granny had never taken pleasure in anything in her life.

Katie fainted at her funeral and then gagged on the brandy the minister gave her to bring her round. Now all she had left of granny was the heavy wooden cross on the living-room mantelpiece. A bare, dark cross, with no representation of the crucified Christ (for such things smelled too much of popish idolatry for granny), it symbolized perfectly the harsh, arid life the old woman had chosen for herself and her granddaughter. Katie hated the thing, but she hadn't been able to pluck up the courage to throw it out. Outbreaks of boils and plagues of locusts would surely follow such a blasphemous act.

So Stephen Collier was right—she was unhappy. There was nothing anyone could do about it, though, except perhaps . . . But no. She had a terrible feeling of apprehension about the future, certain that her only possible escape route was cut off now. Why she should feel that way she didn't know, but everyone was behaving oddly again—Stephen, Sam, John Fletcher. Could it really be a coincidence that Anne Ralston's name had been mentioned to her again so recently? And that so soon after it had come up, there had been another murder in the village?

Shuddering as if someone had just stepped over her grave, Katie walked back up the path and into the house to get on with cleaning the rooms.

III

After leaving the lab, Banks first drove into Wetherby and bought an *A to Z* street atlas of Leeds. He knew the city reasonably well, but had never been to Armley, where Allen's sister lived. He studied the area and planned a route over lunch in a small pub off the main street, where he ate a rather soupy lasagne, and drank an excellent pint of Samuel Smith's Old Brewery Bitter.

He listened to the Donovan tape as he drove. Those old songs certainly brought back memories. Why did the past always seem so much brighter than the present? Because he had been more innocent then? Surely every childhood summer couldn't have been as sunny as he recalled. There must have been long periods of rain, just as there always seemed to be these days. What the hell, he thought, humming along with "Teen Angel" as he drove—today's beautiful, enjoy the sun while it's here. Most of all, he wanted to put out of his mind for as long as possible what he would soon have to tell Bernard Allen's sister.

He lit a cigarette and turned onto the Leeds Inner Ring Road, which skirted the city centre by a system of yellow-lit tunnels affording occasional flashes into the open and glimpses of church spires, tower blocks and rows of dark terrace houses. It still felt warm, but the sun was now only a blurred pearl behind a thin grey gauze of cloud.

He came out onto Wellington Road, by the Yorkshire Post Building, then crossed the River Aire and, immediately afterwards, the Leeds and Liverpool Canal.

There had been a great deal of development in the area, and one or two very colourful red-and-gold barges stood moored by the waterside. But the river and canal banks were still very much of a wasteland: overgrown with weeds, littered with the tires and old prams people had dumped there.

Many of the huge Victorian warehouses still hung on, crumbling and broken-windowed, their red brick blackened by the industrial smoke of a hundred years or more. It was a little like Thameside, Banks thought, where old wharfs and warehouses, like the warrens where Fagin had run his band of child-thieves, were daily being converted into luxury apartment complexes, artists' studios and office space. Because Leeds was in the depressed and abandoned north, though, the process of regeneration would probably take quite a bit longer, if indeed it ever happened at all.

Skilfully manoeuvring the lanes of traffic and a huge roundabout, Banks managed to get on Armley Road. Soon he was at the bottom of Town Street, where the road swung right, past the park, to Bramley and Stanningley. He turned left up Crab Lane, a narrow, winding one-way street by a small housing estate built on a hill, and parked on the street near the library.

Banks soon found Esther Haines's house. It had a blue door, freshly painted by the look of it. In the garden was an overturned plastic tricycle, green with thick yellow wheels.

Banks pressed the bell and a thin-faced woman answered. She was perhaps in her late twenties, but she seemed haggard and tired. Judging from the noise inside the house, Banks guessed that the cares of motherhood had worn her down. She frowned at him and he showed her his identification card. Immediately, she turned pale and invited him in. For people on estates like this, Banks realized, a visit from the police always means bad news. He felt his stomach muscles tighten as he walked inside.

In the living-room, cluttered with children's toys, Mrs Haines had already sat down. Hands clasped in her lap, she perched at the edge of her seat on the sofa. A dark-haired man came through from the kitchen, and she introduced him as her husband, Les. He was wearing only vest and pants. His shoulders and chest were matted with thick black hair, and he had a tattoo of a butterfly on his right bicep.

"We were just having our tea," Esther Haines said. "Les is on the night shift at the yeast factory."

"Aye," her husband said, pulling up a chair and facing Banks aggressively. "What's all this about?"

A child with jam smeared all over his pale grinning face crawled through the open kitchen door and busied himself trying to tear apart a fluffy toy dog.

"I'm sorry," Banks said, "but I've got some bad news for you."

And the rest followed as it always did: disbelief, denial, shock, tears and, finally, a kind of numb acceptance. Banks was relieved to see that the first thing Mr Haines did was light a cigarette. He followed suit. Esther clutched a handkerchief to her nose. Her husband went to make tea and took the child with him.

After Mr Haines had brought in the teapot and cups, leaving the child to play in the kitchen, Banks leaned forward in his seat and said to Esther, "There are some questions I've got to ask."

She nodded. "Are you sure?" she said. "Are you sure it's our Bernie?"

"As sure as we can be at this point," Banks told her. He didn't want to have to tell her what state her brother's corpse had been in. "Your answers will help us a lot. When did you last see him?"

"It was a couple of weeks ago, now," she said. "He stayed with us a week."

"Can you find out the exact date he left here, Mrs Haines? It's important."

Her husband walked over to a calendar of Canadian scenes and ran a stubby finger along the squares. "It was the thirteenth," he said, then looked over at Esther: "Remember, love, that morning he went to the dentist's for that filling he needed?"

Mrs Haines nodded.

"Did he leave immediately after his visit to Dr Jarrett's?"

"Yes," said Les Haines. "He was heading for the Dales, so he had to be off about eleven. He was after taking one of them trains on the Settle–Carlisle route."

"And that was the last time either of you saw him, at eleven o'clock on May thirteenth?"

They both nodded.

"Do you know where he was headed?"

"Of course," Esther said. "He were off back to Swainshead."

"Going back? I don't understand. Is that where he was before he came to stay with you?"

"No, it's where he grew up, it's where we used to live."

Now Banks remembered where he'd heard the name before. Allen. Nicholas Collier had directed Gristhorpe and himself to the ruins of Archie Allen's old farmhouse high on the side of Swainshead Fell.

"Is your father Archie Allen?" he asked.

"Yes, that's right."

"And you lived on the fell-side, worked a farm?"

"Until it went belly-up," Mr Haines cut in.

"Did you live there too?" Banks asked him.

"Me? No. Leeds born and bred. But the missis grew up there."

"How long ago was this, Mrs Haines?" Banks asked Esther, who had started weeping quietly again.

"It's ten years since we moved, now."

"And you came straight here?"

"Not until Les and I got married. We lived in an old back-to-back off Tong Road. It's not far away. Dad got a job at Blakey's Castings. It were all he could get. Then they went to Melbourne— Australia, like—to go live with our Denny after they retired. Oh God, somebody'll have to tell Mum and Dad." She looked beseechingly at her husband, who patted her arm. "Don't worry about that, love," he said. "It'll keep a while."

"As far as I can gather," Banks said when Mrs Haines had regained her composure, "your brother had some connection with Toronto, in Canada. Is that right?"

She nodded. "He couldn't get a job over here. He was a bright lad, our Bernie. Got a degree. But there was no jobs. He emigrated eight years ago."

"What did he do in Toronto?"

"He's a teacher in a college. Teaching English. It's a good job. We was off out to see him next year."

Banks lit another cigarette as she wiped away the tears and blew her nose.

"Can you give me his address?"

She nodded and said, "Be a love, Les." Her husband went to the sideboard and brought out a tattered Woolworth's address book.

"How often did Bernard come home?" Banks asked, writing down the Toronto address.

"Well, he came as often as he could. This was his third trip, but he hadn't been for four years. Proper homesick he was."

"Why did he stay in Canada, then?"

She shrugged. "Money. No work for him here, is there? Not with Thatcher running the country."

"What did he talk about while he was with you?"

"Nothing really. Just family things."

"Did he say anything odd to you, Mr Haines? Anything that struck you as unusual?"

"No. We didn't talk a lot. We'd not much in common really. I'm not a great reader, never did well at school. And he liked his books, did Bernie. We talked about ale a bit. About what the boozers are like over there. He told me he'd found a nice pub in Toronto where he could get John Smith's and Tartan on draught."

"Is that all?"

Haines shrugged. "Like I said, we didn't have much in common."

Banks turned to Mrs Haines again. "What state of mind was he in? Was he upset about anything, depressed?"

"He'd just got divorced about a year ago," she said, "and he were a bit upset about that. I think that's what made him homesick. But I wouldn't say he were really depressed, no. He seemed to think he might be able to come back and live here again before too long."

"Did he say anything about a job?"

"No."

"How could he manage to move back here then?"

Esther Haines shook her head. "I don't know. He didn't say. He just hinted. Maybe it were wishful thinking, like, now he didn't have Barbara any more."

"That was his wife?"

"Yes."

"What happened between them?"

"She ran off wi' another man."

"Where had Bernie been before he visited you?"

Esther took a deep breath and dabbed at her red eyes. "He'd come to England for a month, all told," she said. "First off, he spent a week seeing friends in London and Bristol, then he came up here. He'd be due to go back about now, wouldn't he, Les?"

"Do you know how to get in touch with these friends?" Banks asked.

She shook her head. "Sorry. They were friends of Bernie's from university."

"Which university?"

"York."

"And you didn't know them?"

"No. They'd be in his notebook. He always carried a notebook full of names and stuff."

"We didn't find it. Never mind, we'll find them somehow." If necessary, Banks knew he could check with the university authorities and track down Bernard Allen's contemporaries. "Do you know where he was heading after Swainshead?"

"He were going to see another friend in Edinburgh, then fly back from Prestwick. You can do that with Wardair, he said, fly to London and go back from somewhere else." She put her handkerchief to her nose again and sniffed.

"I don't suppose you have this person's address in Edinburgh?"

She shook her head.

"So," Banks said, stubbing out his cigarette and reaching for the tea, "he left here on May thirteenth to do some fell-walking in the Dales, and then—"

Mrs Haines cut in. "No, that's not right. That's not the reason he went."

"Why did he go, then? Sentimental reasons?"

"Partly, I suppose. But he went to stay with friends."

"What friends?"

"Sam and Katie. They run a guest house—Greenock's. Bernie was going to stay with Sam and Katie."

Struggling to keep his excitement and surprise to himself, Banks asked how Bernard had got to know Sam and Katie. At first, Mrs Haines seemed unable to concentrate for weeping, but Banks encouraged her gently, and soon she was telling him the whole story, pulling at the handkerchief on her lap as she spoke.

"They knew each other from Armley, from after we came to Leeds. Sam lived there, too. We were neighbours. Bernie was always going on about Swainshead and how wonderful it was, and I think it were him as put the idea into Sam's head. Anyways, Sam and Katie scrimped and saved and that's where they ended up."

"Did Bernie have any other close friends in Swainshead?"

"Not really," Esther said. "Most of his childhood mates had moved away. There weren't any jobs for them up there."

"How did he get on with the Colliers?"

"A bit above our station," Esther said. "Oh, they'd say hello, but they weren't friends of his, not as far as I know. You can't be, can you, not with the sons of the fellow what owns your land?"

"I suppose not," Banks said. "Was there any bitterness over losing the farm?"

"I wouldn't say that, no. Sadness, yes, but bitterness? No. It were us own fault. There wasn't much land fit for anything but sheep, and when the flock took sick . . ."

"What was Mr Collier's attitude?"

"Mr Walter?"

"Yes."

"He were right sorry for us. He helped out as much as he could, but it were no use. He were preparing to sell off to John Fletcher anyway. Getting out of farming, he were."

"How would that have affected you?"

"What do you mean?"

"The sale."

"Oh. Mr Walter said he'd write it into the terms that we could stay. John Fletcher didn't mind. He and Dad got on quite well."

"So there was no ill feeling between your family and John Fletcher or the Colliers?"

"No. Not to speak of. But I didn't think much of them."

"Oh?"

She pulled harder at the handkerchief on her lap, and it began to tear along one edge. "I always thought they were a pair of right toffee-nosed gits, but I never said nowt. Stephen thinks he's God's gift to women, and that Nicholas is a bit doolally, if you ask me."

"In what way?"

"Have you met him?"

"Yes."

"He's like a little kid, gets all over-excited. Especially when he's had a drink or two. Practically slavers all over a person, he does. Especially women. He even tried it on with me once, but I sent him away with his tail between his legs." She shuddered. "I don't know how they put up with him at that there school, unless they're all a bit that way."

"What about Stephen?"

Esther shrugged. "Seems a pleasant enough gent on the outside. Bit of a smoothie, really. Got a lot more class than his brother. Bit two-faced, though."

"In what way?"

"You know. All friendly one minute, then cuts you dead next time he sees you. But they can afford to do that, can't they?"

"Who can?"

"Rich folks. Don't have to live like ordinary people, like you and me, do they?"

"I don't imagine they have the same priorities, no," Banks said, unsure whether he approved of being called an ordinary person. "Did he try it on too?"

"Mr Stephen? No. Oh, he liked the girls, all right, but he was too much of a gentleman, for all his faults."

Mrs Haines seemed to have forgotten her grief for a few moments, so absorbed had she been in the past, but as soon as silence fell, her tears began to flow again and her husband put his arm around her. In the kitchen, something smashed, and the child ran wailing into the room and buried his jammy face in Esther Haines's lap.

Banks stood up. "You've been very helpful," he said. "I'm sorry to have been the bearer of such bad news."

Esther nodded, handkerchief pressed to her mouth, and Mr Haines showed him to the door. "What are we to do about . . . you know . . ."

"The remains?"

"Aye."

"We'll be in touch soon," Banks said. "Don't worry."

Upstairs, a baby started crying.

The first thing Banks did was look for a phonebox to call Sandra and tell her when he'd be back. That didn't prove as easy as it sounded. The first three he came across had been vandalized, and he had to drive almost two miles before he found one that worked.

It was a pleasant drive back to Eastvale through Harrogate and Ripon. In a quiet mood, he slipped in Delius's *North Country Sketches* instead of the sixties pop he'd been listening to. As he drove, he tried to piece together all the information he'd got that day. Whichever way he looked at it, the trail led back to Swainshead, the Greenocks, the Colliers and John Fletcher.

FIVE

I

Only the cry of a distant curlew and the sound of water gurgling over rocks in the stream out back broke the silence.

Then Sam Greenock echoed the news: "Bernie? Dead? I can't believe it."

"Believe it," Banks said. It was the second time in two days that he had been the bearer of bad news, but this time it was easier. The investigation proper had begun, and he had more on his mind than Sam Greenock's disbelief, real or feigned.

They sat in the living-room at the back of the house: the Greenocks, Banks, and Sergeant Hatchley taking notes. Katie gazed out of the window, or sometimes she stared at the huge, ugly wooden cross on the mantelpiece. She had said nothing, given no reaction at all.

"It's true he was staying with you, then, is it?" Banks asked.

Sam nodded.

"Why didn't his name show up on the register? We went to a lot of trouble checking every place in Swainsdale."

"It's not my fault," Sam said. "He was staying with us as a friend. Besides, you know as well as I do that those guest books aren't legal requirements—they're only for people to write comments in if they want, show they've been here."

"When our man called and asked if you'd had any Canadians staying recently, why didn't you mention Bernard Allen?"

"He didn't ask me anything. He just looked at the register. Besides, I never thought of Bernie as a Canadian. Oh, I know he lived there, but that's not everything, is it? I've known people who lived in Saudi Arabia for a year working on the oil fields but I don't think of them as Saudis."

"Come off it, Sam. Bernard Allen had been in Canada for eight years, and you hadn't seen him for four. This was only his third trip back."

"Still . . ."

"Did you have any reason to lie about Bernie being here?"

"No. I told you—"

"Because if you did, we can charge you with concealment of information. That's serious, Sam. You could get two years."

Sam leaned forward. "Look, I never thought. That policeman who came, he didn't tell us what he was looking for."

"We can check, you know."

"Bloody check then. It's true."

Sam couldn't remember the officer's name, so Banks asked Hatchley to make a note of the time and date. It would be easy enough to find out who had made the visit and what approach he had taken. He still wasn't sure about Sam Greenock, though.

Banks sighed. "All right. We'll leave that for now. Which room did he stay in?"

Sam looked at Katie. She was staring out on the fell-side, so he had to nudge her and repeat the question.

"Five," she said, as if speaking from a great distance. "Room five."

"We'll need to have a look," Banks told her.

"It was two weeks ago," Sam said. "There's been other people in since then. That's where we took Fellowes after he'd found the body."

"We'll still need to look."

"Do you think he's hidden some secret message there, Inspector? Taped it to the bottom of the dresser drawer, maybe?"

"You've been reading too many espionage novels. And if I were you, I'd cut the bloody sarcasm. You might start me thinking that there's some reason you don't want me to look in Bernie Allen's room. And while we're at it, he's not the first person to get killed after leaving this guest house, is he, Sam?"

"Now wait a minute," said Sam. "If you're trying to imply—"

Banks held his hand up. "I'm not trying to imply anything. What was it the man said: once is happenstance, twice is coincidence? Let's just hope there's not a third time."

Sam put his head in his hands and rubbed his eyes. "I'm sorry," he said. "Really, I am. It's the shock. And now all these questions."

"Look at it from my point of view, Sam. Bernard Allen was killed after he left your guest house. That's given his killer about two whole weeks to cover his tracks, leave the country, arrange for an alibi, whatever. I need everything I can get, and I need it quick. And the last thing I need is for some clever bugger who just might have been withholding information to start playing the comic."

"Look, I've said I'm sorry. What more do you want?"

"First of all you can tell us when he left?"

"About two weeks ago."

"Can you be more specific?"

"Katie?"

Again, with great difficulty, Katie turned her attention to the people in the room. Banks repeated his question.

"It was a Friday," she said.

Hatchley checked the dates against his diary. "That'd be the seventeenth, sir," he said. "Friday, May seventeenth."

"What time?"

"Just after breakfast. About nine-thirty. He said he wanted to get an early start," Sam said.

"Where was he going?"

"He was heading for the Pennine Way, then up to Swaledale."

"Do you know where he was intending to stay?"

Sam shook his head. "No. He just said he'd find somewhere on the way. There are plenty of places; it's a very popular route."

"Did he say anything to you about visiting the hanging valley on his way?"

"No. I wouldn't have been surprised, though. He used to play there when he was a kid, or so he said."

"What did you do after he'd gone?"

"I drove to Eastvale to do some shopping. I always do on a Friday morning."

"What shops did you go to?"

"What is this? Are you trying to tell me I'm a suspect in the murder of my friend?"

"Just answer the bloody question."

"All right, Inspector, there's no—"

"It's Chief Inspector." Banks didn't usually push rank, but Sam Greenock had rubbed him up the wrong way.

"Chief Inspector, then. Where did I go? I went to Carter's for some seeds, peat moss and fertilizer. Katie's trying to get a vegetable patch going in the back garden. It'll save us a bit of money in the long run."

"Is that all?"

"No. But they'll remember me there. I called in at a newsagent's for some magazines—that one on King Street opposite the school road."

"I know it."

"I'm a regular there, too."

"Thanks, that'll do fine for a start. What kind of car do you drive?"

"A Landrover. It's in the garage."

"And you, Mrs Greenock, what did you do after Bernard Allen left?"

"Me? Housework. What else?"

Banks turned back to Sam: "You met Allen in Leeds about ten years ago, is that right?"

"Yes. In Armley. We lived just off Tong Road and the Allens came to live next door after they gave up the farm. Bernie and I were about the same age, so we palled up."

"What was he doing then?"

"Just finishing at university. It was only York, so he was home most weekends and holidays. We used to go for a jar or two every Saturday night."

"How did the family take the move?"

Sam shrugged. "They adapted. At first Mr Allen, Bernie's dad, went around as if he'd been kicked out of paradise. It must have been very hard for him, though, swapping farm work for a crummy factory job. Hard on the pride."

"Is that what he said?"

"Never in so many words, no. You could just tell. He's a tough old bird, anyway, so they survived."

"And Bernard?"

"He tried to fit in. But you know what it's like. He got his degree and all, but he couldn't get the kind of work he wanted. He lived at home and did all kinds of odd jobs—mushroom picking at Greenhill Nurseries, sweeping factory yards, production line . . . all dull routine work."

"Is that when he decided to go to Canada?"

"After a year or so of it, yes. He'd had enough. Someone he knew from university had already gone over and said it wasn't too hard to get teaching jobs in the colleges. He said they paid well, too."

"Who was this?"

"His name was Bob Morgan. I think he and Bernie taught at the same place, Toronto Community College."

"Was Bernie homesick?"

"I suppose so. I mean, you don't forget your roots, do you? But he stayed. One thing leads to another. He made friends over there, got married, divorced."

"What was his state of mind while he was staying here?"

"He was fine. Cheerful. Happy to be back."

"Did he talk about coming home to stay?"

Sam shook his head. "He knew better than that. There aren't any jobs for him."

"So he didn't seem unusually homesick or depressed, and he didn't say he was planning to come back."

"No."

Banks lit a cigarette and studied Katie's profile. She was a blank; he had no idea what she was thinking.

"How long have you been in Swainshead?" he asked Sam.

"Six years."

"And it's going well?"

Sam nodded. "Can't complain. We're hardly millionaires, but we like the life."

"And you, Mrs Greenock?"

Katie turned and focused on him. "Yes. It's better than cleaning rooms at the Queen's Hotel."

"Did Bernie have any other friends in the village apart from you?"

"Not really," Sam answered. "See, most of the kids he grew up with had moved away. A lot do these days. They see the good life on telly and soon as they're old enough there's no stopping them. Like Denny, Bernie's older brother. Off to Australia like a shot, he was."

"Was Bernie friendly with the Colliers?" Esther Haines had said not, but Banks thought she might have been prejudiced by her own opinions of Nicholas and Stephen.

"Well, I'd hardly say they were friends. Acquaintances, more like. But we had an evening or two in the White Rose together. I think Bernie was always a bit uncomfortable around Stephen and Nick, though, them having been his landlords, so to speak, the local gentry and all."

Banks nodded. "Can you think of anyone in the village who might have wanted him out of the way?"

"Bernie? Good Lord, no."

"He had no enemies?"

"None that I know of. Not here."

"What about in Leeds?"

"Not there either, as far as I know. Maybe somebody followed him over from Canada, an enemy he'd made there?"

"Mrs Greenock," Banks said, turning to Katie again, "do you know of anyone with a reason for getting rid of Bernard Allen?"

Katie hesitated before answering. "No. He was harmless. Just a friendly sort of person. Nobody would want to hurt him."

"One more thing: What was he carrying when he left here?"

"Carrying?" Sam said. "Oh, I see. His belongings. A big blue rucksack with his clothes, passport, money, a few books."

"And what was he wearing?"

"I don't really remember. Do you, Katie?"

Katie shook her head. "It was a warm day, though," she said. "That I do remember. I think he was just wearing an open-necked shirt. White. And slacks, not jeans. It's only the amateurs wear jeans for walking."

"They're too heavy, you see," Sam explained. "Especially if they get wet. We try to give a bit of advice to our guests sometimes, and we always make sure we know where they're going if they're due back in the evening. That way, if they don't return, we can let the Mountain Rescue Post know where they were heading."

Banks nodded. "Very sensible. Have you any vacancies at the moment?"

"I think so," Sam said.

"Six and eight," Katie added.

"Good, we'll take them."

"You're staying here?"

"There'll be quite a lot of questions to ask in Swainshead," Banks said, "and it's fifty miles to Eastvale and back. We'll be staying here tonight at least."

"One's a single," Katie said. "The other's a double."

Banks smiled at her. "Fine. Sergeant Hatchley will take the single." It was patently unfair, Banks knew. He was much more slightly built than the well-padded Hatchley, and a good four or five inches shorter. But rank, he reflected, did have its privileges.

"Don't sulk, Sergeant," he said as they walked over to the car to pick up their overnight bags. "My room might be bigger, but it's probably right next to the plumbing. What did you think of Mrs Greenock?"

"Not bad if you like those wand-like figures," Hatchley said. "Prefer 'em with a bit of meat on their bones, myself."

"I wasn't asking you to rate her out of ten on looks. What about her attitude?"

"Didn't say much, did she? Seemed in a bit of a daze to me. Think there might be more to her than meets the eye?"

"I think there might indeed," said Banks. "In fact, I got the distinct impression that she was holding something back."

II

The Greenocks ate their lunch in silence, then Sam dashed out. Katie, who had lost her appetite and merely played with her food, piled the dishes in the washer, set the controls and turned it on. There was still shopping to do and the evening meal to prepare, but she felt she could afford to relax for a few minutes.

As she lay down on the sofa and looked out on the slopes of Swainshead Fell beyond the back garden, she thought of Bernie helping her clear the dishes, talking about Toronto, watching cricket on the telly. She remembered the little presents he had brought each time—no doubt picked up at the airport at the last minute, for Bernie was like that—jars of pure maple syrup, a box of cigars or a bottle of malt Scotch for Sam, Opium perfume or Chanel No 5 for Katie. She'd never had the heart to tell him that she didn't wear perfume, that the one time she had tried she had felt like a tramp, even though it had been White Linen, and had scrubbed it off straight away. Now the three little bottles lay in the dark inside her dresser drawer, untouched.

Bernie had even helped her with the garden sometimes; he might not have had green fingers, but he could wield a trowel or a hoe well enough. Bernie: so considerate, so kind. But the dark images began to crowd out her thoughts. Frowning, she pushed them away. Instead she saw endless prairies of golden wheat swaying in the breeze, heard the sea beating against a rough coastline where redwood forests reared as tall as the sky. Bernie had told her all about Canada, all the places he'd been. She'd never get to see them now, she realized, because Bernie was dead.

Fellowes's words came back to her, what he'd said in his drunken stupor when he grasped her hand by the bed: "Moving," he'd said. "Moving." And she hadn't understood at the time. Now she did. If Bernie had been lying up there for two weeks he would have been like that dead lamb she had seen on Adam's Fell last year. It didn't bear thinking about.

She'd given a bad impression to the police, she knew that, but at the time she had been unable to help herself. The lean, dark one, the one who seemed too short to be a policeman, would want to talk to her again, that was for sure. How could she keep her secret? She pictured her grandmother standing over her, lined face stern and hard, eyes like black pinheads boring into her: "Secrets, girl, secrets are the devil's doing. God loves a pure and open heart." But she had to keep this secret.

There were so many things, it seemed, one had to do in life that went against God's commandments. How could a person live without sinning? She was no longer even sure that she knew what was right or wrong. Sometimes she thought it was a sin to breathe, to be alive. It seemed you had to sin to survive in today's world. It was wrong to keep secrets and tell lies; but was it wrong to keep your word, your promise? And if you had broken it once for a special reason, was it all right to break it again?

Wearily, Katie got up and prepared to go to the shops down in Lower Head. Work and duty: they were the only constants in life. Everything else was a trap, a trick, a temptation to betrayal. The only way to survive was to shun pleasure. She picked up her purse and shopping basket and pulled a face at the nasty, soapy taste in her mouth as she left the house.

III

After Banks and Hatchley had carried their bags to their rooms, they walked over to the White Rose for lunch. The place was busy with Saturday tourists who had let their curiosity lead them to the northern part of Swainshead, but none of the regulars was present. Luckily, Freddie Metcalfe was too busy to chat. They both ordered gammon and chips and carried their pints over to a corner table.

"I want you to get onto Richmond after lunch," Banks said, "and have him check to see if anyone in Swainshead has connections with Canada, specifically with Toronto. I know it sounds like a big job, but tell him to start with the people we already know: the Greenocks, Fletcher, the Colliers. You might also add," he said, lowering his voice, "Freddie Metcalfe over there, and Neil Fellowes, too."

"The bloke who found the body? But he's from Pontefract."

"No matter. Remember, we thought Allen was from Canada at first, then from Leeds. And while we're on the subject, have him check on the brother-in-law, Les Haines. I want to know if he's made any trips to this area in the past few weeks. Ask him to get as much background as he can on all of them. I'm sure the superintendent will be able to get him some help from downstairs. And get someone to go to Carter's and that newsagent's to check Greenock's alibi. Tell them to make sure they get the times as exact as possible."

"Don't you believe him?"

Banks shrugged. "He could be telling the truth. He could also have driven to a convenient spot along the main road and approached the valley from the other side."

The little waitress brought over their food and they ate in silence. At the bar, they could hear Freddie Metcalfe enthralling visitors with examples of Yorkshire humour filched from *The Dalesman*, and at the next table, two middle-aged women from Lancashire were talking about lager louts: "They get right confident after a few drinks, young 'uns do."

When they had finished eating, Banks sent Hatchley to radio in to Richmond, then he stood outside the pub for a moment and took a deep breath of fresh air. It was June 1, another fine day. Nobody knew what the Dales had done to deserve such a long stretch of good weather, but according to a transistor radio Banks overheard, it certainly wasn't any thanks to Yorkshire Cricket Club, currently 74 for 6 at Somerset.

Banks wanted to talk to the Colliers, but first he returned to his room to change his shirt. On his way back down, he spotted Mrs Greenock in the hall, but she seemed to see or hear him coming and scuttled off into the back before he could catch her. Smiling, he walked back out into the street. He knew he could have followed her and confronted her with his suspicions there and then, but decided instead to let her play mouse to his cat until she tired of it.

There were plenty of people on the grassy banks of the River Swain that afternoon. Three children fished for tiddlers with nets at the end of cane rods while their parents sat and watched from lawn chairs, dad with a knotted handkerchief over his head reading the *Daily Mail* and mum knitting, glancing up occasionally to make sure the offspring were still in sight.

The Dales were getting as crowded and noisy as the coast, Banks thought as he crossed the bridge. There was even a small group of teenagers farther down, towards Lower Head, wearing cut-off denim jackets with the names of rock bands inked on the back. Two of them, a boy and a girl, Banks assumed, were rolling on

the grass in an overtly sexual embrace while tinny music rattled out
of a portable stereo placed close to one prostrate youth's ear.

Many of his colleagues, Banks knew, would have gone over and
told them to move on, accused them of disturbing the peace and
searched them for drugs. But despite his personal distaste for some
gangs of youngsters and their music, Banks made it a rule never to
use his power as a policeman to force his own will on the general
public. After all, they were young, they were enjoying life, and
apart from the noise, they were really doing no-one any harm.

Banks passed the old men on the bridge and made a mental
note to have a chat with them at some point. They seemed to be
permanent fixtures; maybe they had seen something.

He met Sergeant Hatchley at the car and they headed for the
Collier house.

"Have you noticed," Banks said, "how Allen seemed to have a
different story for everyone he talked to? He was upset; he was
cheerful. He was coming home; he wasn't."

"Maybe," said Hatchley, "it's just that all the people he talked to
have a different story for us."

Banks gave the sergeant an appreciative glance. Thinking things
out wasn't Hatchley's strong point, but there were times when he
could be quite surprising.

"Good point," Banks said. "Let's see what the Colliers have to
add."

Gristhorpe was right; the Collier house was a Victorian
monstrosity. But it had its own grotesque charm, Banks thought as
he walked up the crazy paving with Hatchley. Most Dales architecture was practical in nature and plain in style, but this place was
for show. It must have been the great-grandfather who had it built,
and he must have thought highly indeed of the Collier status.

Banks rang the bell on the panelled door and Stephen Collier
answered, a frown on his face. He led them through a high-
ceilinged hallway into a sitting-room at the back of the house.
French windows opened onto the patio. In the centre of the large
lawn stood an elaborate stone fountain. White dolphins and cheru-
bim curled about the lip of the bowl.

The room itself contrasted sharply with the exterior of the

house. Off-white walls created a sense of light and space on which
the ultra-modern Swedish pine and chrome and glass furnishing
made hardly any encroachment at all. Abstract paintings hung over
a blue-tiled mantelpiece: bold and violent splashes of colour reminiscent, in their effect on Banks's eyes, of the Jackson Pollocks
Sandra had insisted he look at in a London gallery years ago.

The three of them sat in white wicker chairs around a table on
the patio. Banks half-expected a servant to arrive with a tray of
Margaritas or mint juleps, but Collier himself offered them drinks. It
was warm, so both men eagerly accepted a cold bottle of Beck's lager.

Before he went to fetch the drinks, Stephen Collier rapped on
the French windows of the next room and beckoned to Nicholas.
Banks had wanted to talk to them separately, but it wasn't important
at this point. Stretching, he got up and walked over as Nicholas
emerged onto his half of the patio. He was just in time to catch a
glimpse of a much darker room, all oak panelling, leather-bound
books and oil-paintings of ancestors gleaming on the walls.

Nicholas smiled his horsy yellow smile and held out his hand.

"It's an interesting set-up you've got here," Banks said.

"Yes. We couldn't bear to get rid of the house, however ugly it
might seem from the outside. It's been in the family for years. Lord
knows what prompted my great-great-grandfather to build such a
folly—ostentatious display of wealth and position, I suppose. And
it's so inappropriate for the area." Despite the deprecating tone,
Banks could tell that Nicholas was proud of the house and the
status of his family.

"Do you share the place?" Banks asked Nicholas after they had
sat down at the table.

"Sort of. It's divided into two halves. We thought at first that
one of us could take the upstairs and the other the downstairs, but
it's better like this. We've got the equivalent of two completely
separate houses. Stephen and I have very different tastes, so the
two halves make quite a contrast. You must let me show you around
my half one day."

Stephen returned with the drinks. Dressed all in white, he looked
like a cricketer breaking for tea. Nicholas, however, with his slight
stoop, pale complexion, and comma of black hair over his forehead,

looked more like an ageing umpire. It was hard to believe these two were brothers; even harder to accept that Stephen was the eldest.

After giving both of them time to register surprise and shock at the news of Bernard Allen's death, of which he was certain they knew already, Banks lit a cigarette and asked, "Did you see much of him while he was here?"

"Not a lot," Stephen answered. "He was in the pub a couple of times with Sam, so naturally we talked, but that's about all."

"What did you talk about?"

"Oh, just small talk, really. This and that. About Canada, places we'd both been to."

"You've visited Canada?"

"I travel quite a bit," Stephen said. "You might think a small food-freezing plant in the Dales isn't much, but there are other businesses, connected. Import, export, that kind of thing. Yes, I've been to Canada a few times."

"Toronto?"

"No. Montreal, as a matter of fact."

"Did you ever see Bernard Allen over there?"

"It's a big country, Chief Inspector."

"Did you get the impression that anything was bothering Allen while he was over here?"

"No."

"What about you?" he asked Nicholas.

"No, I can't say I did. I've always found it a bit awkward talking to Bernard, to tell you the truth. One always feels he has a bit of a chip on his shoulder."

"What do you mean?"

"Oh, come on," Nicholas said, grinning. "Surely you know what I mean. His father spent his life working on land rented from my father. They were poor. From where they lived they had a fine enough view of this place, and you can't tell me that Bernard never thought it unfair that we had so much and he had so little. Especially when his father failed."

"I didn't know Bernard Allen or his father," Banks said, peeling the foil from the neck of the Beck's, which he preferred to drink straight from the bottle. "Tell me about him."

"I'm not saying I knew him well, myself, only that he became a bit of a lefty, a socialist. Up the workers and all that." Nicholas grinned again, showing his stained teeth. His eyes were especially bright.

"Are you saying that Bernard Allen was a Communist?"

"I don't know about that. I don't know if he was a party member. All I know is he used to spout his leftist rot in the pub."

"Is this true?" Banks asked Stephen.

"Partly. My brother exaggerates a bit, Chief Inspector. It's a tendency he has. We sometimes had arguments about politics, yes, and Bernard Allen had left-wing views. But that's as far as it goes. I'd hardly say he was a proselytizer or that he toed some party line."

"His political opinions weren't particularly strong, then?"

"I wouldn't say so, no. He said he left the country partly because Margaret Thatcher came into office. Well, we all know about unemployment, don't we? Bernard couldn't find work in England, so he left. You could hardly say he was running from country to country to escape political tyranny, could you?"

"He just used to whine about it, that's all," Nicholas cut in. "Expected the government to do everything for him without him having to lift a finger. Typical socialist."

"As you can gather, Chief Inspector," Stephen said with a strained smile, "my brother's something of a young fogey. That hardly gave either of us reason to do away with Bernard, though."

"Of course not," Banks said. "And I was never suggesting it did. I just want to know as much about the victim as possible. Would you say that there was any real animosity between you—political arguments aside—over the farm?"

"Do you mean did he blame us?" Stephen asked.

"Yes."

"He blamed everyone but himself," Nicholas cut in.

Stephen turned on him. "Oh, shut up Nicky. You're being bloody awkward, you know."

"Did he?" Banks asked Stephen again.

"Not that I ever knew of. It was nothing to do with us, really. As you know, Father was preparing to give up farming anyway, and he certainly hadn't groomed us to take over. Nobody kicked Archie

Allen off the land. He could have stayed there as long as he wanted to. It just wasn't financially viable any more. Ask any farmer, they'll tell you how things have changed over the past twenty years or so. If Bernard was holding a grudge, then it was a very unreasonable one. He didn't strike me as an unreasonable person. Does that answer your question?"

"Yes, thank you," Banks said. He turned to Nicholas again. "I understand you knew Mr Allen's sister, Esther."

Nicholas reddened with anger. "Who said that?"

"Never mind who said it. Is it true?"

"We all knew her," Stephen said. "I mean, we knew who she was."

"More than that," Banks said, looking at Nicholas, whose eyes were flashing. "Nicholas knows what I mean, don't you?"

"Don't be ridiculous," Nicholas said. "Are you trying to suggest that there was anything more to it than a landlord-tenant relationship?"

"Was there?"

"Of course not."

"Didn't you find her attractive?"

"She was hardly my type."

"Do you mean she was of a lower class?"

Nicholas bared his teeth in a particularly unpleasant smile. "If you want to put it that way, yes."

"And what about the servant girl? The one who used to work here."

"I insist you stop this at once, Chief Inspector," Stephen said. "I can't see how it's relevant. And I'm sure I don't have to remind you that the deputy chief constable is a good friend of the family."

"I'm sure he is," Banks said. He wasn't at all put out; in fact, he was enjoying their discomfort tremendously. "Just a couple of minor points, then we'll be on our way. When was the last time you saw Bernard?"

Nicholas said nothing; he appeared to be sulking. Stephen paused for a moment and answered in a business-like manner, "I'd say it was in the White Rose the evening before he left. Thursday. I remember talking to him about Tan Hill in Swaledale."

"Is that where he was heading?"

"Not specifically, no, but it's on the Pennine Way."

"Did he talk about the hanging valley at all, the place where his body was found?"

"No, not that I remember."

"Did either of you see him set off from Swainshead?"

Both the Colliers shook their heads. "I'm usually at the office before nine," Stephen said. "And my brother would have been at Braughtmore."

"So you saw nothing of him after that Thursday evening in the White Rose?"

"Nothing."

"Just one more thing: could you tell us where John Fletcher lives?"

"John? He's a couple of miles north of the village. It's a big farmhouse on the eastern fell-side. You can't miss it, it's the only one in sight."

"Fine, then." Banks nodded to Hatchley and they stood up to leave. Stephen Collier led them out and Nicholas followed, still sulking. As soon as the door closed, Banks could hear them start arguing.

Hatchley turned up his nose in disgust. "What a pair of wankers," he said.

"Aptly put," said Banks. "But we did learn a few things."

"Like what?"

"I never told them what time Allen left Swainshead, so why should Stephen Collier make a point of mentioning nine o'clock?"

"Hmm," said Hatchley. "I suppose he could have just been assuming that Allen would leave after breakfast. Or maybe it had been mentioned the night before?"

"It's possible," Banks said. "Come to that, Sam Greenock could have told them. Nicholas Collier seemed much more annoyed by my reference to Esther Haines than I thought he'd be. There could be much more to that than even she let on."

"I thought you were pushing it a bit there," Hatchley said. "I mean, the super did say to take it easy on them. They're important."

Banks sniffed. "The problem is, Sergeant, that it's all arse backwards, isn't it?"

"What do you mean?"

"Let's say Nicholas Collier might have been messing around with Allen's little sister, or Allen might have been bitter over losing the farm and eventually having to leave England. That gives him a motive for murder, but he's the one who ends up dead. Odd, that, don't you think?"

"Aye, when you put it like that," Hatchley said.

"Get on the radio and see if Richmond has turned up anything yet, will you? I want a word with these blokes here."

Hatchley carried on to the car. Banks neared the bridge and steeled himself for the encounter with the old men. Three of them stood there silently, two leaning on walking sticks. No flicker of interest or concern showed on their weather-beaten faces when Banks approached them. He leaned against the warm stone and introduced himself, then asked if they had been out as early as nine o'clock a couple of weeks ago.

No-one said a word at first, then one of them, a gnarled, misshapen man, turned to face Banks. With his flat cap and dark brown clothing, he looked like some strange plant with the power to uproot itself and walk among people.

He spat in the beck and said, "'Appen."

"Do you know Bernard Allen?"

"Archie Allen's lad? Aye, o'course."

"Did you see him that morning?"

The man was silent for a moment; he screwed up his eyes and contemplated Adam's Fell. Banks took out his cigarettes and offered them around. Only one of them, a man with a huge red nose, took one He grinned toothlessly at Banks, carefully nipped off the filter and put the other end in his mouth.

"Aye," the spokesman said finally.

"Where did he come from?"

The man pointed towards the Greenock Guest House.

"Did he stop anywhere on his way?"

The man shook his head.

"Where did he go?"

"Up there." The man pointed with his stick to the footpath up Swainshead Fell.

"And that was the last you saw of him?"

"Aye."

"What was he wearing?"

"Nay, lad, I don't remember that. 'Ee was carrying one o'them there 'aversacks on 'is back, that's all I recollect. P'raps 'ee was wearing a shirt. I don't remember no jacket."

"Did you notice anyone go after him?"

The man shook his head again.

"Could someone have followed him without you seeing?"

"'Appen. There's plenty o'ways to get up t'fell."

"We know he went to the hanging valley over the fell-top," Banks said. "Are there many other ways to get there?"

"A few. Tha can go from t'main road, 'bout a mile past Rawley Force, and from further up t'valley."

"How could anyone know where he was headed?"

"That's tha job, bobby, in't it?"

He was right. Someone could easily have watched Allen set off up the side of Swainshead Fell then gone up by another route to head him off somewhere out of sight. And Sam Greenock had said he wouldn't have been surprised if Bernard had visited the hanging valley. Anyone else could have known that, too, and gone up earlier to wait for him there.

Typically, as more information came to light the case was becoming more and more frustrating. Clearly it would be necessary to do a house-to-house in the village and ask the people with an eastern view if they had noticed anything that morning. It would also be useful to know if anyone had seen a car parked off the Helmthorpe road near the other access point. The trouble was that May seventeenth was so long ago most people would have forgotten.

And those were only the most obvious ways in. Someone could surely have approached the hanging valley from almost any direction and lain in wait overnight if necessary, especially if he knew Bernard Allen was bound to pass that way. The break, if it came, didn't look so likely to come from establishing opportunity—just about everyone who had no alibi seemed to have had that—but from discovering a motive.

Banks thanked the old men and walked off to find Sergeant Hatchley.

SIX

I

Hatchley started the next day in a bad mood. He grumbled to Banks that not only was his bed too small but the noise of the plumbing had kept him awake.

"I swear there was some bugger in there for a piss every five minutes. Flushed it every time, too. The bloody thing took at least ten minutes to quieten down again."

Banks, who had slept the sleep of the truly virtuous, overlooked the sergeant's spurious arithmetic. "Never mind," he said. "With a bit of luck you'll be snug and warm in your own bed tonight."

"Not if I can help it."

"Carol Ellis?"

"Aye."

"How long's it been now?"

"Over eighteen months."

'It'll be wedding bells next, then?"

Hatchley blushed and Banks guessed he wasn't far from the truth.

"Anyway," Banks went on. "I'm sorry to keep you away from your love-life, but I think we'll be finished here today unless Richmond comes up with anything else."

Hatchley had been onto the detective constable back in Eastvale, but Richmond had discovered nothing of importance except that Sam Greenock's alibi seemed to hold. There remained, however, some doubt about the exact times he had called at Carter's and the newsagent's, so he wasn't entirely out of the running.

Also, Richmond had spoken to PC Weaver, who had called at the Greenocks' to ask about Canadian visitors. Weaver said that in all cases he had both checked the register and made enquiries. It looked like Sam Greenock was lying. Weaver could have been covering himself, but he was a good officer, and Banks tended to believe him.

The previous evening, Banks and Hatchley had gone to interview John Fletcher, but he had been out. On the way back, they called in at the White Rose for a nightcap and had an early night. Mrs Greenock had still been skilfully managing to avoid them.

Breakfast seemed to cheer Hatchley up. Delivered by Katie, who blushed and ran as soon as she put, or almost dropped, the plates in front of them, the main course consisted of two fried eggs, two thick rashers of Yorkshire bacon, Cumberland sausage, grilled mushrooms and tomato, with two slices of fried bread to mop it all up. Before that they had drunk grapefruit juice and eaten cereal, and afterwards came the toast and marmalade. By some oversight, the toast was actually hot, and Hatchley, his equilibrium much restored, recoiled in mock horror.

"What's on after we've talked to Fletcher?" he asked.

"We've got to put it all together, write up the interviews, see what we've got. I'm due for lunch with the super, so as far as I'm concerned you can take the rest of the day off and make an early start in the morning."

Sergeant Hatchley beamed.

"I'll drop you off at home," Banks said. "I've got to go back to Eastvale to pick up Sandra and the kids, anyway."

They finished their tea and left the room to the quiet Belgian couple by the window and the young marrieds in the corner, who hadn't noticed anyone except each other. The Greenocks themselves were nowhere in sight.

Outside, the three men Banks had spoken with the previous day were on the bridge as usual. The one who had acted as spokesman gave him a curt, grudging nod of acknowledgement as he passed.

Hatchley nudged him as they got in the car. "It usually takes an incomer two generations to get any sign of recognition from those characters. What did you do, slip 'em a tenner each?"

"Southern charm, Sergeant," Banks said, grinning. "Sheer charm. That and a lot of luck."

About two miles up the valley, they crossed the low bridge and took a narrow dirt road up the fell-side. Fletcher's farmhouse was a solid, dark-stone construction that looked as if it had been extruded from the earth like an outcrop of rock. Around the back were a number of pens and ditches for dipping and shearing. This time, he was at home.

"I'm sorry I wasn't in," he said when Banks mentioned their previous visit. "I was doing a bit of business over in Hawes. Anyway, come in, make yourselves comfortable."

They followed him into the living-room, a spartan kind of place with bare plastered walls, stiff-backed chairs and a solid table on which rested an old wireless and precious little else. Whatever money Fletcher had in the bank, he certainly didn't waste any on luxurious living. The small window looked out across the valley. With a view like that, Banks thought, you'd hardly need paintings or television.

One thing in particular caught Banks's eye immediately, partly because it just didn't seem to fit in this overtly masculine environment. Propped on the mantelpiece was a gilt-framed photograph of a woman. On closer inspection, which Banks made while Fletcher went to brew tea, the photo proved doubly incongruous. The woman, with her finely plucked eyebrows, gay smile and long, wavy chestnut hair, certainly didn't look as if she belonged in Fletcher's world. Banks could imagine her cutting a fine figure at society cocktail parties, sporting the latest hat at Ascot or posing elegantly at fashion openings, but not living in this godforsaken part of the world with a dark, squat, rough-cheeked sheep-farmer.

When Fletcher came back, Banks pointed to the photograph and asked who she was.

"My wife," he said. "She's been gone two years now." There was a distinct chill in his tone that harmonized with the lonely, brooding atmosphere Banks sensed in the house.

He didn't like to ask, but curiosity, as it often did, got the better of him. "I'm sorry," he said. "Is she dead?"

Fletcher looked sharply at him. "Not dead, no. If you must know, she left me."

And you're still in love with her, Banks thought. At least that explained something of the heaviness that Fletcher seemed to carry around inside himself.

"We've come about Bernard Allen," Banks said, accepting a cup of tea and changing tack quickly.

"Aye, I heard," Fletcher said. "Poor sod."

"Did you know him well?"

"Not really, no. Just used to pass an evening or two in the White Rose when he dropped by for a visit."

"Did you know him before he went to Canada?"

"I met him a few times. Hard not to when I was dealing with Walter Collier. Archie Allen worked some of his land."

"So I heard. What were you going to do about that?"

Fletcher shrugged. "I wasn't going to evict them, if that's what you're getting at. They were quite welcome to stay as far as I was concerned."

"But they couldn't make a go of it?"

"That's right. It's tough, sheep-farming, like I said before. I felt sorry for them, but there was nothing I could do."

"So you only knew Bernard through his father at first?"

"Aye. He was off at university around then, too. And his brother had emigrated to Australia. There was only the young lass left."

"Esther?"

"Aye. How is she? Have you seen her?"

"Yes," Banks said. "She's well. Married. Lives in Leeds. Did you ever hear anything about her and Nicholas Collier?"

Fletcher frowned. "No, I can't say as I did. Though I wouldn't put it past him. She were a nice lass, young Esther. I've often thought things might've worked out different if the others had stuck around, kept the family together, like."

"You mean Bernard and Denny going away might have caused their father's problems?"

"Some of them, perhaps. Not all, mind you. But it costs money to hire men. If you've got a family, there might be more mouths to feed, but there's more hands to help, too."

"Did you have any connection with Bernard other than his father? There can't have been much of an age difference between you."

"Nay, I'm older than I look," Fletcher said, and grinned. "Like I said, we'd pass the time of day in the White Rose now and then. Him and his girlfriend were in there often enough."

"Girlfriend? Who was that, Mr Fletcher?"

"The one who disappeared. Anne Ralston, her name was."

Banks felt a tremor of excitement. "She was Bernard Allen's girlfriend?"

"Aye. Childhood sweethearts. They grew up together. I don't think it was owt serious later, like, or he wouldn't have gone off to Canada and left her. But they were thick as thieves, them two—more like brother and sister, maybe, as they got older."

"And after he'd gone, she took up with Stephen Collier?"

"Aye. Got a job at Collier Foods and, well . . . Stephen's got a way with the women."

"Did Bernard Allen ever say anything about this?"

"Not in my hearing he didn't. You're thinking maybe he was jealous?"

"Could be."

"Then the wrong one got himself killed, didn't he?"

Banks sighed. "It always seems to look that way in this case. But if Allen thought Stephen Collier had harmed her, he might have been out for revenge."

"Waited long enough, didn't he?" Fletcher said.

"I'll be frank with you, Mr Fletcher," Banks said. "We've no idea why Bernard Allen was murdered, none at all. At the moment I'm gathering as much information as I can. Most of it will probably turn out to be useless. It usually does. But right now there's no way of telling what's of value and what isn't. Can you think of any reason why someone in Swainshead would want him out of the way?"

Fletcher paused to think for a few moments, his dark eyebrows knitting together. "No," he said finally. "It's nothing to do with the farming business, I'm sure of that. There's not enough money in it to make murder worthwhile. And there was no animosity between myself and the Allens. Like I said I don't think there was bad feeling between Bernard and the Colliers, but I couldn't swear to it. I know he baited them a bit about being capitalist oppressors, but I don't think anyone took that seriously enough to kill for."

"What was your impression of Bernard Allen?"

"I liked him. As I said, I didn't know him well, and I can't say I agreed with his politics—with him on one side and Nicholas on the other, it was hardly my idea of a peaceful evening's drinking. But he was bright, thoughtful, and he loved the land. He knew he wasn't cut out to be a farmer—few are—but he loved The Head."

"When was the last time you saw him?"

"The evening before he left. We were all in the White Rose. He was getting quite maudlin about coming home. Said if only he could get a job, however little it paid, or maybe a private income, then he'd be back like a shot. Of course, Nicholas jumped on that one—a socialist wanting a private income!"

"Were there any serious arguments?"

"No. It was all playful. The only serious bit was Bernard's senti-mentality. He really seemed to convince himself that he was coming back here to live. But he'd had a few too many, of course. Sam had to help him back to the house. I'm sorry I can't be more useful, Mr Banks. I'd like to, but I don't know anything. I had no reason to harm Bernard and, as far as I know, nor did any of the others. If there are motives, they're hidden from me."

"Did he mention his divorce at all?"

"Oh aye," Fletcher said grimly. "I could sympathize with him over that."

"Did he seem upset about it?"

"Of course. His wife had run off with another man. Wouldn't you be upset? I think that's what set him thinking about coming back home to stay. You get like that when you lose whatever it is that keeps you away."

"Did Mr Allen know your wife?"

Fletcher's face hardened. "What do you mean 'know'? 'Know' in the biblical sense? Are you suggesting there was something between them and I killed him in a fit of jealousy?"

"No," said Banks, "I'm simply trying to get a grasp on the web of relationships."

Fletcher continued to eye him suspiciously. "She didn't know him," he said. "Oh, I'm not saying their paths never crossed, that they wouldn't say hello if they passed one another in the street, but that's all."

"Where is your wife?"

Fletcher looked at the picture. "In Paris," he said, his voice shaking with grief and anger. "In Paris with that bastard she ran off with."

The silence that followed weighed on them all. Finally, Banks gestured to Hatchley and they stood up to leave. "I'm sorry if I upset you," he said. "It wasn't intentional, believe me, but some-times in a murder investigation . . ."

Fletcher sighed. "Aye, I know. You've got to ask. It's your job. No offence taken." And he held out his square, callused hand.

Driving down the fell-side, Banks and Hatchley said very little. Banks had been impressed by Fletcher's solidity; he seemed a man with great integrity and strong foundations. But such a man, he knew, could kill when pushed too far. It was easier to push an earnest man too far than it was a more frivolous one. Although he was inclined to believe Fletcher, he nonetheless made a mental note of his reservations.

"Ideal place, isn't it?" Hatchley said, looking back at Fletcher's farm as they crossed the bridge.

"In a way," Banks answered. "A bit dour and spartan for my tastes, though."

"I didn't mean that, sir." Hatchley looked puzzled. "I meant it's an ideal location for approaching the hanging valley unseen."

Banks slowed down on the narrow road as Sam Greenock's Landrover passed them going in the other direction. Sam waved half-heartedly as he drove by.

"Yes," Banks said absently. "Yes, I suppose it is. I'd just like to stop off at the Greenocks' before we go back to Eastvale. There's something I'd like to do. You use the radio and get onto Richmond. See if anything's come up."

II

Katie flinched and backed towards the wall when she saw Banks appear in the doorway of the room she was cleaning.

"It's all right, Katie," he said. "I'm not going to hurt you. We've got to have a little talk, that's all."

"Sam's out," Katie said, clutching the yellow duster tight over her breast.

"I know he is. I saw him drive off. It's you I want to talk to. Come on, Katie, stop playing games. You've been trying to avoid us ever since we got here. What is it? What are you afraid of?"

"I don't know what you're talking about."

Banks sighed. "Yes you do." He sat down on the corner of the bed. "And I'm prepared to wait until you tell me."

Now, as she stood cringing by the window, Banks realized who she reminded him of: Hardy's Tess Durbeyfield. Physically, she resembled Nastassia Kinski, who had played Tess in the film version, but the similarity went deeper than that. Banks had a sense of Tess as a child in a woman's body, not fully aware of her own beauty and sexuality, or of the effect she might have on men. It wasn't entirely innocence, but it was close—a kind of innocent sensuality. He made a note to look up the description of Tess in the book when he got home.

"Look," he went on, "we can either talk here, or we can go to CID headquarters in Eastvale. It's up to you. I don't really mind at all."

"You can't do that," Katie said, thrusting out her bottom lip. "You can't just take a person away like that. I haven't done anything. I've got my work to finish."

"So have I. You're withholding evidence, Katie. It's a crime."

"I'm not withholding anything."

"If you say so." Banks stood up with exaggerated slowness. "Let's go, then."

Katie stepped back until she was flat against the wall. "No! If you take me away Sam . . . Sam'll . . ."

"Come on, Katie," Banks said, more gently, "don't be silly." He pointed to the chair. "Sit down. Tell me about it."

Katie flopped into the chair by the window and looked down at the floor. "There's nothing to tell," she muttered.

"Let me try and make it a bit easier for you," Banks said. "Judging by the way you behaved when we talked to you and Sam yesterday, I'd guess that something happened between you and Bernard Allen while he was staying here. Maybe it was personal. You might think it's your business and it has nothing to do with his death, but I'm the one to be the judge of that. Do you understand?"

Katie just stared at him.

"You'd known him a long time, hadn't you?"

"Since he came to Leeds. We lived next door."

"You and Sam?"

"With his parents."

"What happened to your own parents?"

"They died when I was a little girl. My grandmother brought me up." Katie lowered her gaze down to her lap, wringing the yellow duster in her hands.

"Did you ever go out with Bernie Allen?"

She looked up sharply, and the blood ran to her cheeks. "What do you mean? I'm married."

"Well, something happened between you, that's clear enough. Why won't you tell me what it was?"

"I've told you," Katie said. "Nothing happened. We were friends, that's all." She went back to twisting the duster on her lap. "I'm thirsty."

Banks brought her a glass of water from the sink.

"Were you lovers, Katie?" he asked. "Did you sleep with Bernard Allen while he was staying here?"

"No!" Tears blurred Katie's clear brown eyes.

"All right." Banks held up his hand. "It's not important. I believe you." He didn't, but he often found it useful to pretend he believed a lie. It was always clear from the teller's obvious relief that it had been a lie. Afterwards it was easier to get at the information that really mattered. And he had a feeling she was hiding something else.

"But you spent some time together, didn't you? Time alone, like friends do?"

Katie nodded.

"And you must have talked. What did you talk about?"

Katie shrugged. "I don't know, just things. Life."

"That's a broad subject. Anything in particular?"

She was chewing on her bottom lip now, and Banks could sense that she was on the verge of talking. He would have to tread carefully to avoid scaring her off again.

"It might be important," he said. "If he was a friend of yours, surely you want his killer caught?"

Katie looked at him as if the idea was completely new to her. "Yes," she said. "Yes, of course I do."

"Will you help me, then?"

"He talked about Canada, his life in Toronto. What it was like there."

"What about it?"

"How wonderful and exciting it was."

It was like drawing a confession out of a naughty child. "Come on," Banks prompted her. "There was something special, wasn't there? You'd have no reason to hide any of this from me, and I know you're hiding something."

"He told me in confidence," she said. "I wasn't to tell anyone. Sam'll kill me if he finds out."

"Why?"

"He doesn't like me talking to people behind his back."

"Look, Katie. Bernard is dead. Somebody murdered him. You can't keep a secret for a dead man, can you?"

"Life doesn't end with death."

"Maybe not. But what he said might be important."

There was a long pause while Katie seemed to struggle with her conscience; each phase of the skirmish flashed across her flawless complexion. Finally, she said, "Annie was there. That's what he told me. Annie was in Toronto."

"Annie?"

"Yes. Anne Ralston. She was a friend of Bernie's from years ago. She disappeared when we had all that trouble here five years back."

"I've heard of her. What exactly did Bernard say?"

"Just that she was living in Toronto now. He'd heard from her about three years ago. She was in Vancouver then. They'd kept in touch, and now she'd moved."

"Did he say anything else about her?"

Katie looked at him blankly. "No. She just asked him not to go telling everyone in Swainshead that he'd seen her."

"This is what Bernard told you?"

"Yes."

"Why did he tell you, do you think, when Anne had told him not to tell anyone?"

"I . . . I . . . don't know," Katie stammered. "He trusted me. He was just talking about people leaving, finding a new life. He said she was happy there."

"Were you talking about wanting a new life for yourself?"

"I don't know what you mean."

Her words lacked conviction. Banks knew he was right. Katie had probably been telling Bernard Allen that she wanted to get away from Swainshead. Why she should want to leave he didn't know, but from what he'd seen and heard of Sam so far, she might have one good reason.

"Never mind," Banks said. "Did he say anything about coming home to stay?"

Katie seemed surprised. "No. Why should he? He had a wonderful new life out there."

"Did he tell you this on the morning he left or before?"

"Before. Just after he arrived."

"And you were the only one he told?"

"Yes."

"You're hesitating, Katie. Why?"

"I . . . I don't know. You're confusing me. You're making me nervous."

"Were you the only one he told?"

"As far as I know, yes."

"And who did you tell?"

"I didn't tell anyone."

"You're lying, Katie."

"I'm not. I—"

"Who did you tell? Sam?"

Katie pulled at the duster so hard it tore. "All right, yes! I told Sam. He's my husband. Wives aren't supposed to keep secrets from their husbands, are they?"

"What did Sam say?"

"Nothing. He just seemed surprised, that's all."

"Did he know Anne Ralston?"

"Not well. It was only about a year after we arrived that she disappeared. We met her with Bernie, and she was going out with Stephen, but Sam didn't know the Colliers as well then."

"Are you sure you told no-one else?"

"No-one," Katie whispered. "I swear it."

Banks believed her.

Sam Greenock, he reflected, was quite a one for passing on news, especially to his cronies in the White Rose, with whom he seemed intent on ingratiating himself. Socially, he was beneath them all. The Colliers were cocks of The Head, and Fletcher owned quite a bit of land. Stephen Collier, as Katie said, had been going out with Anne Ralston around the time she disappeared, which had also been coincidental with the murder of Raymond Addison, the London private-enquiry agent. Somewhere, somehow, Sam Greenock was involved in it all.

What if Sam had told Stephen that Bernard Allen had been in touch with Anne? And what if she was in a position to tell Allen something incriminating about Collier, something to do with the Addison murder? That would certainly give Stephen a motive. And if that was what had happened, to what extent was Sam Greenock an accessory? For the first time, there seemed to be the strong possibility of a link between the murders of Raymond Addison and Bernard Allen. This would certainly interest Superintendent Gristhorpe, who had withdrawn into his usual role because the two cases hadn't seemed connected.

"Thank you, Katie," Banks said, walking to the door. "You'd better keep our rooms for us. I think we'll be back this evening."

Katie nodded wearily. Pale, slumped in the chair, she looked used and abused like a discarded mistress.

III

"Anne Ralston?" Gristhorpe repeated in disbelief. "After all these years?"

He and Banks knelt beside the pile of stones. Usually, when they worked on the wall together they hardly spoke, but today there was pressing police business to deal with. Sandra had taken Brian and Tracy down into Lyndgarth after lunch to see a local craft exhibition, so they were alone with the twittering larks and the cheeky wagtails on the valley-side above the village.

"You can see how it changes things," Banks said.

"I can indeed—if it had anything to do with Bernard Allen's murder."

"It must have."

"We don't even know that Anne Ralston's disappearance was connected with Addison's killing, for a start."

"It's too much of a coincidence, surely?" Banks said. "A private detective is killed and a local woman disappears on practically the same day. If it happened in London, or even in Eastvale, I'd be inclined to think there was no link, but in a small village like Swainshead . . . ?"

"Aye," said Gristhorpe. "Put like that . . . But we need a lot more to go on. No, not that one—it's too flat." Gristhorpe brushed aside the stone Banks had picked up.

"Sorry." Banks searched the pile for something better. "I'm working on the assumption that Anne Ralston knew something about Addison's murder, right?"

"Right. I'll go along with that just for the sake of argument."

"If she did know something and disappeared without telling us, it means one of two things—either she was paid off, or she was scared for her own life."

Gristhorpe nodded. "Or she might have been protecting someone," he added.

"But then there'd be no need to run."

"Maybe she didn't trust herself to bear up under pressure. Who knows? Go on."

"For five years nobody hears any more of her, then suddenly Bernard Allen turns up and tells Katie Greenock he's been seeing the Ralston woman in Toronto. The next thing we know, Allen's dead before he can get back there. Now, Katie said that Bernard had been told not to spread it around about him knowing Anne. Was she protecting him, or herself? Or both? We don't know. What we do know, though, is that she didn't want her whereabouts known. Allen tells Katie, anyway, and she tells her husband. I think we can safely assume that Sam Greenock told everyone else. Allen must have become a threat to someone because he'd met up with Anne Ralston, who might have known something about Addison's murder. Stephen Collier was closely associated with her, so he looks like a good suspect, but there's no reason to concentrate on him alone. It could have been any of them—Fletcher, Nicholas, Sam Greenock, even Katie—they were all in Swainshead at the time both Addison and Allen were killed, and we've no idea what or who that private detective was after five years ago."

"What about opportunity?"

"Same thing. Everybody knew the route Allen was taking out of Swainshead. He'd talked all about it in the White Rose the night before. And most of them also knew how attached he was to that valley. The killer could easily have hidden among the trees up there and watched for him."

"All right," Gristhorpe said, placing a through-stone. "But what about their alibis?"

"We've only got Fletcher's word that he was at home. He could have got to the valley from the north without anyone knowing. He lives alone on the fell-side and there are no other houses nearby. As for the Colliers, Stephen says he was at the office and Nicholas at school. We haven't checked yet, but if Nicholas wasn't actually teaching a class and Stephen wasn't in a meeting, either of them could have slipped out for a while, or turned up later. It would have been easy for Nicholas, again approaching from the north, and Stephen could have got up from a half a mile past Rawley Force. It's not much of a climb, and there's plenty of cover to hide the car off the Helmthorpe Road. I had a look on my way over here."

"The Greenocks?"

"Sam could have got there from the road too. He went to Eastvale for supplies, but the shopkeepers can't say exactly what time he got there. Carter's doesn't open till nine, anyway, and the chap in the newsagent's says Sam usually drops in at about eleven. That gives him plenty of time. He might have had another motive, too."

Gristhorpe raised his bushy eyebrows.

"The woman denies it, but I got a strong impression that some-thing went on between Katie Greenock and Bernard Allen."

"And you think if Sam got wind of it . . . ?"

"Yes."

"What about Mrs Greenock?"

"She says she was home cleaning, but all the guests would have gone out by then. Nobody could confirm that she stayed in."

"Have you checked the Colliers' stories?"

"Sergeant Hatchley's doing it tomorrow morning. There's no-one at the factory on a Sunday."

"Well maybe we'll be a bit clearer when we get all that sorted out."

"I'm going back to Swainshead for another night. I'll want to talk to Stephen Collier again, for one."

Gristhorpe nodded. "Take it easy, though, Alan. I've already had an earful from the DCC about your last visit."

"He didn't waste any time, did he? Anyway, I could do with a bit of information on the Addison case and the Ralston woman's disap-pearance. How did the alibis check out?"

Gristhorpe put down the stone he was weighing in his hand and frowned. Banks lit a cigarette—at least smoking was allowed in the open, if not in the house. He looked at the sky and noticed it had clouded over very quickly. He could sniff rain in the air.

"Everyone said they were at home. We couldn't prove other-wise. It was a cold, dark February evening. We pushed Stephen Collier as hard as we dared, but he had a perfect alibi for the day of the girl's disappearance: he was in Carlisle at a business meeting."

"Was Walter Collier around in those days?"

"No. He was dead by then."

"What was he like?"

"He was quite an impressive man. Complex. He had a lot of power and influence in the dale, some of which has carried over to the sons, as you've already found out. Now, you know how I feel about privilege and such, but you had to respect Walter—he never really abused his position. He was proud, especially of the family and its achievements, but he managed to be kind and considerate without being condescending. He was also a regular church-goer, a religious man, but he liked the ladies and he could drink most villagers under the table. Don't ask me how he managed to square that with himself. It's rare for a Dales farmer, especially one from a family as long-established as the Colliers, to sell up. But Walter was a man of vision. He saw what things were coming to, so he shifted his interests to food processing and encouraged his sons to get good educations rather than strong muscles."

"What was he like as a father?"

"I'd imagine he was a bit of a tyrant," Gristhorpe answered, "though I can't say for certain. Used to being obeyed, getting his own way. They probably felt the back of his hand more than once."

Banks held out his palm and felt the first, hesitant drops of rain. "When Anne Ralston disappeared," he asked, "were there no signs at all of what might have happened to her?"

"Nothing. There were a few clothes missing, that's all."

"What about money, bank accounts?"

"She didn't have one. She got a wage-packet every two weeks from Collier Foods. What she did with the cash, I've no idea. Maybe she hid it under the mattress."

"But you didn't find any in the cottage?"

"Not a brass farthing."

"So she could have packed a few things, a bit of money, and simply run off?"

"Yes. We never found out what happened to her, until now." Gristhorpe stood up and scowled at the grey sky. A flock of rooks wheeled above the valley-side. "Better go inside."

As they walked round to the side door, they saw Sandra and the children come hurrying up the drive with their coats thrown over their heads. Banks waved to them.

"It would be very interesting to have a chat with Anne Ralston, wouldn't it?" he said.

Gristhorpe looked at him and narrowed his eyes. "Aye, it would. But I'm not sure the department would be able to justify the expense."

"Still . . ."

"I'll see what I can do," Gristhorpe said. Then Sandra, Brian and Tracy came racing into the house.

SEVEN

I

Katie finished her cleaning in a daze when Banks had gone, and she was so distracted she almost forgot to put the roast in on time. The Greenock Guest House always served a traditional Yorkshire Sunday dinner, both for guests and non-residents, at two o'clock. It was Sam's idea. Thank God he was in the pub, his usual Sunday lunch-time haunt, Katie thought. He'd be bending elbows with the wonderful Colliers.

Perhaps Sam needn't know what the policeman had made her tell. But the inspector would be sure to question him, she knew, and he would find out; he was bound to accuse her of betraying him.

With a start, she realized she was in room five, where the talk had taken place on the second morning of Bernie's stay. But it wasn't his words she thought of now. The rush of images almost overwhelmed her at first, but she forced herself to re-examine what had happened. Perhaps it hadn't been such a sin, after all? Of course it was, she told herself; it was a double sin, for she was a married woman. But it had happened, she couldn't deny that. The first time in all her married life.

That morning she had been cleaning the rooms as usual, when Bernie had come back to put on his walking-boots. The sky had brightened, he said, and he had decided to go for a good long walk after all. They'd talked for as much time as she dared take off from her chores, then he had sat on the bed while she washed the windows. All the time she had been aware of him watching her. Finally, when she felt his arms around her waist, she told him no. She had her back to him and he bent to kiss her neck where the wisps of blonde hair were swept up and tied while she worked. She struggled, but he held her tight and his hands found her breasts. She dropped the chamois and it fell in the bucket and splashed water on the carpet.

Why did she let him? She had always liked him, but why this? Why let him do what she hated most? She thought perhaps it was because he offered her a chance of escape, and that this was the price she would have to pay. He was gentler than Sam. His mouth moved over her shoulder and his hands slid down along her stomach and over her thighs. She didn't have the heart or the courage to put up a fight; men were so strong. Surely, she thought, it could do no harm as long as she didn't feel pleasure. She couldn't tell Sam. That would mean she'd have to lie, too. She would have to wash her mouth out with soap.

Then he said he loved her, that he'd always wanted her, as his hands unfastened her skirt. She struggled again, but less violently this time, and he backed her towards the bed. There, he finished undressing her. She was trembling, but so was he; even body language speaks ambiguously at times. She held onto the bedposts tightly as he bore down on her, and she knew he thought her groans were sounds of pleasure. Why did men want her like this? Why did they want to do these things to her?

He kissed her breasts and said he would take her back to Canada with him, and suddenly that seemed like the answer. She wanted to get away, she needed to. Swainshead and Sam were stifling her.

So she didn't struggle any more. Bernard talked of the vast prairie skies and of lakes as boundless as oceans as his hands caressed her still body. Yes, he would take her with him, he said, he had always wanted her. Urgently, he drew himself along the length of her body and entered her. She bit her tongue in loathing and self-disgust, and he looked into her eyes and smiled as she made little strangled cries that must have sounded like pleasure.

After, as they dressed, Katie had tried to hide the shame of her nakedness from his gaze. He had laughed and told her he found her modesty very appealing. She said he'd better go, that Sam would be back, and he reminded her about Canada.

"I'll send for you when I get back," he promised. "I'll find a place for us and I'll send for you. Anne's there, too. She wanted to get away, just like you. She's happy now."

"Yes," she had said, anxious to get rid of him. "I'll come with you." Then he had kissed her and left the room.

After that morning, they had hardly spoken to one another— mostly because Sam had been around or Katie had contrived to avoid Bernie—but he kept giving her meaningful glances whenever nobody was looking. She believed him. He would send for her.

Not any more. All for nothing. All gone. All she had left was the guilt. "As ye sow, so shall ye reap," her granny had always said. She had behaved wantonly, like that time she had swayed to the distant music. It didn't matter that she hadn't enjoyed it; now everything was a mess, Bernie was dead, and the police were all over the place. She was reaping what she had sown.

II

Stephen Collier sat in his spacious living-room reading a thick, leather-bound report when Banks and Hatchley called that evening. The French windows were open onto the patio and lawn, and the fountain played against a backdrop of dry-walled fell-side. A brief, heavy shower had cleansed the landscape and in the gentle evening light the grass was lush and green, the limestone outcrops bright as marble.

Stephen seemed surprised and annoyed at a second visit from the police so close on the heels of the first, but he quickly regained his composure and offered drinks.

"I'll have a Scotch, please," Banks said.

"Sergeant Hatchley?"

"Don't mind if I do, sir." Hatchley glanced towards Banks, who nodded his permission. After all, he had spoiled the sergeant's weekend. Hatchley took out his notebook and settled in a corner with his drink.

"What can I do for you this time?" Stephen asked. "Do you want to see my brother, too?"

"Not at the moment," Banks said. "I want to talk to you about Anne Ralston."

Collier frowned. "Anne Ralston? What about her? That was years ago."

"I'd like to know what happened."

"Aren't I entitled to know why?"

"Will you just bear with me for a while?"

"Very well."

"As far as I know," Banks began, "she disappeared the day after the private detective, Raymond Addison, was killed. Am I right?"

"I wouldn't know when he was killed," Stephen said. "Though I do remember Superintendent Gristhorpe saying something about a post-mortem report."

"But it was around that time she disappeared?"

"Yes."

"And she was an employee of Collier Foods?"

"Yes. Your superintendent already knows all this. Please get to the point, Chief Inspector." He tapped the book on his lap. "I have an important report to study for a meeting in the morning."

"I won't keep you long, sir," Banks said, "if you'll just answer my questions. Were you going out with Anne Ralston at the time of her disappearance?"

"Yes. You know I was. But I don't see—"

Banks held up his hand. "Let me finish, please. Can you think of any reason why should she disappear?"

"None."

"What do you think happened to her?"

Collier walked over to the cocktail cabinet and refreshed his drink. He offered Banks and Hatchley cigarettes from a box on the glass-topped coffee-table.

"I thought she might have taken off to see the world," he answered. "It was something she'd often talked about."

"Didn't it worry you?"

"Didn't what worry me?"

"Her disappearance."

"I must admit, in some of my darker moments I thought something might have happened to her—a wandering psychopath or something—especially with the Addison business. But I decided it wasn't so out of character for Anne to just up and go."

"Weren't you bothered that she never got in touch with you? Or did she?"

Collier smiled. "No, Chief Inspector, she didn't. And, yes, it was a bit of a blow to the ego at first. But I got used to it. It wasn't as if we were engaged or living together."

"I noticed you mentioned a moment ago that you linked her disappearance with the Addison killing—a wandering psychopath. Did it occur to you to link the two events in any other way?"

"What do you mean?"

"Could Anne Ralston have had something to do with Addison's visit to Swainshead? He was a private-enquiry agent, after all."

"Yes, I know. But nobody here had any idea why he was in the area. If it was anything to do with Anne, she certainly kept quiet about it. Maybe he was just on holiday. I'm sure private eyes have holidays too."

"Would she have been likely to tell you?"

"I don't know. I don't imagine she told me everything about her life. Ours was a casual relationship. I'd never have expected her to bare her soul."

"Are you sure it wasn't more serious on her part?"

"Not at all. She'd been around."

"And you?"

Stephen smiled. "I wasn't new to the wily ways of the fair sex, no. Another drink?"

Hatchley passed his empty glass and Banks nodded. He lit a Silk Cut and looked out onto the lawn. Two sparrows were taking a bath in the fountain. There was plenty of room, but each defended its territory with an angry flapping of wings, splashing water all over the place. A shadow fell over the patio and Nicholas Collier popped his head around the French windows.

"Hello," he said, stepping into the room. "I thought I heard voices."

"If you don't mind sir . . ." Sergeant Hatchley stood up and blocked the entrance, a task for which he might have been specially designed.

Nicholas tilted his head back and looked down his long nose at Hatchley. "What's going on?"

"I'm just having a little chat with your brother," Banks said. "You're perfectly at liberty to stay, but I'd be obliged if you'd refrain from interrupting."

Nicholas raised his black eyebrows. He seemed to have forgotten his sulking, but he clearly wasn't used to being told what to do. For a moment, anger flashed in his eyes, then he simply nodded and sat by the windows.

"Look," Stephen said, frowning at his brother and coming back with the drinks. "Where on earth is all this leading? Anne Ralston is history now. I haven't seen or heard from her in five years. Quite frankly, it was embarrassing enough at the time having our relationship, such as it was, plastered all over the local papers. I wouldn't like to relive that."

"You mean you didn't know?" Banks said, sipping his Scotch.

"Didn't know what?"

"About Anne Ralston."

"Look here. If this is some kind of a game . . ."

Did he or didn't he? Banks couldn't be sure. Sam Greenock would know the answer to that—when he got home, and if he could be persuaded to talk.

"Anne's turned up again."

"But . . . where?"

"Bernard Allen knew where she was. He told the Greenocks. Surely Sam told you?"

"No. No, I'd no idea. How is she? What happened?"

"I don't know all the details," Banks said. "Just that she's alive and well and living in Canada. Are you sure nobody told you?"

"I've already said so, haven't I? This is a complete surprise to me. Though I was sure she'd turn up somewhere, some day." He went over and poured himself another drink; his hand was shaking. Banks glanced sideways at Nicholas, who sat impassively in his chair. There was no way of telling what he knew or didn't know.

Banks and Hatchley finished their drinks and stood up.

"I'm sorry it came as such a shock, Mr Collier," Banks said. "I just thought you ought to know."

"Yes, of course," Stephen said. "I'm very grateful to you. If you do hear anything else . . ."

"We'll let you know."

"There is just one thing," Stephen said, standing in the doorway. "What has this to do with Bernard Allen's death? Do you see any connection?"

"I don't know, Mr Collier," Banks said. "I really don't know. It does seem like a bit of a coincidence, though—Anne disappearing the day after Addison's killing, then turning up again, so to speak, around the time of Allen's murder. It makes you wonder, doesn't it?"

And they walked back over the bridge, where the three men stood like shadows in the soft light. On impulse, Banks sent Hatchley on ahead and stopped.

"Do you remember Anne Ralston?" he asked the gnarled spokesman.

As was his custom, the man spat in the fledgling River Swain before answering. "Aye. Alus in and out o'there." He nodded over at the Collier house.

"Have you seen her at all over the last few years?"

"Nay. She flitted."

"And she hasn't been back?"

He shook his head.

"Have you seen either Mr or Mrs Greenock go over to the Collier house this afternoon?"

"Aye," the man said. "Sam Greenock went over about three o'clock."

"To see Stephen or Nicholas?"

"It were Mr Stephen's door he knocked on."

"And did Stephen Collier answer it?"

The man scowled. "Aye, course he did."

"How long was Mr Greenock in there?"

"'Baht ten minutes."

"Thank you," Banks said, heading for the guest house. "Thank you very much."

He heard his reluctant informant hack into the beck again, then the murmur of their voices rose up behind him.

III

Katie Greenock hurried away when she saw Banks coming, but he couldn't help noticing that she moved with some difficulty.

"Katie!" he called, hurrying down the hall after her and grasping her elbow.

She spun around and faced him, one hand over her stomach. Her face was white and tense with suppressed pain. "What do you want?" she asked angrily. "Haven't you caused enough trouble?"

"There'll be a lot more before this business is over, Katie. I'm sorry, but there it is. You'll just have to learn to face the world. Anyway, that's not why I called you. What's wrong? You look ill."

"Nothing's wrong."

"You're white as a ghost. And what's wrong with your stomach? Does it ache?"

"What do you care?" she asked, breaking away.

"Is it Sam? Has he hurt you?"

"I don't know what you mean. I've got a tummy-ache, that's all."

"Did you tell Sam you'd told me about Anne?"

"I had to, didn't I? He knew there was something wrong. I'm not good at hiding things."

"And what did he do, beat it out of you?"

"I told you, I've just got a tummy-ache. Leave me alone, I feel sick."

"Where is he?"

She gestured with her head. "In back."

"Will you stay out here for a few minutes, Katie, while I talk to him?"

Katie nodded and edged into the dining-room.

Banks walked down the hall and knocked on the door that separated the Greenocks' part of the house from the rest. Sam let him in.

"Chief Inspector Banks," he said. "What a surprise. I hope nothing's wrong?"

"Has your wife told you we had a little talk earlier today?"

Greenock sat down. "Well, yes. She did right, too. I'm her husband."

"Why didn't you tell me about the Ralston woman earlier, as soon as we found out it was Bernard Allen feeding the maggots up in the hanging valley? This is the second time you've obstructed our investigation, and I'm having serious thoughts about taking you in."

"Now hold on a minute." Sam stood up again and puffed out his chest. "You can't come around here making accusations like that."

"She said she told you that Bernard had met up with Anne Ralston in Canada."

"So?"

"So you should have told me."

"You never asked."

Banks glared at him.

"I didn't think it was relevant. Dammit, Chief Inspector, the woman's been gone for five years."

"You know bloody well how important she is. She's important enough for you to dash out and tell Stephen Collier that Katie had told me what Bernie said. What's going on, Greenock? Just what is your involvement in all this?"

"Nothing," Sam said. "There's nothing going on. I don't know what you're talking about."

"But you did go over to Stephen Collier's this afternoon?"

"So what? We're friends. I dropped by for a drink."

"Did you also dash over a few weeks ago and tell him what Bernie said about Anne Ralston turning up?"

"I didn't tell anyone."

"I think you did. I also think you told him this afternoon that your wife had let the cat out of the bag to me about Anne Ralston. Didn't you?"

"I did no such thing. And you can't prove it either."

"I will prove it," Banks said. "Believe me, I will. And when I do, your feet won't touch the ground."

"You don't scare me," Sam said.

Banks drew closer and Greenock backed towards the wall. They were both about the same size, though Sam was heavier.

"I don't?" Banks said. "Well I bloody well should. Where I come from, we don't always do things by the book. Do you know what I mean?" It was Hatchley's line, Banks knew, but it wasn't as if he was intimidating some scared kid. Sam was a villain, and Banks knew it. His dark eyes glittered with pent-up energy and Sam flinched as he felt his shoulder-blades make contact with the wall.

"Leave me alone!" Sam shouted. "I'll bloody report you, I will."

Banks sneered. "That's a laugh." Then he backed away. "Keep out of my sight, Greenock," he said. "If I want you, I'll know which rock to look under. And when I do, I'll have proof. And if I see or hear any more evidence—even the merest hint—that you've been hurting your wife again, I'll make you bloody sorry you were ever born."

IV

"Will there be anything else, Miss?" the waitress asked, clearing away the empty plate.

"What? Oh, yes. Yes. Another cup of tea, please." Katie Greenock had to pull herself back from a very long way. It would be her third cup, but why not? Let it simply be another part of her little rebellion.

She sat at a table with a red-checked cloth—very clean, she noticed—by the window of the Golden Grill in Eastvale. The narrow street outside was busy with pedestrians, even in the thin drizzle, and almost directly opposite her was the whitewashed building with the black beams and the incongruous white-on-blue sign over the entrance: POLICE.

It was early Monday afternoon, and she didn't know what she was doing in Eastvale. Already she was beginning to feel guilty. It was simply a minor gesture, she tried to convince herself, but her conscience invested it with the magnitude of Satan's revolt.

That morning, at about eleven o'clock, she had felt so claustrophobic cleaning the rooms that she just had to get out—not only out of the house, but out of Swainshead itself for a while. Walking aimlessly down the street, she had met Beryl Vickers, a neighbour she occasionally talked gardening with, and accepted her offer of a ride into Eastvale for a morning's shopping. Beryl was visiting her sister there, so Katie was left free to wander by herself for a few hours. After buying some lamb chops and broccoli at the indoor market for that evening's dinner, she had found the Golden Grill and decided to rest her feet.

She had only been sitting there for fifteen minutes when she saw three men come out of the pub next door and hurry through the rain back into the police station. Two of them she recognized— the lean, dark inspector and his fair, heavy sergeant—but the young athletic-looking one with the droopy moustache and the curious loping walk was new to her. For a moment, she thought they were sure to glance over their shoulders and see her through the window, so she covered the side of her face with her hand. They didn't even look.

As soon as she saw the inspector, she felt again the bruises that Sam had inflicted on her the previous afternoon. She knew it wasn't the policeman's fault—in fact, he seemed like a kind man—but she couldn't help the association any more than she could help feeling one between room five and what she had let Bernie do to her.

"What's wrong with you?" Sam had asked when he came home.

Katie had tried to hide her red-rimmed eyes from him, but he grasped her chin between his thumb and forefinger and asked her again. That was when she told him the police had been back and the inspector had interrogated her so hard she couldn't hide it from him any more.

Sam had hit the roof.

"But it's not that important," Katie protested. "It can't be!"

"That's not for you to say," Sam argued. He threw up his hands. "You stupid bloody bitch, have you any idea what trouble you might have caused?"

Though she was scared, Katie still felt defiant. "What do you mean, trouble?" she asked, her lower lip trembling. "Trouble for who?"

"For everyone, that's for who."

"For your precious Colliers, I'll bet." As she said it, her image was of Nicholas, not Stephen.

And that was when Sam hit her the first time, a short sharp blow to the stomach. She doubled up in pain, and when she was able to stand again he thumped her left breast. That hurt even more. She collapsed on the sofa and Sam stood over her. His face was red and he was breathing funny, in short gasps that seemed to catch in his throat. "If we make something of ourselves in this place," he said, "it won't be any thanks to you."

He didn't hit her any more. He knew when enough was enough. But later that night, in bed, the same cruel hands grasped the same wounded breast. He pulled her roughly to him, and there was nothing she could do about it. Katie shuddered, trying to shake off the memory.

"Will that be all?" the waitress asked, standing over her again.

"Oh, yes. Yes, thank you," Katie said, paying the bill. Awkwardly, aware of the ache in her breast and the Black Forest gâteau sitting uneasily in her sore stomach, she made her way out into the street. She had one more hour of freedom to wander in the rain before meeting Beryl near the bus station at two-thirty. Then she would have to go home and face the music.

V

After a pub lunch in the Queen's Arms and a chat with Hatchley and Richmond about the case, Banks was no further ahead. Back in his office, he sat down, sent for some coffee, and put his feet up on the desk to think things out. When PC Craig arrived with the coffee—looking very put out, no doubt because Susan Gay had coerced him into carrying it up—Banks lit a Silk Cut and went over what he'd got.

Richmond had discovered that Les Haines, Bernie Allen's brother-in-law, had done a brief stretch in Armley Jail for receiving stolen goods (i.e. two boxes of Sony E-120 video cassette tapes). It was his second offence, hot on the heels of an assault charge against a man in the alley outside a Leeds bier-keller. But Haines had been at work on the day of Allen's murder, so he would have had no opportunity to get to Swainshead and back, even if there had been some obscure family motive. Besides, as Banks well knew, just because a man has a record as a petty thief, it doesn't make him a murderer. Esther had been home with the kids, as usual, and

Banks could hardly visualize her trailing them up to the hanging valley and knocking off her brother.

Most interesting of all were the Colliers' alibis, or lack of them. Nicholas never taught classes on Friday mornings, but he usually went in anyway and used the time for paperwork. On the Friday in question, however, the headmaster's administrative assistant remembered seeing him arrive late—at around eleven o'clock. This was nothing unusual—it had happened often enough before—but it did leave him without a valid alibi.

Stephen Collier, it turned out, had no meetings scheduled for that day, again quite normal in itself, and nobody could remember whether he had been in or not. Work days, the world-weary secretary had explained to Sergeant Hatchley, are so much the same that most office workers have difficulty remembering one from another. Mr Collier was often off the premises anyway, and the people who actually ran the business never saw much of him.

PC Weaver from Helmthorpe, who had been questioning people in Swainshead that morning, reported that nobody remembered seeing Bernard Allen out there on the morning in question, let alone noticed anyone follow him.

At about two o'clock, Richmond popped his head around the door. He'd been using the computer to check with various business agencies and immigration offices, but so far he'd found no-one in Swainshead with Canadian connections. Except for Stephen Collier, who dealt with a Montreal-based food-products corporation.

"What's a food product, do you think?" Banks asked Richmond.

"I wouldn't know, sir. Something that's not real food, I'd imagine."

"And I thought he was trading Wensleydale cheese for maple syrup. That reminds me: what time is it in Toronto?"

Richmond looked at his watch. "It'll be about nine in the morning."

"I'd better phone the Mounties."

"Er . . . they won't be Mounties, sir. Not in Toronto." Richmond stroked his moustache.

"Oh? What will they be?"

"The Toronto Metropolitan Police, sir. The RCMP's federal. These days they mostly do undercover work and police the more remote areas."

Banks grinned. "Well, you learn something new every day."

When Richmond had left, he lit a cigarette and picked up the phone. There was a lot of messing about with the switchboard, but after a few minutes of clicks and whirrs, the phone started ringing at the other end. It wasn't the harsh and insistent sound of an English telephone, though; the rings were longer, as were the pauses between them.

When someone finally answered, it took Banks a while to explain who he was and what he wanted. After a few more clicks, he finally got through to the right man.

"Chief Inspector Banks? Staff Sergeant Gregson here. And how's the old country?"

"Fine," said Banks, a little perplexed by the question.

"My father was a Brit," Gregson went on. "Came from Derbyshire." He pronounced the "e" as in "clergy," and "shire" came out as "sheer." "Do you know it?" he asked.

"Oh, yes. It's just down the road."

"Small country."

"Right."

Gregson cleared his throat and Banks could hear papers rustling three thousand miles away. "I can't say we've got any good news for you," the Canadian said. "We've had a look around Allen's apartment, but we didn't find anything unusual."

"Was there an address book?"

"Address book . . . let me see . . ." More paper rustled. "No. No address book. No diary."

"Damn. He must have taken them with him."

"Makes sense, doesn't it? If he was going on vacation he'd be sure to want to send pretty postcards to all his buddies back home."

"What about his friends? Have you seen any of them?"

"We talked to his colleagues at work. There's not many of them around. College finishes in early May, so teachers are pretty thin on the ground at this time of year. Nice work if you can get it, eh? Now they're all off swimming in the lake and sunning themselves on the deck up at their fancy summer cottages in Muskoka."

"Is that like a villa in Majorca?"

"Huh?"

"Never mind. What did they have to say?"

"Said he was a bit aloof, stand-offish. Course, a lot of Brits over here are like that. They think Canada's still part of the Empire, so they come on like someone out of 'The Jewel in the Crown.'"

"Did you find his ex-wife?"

"Yup. She's been in Calgary for the past six months, so you can count her out."

"Apparently, there was a lover," Banks told him. "Someone at the college. That's why they got divorced."

"Have you got a name?"

"Sorry."

Gregson sighed. "I'd like to help you, Chief Inspector, I really would," he said. "But we can't spare the men to go tracking down some guy who ran off with Allen's wife. We just don't have the manpower."

"No, of course not."

"Besides, people don't usually steal a man's wife and then kill him."

"They might if he was causing them problems. But you're right, it's not likely. Did he have any girlfriends?"

"As I said, his colleagues thought he was a bit stuck-up. One of them even thought he was gay, but I wouldn't pay much mind to that. Sometimes, with their accents and mannerisms and all, Brits do seem a bit that way to us North Americans."

"Yes," Banks said, gritting his teeth. "I think that just about covers it all. I can see now why they say you always get your man." And he hung up. Nothing. Still nothing. He obviously couldn't expect any help from across the Atlantic.

Still feeling a residue of irrational anger at Gregson's sarcasm, he stalked over to the window and lit a cigarette. The drizzle had turned into steady rain now and the square below was bright with open umbrellas. As he gazed down on the scene, one woman caught his eye. She walked in a daze, as if she wasn't sure where she was heading. She looked soaked to the skin, too; her hair was plastered to her head and the thin white blouse she wore was moulded to her form so that the outline of her brassiere stood out in clear relief. It took Banks a few moments to recognize Katie Greenock.

He grabbed his raincoat and made a move to go down and make sure she was all right, but when he looked out for her one last time, she was nowhere in sight. She had disappeared like a phantom. There was no sense in searching the town for her just because she was walking in the rain without an umbrella. Still, he was strangely disturbed by the vision. It worried him. For the rest of the wet afternoon he felt haunted by that slight and sensuous figure staring into an inner distance, walking in the rain.

PART TWO:

THE
THOUSAND-DOLLAR
CURE

EIGHT

I

The powerful jet engines roared and Banks felt himself pushed back in his seat. It was his first time in a Jumbo. The plane lumbered along the runway at Manchester International Airport, fixtures and fittings shaking and rattling, as if defying anyone to believe that a machine of such bulk could fly. But it did. Soon, Lancashire was a checkerboard of wet fields, then it was lost completely under the clouds. The NO SMOKING sign went off and Banks lit up.

In a few moments, the blue-uniformed flight-attendant with her shocking pink lipstick and impossibly white teeth—the same one who had managed to put such drama into the routine demonstration of the use of the life-jacket—came around with more boiled sweets and personal headphones in plastic bags. Banks took a set, as he knew there would be a film later on, but he gave the designer music a miss and took out his own Walkman. Soon the plane was over Ireland, an occasional flash of green between the clouds, the Beatles were singing "Dear Prudence," and all was well with the world.

Banks ordered Scotch on the rocks when the trolley came around and relaxed with his miniature Johnny Walker Red. Closing his eyes, he settled back to reconsider the events that had led to his present unnatural position—about 35,000 feet above the Atlantic Ocean, hurtling at a speed of roughly 600 miles an hour towards a strange continent.

It was Saturday, July 3, almost a month since the Bernard Allen case had stalled. Banks had visited Swainshead once or twice and found things relatively quiet. Stephen and Nicholas Collier had remained polite in their arrogant way; Sam Greenock had been surly, as usual; Katie Greenock still seemed troubled and distracted; and John Fletcher had expressed passing interest in the progress of the case.

The problem was that there really wasn't a case any more. Enquiries had turned up neither new witnesses nor motives. A number of people had the opportunity to kill Bernard Allen, but no-one had a clear reason. As long as the suspects stuck to their stories, it didn't matter whether they were lying or telling the truth; there was no solid evidence to break the case. That was why it was vital for Banks to find Anne Ralston—she was the link between the Addison and Allen murders—and he had convinced Gristhorpe he could do it in a week.

"How?" the superintendent had asked. "Toronto's a strange city to you. A big one, too."

"Where would you head if you were an Englishman living abroad?"

Gristhorpe rubbed his chin. "I'd seek out the expatriate community, I suppose. The 'club.' I'd want to be among my own."

"Right. So, given we're not dealing with the gentry, I'd expect Allen to hang around the English-style pubs. Every big city has them. His brother-in-law, Les Haines, told me Allen liked his ale and had found a pub where he could get imported British beer. There can't be all that many of them in Toronto."

"But it's Anne Ralston we're looking for, remember that."

"I know. I'm just assuming that if Allen was a bit stand-offish with his mates at work, he had a crowd of fellow *émigrés* he hung around with in his spare time. The odds are they'd meet up in a pub and stand at the bar quaffing pints. They might know the Ralston woman."

"So you want to go on a pub-crawl of Toronto?"

"Looks like it, doesn't it?"

"Better not tell Jim Hatchley or you'll get nowt out of him for a month or more. Why can't you get the Toronto police to find her?"

"For a start, I got the impression on the phone that they didn't have time or didn't give a damn, or both. And anyway, they wouldn't know how to question her, what to ask. Someone would

have to brief them on two murder investigations, the sociology of
the Yorkshire village, the history of—"

Gristhorpe held up his hand. "All right, all right, I get the
point."

"And I think they'd scare her off, too," Banks added. "She was
nervous enough about what she knew to warn Allen not to spread
it around, so if she thinks the police are after her, the odds are she'll
scarper."

"Have you considered that she might not be using her own
name?"

"Yes. But I've got her photograph from our missing person
files—it's a bit old, but it's all we've got—and I think I know where
to look. Being English myself gives me an advantage in that kind of
environment, too. Do you think it makes sense?"

"It's all a bit iffy, but yes, yes I do, on the whole. If you can track
down Allen's drinking companions, there's a good chance he'll have
told them about Anne Ralston. She might even drop in at his local
herself from time to time, if she's the kind that likes to be among
her own."

"So you'll see what you can do about getting me over there?"

Gristhorpe nodded. "Aye. I'll see what I can do."

About a week later, on a Thursday morning, the superintendent
had asked Banks to drop by his office. Banks stubbed out his cigarette and carried his full coffee mug carefully along the corridor. As
usual, Gristhorpe's door was slightly ajar. Banks nudged it open
with his shoulder and entered the cosy, book-lined room. He took
his usual seat and put his coffee on the desk in front of him.

Gristhorpe pushed a long envelope over the blotter.

"You've done it?"

"Open it."

Inside was a return ticket on a charter flight from Manchester to
Toronto.

"There's an important international conference on policing the
inner city in London, Ontario. I thought you ought to go."

"But this ticket's for Toronto."

"Aye, well, there isn't an international airport in London."

"And Eastvale doesn't have an inner city."

Gristhorpe scratched his hooked nose. "We might have, one day. We did have a riot a few months ago, didn't we? It pays to be prepared."

"Will you be expecting a report?"

"Oh, a brief verbal account will do."

Banks grinned.

"There's one catch, though."

"Oh?"

"Money. All I could scrounge was the ticket and a bit of loose change for meals. You'll have to supply most of your own pocket money."

"That's all right. I'm not likely to be spending a fortune. What about accommodation, though?"

"You'll be staying with my nephew—at least, you can stay in his apartment. He's off to Banff or some such place for the summer. Anyway, I've been in touch and he says he'll be happy to meet you at the airport. I described you to him, so just stand around and look lost. He's rather a lanky lad, as I remember. His hair's a bit too long and he wears those silly little glasses—granny-glasses, I think they're called. He's a nice enough lad—graduate student, organic chemistry or some such thing. He says he lives downtown, what-ever that means. You told me a week, Alan. I'm depending on you."

"I'll do my best," Banks said, pocketing the ticket.

"Find Anne Ralston and discover what she knows. I don't care how you do it, outside of torture. And for Christ's sake keep away from the local police. They wouldn't appreciate your trespassing on their patch. You're a tourist, remember that."

"I've been wondering why you're sending me," Banks said. "You're very much concerned with this case yourself, especially the connection with the Addison murder. Why don't *you* go?"

"I would," Gristhorpe said slowly. "Believe me, I would." He looked sideways towards the open window. "I did my National Service in the RAF. I'd always hero-worshipped fighter pilots in the war and I suppose, in my folly, I wanted to be just like them. First time up one of the engines caught fire. If the pilot hadn't been so damn good we'd have both been dead. Even so . . . I've never fancied the idea since."

"I can't say I blame you," Banks said. "I'll find her, don't worry. At least I've an idea where to look."

And that was that. Sandra and the children were excited and, of course, disappointed that they couldn't go with him. Sergeant Hatchley acted as if Banks had been given a free holiday in an exotic place. And now here he was, high above the Atlantic Ocean, the pink lips and white teeth leaning over him with a tray of cling-wrapped food.

Banks took off his headphones and arranged the tray in front of him. The main course appeared to be a small, shrivelled chicken leg with pale, wrinkled skin, accompanied by tiny potatoes and carrots covered in gravy. On further inspection, Banks discovered that one-half of the meal was piping hot and the other still frozen solid. He called the attendant, who apologized profusely and took it away. When she delivered it again, the frozen side was warm and the other overcooked. Banks took a few mouthfuls and gave up in disgust. He also felt no inclination to investigate the mound of jelly-like substance with a swirl of cream on its top, or the limp, wet lettuce leaves that passed for a salad. Instead, he turned to his cheese and crackers which, being wrapped in cellophane, were at least fresh, and washed them down with a small plastic bottle of harsh red wine.

Feeling the onset of heartburn, Banks declined the offer of coffee and lit a cigarette. After the trays had been cleared, more drinks came. They really were very generous, Banks thought, and wondered what havoc a plane full of drunks might wreak—especially if the booze ran out. But it didn't. He was kept well supplied with Johnny Walker Red—a kind of sedation, he guessed, insurance against restless and troublesome passengers—and soon people were asked to pull down their blinds against the blazing sunlight in preparation for the movie. This turned out to be a dreadful cops-and-robbers affair full of car chases and shoot-outs in shopping precincts. After about ten minutes, Banks put his headset aside, closed his eyes and went over in his mind the questions he wanted to ask Anne Ralston. The jet engines were humming, the Scotch warmed his veins, and soon he fell into a deep sleep. The last thing he remembered was the crackly voice of the pilot saying they were soon going to reach the tip of Newfoundland and would then fly along the St Lawrence River.

II

While Banks was asleep somewhere over Quebec City, Detective Superintendent Gristhorpe sat hunched over a pint of Theakston's bitter and a veal-and-egg pie in the Queen's Arms, waiting for Sergeant Hatchley.

Frowning, he looked at his watch. He'd told Hatchley to arrive no later than seven-thirty. He glanced out of the window at the market square, but saw no sign of the sergeant. It was still raining. That very morning the clouds had closed in again, draining the valley-sides of their lush greens and flattening the majestic perspective of fells and moors.

At last Hatchley burst in and looked anxiously around for the superintendent. His hair was slicked down by the rain, emphasizing the bullet shape of his head, and the shoulders of his beige trench coat were splotched dark with wet patches.

"Sorry, sir," he apologized, sitting opposite Gristhorpe. "The damn weather's slowing traffic down all along the dale."

Gristhorpe could smell the beer on his breath and guessed that he'd probably stopped for a quick one in Helmthorpe on his way— or maybe he had even made a minor diversion to the Black Sheep in Relton, where the landlord brewed his own prize-winning beer on the premises. He said nothing, though. Without Banks around, Hatchley and Richmond were all he had, and he had no wish to alienate the sergeant before putting his plan into action.

Gristhorpe accepted Hatchley's offer of another pint and leaned back in his seat to avoid the drift of smoke when the sergeant lit a cigarette.

"Did you tell them?" Gristhorpe asked.

"Aye, sir. Found them all in the White Rose."

"I hope you weren't too obvious."

Hatchley looked offended. "No, sir. I did it just like you said. When Freddie Metcalfe started probing and prodding about why I was there, I just told him it was a few loose ends I had to tie up, that's all."

"And then?"

"Ah, well. Then, sir, I got myself invited over to the table. It was all very casual, like, chatting about the cricket and the local markets as if we was old mates. Then Sam Greenock asked me where my boss was."

"What did you say?"

"Just what you told me, sir. I said he'd gone off to Toronto to talk to Anne Ralston."

"And?"

"And what, sir?"

"What happened next, man? How did they react?"

Hatchley took a long pull at his beer and wiped his lips with the back of his hairy hand. "Oh, they just looked at one another and raised their eyebrows a bit."

"Can you be a bit more specific, Sergeant? What did Sam Greenock say?"

"He didn't really say anything. Seemed excited to hear the news. I got the impression it made him a bit angry. And Stephen Collier went distinctly a bit pale. That poncy brother of his just looked down his nose like I was something the cat dragged in."

"Who else was there?"

"Only John Fletcher."

"Did he react in any way?"

Hatchley scratched his ear. "I'd say he got a bit tight-lipped. You wouldn't really say he reacted, but it was as if it rang a bell somewhere and sent him off in his own world. More puzzled and worried than anything else."

Gristhorpe thought over the information and filed it away in his mind. "Good work, Sergeant," he said finally. "You did well."

Hatchley nodded and started casually rocking his empty pint glass on the table. "What now, sir?" he asked.

"We keep an eye on them. Tomorrow I'm going to send DC Richmond to stay at the Greenock Guest House for a few days. I don't think his face is well known in Swainshead." Gristhorpe turned up his nose and leaned forward to grind out Hatchley's cigarette butt, which still smouldered in the ashtray. "We keep an eye on them," he repeated. "And we watch very carefully for one of them to make a slip or try and make a run for it. All right, Sergeant. You don't have to break the bloody glass on the table. I know it's my round. Same again?"

III

Somewhere, with maddening metronomic regularity, a bell was ringing. Banks rubbed his eyes and saw the seat-belt sign was lit up. The NO SMOKING sign was still out, so he lit a cigarette immediately to clear his head. Looking out of the window, he saw a vast urban area below. It was too far down to distinguish details, but he could make out the grid system of roads and fancied he could see cars flash in the sun.

The attendant said something over the PA system about a final descent, and passengers were then asked to extinguish their cigarettes. Banks's ears felt funny. He swallowed and yawned to clear them, and the noise of the plane roared in again. All the way down he had to keep repeating the process every few seconds.

The plane banked to the left and now individual buildings and moving vehicles stood out quite clearly. After a long turn, a great expanse of water came into sight on the right and a cluster of tall buildings appeared on the waterside. The plane was dropping quickly now, and within moments it touched the runway smoothly. The loud retro-jets kicked in. They felt like ropes tied to the back of the plane, dragging it to a halt. Several nervous passengers applauded.

After some delay, the doors slid open and the slow line of people left the aircraft, running a gauntlet of fixed smiles from the attendants. Banks negotiated the stairs and corridors, then found himself in a long queue at Immigration. After that, there was another wait until the baggage came around on the carousel. Clutching his small suitcase, duty-free Scotch and cigarettes, he walked past the customs officers, who paid him no mind, and out into the throng of people waiting to welcome friends and relatives.

As Gristhorpe suggested, he stood to one side and looked lost. It was easy.

Soon he noticed an Adam's apple the size of a tennis ball stuck in a long skinny neck below a head covered with long brown hair making its way through the crowd. As the head also wore a pair of ridiculously old-fashioned granny-glasses, Banks risked a wave of recognition.

"Gerry Webb," the man said, shaking hands. "Are you Chief Inspector Banks?"

"Yes. Just call me Alan. I'm not here officially."

"I'll bet," Gerry said. "Come on, let's get out of here."

They pushed their way through the crowds of relatives embracing long-lost children or parents, and took a lift to the multi-storey car-park.

"This is it," Gerry said, pointing proudly to a saffron Volkswagen bug. "I call her 'Sneezy' because she's a bit of a dwarf compared to most of the cars here, and she makes a funny noise when I try to start her in mornings, especially during winter. Still, she gets me around." He patted Sneezy on the bonnet and opened the boot at the front. Case and duty-free securely stored, Banks got in the passenger door after a false start on the left.

"It always happens when people visit from England," Gerry said, laughing. "Without fail. Just wait until you try and cross the road."

The first things Banks noticed as Gerry drove out onto the expressway were the huge cars and the stifling heat. It was like trying to breathe at the bottom of a warm bath. In no time, his shirt was stuck to his skin. He took off his jacket and tossed it on the back seat. Even the draught through the open window was hot and wet.

"You've come in the middle of a heat wave, I'm afraid," Gerry explained. "It's been between thirty-three and thirty-six degrees for the past three days now. Above ninety percent humidity, too."

"What's a hundred like?"

"Funny, that," Gerry said. "We never get a hundred. Not even during a thunderstorm. Summer can be a real bitch here. Toronto's a city of extremes as far as climate is concerned. In winter it's bloody cold, real brass-monkey weather, and in summer it's so hot and humid it's unbearable, as you can tell. Pollution count goes way up, too."

"What about spring?"

"We don't have one. Just a lot of rain and then the sun. Fall's the best. September, October. Warmish days, cool evenings. Beautiful." He glanced sideways at Banks. "I suppose you were expecting icicles and snowmen?"

"Not exactly. But I didn't expect the heat to be this bad."

"You should see the Americans," Gerry said. "I lived in Windsor for a while when I was doing my MSc, and I worked for customs during summer. They'd come over the border from the Detroit suburbs in the middle of July with skis on top of their cars and fur coats on the back seats. What a laugh that was. Americans know bugger all about Canada."

"I can't say I know much, myself," Banks admitted.

"Worry not. Keep your eyes and ears open and all will be revealed." Gerry had an odd accent, part Yorkshire and part North American, with a mixed vocabulary to match.

They swung eastwards around a bay. For a moment, Banks thought they were on the wrong side of the road. He tensed and the adrenalin prickled in his veins. Then, again, he realized he was in Canada.

On the right was Lake Ontario, a ruffled blue sheet with millions of diamonds dancing on it. The white triangular sails of yachts leaned at sharp angles. There seemed to be at least a cooler breeze coming from the water and Banks envied the idle rich who could spend their days sailing like that.

"Those are the Islands over there," Gerry said, pointing towards a low hazy blur of green. "They're just a long sandbar really, but everyone calls them islands. People live on the far ones, Ward's and Algonquin, but the politicians want to chuck them off and make a heliport or a mini golf-course."

"That sounds typical," Banks said, recalling the various schemes for developing adventure playgrounds and safari parks in the Dales.

"A lot of trouble over it," Gerry said. "At first, the islanders even got themselves a Home Guard organized—hard hats, the lot. They were prepared to fight off an invasion."

"What happened?"

"It's still going on really. Oh, various bright sparks come up with ideas for long-term leases and what-not, but there's always trouble brewing. It's jealousy, I think. Most of the people who live there now are academics or artists and a lot of people stuck in the city envy them their lives. They think only the filthy rich ought to be able to afford such a pleasant environment."

"What about you?"

"I don't envy anyone who survives winter after winter out there in not much more than a wooden shack. Look." He pointed ahead.

In front of them a cluster of tall buildings shimmered in the heat like a dot-matrix block-graph. A few were black, others white, and some even reflected the deep gold of the sun. Close to the lake, dominating them all, was a tapering tower with a bulbous head just below its long needle-point summit. It was a phallic symbol of such Olympian proportions that it made the London Post Office Tower look like it had a serious sexual dysfunction.

"The CN Tower," Gerry said. "Toronto's pride and joy. Tallest free-standing structure in the world—or at least it will be until the Japanese build a bigger one. See those elevators going up the outside?"

Banks did. The mere thought of being in one made him feel dizzy. He wasn't afraid of heights up to a certain point, but he'd never felt like risking a meal in a revolving restaurant at the top of a tower.

"What's it for?" he asked.

"Well may you ask. For show really."

"What's at the top?"

"A restaurant, what else? And a disco, of course. This is the height of western civilization. A feat on a par with the great pyramids and Chartres Cathedral."

"A disco?"

"Yes. Honest. Oh, I suppose I'm being flippant. They do use the place as a radio- and TV-signal transmitter, but it's basically just one of man's muscle-flexing exercises. This is downtown."

The expressway, on a kind of elevated ramp, rolled past the backs of warehouses and billboards. Because the buildings were so close, the speed the car was travelling at was exaggerated and Banks felt as if he was on a roller coaster.

Finally, Gerry branched off, drove through an industrial waste-land of dirty old factories with external plumbing, then turned onto a busy street. Most of the buildings seemed quite old and run-down, and Banks soon noticed that nearly all the shop-signs were in Chinese. Roast ducks hung by their feet in shop windows and teeming stalls of colourful fruit and vegetables blocked the pave-ments in front of grocery stores. One shop displayed a handwritten sign offering a mysterious combination of "LIVE CRABS & VIDEOS." The street was bustling with people, mostly Chinese, pushing and shoving to get to the best deals, picking up and examining wares. The rich smell of food gone bad in the heat, mingled with the aroma of exotic spices, drifted into the car along with the suffocating air. A red-and-cream tram rattled along its track beside them.

"Chinatown East," Gerry said. "Not far to go now."

He continued up the street past a prison and a hospital. To the left was a broad green valley. Beside the road, it sloped like a huge lawn down to the broad bottom, where a busy expressway ran beside the brown river. Above the trees on the far side, the down-town towers shimmered, greyish blurs in the heat-haze. Gerry turned right into a tree-lined street and pulled up in the driveway of a small brick house with a green-and-white porch.

"Home," he announced. "I've got the bottom floor and there's a young couple upstairs. They're generally pretty quiet, so I wouldn't worry too much about noise." He put his key in the lock and opened the door. "Come on in. I'm dying for a cold beer."

The place was small and sparsely furnished—apparently with cast-offs bought from second-hand shops—but it was clean and comfortable. Books stuffed every possible shelf and cavity. The Gristhorpe clan certainly seemed to be great readers, Banks thought.

Gerry led him into the small kitchen and took two cans of Budweiser from the fridge. Banks pulled the tab and poured the iced, slightly malty beer down his throat. When Gerry tipped back his can to drink, his Adam's apple bobbed wildly.

"That's better," he said, wiping his lips. "I'm sorry it's so hot in here, too, but I can't afford an air-conditioner. Actually, I've lived in worse places. There's a good through-draft, and it does cool down a bit at night."

"What's this area of town called?" Banks asked.

"Riverdale. It's gone very yuppie in the past few years. Property values have shot up like crazy. You'll see the main drag, the Danforth, if you walk or take a streetcar up to the corner. It used to be all Greek cafés, restaurants and twenty-four-hour fruit-and-vegetable stores. Now it's all health foods, late-night bookshops, and bistros with long-stemmed wineglasses and coral pink table-cloths. All right if you like that kind of thing, I suppose."

"And if you don't?"

"There's a few unpretentious places left. You get some good blues at the Black Swan on Saturday afternoons. And then there's Quinn's, not a bad pub. Some of the old Greek places are still around, but I can't say I've ever been fond of Greek food myself—it's all greasy lamb, eggplant and sticky desserts as far as I'm concerned."

They sat down on the sofa, an overstuffed, maroon fifties monstrosity with arms like wings, and finished their beers.

"Your uncle said you had to go to a conference somewhere," Banks said. "I hope I'm not driving you out?"

"Not at all. Actually, the conference isn't so important, but Banff is a great place—right on the edge of the Rockies—so I'll get a bit of hiking and partying done too."

"How are you getting there?"

"Sneezy."

"How far is it?"

"A couple of thousand miles. But you get used to distances like that here. Sneezy's done it before. She quite likes long journeys. I'll take my tent and camp out on the way. If you need a car . . ."

Banks shook his head. "No. No, I wouldn't dare drive on the wrong side of the road. What's the public transport like?"

"Very good. There's a subway, buses, and the streetcars you've seen. We don't call them trams here."

"I was surprised," Banks said. "I haven't been on one of them since I was a kid."

"Well now's your chance to make up for lost time. I use them a lot myself to get around the city. Often it's not worth the bother of parking in town, and the cops can be pretty sticky about drinking and driving. Oops, sorry."

Banks laughed.

"Anyway," Gerry went on, delving into a drawer and bringing out a couple of maps. "This is the city—easy to find your way about as it's mostly an east-west, north-south grid system. And here's the transit map. It's not as complicated as the London Underground, so you shouldn't have much trouble."

And Gerry went on giving information about subway tokens and free transfers from one mode of transport to another. But after the journey and in the sweltering heat, Banks felt his eyes closing. He could do nothing about it.

"Here," Gerry said, "I'm boring you to death. I don't suppose you're taking any of this in."

"Not much."

"Do you want to go to bed?"

"I wouldn't mind a nap."

Gerry showed him the bedroom.

"Isn't this your room?" Banks asked.

"It's okay. I'll bed down on the couch tonight."

"I can do that."

"Not necessary. I'm off early in the morning anyway. This'll be your room for the next week."

Too tired to argue more and, frankly, grateful for a bed, Banks undressed, sank onto the mattress and fell asleep within seconds.

When he woke he was disoriented at finding himself in an unfamiliar bed. It took him a few moments to remember where he was. It was hot and dark, and the sheets felt moist with sweat. Hearing sounds in the front room, Banks rubbed his eyes, pulled on his pants and walked through. He found Gerry stuffing clothes into a huge backpack. For a moment, it made him think of Bernard Allen.

"Hi," Gerry said. "I thought you were out for the count."

"What time is it?"

"Ten o'clock. Three in the morning, your time."

"I just woke up suddenly. I don't know why."

"Jet lag does funny things like that. It's much worse going the other way."

"Wonderful."

Gerry grinned. "Beer?"

"Any chance of a cup of tea?"

"Sure. We're not all coffee-drinking barbarians out here, you know."

Gerry switched on the TV set and went into the kitchen. Banks sank into the sofa and put his feet up on a battered pouffe. A pretty woman was talking very intensely about a debate in the House of Commons. Again Banks felt the shock of being in a foreign land. The TV newscaster spoke with an odd accent—less overbearing than the Americans he had heard—and he knew none of the politicians' names.

Gerry brought the tea and sat beside him.

"There might be a couple of things you can help me with," Banks said.

"Shoot."

"Where can I find Toronto Community College?"

"Easy. The subway's the quickest." And Gerry told him how to get to Broadview station by streetcar or on foot, where to change trains, and where to get off.

"There's another thing. Do you know anything about the English-style pubs in town? Somewhere that sells imported beer."

Gerry laughed. "You've certainly got your work cut out. There's dozens of them. The Madison, The Sticky Wicket, Paupers, the Hop and Grape, the Artful Dodger, The Jack Russell, The Spotted Dick, The Feathers, Quigley's, not to mention a whole dynasty of Dukes. I'll try and make a list for you. What's it all about, by the way, if that's not top secret?"

"I'm looking for a woman. Her name's Anne Ralston."

"What's she done?"

"Nothing, as far as I know."

"How very secretive. You're as bad as Uncle Eb, you are."

"Who?"

"Uncle Eb. You mean you don't know . . . ?"

Banks shook his head. Gristhorpe had never mentioned his first name, and his signature was an indecipherable scrawl.

"Well maybe I shouldn't tell you. He won't thank me for it, if I know him."

"I won't tell him I know. Scout's honour. Come on."

"It's short for Ebenezer, of course."

Banks whistled through his teeth. "No wonder he never lets on."

"Ah, but that's not all. His father was a grand champion of the labouring man, especially the farm workers, so he called his oldest son Ebenezer Elliott—after the 'Corn Law Rhymer.'"

Banks had never heard of Ebenezer Elliott but made a mental note to look him up. He was always interested in new things to read, look at or listen to.

"Ebenezer Elliott Gristhorpe," he repeated to himself. "Bloody hell."

"Thought you'd like that," Gerry said, grinning. "It does have a certain ring to it, doesn't it? My poor mum got lumbered with Mary Wollstonecraft. Very progressive Grandad was, respected the rights of women, too. But my dad was plain old George Webb, and thank the Lord he'd no hobby-horse to tie his kids to."

On the news, a gang of street kids in Belfast threw stones and tossed Molotov cocktails at police in riot gear. It was night, and orange flames blossomed all along the street. Black smoke rose from burning tires. The world really was a global village, Banks thought, feeling his attention start to slip. Consciousness was fading away again. He yawned and put down his teacup on the low table.

"You can tell me something now," Gerry said. "Where did you get that scar?"

Banks fingered the white scar by his right eye. "This? I passed out from lack of sleep and hit my head on the corner of a table."

Gerry laughed. "I get the point. I'm keeping you up."

Banks smiled. "I'm definitely falling asleep again. See you in the morning?"

"Probably not," Gerry said. "I've got a long way to go and I'm setting off at the crack of dawn. There's coffee and sugar in the cupboard above the sink. Milk and stuff's in the fridge. Here's a spare door-key. Make yourself at home."

Banks shook his bony hand. "Thanks," he said. "I will. And if you're ever in England . . ."

"I'll be sure to visit Uncle Ebenezer. I always do. And we'll have a jar or two in the Queen's Arms. Goodnight."

Banks went back into the bedroom. A light breeze had sprung up to ease the suffocating heat a little, but it was still far from comfortable. He flopped down on the damp sheets. Outside, a short distance away, he heard a streetcar rattle by and remembered exciting childhood trips to big cities when the trams were still running. He thought of the Queen's Arms on the edge of sleep, and pictured the pub on the corner of Market Street and the cobbled square. He felt very far from home. The Queen's Arms was a long, long way away, and there was a lot to do if he was to track down Anne Ralston before the week was over.

NINE

I

They were going to church: the women smiling in their wide-brimmed hats and cotton-print dresses, the men ill at ease in tight ties and pinching waistcoats.

Every Sunday morning Katie watched them as she cleaned the rooms, and every week she knew she should be with them, dragging Sam along with the promise of an hour in the pub for him later while she cooked dinner. But he went to the pub anyway, and she cooked dinner anyway. The only thing missing was the hour in church. And that she couldn't face.

All through her childhood, Katie had been forced to go to the Gospel with her grandmother, and the icy devotion of the congregation had scared her half to death. Though they were praising God, they hardly dared sing so loud for fear He would think they were taking pleasure in the hymns. Katie could never understand the readings or the lessons, but she understood the passionate menace in the tones of those who spoke; she understood the meaning of the spittle that sometimes dribbled over their lips, and the way their eyes glazed over. As she grew older, all her fear affixed itself to the sights, sounds and smells of the church: the chill mustiness rising from worn stone flags; the pews creaking as a bored child shifts position; the unearthly echo of the minister's voice; the wooden board announcing the hymn numbers; the stained glass fragmenting colour like broken souls. Just thirty seconds in a church meant panic for Katie; she couldn't breathe, she started trembling, and her blood turned to stone.

But she knew she should go. It was, after all, God's Mansion on Earth, and she would never escape this Vale of Tears if she didn't

give herself to Him completely. Instead, she watched the rest of the
village go off in their finery and listened to the hymns on the radio
as she dusted, tidied and swept, humming along very quietly under
her breath. Surely, surely, He would approve? She was working,
doing her duty. It was the Sabbath, of course, but there were still
guests to take care of, and she suspected deep in her heart that the
Sabbath was only meant for men anyway. Surely He would
approve. Her work would count in her favour. But it was a sin, she
remembered vaguely, to court His favour, to say, "Look what I've
done, Lord." It was the sin of Pride. At least some said it was. She
couldn't remember who, or whether she had been told to believe or
disbelieve them—there were so many heresies, traps awaiting those
impure in body and mind—but words such as Faith, Works and
Elect circled one another in her thoughts.

Well, Katie concluded dismally, working on Sundays could only
add to the weight of sin she carried already. She picked up the
black plastic bag. There were still three more rooms to do, then
there was dinner to see to. When, she wondered, was it all going to
end?

She went downstairs to put the roast in and immediately recognized the new guest standing over the registration book in the
hallway. He signed himself in as Philip Richmond, from Bolton,
Lancashire, and he told Sam, who was dealing with the details, that
he was simply after a few relaxing days in the country. But Katie
remembered the moustache and the athletic spring in his step; it
was the man she had seen with Chief Inspector Banks and Sergeant
Hatchley the day she had run away to Eastvale.

Seeing him there brought back the whole day. Nothing had
come of it, really, except that she had caught a minor cold. The
housework got done. Not on time, but it got done. Sam never even
found out, so there was no retribution at his hands. Nor were there
any outbreaks of boils, thunderbolts from heaven, plagues of
locusts or other such horrors her grandmother had assured her
would happen if she strayed from the path.

She felt as if she had lost sight of the path completely now.
That was all she really knew about what was happening to her.
The conflicting voices in her mind seemed to have merged into

one incomprehensible rumble, and much of the time she felt as if she had no control over her thoughts or deeds.

There were clear moments, though. Like now. Outside, the landscape was fresh after the previous few days' rain, which was now rising in sun-charmed wraiths of mist from the lower fell-sides and the valley bottom. And here, in their hall, stood a man she recognized as having a close association with the police.

She hadn't seen what all the fuss was about the previous evening, when Sam had stumbled home from the White Rose in a very bad mood.

"He's gone to find her," he had said, scowling. "All the way to bloody Canada. Just to find her."

"Who?" Katie had asked quietly, confused and frightened of him. In moods like this he was likely to lash out, and she could still feel the pain in her breast from the last time.

"Anne Ralston, you silly bitch. That copper's taken off to Toronto after her."

"Well, what does it matter?" Katie had argued cautiously. "If she killed that man all those years ago, they'll put her in jail, won't they?"

"You don't know nothing, woman, do you? Nothing at all." Sam hit out at her and knocked the wooden cross off the mantelpiece.

"Leave it," he snarled, grabbing Katie by the arm as she bent to pick it up. "Can't you think of anything but bloody cleaning up?"

"But I thought you wanted me—"

"Oh, shut up. You don't know nothing."

"Well, tell me. What is it? Why does it matter so much that he's gone chasing after Anne Ralston in Canada? You hardly knew her. Why does it matter to us?"

"It doesn't," Sam said. "But it might to Stephen. She might make things difficult for him."

"But Stephen hasn't done anything, has he? How could she harm him?"

"She was his fancy woman, wasn't she? Then she ran off and left him. She could tell lies about his business, about—hell, I don't know! All I know is that it's all your bloody fault."

Katie said nothing. Sam's initial rage was spent, she could tell, and she knew she would remain fairly safe if she kept quiet. It was tricky, though, because he might get mad again if she didn't give the proper response to his ranting.

Sam sat heavily on the sofa and turned on the television. There was an old black-and-white film about gangsters on. James Cagney shot Humphrey Bogart and ran for it.

"Get me a beer," Sam said.

Katie got him a can of Long Life from the fridge. She knew it was no good telling him he'd had enough already. Besides, on nights like this, when he'd had a bit more than usual, he tended to fall asleep as soon as he got to bed.

"And don't forget the Colliers' party next week," he added, ripping open the can. "I want you looking your best."

Katie had forgotten about the garden party. The Colliers had two or three every summer. She hated them.

In the morning, Sam had a thick head and remembered very little about the night before. He sulked until after breakfast, then managed a welcome for the new guest before disappearing some- where in the Landrover. Katie showed Richmond his room, then went to get on with her work.

So there was a policeman in the house. She wondered why he was there. Perhaps he was on holiday. Policemen must have holi- days too. But if he was from Eastvale, he was hardly likely to travel only twenty-five miles to Swainshead for his yearly vacation. Not these days. He'd be off to Torquay, or even the Costa del Sol. Katie didn't know how much policemen got paid, so she couldn't really say. But he wouldn't come to Swainshead, that was for sure. He was a spy, then. He thought nobody would recognize him, so he could keep an eye on their comings and goings while the little one with the scar was in Toronto and the big one was God knows where.

And Katie knew who he was. The problem now was what to do with her knowledge. Should she tell Sam, put him on his guard? He'd spread the word then, like he always did, and maybe he'd be grateful to her. But she couldn't remember anything about Sam's gratitude. It just didn't stand out in her memory like the other things. Did she need it? On the other hand, if Sam had done some- thing wrong—and she didn't know whether he had or not—then the policeman, Richmond, if that was his real name, might find out and take him away. She'd be free then. It was an evil thought, and it made her heart race, but . . .

Katie paused and looked out of the back window at the gauze of mist rising like breath from the bright green slopes of Swainshead Fell. It would take a bit of thinking about, this dilemma of hers. She knew she mustn't make a hasty decision.

II

"I'm afraid there's hardly anybody here to talk to, Mr . . . er . . . ?"

"Banks. Alan Banks. I was a friend of Bernard Allen's."

"Yes, well the only person I can think of who might be able to help you is Marilyn Rosenberg." Tom Jordan, head of the Communications Department at Toronto Community College, looked at his watch. "She's got a class right now, but she should be free in about twenty minutes, if you'd like to wait?"

"Certainly."

Jordan led him out of the office into a staff lounge just big enough to hold a few chairs and a low coffee-table littered with papers and teaching journals. At one end stood a fridge and, on a desk beside it, a microwave oven. The coffee-machine stood on a table below a connecting window to the secretary's office, beside a rack of pigeon-holes for staff messages. Banks poured himself a coffee and Jordan edged away slowly, mumbling about work to do.

The coffee was strong and bitter, hardly the thing to drink in the thirty-three-degree heat. What he really needed was a cold beer or a gin and tonic. And he'd gone and bought Scotch at the duty-free shop. Still, he could leave it as a gift for Gerry Webb. It would surely come in handy in winter.

It was Monday morning. On Sunday, Banks had slept in and then gone for a walk along the Danforth. He had noticed the signs of yuppification that Gerry had mentioned, but he had found a pleasant little Greek restaurant, which had served him a hearty moussaka for lunch. Unlike Gerry, Banks enjoyed Greek food.

After that, he had wandered as far as Quinn's. Over a pint, he had asked around about Bernie Allen and shown Anne Ralston's photograph to the bar staff and waitresses. No luck. One down, two dozen to go. He had wandered back along the residential streets south of Danforth Avenue and noticed that the small brick house with the green-and-white porch fence and columns was a sort of Toronto trademark.

Too tired to go out again, he had stayed in and watched television that evening. Oddly enough, the non-commercial channel was showing an old BBC historical serial he'd found boring enough the first time around, and—much better—one of the Jeremy Brett "Sherlock Holmes" episodes. The only alternatives were the same American cop shows that plagued British TV.

He had woken at about nine o'clock that Monday morning. Still groggy from travel and culture-shock, he had taken a shower and had had orange juice and toast for breakfast. Then it was time to set off. He slipped a sixties anthology tape of Cream, Traffic and Rolling Stones hits in the Walkman and put it in the right-hand pocket of his light cotton jacket. In the left, he placed cigarettes and Hardy's *Tess of the D'Urbervilles*, the only book he'd brought with him.

Jacket slung over shoulder, he set off, following Gerry's directions. A rolling, rattling streetcar ride took him by the valley-side, rife with joggers. The downtown towers were hazy in the morning heat. Finding the westbound platform at Broadview subway station was every bit as straightforward as Gerry had said, but changing trains at Yonge and getting out to the street at St Clair proved confusing. All exits seemed to lead to a warren of underground shopping malls—air-conditioned, of course—and finding the right way out wasn't always easy.

Still, he'd found St Clair Avenue after only a momentary diversion into a supermarket called Ziggy's, and the college was only a short walk from the station.

Now, from the sixth floor, he looked out for a while on the office buildings opposite and the cream tops of the streetcars passing to and fro below him, then turned to the pile of journals on the table.

Half-way through an article on the teaching of "critical thinking," he heard muffled voices in the corridor, and a young woman with a puzzled expression on her face popped around the door. Masses of curly brown hair framed her round head. She had a small mouth and her teeth, when she smiled, were tiny, straight and pearly white. The greyish gum she was chewing oozed between them like a new gum disease. She carried a worn, overstuffed leather briefcase under her arm, and wore grey cords and a checked shirt.

She stretched out her hand. "Marilyn Rosenberg. Tom tells me you wanted to talk to me."

Banks introduced himself and offered to pour her a cup of coffee.

"No thanks," she said, grabbing a Diet Coke from the fridge. "Far too hot for that stuff. You'd think they'd do something about the air-conditioning in this place, wouldn't you?" She pulled the tab and the Diet Coke fizzed. "What do you want with me?"

"I want to talk about Bernard Allen."

"I've been through all that with the police. There wasn't really much to say."

"What did they ask you?"

"Just if I thought anyone had a reason to kill him, where my colleagues were over the last few weeks, that kind of thing."

"Did they ask you anything about his life here?"

"Only what kind of person he was."

"And?"

"And I told them he was a bit of a loner, that's all. I wasn't the only one they talked to."

"You're the only one here now."

"Yeah, I guess." She grinned again, flashing her beautiful teeth.

"If Bernard didn't have much to do with his colleagues here, did he have a group of friends somewhere else, away from college?"

"I wouldn't really know. Look, I didn't know Bernie that well. . . ." She hesitated. "Maybe it's none of your business, but I wanted to. We were getting closer. Slowly. He was a hard person to get to know. All that stiff-upper-lip Brit stuff. Me, I'm a simple Irish-Jewish girl from Montreal." She shrugged. "I liked him. We did lunch up here a couple of times. I was hoping maybe he'd ask me out sometime but . . ."

"It never happened?"

"No. He was too damn slow. I didn't know how much clearer I could make it without ripping off my clothes and jumping on him. But now it's too late, even for that."

"How did he seem emotionally before he went to England?"

Marilyn frowned and bit her bottom lip as she thought. "He hadn't quite got over his divorce," she said finally. "So I guess he might have been off women for a while."

"Did you know his ex-wife?"

"No, not really."

"What about her lover?"

"Yeah, I knew him. He used to work here. He's a louse."

"In what way?"

"Every way. Strutting macho peacock. And she fell for it. I don't blame Bernie for feeling bad, but he'd have been well rid of her anyway. He'd have got over it."

"But he was still upset?"

"Yeah. Withdrawn, sort of."

"How did he get on with his students?"

"Well enough, considering."

"Considering what?"

"He cared about literature, but most of the students don't give a damn about James Joyce or George Orwell. They're here to learn about business or computers or electrical engineering—you know, useful stuff—and then they think they'll walk into top, high-paying jobs. They don't like it when they find they all have to do English, so it makes our job a bit tough. Some teachers find it harder than others to adjust and lower their expectations."

"And Bernie was one?"

"Yeah. He complained a lot about how ignorant they were, how half of them didn't even know when the Second World War was fought or who Hitler was. And, even worse, they didn't care anyway. Bernie couldn't understand that. He had one guy who thought Shakespeare was a small town in Saskatchewan. That really got to him."

"I don't understand," Banks said. "How could someone like that get accepted into a college?"

"We have an open-door policy," Marilyn said. "It's a democratic education. None of that elitist bullshit you get in England. We don't send our kids away to boarding schools to learn Latin and take a lot of cold showers. All that Jane Eyre stuff."

Banks, who had not attended a public school himself, along with, he suspected, the majority of English children, was confused. "But don't a lot of them fail?" he asked. "Doesn't it waste time and money?"

"We don't like to fail people," Marilyn said. "It gives them a poor self-image."

"So they don't need to know much to get in, and they aren't expected to know much more when they leave, is that it?"

Marilyn smiled like a nurse with a particularly difficult patient.

"What did Bernie think about that?" Banks hurried on.

She laughed. "Bernie loved youth, young people, but he didn't have much respect for their intelligence."

"It doesn't sound like they had much."

"There, you see. That's exactly the kind of thing he'd say. You're so sarcastic, you Brits."

"But you liked him?"

"Yeah, I liked him. We might have disagreed on a few things, but he was cute. And I'm a sucker for an English accent. What can I say? He was a nice guy, at least as far as I could tell. I mean, he might not have thought much of his students, but he treated them well and did his damnedest to arouse some curiosity in them. He was a good teacher. What are you getting at, anyway? Do you think one of his students might have killed him over a poor grade?"

"It sounds unlikely, doesn't it?"

"Not as much as you think," Marilyn said. "We once had a guy come after his English teacher here with a shotgun. Luckily, security stopped him before he got very far. Still," she went on, "I shouldn't think an irate student would go to all the trouble of following him over to England and killing him there."

"What did Bernie do when he went home after work? Did he ever mention any particular place he went to?"

Marilyn shook her head and the curls danced. "No. He did once say he'd had a few pints too many in the pub the night before."

"The pub?"

"Yeah."

"He didn't say which pub?"

"No. He just said he'd had six pints when five was his limit these days. Look, what is all this? What are you after? You're not one of those private eyes, are you?"

Banks laughed. "No. I told you, I'm a friend of Bernie's from England. Swainsdale, where he grew up. I want to piece together as much of his life here as I can. A lot of people over there are hurt and puzzled by what happened."

"Yeah, well . . . me too. He wasn't the kind of guy who gets himself killed. Know what I mean?"

Banks nodded.

"Swainsdale, you said?" she went on. "Bernie was always going on about that place. At least the couple of times we talked he was. Like it was some paradise on earth or something. Especially since the divorce, he started to get homesick. He was beginning to feel a bit lost and out of place here. It can happen, you know. So he took the thousand-dollar cure."

"The what?"

"The thousand-dollar cure. I guess it's gone up now with inflation, but it's when Brits take a trip back home to renew their roots. Used to call it the thousand-dollar cure. For homesickness."

"Did he ever talk of going back to Swainsdale to stay?"

"Yeah. He said he'd be off like a shot if he had a job, or a private income. He said there was nothing for him here after he split up with Barbara. Poor guy. Like I said, he got withdrawn, dwelled on things too much."

Banks nodded. "There's nothing else you can tell me? You're sure he didn't name any specific pub or place he used to hang out?"

"Sorry." Marilyn grinned. "I'd remember if he had because I'd have probably dropped in there one evening. Just by chance, you know."

Banks smiled. "Yes. I know. Thanks anyway. I won't waste any more of your time."

"No problem." Marilyn tossed her empty can into the waste-paper basket. "Hey!" she called, as Banks left the staff lounge. "I think your accent's cute, too."

But Banks didn't have time to appreciate the compliment. Coming along the corridor towards him were two very large police officers.

"Mr Banks?" the taller one asked.

"Yes."

"We'd like you to come with us, if you don't mind."

"What for?"

"Just a few questions. This way, please."

There was hardly room for them to walk three abreast down the hallway, but they managed it somehow. Banks felt a bit like a sardine in a tin. As they turned the corner, he noticed from the corner of his eye Tom Jordan wringing his hands outside his office.

Banks tried to get more out of the officers in the lift, but they clammed up on him. He felt a wave of irrational fear at the situation. Here he was, in a foreign country, being taken into custody by two enormous uniformed policemen who refused to answer his questions. And the feeling of fear intensified as he was bundled into the back of the yellow car. The air smelled of hot vinyl upholstery; a strong wire mesh separated him from the men in the front; and the back doors had no inside handles.

III

"What does tha write, then?" Freddie Metcalfe asked, expertly refilling the empty pint glass with Marston's Pedigree Bitter.

"Science fiction," said Detective Constable Philip Richmond. In his checked Viyella shirt and light-brown cords, he thought he looked the part. Posing as a writer would make him less suspicious, too. He would be expected to spend some time alone in his room writing and a lot of time in the pub, with perhaps the occasional constitutional just to keep the juices flowing.

"I knew a chap used to write books once," Freddie went on. "Books about t'Dales, wi' pictures in 'em. Lived down Lower 'Ead." He placed the foaming pint in front of Richmond, who paid and drained a good half of it in one gulp. "I reckon one of them there detective writers would 'ave a better time of it round 'ere these days."

"Why's that?"

Freddie leaned forward and lowered his voice. "Murder, that's why," he said, then laughed and picked up a glass to dry. "Right baffled, t'police are. It's got that southron little chap wi' a scar by 'is eye—it's got 'im running around like a blue-arsed fly, it has. And t'old man, Gristhorpe—well, we all know he durst hardly show his face around 'ere since t'last one, don't we?"

"Last what?"

"Murder, lad! What's tha think I'm talking about? Sheep-shagging?"

"Sorry."

"Think nowt on it. I'm forgetting tha's a foreigner. Tha sounds Yorkshire to me. Bit posh, mind you, but Yorkshire."

"Lancashire, actually," Richmond lied. "Bolton."

"Aye, well, nobody's perfect. Anyroads, as I were saying—blue-arsed flies, t'lot of 'em."

An impatient customer interrupted Freddie's monologue, and Richmond took the opportunity to sip more beer. It was eight-thirty on Monday evening, and the White Rose was about half full.

"Keep your eyes skinned, lad," Sergeant Hatchley had instructed him. "Watch out for anybody who looks like doing a bolt." The orders couldn't have been more vague. What on earth, Richmond wondered, did someone about to do a bolt look like? Would he have to sit up all night and watch for the culprit stealing down by the fledgling Swain with his belongings tied in a bag on the end of a stick slung over his shoulder, faithful cat at his heels, like Dick Whittington? Richmond had no idea. All he knew was that all the suspects had been told Banks had gone to Toronto.

Richmond also had strict instructions not to identify himself and not to push himself forward in any way that might make the locals suspicious. In other words, he wasn't to question anyone, no matter how casually. He could keep his ears open though, he was relieved to hear, especially for anything Sam Greenock might let slip over breakfast, or some titbit he might overhear in the White Rose. At least he'd pack away a few pints of Marston's tonight. Maybe even smoke a panatella.

"Where was I?" Freddie asked, leaning on the bar again.

"Murder."

"Aye, murder." He nodded in the direction of the table in the far corner and whispered again. "And them there's all t'suspects."

"What makes them suspects?" Richmond asked, hoping he was not exceeding his brief by asking the question.

"'Ow would I know? All I know is that t'police 'ave spent a lot of time wi' 'em. An' since yesterday they've all been on hot coals. Look at 'em now. You wouldn't think they 'ad a big party coming up, would you?"

It was true that the group hardly seemed jolly. John Fletcher chewed the stem of his stubby pipe; his dark brows met in a frown. Sam Greenock was staring into space and rocking his glass on the table. Stephen Collier was talking earnestly to Nicholas, who was trying very hard not to listen. Nicholas, in fact, seemed the only unconcerned one among them. He smiled and nodded at customers who came and went, whereas the other two hardly seemed to notice them.

Richmond wished he could get closer and overhear what they were saying, but all the nearby tables were full. It would look too suspicious if he went and stood behind them.

He ordered another pint. "And I'll have a panatella, too, please," he said. He felt like indulging in a rare treat: a cigar with his beer. "What party's this?" he asked.

"A Collier do. Reg'lar as clockwork in summer."

"Can anyone go?"

"Tha must be joking, lad."

Richmond shrugged and smiled to show he was, indeed, jesting. "What's wrong with them all, then?" he asked. "You're right. They don't look like they're contemplating a booze-up to me."

Metcalfe scratched his mutton-chops. "I can't be certain, tha knows, but it's summat to do wi' that London copper taking off for Canada. Talk about pale! Ashen, they went. But I'll tell tha summat, it were good for business. Double brandies all round!" Freddie nudged Richmond and laughed. "Aye, there's nobody drinks like a murder suspect."

Richmond drew on his cigar and looked over at the table. Outside some enemy back in Toronto, it came down to these four.

Come on, he thought to himself, make a bolt. Run for it, you bugger, just try it!

IV

"I don't know what people do where you come from, but over here we like a bit of advance warning if some foreigner's come to invade our territory."

Banks listened. There was nothing he could say; he had been caught fair and square. Fortunately, Staff Sergeant Gregson of the Toronto Homicide Squad was nearing the end of what had been a relatively mild bollocking, and even more fortunately, smoking was allowed—nay, encouraged—in his office.

It was an odd feeling, being on the carpet. Not that this was the first time for Banks. There had been many occasions at school, and even one or two in his early days on the Metropolitan Force, and they always brought back those feelings of terror and helplessness in the face of authority he had known as a working-class kid in Peterborough. Perhaps, he thought, that fear of authority might have motivated him to become a policeman in the first place. He knew he didn't join in order to inflict such feelings on others, but it was possible that he did it to surmount them, to conquer them in himself.

And now here he was, tongue-tied, unable to say a word in his own defence, yet inwardly seething with resentment at Gregson for putting him in such a position.

"You've got no power here, you know," Gregson went on.

Finally, Banks found his voice. Holding his anger in check, he said, "I wasn't aware that I needed any special power to talk to people—either in England or in Canada."

"You won't get anywhere being sarcastic with me," Gregson said, a smile tugging at the corners of his tightly clamped mouth.

He was a round man with a square head. His grey hair was closely cropped, and a brush-like wedge of matching moustache, nicotine-yellow around the ends of the bristles, sprouted under his squashed nose. As he spoke, he had a habit of running his fingers under the collar of his white shirt as if it was too tight. His skin had a pinkish, plastic sheen, like a balloon blown up too much. Banks wondered what would happen if he pricked him. Would he explode, or would the air hiss out slowly as his features folded in on themselves?

"What have you got against irony, Sergeant?" Banks asked. That felt odd, too: being hauled up before a mere Sergeant.

"You know what they say about sarcasm being the lowest form of wit, don't you?" Gregson responded.

"Yes. But at least it is a form of wit, which is better than none at all."

"I didn't bring you here to bandy words."

"Obviously."

Banks lit another cigarette and looked at the concrete-and-glass office blocks out of the window. His shirt was stuck with sweat to the back of the orange plastic chair. He felt his anger ebb into boredom. They were somewhere downtown in a futuristic, air-conditioned building, but the office smelt of burning rubber and old cigar smoke. That was all he knew.

"What are you going to do, then?" Banks asked. "Arrest me?"

Gregson shrugged. "For what? You haven't done anything wrong."

Banks leaned forward. "Then why the bloody hell did you get Laurel and Hardy out there to bundle me in the back of a car and bring me here against my will?"

"Don't be like that," Gregson said. "When Jordan phoned me and said there was a suspicious Englishman asking questions about Bernard Allen, what the fuck else could I do? What would you have done? Then it turned out to be you, a goddamn police inspector from England. And I hadn't even been advised of your visit. I considered that an insult, which it is. And I didn't find your remark on the phone about getting my man particularly funny, either. I'm not a Mountie."

"Well, I'm sorry for any inconvenience I've caused you, Sergeant," Banks said, standing up, "but I'd like to enjoy the rest of my holiday in peace, if you don't mind."

"I don't mind," Gregson said, making no move to stop him walking over to the door. "I don't mind at all. But I think you ought to bear a few things in mind before you go storming off."

"What things?" Banks asked, his palm slippery on the doorknob.

"First of all, that what I said to you on the phone before is true: we don't have the resources to work on this case. Secondly, yes, you can talk to as many people as you wish, providing they want to talk to you. And thirdly, you should have damn well asked for permission before jumping on that fucking jet and flying here half-cocked. What if you find your killer? What are you going to do then? Have you thought about that? Smuggle him out of the country? You could be getting yourself into a damn tricky legal situation if you're not very careful." Gregson rubbed his moustache with the back of his hand. "All I'm saying is that there are things you can't do acting alone, without authority."

"And you don't have the resources. I know. You told me. Look, this is where I came in, so if you don't mind—"

"Wait!" Gregson jumped to his feet and reached for his jacket.

"Wait for what?"

Gregson pushed past him through the door. "Come on," he said, half-turning. "Just come with me."

"Where?"

"You'll see."

"What for?"

"I'm going to save you from yourself."

Banks sighed and followed the sergeant down the corridor and down the lift to the car-park.

There was enough room for a soccer team on the front seat of Gregson's car. With the open windows sucking in what hot wet air they could, the staff sergeant drove up Yonge Street and turned right at the Hudson's Bay building. On the crowded street-corner, vendors sold ice-cream, T-shirts and jewellery; one man, surrounded by quite a crowd, was drawing large portraits in coloured chalk on the pavement.

Farther along, Banks recognized the stretch of the Danforth he'd walked the previous day: the Carrot Common shopping centre; the little Greek restaurant where he'd eaten lunch; Quinn's pub. They came to an intersection called Coxwell, and Gregson turned left. A few blocks up, he pulled to a halt outside a small apartment building. Sprinklers hissed on the well-kept lawn. Banks was tempted to run under one for a cold shower.

They walked up to the third floor, and Banks followed Gregson along the carpeted corridor to apartment 312.

"Allen's place," the staff sergeant announced.

"Why are you helping me?" Banks asked, as Gregson fitted the key in the door. "Why are you bringing me here? You said your department didn't have the resources."

"That's true. We've got a hunt on for a guy who sodomized a twelve-year-old girl, then cut her throat and dumped her in High Park. Been looking for leads for two months now. Twenty men on the case. But this is personal time. I don't like it that a local guy got killed any more than you do. So I show you where he lived. It's no big deal. Besides, like I said, I'm saving you from yourself. You'd probably have broken in, and then I'd have had to arrest you. Embarrassing all around."

"Thanks anyway," Banks said.

They walked into the apartment.

"Building owner's been bugging us to let him rent it out again, but we've been stalling. He knows he's sitting on a gold mine. We've got a zero vacancy rate in Toronto these days. Still, Allen paid first and last month when he moved in, so I figure he's got a bit of time left. To tell you the truth, we don't know who's gonna take care of the guy's stuff."

There wasn't much: just a lot of books, Swedish assemble-it-yourself furniture, pots and pans, a few withered houseplants, and a desk and typewriter by the window. Bernard Allen had lived simply.

The room was hot and stuffy. There was no sign of an air-conditioner, so Banks went over and opened a window. It didn't make much difference.

"What kind of search did your men do?" Banks asked.

"Routine. We didn't open up every book or read every letter, if that's what you mean. The guy didn't keep much personal stuff around, anyway. It was all in that desk drawer."

Banks extracted a messy pile of bills and letters from the drawer. First, he put aside the bills then examined the sheaf of personal mail. They were all dated within the last six months or so, which meant that he threw his letters out periodically instead of hoarding them like some people. There were letters from his parents in Australia and one brief note from his sister acknowledging the dates of his proposed visit. Banks read these carefully, but found nothing of significance.

It was a postcard from Vancouver dated about two weeks before Allen set off for England that proved the most revealing, but even that wasn't enough. It read:

Dear Bernie,

Wrapping things up nicely out here. Weather great, so taking some time for sunbathing on Kitsilano Beach. It'll be a couple more weeks before I get back, so I'll miss you. Have a great trip and give my love to the folks in Swineshead! (Only joking—best not tell anyone you know me!) See you in the pub when you get back.

Love,
Julie.

It was perfectly innocent on the surface—just a postcard from a friend—so there was no reason why Gregson or his men should have been suspicious about it. But it was definitely from Anne Ralston, and it told Banks that she was going under the name of Julie now.

"Looks like you've found something," Gregson said, looking over Banks's shoulder.

"It's from the woman I'm looking for. I think she knows something about Allen's murder."

"Look," Gregson said, "are we talking about a criminal here? Are there charges involved?"

Banks shook his head. He wasn't sure. Anne Ralston could certainly have murdered Raymond Addison and run for it, but he didn't want to tell Gregson that and risk the local police scaring her off.

"No," he said. "They used to know each other in Swainshead, that's all."

"And now they've met up over here?"

"Yes."

"So?"

Banks told him about Ralston's disappearance and the Addison murder, stressing that she wasn't seriously implicated in any way.

"But she might have known something?" he said. "And told Allen. You think that's what might have got him killed?"

"It's possible. We know that she asked him to keep quiet about meeting her over here, and we know he didn't."

"Who did he talk to?"

"That's the problem. Someone who makes it his business to make sure that everyone who counts knows."

"It won't be easy."

"What?"

Gregson tapped the postcard. "Finding her. No address. No phone number. Nothing."

Banks sighed. "Believe me, I know. And all we've got is her first name. I'm just hoping I can dig out some of the spots she might turn up. She mentioned the pub, so at least I was right about her drinking with him there."

"Know how many pubs there are in Toronto?"

"Don't bother to tell me. I'd only get discouraged. It's the kind of job I should have sent my sergeant on." Banks explained about Hatchley's drinking habits and Gregson laughed.

"Can I have a good look around?" Banks asked.

"Go ahead. I'll be down in the car. Lock up behind you."

After the staff sergeant left, Banks puzzled over him for a moment. He was beginning to warm to Gregson and get some understanding of Canadians, especially those of distant British origin. They behaved with a strange mixture of patronage and respect towards the English. Perhaps they'd had British history rammed down their throats at school and needed to reject it in order to discover themselves. Or perhaps the English had simply become *passé* as far as immigrants went, and had been superseded by newer waves of Koreans, East Indians and Vietnamese.

The next item of interest Banks found was an old photograph album dating back to Allen's university days. There were pictures of his parents, his sister, and of the Greenocks standing outside a typical Armley back-to-back. But the most interesting was a picture dated ten years ago, in which Allen stood outside the White Rose with a woman named as Anne in the careful white print under the photo on the black page. The snap was a little blurred, an amateur effort with a Brownie by the look of it, but it was better than the one he'd got from Missing Persons. Anne looked very attractive in a low-cut T-shirt and a full, flowing Paisley skirt. She had long light-brown hair, a high forehead and smiling eyes. Her face was heart-shaped and her lips curved up slightly at the corners. That was ten years ago, Banks thought, carefully taking the photo from its silver corners and pocketing it. Would she look like that now?

He went on to make a careful search of the rest of the apartment, and he did take out every book and flip through the leaves, but he came up with nothing else. The postcard signed "Julie" and the old photograph: those were all he had to go on. By the time he'd finished, his shirt was stuck to his back.

Outside, Gregson seemed quite at ease smoking in his hot car.

"Find anything?" he asked.

"Only an old photograph. Probably useless. What time is it?"

"Ten after four."

"I suppose I'd better make my way home."

"Where are you staying?"

"Riverdale."

"That's not far. How about a beer first?"

"All right." It was impossible to resist the thought of an ice-cold beer.

Gregson drove back downtown and pulled into a car-park behind a grimy cinder-block building with a satellite dish on the roof.

Despite the warm gold sunlight outside, the bar was dark and it took a while for Banks's eyes to adjust. He did notice, though, that it was cold, gloriously cold. There wasn't any sawdust on the floor, but he got the feeling there ought to be. It was a high-ceilinged room as big as a barn, peppered with black plastic tables and chairs. At one end was the bar itself, a feeble glimmer of light in the distance, and at the other was a stage littered with amps and speakers. At the moment a rather flat-chested young girl was dancing half-naked in a spotlight to the Rolling Stones' "Jumpin' Jack Flash." The volume was way too loud. Against a third wall was a huge TV screen on which a game of baseball was in progress.

A waitress sashayed over, shirt-ends tied in a knot under her ample breasts, and took their orders with a weary smile. Shortly, she returned with the drinks on a tray. As Banks looked around, other figures detached themselves from the gloom and he saw that the place was reasonably full. Smoke swirled and danced in the spot beam. Whatever this bar was, it wasn't one of the English-style pubs where Bernard Allen went for his pint. The four glasses of draft beer in front of them were tiny and tapered to thick heavy stems.

"Cheers." Gregson clinked glasses and practically downed his in one.

"If you have to order two each at a time," Banks asked, leaning over and shouting against the music, "why don't they switch to using bigger glasses?"

Gregson shrugged and licked foam off his moustache. "Tradition, I guess. It's always been like this long as I can remember." He offered Banks a cigarette. It was stronger than the ones he usually smoked.

The music ended and the girl left the stage to a smattering of polite applause.

Gregson nodded towards the TV screen. "Get baseball back home?"

Banks nodded. "We do now. My son likes it, but I'm a cricket man myself."

"Can't figure that game at all."

"Can't say I know much about baseball, either." Banks caught the waitress's attention and put in another order, changing his to a bottle of Carlsberg this time. She smiled sweetly at him and made him repeat himself.

"Likes your accent," Gregson said afterwards. "She heard you the first time. You'll be all right there, if you're interested."

"Married man."

"Ah. Still, while the cat's away . . . And you are in a foreign country, a long way from home."

Banks laughed. "The problem is, I have to take myself with me wherever I go."

Gregson nodded slowly. "I know what you mean." He tapped the side of his square head. "There's a few pictures stuck in here I wish I could throw out, believe me." He looked back at the screen. "Baseball. Greatest game in the world."

"I'll take your word for it."

"Listen, if you've got a bit of time, how about taking in a game next Saturday? I've got tickets. Jays at home to the Yankees."

"I'd like that," Banks said. "Look, don't get me wrong, but I got the impression you were distinctly pissed off with me a few hours ago. Now you're inviting me to a baseball game. Any reason?"

"Sure. You were out of line and I did my duty. Now I'm off duty and someone's got to show you there's more to Canada than snow, Mounties, beavers and maple trees."

"Fair enough. Don't forget the Eskimos."

"Inuit, we call them now."

Banks finished his beer and Gregson ordered more. The spot came on again and an attractive young woman with long, wavy black hair and brown skin came onto the stage.

Gregson noticed Banks staring. "Beautiful, eh? She's a full-blooded Indian. Name's Wanda Morningstar."

She certainly was beautiful, in such an innocent, natural way that Banks found himself wondering what the girl was doing taking her clothes off for a bunch of dirty old men in the middle of a summer's afternoon. And, come to think of it, what the hell was he doing among them? Well, blame Gregson for that.

More drinks came, and more strippers walked on and off the stage, but none could hold a candle to Wanda Morningstar. It was after ten when they finally left, and by then Banks felt unusually merry. Because the beer was ice-cold, it had very little taste and, therefore, he had assumed, little strength. Wrong. It was stronger than what he was used to, and he felt light-headed as he followed Gregson to the car.

Gregson paused as he bent to put his key in the door. "No," he said to himself. "Time to take a cab. You've been leading me astray, Alan. It'd be damned embarrassing if I got done for drunken driving in my own city, wouldn't it?"

They walked out onto the street. It was still busy, and many of the shops were open—all-night groceries and the ubiquitous Mac's Milk. Or was this one Mo's, Mc's or Mick's? You'd never get anything but an off-licence open past five-thirty in Eastvale, Banks reflected.

Gregson waved and a cab pulled up. They piled in the back. The driver, an uncommunicative West Indian, nodded when he heard the directions. He dropped Banks off first outside Gerry's house, then drove on with Gregson waving from the back.

Banks walked into the hot room and slumped in front of the TV. A rerun of "Perry Mason" came on. Finally, a little dizzy and unable to keep his eyes open any longer, he went into the bedroom and lay down. The events of the day spun around chaotically in his mind for a while, but the last image, the one that lulled his consciousness to sleep, was of Wanda Morningstar dancing naked, not on a stage in a seedy bar, but in a clearing somewhere in the wilderness, her dark skin gleaming in firelight.

But the scene shifted, as it does in dreams, and it was no longer Wanda Morningstar dancing, but Anne Ralston running ahead of him in her long Paisley skirt. It was a typical policeman's dream, too, for try as he might, he just couldn't run fast enough. His feet felt as if they were glued to the earth. Every so often, she would pause and beckon him, smiling indulgently when she saw him try to drag himself along. He woke at six, covered with sweat. Outside, the birds were singing and an early-morning streetcar clattered by. He got up and took a couple of Gerry's aspirins with a pint of water, then drifted off to sleep again.

TEN

I

The sun had just gone down behind Adam's Fell, silhouetting the steep hillside against its deep crimson glow. The guests milled around in the Colliers' large garden. Doors to both parts of the house were open, allowing access to drinks and a huge table of cheeses, pâtés, smoked salmon and fresh fruit. Music drifted out from Stephen's stereo. Now it was Mozart, but earlier there had been Motown and some ersatz modern pop. The crowd was mostly early to mid thirties, apart from one or two older landowners and friends of the family. There were a couple of bright young teachers from Braughtmore, several members of Stephen's management staff, and a great assortment of entrepreneurs, some with political ambitions, from all over the dale. The parties were a fairly regular affair; they helped maintain the social status of the Colliers and introduce those who had something to those who might be willing and able to pay for it.

Katie stood alone by the fountain, with a glass of white wine in her hand. She had been holding it so long it was warm. Occasionally a well-dressed young man would approach her and begin a conversation, but after a few minutes of her averted looks, blushes and monosyllabic answers, he would make an excuse to get away.

As usual, Sam had insisted she come.

"I didn't buy you those bloody expensive dresses for nothing, you know," he had railed when she told him at the last minute that she didn't want to go.

"I didn't ask you to buy them," Katie said quietly. "I don't even want them." And it was true. She felt uncomfortable in finery, full of pride and vanity.

"You'll damn well do as I say. There'll be some important people there and I want you to make a good impression."

"Oh, Sam," she pleaded, "you know I never do. I can't talk to people at parties. I get all tongue-tied."

"Have a few drinks like everyone else, for a change. That'll loosen you up. For Christ's sake, can't you let your hair down for once?"

Katie turned away.

Sam grasped her arm. "Look," he said, "you're coming with me and that's that. If you're so worried about talking to people, then just stand around and look decorative. At least you can do that. But you are coming. Got it?"

Katie nodded and Sam let go of her. Rubbing her arm, she went up to her room and picked out a cotton print dress just right for the occasion, gathered at the waist and cut low down the back. It looked particularly good if she tied her hair up. She decided to take a fringed woollen shawl, too; sometimes, even in July, the evenings got chilly. After Sam had approved of her appearance and suggested a bit more eye make-up, they left.

She could see Sam in his white suit talking and laughing with a couple of local businessmen. He had a glass of wine too, though she knew he hated the stuff. He only drank it because that was the thing to do at the Colliers' parties.

Katie looked around for John Fletcher, but she couldn't see him. John was always kind and, of all of them, she found him the easiest to talk to, or even to be silent with. She liked Stephen Collier, but felt more comfortable with John Fletcher. He was a sad and haunted man since his wife ran off—but at least she hadn't gone because he mistreated her. Maureen Fletcher, Katie remembered, had been beautiful, vain, haughty and foolhardy. The small community of Swainshead couldn't hold her. Katie thought John ought to be glad to be rid of her, but she never said anything to him. They never discussed anything personal, but he seemed, beyond the depths of his sadness, a good man.

Katie shivered. The sunset had faded, leaving the sky above Adam's Fell a deep, dark violet colour. Even over the clinking glasses and the Motown music, which had started up again because some people wanted to dance, she could hear the eerie, mournful call of a curlew high on the fell. She began to make her way into Nicholas's part of the house to pick up her shawl where Sam had left it, then decided she wanted to go to the bathroom, too. Pausing on the way, she admired the oak panelling and the old-fashioned style of his living-room, with its water-colours of Nelson and Wellington on the walls, and its rows of leather-bound books. She wondered if he ever read them. On a small teak table by the Adam fireplace stood a bronze bust. Looking closer, Katie saw the name "Oscar Wilde" scratched into the base. She'd heard the name before somewhere, but it didn't mean very much to her. What a beautiful place for a monster like Nicholas Collier to live. It would be difficult to clean, though, she thought, taking in all the nooks and crannies with a professional eye.

Finally, she found the toilet, which was more modern than the rest of the house. There, she poured her drink down the bowl and hid for a while, idly glancing at one of the copies of *Yorkshire Life* so thoughtfully set out by the bathtub. Then she got worried that Sam might be looking for her.

On her way back down the hall, she met Nicholas coming up. He was walking unsteadily, and his bright eyes were glassy. A stubborn lock of hair near his crown stood straight up. He looked like a naughty public schoolboy.

"Ah, Katie my dear," he said, reaching out and holding her shoulders. His voice was slurred and his cheeks were flushed with drink. "Come to me, for thy love is better than wine."

Katie blushed and tried to wriggle free, but Nicholas only tightened his grip. He looked behind him.

"Nobody around," he whispered. "Time for a little kiss, my rose of Sharon, my lily of the valley."

Katie struggled, but he was too strong. He held her head still, brought his mouth closer to hers and seemed to suffocate her with a long, wet kiss. His breath tasted rank with wine, garlicky pâté and Stilton cheese. When he stopped, she gulped in the air. But he didn't let her go. One hand was on her bare back now and the other was feeling her breasts.

"Ah, thy breasts are like two young roes that are twins," he said, breathing hard. "Come on, Katie. In here. In the bedroom."

"No!" Katie shouted. "If you don't let me go I'm going to scream."

Nicholas laughed. "I like a girl with a bit of spirit. Come on, I'll make you scream, sure enough. But not yet." He put one hand over her mouth and started dragging her along the hallway. Suddenly, she heard a familiar voice behind them and Nicholas's grip loosened. She shook herself free and turned to hear John Fletcher tell Nicholas to take his hands off her.

"You go to hell!" Nicholas said, clearly too far gone in temper to pull back. "Who are you to tell me what to do? You're nothing but a jumped-up farm boy."

And suddenly, John hit him. It was a quick, sharp blow to the mouth, and it stopped Nicholas in his tracks. He glared at John as the blood welled to his lips and a thin line trickled down his chin. Out in the garden, a glass smashed and somebody giggled loudly above Mary Wells's "My Guy." Nicholas bared his teeth at John, put his hand over his mouth and stalked off to the bathroom.

Fletcher rubbed his knuckles. "Are you all right, Katie?" he asked.

"Yes, yes, thank you." Katie stared down at the patterned carpet as she spoke. "I—I'm sorry . . . I'm so embarrassed. It's not the first time he's tried to touch me, but he's never been that rough before."

"He's drunk," Fletcher said, then smiled. "Don't worry. I've been wanting to do that for a long time."

"But what will he do? He looked so angry."

"He'll cool off. Come on, let's get back to the others."

Katie picked up her shawl, and they walked back into the garden, which was lit now by strategically placed antique lanterns. Katie excused herself, thanking John again, and sneaked around the side of the house into the street. She felt she needed to be out of there for a while, at least until her heart stopped beating so wildly and she could catch her breath again. Her flesh felt numb where Nicholas's hands had touched her. She shuddered.

There was no-one on the street. Even the old men had gone from the bridge. The lights were on in the White Rose, though, and Katie heard the sound of laughter and talk from inside. She thought the young policeman would be in there, the one nobody knew about but her. He hadn't been invited to the party, of course, so he wouldn't get the chance to spy on them that night. She wondered why he was really in the village. He hadn't asked any searching questions of anyone; he just seemed to be there, somehow, always in sight.

Sighing, Katie crept back into the garden. A slow song was playing and some of the couples held each other close. Suddenly, she felt a hand on her back and flinched.

"It's only me. Dance?"

"B-but I . . . can't. . . ."

"Nonsense," Stephen Collier said. "It's easy. Just follow what I do."

Katie had no choice. She saw Sam looking on and smiling with approval from Stephen's doorway. She felt like she had two left feet, and somehow her body just wouldn't respond to the music at all. It felt like wood. Soon, she began to feel dizzy and everything went dark. At the centre of the darkness was a biting, sooty smell. She stumbled.

"Hey, I'm not as bad as all that." Stephen supported her with one arm and led her to the fountain.

Katie regained her balance. "I'm sorry," she said. "I told you I was no good."

"If I didn't know better," Stephen said, "I'd say you'd had too much to drink."

Katie smiled. "About one sip of white wine. It's too much for me."

"Katie?" Stephen suddenly seemed earnest.

"Yes?"

"I enjoyed our little chat in your kitchen that time. It's good to have someone . . . someone outside to talk to."

"Outside what?"

"Oh, business, family . . ."

The occasion seemed so long ago that Katie could hardly remember. And Stephen had ignored her ever since. She certainly hadn't imagined it as an enjoyable occasion for either of them. But there was something so little-boyish about Stephen, especially now when he seemed so nervous and serious. The muscle in the corner of his left eye had developed a tic.

"Remember what we talked about?" he went on.

Katie didn't, but she nodded.

He looked around and lowered his voice. "I think I've made my mind up. I think I'm going to leave Swainshead."

"But why?"

Stephen noticed a couple of his senior executives heading in their direction. "We can't talk here, Katie. Not now. Can I see you on Friday?"

"Sam goes to—"

"Yes, I know Sam goes to Eastvale on Fridays. I don't want to see Sam, I want to see you. We'll go for a walk."

"I—I don't know."

His tone was urgent and his eyes were pleading with her. The two men had almost reached them. "All right," she said. "A walk. A little one."

Stephen relaxed. Even the tic in his eye seemed to disappear.

"Ah, Stephen, here you are," one of the executives, a plump, florid man called Teaghe, said. "Trust you to corner the prettiest filly at the party, eh?" He cast a lecherous glance at Katie, who smiled politely and made an excuse to leave.

She poured herself another glass of wine for appearance's sake and leaned by the side of the French windows, watching the lantern-lit dancers in relief against the huge black mass of Adam's Fell. The garden was a tangled web of shadows, crossing and knotting like an enormous cat's cradle. As the warm light caught their features at certain angles, some of the dancers looked positively Satanic.

So, although she had never thought of herself as a sympathetic listener—so bound up in her own shyness and discomfort was she—Stephen had asked her to be his confidante and she had agreed to go for a walk with him, to listen to his problems. It was more than Sam ever asked her to do. There were only two things he wanted from her: work and sex.

She trusted Stephen as far as she could trust any man. He hadn't tried anything last time, when he could have, and he'd been distinctly cool towards her since. But why did he want to leave Swainshead? Why did he seem so on edge? Was he running away from something? Still, she thought, if he was going away, and he really liked her, then there was just a chance he might take her with him.

She suspected that it might be a sin to desert her husband, but she had thought so much about it, she decided it was worth the risk. Surely God would forgive her for leaving a man with such vile and lascivious appetites as Sam Greenock? She could make amends, do good works. She might have to give Stephen her body, too, she knew that. If not on Friday, then later, if he took her away with him. But that was one sin nobody could catch her out on. She had learned how to comply with all the things men wanted, but she got no pleasure from them herself. She thought it was just because of Sam, her only lover for years, but when Bernie had forced himself on her and she hadn't had the energy or the power to fight him off, she knew that she could never enjoy the act with any man. Bernie had at least been kind and gentle when he got her where he wanted her, but it made no difference to the way she felt about what he was doing.

She looked at the lantern-lit guests again. Sam was dancing with an attractive brunette, probably from Collier Foods, and Nicholas was back in circulation, talking and laughing by the fountain with a group of commuters who lived in Swainsdale and made their money elsewhere. His lower lip was swollen as if he'd been stung by a bee. When he caught her glance, he glared at her with such lust and hatred that she shivered and pulled her shawl up more tightly around her shoulders.

II

In Toronto, Banks combined sightseeing with his search for Anne Ralston in the English-style pubs. The weather remained uncomfortably hot and humid, and a window-rattling thunderstorm one night only seemed to make things worse the next day.

Banks gave the CN Tower a miss, but he walked around the Eaton Centre, a huge shopping mall with a glass roof and a flock of sculptured Canada geese flying in to land at one end, and he visited Yonge and Dundas after dark to watch the hookers and street kids on the neon strip. He took a ferry to Ward's Island and admired the Toronto skyline before walking along the boardwalk on the south side. Lake Ontario glittered in the sun, as vast as an ocean. He went to Harbourfront, where he sipped Carlsberg on a waterfront patio and watched the white sails of the yachts cut slow as knives through treacle in the haze.

One morning he took a bus to Kleinburg to see the McMichael collection. Sandra, he thought, would love the Lawren Harris mountain-scapes and the native art. Also in the collection was a painting by Emily Carr that he associated with Jenny Fuller, a psychologist friend who sometimes helped with cases in Eastvale. She had a print of it on her living-room wall, and it was at her suggestion that he had made the visit.

Nor could he bear to miss Niagara Falls. If anything, it was even more magnificent than he had expected. He went out on the Maid of the Mist, wrapped up in oilskins, and the boat tossed like a cork when it reached the bottom of the falls. From a certain angle, he could see a rainbow cut diagonally across the water. When the boat got closer, the spray filled his eyes like a mist and he could see nothing; he could hear only the primeval roar of the water.

The rest of the time, he visited pubs. Allowing an hour or so in each, he would sit at the bar, show the photographs and ask after Bernard Allen and Anne Ralston of bar staff and customers.

This part of the job was hard on his liver and kidneys, so he tried to slow down his intake and pace himself. To make the task more interesting—for solo pub-crawling is hardly the most exciting pastime in the world—he sampled different kinds of draft beer, both imported and domestic. Most of the Canadian beers tasted the same, and they were uniformly gassy. The English beers, he found, didn't travel well. Double Diamond and Watney's he determinedly ignored, just as he did back home. By far the best were the few local brews that Gerry Webb had told him about: Arkell Bitter, Wellington County Ale, Creemore Springs Lager and Conner

Bitter. Smooth and tasty, they had body and, when required, boasted fine heads.

Despite good beer, he was heartily sick of pubs. He was smoking too much, drinking too much and eating too much fried food. On Tuesday, after getting back from Kleinburg, he had tried The Sticky Wicket, the Madison and the Duke of York, all close to the university. No luck. On Wednesday, after his return from Niagara Falls, he had started out at The Spotted Dick, then made his way down busy Yonge Street among the shoppers and pleasure-seekers to the Hop and Grape, via the Artful Dodger and The Jack Russell. He had sat in the Hop and Grape, on the ground floor of an office block near Yonge and College, and watched long-haired heavy-metal fans in the street flock towards a rock concert at Maple Leaf Gardens. His clothes were soaked with sweat and his feet hurt. The pub was quiet at that time, as the office workers had gone home and the evening crowds hadn't yet turned up. There were only two days left, and he was very much conscious of time's winged chariot at his rear. Fed up, he had gone back to the house for an early night.

He knew he had to be right, though; Bernard Allen had frequented an English-style pub, and he must have had drinking companions who would be mourning his loss.

On Thursday at about three-fifteen, Banks got off a streetcar outside The Feathers, in the east end of the city. The inside door opened opposite a small darts area: two boards against a green baize backing, pock-marked with miss-shots. To his left was the pub itself, all darkly gleaming wood, polished brass and deep red velvet upholstery. And it was cool.

The wall opposite the bar was covered with framed photographs, mostly of English and Scottish scenes. Banks recognized a pub he knew in York, Theakston's brewery in Masham, a road sign he'd often passed on the way to Ripon and, most surprising of all, a photo of the Queen's Arms in Eastvale's cobbled market square. It was an odd sensation, seeing that. He was in a pub over three thousand miles from home looking at a photo of the Queen's Arms. Eerie.

The place was almost empty. Near the door sat a group of four or five people listening to a silver-haired man with a lived-in face and a Lancashire accent complain about income tax.

Banks stood at the bar close to a very tall man with short, neat hair. He was smoking a pipe and staring abstractedly into space as if musing about the follies of mankind. Behind the bar, above the till, was a small Union Jack.

"I'll have a pint of Creemore, please," Banks said, noticing the logo on one of the pumps.

The barmaid smiled. She had curly auburn hair and brown eyes full of humour and mischief. When she walked over to the end of the bar to fill a waitress's order, Banks noticed she was wearing a very short skirt. It did more than justice to a fine pair of legs.

"Quiet," Banks commented, when she placed the ice-cold pint in front of him.

"It usually is at this time," she said. "We get busy around five when people drop in after work."

Banks took a deep breath and reached for the photographs in his jacket pocket. They were getting dog-eared. He was so used to disappointment that he put hardly any enthusiasm into his question: "I don't suppose you had a regular here by the name of Bernard Allen, did you?"

"Bernie?" she said. "Bernie who got killed over in England?"

Banks could hardly believe his ears. "Yes," he said. "Did you know him?"

The barmaid's eyes turned serious as she spoke. "He was a regular here," she said. "I wouldn't say I really knew him, but I talked to him now and then. You know, like you do when you're waitressing. He was a nice guy. Never made any trouble. It was terrible what happened."

"Did he drink alone?"

"No. There was a group of them—Bernie, Glen, Barry and Ian. They always sat in that corner over there." She pointed to a round table opposite the far end of the bar.

"Was there ever a woman with them?"

"Sometimes. But I never talked to her. Why do you want to know all this? Are you a cop or something?"

Banks decided on honesty. "Yes," he said. "But I'm here unofficially. We think Bernie met an old friend over here who might have some information for us. It could help us find out who killed him."

The barmaid rested her elbows on the bar and leaned forward.

Banks showed her the photographs. "Is this her?"

She looked closely and frowned. "It could be. The shape of the face is the same, but everything else is different. These must be old photos."

"They are," Banks said. "But it could be her?"

"Yes. Look, I'm sorry, I can't stand here talking. I honestly don't know much more. Jack over there used to talk to Bernie sometimes. He might be able to help."

She pointed to a man on the periphery of the group near the entrance. He was a solidly built man with a moustache and a fine head of greyish hair, in his mid to late thirties, Banks guessed. At the moment, he seemed to be poring over a crossword puzzle.

"Thank you." Banks picked up his half-finished pint and walked over to the table. He introduced himself and Jack told him to pull up a chair. The Lancastrian at the next table lit a cigarette and said, "I'll just have another gin and tonic, then I'll go."

"We weren't really close friends," Jack said when Banks had asked about Bernie, "but we had some decent conversations." He had a Canadian accent, which surprised Banks. He'd assumed that apart from the bar staff all the regulars were British.

"What did you talk about?"

"Books, mostly. Literature. Bernie was about the only other guy I knew who'd read Proust."

"Proust?"

Jack gave him a challenging look. "Greatest writer who ever lived. He wrote *Remembrance of Things Past.*"

"Maybe I'll give him a try," Banks answered, not sure what he was letting himself in for. He tended to follow through on most of his self-made promises to read or listen to things other people recommended, though time constraints always ensured he had a huge backlog.

"Do that," said Jack. "Then I'll have someone to talk to again. Excuse me." He got up and went to the washroom.

The Lancastrian belched and said to the waitress, "Gin and tonic please, love. No fruit."

Banks observed the other people at the table: a small, slim youth with an earring and a diamond stud in his left ear; a taller thin-faced

man with a brush-cut and glasses; a soft-spoken man with a hint of
an Irish accent. They were all listening to a Welshman telling jokes.

Jack sat down again and ordered another pint of Black Label.
The waitress, a nicely tanned blonde with a beautiful smile, took
Banks's order for another Creemore, too, and delivered both drinks
in no time. Banks paid, leaving her a good tip—one thing he'd soon
learned to do on his pub-crawl of Toronto.

"Did you know any of Bernie's friends?" he asked.

Jack shook his head. "Self-important Brits, for the most part.
They tend to pontificate a bit too much for my liking. But Bernie
seemed to have transcended the parochial barriers of most English
teachers."

Marilyn Rosenberg, at Toronto Community College, had said
much the same thing in a different way. Whether it was a plus or a
minus in her eyes, Banks hadn't been sure.

"When do they usually come in?"

"About five, most days."

Banks looked at his watch; it was just after four.

"Thanks a lot," he said. "By the way, six across is sculls. 'Rows—
of heads, we hear!' Head . . . skull. To row . . . to scull." Jack raised
his eyebrows and filled in the answer.

They worked at the crossword together for the next hour as the
place filled up. At quarter past five, they were puzzling over "Take
away notoriety and attack someone (6)" when two men in white
shirts and business suits walked in.

"That's them over there," Jack said. "Excuse me if I don't join you."

Banks smiled. "Thanks for your help, anyway."

"Nice meeting you," Jack said, and they shook hands. "Defame.
Of course!" he exclaimed just before Banks moved away. "'Take
away notoriety and attack someone.' Defame. Amazing how you
get so much more done when there are two minds working at it."

Banks agreed. It was the same with police work. He could
certainly have done with some help on this trip. Not Sergeant
Hatchley—he hadn't the self-control to separate work from a
pub-crawl—but DC Richmond would have been fine.

When he got to their table, the two men had already taken the
opportunity to loosen their ties, take off their suit jackets and roll

up their sleeves. One was tall and skinny with a bony face and fine blond hair plastered flat against his skull to cover the receding hairline; the other, who only came up to his friend's shoulders, was pudgy and also balding. What little hair he had stood out like a kind of mist or halo around his head. He wore a fixed smile on his lips, and his dark eyes darted everywhere.

Banks walked over to them and told them why he was in Toronto.

"I'm Ian Grainger," said the tall blond one. "Sit down."

"Barry Clark," the other said, still smiling and looking everywhere but at Banks.

"Glen should be along in a while," Ian said. "How can we help you?"

"I'm not sure if you can. I'm looking for Anne Ralston."

For a moment, both men frowned and looked puzzled.

"You might know her as Julie."

"Oh, Julie. Yes, of course," Barry said. "You lost me there for a second. Sure we know Julie. But what could she have to do with Bernie's murder?" His accent was English, as was Ian's, but Banks couldn't place either of them exactly.

"I don't honestly know if she had anything to do with it," Banks said. "But she's the only real lead we've got." He explained about her disappearance just after the Addison murder.

The drinks arrived just before Glen Tadworth, a dark-bearded, well-padded young man with a pronounced academic stoop and a well-developed beer belly, walked over to join them. His red shirt seemed glued to his skin, and there were wet patches under the arms and across the chest. He carried a battered black briefcase stuffed with papers, which he plonked on the floor as he sat down and sighed.

"Bloody students," he said, running his hand through his greasy black hair. "'Dover Beach'—a simple enough poem, you'd say, wouldn't you?" He looked at Banks as he talked, even though they hadn't been introduced. "One bright spark came up with the theory that it was about Matthew Arnold's hangover. Quite elaborate, it was, too. The 'grating roar' was the poet being sick. And as for the 'long line of spray'. . . . Well, I suppose one should be grateful for their inventiveness, but really . . ." He threw his hands up, then reached over and took a long swig from Ian's pint.

"Don't mind him," Barry said, managing to keep his eyes on Banks for a split second as he spoke. "He's always like this. Always complaining." And he introduced them.

"From Swainsdale, eh?" Glen said. "A breath of fresh air from the old country. Lord, what I'd give to be able to live back there again. Not Swainsdale in particular, though it'd do. I'm from the West Country myself—Exeter. The accent's flattened out a bit over the years here, I'm afraid."

"Why can't you go back if you want to?" Banks asked, reaching for another cigarette. "Surely you weren't sent into permanent exile?"

"Metaphorically, my dear Chief Inspector, metaphorically. You know, some people have got hold of the idea that we expatriates, scattered around the ex-colonies and various watering-holes of Europe and Asia, are all pipe-puffing Tories enjoying life without income tax."

"And aren't you?"

"Far from it. Where is that waitress? Ah, Stella, my dear, a pint of Smithwick's please. Where was I? Exile. Yes. If the government really did seek our proxy votes in the next election, I think they'd bloody well regret it. Most of us feel like exiles. We have skills that no-one back home seems to value any more. It's hard enough getting jobs here, but at least it's possible. And they pay well. But I, for one, would be perfectly happy to do the same work back home for less money. There's hardly a day goes by when I don't think about going back."

"What about Bernie?"

"He was as bad as Glen, if not worse," Barry said. "At least recently he was. Full of nostalgia. It's time-travel they're after really, you know, not just a flight across the Atlantic. All of us baby boomers are nostalgic when it comes down to it. That's why we prefer the Beatles to Duran Duran."

Banks also liked the Beatles better than Duran Duran, a group that his son, Brian, had inflicted on him once or twice before moving on to something new. He thought it was because of the quality of the music, but maybe Barry Clark was right and it was

more a matter of nostalgia than anything else. His own father had
been just the same, he remembered, going on about Glenn Miller,
Nat Gonella and Harry Roy when Banks had wanted to listen to
Elvis Presley, The Shadows and Billy Fury.

"The longer you're away, the more you idealize the image of
home," Barry went on, eyes roving the room. The place was packed
and noisy now. People stood three deep at the bar. Jack, Banks
noticed, had been joined by a small, pretty woman with short, dark
hair laid flat against her skull. The Lancastrian and his friends had left.
"Of course, what people don't realize is that the country's changed
beyond all recognition," Barry continued. "We'd be foreigners there
now, but to us home is still the Queen's Christmas message, the last
night of the Proms, Derby Day, the Test Match at Lords, the FA Cup
Final—without bloodshed!—leafy lanes, a green and pleasant land.
Ordered and changeless. Bloody hell, even the dark Satanic mills have
some sort of olde worlde charm for homesick expatriates."

"Damn right," Glen said. "I'd work in a bloody Woollen mill in
Bingley if it meant being back home. Well, maybe. . . . It's the wist-
fulness of the exile, you see, Chief Inspector. You get it a lot in
poetry. Especially the Irish."

Banks was beginning to see what Jack had meant.

"Bernie was just the same," Ian said. "You should have heard him
going on about Yorkshire. It was bloody Dales this and bloody
Dales that. You'd think he was talking about paradise. You'll never
catch me going back to live over there. Canada's a great place as far
as I'm concerned."

"That's because you're in real estate," Glen said. "You're making
a bloody fortune. Is that all you care about—the material things?
What about your soul, your roots?"

"Oh, shut up, Glen. You're getting tiresome."

"If he could have got a job over there," Banks asked, "do you
think he would have gone back?"

"Like a shot," Ian answered. The others agreed.

"Did he ever mention anything about a job?"

"He did say there was a chance of getting back to stay," Glen
said. "Lucky bastard. But I didn't know whether to believe him or
not."

"What was this chance?"

"He didn't say. Very hush-hush, apparently."

"Why?"

Glen scratched his shoulder and tried to unstick the shirt from his armpit. "Dunno. It was just one of those nights when you've had a few too many, if you know what I mean. Bernie said something about a plan he had to get himself back home."

"But he gave you no details?"

"No. Said he'd let us know after he got back."

"Was it a job he mentioned?"

"Not specifically, no. Just a chance to get back. I assumed it must have been some possible job offer. How else would he be able to live?"

"How attached was he to teaching?"

"He liked it up to a point," Glen answered. "It was something he was good at. He should have been teaching university. He was good enough, but there aren't any jobs. Like most of us, though, he hated the conditions he had to work in and he despised the students' wilful ignorance. They don't know anything and they don't want to know unless it's in a ballpark or on video. They expect you to spoon-feed them knowledge, then ask them to regurgitate it in a test. For that they expect to be given an A-plus, no matter how bad their writing or how inaccurate their answers. I could go on—"

"You usually do, Glen," Barry cut in, "but I don't think Mr Banks wants to hear it."

Banks smiled. "Actually, I am running out of time," he said. "I need to find Julie as quickly as possible. Do you know where she lives?"

"No," said Ian. "She just comes in on a Friday after work for a couple of drinks."

"It's somewhere near here, I think," Barry added. "She mentioned sunbathing in Kew Gardens once."

"Have you any idea what surname she's using?"

"It's Culver, isn't it?" Barry said. "Or Cleaver, Carver, something like that."

None of the others could improve on Barry's contribution.

"Do you know where she works?"

"In one of those towers near King and Bay," Ian answered. "The TD Centre or First Canadian Place. She complained that the elevators made her ears go funny."

"That's a lot of help," Glen said. "Do you know how many businesses operate from those places?"

Ian shrugged. "Well, that's all I know. What about you?"

Glen and Barry both shook their heads.

"She should be in here at about six tomorrow, though," Barry said. "She hasn't missed a week yet."

"Fine. Look, would you do me a favour? If she turns up early or if I'm late, please don't tell her I want to see her. It might scare her off. You know how some people react to the police."

"Are you sure you're not after her for something?" Glen asked suspiciously.

"Information. That's all."

"All right," Glen agreed. "If it's going to help catch Bernie's killer, we'll do whatever you want." He paused to pick up his pint glass and raise it for a toast. "There is one good thing in all this, you know. At least Bernie died in the place he wanted to live."

"Yes," Banks said. "There is that."

And they all drank to dying where they wanted to live.

ELEVEN

I

"John told me about Nick's behaviour at the party the other night," Stephen Collier said. "I'm sorry. I warned you to stay away from him."

Katie looked down at the stony path and blushed. "I didn't go seeking him," she said. "He's an animal, a filthy animal."

"But he is my brother, Katie. He's the only family I've got left. I know he acts outrageously sometimes, but . . . I promise it won't happen again."

Katie remembered a phrase from the Bible: "Am I my brother's keeper?" Could Stephen keep Nicholas like an animal in a zoo? He looked strained, she thought. He poked at the stones and sods with his ashplant stick as they walked; his face was pale and the tic in his eye was getting worse.

It was fine walking weather: warm but not hot, with a few high, white clouds and no sign of rain. Sam was in Eastvale for the day— not that Katie's walking out with Stephen would have mattered to him, she thought; he practically threw her at the Colliers as if she were his membership ticket to some exclusive club.

They took the diagonal path up the side of Swainshead Fell, heading for the source of the river. The air was clear, and after a few minutes walking even Stephen's pallid cheeks began to glow like embers.

At last they reached their destination. The source of the River Swain was an unspectacular wet patch on the side of Swainshead Fell. All around it, the grass was greener and grew more abundantly than anywhere else. Only yards away was the source of another river, the Gaiel, which, when it reached the valley below, perversely turned north towards Cumbria.

Stephen had brought a flask of coffee and some dark chocolate. They sat down to eat on the dry grass above the source and looked back on Swainshead. A tewit went into his extended "pee-wit" song as he wove through the air, plummeted and levelled out just before hitting the ground. His wings beat like sheets flapping in a gale.

"He must be trying to attract a mate," Stephen said.

"Or scare us away."

"Perhaps. Coffee? Chocolate?"

Katie accepted the plastic cup of black coffee. She usually liked hers with plenty of cream and a spoonful of sugar, but she took it as it came without complaint. The dark, bitter chocolate puckered her taste buds.

"I shouldn't be here, you know," she said, pushing back a stray wisp of fair hair behind her ear.

"Relax," Stephen said. "Sam's in Eastvale."

"I know. But that's not the point. People will talk."

"Why should they? There's nothing to talk about. Everybody knows we're all friends. You're so old fashioned, Katie."

Katie flushed. "I can't help it. I wish I could," she added in a whisper.

"Look," Stephen went on in a soothing voice, "we've just gone for a short walk up the fell-side, as many people do. Where's the harm in that? We're not hiding from anyone, we're not sneaking off. You act as if we're guilty of something terrible."

"It just feels wrong," Katie said, managing a brief smile. "Oh, don't mind me. I'm trying, I really am. I'm just not very good with people."

"Don't you feel comfortable with me?"

Katie fidgeted with the silver paper from the chocolate wrapper, folding it into a neat, shiny square. "I don't know," she said. "I don't feel afraid."

Stephen laughed. "At least that's a start. But seriously, Katie, sometimes it's necessary to talk. I told you the other night I've got nobody. Nick's hardly the type to make a good listener, and the people at work are just that: employees, colleagues, not friends."

"What about all those guests at the party?"

"Nick's people, most of them. Or from work, business acquaintances. Don't you ever need to talk to someone real, Katie? Don't you ever have problems you want to let out and share?"

Katie frowned and stared at him. "Yes," she said. "Yes, of course I do. But I'm no good at it. I don't know where to start."

"Start with your life, Katie. Are you happy?"

"I don't know. Am I supposed to be?"

"That's what life's for, isn't it, to be enjoyed?"

"Or suffered."

"Are you suffering?"

"I don't think I'm happy, if that's what you mean."

"Why don't you do something about it?"

"There's nothing I can do."

"But there must be. You must be able to change things if you want."

"I don't see how. What would I do? Without the guest house I've got nothing. Where would I go? I don't know anywhere outside Leeds and Swainsdale." She toyed with a stray tress of hair. "I could just see me down in London or somewhere like that. I wouldn't last five minutes."

"Cities aren't quite as bad as you think they are. You only see the worst on television. Many people live happy lives there."

"Still," Katie said, "I'd be lost." She finished the coffee and wiped her lips with the back of her hand.

"Perhaps by yourself you would be."

"What do you mean?"

Suddenly Stephen seemed closer, and somehow he seemed to be holding her hand. Katie tensed. She didn't want to upset him. If he wanted to touch her she would have to let him, but her stomach clenched and the wind roared in her ears. His touch was oddly chaste, though; it didn't seem to threaten her at all.

"I don't know, Katie," he said. "I'm not sure what I'm saying. But I've got to go away. I can't stay around here any longer."

"But why not?"

She felt him trembling as he moved even closer and his grip tightened on her hand. "There are things you don't know anything about, Katie," he said. "Dear, sweet Katie." And he brushed his fingers down her cheek. They felt cold.

Katie wanted to move away, but she didn't dare struggle. "I don't know what you mean," she burst out. "Sam's always telling me I know nothing, too. What is it? Am I so blind or so stupid?" There were tears in her eyes now, blurring her vision of the valley below and the water that bubbled relentlessly from the source.

"No," Stephen said. "No, you're not blind or stupid. But things aren't always what they seem, people aren't what they pretend to be. Listen, let me tell you . . ."

II

The woman who sat opposite Banks in the dining section of The Feathers had changed considerably from the one in Bernard Allen's photograph, but it was definitely the same person. She wore her hair cut short and tinted blonde now, and dressed in a cream business suit. When she sat down and fished in her bag for a cigarette, Banks also noticed that the carefree laughter in her eyes had hardened into a wary, suspicious look. Her long cigarette had a white filter which soon became blotched with lipstick; she had a habit of tapping it on the edge of the ashtray even when there was no ash, and she held it straight out between the V of her first two fingers like an actress in an old movie, pursing her lips to inhale. Her nails were long and painted red.

She had turned up at six, as Glen had said, and she and Banks had left the others to go and talk privately over dinner. There wasn't much separation between the two areas of the pub except for the way the seating was arranged, and they could still hear the conversations at the bar and the tables.

The waitress, a petite brunette with a twinkle in her eye and a cheeky smile, came up and gave them menus. "Something to drink?" she asked.

Julie ordered a White Russian and Banks a glass of red wine, just for a change.

"I need to know why you left Swainshead in such a hurry," he said, when the waitress had gone for the drinks.

"Can't a woman do as she pleases? It's not a police state, you know. Or it wasn't when I was last there."

"Nor is it now. It was your timing that interested us."

"Oh? Why?"

"We tend to be suspicious of someone who disappears without a trace the day after a murder."

"That was nothing to do with me."

"Don't play the innocent. What did you expect us to think? You could have been in danger yourself, or you could have been the killer. For all we knew you could have been buried down a disused mine shaft. You didn't stop to let anyone know what had happened to you."

"Well, I'm telling you now. That killing had nothing to do with me."

"How do you know about it? You don't seem at all surprised at my mentioning it, but the body wasn't discovered until after you'd left."

Julie ground her cigarette into the ashtray. "Don't try your tricks on me," she said. "I read the papers. I know what happened."

The waitress arrived with the drinks and asked if they were ready to order. Banks asked for a few more minutes and she smiled and went away. Julie turned to her menu.

"What would you recommend?" Banks asked.

She shrugged. "The food's always good here. It depends what you fancy. The prime-rib roast and Yorkshire pudding on special is excellent, if you don't mind being reminded too much of home."

Banks looked around at the decor and the photos on the walls. "Not at all," he said, smiling.

This time a different waitress came for their orders, an attractive woman with reddish blonde hair and a warm manner. Banks hoped he hadn't offended the other.

"Where did you go?" he asked Julie, as soon as they'd ordered their meals.

"None of your damn business." She sipped her White Russian.

"A week after you left," Banks pressed on, "the body of a London private-enquiry agent called Raymond Addison was discovered in Swainshead. He'd been murdered. Did you know anything about that?"

"No."

"We've got good reason to think you did. Listen, if you want to make things difficult Miss Ralston—"

"It's Culver, Mrs. Mrs Julie Culver. And it's quite legal. Julie's my middle name and Culver is my husband's. Ex-husband's, I should say."

"Why change your name if you've nothing to hide?"

She shrugged. "It was a new start. Why not a new name?"

"Not very convincing. But Mrs Culver it is. We're on good terms with the Canadian government. We have extradition arrangements and a mutual help policy. If I wanted to, I could make enough fuss to have you sent back to England to answer my questions. This is the easy way."

Julie lit another cigarette. "I don't believe you. I'm a Canadian citizen now. You can't touch me at all."

"That doesn't matter," Banks said. "You're connected to a murder in England. Don't expect your government to protect you from that."

"But you can't prove I had anything to do with it. It's just a coincidence I went away then."

"Is it? What about your involvement with Stephen Collier?"

Julie paled. "What about it? What's he been telling you?"

"Nothing. What does he know?"

"How should I know?"

Banks sighed. "A few weeks ago a friend of yours, Bernard Allen, was murdered in the hanging valley just over Swainshead Fell."

"I know the place," Julie said sadly. "I've been there with him. It always looked like autumn. But what makes you think his death had anything to do with me? I wasn't even in the country. I was here. It could have been a thief or a psycho . . . or a . . . a . . ."

There was something in her tone that let Banks know she was interested now, no longer so hostile. "In the first place," he said, "we know that you told him not to let anyone know he'd met you here, which is suspicious enough in itself. And in the second place, he did tell someone: a woman called Katie Greenock. Her heart seems to be in the right place, but she told her husband, Sam, who soon broadcasted it to the whole White Rose crowd. In the third place, Bernard had been talking about going home to stay, and there's no evidence he had a job lined up. Then Bernard got killed before he had a chance to leave the dale. What does all that indicate to you?"

"You're the sleuth. You tell me." Julie blew cigarette smoke down her nose.

Banks leaned forward. "The way I read it," he said, "is that you knew something about Raymond Addison's murder. Something incriminating. I'm not sure who else was involved, or why, but it had to be someone with money. I'd guess that Stephen Collier played a large part. I think you told Bernard what you knew and he intended to use that knowledge to blackmail his way to what he wanted most—his return to Swainshead."

"My God! I . . . Are you trying to say I'm responsible for Bernie's death?"

"I'm not placing any blame, Mrs Culver. I simply want to know what happened. I want to nail Bernie's killer."

Julie seemed to be thinking fast. Conflicting emotions flashed across her face. "I'm not guilty of anything," she said finally. "I've nothing to be afraid of. And I don't believe you. Bernie could never have been a blackmailer."

The waitress brought their food. Before she left, they ordered another round of drinks, then Banks tucked into his roast, while Julie picked at a Caesar salad. They remained silent while they ate. It wasn't until they both pushed their plates aside and reached for their cigarettes that Julie started to talk again.

"It's been such a long time, you know," she began. "A lot's happened. There's been long stretches when I haven't thought about Swainshead at all."

"Not homesick?"

"Me? I'm at home anywhere. Almost anywhere. Though I can't say I cared for the Middle East much."

"Bernie was homesick."

"He was the type, though, wasn't he? If you'd known him you'd have understood. The place was in his blood. He couldn't even really settle down in Leeds. Yes, Bernie wanted to go back. Which was a shame. I'd kind of been hoping . . ."

"You and Bernie? Again?"

She raised a thin, dark-pencilled eyebrow. "You know about that?"

"It was hardly a state secret."

"True. Anyway, why not? We were both free agents again."

"Tell me what happened five years ago that sent you running off around the world."

The waitress came to pick up their plates. Banks ordered a pint of Creemore this time and Julie asked for a coffee and a double Cognac. All the spaces were occupied now. Next to them, a group of about eight people had pulled two tables together.

"It seems more like a million years ago," Julie said when she got her drink. "I suppose I was a naïve young thing back then. My education really began after I left."

She was stalling for time, Banks thought, telling the story her own way. Perhaps she wasn't sure yet whether she was going to tell him the truth or not. The best thing for now, he decided, was to let her go with it and subtly steer her in the right direction. "Where did you go?" he asked.

"First I went to Europe. I'd been saving up for quite a long time—kept my money under the mattress, believe it or not—just waiting for the day when I knew I would take off and never come back. I took a boat over to Holland and ended up in Amsterdam for a while. Then I bummed around France, Italy, Germany. To cut a long story short, I met a man. A Canadian. This'd be about a year later. He took me back to Vancouver with him and we got married." Julie blew out a steady stream of smoke. "Life was fine for a while . . . then he decided I wasn't enough for him. Two can play at that game, I thought. . . . Anyway, it ended."

"When did you first get in touch with Bernie?"

"About eighteen months ago. That was after I split up with Charles. Bernie was having marriage problems of his own, I soon found out, and he seemed happy enough to hear from me. I might have got in touch with him earlier, but I'd been wary about doing so. I knew he was here, of course. He left Swainshead before I did. But I felt that I'd burned all my bridges."

"What made you contact him, then?"

"Circumstances, really. I'm a freelance publicity agent. I started the business in Vancouver because I liked the idea and it gave me something to do while my husband was . . . not around." She tapped her cigarette against the glass ashtray. "It turned out I had a knack, a flair, so I decided to open an office in Toronto as well. I don't know how much you understand about Canada, but Toronto is pretty much the centre of the universe here. I knew Bernie lived in the city, so I thought what the hell. Any trouble I might have caused would have blown over by now anyway."

"Trouble?"

She narrowed her eyes and looked at him closely. "I had thought Bernie might not want to see me."

"I don't understand."

"I went out with Stephen Collier."

"But Bernard was over here by then. What was that to him?"

"It's not that. Bernie and I were never much more than child-hood sweethearts anyway. But we were close friends, like brother and sister. I was hoping that might change here . . ." She sighed. "Anyway, it's just that Stephen . . . well . . . he's a Collier."

"And Bernie was very class conscious?"

"Yes."

"So he'd feel betrayed."

"Something like that."

"And did he?"

"He wrote me some pretty nasty letters at the time. Then, when I went away, we lost touch for a while. But when we met up again here it had all blown over. Bernie was compassionate. He understood. That's why I can't believe he was a blackmailer."

"He might not have been. I can't be sure. He might just have opened his mouth out of turn."

Julie smiled. "That sounds more like him."

"What about Nicholas Collier?" Banks asked. "Were you ever involved with him?"

Julie raised her eyebrows. "What on earth do you think I am?" she asked, smiling. "I didn't get around that much. And credit me with some taste. Nicky really did nothing for me, though I caught him giving me the eye once or twice."

"Sorry," Banks said. "I'm not trying to insinuate you're a—"

"Tart? Slut? Harlot? Jezebel? Loose woman? Believe me, I've been called much worse." The old laughter lit up Julie's eyes for a moment. "Do you know the difference between a slut and a bitch?"

Banks shook his head.

"A slut is a woman who sleeps with anyone; a bitch is a woman who sleeps with anyone but you."

Banks laughed. "That's from the man's point of view, of course."

"Of course."

"So what happened?" he asked. "What made you leave when you did?"

"You're a persistent man, Mr Banks," Julie said, lighting another long, white cigarette. "Even my tasteless jokes don't seem to deflect you for very long. But I'm still not sure I ought to tell you."

Banks caught her eyes and held them. "Mrs Culver," he said quietly, "Bernard Allen—your childhood sweetheart, as you called him—was murdered. All murders are cruel and vicious, but this one was worse than many. First he was stabbed, and then his face was slashed and beaten in with a rock so nobody could recognize him. When we found him he'd been hidden away in the hanging valley for nearly two weeks and there were maggots crawling out of his eye sockets."

Julie turned pale and gripped her Cognac glass so tightly Banks thought she was going to shatter it. Her jaw was clenched and a muscle just below her ear twitched. "Bastard," she whispered.

The silent tension between them seemed to last for hours. Banks could hear the aimless chatter around him as if it were from a distant movie soundtrack: snippets of conversation about marathon running, beer, cricket and teaching native children up north, all in a medley of Canadian, Yorkshire, London and Scottish accents. Julie didn't even seem to realize he was there any more. She was staring at the wall just to the left of him. He half-turned and saw a photograph of a wooded valley. The leaves were russet, yellow and orange.

He lit a cigarette. Julie finished her Cognac and a little colour returned to her cheeks. The waitress came by and they ordered another round.

When they had their drinks, Julie shook her head and regarded Banks with something close to hatred. "For Bernie, then," she said, and began: "The night before I left I was supposed to see Stephen. We'd arranged to go to dinner at the Box Tree in Ilkley. He picked me up about half an hour late and he seemed unusually agitated— so much so that he pulled into a lay-by after we'd not gone more than four or five miles. And then he told me. He said there'd been some trouble and someone had got hurt. He didn't say killed at that time, just hurt. He was in a terrible state. Then he said something about the past catching up, that it was connected with something that had happened in Oxford."

"When he was at university there?"

"I suppose so. He did go to Oxford. Anyway, this man, a private investigator, had turned up out of the blue and was intent on causing trouble. Stephen told me that Sam Greenock called and said there was someone looking for a Mr Collier. Sam was a bit suspicious about the newcomer asking questions and didn't give anything away. The man said he was going for a short evening walk up the valley. Stephen said he went after him and they talked and the man was going to blackmail the family."

"About this event that had occurred in Oxford?"

"Yes. According to Stephen, tempers were raised, they fought and the man was hurt—badly hurt. I told Stephen he should call an ambulance.

"He got angry then and told me I didn't understand. That was when he said the man was dead. He went on to say there was nothing to connect them. Sam would keep quiet if they humoured him and let him play the local squire. Stephen just had to tell someone, to unburden himself, and he didn't really have anyone else he felt he could talk to but me."

"What was your reaction?"

Julie lit a fresh cigarette from the stub of her old one. "You have to understand Stephen," she said. "In many ways he's a kind, considerate, gentle man. But he's also a businessman and he can be ruthless when he feels the need. But more than all that, he's a Collier. There are few things more important to him than the good name of his family and its history. I wouldn't say I was in love with him, but I thought a lot of him and I didn't want to see him suffer. Needless to say, we didn't have dinner that night. We stopped at the nearest pub and had a bit too much to drink, then we—" Julie stopped. "The rest is of no interest. I never saw him again after that night."

"Why did you leave the next day? Did he suggest it to you?"

"No. I think he trusted me. He knew I was on his side."

"So why did you go?"

"For my own reasons. First, and perhaps least, I'd been thinking about making a break for a while. I've no family. My parents died ten years ago and I just kept on at the cottage. I had no real ambitions, no plans for my life. I was getting bored with my job and I was realistic enough not to see myself as the future Mrs Stephen Collier. Stephen wasn't going to propose, and I'd had hints from him that Nicholas didn't consider me to be of the right class, as if I wasn't aware of that already. These new events just hurried me along a bit. Secondly, I didn't trust myself. I thought if the police came around and started asking me questions, they'd know something was wrong and they'd keep pressuring me until I gave Stephen away. I didn't want to let that happen. I'm not a good liar, Mr Banks, as you can see."

"And third?"

"Fear."

"Of Stephen?"

"Yes. As I said, he's a complex man. There's a dark side to him. He's vulnerable in some ways, but very practical in others. Sentimental and pragmatic. It can sometimes make for a frightening combination. Didn't someone once say that Mafia dons are very sentimental people? Don't they send flowers to the widow when they've killed someone? And weren't the Nazis sentimental too? Anyway, he'd done it before, confided in me one day then cut me dead the next—no pun intended—just pretended we'd never been intimate at all. Basically, Stephen couldn't get close to anyone. He'd try, and one of the ways he did it was by confiding. But then he'd regret it the next day and turn cold. What worried me was the importance of this confidence. It was the kind of thing he might not be able to live with, someone as weak as me knowing his secret."

"In other words, you were worried you might become his next victim."

"I know it sounds a horrible thing to say about someone you basically like and respect—even loved, perhaps, once—but yes, it did cross my mind. Much easier to disappear, as I'd been thinking of it anyway. And there was no-one to make a fuss about my going."

"What kind of things did he confide in you about before?"

"Oh, nothing much. Perhaps a slightly shady business deal—he was pleased if he'd put one over on somebody. Or an income-tax fiddle. He hated the inland revenue."

"Nothing more?"

"No. Not until that time."

They sipped their drinks and let the conversations flow around them. Julie seemed more relaxed now she had told her story, and Banks could see no traces of that hateful look left in her eyes.

"Did he say anything else about this incident in Oxford?" he asked.

Julie shook her head. "Nothing."

"So you don't know what happened there, or who else might have been involved?"

"No. I'm sorry. At the time I never even thought to ask. It was all hard enough to take in as it was."

Banks sighed. Still, even if he hadn't uncovered the whole story yet, he'd done well. The trip had been worthwhile. Julie rejoined the others. Banks said his farewells and left. It was about nine o'clock, a hot, humid evening. Instead of taking the bus, he crossed Kingston Road and started walking towards the lake. The road sloped steeply at one point, crossed another main street with tram rails, then a hundred yards or so farther on ended at a beach.

Couples walked hand in hand along the boardwalk or sat on benches and stared out at the water. Some people jogged by, sweating, and others ambled along with dogs on leashes. Banks made his way over the soft sand to where a group of rocks stuck out into the lake. He clambered as far forward as he could and sat down on the warm stone. Water slopped around just below his feet. The horizon was a broad mauve band; above it, the sky's pink was tinged with misty grey. Banks lit a cigarette and wondered if it was the United States he could see in the distance or just a low, narrow layer of mist.

He'd got what he came for, though he still couldn't put everything together. At least when he got back he would be able to question Stephen Collier more thoroughly, no matter what the man's influence with the deputy chief constable. Collier had killed Raymond Addison, and he might even have killed Bernard Allen too. There was no proof as yet, but Banks would find some if it took him a lifetime. Collier wasn't going to escape justice because of influence or social position; of that Banks would make sure.

By the time he had finished his cigarette, the sun had gone down much lower and the sky had changed. The horizon was now grey, and the mauve band much higher in the sky. The lake seemed scattered with pink, as if the colour had transformed itself into raindrops and shattered the ice-blue surface of the water. Carefully, Banks got to his feet on the angled rock and made his way back towards a streetcar stop.

III

Earlier that day, back in Swainsdale, Detective Constable Philip Richmond had sat on a knoll high on Adam's Fell and unwrapped his cheese-and-pickle sandwiches. He flicked away the flies that gathered and poured some coffee from his flask. Up there, the air was pure and sharp; below, the sun glinted on the steel kegs in the backyard of the White Rose and flashed in the fountain playing in the Colliers' huge garden behind the ugly Gothic mansion. The old men stood on the bridge, and the Greenocks' front door was closed.

Sam had driven off on one of his regular jaunts to Leeds or Eastvale, and Katie had gone for a walk with Stephen Collier up Swainshead Fell. He thought he could see them across in the northeast, near a patch of grass that was greener than that around it, but it could have been someone else.

Sipping the bitter, black coffee, Richmond had reminded himself that tomorrow was his last day in Swainshead. He was expected back at the station with a report on Sunday morning. Not that he hadn't enjoyed himself—it had been very much like a week's holiday—but he longed to get back to his Eastvale mates. Tomorrow the rugby team was playing Skipton, a game he would have to miss. There was always a good booze-up and sing-song after the match, and it would be a shame to miss that too. Jim Hatchley was usually there for the booze, of course. An honorary member they called him now he wasn't fit enough to play any more. But even the sergeant's presence didn't spoil Richmond's fun: a few jars, a good sing-song, then, with a bit of luck, a kiss and a cuddle with Doreen on the way home. He prided himself on being a man of simple tastes, yet he also liked to think that nothing else about him was simple.

Finishing his sandwich, he unwrapped a Kit-Kat and picked up *The Three Stigmata of Palmer Eldritch*, the last of the four Philip K. Dick books he'd brought along. But he couldn't concentrate. He began to wonder why nothing had happened during Banks's absence. Was the killer certain that the chief inspector would find out nothing in Toronto? Or was there, perhaps, no connection at all between the Addison and Allen murders?

Certainly there had been a bit of a fuss or flap, as Freddie Metcalfe had said, earlier in the week. But it had soon died down and everyone carried on as normal. Was it a false sense of security? The lull before the storm. Perhaps they knew who Richmond was and were being especially careful? He certainly couldn't keep an eye on all of them.

He stroked his moustache and turned back to his book. Not ours to reason why . . . But still, he thought, an arrest would have helped his career. A thrilling car chase, perhaps, or a cross-country marathon. He pictured himself bringing in the killer, arm twisted up his back, and throwing him in Eastvale nick under Banks's approving smile. Then he laughed at himself, brushed a persistent wasp away and went back to Philip K. Dick.

IV

That Saturday, the afternoon of his last day in Toronto, Banks went to his first baseball game. The retractable roof was open, and a breeze from the lake relieved some of the humidity at the SkyDome, where the Toronto Blue Jays were playing the New York Yankees, but the temperature was still almost thirty degrees. In England, people would have been fainting from the heat.

Banks and Gregson sat in the stands, ate hotdogs and drank beer out of flimsy plastic cups.

"Lucky to be drinking it at all," Gregson said when Banks complained. "It took a lot of doing, getting drinking allowed at ball games."

A fat boy of about twelve sitting next to Banks stopped shovelling barbecue-flavoured potato crisps into his maw to stand up and hurl obscene death-threats at the Yankees' pitcher. His equally obese mother looked embarrassed but made no attempt to control him.

Banks wished his son, Brian, could be there. Unlike Banks, he had watched enough baseball on Channel 4 to be able to under-stand the game. When Banks first took his seat, the only baseball term he knew was "home run," but by the end of the third inning, Gregson had explained all about RBIs, the tops and bottoms of the innings, designated hitters, knuckle balls, the bullpen, bunting, the balk rule, pinch hitters and at least three different kinds of pitches.

The game mounted to an exciting conclusion, and the boy next to him spilled his crisps all over the floor.

Finally, the home crowd went wild. Down five-four at the bottom of the ninth, with two out, the sixth Blue Jay up drove one home with all the bases loaded—a grand slam, Gregson called it. That made the score eight-five, and that was how the game ended.

They pushed their way out of the stadium, and Gregson nego-tiated the heavy traffic up Spadina to Bloor, where they stopped in at the Madison for a farewell drink.

"Are you planning to do anything about the Culver woman?" Gregson asked.

Banks sipped his pint of Conner bitter. They were out on the patio, and the late afternoon sun beat down on his shoulders.

"No," he answered. "What did she do, after all?"

"From the sound of it, she withheld evidence. She was a material witness. If she'd spoken up, this new homicide might never have happened."

Banks shook his head. "She didn't have much choice really. I know what you mean, but you've got to understand what things are like around Swainshead. It's not like Toronto. She couldn't tell what she knew. There was loyalty, yes, but there was also fear. The Colliers are a powerful family. If she'd stayed we might have got something out of her, but on the other hand something might have happened to her first."

"So she left under threat?"

"That's the way I'd put it, yes."

"And you think this Collier guy killed Allen because he knew too much?"

"I think it was more to do with what Allen intended to do with his knowledge. I can't prove it, but I think he was going to blackmail Stephen Collier. Julie Culver disagrees, but from what one of Allen's boozing buddies told me, he had some plan to get back home to England. I think he asked Collier for the money to come home and live in Swainshead again, or maybe to fix him up with a job. Collier's brother teaches at a small public school, and Allen was a teacher. Maybe he suggested that Stephen tell Nicholas to get him a job there. Instead, Stephen decided to get rid of Allen the same way he did with Addison."

"Shit," said Gregson, "I'd no idea Toronto was so bad that people would stoop to blackmail to get out of here."

Banks laughed. "Maybe it's just that Swainsdale is so beautiful people would do anything to get there. I don't know. Allen was seriously disturbed, I think. A number of things took their toll on him: the divorce, the distance from home, the disappointment of not getting the kind of job that would really challenge his mind. Someone told me that he had gone beyond the parochial barriers of most English teachers, but he found himself in a system that placed no value on the exceptional, a system that almost imposed such barriers. The teaching he was doing was dreary, the students were ignorant and uninterested, and I think he tended to blame it on the local educational system. He thought things would be better in England. He probably remembered his own grammar-school days when even poor kids got to learn Latin, and he thought things were still like that. Perhaps he didn't even think he was doing anything really bad when he approached Collier. Or maybe he did. He had plenty of cause to resent him."

"That old British class system again?"

"Partly. It's hard to figure Allen out. Mostly, he seems like a decent person gone wrong, but he also had a big chip on his shoulder all along. I don't suppose we'll ever know what really motivated him."

"But you do have your killer."

"Yes—if he hasn't done a bunk. But we've no proof yet."

"He knows you're here, onto the girl?"

"The whole village knows. We've got a man there."

"Well, then . . . What time's your flight?"

"Nine o'clock." He looked at his watch. "Christ, it's six now. I'd better get back and pick up my stuff."

"I'll drive you," Gregson said. "I'm off duty all day, and it can be a real hassle getting to the airport."

"Would you? That's great."

At the house, Banks packed his meagre belongings and the presents he had bought for his family, then left a thank-you note with the bottle of Scotch for Gerry. In a way, he felt sad to leave the house and neighbourhood that had become familiar to him over the past week: the sound of streetcars rattling by; the valley with its expressway and green slopes; the downtown skyline; the busy, overflowing Chinese shops at Broadview and Gerrard.

The traffic along Lakeshore Boulevard to the airport turn-off wasn't too heavy, and they made it with plenty of time to spare. The two policemen swapped addresses and invitations outside the departures area, then Gregson drove straight off home. Banks didn't blame him. He'd always hated hanging around airports himself if he didn't have a plane to catch.

After the queue at the check-in desk, the trip to the duty-free shop, and the passage through security and immigration, it was almost time to board the plane. As they took off, Banks looked out of the window and saw the city lit up in the twilight below him: grids and figure-eights of light as far as he could see in every direction except south, where he could pick out the curve of the bay and the matt silver-grey of Lake Ontario.

Once in the air, it was on with the Walkman—Kiri te Kanawa's soaring arias seemed most appropriate this time—down the hatch with the Johnny Walker, and away with the food. A seasoned traveller already. This time even the movie was tolerable. A suspense thriller without the car chases and special effects that so often marred that type of film for Banks, it concentrated on the psychology of policeman and victim.

He slept for a while, managed to choke down the coffee and roll that came for breakfast, and looked out of the window to see the sun shining over Ireland.

It was going on for ten o'clock in the morning, local time, when he'd cleared customs and reclaimed his baggage. Among the crowd of people waiting to welcome friends and relatives stood Sandra, who threw her arms around him and gave him a long kiss.

"I told Brian and Tracy they should come, too," she said, breaking away and picking up the duty-free bag, "but you know what they're like about sleeping in on Sunday mornings."

"So it's not that they don't love me any more?"

"Don't be silly. They've missed you as much as I have. Almost."

She kissed him again, and they set off for the car.

"It's a bloody maze, this place," Sandra complained, "and they really fleece you for parking. Then there's roadworks everywhere on the way. They're still working on Barton bridge, you know. It was misty, too, high up in the Pennines. Oh, I am going on, aren't I? I'm just so glad to see you. You must be tired."

Banks stifled a yawn. "It's five in the morning where I am. Where I was, rather. And I can't sleep on planes. Anything interesting happen while I was away?"

Sandra frowned and hesitated. "I wasn't going to tell you," she said, loading the small case and the duty-free bag into the boot of the white Cortina, "at least not until we got home. Superintendent Gristhorpe called this morning just before I set off."

"On a Sunday morning? What about?"

"He said he wants to see you as soon as you get back. I told him what state you'd be in. Oh, he apologized and all that, but you've still got to go in."

"What is it?" Banks lit cigarettes for both Sandra and himself as she drove down the spiral ramp from the fourth floor of the multi-storey car-park out into the sunlit day.

"Bad news," she said. "There's been another death in Swainshead."

PART THREE:

THE
DREAMING SPIRES

TWELVE

I

"Accidental death! Don't you think that's just a bit too bloody convenient?"

Sergeant Hatchley shrugged as if to imply that perhaps if Banks didn't go gallivanting off to the New World such things might not happen. "Doc says it could have been suicide," he said.

Banks ran his hand through his close-cropped black hair. It was twelve-thirty. He was back in his office only an hour after arriving home, jet-lagged and disoriented. So far, he hadn't even had a chance to admire his favourite view of the cobbled market square. The office was smoky and a cup of black coffee steamed on the desk. Superintendent Gristhorpe was keeping an appointment with the deputy chief constable, whose personal interest in events was a measure of the Colliers' influence in the dale.

"And where the hell was Richmond?" Banks went on. "Wasn't he supposed to be baby-sitting the lot of them while I was away?"

"Yes, sir."

"Where was he then?"

"Asleep at the Greenocks', I suppose. He could hardly invite himself to spend the night with the Colliers, could he?"

"That's not the point. He should have known something was wrong. Send him in."

"He's just gone off duty, sir."

"Well bloody well bring him back again!"

"Yes, sir."

Hatchley stalked out of the office. Banks sighed, stubbed out his cigarette and walked over to the window. The cobbled market square was still there, a bit rain drenched, but still there. Tourists posed for photographs on the worn plinth of the ancient market cross. The church door stood open and Banks could hear the distant sound of the congregation singing "Jerusalem."

So he was home. He'd just had time to say hello to Brian and Tracy, then he'd had to hurry down to the station. He hadn't even given them their presents yet: a Blue Jays sweatshirt for Brian, the *Illustrated History of Canada* for his budding historian daughter, Tracy, and a study of the Group of Seven, with plenty of fine reproductions, for Sandra. They were still packed in his suitcase, which stood next to the duty-free cigarettes and Scotch in the hall.

Already Toronto was a memory with the quality of a dream— baseball, the community college, Kleinburg, Niagara Falls, the CN Tower, and the tall downtown buildings in black and white and gold. But Staff Sergeant Gregson, the Feathers crowd and Anne Ralston/Julie Culver weren't a dream. They were what he had gone for. And now he'd come back to find Stephen Collier dead.

There was no suicide note; at least nobody had found one so far. According to Nicholas Collier, John Fletcher and Sam Greenock, who had all been with Stephen on his last night at the White Rose, Stephen, always highly strung and restless, had seemed excessively nervous. He had got much more drunk than usual. Finally, long beyond closing time, they had had to help him home. They had deposited Stephen fully clothed on his bed, then adjourned to Nicholas's half of the house, where they had a nightcap. John and Sam then left, and Nicholas went to bed.

In the morning when he went to see how his brother was, Nicholas had discovered him dead. The initial findings of Dr Glendenning indicated that he had died of suffocation. It appeared that Stephen Collier had vomited while under the influence of barbiturates and been unable to wake up. Such things often happened when pills and booze were mixed, Glendenning had said. All that had to be determined now was the amount of barbiturate in Stephen's system, and that would have to wait until the post-mortem. He had suffered from insomnia for a long time and had a prescription for Nembutal.

So what had happened? According to Hatchley, Stephen must

have got up after the others left and taken his sleeping pills as usual, then gone downstairs and played a record—Mozart's *Jupiter* symphony was still spinning on the turntable—had another drink or two of Scotch from a tumbler, which was still half full, gone back upstairs, taken some more sleeping pills and passed out. By that time, given how much he'd had to drink, he probably wouldn't have remembered taking the first lot of pills. The only question was, did he do it deliberately or not and the only person who could answer that was Stephen himself.

It was damned unsatisfactory, Banks thought, but it looked like an end to both the Addison and Allen cases. Stephen Collier had certainly confessed to Anne Ralston. He knew that Banks would find her and that when she heard Bernie had been killed, she would pass on the information. He must have gone through a week of torment trying to decide what to do—make a run for it or stay and brazen it out. After all, it was only her word against his. The strain had finally proved too much for him, and either accidentally or on purpose—or accidentally on purpose—he had put an end to things, perhaps to save himself and the family name the ignominy of a trial and all the publicity it would bring down on them.

Feeling calmer, Banks lit another cigarette. He finished his coffee and determined not to haul Richmond over the coals. After all, as Hatchley had said, the constable couldn't be everywhere at once. He still felt restless, though; his nerves were jangling and his eyes ached. He had that strange and disturbing sensation of wanting to sleep but knowing he couldn't even if he tried. When he rubbed his chin, he could feel the bristles. He hadn't even had time for a shave.

When Richmond arrived, they walked over to the Queen's Arms. After the morning sunshine, it had turned cool and rainy: a wonderful relief after the hellish steam-bath of Toronto, Banks thought as he looked up and let the rain fall on his face. Cyril, the landlord, rustled them up a couple of ham-and-tomato sandwiches. They found an empty table in a corner, and Banks got the drinks in.

"Look, I'm sorry for dragging you back, Phil," he said, "but I want to hear your version of what happened."

"In the White Rose, sir?"

"The whole week. Just tell me what you saw and thought."

"There's not very much to tell, really," Richmond said, and gave Banks his version of the week's events in as much detail as he could.

"Katie Greenock went off with Stephen Collier on Friday after-noon, is that right?"

"Yes, sir. They went for a walk up Swainshead Fell. I took a walk up Adam's Fell and I could see them across the dale."

"Did they go towards the hanging valley?"

"No, sir, they didn't go over the top—just diagonal, as far as the river's source. It's about half-way up and a bit to the north."

Banks wondered if anything had gone on between Katie and Stephen Collier. It seemed unlikely, given the kind of woman she seemed, but he was sure that she had surrendered to Bernard Allen. And in her case, the old-fashioned term "surrendered" was the right word to use. Banks recalled the image of Katie standing in the market square, soaked to the skin, just before he'd left, and he remembered the eerie feeling he'd had that she was coming apart at the seams. It would certainly be worth talking to her again; at the very least she would be able to tell him something more about Collier's state of mind on the day before he died.

"What about Saturday night in the White Rose? How long were you there?"

"From about nine till closing time, sir. I tried to pace myself, not drink too much."

Banks grinned, remembering his own nights in the Toronto pubs. "A tough job, eh? Never mind. Notice anything?"

"Like I told the super and Sergeant Hatchley, sir, it seemed pretty much of a normal night to me."

"You didn't think Stephen Collier was drinking more than usual?"

"I don't know how much he usually drank, sir. I'd say from the other three nights I saw him in the White Rose during my stay, he did drink more on Saturday. But it was Saturday night. People do overdo it a bit then, don't they? No work in the morning."

"Unless you're a copper."

Cyril called last orders and Banks hurried to the bar for another two pints.

"What was the mood like at the table?" he asked when he got back.

"A bit festive, really."

"No arguments, no sullen silences?"

"No. Everyone seemed to be enjoying themselves. There was one thing . . ."

"Yes?"

"Well, I couldn't hear anything because Sam and Stephen were talking quite loudly, but I got the impression that at one point John Fletcher and Nicholas Collier were having a bit of a barney."

"What do you mean?"

"I'm just going by the expressions on their faces, sir. It looked like Nicholas was mad at Fletcher for some reason and Fletcher just brushed him aside."

"Did the others appear to notice?"

"No. Like I said, sir, they were talking, arguing about politics or something."

"And this was Nicholas Collier and John Fletcher, not Stephen?"

"Yes, sir."

"Odd. How did Stephen seem?"

"I'd say he was a fairly happy drunk. Happier than he ever seemed sober."

"What was he drinking?"

"They were all drinking beer."

"How many pints would you say Stephen had?"

Richmond flushed and fiddled with his moustache. "I wasn't really counting, sir. Perhaps I should have been . . . but . . ."

"You weren't to know he'd be dead in the morning. Don't worry. It's the bane of our lives. If we all had twenty-twenty hindsight our job'd be a lot easier. Just try and remember. Picture it as clearly as you can."

Richmond closed his eyes. "At a guess, I'd say about five or six, sir."

"Five or six. Not a lot, really, is it? Not for a Yorkshireman, anyway. And he was practically legless?"

"Yes, sir. Maybe he was drinking the vodka as well."

"What vodka?"

"I'm not clear on it, but I remember Freddie Metcalfe, the land-lord, muttering something about having to change the bottle after one of them had been up and bought a round. It was busy and he said he needed eight hands to do his job."

"But you never saw Stephen put a shorts glass to his lips?"

"No, sir."

"Did anyone?"

"Not that I remember."

"Odd, that, isn't it? What happened to the vodka, then?"

"Perhaps whoever bought it just drank it down at the bar."

"Hmm. It's possible. But why? Let's leave it for the moment, anyway. Did you hear any mention at all of Oxford during the week?"

"You mean the university, sir?"

"Any mention at all. The name: Oxford."

Richmond shook his head.

"All right, that'll do for now." Banks rubbed his eyes.

They drifted out into the street with the others as Cyril prepared to lock up for the afternoon. There was a lot more to think about now. Nothing that Banks had heard since he got back had been at all convincing. Something was wrong, he felt, and the case was far from over. Sending Richmond back home, he decided on a short walk in the rain to freshen himself up before returning to the station.

II

Katie watched the rain swell the becks that rushed down Swainshead Fell as it got dark that night. The rhythmic gurgle of water through the half-open window calmed her. All day she had been agitated. Now it was after ten; Sam was still at the pub, and Katie was brooding over the day's events.

If only she had told Sam that their guest was a policeman, prob-ably sent to spy on them. Then he'd have informed all and sundry, and maybe things would have been different. But now Stephen had to die, too: another escape route cut off. Had the policeman noticed anything? Katie didn't think so. There had been nothing really to notice.

Ever since morning, when Stephen's body had been discovered, Upper Head had been stunned. Women gathered in the street after church and lowered their voices, looking over at the Gothic house and shaking their heads. The Colliers were, when all was said and done, still regarded as lords of the manor.

All the curtains of their spooky Victorian mansion across the river had been drawn since morning, when the police and doctors had finished and taken Stephen's body away. One or two people had dropped by to offer condolences, including John Fletcher, who'd have got a rude reception from Nicholas, Katie thought, under any other circumstances. Sam, of course, had been one of the first, keen to establish himself with the new squire now that the more approachable Stephen was gone. Now Sam and John were no doubt getting maudlin drunk in the White Rose. Katie hadn't gone across to the house; she couldn't face Nicholas Collier alone again after the incident at the party.

Rain spilled in over the window-sill. Katie dipped a finger in it and made patterns on the white paintwork. The water beaded on the paint no matter what she tried to make it do. A breeze had sprung up and it brought the scent of summer rain indoors; shivering, she pulled her grey lamb's-wool cardigan around her shoulders.

"Be sure your sins will find you out," another of her grandmother's favourite maxims, sprang into her mind. With it came the dim and painful memory of a tell-tale boy's hair on her collar when she had come home from her one and only visit to the church-run youth club. It must have got there in the cloakroom, somehow, but her grandmother had thrust it forward as irrefutable evidence of Katie's lewd and lascivious nature before making her stand "naked in her shame" in the corner of the cold, stone-flagged kitchen all evening. She had been supposed to repeat "Be sure your sins will find you out" under her breath all the time she stood there, but she hadn't. That was another sin: disobedience. The vicar had got an earful, too, about running a house of ill-repute and corrupting local youth. That had pleased Katie; she didn't like him anyway because his breath smelled like the toilet when he came close, which he always did. Taking pleasure in the misfortunes of others was another sin she had been guilty of that day.

Katie closed the window and turned to get into bed. It was after ten-thirty. Sam would probably be back soon. There was a chance that if she pretended to be asleep . . .

But sleep didn't come easily. She thought of Stephen again, of his chaste touch. Life might not have been so bad if he had taken her away with him. She knew he would want to have her eventually—it would be part of the price—but he seemed a gentle person, like Bernard had been, and perhaps he wouldn't be too demanding. The images blurred in her mind as sleep came closer: her grandmother brandishing the hairbrush, black eyes flashing, Bernard breathing hard as he pulled at her clothes. . . . She heard the back door open and close noisily. Sam. Quickly, she turned over and pulled the covers up to her ears. Her feet were cold.

III

"What do you think, then, Alan?"

Banks and Gristhorpe sat at the dining-room table later that night and sipped duty-free Bell's. The children were in bed and Sandra was leafing through the book Banks had brought her from Toronto. Banks felt better after the short nap he had taken late in the afternoon.

"It stinks. I track down Anne Ralston in Toronto and she tells me Stephen Collier practically confessed to killing Addison because of some scandal he was involved in at Oxford. Then, when I get back I find Collier's conveniently dead—accidental death. It's too pat."

"Hmm." Gristhorpe sipped his Scotch. "It could be true. But let's suppose it's not. What else could have happened? I'm sorry, I know you're still tired, Alan. Maybe tomorrow would be better?"

Banks lit a cigarette. "No, it's all right. What do I think happened? I don't know. I thought I'd got it all worked out but now everything's gone haywire. I know it makes sense that Collier killed himself rather than face the trouble he knew he'd be in for when I got back. Maybe the pressure built in him over the week. On the other hand, what if he didn't kill Allen? What if he knew who did, and whoever it was was afraid he'd crack under pressure and give it away. That would have given someone enough motive to get rid of him, wouldn't it? We still don't have a clear connection between Addison and Allen, though."

"Except the Ralston girl."

"What if there's something else? An angle we haven't really considered."

"Such as?"

"That's the trouble. I've no idea."

Gristhorpe swirled the Bell's in his glass. "Then it has to be connected with Addison and Ralston."

"I'd like to go down to Oxford as soon as possible and dig around. Ted Folley's in the local CID there. We were at training school together."

Gristhorpe nodded. "That's no problem."

"Maybe Addison found something out and was going to blackmail Collier."

"He had a clean record."

"True. But you know as well as I do what private investigators are like—especially solo operators. We can also assume that Bernard Allen had the same information, or part of it, and that he too was blackmailing Collier."

Gristhorpe rubbed his whiskery chin. "Aye. But if Collier did kill Allen for that reason, who killed Collier—and why?"

"That's what we have to find out."

"So we're still looking at the lot of them?"

"It seems that way. Any one of them could have gone back to the house—the French windows at the back weren't locked—and given him another drink with the barbiturates. Or someone could have mixed a few nembies with his drinks earlier. He was so far gone he probably wouldn't have noticed."

"Risky, though."

"Yes. But what murder isn't?"

"Aye."

"And then there's the matter of the vodka. I want to talk to Freddie Metcalfe about that."

"What vodka?"

"Someone in the party was buying vodka that night, but Richmond never actually saw anyone drink it."

"So you think someone was spiking Collier's drinks with vodka, making sure he got really drunk?"

"It's a strong possibility, yes. Vodka's pretty much tasteless in a pint."

"Aye, in more ways than one," Gristhorpe said.

"The trouble is," Banks went on, "it was such a busy night that I can't rely on anyone remembering. It could have been Sam Greenock, John Fletcher or Nicholas Collier—any one of them. I'm assuming they all bought rounds."

"What about the Greenock woman?"

Banks saw again in his mind's eye the image of Katie standing soaked to the skin in the market square. "Katie? I suppose she could play some part in all this. As far as I can tell, though, she's in a world of her own. There's something not quite right about her. I thought it was just her marriage. Sam's a real bastard— thrashes her every now and then—but I think there's more to it than that. According to Richmond, though, she wasn't in the White Rose that night."

Gristhorpe looked at his watch and stood up. "Good Lord, is that the time? I'd better be off. Don't worry about being in early tomorrow."

"I probably will be," Banks said. "I want to go to Swainshead and see a few people. Then I'll go to Oxford. Mind if I take Sergeant Hatchley? There might be a bit of legwork, and I'd rather have Richmond up here taking care of business."

"Aye, take him. He'll feel like a fish out of water in Oxford. Do him good, though. Broaden his horizons."

Banks laughed. "I'm afraid Sergeant Hatchley's horizons are firmly fixed on beer, idleness, sports and sex—in that order. But I'll try."

Gristhorpe drained his glass and left. Banks sat beside Sandra and looked at some of the pictures with her, but his eyes began to feel suddenly prickly and heavy. He'd been wondering whether to let the superintendent know that Gerry Webb had revealed his full name, but decided against it. Names were, after all, a kind of power. He would tell no-one at the station, but it was too good to keep to himself.

"Do you know," he said, slipping his arm around Sandra's shoulders, "I found out a very interesting thing about Superintendent Gristhorpe in Toronto."

"It sounds like you discovered a lot of interesting things there," Sandra said, raising an arched black eyebrow. Her eyebrows contrasted sharply with her natural blonde hair, and that was one of the features Banks found sexy about her. "Go on," she urged him. "Give."

"I've missed you," Banks said, moving closer. "I'll tell you in bed, later."

"I thought you were tired."

"Only my eyes."

"Is it worth knowing?"

"It's worth it."

"Right, then." Sandra turned towards him. "Let's not waste time and energy climbing upstairs. It has been a whole week, after all."

IV

It was good to be home, Banks thought, as he drove the white Cortina along the dale. The sun was out, the water glittered silver, the valley sides shone vibrant green, and the Beatles were singing "And Your Bird Can Sing" on the cassette. He lit a cigarette and slowed down to pass a colourful group of hikers. They clustered together in the deep grass by the dry-stone wall and waved as he drove by.

Who to visit first? That was the question. It was still only ten-thirty, so perhaps he'd best leave Freddie Metcalfe till the White Rose opened at eleven and call on Nicholas Collier—the interview he was least looking forward to.

Accordingly, he carried on past the pub and pulled up on the verge outside the Collier house. Nicholas opened the door at the first ring of the bell.

"Chief Inspector Banks," he said. "Long time, no see. Come in."
He looked tired; his usually bright eyes had lost their sparkle and
there were dark pouches under them. "Please, sit down." He
pointed towards a leather upholstered armchair by the open French
windows. "I'm not in a mood to sit in the sun today, but I feel I must
remind myself of its presence."

"I'm sorry about what happened," Banks said. "I'd been hoping to
talk to Stephen when I got back."

Nicholas turned to look at the fountain outside and said
nothing. Banks thought he could see a fading bruise at the side of
his mouth.

"I hope you're not going to ask me to go through it all again,"
Nicholas said at last, taking a cigarette from the porcelain box on
the low table beside him. "Policemen always seem to be asking
people to repeat their stories."

"There's a good reason for that," Banks said. "Sometimes people
remember things. Little things they thought insignificant at the
time."

"All the same, I very much doubt that I can help you."

"I was wondering if you had any knowledge of your brother's
problems?"

"Stephen's problems? No, I can't say I did. Though he seemed a
bit edgy this past week or two, as if he had something on his mind."

"Did you ask him what it was?"

"No. Does that surprise you? Well, it shouldn't. Stephen wasn't
the most forthcoming of people. If he wanted to talk, he would, to
whoever struck his fancy at the moment. But if you asked him, you
got nowhere. Certainly I never did."

"I see. So you've no idea what he was worried about?"

"Not at all. I take no interest in the business, so I wouldn't know
about that side of things. Did he have business problems? Trouble
at t'mill?"

"Not that I know of, no, Mr Collier. His problem was that we
think he may have killed a man over five years ago because of
something that happened at Oxford. We also think he might
have been responsible for the murder of Bernard Allen more
recently."

"Stephen! You're joking, Chief Inspector, surely?"

Banks shook his head. "When was St phen at Oxford?"

"He went there nine years ago. But nothing untoward happened to him in Oxford as far as I know." He paused and his eyes turned hard. "You're not joking, are you?"

"I'm afraid not."

"Well, what can I say? Your wording would seem to indicate that this is mere supposition, that you have no proof."

"Only the testimony of Anne Ralston."

"That woman Stephen was seeing all those years ago?"

"Yes. I found her in Toronto."

"And you'd take a slut's word that Stephen was a murderer?"

"She'd no reason to lie. And I don't believe she's a slut."

Nicholas shrugged dismissively. "As you like. She certainly wasn't the type of woman I'd want for a sister-in-law. But haven't you considered that she might have been the guilty party? As I remember, she disappeared the morning after the man was killed."

"Yes, she did."

"So she'd have everything to gain by trying to put the blame on Stephen."

"It's possible, yes. But there's Bernard Allen's murder to take into account, too. She wasn't in Swainshead at the time. She was in Toronto."

"So?"

"So she couldn't have killed Allen."

"I'm sorry but I don't see the connection. You admit she could have killed the other man, but not Bernard Allen. What I don't see is why you should even think the same person killed both of them. What had Allen and that private detective chappie got in common?"

"Nothing, as far as we can tell. Except that they were both killed in Swainshead." Banks lit a cigarette. "There are too many coincidences, Mr Collier. One of the most interesting ones is that Bernard Allen was friendly with Anne Ralston in Toronto. That would make him the only person from Swainshead to see her since she disappeared. And the whole village was aware of that, thanks to Sam Greenock. It's also a coincidence that Stephen was going out with Anne Ralston at the time she left Swainshead, and that she told me he confessed to her about killing Addison. It's another coincidence that Stephen is dead when I return."

"I can't argue with your logic, Chief Inspector. There certainly are a lot of coincidences. But they *are* coincidences, aren't they? I mean, you've no real evidence to link them or to back up your suppositions, have you?"

"Are you sure you knew nothing about your brother's problems?" Banks asked.

"I've told you," Collier sighed. "We just weren't that close. You can see for yourself how we've split the house—into two very different halves, I might add. All we had in common was family. Even if he had been a murderer, which I don't believe for a moment, Stephen would have hardly told me."

"But he told Anne Ralston."

"So you say. I can only repeat that the woman must be lying to save her own skin." He leaned forward to stub out his cigarette but didn't slouch back in the chair again. "Chief Inspector," he said, folding his hands on his lap, "I hope you're not going to spread these accusations about my brother around the dale. After all, you admit you've no proof. You could do untold damage to the family name—not to mention my career."

"Rest assured, Mr Collier. I'm not in the habit of spreading unfounded accusations."

"And might I suggest," Nicholas added, "that even if Stephen had been guilty, he's certainly suffered adequate penalty for his sin, and no useful purpose would be served by going poking around in his past affairs."

"Ah, that's where we differ," Banks said. "I'm not judge or jury, Mr Collier. I just try to dig out the truth. And until there are answers to a number of questions, Stephen's file remains open— wherever Stephen himself may be." Nicholas opened his mouth to protest but Banks ignored him and went on. "I don't care who you are, Mr Collier. You can threaten, you can pull strings, you can do what you bloody well want. But I'm going to get to the bottom of this." He stood up and walked over to the door. Nicholas sat where he was and stared coldly at him.

"One more question," Banks said. "Which one of you was drinking vodka in the White Rose on Saturday night?"

"Vodka?" Nicholas grunted. "None of us, I shouldn't think. Can't stand the stuff, myself."

"Did you see your brother drink any?"

Nicholas walked over to the door and grasped the handle. "No, I didn't. Stephen never drank vodka." He opened the door. "Now would you mind leaving? And you can be damn sure you haven't heard the last of this."

Was he lying? Banks found it hard to tell. People of Nicholas Collier's class had so much self-confidence bred into them that they could carry most things off.

"What was your argument with John Fletcher about?" he asked, leaning against the open door.

"What argument?"

"You didn't have words?"

Nicholas flicked his wrist. "We may have done, but I can't remember why. A trifle, I should imagine. Now . . ." he nodded towards the path.

Banks set off.

It hadn't been satisfactory at all. Banks swore under his breath as he headed down the path. He should have pushed Nicholas even harder. Still, there would be time later. Plenty of time. There was still Oxford. And Katie Greenock and Freddie Metcalfe. He looked at his watch and walked into the White Rose.

"I understand tha's been globe-trotting," Freddie Metcalfe said, pouring out a pint of Marston's Pedigree.

"That's right," Banks answered. "Been to visit the New World." He counted out his change and put it on the damp bar-towel.

"I don't 'old wi' Americans," Freddie said, screwing up his face. "Get plenty on 'em in 'ere, tha knows. Alus asking for fancy drinks—bourbon and branch water and t'like. Can't understand none on 'em. And Perrier. Bloody Perrier wi' a twist o' lemon them purple-haired old women want. Mutton dressed up as lamb, if y'ask me." He sniffed and carried the money to the till.

Banks thought of pointing out that Canada was not the same as the USA, but he didn't want to miss a good opening. "Not get a lot of fancy drinks orders in here, then? Not many drink shorts?" he asked.

"Nah," said Freddie, ambling back. "Most tourists we get's fell-walkers, and they like a good pint, I'll say that for 'em. T'lasses sometimes ask for a brandy and Babycham, like, or a Pony or Cherry B. But mostly it's ale."

"What about vodka?"

"What about it?"

"Get through much?"

"Nah. Bloody Russkie muck, that is. Can't taste it. We get through a good bit o' single malt Scotch, but vodka . . . nah."

"I understand you had a vodka drinker on Saturday night?"

"What makes tha think that? Tha weren't 'ere then."

"Never mind that. Did you?"

Freddie scratched his mutton-chop whiskers. "Aye, come to think on it, I do remember 'aving to change t'bottle, so somebody must've been at it."

"Who, Freddie, who?"

"I can't rightly say. It might not've been me who served 'im. I don't recollect as I did. Lot o' strangers in last weekend cos t'weather brightened up, like. It were a busy night, Sat'day, and that gormless lass from Gratly never showed up. S'posed to give me an 'and behind t'bar. No, I'm sorry, lad. It's no good. I know I changed t'bottle, but I were alus serving four orders at once. Need eight bloody arms on this job, specially on a Sat'day night. And I only 'ad young Betty to 'elp me."

"Were there any arguments in the pub that night?"

Freddie laughed. "Well, it'd 'ardly be a Sat'day night wi'out a few 'eated words, would it?"

"I suppose not. What about at the Collier table?"

"I don't recollect owt. Billy Black and Les Stott were barneying about whippets, and Wally Grimes—Wally's a local farmer, like— 'ad a little disagreement wi' some walkers about National Trust foot-paths. But that's all I can remember."

"You don't remember anything between Nicholas Collier and John Fletcher?"

"Nah. But that wouldn't be nowt new. Now John and Mr

Stephen, they understood each other. But John Fletcher never did 'ave time for young Nicholas, even when 'e were a lad."

"But you heard nothing on Saturday?"

"Nay. Too much bloody noise. I only 'eard t'others because they were standing at t'bar right a-front o'me."

"Did you clear the tables later?"

"Nay, Betty did that." He pointed towards a buxom rosy-cheeked girl washing glasses.

"Can I talk to her?"

"Aye. Betty, lass, come over 'ere. T'Inspector wants a word wi' thee."

The roses quickly spread over Betty's entire complexion, and down as much of her throat and chest as was exposed. She lowered her big brown eyes and stood in front of Banks like a schoolgirl before the head.

"It's all right, Betty," Banks said, "I just want to ask you a couple of questions about Saturday night when you worked here."

She nodded but still didn't look up.

"Do you remember serving Mr Collier's group at all?"

"Aye," she said. "Well . . . no . . . I mean, I did serve them, but it were that busy I don't remember nothing about it."

"And you collected all the glasses later?"

"Aye."

"Do you remember picking up any shorts glasses from Mr Collier's table?"

Betty thought for a moment—a process Banks fancied he could almost hear—and then shook her head. "I remember picking up some shorts glasses off t'bar," she said, "but I can't say who drank 'em."

"Is this the part of the bar the Collier group came to for their orders?"

"Aye, it would've been," Freddie said.

"But neither of you can say which member of the Collier group was ordering vodka?"

They both shook their heads glumly.

Banks sighed, then finished his pint philosophically and lit a cigarette.

"What's it all about, then?" Freddie asked.

"Eh? Oh, never mind for now," Banks said. "Probably nothing."

"They were all a bit merry, like."

"The Collier group?"

"Aye. All on 'em. But Mr Stephen were t'worst."

"Did he drink more than the rest?"

Freddie shook his head. "I can't say. Shouldn't think so, though. They was drinking rounds. Unless . . ." Then comprehension dawned on his round red face. "Unless 'e were drinking vodka as well as pints."

"And was he?"

Again, Freddie shook his head. "I can't say."

Suddenly Betty, who had remained standing there as if she were waiting to be dismissed, raised her head. Brown curls bobbed around her chubby cheeks. "I can tell yer!" she said excitedly. "I can tell yer."

"What?" Banks asked.

"It can't've been Mr Stephen buying vodka."

"Why on earth not, lass?" Freddie said.

"Well, yer know," Betty spluttered, "'e alus used to say, 'ello, like, Mr Stephen. Proper gentleman. And 'e'd ask me 'ow I was. Well once on Sat'day night 'e were on is way to t'loo and 'e nearly bumped into me, and me carrying a trayful o'—"

"Get on wi' it, lass!" Freddie bellowed. "T'Inspector dun't want to know what tha et for breakfast an' all, tha knows."

Betty cast him a dark glance and announced, "'E'd forgotten 'is wallet."

"'E'd what?"

"'E sometimes slips me a quid—a tip, like," she added proudly. "But on Sat'day 'e patted 'is pockets and said 'e was sorry 'e 'ad no change and 'e'd left 'is wallet at 'ome. 'E was 'aving to depend on t'generosity of 'is friends." She turned to Banks. "Those were 'is very words, 'the generosity of my friends.' 'E'd 'ad a few, like, when 'e said it. . . ."

"Thank you, Betty," Banks said. "I don't suppose you overheard Nicholas Collier and John Fletcher having an argument?"

Betty's face dropped. "No. Not while I were picking t'glasses up. Is it important?"

"It might be. But it's not as important as what you've just told me."

It wasn't a great help, but if Stephen Collier hadn't been up to the bar to buy rounds, and if Freddie had found empty shorts glasses at the spot where the orders had been placed, then one of the party might have been spiking Stephen's beer with vodka. Of course, he realized, anyone could have left the glasses there, and any member of the group could have tipped back a quick shot while waiting for Freddie to pull the pints. But it was a start.

Betty beamed as if she'd solved the case. Freddie sent her back to her glass-cleaning and turned to face Banks.

"There," he said, "Any 'elp?"

"I hope so."

"Well, so do I. Tha's taking tha bloody time, I'll say that about thee. Does tha know, t'last Yankee we 'ad in 'ere . . ."

Banks left Freddie mid-sentence and almost bumped into Katie Greenock as he was leaving the pub.

"Ah," he said, holding the door for her, "just the person I want to see."

But she turned and started to hurry away.

"What is it?" Banks asked after her. He could sense her fear; it was more than just the adrenaline produced by a shock.

"It's nothing," she said, half-turning. "I was just looking for Sam, that's all." He could see a tear streaking down her flushed cheek.

"Katie, have you got something to tell me?" Banks asked, approaching her.

She carried on walking away. Banks put his hand gently on her shoulder. "Katie?"

"No!" she recoiled and started running down the empty street. Banks dashed after her and soon she slowed, dazed, to a halt.

"Come on, Katie," he said. "Let's talk." He offered his hand, but she wouldn't take it. Instead, she walked obediently beside him back to the car. She was shaking.

"A drink?" Banks suggested.

She shook her head. Her fair hair was tied back, but a few strands freed themselves and stuck to her damp cheeks.

"Let's go for a ride, then."

She got in the Cortina beside him and he drove north out of Swainshead. Thinking it might help her relax, he took out the Beatles cassette and put on Vivaldi's *Four Seasons,* turning the volume low.

"I was lying," Katie blurted out as they passed the bridge to John Fletcher's farmhouse. Then she said something else that Banks didn't quite catch. It sounded like "wash my mouth out with soap."

"What about?" he asked.

"I wasn't looking for Sam. I saw you go in there. I saw you leave Nicholas Collier's, too. I was trying to get my courage up."

"For what? Are you sure a drink wouldn't help?"

"No, I don't take alcohol."

"What is it, Katie?"

"You've got to help me," Katie said, staring down into her lap and twisting her hands. "I did it . . . I killed them . . . I killed them all."

THIRTEEN

I

Looking at the ornate limestone building, Banks realized he had never seen Braughtmore school before. Built in the mid-nineteenth century after the previous building had burned down, it had oriels projecting from the first floor, then two floors of tall sash windows topped by dormers and a red pantile roof. It stood at the mouth of a small valley which a tributary had carved on its way down to the Gaiel, and enough flat ground had been cleared around it for rugby and cricket fields.

Banks pulled into a lay-by across the road, lit a cigarette and turned to Katie.

"Tell me about it," he said.

"I did it," Katie repeated. "I killed them."

"Who did you kill?"

"Bernie and Stephen."

"Why?"

"Because I . . . because they . . . It was God's judgment."

"God's judgment for what, Katie?"

"My sins."

"Because you made love to them?"

Katie turned and glared at him through her tears. "Not love," she said. "They were going to take me away, take me away from here, from my husband."

"But you made love with Bernard Allen. Did you sleep with Stephen, too?"

"Bernie took me in his room. It was the price. I found no pleasure in it. He said he'd send for me when he got back."

Banks didn't have the heart to tell her that Bernie was bent on returning to Swainshead, not staying in Canada.

"And Stephen?" he asked.

"He . . . he kissed me. I knew I would have to pay, but later. And now . . ."

"Did you kill him so that you wouldn't have to pay?"

Katie shook her head. "He was going to take me away, like Bernard. He had to die."

"How did you kill him?"

"Everyone who wants to help me dies."

"But how did you kill him?"

"I don't know, don't remember."

"Katie, you didn't kill Stephen Collier or Bernard Allen, did you?"

"They died because of me. The Lord's vengeance. Nicholas was the Lord's vengeance, too. Against me. To show me my vile nature."

"Nicholas? What happened with Nicholas?"

"He put his hands on me. His filthy hands. The Hands of the Beast."

"When was this? Where?"

"At his house. The party Sam made me go to. I didn't want to go, I told him. I knew it would be bad."

"What happened?"

"John came and they fought."

"John and Nicholas?"

"Yes."

At least that explained their argument in the White Rose, Banks thought. "Did Sam know? Did you tell Sam?"

Katie shook her head. "Sam doesn't care anyway. Not where his precious Colliers are concerned."

"But you didn't kill anyone, did you?"

She put her head in her hands and wept. Banks moved to put his arm around her, but she stiffened and jerked away towards the door. She rested her cheek against the window and stared ahead up the dale.

"Are you protecting Sam, Katie? Is that what you're doing? Do you think Sam killed them because they were going to take you away?"

"I killed them. I told you."

"Maybe you think you're responsible, Katie, but you didn't kill anyone. There's a big difference between feeling guilty and taking someone's life, you know. You haven't done anything wrong."

"I wanted to escape my husband, didn't I?"

"He beats you. He's not a good man."

"But he's my husband." She started to sob again. "I must serve him. What else can I do? I can't leave him and go away by myself. I don't know how to live."

Banks wound down his window and tossed out his cigarette end.

"Do you want to walk a while?" he asked.

Katie nodded and opened her door.

There was a pathway worn in the hillside opposite the school, and they set off slowly up towards the ridge. About half-way, they sat on warm grass among limestone boulders and gazed down on the scene. The building glowed like mother-of-pearl, and the red S-shaped tiles shone bright in the sun. Some pupils dressed in whites were practising in the cricket nets by one of the mowed fields, and a group in shorts and vests were running around the cinder track. Plenty of exercise and cold showers, Banks thought. Cross-country runs and Latin unseens to keep their minds off sex—and perhaps a bit of masturbation in the dorms, a little buggery in the bushes, sodomy in the cycle sheds. It was every outsider's version of public-school life. Probably the reality was much more innocent. After all, these people were being groomed to run the country, the government. Still, look how many of them ended up on the front pages of the tabloid press. Perhaps the outsider's version wasn't so far from the truth.

Katie plucked blades of grass and scattered them on the light breeze.

"Tell me what happened with Stephen," Banks said.

"We walked up to the source. He said he was going away. I thought he would take me with him if I let him kiss me. That's all."

"What else did he say? You must have talked about things."

"Oh, yes." Katie's voice sounded like it was coming from a great distance.

"Why was he going away?"

"He said he'd had enough, he couldn't stand being here any longer. He said something about getting away from the past and from who he was."

"What did he want to get away from?"

For the first time, Katie looked directly at him. Her eyes were red-rimmed with crying but still shone warm brown in the sunlight. Banks could feel her attraction. The desire to protect her merged with the impulse to touch her. She made him want to reach out and brush the blonde hairs away from her cheeks, then kiss her white throat and explore the gentle curves and mounds of her body. And he also knew that she was largely unaware of the effect she had; it was as if she couldn't understand the natural sexual instinct that draws people to one another. She knew what men wanted, yes, but she didn't know why or what it was all about. She was innocent, a unique and vulnerable wild flower growing here at the edge of the moorland.

"What did he want to get away from?" she echoed, shattering his illusion. "What we all want to get away from. The traps we make for ourselves. The traps God makes for us."

"It's not such a terrible thing to want to escape a bad marriage, Katie," Banks said. But he felt he couldn't get the tone right, couldn't find the way to talk to this woman. What he said came out as patronizing when he didn't intend it to.

"It's a woman's duty," Katie answered. "Her cross to bear."

"What was Stephen running away from? Was it me? Did he mention me?"

Katie seemed surprised. "No," she said. "Not you. His past, the life he led."

"Did he mention anything in particular?"

"He said he'd been bad."

"How?"

"I don't know. He just talked. I didn't understand it all. I was thinking about something else. The river bubbling up from the grass, how green and shiny the grass was where the water always flowed over it and in it."

"Can you remember anything? Anything at all?"

"He talked about Oxford. Something bad happened at Oxford."

"Did he say what it was?"

"A girl. A girl died."

"Is that all he said?"

"Yes. That's how it started, he said. The nightmare."

"With a girl dying at Oxford?"

"Yes."

"How was he involved with this girl?"

"I don't know. Just that she died and it was bad."

"And now he'd had enough and he was going away to escape the past, the consequences?"

Katie nodded, then she stared at him sharply. "But you can't escape consequences, can you? Bernie couldn't. Stephen couldn't. I can't."

"Was Stephen unhappy?"

"Unhappy? I don't think so. He was worried, but not unhappy."

"Do you think he would have harmed himself?"

"No. Stephen wouldn't have done that. He had plans for the future. He was going to take me with him. But his future killed him."

"I thought it was his past?"

"It was me," she said calmly. "Whatever you say, I know it was me who killed him."

"That's not true, Katie. I wish I could get you to believe it." Banks took out his cigarettes and offered her one. She said no and carried on plucking blades of grass and rubbing them between her fingers.

"Why didn't he go away before?" Banks asked. "He had plenty of time, plenty of opportunity."

"I don't know. He said it was hard for him—the family name, the house, the business. He seemed to be trying to find the courage to make a break, like me. I didn't tell him, if that's what you're thinking."

"Didn't tell him what?"

"About the policeman you sent to spy on everyone. I saw him with you one day in Eastvale, but I didn't tell Stephen."

"Did you tell Sam?"

Katie shook her head slowly. "No," she said. "Not this time."

So Stephen had been struggling with himself over whether to run or whether to stay and brazen it out. After all, he probably knew that the police could have no real proof of his guilt, just hearsay—Anne Ralston's word against his.

"If he'd gone," Katie said, as if she'd been reading his mind, "it would have been like admitting his guilt, wouldn't it?"

"Perhaps." Banks stood up and brushed the grass from his pants. "Come on." He held out his hand and Katie took it. As soon as she'd stood up, though, she let go and followed him back to the car in silence.

II

"What else did she say?" Sergeant Hatchley asked, as the white Cortina, with Banks at the wheel, hurtled down the M1.

"Nothing," Banks answered. "I told her to get in touch with us if she remembered anything else at all, then I drove her home. She went in without a word. To tell you the truth, I'm worried about her. She's so bloody fragile and she's close to breaking-point. The woman needs help."

Hatchley shrugged. "If she doesn't like her nest she can always change it."

"It's not as easy as that for some people. They get stuck, they don't know where to turn, how to take care of themselves. Katie Greenock's like that."

They passed Sheffield's cooling towers, shaped like giant whale-bone corsets by the motorway. Even with the windows and many of the factories closed, the sulphurous smells of steelworks seeped into the car.

"What exactly will we be doing in Oxford?" Hatchley asked.

"We'll be trying to track down an incident involving the death of a girl about nine years ago, maybe two or three years later. Undergraduate courses are usually three years long, so that's a welcome limit."

"Unless Collier wasn't actually a student when it happened."

"That's bloody helpful," Banks said. "We'll deal with that if we draw a blank on the other."

"What kind of incident?"

"It strikes me we're looking for an unsolved crime, or a freak accident. Could have been hit and run, drug overdose, anything."

"Then what? Whoever this lass was, she won't be doing much talking now."

"I don't know," Banks admitted. "We try and link her to Stephen Collier."

"And what if we come up blank?"

Banks sighed and reached for a cigarette. He swerved quickly to avoid a Dutch juggernaut meandering on the centre lane. "You're being bloody negative today, Sergeant," he said. "What's the matter, did you have something planned for tonight? A date with Carol, maybe?"

"No. Carol understands my job. And I like a nice ride out. I'm just trying to cover all the angles, that's all. I find the whole damn thing confusing. I'm not even sure we've got a case. After all, Collier is dead, whether he died accidentally or offed himself."

"It is confusing," Banks agreed. "That's why I don't believe we're at the bottom of it yet. That's why we're off to Oxford, to try and make it simpler."

"Oh, I see." Hatchley wound down his window a couple of inches. With the two of them smoking, the fug in the car was making his eyes water. "I suppose it's full of silly-looking buggers in caps and gowns, Oxford?"

"Maybe so," Banks said. "Never been there, myself. They say it's a working town, though."

"Aye. It might have been at one time. But there's not many left making cars these days. Some nice buildings there, though. I saw those on telly as well. Christopher Wren, Nicholas Hawksworth."

"Bloody hell, Jim, have you been watching BBC2 again? We'll not have much time for sightseeing. Except for what you can take in on the job. Anyway, it's Hawksmoor. Nicholas Hawksmoor."

He realized with a shock that it was the first time he had called Sergeant Hatchley by his first name. It felt strange, but Hatchley said nothing.

Banks drove on in silence and concentrated on the road. It was after five o'clock and the stretches of motorway that passed close to urban areas were busy with rush-hour traffic. By the time they got to Oxford they wouldn't have time to do much but check in at the police station, say hello to Ted Folley, and maybe discuss the case over a pint—which would certainly appeal to Hatchley—before bed. Banks had booked them in at a small hotel recommended by Ted on the phone. In the morning the real work would begin.

Holding the wheel with one hand, Banks sorted through the cassettes. "Do you like music?" he asked. It was odd; he knew Gristhorpe was tone deaf—he couldn't tell Bach from the Beatles—but he had no idea what Hatchley's tastes ran to. Not that it would affect his choice. He knew what he wanted to hear and soon found it—the Small Faces' greatest hits.

"I like a good brass band," Hatchley mused. "A bit of country-and-western now and then."

Banks smiled. He hated country-and-western and brass bands. He lit another cigarette and edged up the volume. The swirling chords of "All or Nothing" filled the car as he turned off near Northampton onto the road for Oxford. The music took him right back to the summer of 1966, just before he started in the sixth form at school. Nostalgia. A sure sign he was pushing forty. He caught Hatchley looking at him as if he were mad.

III

There weren't many caps and gowns in evidence on High Street in Oxford the following morning. Most of the people seemed to be ambling along in that lost but purposeful way tourists have. Banks and Hatchley were looking for somewhere to eat a quick breakfast before getting down to work at the station.

Hatchley pointed across the street. "There's a McDonald's. They do quite nice breakfasts. Maybe . . ." He looked at Banks apprehensively, as if worried that the chief inspector might turn out to be a gourmet as well as a southerner and a lover of sixties music. Despite all the times they'd enjoyed toasted teacakes and steak pies together, maybe Banks would insist on frogs' legs with anchovy sauce for breakfast.

Banks glanced at his watch and scowled. "At least they're fast. Come on, then. Egg McMuffin it is."

Astonished, Hatchley followed him through the golden arches. Most of the places Banks had eaten in on his trip to Toronto had provided quick, friendly service—so much so that it had been one of the things that had impressed him—but it seemed that even McDonald's could do nothing to alter the innate sloth and surliness of the English catering industry. The look they got from the uniformed girl behind the counter immediately communicated that they were being a bloody nuisance in placing an order, and, of course, they had to wait. Even when she slung the food at them, she didn't say, "Thank you, please come again."

Finally, they sat by the window and watched people walk in and out of W.H. Smith's for the morning papers. Hatchley ate heartily, but Banks picked at his food, then abandoned it and settled for black coffee and a cigarette.

"Nice bloke, that Ted Folley," Hatchley said with his mouth half full of sausage. "Not what I expected."

"What did you expect?"

"Oh, some toffee-nosed git, I suppose. He's real down-to-earth, though. Dresses like a toff, mind you. They'd have a bit of a giggle over him in The Oak."

"Probably in the Queen's Arms, too," Banks added.

"Aye."

They had found time for a few drinks with Folley before returning to their hotel for a good night's sleep, and Banks wondered whether it was Ted's generosity that won Hatchley over, or his store of anecdotes. Either way, the sergeant had managed to down a copious amount of local ale (which he pronounced to be of "passable" quality) in a very short time.

They had stood at the bar of a noisy Broad Street pub, and Ted—a dapper man with Brylcreemed hair and a penchant for three-piece pin-stripe suits and garish bow-ties—had regaled them with stories of Oxford's privileged student classes. Hatchley had been particularly amused by the description of a recent raid on an end-of-term party: "And there she was," Folley had said, "Deb of the Year with her knickers round her ankles and white powder all over her stiff upper lip." The sergeant had laughed so much he had got hiccups, which kept returning to haunt him for the rest of the evening.

"Come on," Banks said. "Hurry up. It can't be so bloody delicious you need to savour every mouthful."

Reluctantly, Hatchley ate up his food and slurped his coffee. Ten minutes later they were in Ted Folley's office on St Aldates.

"I've got the files out already," Ted said. "If you can't find what you're after there, come and see me. I think you will, though. They cover all unsolved crimes, including hit and runs, involving women during the three-year period you mentioned."

"Thank God there aren't many," Banks said, picking up the slim pile.

"No," Folley said. "We're lucky. The students keep us busy enough but we don't get all that many mysterious deaths. They're usually drug related."

"These?"

"Some of them. Use that office over there." Folley pointed across to a small glass-partitioned area. "Doug's on holiday, so you won't be disturbed."

Most of the cases were easily dealt with. Banks or Hatchley would phone friends or parents of the deceased, whenever phone numbers appeared in the files, and simply ask if the name Stephen Collier meant anything. On the off chance, they also asked if anyone had hired a private investigator named Raymond Addison to look into the unsolved crime. In the cases where no numbers were given, or where people had moved, they made notes to follow up on later. In some of those cases, the phone directory told them what they needed to know, and Ted also proved as helpful as ever.

By mid-afternoon, after a short lunch-break, they had only three possibilities left. Folley was able to rule one of those out—the girl's parents had died tragically in a plane crash less than a year after their daughter's death—which left one each for Banks and Hatchley. They tossed for it, and Banks drew the phoneless family in Jericho, Hatchley the paraplegic father in Woodstock.

Wedged between Walton Street and the canal, Jericho is a maze of small nineteenth-century terraced houses, originally built for the foundry workers and navvies of the city. Most of the streets are named after Victorian battles or military heroes. It is as far away in spirit and appearance from the magnificent architectural beauty of the old university city as is Eastvale's East End Estate from its cobbled market square and Norman church.

Banks drove slowly down Great Clarendon Street until he found the turning he wanted. His car attracted the attention of two scruffy children playing jacks on the pavement, and he was manoeuvred into paying them fifty pee to "protect" it for him.

At first no-one answered the cracked blue door, but eventually, Banks heard someone move inside and when the door opened, an old, haggard face stared out. He couldn't tell whether it was male or female until a deep man's voice asked him roughly what he wanted.

"It's about your daughter, Cheryl," he said. "May I come in?"

The man blinked and opened the door a bit wider. Banks could smell boiled turnip and stale pipe smoke.

"Our Cheryl's been dead six years or more," the man said. "Nobody did anything then; why should they bother now?"

"If I could just come in . . . ?"

The man said nothing, but he opened the door wider to admit Banks. There was no hallway; the door opened directly into a small living-room. The curtains were half-closed, cutting out most of the light, and the air felt hot and cloying. From what Banks could see, the place wasn't dirty, but it wasn't exactly clean, either. A grey-haired old woman with a blanket over her knees sat in a wheelchair by the empty grate. She looked around as he came in and gave him a blank smile.

"It's about our Cheryl," the man said, reaching for his pipe.

"I heard."

"Look, Mrs Duggan," Banks said, perching on the arm of the settee, "I know it's a long time ago, but something might have come up."

"You've found out who killed her?"

"It's possible. But I still don't know that she was killed. You'll have to help me."

The file was still fresh in his mind. Cheryl Duggan had been fished out of the River Cherwell not too far from Magdalen Bridge and St Hilda's College on a foggy November Sunday morning over six years ago. The coroner's inquest said that death was due to drowning, or so it appeared. Several odd bruises indicated that her head may have been held under the water until she drowned. She had had sexual intercourse shortly before death, and the stomach contents indicated that she had been drinking heavily the previous evening. In view of all this, an open verdict was recorded and a police investigation was ordered.

To complicate matters, Cheryl Duggan, according to Folley, had been a well-known local prostitute since the age of fifteen. She had been only seventeen when she died. The investigation, Folley admitted, had been cursory. This was due to other pressures—in particular the drug-related death of a peer's daughter, in which the heir to a brewery fortune was implicated as a pusher.

"It could have been an accident," Banks said.

"It warn't no accident, Mr Banks," Mrs Duggan insisted.

"There was water in the lungs," Banks countered weakly.

Mr Duggan snorted. "You'd think she were a mermaid, our Cheryl, the way she took to water."

"She'd been drinking."

"Yes, well, nobody's saying she was perfect."

"Did you ever hear her mention a man by the name of Stephen Collier?"

Mr Duggan shook his head slowly.

There was a sense of defeat about the Duggans that weighed heavily in the dim and stuffy room and made Banks feel sick. Their voices were flat, as if they had repeated their stories a hundred times and nobody had listened; their faces were parchment dry and drawn, the eyes wide and blank, with plenty of white showing between the lower lashes and the pupils. Dante's words came into Banks's mind: "Abandon all hope, ye who enter here." This was a house of defeat, a place without hope.

Banks lit a cigarette, which would at least give him a more concrete reason to feel sick and dizzy, and went on. "The other thing I'd like to know," he asked, "is if you hired anyone to look into

Cheryl's death. I know you didn't think much of the police investigation."

Mr Duggan spat into the grate. His wife frowned at him. "Why does it matter?" she asked.

"It could be important."

"We did hire someone," she said. "A private investigator from London. We looked him up in the phone book at the library. We were desperate. The police hadn't done anything for more than a year, and they were saying such terrible things about Cheryl. We took out all our savings."

"What happened?"

"He came from London, this man, and he asked us about Cheryl—who her friends were, where she liked to go out and everything, then he said he'd try and find out what happened."

"He never came back," Mr Duggan cut in.

"You mean he ran off with your money?"

"Not all of it, Alf," Mrs Duggan said. "Only a retainer, that's all he'd take."

"He took off with the money, Jesse, let's face it. We were had. He never meant to do anything about our Cheryl, he just took us for what he could get. And we let him."

"What was his name?"

"Don't remember."

"Yes you do, Alf," said Mrs Duggan. "It was Raymond Addison. I haven't forgotten."

"So what did you do?"

"What could we do?" she said. "He'd got most of our money, so we couldn't hire anyone else. The police weren't interested. We just tried to forget, that's all." She pulled the tartan blanket up higher around her hips.

"Mr Addison didn't report back to you at all, then, after the first time you saw him?"

"No," Mr Duggan said. "We only saw him the once."

"Can you remember the date?"

The old man shook his head.

"I can't remember the exact day," his wife said, "but it was in February, about fifteen months after Cheryl was killed. The police seemed to have given up and we didn't know where to turn. We found him, and he let us down."

"If it's any consolation, Mrs Duggan, I don't think Mr Addison did let you down."

"What?"

"He was found killed himself, probably no more than a day or so after you saw him, up in Yorkshire. That's why you never heard from him again, not because he'd run off with your money."

"In Yorkshire? What was he doing there?"

"I think he did find out something about Cheryl's death. Something the police had missed. You've got to understand that we don't have enough time or men to devote ourselves full time to every single case, Mrs Duggan. I don't know the circumstances, but maybe the police here weren't as active as you think they should have been. It's only in books that policemen find the killer every time. But Mr Addison had only the one case. He must have visited every possible place Cheryl might have been that night, talked to everyone who knew her, and what he found out led him to a village in Yorkshire, and to his death."

Mrs Duggan bit her knuckles and began to cry silently. Her husband moved forward to comfort her.

"It never does any good raking up the past," he snapped at Banks. "Look how you've upset her."

"I can understand that you're angry, Mr Duggan," Banks said, "but if I'm right, then we know who killed your daughter."

Duggan looked away. "What's it matter now?"

"Maybe it doesn't, at least not to you. But I think it ought to mean something that Addison didn't let you down, didn't run off with your money. He found a lead, and instead of reporting in, he set off while the trail was hot. I think you owe his memory some kind of apology if you've been blaming him and thinking ill of him all these years."

"Maybe so," Duggan admitted. "But what use is it now? Two people dead. What use?"

"More than two," Banks said. "He had to kill again to cover his tracks. First Addison, then someone else."

"All over our Cheryl?" Mrs Duggan said, wiping her eyes.

Banks nodded. "It looks like that's where it started. Is there anything else you can tell me? Did Cheryl ever talk about anyone at all she knew from Yorkshire? A student she was seeing, perhaps?"

They both shook their heads, then Mrs Duggan laughed bitterly. "She said she was going to marry a student one day, a lord's son, or a prime minister's. She was very determined, our Cheryl. But she'd too much imagination. She was too flighty. If only she'd done as I said and stuck to her station."

"Did she hang around with students much?"

"She went to the same pubs as they did," Mr Duggan said. "The police said she was a prostitute, Mr Banks, that she sold herself to men. We didn't know nothing about that. I still can't believe it. I know she liked to tart herself up a bit when she went out, but what girl doesn't? And she wasn't really old enough to drink, but what can you do . . . ? You can't keep them prisoners, can you? She was always talking about what fun the students were, how she was sure to meet a nice young man soon. What were we to do? We believed her. Our Cheryl could make you believe she could do anything if she set her mind to it. Every day she woke up with a smile on her face, and that's no lie. Happiest soul I've ever known. What did we do wrong?"

Banks had no answer. He dropped his cigarette in the grate and walked to the door. "If you think of anything, let the local police know," he said.

"Wait a minute." Mrs Duggan turned to him. "Aren't you going to tell us?"

"Tell you what?"

"Who did it. Who killed our Cheryl."

"It doesn't matter now," Banks said. "It looks like he's dead himself." And he closed the door on their hopelessness and emptiness.

IV

"I'm sorry, Alan," Ted Folley said when he'd heard the story. "I told you it wasn't much of an investigation. We looked into it, but we got nowhere. We were sure the girl drowned. She'd been drinking, and there was water in her lungs. The bruises could have been caused by a customer; it's a rough trade she was in. She didn't have a ponce, so we'd no-one we could jump on right from the start."

Banks nodded and blew smoke rings. "We got nowhere with the Addison case, either," he said. "There was nothing to link him with Oxford, and we couldn't find out why he was in Swainshead. Not until now, anyway. What on earth could he have found out?"

"Anything," Folley said. "Maybe he found the last pub she'd been in, tracked down a pusher who'd run a mile if he even smelled police."

"Was she on drugs?"

"Not when she died, no. But there had been trouble. Nothing serious, just pills mostly. If Addison trailed around all her haunts and talked to everyone who knew her, showed a photo, flashed a bit of money . . . You know as well as I do, Alan, these blokes who operate outside the law have a better chance. He must have picked up your man's name somewhere and set off to question him."

"Yes. It's just a damn shame he wasn't more efficient."

"What do you mean?"

"If he'd gone back and told the Duggans what he'd found before rushing off to Yorkshire. If he'd just filed some kind of report . . ."

"He must have been keen," Folley said. "Some of them are, you know."

At that moment, Sergeant Hatchley came in from Woodstock. "Bloody waste of time," he grumbled, slouching in a chair and fumbling for a cigarette.

"Nothing?" Banks asked.

"Nowt. But judging by the expression on your face, you're that cat that got the cream. Am I right?"

"You are." He told Hatchley about his interview with the Duggans.

"So that's it, then?"

"Looks like it. Stephen Collier must've met up with this young girl, Cheryl Duggan, gone drinking with her then taken her to the meadows by the riverside for sex. It was unusually warm for that time of year. He got a bit rough, they fought, and he drowned her.

Or she fell in and he tried to save her. It could have been an accident, but it was a situation he couldn't afford to be associated with. Maybe he was on drugs; we'll never know. He might not even have been responsible for the bruising and the rough sexual treatment she'd received. That could have been a previous customer. Collier might even have been comforting her, trying to persuade her back onto the straight and narrow. I suppose the version will vary according to what kind of person you think Stephen was. One mistake—one terrible mistake—and three deaths have to follow. Christ, it could even have been some silly student prank."

"Do you think he killed himself?"

Banks shook his head. "I don't know. In his state of mind, if he'd been carrying the guilt all this time and feeling the pressure build, suicide and accidental death might have been much the same thing. It didn't matter any more, so he just got careless. Katie Greenock said he was planning to leave Swainshead, and I guess he didn't much mind how he went."

"What do we do now?" Hatchley asked.

Banks looked at his watch. "It's three-thirty," he said. "I suggest we go pay Stephen's old tutor a visit and see if we can find out whether he was in the habit of taking up with young prostitutes. We might find some clue as to what really happened, who was responsible for what. Then we'll head back home. We should be able to make it before nine if we're on the road soon." He turned to Folley and held out his hand. "Thanks again, Ted. We appreciate all you've done. If I can ever return the favour . . ."

Folley laughed. "In Swainsdale? You must be joking. But you're welcome. And do pay us a social call sometime. A few days boating on the Thames Valley would be just the ticket for the wife and kids."

"I will," Banks said. "Come on, Jim lad, time to hit the road again."

Hatchley dragged himself to his feet, said goodbye to Folley and followed Banks out onto St Aldates.

"There you are," Banks said, near Blackwell's on Broad Street. "Caps and gowns."

True enough, students were all over the place: walking, cycling, standing to chat outside the bookshops.

"Bloody poofdahs," Hatchley said.

They got past the porter, crossed the quadrangle, and found Dr Barber in his office at Stephen's old college.

"Sherry, gentlemen?" he asked, after they had introduced themselves.

Banks accepted because he liked dry sherry; Hatchley took one because he had never been known to refuse a free drink.

Barber's study was cluttered with books, journals and papers. A student essay titled "The Dissolution of the Monasteries: Evidence of Contemporary Accounts" lay on the desk, but it didn't quite obscure an old green-covered Penguin crime paperback. Banks tilted his head and glanced sideways at the title: *The Moving Toyshop*, by Edmund Crispin. He had never heard of it, but it wasn't quite the reading material he'd have expected to find in the office of an Oxford don.

While Dr Barber poured, Banks stood by the window and looked over the neat, clipped quadrangle at the light stone façades of the college.

Barber passed them their drinks and lit his pipe. Its smoke sweetened the air. In deference to his guests, he opened the window a little, and a draught of fresh air sucked the smoke out. In appearance, Barber had the air of an aged cleric, and he smelled of Pears soap. He reminded Banks of the actor Wilfrid Hyde-White.

"It was a long time ago," Barber said, when Banks had asked him about Collier. "Let me check my files. I've got records going back over twenty years, you know. It pays to know whom one has had pass through these hallowed halls. As a historian myself, I place great value on documentation. Now, let me see . . . Stephen Collier, yes. Braughtmore School, Yorkshire. Is that the one? Yes? I remember him. Not terribly distinguished academically, but a pleasant enough fellow. What's he been up to?"

"That's what we're trying to find out," Banks said. "He died a few days ago and we want to know why."

Barber sat down and picked up his sherry. "Good Lord! He wasn't murdered, was he?"

"Why would you think that?"

Barber shrugged. "One doesn't usually get a visit from the Yorkshire police over nothing. One doesn't usually get visits from the police at all."

"We don't know," Banks said. "It could have been accidental, or it could have been suicide."

"Suicide? Oh dear. Collier was a rather serious young man—a bit too much so, if I remember him clearly. But suicide?"

"Possibly."

"A lot can change in a few years," Barber said. He frowned and relit his pipe. Banks remembered his own struggles with the infernal engines, and the broken pipe that now hung on his wall in Eastvale CID Headquarters. "As I said," Barber went on, "Collier seemed a sober, sensible kind of fellow. Still, who can fathom the mysteries of the human heart? *Fronti nulla fides.*"

"There's no real type for suicide," Banks said. "Anyone, pushed far enough—"

"I suppose you're the kind of policeman who thinks anyone can become a murderer, too, given the circumstances?"

Banks nodded.

"I'm afraid I can't go along with that," Barber said. "I'm no psychologist, but I'd say it takes a special type. Take me, for example, I could never conceive of doing such a thing. The thought of jail, for a start, would deter me. And I should think that everyone would notice my guilt. As a child, I once stole a lemon tart from the school tuck-shop while Mrs Wiggins was in the back, and I felt myself turn red from head to toe. No, Chief Inspector, I'd never make a murderer."

"I'm thankful for that," Banks said. "I don't need to ask you for an alibi now, I suppose."

Barber looked at him for a moment, unsure what to do, then laughed.

"Stephen Collier," Banks said.

"Yes, yes. Forgive me. I'm getting old; I tend to ramble. But it's coming back. He was the kind who really did have to work hard to do well. So many others have a natural ability—they can dash off a good essay the night before. But you'd always find Collier in the library all week before a major piece of work was due. Conscientious."

"How did he get on with the other students?"

"Well enough, as far as I know. Collier was a bit of a loner, though. Kept himself to himself. I hardly need to tell you, Chief Inspector, that quite a number of young lads around these parts go in for high jinks. It's always been like that, ever since students started coming here in the thirteenth century. And there's always been a bit of a running battle between university authorities and the people of the city: town and gown, as we say. The students aren't vindictive, you realize, just high spirited. Sometimes they cause more damage than they intend."

"And Collier?"

"I'm sure he didn't go in for that kind of thing. If there had been any incidents of an unsavoury nature, they would have appeared in my assessment file."

"Did he drink much?"

"Never had any trouble with him."

"Drugs?"

"Chief Inspector Banks," Barber said slowly. "I do realize that the university has been getting a bad reputation lately for drugs and the like, and no doubt such things do happen. But if you take the word of the media, you'd be seriously misled. I don't think Stephen Collier was involved in drugs at all. I remember that we did have some trouble with one student selling cannabis around that time— most distressing—but there was a full investigation, and at no point was Stephen Collier implicated."

"So as far as you can say, Collier was a model student, if not quite as brilliant as some of his fellows?"

"I know it sounds hard to believe, but yes, he was. Most of the time you'd hardly have known he was here. I'm having great difficulty trying to guess what you're after. You say that Stephen Collier's death might have been suicide or it might have been an accident, but, if you don't mind my saying so, the questions you're asking seem preoccupied with unearthing evidence that Collier himself was some kind of hellraiser."

Banks frowned and looked out of the window again. The shadow of a cloud passed over the quadrangle. He drained his sherry and lit a cigarette. Sergeant Hatchley, quietly smoking in a chair in the corner, had emptied his glass a while ago and sat fidgeting with it as if he hoped Barber would notice and offer a refill. He did, and both policemen accepted. Banks liked the way the dry liquid puckered his taste buds.

"He's a suspect," Banks said. "And I'm afraid that's all I can tell you. We have no proof that Collier was guilty of anything, but there's a strong possibility."

"Does it matter," Barber asked, "now that he's dead?"

"Yes, it does. If he was guilty, then the case is closed. If not, we still have a criminal to catch."

"Yes. I see. Well I'm afraid I can't offer you any evidence at all. Seemed a thoroughly pleasant, hard-working, nondescript fellow to me as far as I can remember."

"What about six years ago? It would have been his third year, his last. Did anything unusual happen then, around early November?"

Barber frowned and pursed his lips. "I can't recall anything. . . . Wait a minute . . ." He walked back over to his ancient filing cabinet and riffled through the papers. "Yes, yes, I thought so," he announced finally. "Stephen Collier didn't finish his degree."

"What?"

"He didn't finish. Decided history wasn't for him and left after two years. Went to run a business, as far as I know. I can confirm with the registrar's office, of course, but my own records are quite thorough."

"Are you saying that Stephen Collier wasn't here, that he wasn't in Oxford in November six years ago?"

"That's right. Could it be you've got him mixed up with his brother, Nicholas? He would have just been starting his second year then, you know, and I certainly remember him, now I cast my mind back. Nicholas Collier was a different kettle of fish, a different kettle of fish entirely."

FOURTEEN

I

Katie stared at her reflection in the dark kitchen window as she washed the crystal glasses she couldn't put in the machine. The transistor radio on the table played soothing classical music, quiet enough that she could even hear the beck at the bottom of the back garden rippling over its stones.

Now that Stephen was dead and she had unburdened herself to Banks, she felt empty. None of her grandmother's maxims floated around her mind, as they had been doing lately, and that tightness in her chest that had seemed to squeeze at her very heart itself had relaxed. She even noticed a half-smile on her face, a very odd one she'd not seen before. Nothing hurt now; she felt numb, just like her mouth always did after an injection at the dentist's.

Chief Inspector Banks had told her that if she remembered anything else, she should get in touch with him. Try as she might, though, she couldn't remember a thing. Looking back over the years in Swainshead, she had noticed hints that all wasn't well, that some things were going on about which she knew nothing. But there was no coherent narrative, just a series of unlinked events. She thought of Sam's behaviour when Raymond Addison first appeared. She hadn't heard their conversation, but Sam had immediately left everything to her and gone running off across the street to the Collier house. Later, Addison had gone for a walk and never returned. When they found out the man had been murdered, Sam had been unusually pale and quiet for some days.

She remembered watching Bernie pause and glance towards the Collier house before going on his way the morning he left. She had also seen him call there one evening shortly after he'd arrived and thought it odd because of the way he usually went on about them being so rich and privileged.

None of it had meant very much at the time. Katie wasn't the kind of woman to look for bad in anyone but herself. She had had far more pressing matters to deal with and soon forgot the suspicious little things she'd noticed. Even now, she couldn't put it all together. When she told Banks that she had killed Bernie and Stephen, she meant it. She hadn't physically murdered them, but she knew she was responsible.

The things she remembered often seemed as if they had happened to someone else. She could view again, dispassionately, Bernard Allen sating himself on her impassive body, as if she were watching a silent film from the ceiling. And Stephen's chaste kiss left no trace of ice or fire on her lips. Sam had taken her roughly the previous evening, but instead of fear and loathing, she had felt a kind of power in her subservience. It wasn't pleasure; it was something new, and she felt that if she could only be patient enough it would make itself known to her eventually. It was as if he had possessed her body, but not her soul. She had kept her soul pure and untainted, and now it was revealing itself to her. Somehow, these new feelings were all connected with her sense of responsibility for the deaths of Bernie and Stephen. She had blood on her hands; she had grown up.

The future still felt very uncertain. Life would go on, she supposed, much as it had done. She would clean the rooms, cook the meals, submit to Sam in bed, do what she was told, and try to avoid making him angry. Everything would continue just as it had done, except for the new feelings that were growing in her. If she stayed patient, change would come in its own time. She wouldn't have to do anything until she knew exactly *what* to do.

For the moment, nothing touched her; nothing ruffled the calm and glassy surface of her mind. Caught up in her dark reflection, she dropped one of a set of six expensive crystal glasses. It shattered on the linoleum. But even that didn't matter. Katie looked down at the shards with an indulgent, pitying expression on her face and went to fetch the brush and dustpan.

As she moved, she heard a sound out back. Hurrying to the window, she peered through her own reflection and glimpsed a shadow slipping past her gate. A moment later—before she could get to the unlocked door—she heard a cursory tap. The door opened and Nicholas Collier popped his head around and smiled: "Hello, Katie. I've come to visit."

II

The sun was a swollen red ball low on the western horizon. It oozed its eerie light over the South Yorkshire landscape, silhouetted motionless pit-wheels and made the slag-heaps glow. On the cassette, Nick Drake was singing the haunting "Northern Sky."

Much of the way, the two had sat in silence, thinking things out and deciding what to do. Finally, Hatchley could stand it no longer: "How can we nail the bastard?" he asked.

"I don't know," Banks answered. "We don't have much of a case."

Hatchley grunted. "We might if we hauled him in and you and me had a go at him."

"He's clever, Jim," Banks said. The sergeant's first name didn't feel so strange to his lips after the first few times. "Look how he's kept out of it so long. He's not going to break down just because you and me play good cop-bad cop with him. That'll be a sign of our weakness to him. He'll know we need a confession to make anything stick, so it only strengthens his position. No, Nicholas Collier's a cool one. And don't forget, he's got pull around Swainsdale. We'd no sooner get started than some fancy lawyer would waltz in and gum up the works."

"What I'd give for a bloody good try, though!" Hatchley thumped the dashboard. "Sorry. No damage done. It just makes me angry, a stuck-up bastard like Nicholas Collier getting away with it. How many people has he killed?"

"Three, maybe four if we count Stephen. And he hasn't got away with it yet. The trouble is, we don't know if he killed anyone apart from the girl, Cheryl Duggan. We can't even prove that he killed her. Just because Dr Barber told us he had a reputation for pestering the town's working girls doesn't make him guilty. It certainly doesn't give us grounds for a conviction."

"But it was Cheryl Duggan's death that sent Addison up to Swainshead."

"Yes. But even that's circumstantial."

"Who do you think killed Addison and Allen?"

"At a guess, I'd say Stephen. He'd do it to protect his little brother and his family's reputation. But we don't know, and we never will if Nicholas doesn't talk. I'll bet, for all his cleverness, Nicholas is weak. I doubt he has the stomach for cold-blooded murder. They might both have been at the scene—certainly neither had a good alibi—but I'd say Stephen did the killing."

"What do you think happened with the Duggan girl?"

Banks shifted lanes to overtake a lorry. "I think he picked her up in a pub and took her down by the river. She was just a prostitute, a working-class kid, and he was from a prominent family, so what the hell did it matter to him what he did? I think he got over-excited, hurt her perhaps, and she started to protest, threatened to scream or tell the police. So he panicked and drowned her. Either that or he did it because he enjoyed it."

The tape finished. Banks lit a cigarette and felt around in the dark for another cassette. Without looking at the title, he slipped in the first one he got hold of. It was the sixties anthology tape he'd taken to Toronto with him. Traffic came on singing "No Face, No Name and No Number."

"I think Addison was a conscientious investigator," Banks went on. "He more than earned his money, poor sod. He did all the legwork the police didn't do and found a connection between Cheryl Duggan and Nicholas Collier. Maybe they'd been seen leaving a pub together, or perhaps her friends told him Collier had been with her before. Anyway, Addison prised the name out of someone, or bought the information, and instead of reporting in he set off for Swainshead. That was his first mistake.

"His second was to ask Sam Greenock about Nicholas Collier. Greenock was anxious to get in with the local gentry, and he was a bit suspicious of this stranger asking questions, so he stalled Addison and took the first opportunity to run over the bridge and tell Collier about it. There must have been real panic in the Collier house that evening. Remember, it was about fifteen months after the girl's death, and the Colliers must've thought all was well. I don't know the details. Maybe Sam arranged for Addison to go over to the house when the village was quiet, or maybe he even arranged for the Colliers to go up to Addison's room and kill him there. I don't know how it happened, but I think it was Stephen who struck the blow. That would explain the state he was in when he met Anne Ralston later that night."

"What about Bernard Allen?" Hatchley asked.

"At first I thought he was just unlucky," Banks said. "He told Katie Greenock that he knew Anne Ralston in Toronto. She told Sam, who did his usual town-crier routine. Not that it mattered this time, if Allen was intent on blackmail. Stephen Collier was an odd kind of bloke, from what I can make out—a real combination of opposites. When he'd killed Addison, he had to unburden himself to his girlfriend, but I'm sure he soon regretted it. He must have had a few sleepless nights after Anne first disappeared. Anyway, Bernard Allen knew that Stephen was involved in Addison's murder and that it was something to do with an incident back in Oxford. He obviously assumed that if the police knew that they could put the whole thing together. Which we did, rather too late."

"You said you thought Allen was unlucky at first," Hatchley said. "What about now?"

"I think he was going to blackmail the Colliers. I've not had time to tell you much about Toronto, but I met a few people there who said that Bernard Allen really wanted to come home to Swainshead. His sister mentioned it, too, but the others all played it down. He'd even let on to Katie Greenock that he'd send for her when he got back to Canada. That was because she wanted to escape Swainsdale and he wanted to get into her pants.

"I wondered why I was getting so many conflicting pictures of Allen's state of mind, so many contradictions. But that was his motive. He was blackmailing the Colliers to get himself home. A job at the school, money in the bank—I don't know what he'd asked for, but I'm certain that was his reason. And it got him killed. I doubt that whoever said 'you can't go home again' meant it as literally as that. Anyway, the Colliers decided they couldn't live with the threat, so one or both of them waited for him in the hanging valley that morning. They knew he'd be there because he'd often talked about it and he was heading that way."

"And what happened to Stephen? Why would Nicholas kill him, if he did?"

"Stephen was getting too jittery. Nicholas knew it was just a matter of time before his brother broke down completely, and he couldn't allow him to remain alive when I got back from Toronto after talking to Anne Ralston. Stephen must have told his brother that he didn't give anything away to Anne about the Oxford business, but that he'd made a serious mistake in hinting at his own involvement in Addison's killing. Nicholas knew that what Anne had to tell me would give me enough grounds to bring Stephen in, and he couldn't trust his brother to stand up under questioning. If we could discover the motive behind Addison's murder, then we'd know everything. Nicholas couldn't allow that.

"What he did was risky, but there was a lot at stake—not just the family name, now, but Nicholas's own freedom, his home, his career. He had to kill his own brother to survive. And if he succeeded, it would look like the accidental death of a disturbed man or the suicide of a guilty one."

It was dark when Banks negotiated the tricky connections onto the A1 east of Leeds. Cream were singing "Strange Brew" on the tape and Hatchley had fallen silent.

Banks still didn't understand it all. Stephen had killed to preserve what was important to him, but Nicholas Collier remained something of an enigma. In all likelihood, he had drowned Cheryl Duggan, but what bothered Banks was why. Had he done it from pleasure, accident or desperation? And was he also responsible for the bruising and marks of sexual abuse found on her body? Dr Barber had said that Nicholas had been in trouble once or twice over consorting with prostitutes and offering Oxford factory girls money for sex. Banks wondered why. Nicholas had all the advantages. Why hadn't he hung around with his own set, girls of his own social class?

"Let's call in at the station first," Banks said. "Something might have turned up." They were approaching the turn-off onto a minor road that would take them over the moors to Helmthorpe and the main valley road. "We can always drive to Swainshead later if there's nothing new." He looked at his watch. "It's not late, only nineish."

Hatchley nodded and Banks drove past the exit ramp and on to the Eastvale road.

The station was quiet. There had been no serious crimes while Banks and Hatchley had been gone. There was, however, a message from John Fletcher timed at five o'clock that evening asking them if they would call and see him as soon as possible. He said it was important—something to do with Stephen Collier's death—and he would be at home all evening.

There was also a copy of Dr Glendenning's preliminary post-mortem report on Stephen Collier. The doctor had found the equivalent of about five capsules of Nembutal in Collier's system—not enough in itself to cause death, but potentially lethal when mixed with alcohol. And his alcohol level had been far higher than the amount five or six pints would account for. It looked as if Banks was right and Collier had been slipped vodka in the pub and more drinks back at the house.

"Should we go to see Fletcher tonight?" Banks asked Hatchley. "Or leave it until tomorrow?"

Under normal circumstances he would have expected Hatchley to take any opportunity to get off work for a pint or a session on the sofa with Carol Ellis, but this time the sergeant was angry.

"Let's go," he said. "Maybe Fletcher's got the answer. I wouldn't want to leave it till he went and got himself killed, too. And I wouldn't mind paying a call on Nicholas bloody Collier either."

III

"Go away!" Katie said, rushing forward and trying to close the door.

But Nicholas had his foot wedged in. "Let me in, Katie," he said. "I want to talk to you about Stephen. He was very fond of you, you know."

"He's dead," Katie said, still pushing at the door with her shoulder. But Nicholas was too strong for her and the door knocked her backwards against the kitchen table as he entered. He shut the door behind him and walked towards her.

"I won't hurt you," he said. "I know you were talking to Stephen the day before he died. I just wondered if he'd been saying anything silly. He wasn't well, you know." He reached out and grabbed Katie's arm as she tried to slip away. "There's no need to be afraid of me," he said, relaxing his grip a little. "No need to run away. I won't hurt you. I just want to talk to you."

"I don't know what you mean," Katie said. "There was nothing wrong with Stephen."

"He was upset. He might have said things he didn't mean."

"What things?"

"I don't know. That's what I'm asking you, you stupid bitch," Nicholas shouted, then lowered his voice again. "Just tell me what you talked about. Aren't you going to offer me a drink?"

"I don't have anything."

"Liar." Nicholas opened Sam's liquor cabinet and poured a large shot of gin. "I've been here before, remember? With Sam." He held out the glass. "Go on, have some. You like gin, don't you?"

Katie shook her head. Nicholas hooked the back of her neck with one hand, put the glass to her closed lips, and tipped it forwards. The vile-smelling spirit spilled down Katie's chin and onto the front of her dress. It burned her throat and made her gag.

"Stop it!" she cried, spluttering and pushing him away.

Nicholas laughed, showing his yellowed teeth, and put the glass down. He went back to the cabinet and poured himself some Scotch.

"What did Stephen tell you?" he asked.

"Nothing." Katie coughed and rubbed at her lips with the back of her hand.

"He must have said something. He was quite a one for confiding in the wrong people, Stephen was—especially women. And I saw you talking to that policeman. Where is he now? What's he doing?"

"I don't know. I haven't seen him since yesterday."

"What did he ask you? What did you say to him?"

"Nothing. He doesn't know anything."

"Stop lying, Katie. Did you do it with him too, just like you do with all the others?"

Katie turned pale. "What do you mean?"

Nicholas grinned. The dark comma of hair had flopped over his brow and his cheeks were flushed. "You know what I mean. Just like you did with Stephen and everyone else. Did you let him do it to you, Katie, that policeman?"

"No!"

"Oh, don't be shy. You do it with everyone, don't you? You know you're nothing but a slut. A filthy whore. Tell me you're a filthy whore, Katie, say it."

"I'm not."

Katie rushed desperately for the connecting door, but Nicholas got there before her.

"There's no way out," he said. "All your guests are in the White Rose. I saw them. And Sam's off with his fancy women as usual."

"He's what?"

"Didn't you know? Oh, don't tell me you didn't know. All those times he goes off to see his friends in Leeds or Eastvale. It's women, Katie. Loose women. Can't you smell them on his skin when he comes home? Or do you like it when he comes straight from another woman and takes you? Do you like to smell other women on your husband's skin?"

Katie put her hands to her ears. "Stop it! Stop it!" she screamed. "You're evil."

Nicholas applauded quietly. "Oh, Katie, what an act."

Katie dropped her hands to her side. "What are you going to do?"

"Do? Why, I'm going to take you away from here. I don't trust you, Katie. There's no telling what you know and what you might say."

"I don't know anything."

"I think you do. Stephen told you, didn't he?"

"Told me what?"

"About Oxford."

Katie could think of nothing to say.

"Look at you blushing," Nicholas said, pointing at her. "You know, don't you? I can tell. Be sure your sins will find you out."

Suddenly, Katie realized what he meant and a terrible thought dawned on her.

"You killed him," she said quietly. "You killed Stephen."

Nicholas shrugged and spoke in a cold, passionless voice. "I couldn't trust him any more. He was falling apart on me."

Katie stiffened. She felt like a trapped animal. "What are you going to do?"

"I'm going to take you away, far away. What did he tell you about Oxford?"

"Nothing."

"Did he tell you about that girl, that stupid slut?"

Katie shook her head.

"He did, didn't he?"

"No! He told me nothing."

Nicholas leaned against the table. His bright eyes glittered and his breath came in short, sharp gasps. He looked like a madman to Katie. A wild, terrifying madman.

"She was nothing but a prostitute, Katie," he said. "A fallen woman. She sold herself to men. And when I . . . when I took her, she didn't . . . She told me I was too rough and she tried to make me stop. Me! Nicholas Collier. But I didn't. I couldn't. I knew that was the way she really wanted it. A common tart like her. Like you."

"No!" Katie said. "I'm not."

"Yes you are. I've had my eye on you. You do it with everyone. Do they pay you, Katie, or do you do it for nothing? I know you like to struggle. I'll pay you if you want."

"I don't know what you're talking about."

"I want you to say it for me. Say you're a filthy whore."

"I'm not."

"What's wrong? Why won't you say it? I bet you even let that policeman do it. I'm better than the lot of them, Katie. Say it."

"No! I won't."

He spoke very softly, so quiet she could hardly hear. "I want you to go down on your knees, Katie, and tell me you're a filthy whore and you want me to do it to you like an animal. Like a dog. I want you to lift your dress up and crawl, Katie."

He was moving towards her now, and his eyes held hers with a power that seemed to sap what little strength she had. She felt her shoulders hit the wall by the mantelpiece. There was nowhere else to go. But Nicholas kept coming closer, and when he was near enough he reached out and grabbed the front of her dress.

IV

Banks drove fast along the dark dale by the River Swain, passed through Helmthorpe and into the darker fell-shadowed landscape beyond. He turned sharp right at Swainshead, tires squealing, and carried on up the valley to Upper Head. He slowed down as they passed the Collier house, but the lights were out.

"I hope the bastard hasn't done a bunk," Hatchley said.

"No, he's too cool for that. We'll get him, don't worry."

The glimmer of light high on the fell-side about two miles north of the village came from Fletcher's isolated cottage. It was a difficult track to manage in the dark, but they finally pulled up outside the squat, solid house with its three-foot-thick walls. Fletcher had heard them coming and stood in the doorway. Again, they were ushered into the plain whitewashed room with its oak table and the photograph of Fletcher's glamorous ex-wife.

Fletcher was ill at ease. He avoided looking at them directly and fussed around with glasses for beer. Hatchley stood by the window looking out into the darkness. Banks sat at the table.

"What is it?" he asked, when Fletcher had sat down opposite him.

"It's about Stephen's death," Fletcher began hesitantly. "He was my friend. It's gone too far, now. Too far."

Banks nodded. "I know. I understand there was no love lost between you and Nicholas."

"You've heard about that? Well, it's true enough. I never had much time for him. But old Mr Walter was like a father to me, and I always felt like an older brother to Stephen."

Banks passed around the cigarettes.

"Saturday night," Fletcher burst out suddenly. "I thought nothing of it at the time—it was just the kind of silly trick Nicholas would play—but when he went to buy a round, I saw him pour a shot of clear spirits into Stephen's drink. As I said, I thought nothing of it. I knew Stephen was upset about something—what it was, I don't know—and he seemed to want to get drunk and forget his problems anyway. No point causing trouble, I thought, so I kept quiet.

"That family has a secret, Mr Banks, a dark secret. Stephen's hinted at it more than once, and I reckon it's something to do with Nicholas and the ladies, though ladies is too dignified a term. Did you know he once forced himself on Molly Stark from over Relton way?"

"No, I didn't."

"Aye. Well, it was hushed up, like most things Nicholas got up to. All neat and business-like."

"Wasn't there also some trouble with a servant-girl when his father was alive?" Banks asked.

"Aye," said Fletcher "Got her in the family way. But money changed hands and shut mouths. It was all arranged for, no expense spared, and she did away with it. He had a lust for lasses below his station, as they used to say. Working-class girls, servants, factory-girls, milkmaids . . . I even caught him mauling Katie Greenock at Stephen's party last week."

At last it made sense to Banks. Nicholas Collier couldn't keep away from women of a lower social class: Cheryl Duggan, Esther Haines, Katie Greenock, Anne Ralston, the servant-girl, Molly Stark—they were all beneath him socially. Although the term had lost a lot of its meaning over the past few years, they might still be called working-class women. Obviously it didn't matter who they were as individuals; that didn't interest Collier. He probably had some Victorian image of the working classes as a seething, gin-drinking, fornicating, procreating mass. He thrust himself on them and became violent when they objected. No doubt like most perverse sexual practices, his compulsion had a lot to do with power and humiliation.

"I knew something serious was up when we had those two murders here," Fletcher went on, refilling their beer glasses. "That detective and young Bernard Allen. I knew it, but I didn't know what. Whenever I asked, Stephen clammed up, told me to leave it be and I'd be better off not knowing." He took a sip of beer. "Maybe I should've pushed a bit harder. Maybe Stephen would still be alive. . . . But I don't think he killed himself. That's what I wanted to tell you. I saw Nicholas putting something into his drink, and he was in a hell of a state at closing-time, worse than if he'd just had a few jars. And the next thing I hear, he's dead. An overdose, they said. I knew he took sleeping tablets, but an overdose . . . ?"

"Yes, barbiturates," Banks said. "Usually fatal, mixed with as much alcohol as Stephen Collier had in his system."

"So it's murder, isn't it? That bastard brother of his murdered him."

"It looks like it, Mr Fletcher, but we've got to tread carefully. We've got no evidence, no proof."

"I'll testify to what I saw. I'll help put him away, as God's my witness."

Banks shook his head. "It'll help, but it's not enough. What if Nicholas was putting vodka in his brother's beer? As you said, it could have been a simple prank, and that's exactly what he'll say. It's all circumstantial and theoretical. We need more solid evidence, or a confession."

"Then I'll bloody well beat it out of him," Fletcher said, grasping the table and rising to his feet.

"Sit down," said Banks. "That's not going to help at all."

"Then what are you going to do?"

"I honestly don't know yet," Banks said. "We might just be able to put together a case, especially if we bring in Anne Ralston, but I don't want to risk it. Even if we could convince the court it's worth a trial, I don't want to take the chance of him getting off, which he might well do on what we've got so far."

"I know I should've spoken up earlier," Fletcher said. "I knew there was something wrong. If I'd told you before you went to Toronto, you might have had something to push at Stephen with, and he just might have told you the truth. He was on the edge, Mr Banks. That's why Nicholas had to get rid of him, I suppose."

"I think you're right," Banks said. "But we still can't prove it. You shouldn't blame yourself, though. You might have thought you were going to get Stephen in trouble. I imagine you were protecting him?"

Fletcher nodded. "I suppose I was. Him and his father's memory."

"To get Nicholas, you'd have had to betray Stephen. He was protecting his brother, or his father, like you were."

"What'll happen to me? Will you prosecute?"

"For what?"

"Withholding evidence? Accessory after the fact?"

Banks laughed. "You have a very thin grasp of the law, Mr Fletcher. Sure, you could have spoken earlier, as could a number of other people around Stephen Collier. But he kept everyone just enough in the dark so there was nothing, really, to say—nothing but vague fears and suspicions. Believe me, few people come to us with those—they don't want to look silly."

"So nothing's going to happen to me?"

Banks stood up and gestured to Hatchley it was time to leave. "No. You've helped us. It's up to us now to put a case together, or set a trap."

"I'll do anything to help," Fletcher said. "Tell the bastard I know something and let him come and try to bump me off."

"I hope it doesn't come to that," Banks said, "but thanks for the offer."

They sat in the car for a few minutes and lit cigarettes. It was pitch black, and far down in the valley below, the lights of Swainshead glittered like an alley of stars.

"How hard should we push Collier?" Hatchley asked.

"We don't push," Banks said. "At least not the first time. I told you, he's clever. He'll see we're desperate."

"So what do we do?"

"We confront him with what we've got and try to trip him up. If he's too clever to fall for that, and I suspect he is, then we try again and keep trying." He started the engine and broke the fell-side silence.

"You can't help admiring the bastard's nerve, though, can you," Hatchley said. "What if Freddie Metcalfe and Richmond had remembered seeing him order vodka and pour it in Stephen's pints?"

"Then all he'd have had to say was that he played a practical joke, like Fletcher said. There's nothing illegal about chasers. As things stand, it's only Fletcher's word against his, and a good defence lawyer would soon prove that John Fletcher had more than just cause to want to incriminate Collier. They'd bring up the incident at the party, for a start. Could you imagine Katie Greenock on the stand?"

Hatchley shook his head. "That lass never seems to know whether she's coming or going."

For some reason, Banks began to feel uneasy at the thought of Katie. What if she really did know more than she was telling? And what if Nicholas Collier suspected she knew? He might easily have seen her talking to Stephen. And Katie was exactly the kind of woman to set off his violent sexual behaviour.

He turned on to the road and headed south for Swainshead. There was still no light on in Collier's house. Hatchley hammered at the door but got no answer.

"Let's try the pub," Banks suggested.

Hatchley brightened up at that. He hadn't completely forgotten his priorities in a burst of professional zeal.

"Well, if it isn't Chief Inspector Banks," Freddie Metcalfe greeted them. "And Sergeant Hatchley, isn't it? What can I do you for?"

Banks ordered two pints of Pedigree and lit a Silk Cut. Maybe a pint would calm down his jangling nerves. The hairs at the back of his neck were bristling.

"Seen Nicholas Collier tonight?" he asked.

"No, he's not been in," Freddie said. "Has tha got any further wi' t'murder?"

"We're getting there, we're getting there," Banks said.

"Aye, and pigs can fly," Freddie said, passing their drinks.

"None of the usual lot been in tonight?"

"Nope. It's been as quiet as this since opening time," Freddie answered miserably and loped off to serve a youth in hiking boots.

"You know," Banks said, "I've been thinking about what to do next, and there's someone else we might profit from leaning on in this case."

"Sam Greenock?" Hatchley said.

"Yes. Threaten him with arrest as an accessory, and we might just get him to open up. He's cocky, but I don't think he's as cool as Nicholas. Stephen Collier's dead now. If we can convince Sam that Nicholas will fall from grace with or without his help, we might be able to strike a bargain. After all, without gentry to suck up to, what's Sam going to get out of it? Nicholas might well have sawn off the branch he was sitting on by killing Stephen."

"It's an idea," Hatchley said.

"And Greenock's a bully," Banks said. "Bullies are the easiest of the lot to lean on, especially men who beat up their wives."

"I think I might be able to work up a bit of enthusiasm," Hatchley said, grinning.

"Good. Let's go."

"What? Now? But we haven't finished our drinks."

"I've just got a feeling, that's all. We can come back to them. Let's see if Sam's in."

They left the White Rose and crossed the bridge. There were no lights on in the front lower or upper rooms of the Greenock Guest House.

"He's not in," Hatchley said. "Let's go back to the pub and call again later."

"It looks like there's nobody in at all," Banks said. "That's odd." He couldn't explain why he felt disturbed by the dark silent house, but he couldn't ignore the feeling. "No," he said. "I'm going in."

Hatchley sighed and followed. "I'll bet the bloody door's locked."

Before they could close the gate behind them, they heard a car coming. It was Sam's Landrover. He parked near the pub across the narrow Swain, as there was no road on the Greenocks' side of the river, and came bounding over the bridge.

"Evening, gents," he called out. "And what can I do . . . Oh, it's you."

"Don't sound so disappointed," Banks said. "We might be able to do something for you."

"Oh?" Sam's boyish face looked puzzled. He patted his curly hair. "All right. Never turn down a favour from a copper, that's me."

"Can we go in?"

"Of course. I'll get the missis to brew a pot of tea." He dug in his pocket for his keys, finally found the right one and stuck it in the lock, where he poked and twisted it for a while, then turned to Banks and frowned. "That's odd. It was already open. Katie usually locks up at ten sharp and the guests let themselves in with their own keys. And it's not usually as dark as this. She puts the hall light on for the guests. They're probably still in the pub, but I can't imagine where she is."

Banks and Hatchley followed him through the front door into the dark hall. Sam turned the light on. The guest book lay open on its varnished table by a stack of tourist guides, maps and brochures advertising local businesses and leisure pursuits. Automatically, Sam looked at himself in the mirror over the phone and patted his curly hair again.

"Katie!" Sam called.

No answer.

He went into the dining-room and flicked the light switch on. "Bloody hell!"

Banks followed him inside. "What is it?" All he could see was the room where he and Hatchley had eaten breakfast. The varnished tables gleamed darkly in the shaded light.

"She's not set the tables for the morning. She's not even put the bloody cloths on," Sam said. He sounded more angry than worried about why or where Katie might have gone.

They paused at the foot of the stairs, where Sam called again and got no answer. "It doesn't look like she's home," he said, puzzled. "I can't imagine where she'd be at this time."

"Maybe she's left you," Banks suggested.

"Don't be daft. Where would she go? Why would she do a thing like that anyway?"

They carried on to the door that separated the Greenocks' living-quarters from the rest of the house.

"Katie!" Sam called once more, hand on the knob.

Still no reply. The absolute silence in the house made Banks's hackles rise.

Sam opened the door and walked along the short, narrow corridor that linked the two parts of the house. Banks and Hatchley followed close behind. Coats on hooks on either side brushed against them as they walked in single file behind Sam. The only faint illumination was at the end of the passage.

"At least she's left this light on," Sam said.

The light came from the pane of frosted glass on the door that led into the Greenocks' living-room. Sam called his wife's name again but got no answer. He walked into the room and stopped dead in his tracks.

"Jesus Christ," he gasped, then stumbled backwards into Banks and started to slide slowly down the wall, hands over his eyes.

Banks regained his balance, pushed past Sam and went in, Hatchley close behind. They stopped in the doorway, awed and horrified by the scene before them. Banks heard Hatchley mutter a prayer or a curse.

There was blood all over the room: on the carpet, the sofa, the hearth, and even splashed like obscene hieroglyphs over the wall above the mantelpiece. Nothing moved. Nicholas Collier lay awkwardly, half on the sofa and half on the carpet, his head bashed in, his face a bloody pulp. He wouldn't even have been recognizable if it hadn't been for the prominent, yellowish teeth splintered and bared in agony and shock.

Katie sat on the arm of the settee still holding the heavy wooden cross of her granny's that had stood on the mantelpiece. Her beautiful brown eyes were looking at things nobody else could see. The front of her dress was ripped open at one side and a few drops of blood glistened against the pale skin of her blue-veined breast.

PAST REASON HATED

This one is for the
Usual Suspects

ONE

I

Snow fell on Swainsdale for the first time that year a few days before Christmas. Out in the dale, among the more remote farms and hamlets, the locals would be cursing. A heavy snowfall could mean lost sheep and blocked roads. In past years, some places had been cut off for as long as five weeks. But in Eastvale, most of those crossing the market square on the evening of December 22 felt a surge of joy as the fat flakes drifted down, glistening in the gaslight as they fell, to form a lumpy white carpet over the cobble-stones.

Detective Constable Susan Gay paused on her way back to the station from Joplin's newsagents. Outside the Norman church stood a tall Christmas tree, a gift from the Norwegian town with which Eastvale was twinned. The lights winked on and off, and its tapered branches bent under the weight of half an inch of snow. In front of the tree, a group of children in red choir-gowns stood singing "Once in Royal David's City." Their alto voices, fragile but clear, seemed especially fitting on such a beautiful winter's evening.

Susan tilted her head back and let the snowflakes melt on her eyelids. Two weeks ago she would not have allowed herself to do something so spontaneous and frivolous. But now that she was *Detective* Constable Gay, she could afford to relax a little. She had finished with courses and exams, at least until she tried for sergeant. Now there would be no more arguing with David Craig over who made the coffee. There would be no more walking the beat, either, and no more traffic duty on market day.

The music followed her as she headed back to the station:

And He leads His children on
To the place where He is gone.

Directly in front of her, the new blue lamp hung like a shop-sign
over the doorway of the Tudor-fronted police station. In an attempt
to change the public image of the force, tarnished by race riots, sex
scandals and accusations of high-level corruption, the government
had looked to the past: more specifically, to the fifties. The lamp
was straight out of "Dixon of Dock Green." Susan had never actually seen the program, but she understood the basic idea. The
image of the kindly old copper on the beat had caused many a
laugh around Eastvale Regional Headquarters. Would that life were
as simple as that, they all said.

Her second day on the job and all was well. She pushed open
the door and headed for the stairs. Upstairs! The inner sanctum of
the CID. She had envied them all for so long—Gristhorpe, Banks,
Richmond, even Hatchley—when she had brought coffee or
messages, or stood by taking notes while they interrogated female
suspects. No longer. She was one of them now, and she was about
to show them that a woman could do the job every bit as well as a
man, if not better.

She didn't have her own office; only Banks and Gristhorpe were
allowed such luxuries. The hutch she shared with Richmond would
have to do. It looked over the car-park out back, not the market
square, but at least she had a desk, rickety though it was, and a
filing cabinet of her own. She had inherited them from Sergeant
Hatchley, now exiled to the coast, and the first thing she had had
to do was rip down the nude pin-ups from the cork bulletin board
above his desk. How anybody could work with those bloated
mammaries hanging over them was beyond her.

About forty minutes later, after she had poured herself a cup of
coffee to keep her awake while she studied the latest regional crime
reports, the phone rang. It was Sergeant Rowe calling from the
front desk.

"Someone just phoned in to report a murder," he said.

Susan felt the adrenalin flow. She grasped the receiver tighter.
"Where?"

"Oakwood Mews. You know, those tarted-up *bijou* terraces back of King Street."

"I know them. Any details?"

"Not much. It was a neighbour that called. Said the woman next door went rushing into the street screaming. She took her in but couldn't get much sense out of her except that her friend had been murdered."

"Did the neighbour take a look for herself?"

"No. She said she thought she'd better call us right away."

"Can you send PC Tolliver down there?" Susan asked. "Tell him to check out the scene without touching anything. And tell him to stay by the door and not let anyone in till we get there."

"Aye," said Rowe, "but shouldn't—"

"What's the number?"

"Eleven."

"Right."

Susan hung up. Her heart beat fast. Nothing had happened in Eastvale for months—and now, only her second day on the new job, a murder. And she was the only member of the CID on duty that evening. Calm down, she told herself, follow procedure, do it right. She reached for her coat, still damp with snow, then hurried out the back way to the car-park. Shivering, she swept the snow off the windscreen of her red Golf and drove off as fast as the bad weather allowed.

II

Four and twenty virgins
Came down from Inverness,
And when the ball was over
There were four and twenty less.

"I think Jim's a bit pissed," Detective Chief Inspector Alan Banks leaned over and said to his wife, Sandra.

Sandra nodded. In a corner of the Eastvale Rugby Club banquet room, by the Christmas tree, Detective Sergeant Jim Hatchley stood with a group of cronies, all as big and brawny as himself. They looked like a parody of a group of carol-singers, Banks thought, each with a foaming pint in his hand. As they sang, they swayed. The other guests stood by the bar or sat at tables chatting over the noise. Carol Hatchley—*née* Ellis—the sergeant's blushing bride, sat beside her mother and fumed. The couple had just changed out of their wedding clothes into less formal attire in readiness for their honeymoon, but Hatchley, true to form, had insisted on just one more pint before they left. That one had quickly turned into two, then three. . . .

The village butcher, he was there,
Chopper in his hand.
Every time they played a waltz,
He circumcised the band.

It didn't make sense, Banks thought. How many times could you circumcise one band? Carol managed a weak smile, then turned and said something to her mother, who shrugged. Banks, leaning against the long bar with Sandra, Superintendent Gristhorpe and Philip Richmond, ordered another round of drinks.

As he waited, he looked around the room. It was done up for the festive season, no doubt about that. Red and green concertina trimmings hung across the ceiling, bedecked with tinsel, holly and the occasional sprig of mistletoe. The club tree, a good seven feet tall, sparkled in all its glory.

It was twenty past eight, and the real party was just beginning. The wedding had taken place at Eastvale Congregationalist Church late in the afternoon, and it had been followed by a slap-up meal at the rugby club at six. Now the speeches had been made, the plates cleared away and the tables moved for a good Yorkshire knees-up. Hatchley had hired a DJ for the music, but the poor lad was still waiting patiently for a signal to begin.

Singing "Balls to your father,
Arse against the wall.
If you've never been shagged on a Saturday night,
You've never been shagged at all."

"Four and Twenty Virgins" was coming to a close, Banks could tell. There would be a verse about the village schoolmistress (who had unusually large breasts) and one about the village cripple (who did unspeakable things with his crutch), then a rousing finale. With a bit of luck, that would be the end of the rugby songs. They had already performed "Dinah, Dinah, Show Us Yer Leg (A Yard Above Your Knees)," "The Engineer's Song" and a lengthy, improvised version of "Mademoiselle from Armentieres." The sulky DJ, who had been pretending to set up his equipment for the past hour, would soon get his chance to shine.

Banks passed the drinks along to the others and reached for a cigarette. Gristhorpe frowned at him, but Banks was used to that. Phil Richmond was also smoking one of his occasional panatellas, so the superintendent was having a particularly hard time of it. Sandra had stopped smoking completely, and Banks had agreed not to smoke in the house. Luckily, although most of the police station had been declared a non-smoking area, he was still permitted to light up in his own office. Things had got so bad, though, that even alleged criminals brought in for interrogation could legally object to any police officer smoking in the interview rooms. It was a sorry state of affairs, Banks mused: you could beat them to your heart's content, as long as the bruises didn't show, but you couldn't smoke in their presence and get away with it.

Sandra raised her dark eyebrows and breathed a sigh of relief when "Four and Twenty Virgins" came to an end. But her joy was short-lived. The choir of rugby forwards refused to leave the stage without giving their rendition of "Good King Wenceslas." Despite groans from the captive audience, a dirty look from the DJ and a positive flash of fury from Carol's eyes, Sergeant Hatchley led them off:

Good King Wenceslas looked out
Of his bedroom window.
Silly bugger, he fell out . . .

Gristhorpe looked at his watch. "I think I'll be off after this one. I just overheard someone say it's snowing pretty heavily out there now."

"Is it?" Sandra said. Banks knew she loved snow. They walked over to the window at the far end of the room and glanced out. Clearly satisfied with what she saw, Sandra pulled the long curtains open. It had been snowing only lightly when they had arrived for pre-dinner drinks at about five, but now the high window framed a thick swirl of white flakes falling on the rugby field. Others turned to look, oohing and aahing, touching their neighbours on the arm to tell them what was happening. As they walked back, Banks took Sandra in his arms and kissed her.

"Got you," he said, then he looked up and Sandra followed his gaze to the mistletoe hanging above them.

Sandra took his arm and walked beside him back to the bar. "I don't mean to be rude or anything," she said, "but when's this racket going to end? Don't you think someone should have a word with Jim? After all, it *is* Carol's wedding day. . . ."

Banks looked at Hatchley. Judging by his flushed face and the way he swayed, there wouldn't be much of a wedding night for the bride.

Brightly shone his arse that night,
Though the frost was cruel . . .

Banks was just about to walk across and say something—only concerned that he might sound too much like the boss when he was just a wedding guest—when he was saved by the DJ. A long and loud blast of feedback issued from the speakers and stopped Hatchley and his mates in their tracks. Before they could regather their wits for a further onslaught, several quick-thinking members of the party applauded. At once, the singers took this as their cue for a bow and the DJ as his opportunity to begin the real music. He adjusted a couple of dials, skipped the patter, and before Hatchley and his mob even knew what had hit them the hall was filled with the sound of Martha and the Vandellas singing "Dancing in the Street."

Sandra smiled. "That's more like it."

Banks glanced over at Richmond, who looked very pleased with himself. And well he might. There had just been a big change-around at Eastvale Regional Police Headquarters. Sergeant Hatchley had been a problem for some time. Not suitable material for promotion, he had stood in Richmond's way, even though Richmond had passed his sergeant's examination with flying colours and shown remarkable aptitude on the job. The trouble was, there just wasn't room for two detective sergeants in the small station.

Finally, after months of trying to find a way out of the dilemma, Superintendent Gristhorpe had seized the first opportunity that came his way. Official borders had been redrawn and the region had expanded eastwards to take in a section of the North York Moors and a small stretch of coastline between Scarborough and Whitby. It seemed a good idea to place a small CID outpost on the coast to deal with the day-to-day matters that might arise there, and Hatchley came to mind as the man to head it. He was competent enough, just lazy and inattentive to detail. Surely, Gristhorpe had reasoned to Banks, he couldn't do much damage in a sleepy fishing village like Saltby Bay?

Hatchley had been asked if he fancied living by the seaside and he had said yes. After all, it was still in Yorkshire. As the time of the move coincided with his impending marriage, it had seemed sensible to combine the two celebrations. Though Hatchley remained a sergeant, Gristhorpe had managed to wangle him a small pay increase, and—more important—he would be in charge. He was to take David Craig, now a detective constable, with him. Craig, soaking up the ale at the other end of the bar, didn't look too pleased about it. Hatchley and his wife were off to Saltby Bay that night—or, the way things were going, the next morning—where he was to take two weeks' leave to set up their cottage by the sea. His only complaint was that it wouldn't be summer for a long time. Apart from that, Hatchley seemed happy enough with the state of affairs.

In Eastvale, Richmond had got his promotion to detective sergeant at last, and Susan Gay had been brought upstairs as their new detective constable. It was too early to know whether the arrangement would work, but Banks had every confidence in both Richmond and Gay. Still, he felt sad. He had been in Eastvale

almost three years, and during that time he had grown to like and
depend on Sergeant Hatchley, despite the man's obvious faults. It
had taken Banks until last summer to call the sergeant by his first
name, but he felt that Hatchley, with Superintendent Gristhorpe,
had been responsible for helping him adapt to Yorkshire ways after
his move from London.

The music slowed down. Percy Sledge started singing "When a
Man Loves a Woman." Sandra touched Banks's arm. "Dance?"

Banks took her hand and they walked towards the dance-floor.
Before they got there, someone tapped him gently on the shoulder.
He turned and saw DC Susan Gay, snowflakes still melting on the
shoulders of her navy coat and in her short, curly blonde hair.

"What is it?" Banks asked.

"Can I have a word, sir? Somewhere quiet."

The only quiet places were the toilets, and they could hardly go
charging off into the gents' or ladies'. The alternative was the corner
opposite the DJ, which seemed to be deserted. Banks asked Sandra
if she minded missing this one. She shrugged, being used to such
privations, and went back to the bar. Gristhorpe, Banks noticed,
gallantly offered her his arm, and they went onto the dance-floor.

"It's a murder, at least a possible murder," DC Gay said, as soon
as they had found a quieter spot. "I didn't see the superintendent
when I came in, so I went straight to you."

"Any details?"

"Sketchy."

"How long ago was this?"

"About ten minutes. I sent PC Tolliver to the house and drove
straight over here. I'm sorry to spoil the celebrations, but I couldn't
see what else—"

"It's all right," Banks said, "you did fine." She hadn't, but that was
hardly her fault. She was new to the job and a murder report had
cropped up. What should she have done? Well, she could have
gone to check out the scene herself, and she might have found, as
nine times out of ten one did, that there had been some mistake, or
a prank. Or she might have waited for the PC to call in and let her
know the situation before running off and dragging her chief
inspector away from his ex-sergeant's wedding celebration. But

Banks didn't blame her. She was young yet, she would learn, and if they really were dealing with a murder, the time saved by Susan's direct action could prove invaluable.

"I've got the address, sir." She stood there looking at him, keen, expectant. "It's on Oakwood Mews. Number eleven."

Banks sighed. "We'd better go then. Just give me a minute."

He went back to the bar and explained the situation to Richmond. The music speeded up again, into the Supremes' "Baby Love," and Gristhorpe led Sandra back from the dance-floor. When he heard the news, he insisted on accompanying Banks to the scene, even though it was by no means certain they would find a murder victim there. Richmond wanted to come along, too.

"No, lad," said Gristhorpe, "there's no point. If it's serious, Alan can fill you in later. And don't tell Sergeant Hatchley. I don't want it spoiling his wedding day. Though judging by the look on young Carol's face he might have already done that himself."

"Are you taking the car?" Sandra asked Banks.

"I'd better. Oakwood Mews is a fair distance from here. There's no telling how long we'll be. If there's time, I'll come back and pick you up. If not, don't worry, Phil will take good care of you."

"Oh, I'm not worried." She slipped her arm in Richmond's and the new detective sergeant blushed. "Phil's a lovely mover."

Banks kissed her quickly and set off with Gristhorpe.

Susan Gay stood waiting for them by the door. Before they got to her, one of Hatchley's rugby club cronies lurched over and tried to kiss her. From behind, Banks saw him put his arms around her, then double up and stagger back. Everyone else was too busy dancing or chatting to notice. Susan looked flushed when Banks and Gristhorpe got there. She put her hand to mouth and muttered, "I'm sorry," while the rugby player pointed, with a hurt expression on his face, to the sprig of mistletoe over the door.

III

It was no false alarm; that much, at least, was clear from the expression on PC Tolliver's face when Banks and the others reached

number eleven Oakwood Mews. After Gristhorpe had issued
instructions to send for Dr Glendenning and the scene-of-crime
team, the three detectives went inside.

The first thing Banks noticed when he entered the hall was the
music. Muffled, coming from the front room, it sounded familiar: a
Bach cantata, perhaps? Then he opened the living-room door and
paused on the threshold. The scene possessed a picturesque quality,
he felt, which even extended, at first, to masking the ugliness of the
corpse on the sofa.

A log fire crackled in the hearth. Its flames tossed shadows on
the sheepskin rug and over the stucco walls. The only other light
came from two red candles on the polished oak table in the far
corner, and from the Christmas tree lights in the window. Banks
stepped into the room. The flames danced and the beautiful music
played on. On the wall above the stereo was a print of one of
Gauguin's Tahitian scenes: a coffee-skinned native woman, naked
to the waist, carrying what looked like a bowl of red berries as she
walked beside another woman.

As he approached the sofa, Banks noticed that the sheepskin rug
was dotted with dark blotches, as if the fire had spat sparks, which
had seared the wool. Then he became aware of that sickly, metallic smell he had come across so often before.

A log shifted on the fire; flames leapt in all directions and
their light played over the naked body. The woman lay stretched
out, head propped up on cushions in what would have been a
very inviting pose had it not been for the blood that had flowed
from the multiple stab wounds in her throat and chest and
drenched the whole front of her body. It glistened like dark satin
in the firelight. From what Banks could see, the victim was young
and pretty, with smooth, olive skin and shoulder-length, jet-
black hair. Bending over her, he noticed that her eyes were blue,
the intense kind of blue that makes some dark-haired people all
that much more attractive. Now their stare was cold and lifeless.
In front of her, on the low coffee table, stood a half-empty
teacup on a coaster and a chocolate layer-cake with one slice
missing. Banks covered one fingertip with his handkerchief and
touched the cup. It was cold.

The spell broke. Banks became aware of Gristhorpe's voice in the background questioning PC Tolliver, and of Susan Gay standing silent beside him. It was her first corpse, he realized, and she was handling it well, better than he had. Not only was she not about to vomit or faint, but she, too, was glancing around the room, observing the details.

"Who found the body?" Gristhorpe asked PC Tolliver.

"Woman by the name of Veronica Shildon. She lives here."

"Where is she now?" Banks asked.

Tolliver nodded towards the stairs. "Up there with the neighbour. She didn't want to come back in here."

"I don't blame her," said Banks. "Do you know who the victim is?"

"Her name's Caroline Hartley. Apparently, she lived here too."

Gristhorpe raised his bushy eyebrows. "Come on, Alan, let's go and hear what she has to say. Susan, will you stay down here till the scene-of-crime team arrives?"

Susan Gay nodded and stood aside.

There were only two rooms and a bathroom-toilet upstairs. One had been converted into a sitting room, or a study, with bookcases covering one wall, a small roll-top desk under the window and a couple of wicker armchairs arranged below the track-lighting. The bedroom, Banks noticed from the landing, was done out in coral and sea-green, with Laura Ashley wallpaper. If two women lived in the house and there was only one bedroom, he reasoned, then they must share it. He took a deep breath and went into the study.

Veronica Shildon sat in one of the wicker chairs, head in hands. The neighbour, who introduced herself as Christine Cooper, sat beside her. The only other place to sit was the hard-backed chair in front of the desk. Gristhorpe took it and leaned forward, resting his chin on his fists. Banks stood by the door.

"She's had a terrible shock," Christine Cooper said. "I don't know if she'll be able to tell you much."

"Don't worry, Mrs Cooper," Gristhorpe said. "The doctor will be here soon. He'll give her something. Is there anyone she can stay with?"

"She can stay with me if she wants. Next door. We've got a spare room. I'm sure my husband won't mind."

"Fine." Gristhorpe turned towards the crying woman and introduced himself. "Can you tell me what happened?"

Veronica Shildon looked up. She was in her mid-thirties, Banks guessed, with a neat cap of dark brown hair streaked with grey. Handsome rather than pretty, her thin face and lips, and everything in her bearing, spoke of dignity and refinement, perhaps even of severity. She held a crumpled tissue in her left hand and the fist of her right was clenched so tightly it was white. Even as he admired her appearance, Banks looked for any signs of blood on her hands or her clothing. He saw none. Her grey-green eyes, red around the rims, couldn't quite focus on Gristhorpe.

"I just got home," she said. "I thought she was waiting for me."

"What time was this?" Gristhorpe asked.

"Eight. A few minutes after." She didn't look at him when she answered.

"Where had you been?"

"I'd been shopping." She looked up, but her eyes appeared to be staring right through the superintendent. "That's just it, you see. I thought for a moment she was wearing the present I'd bought her, the scarlet camisole. But she couldn't have been, could she? I hadn't even given it to her. And she was dead."

"What did you do when you found her?" Gristhorpe asked.

"I . . . I ran to Christine's. She took me in and called the police. I don't know. . . . Is Caroline really dead?"

Gristhorpe nodded.

"Why? Who?"

Gristhorpe leaned forward and spoke softly. "That's what we have to find out, love. Are you sure you didn't touch anything in the room?"

"Nothing."

"Is there anything else you can tell us?"

Veronica Shildon shook her head. She was clearly too distraught to speak. They would have to leave their questions until tomorrow.

Christine Cooper accompanied Banks and Gristhorpe to the study door. "I'll stay with her till the doctor comes, if you don't mind," she said.

Gristhorpe nodded and they went downstairs.

"Organize a house-to-house, would you?" Gristhorpe asked PC Tolliver before they returned to the living-room. "You know the drill. Anyone seen entering or leaving the house." The constable nodded and dashed off.

Back inside the front room, Banks noticed for the first time how warm it was and took off his overcoat. The music stopped, then the needle came off the record, returned to the edge of the turntable and promptly started on its way again.

"What *is* that music?" Susan Gay asked.

Banks listened. The piece—elegant, stately strings accompanying a soprano soloist singing in Latin—sounded vaguely familiar. It wasn't Bach at all, Italian in style rather than German.

"Sounds like Vivaldi," he said, frowning. "But it's not what it is bothers me so much, it's why it's playing, and especially why it's been set to repeat."

He walked over to the turntable and knelt by the album cover lying face down on the speaker beside it. It was indeed Vivaldi: *Laudate pueri*, sung by Magda Kalmár. Banks had never heard of her, but she had a beautiful voice, more reedy, warm and less brittle than many sopranos he had heard. The cover looked new.

"Should I turn it off?" Susan Gay asked.

"No. Leave it. It could be important. Let the scene-of-crime boys have a look."

At that moment the front door opened and everyone stood aghast at what walked in. To all intents and purposes, their visitor was Santa Claus himself, complete with beard and red hat. If it hadn't been for the height, the twinkling blue eyes, the brown bag and the cigarette dangling from the corner of his mouth, Banks himself wouldn't have known who it was.

"I apologize for my appearance," said Dr Glendenning. "Believe me, I have no wish to appear frivolous. But I was just about to set off for the children's ward to give out their Christmas presents when I got the call. I didn't want to waste any time." And he didn't. "Is this the alleged corpse?" He walked over to the sofa and bent over the body. Before he had done much more than look it over, Peter Darby, the photographer, arrived along with Vic Manson and his team.

The three CID officers stood in the background while the specialists went to work collecting hair and fabric samples with tiny vacuum cleaners, dusting for prints and photographing the scene from every conceivable angle. Susan Gay seemed enthralled. She must have read about all this in books, Banks thought, and even taken part in demonstration runs at the police college, but there was nothing like the real thing. He tapped her on the shoulder. It took her a few seconds to pull her eyes away and face him.

"I'm just nipping back upstairs," Banks whispered. "Won't be a minute." Susan nodded and turned to watch Glendenning measure the throat wounds.

Upstairs, Banks knelt in front of the armchair. "Veronica," he said gently, "that music, Vivaldi, was it playing when you got home?"

With difficulty, Veronica focused on him. "Yes," she said, with a puzzled look on her face. "Yes. That was odd. I thought we had company."

"Why?"

"Caroline . . . she doesn't like classical music. She says it makes her feel stupid."

"So she wouldn't have put it on herself?"

Veronica shook her head. "Never."

"Whose record is it? Is it part of your collection?"

"No."

"But you like classical music?"

She nodded.

"Do you know the piece?"

"I don't think so, but I recognize the voice."

Banks stood up and rested his hand on her shoulder. "The doctor will be up soon," he said. "He'll give you something to help you sleep." He took Christine Cooper's arm and drew her onto the landing. "How long have they been living here?"

"Nearly two years now."

Banks nodded towards the bedroom. "Together?"

"Yes. At least I . . ." She folded her arms. "It's not my place to judge."

"Ever any trouble?"

"What do you mean?"

"Rows, threats, feuds, angry visitors, anything?"

Christine Cooper shook her head. "Not a thing. You couldn't wish for quieter, more considerate neighbours. As I said, we didn't know each other very well, but we've passed the time of day together now and then. My husband . . ."

"Yes?"

"Well . . . he was very fond of Caroline. I think she reminded him of our Corinne. She died a few years ago. Leukaemia. She was about Caroline's age."

Banks looked at Christine Cooper. She seemed to be somewhere in her mid-fifties, a small, puzzled-looking woman with grey hair and a wrinkled brow. That would make her husband about the same age, or a little older perhaps. A paternal attachment, most likely, but he made a mental note to follow it up.

"Did you notice anything earlier this evening?" he asked.

"Like what?"

"Any noise, or anyone calling at the house?"

"No, I can't really say I did. The houses are quite solid, you know. I had my curtains closed, and I had the television on until eight o'clock, when that silly game show came on."

"You heard nothing at all?"

"I heard doors close once or twice, but I couldn't be sure whose doors."

"Can you remember what time?"

"When I was watching television. Between seven and eight. I'm sorry I'm not more use to you. I just didn't pay attention. I didn't know it would be important."

"Of course not. Just one more small point," Banks said. "What time did Mrs Shildon arrive at your house?"

"Ten past eight."

"Are you sure?"

"Yes. I was in the kitchen then. I looked at the clock when I heard someone shouting and banging on my door. I hadn't heard any carol-singers, and I wondered who could be calling at that time."

"Did you hear her arrive home?"

"I heard her door open and close."

"What time was that?"

"Just after eight—certainly not more than a minute or two after. I'd just switched the television off and gone to start on Charles's dinner. That's why I heard her. It was quiet then. I thought it was my door at first, so I glanced up at the clock. It's a habit I have when I'm in the kitchen. There's a nice wall-clock, a present . . . but you don't want to know about that. Anyway, I wasn't expecting Charles back so early so I . . . Just a minute! What are you getting at? Surely you can't believe—"

"Thank you very much, Mrs Cooper, that'll be all for now."

When Mrs Cooper had gone back into the study, Banks had a quick look through the bedroom for any signs of blood-stained clothing, but found nothing. The wardrobe was clearly divided into two halves: one for Veronica's more conservative clothes and the other for Caroline's, a little more modern in style. At the bottom sat a carrier bag full of what looked like unwrapped Christmas presents.

The whole house would have to be searched thoroughly before the night was over, but the scene-of-crime team could do that later. What bothered Banks for the moment was the gap of almost ten minutes between Veronica Shildon's arriving home and her knocking on her neighbour's door. A lot could be accomplished in ten minutes.

Back downstairs, Banks led Vic Manson over to the turntable.

"Can you get this record off and dust the whole area for prints? I want the cover and the inside sleeve bagged for examination, too."

"No problem." Manson set to it.

Everyone looked up when the music stopped. It had cast such a spell over the scene that Banks felt like a dancer cut off in the middle of a stately pavan. Now everyone seemed to notice for the first time exactly what the situation was. It was harsh and ugly, especially with all the lights on.

"Have they found anything interesting yet?" Banks asked Gristhorpe.

"The knife. It was on the draining-board in the kitchen, all washed, but there are still traces of blood. It looks like one of their own, from a set. Did you notice that cake on the table in front of the sofa?"

Banks nodded.

"It's possible she'd used the knife to cut herself a slice earlier."

"Which would make it the handiest weapon," Banks said, "if it was still on the table."

"Yes. And there's this." The superintendent held out a crumpled sheet of green Christmas wrapping paper with silver bells and red holly-berries on it. "It was over by the music centre." He shrugged. "It might mean something."

"It could have come from the record," Banks said, and told Gristhorpe what Veronica had said.

Dr Glendenning, who had taken off his beard and hat and unbuttoned the top half of his Father Christmas outfit, walked over to them and stuck another cigarette in his mouth.

"Dead three or four hours at the most," he said. "Bruise on the left cheek consistent with a hard punch or kick. It might easily have knocked her out. But cause of death was blood loss due to multiple stab wounds—at least seven, as far as I can count. Unless she was poisoned first."

"Thanks," Gristhorpe said. "Any way of telling how it happened?"

"At this stage, no. Except for the obvious—it was a bloody vicious attack."

"Aye," said Gristhorpe. "Was she interfered with sexually?"

"On a superficial examination, I'd say no. No signs of it at all. But I won't be able to tell you any more until after the post-mortem, which I'll conduct first thing tomorrow morning. You can have the lads cart her to the mortuary whenever they're ready. Can I be off now? I hate to keep those poor wee kiddies waiting."

Banks asked him if he would drop in on Veronica Shildon first and give her a sedative. Glendenning sighed but agreed. The ambulance men, who had been waiting outside, came in to take away the body. Glendenning had covered the hands with plastic bags to preserve any skin caught under the fingernails. As the ambulance men lifted her onto the stretcher, the cuts around her throat gaped open like screaming mouths. One of the men had to put his hand under her head so that the flesh didn't rip back as far as the spine. That was the only time Banks saw Susan Gay visibly pale and look away.

With Caroline Hartley's body gone, apart from the blood that had sprayed onto the sheepskin and the sofa cushions, there was very little left to indicate what horror had occurred in the cosy room that night. The forensic team bundled up the rug and cushions to take with them for further examination, and then there was nothing left to show at all.

It was after ten-thirty. PC Tolliver and another two uniformed constables were still conducting house-to-house enquiries in the area, but there was little else the CID could do until morning. They needed to know Caroline Hartley's movements that evening: where she had been, who she had seen and who might have had a reason to want her dead. Veronica Shildon could probably tell them, but she was in no state to answer questions.

Gristhorpe and Susan Gay left first. Then, after leaving instructions for the scene-of-crime team to search the house thoroughly for any signs of blood-stained clothing, Banks returned to the rugby club to see if Sandra was still there. Snow swirled in front of his headlights and the road was slippery.

When Banks pulled up outside the rugby club in the northern part of Eastvale it was almost eleven o'clock. The lights were still on. In the foyer, he kicked the clinging snow off his shoes, brushed it from his hair and the shoulders of his camel-hair overcoat, which he hung up on the rack provided, and went inside.

He stood in the doorway and looked around the softly lit banquet hall. Hatchley and Carol had finally left, but plenty of others remained, still holding drinks. The DJ had taken a break and someone sat at the piano playing Christmas carols. Banks saw Sandra and Richmond sitting on their stools at the bar. He stood and watched them sing for a few moments. It was a curiously intimate feeling, like watching someone sleep. And like sleepers, their faces wore innocent, tranquil expressions as their lips mouthed the familiar words:

Silent night, holy night
All is calm, all is bright

TWO

I

"What have we got so far?" Gristhorpe asked at eight o'clock the
following morning. As Banks knew from experience, the superintendent liked to call regular conferences in the early stages of an
investigation. Although he had been at the scene the previous
evening, he would now leave the fieldwork to his team and concentrate on co-ordinating their tasks and dealing with the press.
Gristhorpe, unlike some supers Banks had worked with, believed in
letting his men get on with the job while he handled matters of
politics and policy.

In the conference room, the four of them—Gristhorpe, Banks,
Richmond and Susan Gay—reviewed the events of the previous
evening. Nothing had come in yet from forensics or from Dr
Glendenning, who was just about to start the post-mortem. The
only new information they had obtained had resulted from the
house-to-house enquiry. Three people had been seen visiting
number eleven Oakwood Mews separately that evening. Nobody
could describe them clearly—after all, it had been dark and
snowing, and the street was not well lit—but two independent
witnesses seemed to agree that one man and two women had called
there.

The man had called first, around seven o'clock, and Caroline
had admitted him to the house. Nobody had seen him leave. Not
very long after, a woman had arrived, talked briefly to Caroline on
the doorstep, then left without entering the house. One witness said
she thought it might have been someone collecting for charity, what
with it being Christmas and all, but then a collector wouldn't have

missed the opportunity of knocking on everyone else's door as well, would she? And no, there had been no obvious signs of a quarrel.

The final visitor—according to the sightings—called shortly after the other woman left and went inside the house. Nobody had noticed her leave. That, as far as they could pin down, was the last time Caroline Hartley had been seen alive by anyone but her killer. Other visitors may have called between about half past seven and eight, but nobody had seen them. Everybody had been watching "Coronation Street."

"Any ideas about the record?" Gristhorpe asked.

"I think it might be important," Banks said, "but I don't know why. According to Veronica Shildon, it wasn't hers, and the Hartley girl didn't like classical music."

"So where did it come from?" Susan Gay asked.

"Tolliver said that one of the witnesses thought the man who called was carrying a shopping bag of some sort. It could have been in there—a present, say. That would explain the wrapping paper we found."

"But why would anyone bring a woman a present of something she didn't like?" Susan asked.

Banks shrugged. "Could be any number of reasons. Maybe it was someone who didn't know her tastes well. Or it might have been intended for Veronica Shildon. All I'm saying is that it's odd and I think we ought to check it out. It's also strange that someone should put it on the turntable and deliberately leave it to repeat *ad infinitum*. We can be reasonably certain that Caroline wouldn't have played it, so who did, and why? We might even be dealing with a psycho. The music could be his calling card."

"All right," Gristhorpe said after a short silence. "Susan, why don't you get down to Pristine Records and see if they know anything about it."

Susan made a note in her book and nodded.

"Alan, you and Detective Sergeant Richmond here can see what you can get out of Veronica Shildon." He paused. "What do you make of their relationship?"

Banks scratched the little scar by the side of his right eye. "They were living together. And sleeping together, as far as I could tell.

Nobody's spelled it out yet, but I'd say it's pretty obvious. Christine Cooper implied much the same."

"Could that give us an angle?" Gristhorpe suggested. "I don't know much about lesbian relationships, but anything off the beaten track could be worth looking into."

"A jealous lover, something like that?" Banks said.

Gristhorpe shrugged. "You tell me. I just think it's worth a bit of scrutiny."

The meeting broke up and they went their separate ways, but not before Sergeant Rowe came up to them in the corridor with a form in his hand.

"There's been a break-in at the Community Centre," he said, waving the sheet. "Any takers?"

"Not another!" Banks groaned. It was the third in two months. Vandalism was becoming as much of a problem in Eastvale as it seemed to be everywhere else in the country.

"Aye," said Rowe. "Dustbin men noticed the back door broken open when they picked up the rubbish half an hour ago. I've already notified the people involved with that Amateur Dramatic Society. They're the only ones using the place at the moment— except for your wife, sir."

Rowe was referring to Sandra's new part-time job managing Eastvale's new gallery, where she arranged exhibitions of local art, sculpture and photography. The Eastvale Arts Committee had applied as usual for its grant, fully expecting significant cuts, if not an outright refusal. But that year, whether due to some bureaucratic blunder or a generous fiscal whim, they had been given twice what they had asked for and found themselves looking for ways to spend the money before someone asked for it back. The cheque didn't bounce; months passed and they received no letter beginning, "Due to a clerical oversight, afraid. . . ." So the large upstairs room of the Community Centre was set aside and redecorated for gallery space.

"Any damage upstairs?" Banks asked.

"We don't know yet, sir."

"Where's the caretaker?"

"On holiday, sir. Gone to the in-laws in Oldham for Christmas."

"All right, we'll take care of it. Susan, drop by there before you
go to the record shop and see what's going on. It shouldn't take
long."

Susan Gay nodded and set off.

Banks and Richmond turned down by the side of the police
station towards King Street. The snow had stopped early in the
morning, leaving a covering about six inches thick, but the sky was
still overcast, heavy with more. The air was chill and damp. On the
main streets cars and pedestrians had already churned the snow into
brownish-grey slush, but in those narrow, winding alleys between
Market Street and King Street it remained almost untouched except
for the odd set of footprints and the patches that shopkeepers had
shovelled away from the pavement in front of their doors.

This was the real tourist Eastvale. Here, the antique dealers
hung up their signs and antiquarian booksellers advertised their
wares alongside numismatists and bespoke tailors. These weren't
like the cheap souvenir shops on York Road; they were specialty
shops with creaking floors and thick, mullioned windows, where
unctuous, immaculately dressed shopkeepers called you "Sir" or
"Madam."

Oakwood Mews was a short cul-de-sac, a renovated terrace
with only ten houses on each side. Black-leaded iron railings separated each small garden from the pavement. In summer, the street
blossomed in a profusion of colours, with many houses sporting
bright hanging baskets and window boxes. It had even won a "prettiest street in Yorkshire" prize several years ago, and the plaque to
prove it was affixed to the wall of the first house. Now, as Banks and
Richmond approached number nine, the street looked positively
Victorian. Banks almost expected Tiny Tim to come running up to
them and throw his crutches away.

Banks knocked on the Coopers' door. It was made of light,
panelled wood, and the shiny knocker was a highly polished brass
lion's head. A wealthy little street this, obviously, Banks thought,
even if it was only a terrace block of small houses. They were brick
built, pre-war, and had recently been restored to perfection.

Christine Cooper answered the door in her dressing-gown and
invited them in. Unlike the more cosy, feminine elegance of

number eleven, the Cooper place was almost entirely modern in decor: assemble-it-yourself Scandinavian furniture and off-white walls. The kitchen, into which she led them, boasted plenty of shelf- and surface-space and every gadget under the sun, from microwave to electric tin-opener.

"Coffee?"

Banks and Richmond both nodded and sat down at the large pine breakfast table. It had been set close to a corner to save space, and someone had fixed bench-seating to the two adjacent walls. Both Banks and Richmond sat on the bench with their backs to the wall. Banks had no trouble fitting himself in, as he was only a little taller than regulation 172 centimetres, but Richmond had to shift about to accommodate his long legs.

Mrs Cooper faced them from a matching chair across the table. The electric coffee-maker was already gurgling away, and they had to wait only a few moments for their drinks.

"I'm afraid Veronica isn't up, yet," Mrs Cooper said. "Your doctor gave her a sleeping pill and she was out like a light as soon as we got her into bed. I explained everything to Charles. He's been very understanding."

"Where is your husband?" Banks asked.

"At work."

"What time did he get home last night?"

"It must have been after eleven. We sat up and talked about . . . you know . . . for a while, then we went to bed about midnight."

"He certainly works long hours."

Mrs Cooper sighed. "Yes, especially at this time of year. You see, he runs a chain of children's shops in North Yorkshire, and he's constantly being called from one crisis to another. One place runs out of whatever new doll all the kids want this year and another out of jigsaw puzzles. I'm sure you can imagine the problems."

"Where was he yesterday evening?"

Mrs Cooper seemed surprised at the question, but she answered after only a slight hesitation. "Barnard Castle. Apparently the manager of the shop there reported some stock discrepancies."

There was probably nothing in it, Banks thought, but Charles Cooper's alibi should be easy enough to check.

"Maybe you can give us a bit more background on Caroline Hartley while we're waiting for Mrs Shildon," he said.

Richmond took out his notebook and settled back in the corner seat.

Mrs Cooper rubbed her chin. "I don't know if I can tell you much about Caroline, really. I knew her, but I didn't feel I *really* knew her, if you know what I mean. It was all on the surface. She was a real sparkler, I'll say that for her. Always full of beans. Always a smile and a hello for everyone. Talented, too, from what I could gather."

"Talented? How?"

"She was an actress. Oh, just amateur like, but if you ask me, she'd got what it takes. She could take anybody off. You should have seen her impression of Maggie Thatcher. Talk about laugh!"

"Was this theatrical work local?"

"Oh, yes. Only the Eastvale Amateur Dramatic Society."

"Was this her first experience with theatre?"

"I wouldn't know that. It was only a small part, but she was excited about it."

"Where does she come from?"

"Do you know, I can't say. I know nothing about her past. She could be from Timbuktu for all I know. As I said before, we weren't *really* close."

"Do you know if she had any enemies? Did she ever tell you about any quarrels she might have had?"

Mrs Cooper shook her head, then blushed.

"What is it?" Banks asked.

"Well," Mrs Cooper began, "it's nothing really, I don't suppose, and I don't want to go getting anybody into trouble, but when two women live together like . . . like they did, then somebody some-where's got to be unhappy, haven't they?"

"What do you mean?"

"Veronica's ex-husband. She was a married woman before she came here. I shouldn't think he'd be very happy about things, would he? And I'll bet there was someone in Caroline's life, too—a woman or a man. She didn't seem the kind to be on her own for too long, if you know what I mean."

"Do you know anything about Veronica Shildon's ex-husband?"

"Only that they sold the big house they used to have outside town and split the money. She bought this place and he moved off somewhere. The coast, I think. The whole thing seemed very hush-hush to me. She's never even told me his name."

"The Yorkshire coast?"

"Yes, I think so. But Veronica can tell you all about him."

"You didn't see him in the neighbourhood yesterday evening, did you?"

Mrs Cooper pulled her robe together at the front, looking down and making a double chin as she did so. "No. I told you all I saw or heard last night. Besides, I wouldn't recognize him from Adam. I've never seen him."

Banks heard stairs creak and looked around to see Veronica Shildon standing in the doorway. She was dressed as she had been the previous evening—tight jeans, which flattered her slim, curved hips, trim waist and flat stomach, and a high-necked, chunky-knit green sweater, which brought out the colour in her eyes. She was tall, about five foot ten, and poised. Banks thought there was something odd about seeing her in such casual wear; she looked as if she belonged in a pearl silk blouse and a navy business suit. She had taken the time to brush her short hair and put a little make-up on, but her face still looked drawn underneath it all, and her eyes, disarmingly honest and naked, were still red from crying.

Banks tried to stand up, but he was too closely wedged in by the table.

"I'm sorry to bother you so soon," he said, "but the quicker we get moving the more chance we have."

"I understand," she said. "Please don't worry about me. I'll be all right."

She swayed a little as she walked towards the table. Mrs Cooper took her elbow and guided her to a chair, then brought her some coffee and disappeared, muttering something about things to attend to.

"In cases like this," Banks began, "it helps if we know what the person was doing, where she was, previous to the incident." He knew he sounded trite, but somehow he couldn't bring himself to say "victim" and "murder."

Veronica nodded. "Of course. As far as I know Caroline went to work, but you'll have to check that. She runs the Garden Café on Castle Hill Road."

"I know it," Banks said. It was an elegant little place, very up-market, with a stunning view of the formal gardens and the river.

"She usually finishes at three on a weekday, after the lunchtime crowd. They don't open for tea off-season. On a normal day she'd come home, do some shopping, or perhaps drop by at the shop for a while to help out."

"Shop?"

"I own a flower shop—or rather my partner and I do. It's mostly a matter of his money and my management. It's just round the corner from here, down King Street."

"You said on a 'normal' day. Was yesterday not normal?"

She looked straight at him and her eyes let him know that his choice of words had been inappropriate. Yesterday, indeed, had not been normal. But she simply said, "No. Yesterday after work they had a rehearsal. They're doing *Twelfth Night* at the Community Centre. It's quite a heavy rehearsal schedule as the director's set on actually opening on twelfth night."

"What time did rehearsals run?"

"Usually between four and six, so she would have been home at about quarter past six, if she'd come home immediately."

"And was she likely to?"

"They often went for a drink after, but yesterday she came straight home."

"How do you know?"

"I phoned to see if she was there and to tell her I'd be a bit late because I was doing some shopping."

"What time?"

"About seven."

"How did she sound?"

"Fine . . . she sounded fine."

"Was there any special reason for her not going for a drink with the others yesterday?"

"No. She just said she was tired after rehearsal and she . . ."

"Yes?"

"We've both been so busy lately. She wanted to spend some time with me . . . a quiet evening at home."

"Where had you been that evening?"

Veronica didn't show a flicker of resentment at being asked for an alibi. "I closed the shop at five-thirty, then I went for my six o'clock appointment with Dr Ursula Kelly, my therapist. She's Caroline's too. Her office is on Kilnsey Street, just off Castle Hill. I walked. We do have a car but we don't use it much in town, mostly just for trips away." She blew on her coffee and took a sip. "The session lasted an hour. After that, I went to the shopping centre to buy a few things. Christmas presents mostly." She faltered a little. "Then I walked home. I . . . I got here about eight o'clock."

No doubt it would be possible to check her alibi in the shopping centre, Banks thought. Some shopkeepers might remember her. But it was a busy time of year for them, and he doubted that any would be able to recollect what day and what time they had last seen her. He could examine the receipts, too. Sometimes the modern electronic cash registers gave the time of purchase as well as the date.

"Can you tell me exactly what happened, what you did, from the moment you left the shops and walked home last night?"

Veronica took a deep breath and closed her eyes. "I walked home," she began, "in the snow. It was a beautiful evening. I stopped and listened to the carol-singers in the market square for a while. They were singing 'O, Little Town of Bethlehem.' It's always been one of my favourites. When I got home I . . . I called out hello to Caroline, but she didn't answer. I thought nothing of it. She could have been in the kitchen. And then there was the music . . . well, that was odd. So I took the opportunity and crept upstairs to hide the presents in the wardrobe. Some were for her, you see, the . . ." She paused, and Banks noticed her eyes fill with tears. "It seemed so important just to put them out of sight," she went on. "I knew there would be plenty of opportunity to wrap them later. While I was up there, I washed and changed and went back downstairs.

"The music was still playing. I opened the door to the living room and . . . I . . . at first I thought she was wearing the new scarlet camisole. She looked so serene and so beautiful lying there like that. But it couldn't be. I told you last night, I hadn't given it to her then. I'd just bought her the camisole for Christmas and I'd put it in the bottom of the wardrobe with everything else. Then I went closer and . . . the smell . . . her eyes . . ." Veronica put her mug down and held her head in her hands.

Banks let the silence stretch for a good minute or two. All they could hear was the soft ticking of Mrs Cooper's kitchen wall-clock and a dog barking in the distance.

"I understand you were married," Banks said, when Veronica had wiped her eyes and reached out for her coffee again.

"I still am, officially. We're only separated, not divorced. He didn't want our personal life splashed all over the newspapers. As you may have gathered, Caroline and I lived together."

Banks nodded. "Why should the newspapers have been interested? People get divorced all the time for all kinds of reasons."

Veronica hesitated and turned her mug slowly in a circle on the table. She wouldn't meet his eyes.

"Look," Banks said, "I hardly need remind you what's happened, how serious this is. We'll find out anyway. You can save us a lot of time and trouble."

Veronica looked up at him. "You're right, of course," she said. "Though I don't see how it can have anything to do with all this. My husband was—is, Claude Ivers. He's not exactly a household name, but enough people have heard of him."

Banks certainly had. Ivers had once been a brilliant concert pianist, but several years ago he had given up performance for composition. He had received important commissions from the BBC, and a number of his pieces had been recorded. Banks even had a tape of his two wind quintets; they possessed a kind of eerie, natural beauty—not structured, but wandering, like the breeze in a deep forest at night. Veronica Shildon was right. If the press had got hold of the story she would have had no peace for weeks. *News of the World* reporters would have been climbing the drainpipes and spying in bedroom windows, talking to spiteful neighbours and slighted lovers. He could just see the headlines: "HIGH-BROW MUSICIAN'S WIFE IN LESBIAN LOVE-NEST."

"Where is your husband now?" Banks asked.

"He lives in Redburn, out on the coast. He said the seclusion and the sea would be good for his work. He always did care about his work."

Banks noticed the bitterness in her tone. "Do you ever see one another?"

"Yes," she said. A smile touched her thin lips. "It was an acrimonious parting in many ways, but there *is* some affection left. We don't seem able to stamp that out, whatever we do."

"When did you last see him?"

"About a month ago. We occasionally go for dinner if he's in town. I rarely visit the coast, but he comes here from time to time."

"To the house?"

"He's been here, yes, though he's always worried someone will see him and know who he is. I try to tell him that people don't actually recognize composers in the street any more than they do writers, that it's only television and film stars have to put up with that, but . . ." She shrugged.

"Did he know Caroline?"

"He could hardly *help* knowing her, could he? They'd met a few times."

"How did they get on?"

Veronica shrugged. "They never seemed to have much to say to one another. They were different as chalk and cheese. He thought she was a scheming slut and she thought he was a selfish, pompous ass. They had nothing in common but affection for me."

"Was there any open antagonism?"

"Open? Good lord, no. That isn't Claude's way. He sniped from time to time, made sarcastic comments, cruel remarks, that kind of thing."

"Directed towards Caroline?"

"Directed towards both of us. But I'm sure he blamed Caroline for leading me astray. That's how he saw it."

"Was it that way?"

Veronica shook her head.

"Was Caroline ever married?"

"Not that I know of."

"Was she living with anyone before she met you?"

Veronica paused and gripped her coffee mug in both hands as if to warm them. Her fingers were long and tapered and she had freckles on the backs of her hands. She wore a silver ring on the middle finger of her right hand. As she spoke, she looked down at the table. "She was living with a woman called Nancy Wood. They'd been together about eight months. The relationship was going very badly."

"Where does Nancy Wood live?"

"In Eastvale. Not too far from here. At least, she did the last I heard."

"Did Caroline ever see her after they split up?"

"Only by accident once or twice in the street."

"So they parted on bad terms?"

"Doesn't everyone? Much as I admire Shakespeare, I've often wondered where the sweetness is in the sorrow."

"And before Nancy Wood?"

"She spent some time in London. I don't know how long or who with. A few years, at least."

"What about her family?"

"Her mother's dead. Her father lives in Harrogate. He's an invalid, been one for years. Her brother Gary looks after him. I told one of your uniformed men last night. Will someone have called?"

Banks nodded. "Don't worry, the Harrogate police will have taken care of it. Is there anything else you can tell me about Caroline's friends or enemies?"

Veronica sighed and shook her head. She looked exhausted. "No," she said. "We didn't have a lot of close friends. I suppose we tried to be too much to one another. At least that's how it feels now she's gone. You could try the people at the theatre. They were her acquaintances, at least. But we didn't socialize very much together. I don't think any of them even knew about her living with me."

"We're still puzzled about the record," Banks said. "Are you sure it isn't yours?"

"I've told you, no."

"But you recognized the singer?"

"Magda Kalmár, yes. Claude and I once saw her in *Lucia di Lammermoor* at the Budapest Opera. I was very impressed."

"Could the record have been intended as a Christmas present from your husband?"

"Well, I suppose it could . . . but that means . . . no, I haven't seen him in a month."

"He could have called last night, while you were out."

She shook her head. "No. I don't believe it. Not Claude."

Banks looked over at Richmond and nodded. Richmond closed his notebook. "That's all for now," Banks said.

"Can I go home?" she asked him.

"If you want." Banks hadn't imagined she would want to return to the house so soon, but there was no official objection. Forensics had finished with the place.

"Just one thing, though," he said. "We'll need to have another good look through Caroline's belongings. Perhaps Detective Sergeant Richmond can accompany you back and look over them now?"

She looked apprehensive at first, then nodded. "All right."

They stood up to leave. Christine Cooper was nowhere in sight, so they walked out into the damp, overcast day and shut the door behind them without saying goodbye.

Veronica opened her front door and went in. Banks lingered at the black iron gate with Richmond. "I'm going to the Community Centre," he said. "There should be someone from the theatre group there since they've been notified of the break-in. How about we meet up at the Queen's Arms, say twelve or twelve-thirty?" And he went on to ask Richmond to check Veronica Shildon's purchases and look closely at the receipts for corroboration of her alibi. "And check on Charles Cooper's movements yesterday," he added. "It might mean a trip to Barnard Castle, but see if you can come up with anything by phone first."

Richmond went into the house and Banks set off up the steep part of King Street with his collar turned up against the cold. The Community Centre wasn't very far; the walk would be good exercise. As he trudged through the snow, he thought about Veronica Shildon. She presented an odd mixture of reserve and frankness, stoical acceptance and bitterness. He was sure she was holding something back, but he didn't know what it was. There was something askew about her. Even her clothes didn't seem to go with the rather repressed and inhibited essence that she projected. "Prim and proper" was the term that sprang to mind. Yet she had left her husband, had gone and set up house with a woman.

All in all, she was an enigma. If anything, Banks thought, she seemed like a woman in the process of great change. Her reference to the analyst indicated that she was at least concerned with self-examination.

It seemed to Banks as if her entire personality had been dismantled and the various bits and pieces didn't quite fit together; some were new, or newly discovered, and others were old, rusted, decrepit, and she wasn't sure whether she wanted to discard them or not. Banks had an inkling of what the process felt like from his own readjustment after the move from London. But Veronica's changes, he suspected, went far deeper. He wondered what she had been like as a wife, and what she would become in the future now that Caroline Hartley had been so viciously excised from her life. For the younger woman had had a great influence on Veronica's life; Banks was certain of that. Was Veronica a killer? He didn't think so, but who could say anything so definite about a personality in such turmoil and transition?

II

On her way to the Community Centre, DC Susan Gay thought over her behaviour of the previous day and found it distinctly lacking. She had felt even more miserable than usual when she went home from Oakwood Mews that night. Her small flat off York Road always depressed her. It was so barren, like a hotel room, so devoid of any real stamp of her presence, and she knew that was because she hardly spent any time there. Mostly she had been working or off on a course somewhere. For years she had paid no attention to her surroundings or to her personal life. The flat was for eating in, sleeping in and, occasionally, for watching half an hour of television.

It seemed like a lifetime since she'd last had a boyfriend, or anyone more than a casual date, anyone who *meant* something to her. She accepted that she wasn't especially attractive, but she was no ugly sister, either. People had asked her out; the problem was that she always had something more important to do, something related to her career. She was beginning to wonder if the normal sexual impulse had somehow drained away over the years of toil. That incident with the rugby player last night, for example. She knew she shouldn't have responded with such obvious revulsion. He was only being friendly, even if he was a bit rough about it. And wasn't that what mistletoe was for? But she had to overreact. Banks and Gristhorpe had both noticed, she was certain. She wondered what they must think of her.

Damn! The front doors of the Community Centre, a Victorian sandstone building on North Market Street, were still locked. That meant Susan would have to double back to the narrow street behind the church. Shivering, she hunched up against the cold and turned around.

It seemed now that the whole of yesterday evening had been a nightmare. First she had run off half-cocked out of the station at the first sign of trouble, without even bothering to check if the call was genuine or not. Then she had gone straight to Banks. She had seen Gristhorpe by the bar, of course, but she hadn't approached him because she was terrified of him. She knew he was said to be a softie, really, but she couldn't help herself. He seemed so self-contained, so sure of himself, so *solid*, just like her father.

The only thing she was proud of was her reaction at the scene. She hadn't fainted, even though it was her first corpse, and a messy one at that. She had managed to maintain a detached, clinical view of the whole affair, watching the experts at work, getting the feel of the scene. There had been only one awkward moment, as the body was being carried away, but anyone could be forgiven for paling a bit at that. No, her behaviour at the scene had been exemplary. She hoped Banks and Gristhorpe had noticed that, and not only her faults.

And now she was on her way to investigate a case of vandalism while the others got to work on the murder. It wasn't fair. She realized she was the new member of the team, but that didn't mean she always had to be the one to handle the petty crimes. How could she get ahead if she didn't get to work on important cases? She already had sacrificed so much to her career that she couldn't bear to contemplate failure.

Finally, she got to the back entrance, down an alley off the northern part of York Road. The back door had obviously been jemmied open. Its meagre lock was bent and the wood around the jamb had cracked. Susan walked down the long corridor, lit only by a couple of bare sixty-watt bulbs, to where she could hear voices. They came from a room off to her right, a high-ceilinged place with exposed pipes, bare brick walls pied with saltpetre, and more dim lighting. The room smelled of dust and mothballs. There she found a man and a woman bent over a large trunk. They stood up as she walked in.

"Police?" the man asked.

Susan nodded and showed her new CID identification card.

"I must admit, I didn't expect a woman," he said.

Susan prepared to say something withering, but he held up a hand. "Don't get me wrong. I'm not complaining. I'm not a sexist pig. It's just a surprise." He peered at her in the poor light. "Wait a minute, aren't you . . . ?"

"Susan Gay," she said, recognizing him now that her eyes had adjusted to the light. "And you're Mr Conran." She blushed. "I'm surprised you remember me. I was hardly one of your best students."

Mr Conran hadn't changed much in the ten years since he had taught the sixteen-year-old Susan drama at Eastvale Comprehensive. About ten years older than her, he was still handsome in an artsy kind of way, in baggy black cords and a dark polo-neck sweater with the stitching coming away at the shoulder seam. He still had that vulnerable, skinny, half-starved look that Susan remembered so well, but despite it he looked healthy enough. His short fair hair was combed forward, flat against his skull; beneath it, intelligent and ironic grey eyes looked out from a pale, hollow-cheeked face. Susan had hated drama, but she had had a crush on Mr Conran. The other girls said he was a queer, but they said that about everyone in the literature and arts departments. Susan hadn't believed them.

"James," he said, stretching his hand out to shake hers. "I think we can dispense with the teacher-pupil formalities by now, don't you? I'm directing the play. And this is Marcia Cunningham. Marcia takes care of props and costumes. It's she you should talk to, really."

As if to emphasize the point, Conran turned away and began examining the rest of the storage room.

Susan took her notebook out. "What's the damage?" she asked Marcia, a plump, round-faced woman in grey stretch slacks and a threadbare alpaca jacket that looked at least one size too large for her.

Marcia Cunningham sniffed and pointed to the wall. "There's that, for a start." Crudely spray-painted across the bricks were the words "FUCKING WANKERS." "But that'll wash off easy enough," she went on. "This is the worst. They've shredded our costumes. I'm not sure if I can salvage any of them or not."

Susan looked into the trunk. She agreed. It looked like someone had been to work on them with a large pair of scissors, snipping the different dresses, suits and shirts into pieces and mixing them all together.

"Why would anyone do that?" Marcia asked.

Susan shook her head.

"At least they left the shoes and wigs alone," she said, gesturing towards the other two boxes of costumes.

"Has anyone checked upstairs?" Susan asked.

Marcia looked surprised. "The gallery? No."

Susan made her way down the corridor to the stairs, cold stone with metal railings. There were several rooms upstairs, some of them used for various groups such as the Philately Society or the Chess Club, others for local committee meetings. All of them were locked. The glass doors to the new gallery were locked too; no damage had been done there. She went back down to the props room and watched Marcia picking up strands of slashed material and moaning.

"All that work, all those people who gave us stuff. Why do they do this?" Marcia asked again. "What bloody point is there?"

Susan knew numerous theories of hooliganism, from poor potty-training to the heartlessness of modern England, but all she said was, "I don't know." People don't want to hear theories when something they value has been destroyed. "And short of catching them red-handed, we can't promise much, either."

"But this is the *third* time!" Marcia said. "Surely by now you must have some kind of lead?"

"There are a few people we're keeping our eye on," Susan told her, "but it's not as if they've stolen anything."

"Even that would be more understandable."

"What I mean is, we'd find no evidence even if we suspected someone. There's no stolen property to trace to them. Have you thought of employing a night-watchman?"

Marcia snorted. "A night-watchman? How do you think we can afford that? I know we got a bonanza grant this year, but we didn't get that much. And most of it's gone already on costumes and stuff."

"I'm sorry," Susan said. She realized this was an inadequate response, but what else was there to say? A constable walked the beat, but he couldn't spend his whole night in the alley at the back of the Community Centre. There had been other break-ins, too, and other incidents of vandalism. "I'll make out a report," she said, "and let you know if we come up with anything."

"Thanks a lot."

"Don't be so rude, Marcia." James Conran reappeared and put his hand on Marcia's shoulder. "She's only trying to help." He smiled at Susan. "Aren't you?"

Susan nodded. His smile was so infectious she could hardly keep from responding, and the effort to maintain a detached expression made her flush.

Marcia rubbed her face until her plump cheeks shone. "I'm sorry, love," she said. "I know it's not your fault. It's just so bloody frustrating."

"I know." Susan put her notebook back in her handbag. "I'll be in touch," she said.

Before she could turn to leave, they heard footsteps coming along the corridor. Conran looked surprised. "There's nobody else supposed to be coming here, is there?" he asked Marcia, who shook her head. Then the door creaked open and Susan saw a familiar face peep around. It was Chief Inspector Banks. At first she was relieved to see him. Then she thought, why the hell is he here? Checking up on me? Can't he trust me to do a simple job properly?

III

Detective Sergeant Philip Richmond was glad that Veronica Shildon had not wanted to stand over him as he searched the two upper rooms. He never could tolerate the feel of someone looking over his shoulder. Which was one of the reasons he liked working with Banks, who usually left him to get on with the job his own way.

The bedroom smelled of expensive cologne or talcum. As he looked at the large bed with its satiny coral spread, he thought of the two women in there together and the things they did to each other. The images embarrassed him and he got back to work.

Richmond took the bag of presents out of Veronica's half of the wardrobe and spread them on the bed: a Sheaffer fountain-pen and pencil set, a green silk scarf, some Body Shop soaps and shampoos, a scarlet camisole, the latest Booker Prize winner . . . all pretty ordinary stuff. The receipts were dated but none of them gave the time the purchase had been made. Richmond made a list of items and shops so the staff could be questioned.

The dresser drawers contained mostly lingerie. Richmond picked his way through it methodically, but found nothing hidden away, nothing that shouldn't be there. He moved on to the study.

In addition to the books—none of them inscribed—there was also a roll-top desk in the corner under the window. There was nothing surprising in it: letters to Veronica Shildon, some from her husband, about practical and financial matters; a few bills; Veronica's address book, mostly empty; a house insurance policy; receipts and guarantees for the oven, the fridge and items of furniture, and that was about all. None of it any use to Richmond.

Just when he was beginning to wonder whether Caroline Hartley had had any possessions at all, he came across a manila envelope with "Caroline" written on the front. Inside were a pressed flower, her birth certificate (which showed she had been born in

Harrogate twenty-six years ago), an expired passport with no stamps or visas, and a black-and-white photograph of a woman he didn't recognize. She had piercing, intelligent eyes, and her head was slightly tilted to one side. Her medium-length hair was swept back, revealing a straight hairline and ears with tiny lobes. Her lips were pressed tight together, and there was something about the arrogant intensity of her presence that Richmond found disturbing. He wouldn't have described her as beautiful, but striking, certainly. Across the bottom were the words "To Carrie, Love Ruth," written with a flourish.

Making sure he hadn't missed anything, Richmond went back downstairs, taking the envelope of Caroline's possessions with him. Veronica Shildon turned on the small electric fire in the front room when he entered.

"I'm sorry," she said, "I can't be bothered to light a real fire now. We use this most of the time anyway. It seems to be warm enough. Some tea?"

"Yes, please, if it's no trouble."

"It's already made."

Richmond sat down, avoiding the cushionless sofa in favour of an armchair. After Veronica had poured, he held out the photograph to her. "Who's this woman?" he asked. "Can you tell me anything about her?"

Veronica glanced at the photograph and shook her head. "It's just someone Caroline used to know in London."

"Surely she must have told you something about her."

"Caroline didn't like to talk about her past very much."

"Why not?"

"I don't know. Perhaps it was painful for her."

"In what way?"

"I told you. I don't know. I've seen the picture before, yes, but I don't know who it is or where you can find her."

"Is it an old girlfriend?" Richmond felt embarrassed as he asked the question.

"I should think so, wouldn't you?" Veronica said evenly.

"Mind if I take it with me?"

"Not at all."

"Caroline didn't seem much of a one for possessions," Richmond mused. "There's hardly anything of hers but clothes. No letters, nothing."

"She liked to travel light, and she had no sentimental regard for the past. Caroline always looked ahead."

It was a simple statement, but Richmond heard the irony in Veronica Shildon's voice.

She shrugged. "A few of the books are hers. Some of the jewellery. All the non-classical records. But she didn't go in much for keepsakes."

Richmond tapped the photograph. "Which makes it all the more odd she should have hung onto this. Thank you, Ms Shildon. I'd better be off now."

"Aren't you going to finish your tea?"

"Best not," he said. "I'll have to get back to work or my boss'll skin me alive. Thanks very much anyway." Richmond could sense her unease. She looked around the room before glancing at him again and nodding.

"All right, if you must."

"Will you be all right?" he asked. "You could always go back to Mrs Cooper's, if you feel—"

"I'll be all right," she said. "I'm still in a bit of a daze. I can't believe it's really happened."

"Is there no-one you can go to, until you're feeling better?"

"There's my therapist. She says I can call her anytime, day or night. I might do that. We'll see. But do you know the oddest thing?"

Richmond shook his head.

She folded her arms and nodded towards the room in general. "I can take all this. The room where it happened. I didn't think I'd be able to bear it after last night, but it doesn't bother me in the slightest to be here. It just feels empty. Isn't that strange? It's the loneliness, Caroline's absence, that hurts. I keep expecting her to walk in at any moment."

Richmond, who could think of no reply, said goodbye and walked out into the snow. He still had about an hour before his lunchtime meeting with Banks in the Queen's Arms. He could use that time to check on Charles Cooper's movements the previous evening and perhaps see if he could find out anything about the mysterious Ruth.

THREE

I

The gears screeched as Susan Gay slowed to turn onto the Harrogate road. Luckily, the snow hadn't been so heavy south of Eastvale. It lay piled up against the hedgerows, but the roads had been cleared and the temperature hadn't dropped low enough to make the surface icy. She was out of the Dales now, in the gently rolling country south of Ripon. Nothing but the occasional stretch of stone wall, or a distant hamlet, showed through the thin white veil of snow.

She still felt angry at herself for being so damn jumpy. Banks had only dropped by the Community Centre to break the news of Caroline Hartley's death and to discover what time she had left the rehearsal the previous evening. But Susan hadn't known anything about Caroline's part in the play, so how could she help assuming that Banks was checking up on her? Anyway, she had kept quiet and matters had soon become clear to her.

When Banks had gone, she'd walked to Pristine Records in the shopping centre by the bus station. The girl with the white-face make-up and hair like pink champagne pointed out the small classical section and, when pushed, leafed idly through the stock cards. No, they hadn't sold a copy of *Lousy whatsit* lately; they hadn't even had a copy in. Ever. Using her own initiative, Susan also checked Boots and W.H. Smith's, both of which had small record departments, but she had no luck there either. The record was imported from Hungary, and whoever had bought it hadn't done so in Eastvale.

Over lunch at the Queen's Arms, information had been pooled and tasks assigned by Superintendent Gristhorpe. According to

Banks, Caroline had left the Garden Café just after three o'clock, as usual, probably done a bit of shopping, then attended rehearsal at four. James Conran said they had finished at ten to six and everyone had left by five to. He himself had been the last to leave. He had gone out the back way, as usual, locked up and strolled over to the Crooked Billet on North York Road for a couple of drinks. In the caretaker's absence, he and Marcia Cunningham were the only ones in the drama group to have keys to the centre, although an extra one had been lodged at the police station in case of emergencies. Members of the other societies housed in the centre also had keys, including Sandra Banks.

Presumably, Caroline had gone straight home, because a neighbour across the street told one of the constables that she had seen Miss Hartley enter the house. It had happened at the same time the neighbour had gone over to her window to close a chink in the curtains during the commercial break in "Calendar," which would have been about six-fifteen.

Richmond had not been able to find out much about Charles Cooper's movements. The clerk who had been at the Barnard Castle shop on the evening in question had the day off today. He planned to visit Barnard Castle and ask around some more after he had talked to Veronica Shildon's therapist and made a start on tracking down Ruth. Banks was off to visit Claude Ivers, Veronica's estranged husband, and Susan herself had drawn the job of talking to Caroline's family in Harrogate. In addition to keeping tabs on the break-in, she was still on the murder team. Thank God the Harrogate police had at least broken the news of Caroline's death. That was one distasteful task she had been spared.

She drove up Ripon Road by the huge Victorian hotels—the Cairn, the Majestic, the St George—dark stone mansions set back behind vast walled lawns and croquet greens. As she kept an eye on the road, Susan found herself hoping that the Hartley case wouldn't be solved by Christmas. That way she could legitimately beg off visiting her parents in Sheffield. Home visits were always tense. Susan found herself regaled with stories about her brother the stockbroker and her sister the lawyer. Of course, neither of them could ever make it home for Christmas; her brother lived in

London and her sister in Vancouver. But she had to hear all about them, nonetheless. And whatever Susan herself achieved was always belittled by her siblings' success stories, pieced together from occasional letters and the odd newspaper clipping, and by her parents' disapproval of the course she had chosen. She could make chief constable and they would still look down on her. With a bit of luck, Caroline Hartley's murder would keep her busy well into the new year. Susan had a feeling they might be dealing with a nutter—the violence of the wounds and the music left playing seemed to point that way—and nutters, she remembered from her training, were always difficult to catch.

The town of Harrogate soon banished thoughts of psychopaths. All formal gardens and elegant Victorian buildings, it was a spa town, like Bath, a place people retired to or visited to attend business conventions. Ripon Road became Parliament as she drove past the Royal Baths and Betty's Tea Room, then its name changed again to West Park. She turned left onto York Place, the road that ran by the Stray, a broad expanse of parkland in the town centre renowned for its vibrant flower displays in spring. Now it looked cool and serene under its layer of snow.

The Hartleys lived in a large house off Wetherby Road on the southern outskirts of the town. From the outside, it looked like something out of Edgar Allan Poe: the House of Usher, Susan thought, the way it appeared in that Roger Corman film that used to scare her when she was a little girl. The black stone was rough and pitted like coke, and the upper oriels seemed to stare out like bulging eyes. When Susan rang the doorbell she half expected an enormous manservant with a green complexion to answer and say "You rang?" in a deep voice. But the boy who came to the door was far from enormous. He was in his late teens, judging by the pale, spotty face, the spiky hair and the look of dazed contempt for the world on his face, and he was as skinny as a rake.

"What is it?" he asked in an edgy, high-pitched voice. "We don't want anything. There's been a death in the family."

"I know," Susan said. "That's why I'm here." She showed her card and he stepped back to let her in. She followed him down the gloomy hallway to a room that must once have been a study or library. The ceiling was high, with curlicues at the corners and an ornate fixture at the centre from which the chandelier had once hung. Dark wainscotting came waist-high.

But the room was a mess. Much of the fine oak panelling was scratched with graffiti and pitted where darts had been thrown. The huge windows, framed by heavy, moth-eaten drapes, were filmed with cobwebs and grime. Magazines and newspapers lay scattered all over the threadbare carpet. Beer cans and cigarette ends littered the hearth and the old stone fireplace, and the stuffing was coming out of the huge green velvet-upholstered settee. The room was an elegant Victorian sanctuary reduced to a teenager's private wasteland.

The boy didn't ask Susan to sit down, but she found a chair that looked in reasonable condition. Before she sat, she began to undo her coat, but as she did so she realized that it was freezing in the room, as it had been in the hall. There was no heat at all. The boy didn't seem to notice or care, even though he was only wearing jeans and a torn T-shirt. He lit a cigarette and slumped on the settee. More stuffing oozed out, like foam from a madman's mouth.

"So?" he said.

"I'd like to see your father."

The boy laughed harshly. "You must be the first person to say that in five years. People don't usually *like* to see my father. He's a very depressing man. He makes them think of death. The grim reaper."

The boy's thin face, only a shade less white than the snow outside, certainly made Susan think of death. He looked in urgent need of a blood transfusion. Could he really be Caroline Hartley's brother? It was hard to see a resemblance between the boy and his sister. Caroline, when she was alive, must have been a beautiful woman. Even in death she had looked more alive than her brother.

"Can I see him?"

"Be my guest." The boy pointed towards the ceiling and flicked his ash towards the littered fireplace.

Susan walked up the broad staircase. It must have been wonderful once, with thick pile carpeting and guests in evening dress standing around sipping cocktails. But now it was just bare, creaky wood, scuffed and splintered in places, and the banister looked liked someone had been cutting notches in it. There were pale squares on the walls showing where pair ings had been removed.

Without a guide or directions, it took Susan three tries before she opened the right door. Her first try had led her into a bathroom, which seemed clean and modern enough; the second revealed the boy's room, where the curtains were still closed and faint light outlined messy bedsheets and last week's underwear on the floor; and the third took her into a warm, stuffy room that smelled of cough lozenges, camphor and commodes. A one-element electric fire radiated its heat close to the bed, and there, in a genuine four-poster with the curtains open, a shadow of a man lay propped upon pillows. The bags under his eyes were so dark they looked like bruises, his complexion was like old paper, and the hands that grasped the bedclothes around his chest were more like talons. His skin looked as if it would crack like parchment if you touched it. As she approached, his watery eyes darted towards her.

"Who are you?" His voice was no more than a frightened whisper.

Susan introduced herself and he seemed to relax. "About Caroline?" he said. A faraway look came into his ruined eyes, pale yokes floating in glutinous albumen.

"Yes," Susan said. "Can you tell me anything about her?"

"What do you want to know?"

Susan wasn't sure. She had taken statements as a uniformed constable and studied interview techniques at police college, but it had never seemed as haphazard as this. Superintendent Gristhorpe hadn't been much help either. "Find out what you can," he had told her. "Follow your nose." Clearly it was a matter of sink or swim in the CID. She took a deep breath and wished she hadn't; the warmed-up smell of terminal illness was overpowering.

"Anything that might help us find her killer," she said. "Did Caroline visit you recently?"

"Sometimes," he muttered.

"Were you close?"

He shook his head slowly. "She ran away, you know."

"When did she run away?"

"She was only a child and she ran away."

Susan repeated her question and the old man stared at her. "Pardon? When did she go? When she was sixteen. Only a child."

"Why?"

A look of great sadness came into his eyes. "I don't know. Her mother died, you know. I tried the best I could, but she was so hard to manage."

"Where did she go?"

"London."

"What did she do there?"

He shook his head. "Then she came back. That's when she came to see me."

"And again since?"

"Yes."

"How often?"

"When she could. When she could get away."

"Did she ever tell you anything about her life down in London?"

"I was so happy to see her again."

"Do you know where she lived, who her friends were?"

"She wasn't a bad girl, not really a *bad* girl."

"Did she write from London?"

The old man shook his head slowly on the pillow.

"But you still loved her?"

"Yes." He was crying now, and the tears embarrassed him. "I'm sorry . . . could you please . . . ?" He pointed to a box of tissues on the bedside table and Susan passed it to him.

"She wasn't *bad*," he repeated when he'd settled down again. "Restless, angry. But not *bad*. I always knew she'd come back. I never stopped loving her."

"But she never talked about her life, either in London or in Eastvale?"

"No. Perhaps to Gary. . . . I'm tired. Not a *bad* girl," he repeated softly.

He seemed to be falling asleep. Susan had got nowhere and could think of no more questions to ask. Clearly, the old man had not jumped out of bed, hurried over to Eastvale and murdered his daughter. Maybe she would get more out of the son. At least he seemed angry and bitter enough to give something away if she pushed him hard enough. She said goodbye, though she doubted that the old man heard, and made her way back downstairs. The boy was still sprawled on the sofa, a can of lager open beside him on the floor. Despite the cold, she could still smell, underlying the smoke, a faint hint of decay, as if pieces of meat lay rotting under the floorboards.

"When did you last see your sister?" she asked.

He shrugged. "I don't know. A week, two weeks ago? She came when she felt like it. Time doesn't have much meaning around this place."

"But she had visited you recently?"

Gary nodded.

"What did she talk about?"

He lit a cigarette and spoke out of the corner of his mouth. "Nothing. Just the usual."

"What's the usual?"

"You know . . . job, house . . . relationships. . . . The usual crap."

"What's wrong with your father?"

"Cancer. He's had a couple of operations, chemotherapy, but . . . you know."

"How long has he been like this?"

"Five years."

"And you look after him?"

The boy tensed forward and points of fire appeared in his pale cheeks. "Yes. Me. All the fucking time. It's bring me this, Gary, bring me that. Go get my prescription, Gary. Gary, I need a bath. I even sit him on the fucking toilet. Yes, I take care of him."

"Does he never leave his room?"

He sighed and settled back on the sofa. "I told you, only to go to the bathroom. He can't manage the stairs. Besides, he doesn't want to. He's given up."

That explained the state of the place. Susan wondered if the father knew, suspected, or even cared that his son had taken over the huge cold house to live whatever life of his own he could scrounge from the responsibilities of the sick-room. She wanted to ask him how he put up with it, but she already knew the scornful answer she would get: "Who else is there to do it?"

Instead, she asked, "How old were you when your sister ran away?"

He seemed surprised by the change in direction and had to think for a moment. "Eight. There's eight years between us. She'd been a bitch for years, had Caroline. The atmosphere was always tense. People were always rowing or on the verge of rows. It was a relief when she went."

"Why?"

He turned away so she couldn't see his eyes. "Why? I don't know. She was just like that. Full of poison. Especially towards me. Right from the start she tormented me, when I was a baby. They found her trying to drown me in my bath once. Of course they said she didn't realize what she was doing, but she did."

"Why should she want to kill you?"

He shrugged. "She hated me."

"Your father says he loved her."

He cast a scornful glance towards the ceiling and said slowly, "Oh yes, she always was the apple of his eye, even after she took off to London to become a tramp. Caroline could do no wrong. But who was the one left looking after him?"

"Why did you say tramp? How do you know?"

"What else would she do? She didn't have any job skills, but she was sixteen. She had two tits and a cunt like any other bird her age."

If Susan was expected to be shocked by his crudity, she was determined not to show it. "Did you ever see her during that period?"

"Me? You must be joking. It was all right for a while till mum got sick and died. It didn't take her longer than a month or two, not five years like that miserable old bastard upstairs. I was thirteen then, when he started. Took to his bed like a fish to water and it's been the same ever since."

"What about school?"

"I went sometimes. He sleeps most of the time, so I'm okay unless he has one of his awkward phases. I left last year. No jobs anyway."

"But what about the Health Service? Don't they help?"

"They send a nurse to look in every once in a while. And if you're going to mention a home, don't bother. I'd have him in one before you could say Jack Robinson if I could, but there's no room available unless you can pay." He gestured around the crumbling house. "As you can see, we can't. We've got his pension and a bit in the bank and that's it. I've even sold the bloody paintings, not that they were worth much. Thank God the bloody house is paid for. It must be worth a fortune now. I'd sell it and move somewhere cheaper if I could but the old bastard won't hear of it. Wants to die in his own bed. Sooner the better, I say."

Susan realized that Gary was drunk. As he'd been talking he'd finished one can of lager and most of a second, and he had obviously drunk a few before she arrived.

"Did you know anything at all about Caroline's life?" she asked.

His bright eyes narrowed. "I knew she was a fucking dyke, if that's what you mean."

"How did you know that?"

"She told me. One of her visits."

"But your father doesn't know?"

"No. It wouldn't make a scrap of difference if he did, though. It wouldn't change his opinion. As far as he's concerned the sun shone out of her arse and that's all there is to it." He tossed the empty can aside and picked up another from the low, cigarette-scarred table.

"How do you feel about her death?"

Gary was silent for a moment, then he looked directly at Susan. "I can't say I feel much at all. If you'd asked me a few years ago, I'd have said I felt glad. But now, nothing at all. I don't really care. She made my life a misery, then she left and lumbered me with the old man. I never had a chance to get out like her. And before that, she made everyone's life miserable at home. Especially mum's. Drove her to an early grave."

"Did you talk to her much when she visited?"

"Not by choice," he said, reaching for another cigarette. "But sometimes she wanted to talk to me, explain things, like she was taking me into her confidence. As if I cared. It was funny, almost like she was apologizing for everything without ever quite getting around to it. Do you know what I mean? 'I want you to know, Gary,' she says, 'how much I appreciate what you're doing for Dad. The sacrifices you're making. I'd help if I could, you know I would . . .' and all that fucking rubbish." He imitated her voice again: "'I want you to know, Gary, that I'm living with a woman in Eastvale and I'm happy for the first time in my life. I've really found myself at last. I know we've had problems in the past . . .' Always that 'I want you to know, Gary . . .' as if I fucking cared what she did, the slut. So she's dead. I can't say I care one way or another."

Susan didn't know whether to believe him. There was more pent-up passion and rage in his tone than she could handle, and she wasn't sure where it was coming from. All she knew was that she had to get out of this oppressive house, with its vast cold and crumbling spaces. She was beginning to feel dizzy and nauseated listening to Gary Hartley's high-pitched vitriol, which, she suspected, had as much to do with self-pity at his own weakness as anything else. Quickly, she muttered her farewell and headed for the door. As she walked down the hallway she heard an empty lager can crash against the wainscotting, followed by the screech of the top being ripped off another.

Outside, she breathed in the cold damp air and leaned against the roof of her car. Her gaze fixed on the melting snow that dripped from the branches of a tall tree. Her hands were shaking, but not from the cold.

Before she had driven far, she realized that she needed a drink. She pulled into the parking lot of the first decent-looking pub she saw outside town. There, in a comfortable bar lit and warmed by a real coal fire, she sipped a small brandy and thought about the Hartleys. She felt that her visit had barely scraped the surface. There was so much bitterness, anger and pain festering underneath, so many conflicting passions, that it would take years of psychoanalysis to sort them out.

One thing was clear, though: whatever the reasons for the family's strife, and whatever Caroline's reasons for running away, Gary Hartley certainly had a very good motive for murder. His sister had ruined his life; he even seemed to blame her for his mother's death. Had he been a different kind of person, he would have handled the burden some other way, but because he was weak and felt put upon, blood had turned to vinegar in his veins. As Susan had just seen, it didn't take more than a few drinks to bring the acid to the surface.

It would be very interesting to know what Gary Hartley had been doing between seven and eight o'clock the previous evening. As he had told her, the old man slept most of the time, so it would have been easy for Gary to nip out for a while without being missed. She hadn't asked him for an alibi, and that was an oversight. But, she thought, taking another sip of brandy and warming her hands by the fire, before we start to get all paranoid again, Susan, let's just say that this was only a preliminary interview. It would be a good idea to approach Gary Hartley again with someone else along. Someone like Banks.

As she tilted her head back and finished the rest of her drink, she noticed the bright Christmas decorations hung across the ceiling and the string of cards on the wall above the stone fireplace. That was another thing she remembered about the Hartley house. In addition to the cold and the overwhelming sense of decay, there had been nothing at all in the entire huge place to mark the season: not a Christmas tree, not a card, not a sprig of holly, not a cut-out Father Christmas. In that, she realized bitterly, the place resembled her own flat all too closely. She shivered and walked out to the car.

II

Banks drove carefully down the hill into Redburn as his tape of Bartok's third string quartet neared its end. The gradient wasn't quite as steep as at Staithes, where you had to leave your car at the top and walk, but it was bad enough. Luckily, the snow had petered out somewhere over the heathered reaches of the North York Moors and spared the coast.

The narrow hill meandered alongside the beck down to the sea, and it wasn't until he turned the final corner that Banks saw the water, a heaving mass of grey sloshing against the sea-wall and showering the narrow promenade with silver spray. Redburn was a small place: just the one main street leading down to the sea, with a few ginnels and snickets twisting off it where cottages were hidden away, half dug into the hillside itself, all sheltered in the crescent of the bay. In summer the jumble of pastel colours would make a picturesque scene, but in this weather they seemed out of place, as if a piece of the Riviera had been dug up and transported to a harsher climate.

Banks turned left at the front, drove to the end of the road and parked outside the Lobster Inn. Where the road ended, a narrow path led up the hillside, providing the only access to the two or three isolated cottages that faced the sea about half-way up: ideal places for artists.

The cold whipped the breath out of him and the air seemed full of sharp needles of moisture, but Banks finally reached his goal, the white cottage with the red pantile roof. Like the rest of the village, it would look pretty in summer with its garden full of flowers, he thought, but in the dull grey air, with the wind curling smoke from the red chimney, it took on a desolate aspect. Banks knocked at the door. Somewhere the wind was whistling and banging a loose shutter. He thought of Jim Hatchley and wondered how much he was enjoying the seaside not many miles away.

The woman who answered his knock had the kind of puzzled expression on her face that he'd expected. There couldn't be many people dropping in on such a day in such an isolated place.

She raised her dark eyebrows. "Yes?"

Banks introduced himself and showed his card. She stood aside to let him in. The room was a haven from the elements. A wood fire crackled in the hearth and the smell of fresh-baked bread filled the air. The wooden furniture looked primitive and well-used, but homely. The woman herself was in her mid-twenties, and the long skirt and blouse she wore outlined her slender figure. She had a strong jaw and full, red lips. Beneath her fringe of dark hair, two large brown eyes watched him go over and rub his hands in front of the fire.

Banks grinned at her. "No gloves. Silly of me."

She held out her hand. "I'm Patsy Janowski. Pleased to meet you." Her grip was firm and strong. Her accent was American.

"I'm here to see Mr Ivers," he said. "Is he at home?"

"Yes, but he's working. You can't see him now. He hates to be disturbed."

"And I would hate to disturb him," Banks said. "But it's important."

She gave him a thoughtful look, then smiled. It was a radiant smile, and she knew it. She looked at her watch. "Why don't I make us some tea and you can try some of my bread. It's fresh from the oven. Claude will be down in twenty minutes or so for a short break."

Banks considered the options: Either way he would have surprise on his side, and if he let Ivers finish his session, the man would probably be better disposed towards him. Was that what he wanted? At this stage, he decided, it would be helpful. He also felt a great sense of respect for the music the man created and would have been loath to interrupt the creative process. In addition, he had to admit that the prospect of tea and fresh bread was one that appealed very strongly.

He smiled back at Patsy Janowski. "Sounds good to me. Mind if I smoke?"

"Go ahead. I don't myself, but Claude's a pipe man. I'm used to it. I won't be a minute."

Banks sat in front of the fire and lit up. The chair was hard and creaked whenever he shifted position, but in an odd way it was comfortable. A few minutes later, Patsy came back in with a plate full of warm bread and a steaming teapot covered with a pink quilted cosy. She put them on the low table in front of the fire then fetched butter and strawberry jam. That done, she sat opposite Banks.

"Nice place," he said, buttering the bread.

"Yes. Claude bought it after he split up with his wife. They had this enormous mansion near Eastvale, and you know what prices are like these days. This was comparatively cheap. Needed a bit of work. And he always wanted to live by the sea. He says it inspires his work. You know, the sea's rhythms, its music."

As she spoke, Banks noticed, her lively eyes flitted from one thing to another: his wedding ring, the scar by his right eye, his left foot, the middle button on his shirt. It wasn't as if she were avoiding eye-contact, more as if she were conducting an inventory.

Banks nodded at what she said. He had noticed musical imita-
tions of the ebb and flow of waves in Ivers's previous work. Perhaps
such effects would be even more prevalent in the future. Certainly
between the hiss and crackle of the fire he could hear waves pounding the rough sea-wall.

"What about you?" Banks asked.

"What about me?"

"What do you do? It's a bit out of the way here, isn't it?"

She shrugged. "Why should you assume I'd prefer the city? Do
you think I like cruising the bars, going to discos, taking my credit
cards shopping?" She smiled before he could answer. "I love it here.
I can amuse myself. I read, I draw a little. I like to cook and go for
long walks. And I'm working on my PhD dissertation. That keeps
me busy."

"Consider me suitably chastised," Banks said.

"Thank you." She treated him to the radiant smile again, then
frowned. "What is it you want with Claude?"

"It's a personal matter."

"We do live together, you know. It's not as if I was just a neighbour dropping in for gossip."

Banks smiled. She had at least answered a question before he'd
had to ask it. "Do you know his ex-wife, Veronica Shildon?"

"I've met her. Why, has anything—?"

Banks held up a hand. "Don't worry, nothing's happened to her,"
he said.

"And she's not really his ex-wife," Patsy said. "They're still
married." She sounded as if she didn't like that state of affairs.
"Wanted to avoid the scandal. More bread?"

"Mmm, I think I will." Banks reached forward. "A drop more tea
as well, if there is any."

"Sure."

"How did you meet Claude Ivers?"

Patsy looked at the pen in Banks's top pocket. "I was studying at
York when he was teaching a music appreciation course. I took it
and kind of . . . well, he noticed me. We've been living together
here for a year now."

"Happily?"

"Yes."

"How often have you met Veronica?"

"Three or four times. They were very civilized about things. At least they were by the time I came onto the scene."

"What about Caroline Hartley?"

Her jaw set. "You'll have to ask Claude about her. I've met her once or twice, but I can't say I know her. Look, if it's—"

At that moment they heard a creaking on the stairs and both turned in unison to see Claude Ivers duck under the low lintel and walk into the room. He made an imposing figure—tall, gaunt, stooped—and there was no doubt about the power of his presence. He wore a jersey and baggy jeans, and his grey hair stuck up in places as if he had been running his hand through it. His skin was reddish and leathery, like that of a man who has spent a lot of time in the wind and sun, and a deep "V" of concentration furrowed the bridge of his nose. He looked to be in his early fifties. An inquisitive glance passed between Ivers and Patsy before she introduced Banks. Ivers shook hands and sat down. Patsy went to see to his coffee.

"What do you want to see me about?" he asked.

Banks repressed a childish urge to tell him he liked his music. "Bad news, I'm afraid," he said. "Caroline Hartley, your wife's companion. She's dead."

Ivers lurched forward and gripped the sides of his chair. "Good God! What? How?"

"She was murdered."

"But that's absurd. Things like that don't happen in real life."

"I'm sorry. It's true."

He shook his head. "Is Veronica all right?"

"She's very upset, obviously, but apart from that she's okay. I take it you still care?"

"Of course I do."

Banks heard something crash down heavily in the kitchen.

"If you don't mind my saying so, Mr Ivers," he went on, "I find that very difficult to understand. If my wife—"

He waved Banks's comparison aside. "Listen, I went through everything any normal man would go through. Everything. Not just anger and rage, but disbelief, disgust, loss of self-esteem, loss of self-confidence. I went through hell. Christ, it's bad enough when your wife runs away with another man, but another woman . . ."

"You forgave her?"

"If that's the right word. I could never entirely blame Veronica in the first place. Can you understand that? It was as if she'd been led astray, fallen under someone else's influence."

"Caroline Hartley's?"

He nodded.

"Would you tell me what happened?"

For several moments there was silence but for the fire, the sea and muted sounds from the kitchen. Finally, Ivers stared at Banks, then cracked his fingers and stretched back in the chair.

"All right," he said. "You're a stranger. Somehow that makes it easier. And we don't get many people to talk to around here. Sometimes I get a bit stir-crazy, as Patsy puts it. There's not a lot to it, really. One day everything was fine. She was happy, we were happy. At least I thought so. Maybe she got a bit bored from time to time, got depressed now and then, but we had a good solid marriage, or so I thought. Then she started seeing a therapist, didn't tell me why. I don't think she knew herself, but I suspect it was a bit of a trend among bored, middle-class housewives. It didn't seem to be doing her much harm at first so I didn't object, but then, out of the blue, there's this new friend. It's all 'Caroline says this' and 'Caroline says that.' My wife starts to change in front of my eyes. Can you believe that? She even started using this other girl's language, saying things she would never say herself. She started calling things she liked 'neat.' 'Really neat,' she'd say! That wasn't Veronica. And she started dressing differently. She'd always been a bit on the formal side, but now she'd wear jeans and a sweatshirt. And there was all that interminable talk about Jung and self-actual-ization. I think she once told me I was too much the thinking type, or some such rot. Said my music was too intellectual and not emotional enough. And she got interested in stuff she'd never cared about when I'd tried to interest her—theatre, cinema, literature. She was never in, always around at Caroline's. Then she even started suggesting that *I* should go to therapy too."

"But you didn't?"

He stared into the fire and paused, as if he realized he had already given too much away, then he said quietly, "I have my demons, Mr Banks, but they also fire me. I'm afraid that if I subjected them to therapy I'd have no more fuel, no more creativity. Whatever Veronica might say, my music's born from conflict and feeling, not just technical skill." He tapped his head. "I really hear those things. And I was afraid if I opened my head to some shrink all the music would escape and I would be condemned to silence. I couldn't live like that. No, I didn't go."

Patsy returned with the coffee. Ivers took it, smiled at her, and she sat on the floor beside him with her legs curled under her and her hand resting on his thigh.

"Did you know at the start of the friendship that Caroline was a lesbian?" Banks asked.

"Yes. Veronica told me Caroline was living with a woman called Nancy Wood. Fair enough, I thought. Live and let live. I'm a musician, not the bohemian type, perhaps, but I've been around enough oddballs in my time not to worry about them too much. And I'm fairly broad-minded. So Caroline was a lesbian. I never for a moment thought that my wife . . ."

"So if you blamed anyone it was Caroline?"

"Yes." He hesitated, realizing what he'd said. "But I didn't kill her, if that's what you're getting at."

"What did you do yesterday evening?"

He sipped his coffee and spoke, half into the mug. "Stayed in. With Patsy. We don't go out all that much."

Patsy looked at Banks and nodded in agreement. He saw shadows behind her eyes. He wasn't sure he believed her. "Do you own a car?" he asked.

"We both do."

"Where do you park?"

"We've got spots reserved in the village, behind the pub. Obviously there's no parking up here."

"When did you last see your wife?"

He thought for a moment. "About a month ago. I was in Eastvale on business and I dropped in to see how Veronica was doing. I called at the shop first. I usually do that to avoid meeting

Caroline, but sometimes if it's evening I just have to face it out."

"How did Caroline react to these visits?"

"She'd leave the room."

"So you never spoke to her."

"Not much, no. And Veronica would be tense. I'd never end up staying long if Caroline was around."

"Are you sure that was the last time you visited the house, a month ago?"

"Yes, of course I am."

"You didn't go there yesterday evening?"

"I told you. We stayed in."

"You're a musician," Banks said. "You must know Vivaldi's work."

"I—of course I do."

"Do you know the *Laudate pueri?*"

Ivers turned aside and reached for some bread and butter. "Which one? He wrote four, you know."

"Four what?"

"Four settings for the same liturgical piece. I think it's Psalm 112, but I can't be sure. Why do you ask?"

"Have you heard of a singer called Magda Kalmár?"

"Yes. But I—"

"Did you usually buy your wife a Christmas present?"

"I did last year."

"And this year?"

He buttered his bread as he spoke. "I was going to. Am. I just haven't got round to it yet."

"Better hurry up, then," Banks said with a smile. "Only one more shopping day to Christmas." He put his cup down on the hearth and stood up to leave. "Thank you very much for the tea and bread," he said to Patsy, "and it was an honour to meet you Mr Ivers. I've enjoyed your music for a long time."

Ivers raised an eyebrow. Banks was thankful he just nodded and didn't say anything about being surprised that policemen listened to music.

Banks walked over to the door and Ivers followed him. "About Veronica," he said. "She must be in a terrible state. Do you think she needs me?"

"I don't know," Banks said. He honestly didn't. Did a wife who lost her female lover turn back to her husband for comfort? "Maybe you should ask her."

Ivers nodded, and the last thing Banks noticed before the door closed was the darkening expression in Patsy Janowski's eyes, fixed on the pipe in Ivers's hand.

He made his way against the wind back to the car and drove up the hill again. The Ivers household had left him with a strange feeling. However rustic and cosy it was, he couldn't help but suspect that all was not well, and that nobody had told him the complete truth. He had little doubt that Ivers had bought the record for Veronica and had more than likely delivered it, too. But he couldn't prove it. As soon as he could, he would go back to visit Claude Ivers again.

III

The Queen's Arms was never very busy at five o'clock on a winter's afternoon. It was too late for the lunch-time drinkers and too early for the after-work crowd. The only other customers, apart from Banks, Richmond and Susan Gay, were three or four people with shopping bags full of Christmas presents.

The three of them sat in the deep armchairs around the fire. Banks and Richmond were drinking pints and Susan had accepted a brandy and soda. They had pooled their notes and still had nothing concrete to go on. Richmond had discovered that Nancy Wood had left Eastvale for an extended trip to Australia. A phone call to immigration had established that she was indeed there. Richmond followed with a call to the Sydney police, who got back to him a couple of hours later with positive confirmation. That was one serious suspect eliminated.

Richmond had so far got nowhere with the photograph of Ruth, the mystery woman. The record, too, remained unexplained. They would have to start canvassing classical record shops all over England, and that would take time. Veronica Shildon's therapist had confirmed that Veronica had left her office at about seven o'clock the previous evening, as usual, and that she had mentioned going shopping.

"You said that Caroline ran off to London when she was sixteen?" Banks said to Susan.

"That's what her brother told me."

"And she was down there for about six years before she came up to Eastvale. A lot can happen in that time. Any idea where she was?"

"Sorry, sir, they didn't seem to know anything. Either that or they weren't saying."

"Was that the feeling you got?"

"There was certainly something weird about them." Susan shuddered as she spoke.

"Never mind. We'll find out when we talk to them again. Maybe you can get a print-out from the PNC, Phil? Caroline Hartley might have a record down there. Runaways often get in trouble with the law."

Richmond nodded.

"Any other leads?" Banks asked.

They shook their heads. He smiled. "Don't look so bloody despondent, Susan. At least it means you'll get Christmas Day at home."

"Sir?"

"If we don't solve a murder in twenty-four hours, the odds are we'll be at it a long time. A day here or there isn't going to make a lot of difference unless we come up with a hot lead tomorrow. And it *is* Christmas. Things slow down. You know as well as I do it's impossible to get anything done for a couple of days. Nobody's around, for a start. All we can do is get the statements sorted out and see if we can build up a clear picture of the victim. You find often enough that the seeds of the death are in the life, so to speak, and given the life Caroline Hartley led that may be even more apt in her case. We'll do what we can with the photo, the record and the London connection, and in a day or two we'll visit her family again and push a bit harder. Maybe you and I could have a bit of a chat with the Amateur Dramatic Society again, too, Susan. There might be some connections there—jealousy, rivalry, something like that."

Susan nodded.

"And I don't think Veronica Shildon's coming clean with us, either," Banks went on. "But then she's not likely to. She'll be protecting Caroline's memory, especially if there's any shady business in the girl's past. Her alibi checks out, but there are ten minutes unaccounted for between her return home and going to Christine Cooper's. She could have nipped back earlier, too, say between seven and half-past, if she'd wanted to, and only pretended to arrive later. Then there's Cooper himself, and his wife for that matter. If there was anything odd going on between those two households, who knows what kind of can of worms it might have opened. All I'm saying is that we should keep an open mind while we let them all stew for a while. Let them enjoy Christmas. Maybe we'll do the rounds again on Boxing Day when they're all full and comfy. An old sparring partner of mine from the Met, Dirty Dick Burgess, always used to prefer Sundays for surprise raids. Boxing Day's probably even better."

Richmond raised his eyebrows at the mention of Burgess. Banks and Dirty Dick had locked horns over a politically sensitive case in Eastvale last spring, and they had hardly parted on the best of terms. Apart from Banks and Burgess, only Richmond knew the full story.

Banks looked at his watch and finished his pint. "Right. I'd better be off now. I want to see if that post-mortem report's turned up yet." It was already dark outside and the snow had just started falling again.

The report had indeed turned up. Banks skipped the technical details for the layman's synopsis that Dr Glendenning always courteously provided.

There was nothing new at first. She had been hit, probably punched, on the cheek, and the blow could have rendered her unconscious. After that, she had been viciously and repeatedly stabbed with her own kitchen knife. The only blood found at the scene was hers. Her dressing-gown had no blood-stains on it, so it had been removed—or Caroline herself had removed it—before the stabbing. Glendenning had found no signs at all of sexual interference. He had, however, found crumbs of chocolate cake in several of the wounds, which led him to believe that the knife had been lying by the cake on the table. If so, Banks thought, they were probably dealing with a spur-of-the-moment attack, a weapon at hand, grabbed and used in anger. There were no signs of skin or blood under her fingernails, which meant she hadn't had a chance to fight off her attacker.

And that was it, apart from the general information. Banks read idly through—health basically sound, appendix scar, gave birth to a child. . . . He stopped and read that part over again. According to Glendenning, who had been as thorough as usual, the cervix showed a multiparous os, which meant the deceased had, at some point, had a baby.

That cast an interesting new light on things. Not only did it mean she had had at least one heterosexual relationship, it might also explain why she went to London, or what might have happened to her down there. All the more imperative, therefore, to find out exactly where she'd been and what she'd done. Banks felt that the photograph was a clue. Given that it was the only memento she'd kept, apart from a pressed flower, Ruth was obviously someone important from Caroline's past.

Banks walked over to the window and looked out on the market square. It looked like one of Brueghel's winter scenes. The tree was lit up and shoppers crossed the whitened cobbles to and fro with their packages. Banks was glad he'd done his Christmas shopping a week ago. The only thing that remained was the booze. He'd buy that tomorrow: a bottle of port, a nice dry sherry, perhaps some Ciardhu single-malt, if he could afford it. Then his thoughts drifted back to Caroline Hartley. A baby. What a bloody turn-up! And if there was a baby, somewhere there had to be a father. Maybe a father with a grudge.

Eager to find out if there had been any progress on the record and the scrap of wrapping paper, he phoned the forensic lab and asked for Vic Manson.

Manson was slightly breathless when he came on the line. "What is it? I'd just this minute put my overcoat on. I was on my way out."

Banks smiled to himself and lit a cigarette. Manson was always on his way somewhere. "Sorry, Vic. I won't keep you long. Just wanted to know if you've got anything for us on the Hartley murder."

Manson sighed. "Not a lot. No dabs we can't account for. The knife was washed, but we found traces of blood and crumbs where the blade meets the handle."

"What about the record?"

"Nothing. Besides, people usually hold records by the edge. No room for prints there. The cover and inside sleeve were clean, too."

"Anything else?"

"It looked new, the record. As far as we can tell it was in mint condition, only been played a few times."

"How many?"

"Can't tell for sure—two or three at the most—but take our word, it was new."

"The paper?"

"Common or garden Christmas wrapping paper. Could have come from anywhere. It does look like it had been wrapped around the record, though. It fits to a tee. But there's no gift tag with the murderer's name on, unfortunately."

"Well, at least we've got something. Thanks, Vic. Look, can you send the record over to me when you've done with it?"

"Of course. Tomorrow okay?"

"Fine. Don't let me keep you any longer. And have a good Christmas."

"You too."

Banks hung up, walked back to the window and lit a cigarette. What the hell was it about the music that bothered him? Why did it have to mean something? He would find out as much as he could about Vivaldi's *Laudate pueri*, all four versions. Claude Ivers admitted he knew them, but that didn't mean anything. He must have known that if he'd feigned ignorance, given his musical reputation, Banks would have immediately become even more suspicious. But Ivers knew more than he let on, that was for certain. And so did Patsy Janowski, she of the wandering eyes. Well, give them time, he thought, as he smoked and looked down on the Brueghel scene, they're not going anywhere. Let them think they're safe, then . . .

FOUR

I

James Conran lived in a small terrace house on the north-west edge of town, where Cardigan Drive met North Market Street and turned into the main Swainsdale road. At the far end of his living room, a manual typewriter sat on a table by the window. The view to the west along snow-shrouded Swainsdale was superb. Bookcases flanked the table on both sides with books on all subjects. Banks took a quick glance: history, theatre, music, but hardly any fiction. A small sofa and two matching armchairs formed a semicircle around the hearth, where a peat fire smouldered. On the wall above the mantelpiece hung a poster advertising a performance of *The Duchess of Malfi* at Stratford. There was no television set, but a music centre with a compact-disc player stood opposite the fireplace. Banks ran his eyes over the records and discs, most of them the works of classical composers: Beethoven, Zelenka, Bax, Stanford, Mozart, Elgar. There was some Vivaldi, including the *Stabat Mater*, but not the *Laudate pueri*.

Conran, having explained to Banks how Susan had once been one of his pupils, was now fussing over her and offering to make tea. Both she and Banks accepted.

"Nice collection of discs," Banks observed. "Are you a musician?"

"Merely a dabbler," Conran said. "I sang with the church choir when I was a boy, then with an amateur outfit in York. I also directed the choir at Eastvale Comprehensive for a few years—mostly, I might add, because no-one else would take on the job. But that's just about the limit of my musical abilities. I *am* a good listener, however."

As Conran made tea in the kitchen, Banks continued reading book and record titles. It helped get a sense of people, he always thought, to discover their tastes in literature and music. Conran definitely read to learn, not for pleasure, which hinted at a certain amount of intellectual and artistic ambition. His record collection, while fairly eclectic, favoured choral works, perhaps an unconscious left-over from his choir days. The fact that he owned a compact-disc player showed he was serious about his listening. Though she said she liked classical music, Veronica Shildon only had an old stereo system, a turntable complete with arm and spindle for stacking records. No one who genuinely loved music would play it on such antiquated equipment, especially if they could afford better. No, Veronica Shildon's priorities lay elsewhere than music—in decor, perhaps, in creating the sense of a cosy and comfortable home. But Conran clearly valued his artistic pleasures over material ones.

Banks warmed his hands by the fire. "I should imagine you got to know Caroline Hartley pretty well during rehearsals for *Twelfth Night*," he said. "Can you tell us anything about her?"

"Such as what?"

"Anything at all. Her habits, moods, your impression of her. Believe me, every little bit helps."

"It's very difficult," Conran said. "I mean, I didn't know her that well. None of us did, really."

"What was your relationship with her?"

Conran frowned. "Relationship? I'd hardly say we had a relationship. What are you implying?"

"You were directing her in a theatrical production, isn't that so?"

"Well, yes . . . but—"

"That's a relationship."

"I see . . . I . . . I thought. Anyway, yes, I directed her on stage. It was a purely working relationship. You don't really find out much about people when you're busy telling them where to stand and how to speak, you know."

"What did you think of her?"

"She was a very talented and attractive girl, a natural. It's a real tragedy. She'd have gone far had she lived."

"Yet you only gave her a small part."

"It was her first performance. She needed more experience. But she was quick. It wouldn't have taken her long to get to the top if she'd put her mind to it. *Mercurial*. I think that's the best word to describe her talent."

"How did she get on with the rest of the cast?"

Conran shrugged. "All right, I suppose."

"Did she form any special relationships? Was she close to anyone in particular?"

"Not that I know of. We're all pretty chummy, really, when it comes down to it. After all, this isn't the West End. It's meant to be fun. That's the reason I'm involved."

"She did join you for drinks after rehearsals sometimes, didn't she?"

"Yes, usually. But you can hardly get to know somebody in a group situation like that."

"Who did she talk to?"

"Everyone, really."

"How did she behave?"

"I don't understand."

"Was she comfortable with the group?"

"As far as I could tell."

"Did you know she was a lesbian?" Banks asked.

"Caroline?" He shook his head. "I don't believe it."

"Do you have evidence to the contrary?"

"Of course not," Conran snapped. "Stop twisting everything I say. What I mean is I'm surprised. She . . ."

"She what?"

"Well, you don't expect things like that, do you? She seemed quite normal to me."

"Heterosexual?"

Conran looked at Susan as if pleading for support. "You're doing it again. I've no knowledge of her sex life at all. All I'm saying is she *seemed* normal to me."

"So she didn't tell you anything about her private life?"

"No. She kept herself to herself. I knew nothing at all about what she did when she left the hall or the pub."

"Oh, come on! Surely some of the men in the cast must have tried it on with her. Maybe you even tried yourself. Who wouldn't? How did she respond?"

"I'm not sure what you mean."

"It's obvious enough. Was she cold, polite, friendly, rude . . . ?"

"Oh, I see. Well, no, she certainly wasn't cold. She'd joke and flirt like the rest, I suppose. It's not something I actually thought about. She was always friendly and cheerful, or so it seemed to me."

"Terrible waste, don't you think? A beautiful woman like that, and no man stood a chance with her."

Conran glanced down into his mug and muttered, "It takes all sorts, Chief Inspector."

"Who did she usually sit next to?"

"It varied."

"Did you notice anything at all that hinted at a more than superficial relationship with anyone in the cast, male or female?"

"No."

Banks sipped some tea and leaned back in his chair. "In a close group like that, you must get all sorts of pressures. I've heard that actors sometimes have very fragile egos. Did you get many tantrums or rows? Any professional jealousies?"

"Only over petty matters," Conran, "like you'd get in any team situation. As I said, we're in it for pleasure, not ambition or fame."

"'Petty matters'? Can you be a bit more specific?"

"I honestly can't remember any examples."

"Anything involving Caroline Hartley?"

He shook his head.

"Was there any special reason why Caroline didn't join you all for a drink after rehearsal on December twenty-second?"

"Nobody went to the pub that evening. We didn't always go, you know. It was a very casual thing."

"But you went?"

"Yes. Alone. I wanted to mull over the rehearsal. I seem to be able to think better about things like that when there's a bit of noise and festive activity around me."

"Drink much?"

"A bit. I wasn't drunk, if that's what you mean."

"Had anything odd happened between four and six? Any fights, threats, arguments?"

"There was nothing unusual, no. Everybody was tired, that's all. Or they had shopping to do. Surely you can't think one of the cast—"

"Right now, I'm keeping an open mind." Banks put down his mug. "Why did you give up teaching, Mr Conran?"

If Conran was surprised by the abrupt change in questioning, he didn't show it. "I'd always wanted to write. As soon as I had a little success I decided to burn my bridges. Much as I enjoyed it, teaching made too many demands on my time and energy."

"How do you make your living now? Surely not from the Eastvale Amateur Dramatic Society?"

"Good lord, no! That's just a hobby, really. I work as a freelance writer. I've also had a few plays produced on television, some radio work."

Banks looked around the room again. "Don't you even watch your own work?"

Conran laughed. "I *do* have a television, as a matter of fact. I don't watch it very often so I keep it upstairs in the spare room. One of the advantages of being a bachelor. Plenty of space."

"Are you working on anything right now?"

Conran beamed and sat forward, hands clasped in his lap. "As a matter of fact, I am. I've just got this wonderful commission from the BBC to dramatize John Cowper Powys's novel, *Weymouth Sands*. It'll be a hard task, very hard, but it pays well, and it's an honour to be involved. I'm not the only writer in the project, of course, but still . . ."

"You're a long way from Weymouth," Banks remarked. "Come from down there?"

"Litton Cheney, actually. You won't have heard of it. It's a small village in Dorset."

"I thought I could spot a trace of that Hardy country burr. Well, Mr Conran, sorry to have bothered you on Christmas Eve. Hope we haven't kept you from your family."

"I have no family," Conran said, "and you haven't kept me from anything, no." He stood up and shook hands, then helped Susan on with her coat.

Back outside at the car, Banks turned to Susan and said, "Do you know, I think he fancies you."

Susan blushed. "He probably fancies anything in a skirt."

"You could be right. He seemed a bit edgy, didn't he? I wonder if there's more to this dramatic society than meets the eye? You know the kind of thing, fiery passions lurking beneath the surface of dull suburban life."

Susan laughed. "Could be," she said. "Or perhaps he's just shaken up."

"And did I miss something," Banks said, "or did he tell us nothing at all?"

"He told us nothing," Susan agreed. "But I certainly got the impression he knew much more than he let on."

Banks opened the car door. "Yes," he said. "Yes, I think he did, didn't he. That's the trouble with cases like this. Everybody's got something to hide."

II

On Christmas Eve at four o'clock the Queen's Arms was packed. Businessmen, off work early for the holidays, loosened their ties, smoked cigars and laughed themselves red in the face at dirty jokes; friends met for a last few drinks before parting to spend the holidays with their families; groups of female office workers drank brightly coloured concoctions and laughed about the way the mail-room boy's hands had roamed during the office party. A large proportion of the Eastvale police force, denied their favourite spot by the fire, had pulled together two round tables with dimpled copper tops and cast-iron legs for their own party. It was a movable feast; men nipped over from the station for a quick one, then returned to cover for others. Even Fred Rowe managed to drop by for a couple of pints while young Tolliver took over the front desk. The only real continuity was provided by the CID—Gristhorpe, Banks, Richmond and Susan Gay— who had managed to hang onto their chairs amidst the chaos around them.

Everyone seemed to be having a good time. The atmosphere was cheery with its blazing fire and green-and-red decorations. The only thing Banks found objectionable, especially after a couple of pints, was the music that Cyril, the landlord, had piped in for the occasion. It sounded like airport-music versions of Christmas carols. Gristhorpe didn't seem to mind, but he was tone-deaf.

After the visit to Conran's, they had achieved very little that day, and nothing more would be achieved by working longer. By mid-afternoon it had been almost impossible to reach anyone on the phone. If you did happen to be lucky enough, all you got for your trouble was a drunken babble in the earpiece. Police work may never stop completely, but it does slow down at times. The only coppers working harder than ever now would be the road patrols chasing after drunken drivers.

Richmond had talked to Caroline's staff at the Garden Café, but found out nothing more about her. No, they had never suspected she might be a lesbian; she had kept her private life to herself, just as Conran had said. She was cheerful and friendly, yes, good with customers, but a closed book when it came to her personal life. She never talked about boyfriends or shared her problems, as some of the other women did.

Richmond had also dropped in on Christine Cooper and taken her through her story again. The details matched word for word. He had first taken the initiative of phoning his mother and asking her what had happened on the December 22 broadcasts of "Emmerdale Farm" and "Coronation Street." Passing himself off as a fan who had missed his favourite programs, he asked Christine Cooper to give him a blow-by-blow description of them, which she did. That accounted for her whereabouts between seven and eight o'clock. Caroline Hartley had last been seen alive around seven-twenty, answering the door to a female visitor. Unless Christine Cooper had nipped out during the commercials and stabbed her with the handy kitchen knife, or unless she was such a cunning killer she had videotaped the television programs in case someone asked about them, then it looked as if she was out of the running. So far, Richmond had not been able to satisfy himself about her husband's alibi, but he planned to pay a visit to Barnard Castle after Christmas, when the shop reopened.

The only new fact he had discovered, via the PNC, was that Caroline Hartley had been arrested for soliciting in London five years ago. That seemed to back up what her brother, Gary, had said about her life there, but it still left a lot unsaid. Had Gary actually known what she was doing, or had he made an inspired guess? Both he and Caroline's father said that Caroline had never contacted them during her time in London. Were they lying? If so, why?

For the moment, though, the festive season chased away day-to-day concerns. Even Susan Gay was knocking back the Old Peculier and chatting with the others more easily than she usually did.

"What are you doing over the holidays?" Banks asked her over the racket.

"Going home."

"Because if you're stuck for somewhere," he went on, "you can always join us for Christmas dinner. I know you don't get enough time off to really go anywhere."

"Thanks," Susan said, "but it's all right. Sheffield's not that far."

Banks nodded. Richmond, he knew, would be spending the day with his family in town. Gristhorpe was coming to the Banks's this year. For their first two Christmases up north, Banks and his family had gone out to his farmhouse where Mrs Hawkins, the woman "what did for him," had done them proud. This year, however, Mrs Hawkins and her husband had been invited to their daughter's in Cambridge. It would be the first Christmas away for them, but as the daughter had recently borne them a grandchild, they could hardly refuse. Gristhorpe had played hard-to-get at first, but succumbed without too much of a fight at Banks's third invitation. Banks suspected that it was actually Sandra's telling Gristhorpe that the house was now a "smoke-free environment" that finally tipped the balance.

At five o'clock, Banks decided it was time to leave. He had had three pints of Theakston's bitter, just about the right amount to work up an appetite. Sandra would be expecting him for dinner. He was due to help with the big meal tomorrow—mostly the dull stuff, he imagined, chopping vegetables and setting the table, as his cooking skills were limited—but tonight was Sandra's treat.

He said his goodbyes and wandered out into the snow, which had been falling on and off all day. Opposite, the blue lamp outside the police station shed its avuncular light. Banks didn't know why he hated it so much, but he did. It was phoney, a kind of cheap nostalgia for a time when things were simpler—or at least we fooled ourselves into believing they were simpler—when the goodies wore white and the baddies wore black. Maybe it really had been like that, but Banks doubted it. Certainly nothing could ever have been simple for the Caroline Hartleys and Veronica Shildons of this world.

Anyway, he told himself, no more gloomy thoughts. He stuck on his headphones and fiddled with the Walkman in his pocket. The music he'd chosen was his own tribute to the season: Benjamin Britten's *A Ceremony of Carols*. It was difficult, though, to put the case out of his mind: not the investigation, the details or the leads, but the sheer fact of Caroline Hartley's brutal murder. Even at the pub he had felt at times like a spectator, watching everyone celebrate, but held back from joining in by what he had seen at number eleven Oakwood Mews. Still, it was Christmas Eve and he had to make an effort to be jolly for his family's sake.

The snow was crisp and squeaky. At last Eastvale had the white Christmas it had been screaming for during the past three or four rainy ones. Coloured lights winked on and off in windows, and Banks felt for a moment that fleeting sense of peace and relaxation in the air that seems to arise and flourish briefly when the commercial fervour of the season begins to abate.

He remembered his own childhood Christmases: the sleepless nights before the big day; the early mornings opening presents; the disappointment the year his parents hadn't been able to buy him the bicycle he wanted because his father was out of work; the joy two years later when he got an even better one than he had expected.

At home, the trimmings were up, the lights were on and the children were brimming with excitement and curiosity about their presents. At least Tracy was. Brian, being seventeen, was much more cool about the whole thing.

"No, you can't open them tonight," Banks told his daughter.

"But Laura Collins says they do at her house. Oh, go on, Dad. Please!"

"No!" Banks wasn't about to have a lifetime's tradition changed because of Laura Collins. Tracy pouted for a while, but she wasn't the kind to sulk for long.

Brian kept quiet, as though he didn't even care whether he got a present. All that interested him was pop music, and Banks had bought him a second-hand guitar he'd spotted in a shop window. Of course, it would mean a bit of noise to put up with. Banks didn't have much regard for his son's taste, but far be it for him to stand in the way of the lad's musical ambitions. Euterpe, like God, works in mysterious ways; raucous pop music might inspire someone to learn the guitar, but tastes change, and the talent might well end up in the service of jazz, blues or classical music.

Tracy had been a good deal less specific in her demands, but both Banks and Sandra had thought it a good idea to acknowledge that she was no longer a little girl. She was, after all, fifteen, and though her interest in history remained steady, and had even extended to take in literature, she had a new look in her eyes when the subject of boys came up. Banks had also noticed the odd pop star poster surreptitiously making its way onto her bedroom wall. So rather than books, they had bought her some fashionable new clothes and a make-up kit. When Banks looked at his children now, it was with a tinge of sadness in his heart. Next year he would be forty, and soon he would lose them to their own lives completely.

After a tasty beef stew with dumplings—a frugal dinner to counterbalance tomorrow's blow-out—came that time of evening when Banks could start to relax: the children out or occupied in their rooms, the television turned off, a tumbler of good Scotch, quiet music and Sandra beside him on the sofa. When he went for his refill, he remembered the photograph he had brought home in his briefcase along with the record Vic Manson had sent over that afternoon. He had hardly looked at it, but something about it rang a bell. Sandra, with her knowledge of photography, should be able to help him. He took the photograph out and handed it to her.

"What do you think of that?"

Sandra examined it close up, then held it at arm's length. "Do you mean technically?"

"Any way you like."

"Well, it's obviously good, a professional job. You can tell that by the lighting and the way he's made it seem like a relaxed pose. She looks very studious. A striking woman. Good quality paper, too."

"Why would someone have a photograph like that taken?"

"Well, lots of people have portraits done . . . but I see what you mean."

"There's something about it I can't put my finger on," Banks said. "Somehow, I think it's more than a portrait. I just wondered if you had any ideas."

"Hmm. That look in her eyes. Very intelligent, a bit haughty. I wonder if that was her or the photographer."

"What do you mean?"

"Some photographers really capture a person's essence in their portraits, but some create an image—you know, for pop stars or advertising. I'm just not sure what this is."

"That's it!" Banks slapped the chair arm. "An image. A pose. Why would someone want a photographer to create an image?"

Sandra put the photograph carefully aside on the coffee-table. "For publicity, I suppose."

"Right. That's what was bothering me. It must be a publicity picture of some kind. That gives us a chance of tracking her down."

"You need to find this woman?"

"Yes."

"You'll still have a hell of a job. It could be for anything—modelling, movies, theatre."

Banks shook his head. "Caroline had an interest in theatre, but I get the impression that's more of a recent passion. Still, she could be an actress. She's attractive, yes, but she's no model. You said it yourself—look at the intelligence, the arrogance in that tilt of the head and the eyes. And Veronica Shildon said the woman wrote poetry."

"A book jacket?"

"Those are the lines I was thinking along. It could be a publicity still for an author's tour or something. That should narrow things down a bit. We can check with publishers and theatrical agents." Banks paused for a moment, then went on. "Speaking of Caroline Hartley, did you ever meet her?"

"I met her a couple of times with the group, when I went for a drink with Marcia after working late in the gallery. But I didn't know her. I never even spoke to her."

"What was your impression?"

"I can only tell you how she acted as part of a group in a pub. She was very beautiful. You couldn't help but notice her smooth complexion and her eyes. Notice and envy." Sandra put her hand to her own cheek, which Banks had always thought of as soft and unblemished. "In looks, she reminded me a bit of that actress who played Juliet in the old film. What's her name? . . . Olivia Hussey. And mostly she was vivacious, sparkling. Though she did seem to have her quiet periods, as if the energy was a bit of a hard act to keep up sometimes."

"Quiet periods?"

"Yes. I just remember her staring into space sometimes, looking a bit lost. Never for long, because there was always somebody wanting to attract her attention, but it was noticeable."

"Did she seem especially close to anyone else in the group?"

"I don't know. She chatted and laughed with them all, but only in a general, friendly way."

"You never saw her arguing with anyone?"

"No."

"Did you know she was a lesbian?"

"Not until you told me. But why would I?"

"I don't know. I just wondered if it was in any way obvious to you."

"No—to both questions."

"Did you ever notice anyone obviously chatting her up?"

Sandra laughed. "Well, most of the men did, yes."

"How did she react?"

"I'd say she played them along nicely. If anything, I'd have said she was a flirt, a bit of a tease, really. But now I know the truth . . ."

"Self-protection, I suppose. What about the women?"

Sandra shook her head. "I didn't notice anything."

"Did James Conran usually turn up for a drink? He's the only one I've met apart from Marcia, the costume manager."

"Usually, yes. He seems like a pleasant fellow. A bit theatrical, highly strung. Drinks a fair bit. I mean, a lot of actors are really shy, aren't they? They have to get themselves tanked up and play parts to express themselves. And he's a bit of a practical joker. Nothing serious, he just likes arranging for someone's drink to be all tonic and no gin, for example, or having the barman tell someone there's none of their favourite pub grub left. I'd say he's a bit of a ladies' man, too. You know, that vulnerable look, the dedicated, suffering artist. He's pretty sure of himself really, I'll bet. He just finds the act useful. And I know for a fact he's been having it off with Olivia."

"Olivia who?"

"I don't know her real name. The actress who's playing Olivia. They had a bit of a tiff in the pub one night, in the corridor that leads to the toilets, and I happened to overhear them arguing. She seemed to think now he'd got what he wanted he wasn't interested any more, and she told him that was fine with her, because she hadn't liked it much anyway."

"When was this?"

"Quite early on in rehearsals. I can't remember exactly. Mid-November, maybe?"

"Did he ever make a pass at you?"

"No. He knew I was married to a tough detective who'd beat him to a pulp if he did."

Banks laughed. "What about Caroline?"

"You mean did he come on to her?"

"Yes."

"Well, he contrived to sit next to her often enough and arrange for the occasional bit of accidental body contact. I'd say he was putting the moves on her, yes."

No wonder Conran had been so tetchy when Banks had asked about his relationship with Caroline. People often denied their true relationships with victims, especially with murder victims.

"How did she react?" he asked.

"She pretended she didn't notice, but she was always polite and friendly towards him. After all, he *is* the director."

"I should hardly think directors of local amateur dramatic societies have casting couches."

"No, but they could make a person's life difficult if they wanted."

"I suppose so. What about this Olivia? Might she have had good reason to resent Caroline's presence?"

"Not that I noticed. Look, Alan, do you think you could pack it in for a while? It's Christmas Eve. I'm not used to being interrogated in my own home. You know I'm glad to be of help whenever I can, but I didn't know Caroline Hartley was going to get herself murdered, so I didn't pay a lot of attention to who she did or didn't talk to."

Banks scratched his head. "Sorry love. I can't seem to let it drop, can I? Another drink?"

"Please. I don't mean to be—"

Banks held up his hand. "It's okay. You're right. Not another word."

He brought the drinks and turned out the main lights. All they had left was the light from the Christmas tree, from the fake log in the electric fire and a red candle he lit and placed on the low table. He could hear a monotonous pop song playing upstairs on Brian's portable cassette player.

When he sat down again, he put his arm around Sandra.

"That's more like it," she said.

"Mmm. Tell me something. Do you think you could ever see yourself going to bed with another woman?"

"What do you have in mind? Inviting Jenny Fuller over for a threesome?"

"Unfortunately Jenny's away for Christmas."

Sandra hit him gently on the chest. "Beast."

"No, seriously. Could you?"

Sandra was quiet for a moment. Her dark eyebrows knit together and tiny candle flames burned in her blue eyes. Banks sipped his drink and wished he could have a cigarette. Maybe later, while Sandra was getting ready for bed, he could nip outside in the cold and have a few quick drags. That should soon cure him of the habit.

"Well, hypothetically, the idea doesn't offend me," Sandra said finally. "I mean, it's nothing I think about much, but it doesn't disgust

me. It's hard to explain. I've had crushes, what schoolgirl or schoolboy hasn't, but they never led to anything. I can't say I've thought
about it a lot over the years, but there's something about the idea of
being with another woman that's sort of comforting in a way. It
doesn't feel threatening to me, when I think about it. I'm probably
not making much sense, but I've had a few drinks, and you did ask."

"I think I understand," Banks said.

"Men always like the idea of two women together, don't they? It
excites them."

Banks had to admit that it did, but he didn't know why. So far,
he hadn't allowed himself to picture the sexual side of Veronica's
relationship with Caroline, though he guessed they had been a
passionate couple. And where there's passion, he mused, snuggling
closer to Sandra, there's often likely to be violence, even murder.

III

Susan left the pub shortly after Banks, and as soon as she got home
to the bare, empty flat, she felt dizzy. First she drank a large glass
of water, then she turned on the television and lay down on the
sofa. The picture looked blurred. Suddenly she started to feel horribly depressed and nauseated. She remembered the lies she had
told Banks about going home to Sheffield for Christmas. She
had no intention of going. She would phone and tell her parents
she couldn't make it because she was working on an important
case. A murder. And she would spend the day in her flat doing a
few domestic chores and reading that new American book on
homicide investigation. She had enough food—a tin of spaghetti,
a frozen chicken dinner—so she didn't need to go out and risk
being seen by someone. Because she only lived half a mile or so
from Banks, she would have to be careful.

She had bought and wrapped her presents days ago. She would
try to pay a visit home next week or early in the new year.
Somehow, it was easier on non-festive occasions. The forced enjoy-
ment of the season only exacerbated her discomfort. For the same
reason, she had always hated and avoided New Year's Eve parties.

The TV picture still looked blurred. When she closed her eyes, the world spun around and seemed to pull her into a swirling vortex that made her stomach heave. She opened her eyes again quickly. She felt sick but didn't want to get up. The third time she tried, her thoughts settled down and she fell into an uneasy sleep.

In her dream she moved into a room like the one Gary Hartley lived in, and she called it home. A high-ceilinged, dark, cold place crumbling around her as she stood there. And when she looked at the far wall it wasn't a wall at all but a mesh of cobwebs beyond which more ruined rooms with dusty floorboards and walls of flaking plaster stretched to infinity. When she went over to investigate, a huge fat spider dropped from the ceiling and hung inches from her nose. It seemed to be grinning at her.

Susan's own scream woke her. As soon as she came to consciousness she realized that she had been struggling for some time to get out of the nightmare. Her clothes were mussed up and a film of cold sweat covered her brow. Frantically, she looked around her at the room. It was the same, thank God. Dull, empty, characterless, but the same.

She staggered to the kitchen and splashed her face with cold water. Too much to drink. That Old Peculier was powerful stuff. And Richmond had insisted on buying her a brandy and Babycham. No wonder she felt the way she did. She cursed herself for the fool she was and prayed to God she hadn't made an idiot of herself in front of the others.

She looked at her watch: seven o'clock. Her head felt a little clearer now, despite the dull ache behind her eyes.

She couldn't shake the dream, though, or the sense of panic it had caused in her. She made tea, paced about the room while the kettle boiled, switched TV channels; then, suddenly, she knew she had to do something about her bare, joyless flat. She couldn't go home, but neither could she spend Christmas Day in such a miserable place. The visit to Gary Hartley had shaken her up even more than she'd realized.

Panicking that it might be too late, she looked at her watch again. Twenty to eight. Surely some places in the shopping centre would be staying open extra hours tonight? Every year, Christmas seemed to get more and more commercial. They wouldn't miss a business opportunity like Christmas Eve, all those last-minute, desperate shoppers, guilty because they've forgotten someone. Susan hadn't forgotten anyone except herself. She grabbed her coat and dashed for the door. Still time. There had to be.

FIVE

I

Christmas Day in the Banks household passed the way Christmas Days usually pass for small families: plenty of noisy excitement and too much to eat and drink. Downstairs at nine o'clock—a great improvement over the ridiculously early hours they had woken up on Christmas mornings past—Brian and Tracy opened their presents while Sandra and Banks sipped champagne and orange juice and opened theirs. Outside, framed in the bay window, fresh snow hung heavy on the roofs and eaves of the opposite houses and formed a thick, unmarked carpet across street and lawns alike.

Banks and Sandra were happy with their presents—mostly clothes, book or record tokens and the inevitable aftershave, perfume and chocolates. Brian quickly disappeared upstairs with his guitar, and Tracy spent an hour in the bathroom preparing herself for dinner.

Gristhorpe arrived about noon. They ate at one-thirty, got the dishes out of the way as quickly as possible, then watched the Queen's Message, which Banks found as dull and pointless as ever. The rest of the afternoon the adults spent variously chatting, drinking and dozing. Around tea-time, Banks and Sandra made a few phone calls to their parents and distant friends.

In deference to Gristhorpe's tin ear, Banks refrained from playing music most of the time, but later in the evening, when Brian and Tracy had gone up to their rooms and the three adults sat enjoying the peace, he couldn't restrain himself. Off and on, he had been thinking about Caroline Hartley and was anxious to check out the music. He was sure that it had some connection with the murder. Now he could hold back no longer. He searched through his cassette collection for the Vivaldi he thought he had. There it was: the *Magnificat*, with *Laudate pueri* and *Beatus vir* on the same tape.

First he put on the record that Vic Manson had sent over from forensics. The familiar music, with its stately opening and pure, soaring vocal, disturbed him with the memory of what he had seen in Veronica Shildon's front room three days ago. He could picture again the macabre beauty of the scene: blazing fire, Christmas lights, candles, sheepskin rug, and Caroline Hartley draped on the sofa. The blood had run so thickly down her front that she had looked as if she were wearing a bib, or as if an undergarment had slipped up over her breasts. Carefully, he removed the needle.

"I was enjoying that," Sandra said. "Better than some of the rubbish you play."

"Sorry," Banks said. "Try this."

He put the cassette in the player and waited for the music to start. It was very different. The opening was far more sprightly, reminiscent of "Spring" from *The Four Seasons*.

"What are you after?" Sandra asked.

Banks stopped the tape. "They've got the same title, by the same composer, but they're different."

"Any fool can hear that."

"Even me," Gristhorpe added.

"Claude Ivers was right then," Banks muttered to himself. He could have sworn he had a piece by Vivaldi called *Laudate pueri*, but he hadn't recognized the music he heard at the scene.

The sleeve notes for the record told him very little. He turned to the cassette notes and read through the brief biographical sketch: Vivaldi—affectionately called *"il prete rosso"* because of his flaming red hair—had taken holy orders, but ill health prevented him from working actively as a priest. He had served at the *Pietà*, a kind of orphanage-cum-conservatory for girls in Venice, from 1703 to 1740 and would have been asked to compose sacred music when there was no choirmaster.

The blurb went on, outlining the composer's career and trying to pin down dates of composition. The *Laudate pueri* had probably been written for a funeral at the Pietà. One of its sections—the antiphon, *"Sit nomen Domini"*—revealed the liturgical context as a burial service for very young children. There was more about Vivaldi's setting being hardly solemn enough for a child's funeral, but Banks was no longer paying attention. He went back to the word sheet enclosed in the record sleeve and read through the translation: so few words, so much music.

According to the translator, *"Sit nomen Domini benedictum ex hoc nunc et usque in saeculum"* meant, "Blessed be the name of the Lord; from henceforth now and for ever." What that had to do with funerals or children Banks had no idea. He realized he didn't know enough about the liturgy. He would have to talk to a churchman if he really wanted to discover the true relevance of the music.

The main point, however, was that what Banks now knew about the music tied in with the information he had got from Glendenning's post-mortem. Caroline Hartley had given birth to a child. According to Banks's theories so far, this had either been the reason for her flight to London or it had occurred while she had been there. Another chat with Veronica Shildon might clear that up.

Where was the child? What had happened to it? And who was the father? Perhaps if he could answer some of those questions he would know where to begin.

As far as musical knowledge went, Claude Ivers certainly seemed the most likely candidate to have brought the record. Already Banks was far from satisfied with his account of himself. Naturally, Ivers would deny having called at Veronica's house on the night of the murder; he was known to have a grudge against Caroline Hartley. But he must have realized he had left the record. Why take such a risk? Surely he must understand that the police would have ways of finding out who had bought the record, even if there was no gift tag on the wrapping? Or did he? Like many geniuses, his connection with the practical realities of life was probably tenuous. And Ivers couldn't have had anything to do with Caroline Hartley's baby unless they had known one another some time ago. Very unlikely.

"Put some carols on," Sandra said, "and stop sitting on the floor there staring into space."

"What? Oh, sorry." Banks snapped out of it and got up to freshen the drinks. He searched through the pile of records and tapes for something suitable. Kathleen Battle? Yes, that would do nicely. But even as "O Little Town of Bethlehem" began, his mind was on Vivaldi's requiem for a dead child, Caroline Hartley's baby and the photograph of Ruth, the mystery woman; Christmas or not, Veronica Shildon was going to get another visit very soon. He went into the hall, took his cigarettes and lighter from his jacket pocket and slipped quietly out into the backyard for a peaceful smoke.

II

"Veronica Shildon, this is Detective Constable Susan Gay."

It was an embarrassing introduction, but it had to be made. Banks was well aware of the modern meaning of "gay," but he was no more responsible for the word's diminishment than he was for Susan's surname.

Banks noticed the ironic smile flit across Veronica's lips and saw Susan give a long-suffering smile in return—something she would never have done in other circumstances.

Veronica stretched out her hand. "Good to meet you. Please sit down." She sat opposite them, back straight, legs crossed, hands folded in her lap. The excessive formality of her body language seemed at odds with the casual slacks and grey sweatshirt she was wearing. She offered them some sherry, which they accepted, and when she went to fetch it she walked as if she'd put in a lot of time carrying library books on her head.

Finally, when they all had their glasses to hide behind, Veronica seemed ready for questions. Starting gently, Banks first asked her about the furniture, whether she wanted the sofa cushions and the rug back. She said no, she never wished to see them again. She was going to redecorate the room completely, and as soon as the holidays were over and the shops had reopened, she was going to buy a new suite and carpet.

"How are you managing with the flower shop?" he asked.

"I have a very trustworthy assistant, Patricia. She'll take care of things until I feel ready again."

"Did Caroline ever have anything to do with your business? The shop, your partner . . . ?"

Veronica shook her head. "David, my partner, lives in Newcastle and rarely comes here. He was a friend of Claude's, one of the few that stuck with me when . . . Anyway, he regards the shop more as an investment than anything else."

"And Patricia?"

"She's only eighteen. I assume she has her own circle of friends."

Banks nodded and sipped some sherry, then he slipped the signed photograph from his briefcase.

"Are you sure you can't tell me any more about this woman?"

Veronica looked at the photograph again. "It was something personal to Caroline," she answered. "I never pried. There were parts of her she kept hidden. I could accept that. All I know is that her name was Ruth and she wrote poetry."

"Where does she live?"

"I've no idea, but Caroline lived in London for some years before she came up here."

"And you've never met this Ruth, never seen her?"

"No."

Banks bent to slip the photograph back into his briefcase and said casually, before he had even sat up to face her again, "Did you know that Caroline had a conviction for soliciting?"

"Soliciting? I . . . I . . . ." Veronica paled and looked away at the wall so they couldn't see her eyes. "No," she whispered.

"Is there anything at all you can tell us about Caroline's life in London?"

Veronica regained her composure. She sipped some sherry and faced them again. "No."

Banks ran his hand through his cropped black hair. "Come on, Ms Shildon," he said. "You lived with her for two years. She must have talked about her past. As I understand it, you were undergoing therapy. Caroline too. Do you seriously expect me to believe that two people digging into their psyches like that never spoke to one another about important things?"

Veronica sat up even straighter and gave Banks a look as cold and grey as the North Sea. "Believe what you want, Chief Inspector. I've told you what I know. Caroline lived in London for a number of years. She didn't have a very happy time there. What she was working through in analysis was private."

"How was she when you met her?"

"When I . . . ?"

"When you first met."

"I've told you. She was living with Nancy Wood. She seemed happy enough. It wasn't a . . . it was just a casual relationship. They shared a flat, I believe, but there was no deep commitment. What else can I say?"

"Was she more, or less, disturbed back then than she has been lately?"

"Oh, more. Definitely more. As I said, she seemed happy enough. At least on the surface. But she had some terrible problems to wrestle with."

"What problems?"

"Personal ones. Psychological problems, like the ones we all have. Haven't you read the poem: 'They fuck you up, your mum and dad. / They don't mean to, but they do.'" She reddened when she'd finished, as if just realizing there had been a four-letter word in the literary quotation. "Philip Larkin."

Banks, who had heard from Susan all about the Hartley home, could certainly believe that. He knew something about Larkin's poetry, too, through Gristhorpe and a recent Channel Four special, and made a mental note to have another look at the poem later.

"But she was making progress?" he asked.

"Yes. Slowly, she was becoming whole. The scars don't go away, but you recognize them and learn to live with them. The better you understand why you are what you are, the more you're able to alter destructive patterns of behaviour." She managed a wry smile at herself. "I'm sorry if I sound like a commercial for my therapist, but you did ask."

"Was anything bothering her lately? Was she especially upset about anything?"

Veronica thought for a moment and drank more sherry. Banks was coming to see this as a signal of a forthcoming lie or evasion.

"Quite the opposite," Veronica said finally. "As I told you, she was making great progress with regard to her personal problems. Our life together was very happy. And she was excited about the play. It was only a small part, but the director led her to believe there would be better ones to follow. I don't know if Mr Conran was leading her to expect too much, but from what she told me, he seemed convinced of her talent."

"Did you ever meet James Conran?"

"No. Caroline told me all this."

"Did she ever tell you that he fancied her?"

Veronica smiled. "She said he chatted her up a lot. I think she knew he found her attractive and felt she could use it."

"That's a bit cold-blooded, isn't it?"

"Depends on your point of view."

"How far was she willing to go?"

Veronica put her glass down. "Look, Chief Inspector. I don't mind answering your questions when they're relevant, but I don't see how speaking or implying ill of the dead is going to help you at all."

Banks leaned forward. "Now you listen to me for a moment, Ms Shildon. We're looking for the person who killed your companion. At the moment we've no idea who this person might be. If Caroline did *anything* that might have led to her death, we need to know, whether it reflects well or badly on her. Now how far was she willing to go with James Conran?"

Veronica, pale and stiff, remained silent a while. When she spoke, it was in a quiet, tired voice. "It was only an amateur dramatic society," she said. "The way you speak, anyone would think we were talking about a movie role. Caroline could flirt and flatter men's egos easily enough, but that's as far as she'd go. She wasn't mercenary or cold."

"But she did lead men on?"

"It was part of her way of dealing with them. If they were willing to be led . . ."

"She didn't sleep with them?"

"No. And I would have known, believe me."

"So everything seemed to be going well for Caroline. There was nothing to worry or upset her?"

Again, the hesitation, the lady-like sip of sherry. "No."

"It's best not to hold anything back," he said. "I've already told you, you can't have any idea what information might be valuable in an investigation like this. Leave decisions like that to us."

Veronica looked directly at him. He could see courage, pain and stubborn evasion in her eyes. He let the silence stretch, then gave Susan, who had been busy taking notes, a discreet signal to go ahead.

"Veronica," Susan asked softly, "did you know about Caroline's baby?"

This time the reaction was unmistakably honest. She almost spilled her sherry and her eyes widened. "What?"

Veronica Shildon certainly hadn't known about Caroline's baby, and the fact that she hadn't known surprised her. Which meant, Banks deduced, that she probably *did* know a lot more about Caroline than she was willing to let on.

"Caroline had a baby some years ago," Susan went on. "We can't say exactly when, but we were hoping you might be able to help."

Veronica was able only to shake her head in disbelief.

"We're assuming she had it in London," Banks said. "That's why anything you can tell us about Caroline's life there would be a great help."

"A baby," Veronica echoed. "Caroline? She never said a word . . ."

"It's true," Susan said.

"But what happened to it? Where is it?"

"That's what we'd like to know," Banks said. "Did you know that music, the *Laudate pueri*, was used at burial services for children?"

Veronica looked at him as if she didn't understand. Her thin, straight lips pressed tight together and a frown spread over her brow from a deep V at the top of her nose. "What does that have to do with it?" she asked.

"Maybe nothing. But someone put that record on and made sure it was going to stay on. You say it wasn't yours, so someone must have brought it. Perhaps the killer. You said you like classical music?"

"Of course. I could hardly have lived with Claude for ten years if I didn't, could I?"

Banks shrugged. "I don't know. People make the strangest sacrifices for comfort and security."

"I might have sacrificed my independence and my pride, Chief Inspector, but my love for music wasn't feigned, I assure you. I did then and still do enjoy all kinds of classical music."

"But Caroline didn't."

"What does it matter? I was quite happy to enjoy my records when she was out."

Banks, who had often suffered Sandra's opposition to some of the music he liked, understood that well enough. "Is it," he asked, "the kind of present your husband might have given you?"

"If you're expecting me to implicate Claude in this, I won't do it. We may have separated, but I wish him no harm. Are you trying to suggest that there is some obscure link between this music, the baby and Caroline's death?"

"The link seems obvious enough between the first two," Banks said, "but as for the rest, I don't know. If you'd never seen the record before, someone must have brought it over that evening. It would help a lot if we knew who the father of Caroline's child was."

Veronica shook her head slowly. "I didn't know. I really didn't know. About the baby, I mean."

"Does it surprise you to discover that Caroline wasn't exclusively lesbian?"

"No, it's not that. After all, I've hardly been exclusively so myself, have I? Most people aren't. Most people like us." She tilted her head back and fixed him with a cool, grey look. "It might interest you to know, Chief Inspector, just for the record, that I'm not ashamed of what I am, and neither was Caroline. But we weren't crusaders. We didn't go around holding hands and mauling one another in public. Nor did we proselytize on behalf of groups or causes that seem to think sexual preference is an important issue in everything from ordination as a Church minister to what kind of breakfast cereal one buys. Like most people's sex lives, ours was an intimate and private matter. At least it was until the papers got hold of this story. They soon discovered I was married to Claude, and why we parted, and it hasn't taken them long to guess at the nature of my relationship with Caroline."

"I shouldn't worry too much," Banks offered. "People pay much less attention to the gutter press during the Christmas season. Do you know if Caroline had any affairs while she was living with you? With men or women?"

Veronica fingered the neckline of her sweatshirt. "You're very forthright, aren't you?"

"I sometimes have to be. Can you answer the question?"

Veronica paused, then said, "As far as I know she didn't. And I think I would have known. Of course, she was attractive to men, and she knew it. She dealt with it as best she could."

"What were her feelings about men?"

"Fear, contempt."

"Why?"

Veronica looked down into her glass and almost whispered. "Who can say where something like that starts? I don't know."

"What about you?"

"My feelings towards men?"

"Yes."

"I can't see how that's relevant, Chief Inspector, but I certainly don't hate men. I suppose I fear them somewhat, like Caroline, but perhaps not as much. They threaten me, in a way, but I have no trouble dealing with them in the course of business. Mostly they confuse me. I certainly have no desire ever to live with one again." She had finished her sherry and put the glass down on the low table as though announcing the end of the interview.

"Are you sure she wasn't involved with any members of the cast? Things like that do happen, you know, when people work together."

Veronica shook her head. "All I can say is that she never came home late or stayed out all night."

"Did Caroline's brother ever visit you here?" Susan asked.

"Gary? He hardly left the house as far as I know."

"You never met him?"

"No."

"But did he know where the two of you lived?"

"Of course he did. Caroline told me she gave him the address in case of emergency. She'd drop by every nce in a while to see how things were with her father."

"You never went with her?"

"No. She didn't want me to."

Banks could understand why. "Did anyone know you were going shopping after your therapy session the other evening?" he asked.

"Nobody. At least, I . . . I mean, Caroline knew."

"Apart from Caroline."

"She might have told someone, though I can't think why. I certainly don't announce such domestic trivia to the world at large."

"Of course not. But you might have mentioned it to someone?"

"I might have. In passing."

"But you can't remember to whom?"

"I can't even remember mentioning it to anyone other than Ursula, my therapist. Why is it important?"

"Did your husband know?"

She uncrossed her legs and shifted in her chair. "Claude? Why would he?"

"I don't know. You tell me."

Veronica shook her head. "I told you, I've not seen him for a while. He phoned me yesterday to offer his condolences, but I don't think it would be a good time for us to meet again. Not for a while."

"Tell me, is there any chance that your husband knew Caroline Hartley before you introduced them?"

"What a strange question. No, of course he didn't. How could he, without my knowing?"

Banks shook his head and gestured to Susan that they were about to leave. They stood up.

"Thanks for your time," Banks said at the door. "I hope it wasn't too painful for you."

"Not too much, no. Incomprehensible, perhaps, but the pain was bearable."

Banks smiled. "I told you, it's best to leave the sorting out to us."

She looked away. "Yes."

As he turned, she suddenly touched his arm and he swung around to face her again. "Chief Inspector," she said. "This woman, Ruth. If you do find her, would you tell me? I know it's foolish, but I'd really like to meet her. From what Caroline told me, Ruth had quite an influence on her, on the kind of life she'd begun to make for herself. I'm being honest with you. I know nothing more about her than that."

Banks nodded. "All right, I'll see what I can do. And if you remember anything else, please call me."

She started to say something, but it turned into a quick "Goodbye" and a hastily closed door.

The chill hit them as soon as they walked out into Oakwood Mews. Banks shivered and slipped on his black leather gloves, a Christmas present from Sandra. The sky looked like iron and the pavement was slick with ice.

"Well," Susan said, as they walked carefully down the street, "she didn't have much to tell us, did she?"

"She's holding back. I think she's telling the truth about not knowing the woman in the photograph, but she's holding back about almost everything else. Maybe you could pick up the key from the station and drop in at the Community Centre. Caroline may have left some of her things there, in a locker maybe, or a dressing-table drawer."

Susan nodded. "Do you think we should bring her in to the station and press her a bit harder? I'm sure she knows something. Maybe if we kept at her for a while, wore down her resistance . . . ?"

Banks looked at Susan and saw a smart young woman with earnest blue eyes, tight blonde curls and a slightly snub nose gazing back at him. Good as she is, he thought, she's got a long way to go yet.

"No," he said. "It won't do any good. She's not holding back for reasons of guilt. It's a matter of pride and privacy with her. You might break her, given time, but you'd have to strip her of her dignity to do so, and she doesn't deserve that."

Whether Susan understood or not, Banks didn't really know. She nodded slowly, a puzzled look clouded her eyes, then she shoved her hands deep in the pockets of her navy-blue coat and marched up King Street beside him. The crusted ice crackled and creaked under their winter boots.

III

There were certainly no dressing-rooms at the Community Centre, not even for the lead players; nor were there any lockers. Susan wondered how they would manage when the play opened and they had to wear costumes and make-up. As she nosed around idly, she reflected on her Christmas.

On Christmas morning she had weakened and considered going to Sheffield, but in the end she had phoned and said she couldn't make it because of an important murder investigation. "A murder?" her mother had echoed. "How lurid. Well, dear, if you insist." And that was that. She had spent the day studying and watching the old musicals on television. But at least, she remembered with a smile, she had been in time on Christmas Eve to buy a small tree and a few decorations. At least she had made the flat look a bit more like a home, even if there were still a few things missing.

There was not much else they could do about identifying the three visitors Caroline Hartley had received on the evening of her death until they had more information about the record and the woman in the photograph. They wouldn't get that until the shops and businesses were back into the swing of things again in a day or two. Banks had suggested a second visit to Harrogate for the following day, and though Susan was hardly looking forward to that, she was interested in what Banks would make of the set-up there.

Susan wasn't sure about Veronica Shildon at all, especially now that she had met her. The woman was too stiff and thin-lipped— the kind one could imagine teaching in an exclusive girls' school— and her posh accent and prissy mannerisms stuck in her craw. The idea of the two women in bed together made Susan's flesh crawl.

As she poked around, looking for anything that might have been connected with Caroline, she thought she heard a noise down the hallway. It could have come from anywhere. The backstage area, she had quickly discovered, was a warren of store-rooms and cubby-holes. Slowly, she walked towards the stage entrance and peeked through a fire-door. The lights were on in the auditorium, which seemed odd, but it was silent and she saw no-one. Puzzled, she went to the props room.

Marcia had scrubbed the graffiti from the walls, Susan noticed, leaving only garish smears in places. The trunk of tattered costumes had gone. It was a shame about the vandals, she thought, but there was nothing, really, she could do. As she had told Conran and Marcia, the police had a good idea who the culprits were, but they didn't have the manpower to put a round-the-clock watch on them and could hardly arrest them with no evidence at all. PCs Tolliver and Bradley had had a word with the suspected ringleaders, but the kids were so cool and arrogant they had given nothing away.

Again, Susan thought she heard a noise like something being dragged across a wood floor. She stood still and listened. It stopped, and all she could hear was her own heart beating. Not even a mouse stirred. She shrugged and went on poking about the room. It was no use. She would pick up nothing about Caroline Hartley here by osmosis.

The door creaked open slowly behind her. She turned, ready to defend herself, and saw a uniformed policeman silhouetted in the doorway. What the hell? As far as she knew, they hadn't put a guard inside the place. She couldn't make out who it was; his helmet was too low over his brow and its strap covered his chin. The light behind her in the store-room was too dim to be much help.

He stood with his hands clasped behind his back and bent his knees. "Hello, hello, hello! What have we here?"

It was an assumed voice, she could tell that. Pretentiously deep and portentous. For a moment she didn't know what to do or say. Then he walked into the room and closed the door.

"I'm afraid," he said, "I shall have to ask you to accompany me to the Crooked Billet for a drink, and if you don't come clean there, we'll proceed to Mario's for dinner."

Susan squinted in the poor light and saw that under the ridiculous helmet stood James Conran himself. Out of angry relief, she said, "What the hell are you doing here?"

"I'm sorry," he said, taking off the helmet. "Couldn't resist playing a little joke. I saw you when you peeked into the auditorium. I'd just dropped by to check out some blocking angles from the floor."

"But the uniform," Susan said. "I thought the costumes had all been destroyed."

"This? I found it under the stage with a lot more old stuff. Been there for years. I suppose our previous incarnation must have left it all behind."

Susan laughed. "Do you always dress the part when you ask someone out to dinner?"

Conran smiled shyly. "I'm not the most direct or confident person in the world," he said, unbuttoning the high-collared police jacket. "Especially when I'm talking to an ex-pupil. You may be grown-up now, but you weren't the last time I saw you. Maybe I need a mask to hide behind. But I did mean what I said. Would you consider at least having a drink with me?"

"I don't know." Susan had nothing to do, nowhere to go but home, but she felt she couldn't just say yes. It was partly because he made her feel like that sixteen-year-old schoolgirl with a crush on the teacher again, and partly because he was connected, albeit peripherally, with a case she was working on.

"I think I should arrest you for impersonating a police officer," she said.

He looked disappointed, and a faint flush touched his cheeks. "At least grant the condemned man his last wish, then. Surely you can't be so cruel?"

Still Susan deliberated. She wanted to say yes, but she felt as if a great stone had lodged in her chest and wouldn't let out the air to form the words.

"Some other time, perhaps, then?" Conran said. "When you're not so busy."

"Oh, come on," Susan said, laughing. "I've got time for a quick one at the Crooked Billet at least." To hell with it, she thought. Why not? It was about time she had some fun.

He brightened. "Good. Just a minute then. Let me change back into my civvies."

"One thing first," Susan said. "Did Caroline or any of the cast keep any of their private things here? I can't seem to find any lockers or changing areas."

"We just have to make do with what we have," Conran said. "It's all right at the moment, as we're not bothering with make-up and costumes, but at dress rehearsal and after . . . well, we'll see what we can do about some of those little cubbyholes off the main corridor."

"So there's not likely to be anything?"

"Afraid not. If people brought their handbags or briefcases to rehearsal, we just left them in here while we were on stage. The back door was locked, so nobody could sneak in and steal anything. Don't go away," he said, and backed out of the room.

Susan put her hand over her mouth and laughed when he had gone. How shy and clumsy he seemed. But he did have charm and a sense of humour.

"Right," he said, peeping around the door a couple of minutes later. "Ready."

They left the Community Centre by the back door, locked up and made their way down the alley to York Road. There, midway between the bus station and the pre-Roman site, stood the Crooked Billet. Luckily it wasn't too busy. They found a table by a whitewashed wall adorned with military emblems, and Conran went to fetch the drinks.

Susan watched him. His shirt hung out of the back of his pants, under his sweater, he had rather round shoulders and his hair could have done with a trim at the back. Apart from that he was presentable enough. Slim, though more from lack of proper diet than exercise, she guessed; tall, and if not straight at least endearingly stooped. Very artistic, really. His eyes, she noticed as he came back, were two slightly different shades of blue-grey, one paler than the other. Funny, she had never noticed that at school.

"Here," he said, putting a half of mild in front of her and holding out his pint. "Cheers." They clinked glasses.

"How's the investigation going?" he asked.

Susan told him there was nothing to report on the vandalism. "I'm sorry about Caroline Hartley," she went on. "I noticed how upset you were when the Chief Inspector mentioned her death."

Conran looked down and swirled the beer in his glass. "Yes. As I told you on Christmas Eve, I can't say we were great friends. This was her first role with the company. I hadn't known her very long. Obviously, I didn't know her at all, really. But she was a joy to have around. Such childlike enthusiasm. And what talent! Untrained, but very talented. We've lost an important member of the cast. Not that that's why I was upset. A Maria can easily be replaced."

"But not a Caroline Hartley?"

He shook his head. "No."

"Are you sure you weren't in love with her?"

Conran started as if he'd been stung. "What? What on earth makes you ask that?"

"I don't know," Susan said. And she didn't. The question had just risen, unbidden, to her lips. "Just that everyone says she was so attractive. After all, you are a bachelor, aren't you?"

He smiled. "Yes. I'm sorry. It's just that, well, here we are, having a drink together for the first time—our first date, so to speak—and you ask me if I was in love with another woman. Don't you think that's a bit odd?"

"Maybe. But were you?"

Conran smiled from the corner of his mouth and looked at her. "You're very persistent. I'd guess that's something to do with your job. One day you must tell me all about it, all about your last ten years, why you joined the police."

"And the answer to my question?"

He held his hands out, as if for handcuffs, and said in a Cockney voice, "All right, all right, guv! Enough's enough! I'll come clean."

The people at the next table looked over. Susan felt embarrassed, but she couldn't help smiling. She leaned forward and put her elbows on the table. "Well?" she whispered.

"I suppose every man's a little bit in love with every beautiful woman," Conran said quietly.

Susan blushed and reached for her drink. She didn't consider herself beautiful, but did he mean to imply that she was? "That's a very evasive answer," she said. "And besides, it sounds like a quote."

Conran grinned. "But it's true, isn't it? Depending on one's sexual preference, I suppose."

"I think it's disgusting, the way she lived," Susan said. "It's abnormal. Not that I mean to speak ill of the dead," she blustered on, reddening, "but the thought of it gives me the creeps."

"Well, that was her business," Conran said.

"But don't you think it's perverted?"

"I can think of worse things to be."

"I suppose so," Susan said, feeling she'd let too much out. What was wrong with her? She had been so hesitant about going out with him in the first place, and now here she was, exposing her fears. And to him, of all people. Surely, being in the arts, he must have come across all kinds of perverts. But she hadn't been able to help herself. The image of the two women in bed together still tormented her. And it was especially vivid as she had just come from talking to the cool, elegant Veronica Shildon. Slow down, Susan, she warned herself.

"Do you have any idea who the killer is?" Conran asked.

Susan shook her head.

"And what about your boss?"

"I'm never sure I know what he thinks," Susan said. She laughed. "He's an odd one is Chief Inspector Banks. I sometimes wonder how he gets the job done at all. He likes to take his time, and he seems so sensitive to other people and their feelings. Even criminals, I'll bet." She finished her drink.

"You make him sound like a wimp," Conran said, "but I doubt very much that he is."

"Oh no, he's not a wimp. He's . . ."

"Sympathetic?"

"More like empathetic, compassionate. It's hard to explain. It doesn't stop him from wanting to see criminals punished. He can be tough, even cruel, if he has to be. I just get the impression he'd rather do things in the gentlest way."

"You're more of a pragmatist, are you?"

Susan wasn't sure if he was making fun of her or not. It was the same feeling she often had with Philip Richmond. Her eyes narrowed. "I believe in getting the job done, yes. Emotions can get in the way if you let them."

"And you wouldn't?"

"I'd try not to."

"Another drink?" Conran asked.

"Go on, then," she said. "On two conditions."

"What are they?"

"One, I'm buying. Two, no more shop talk. From either of us."

Conran laughed. "It's a deal."

Susan picked up her handbag and went to the bar.

IV

"I've told you," Detective Sergeant Jim Hatchley said to his new wife. "It's not exactly *work*. You ought to know me better than that, lass. Look at it as a night out."

"But what if I didn't want a night out?" Carol argued.

"I'm buying," Hatchley announced, as if that was the end of it.

Carol sighed and opened the door. They were in the car-park at the back of the Lobster Inn, Redburn, about fifteen miles up the coast from their new home in Saltby Bay. The wind from the sea felt as icy as if it had come straight from the Arctic. The night was clear, the stars like bright chips of ice, and beyond the welcoming lights of the pub they could hear the wild crashing and rumbling of the sea. Carol shivered and pulled her scarf tight around her throat as they ran towards the back door.

Inside, the place was as cosy as could be. Christmas decorations hung from beams that looked like pieces of driftwood, smoothed and worn by years of exposure to the sea. The murmur of conversations and the hissing of pumps as pints were pulled were music to Hatchley's ears. Even Carol, he noticed, seemed to mellow a bit once they'd got a drink and a nice corner table.

She unfastened her coat and he couldn't help but look once again at the fine curve of her bosom, which stood out as she took off the coat. Her shoulder-length blonde hair was wavy now, after a perm, and Hatchley relished the memory of seeing it spread out on the pillow beside him that very morning. He couldn't get enough of the voluptuous woman he now called his wife, and she seemed to feel the same way. His misbehaviour at the reception had soon been forgiven.

Carol spotted the way he was looking at her. She blushed, smiled and slapped him on the thigh. "Stop it, Jim."

"I weren't doing anything." His eyes twinkled.

"It's what you were thinking. Anyway, tell me, what did Chief Inspector Banks say?"

Hatchley reached for a cigarette. "There's this bloke called Claude Ivers lives just up the road from here, some sort of high-brow musician, and he parks his car at the back of the pub. Banks wants to know if he took it out at all on the evening of December twenty-second."

"Why can't he find out for himself?"

Hatchley drank some more beer before answering. "He's got other things to do. And it'd be a long way for him to come, especially in nasty weather like this. Besides, he's the boss, he delegates."

"But still, he needn't have asked *you*. He knows we're supposed to be on our honeymoon."

"It's more in the way of a favour, love. I suppose I could've said no."

"But you didn't. You never do say no to a night out in a pub. He knows that."

Hatchley put a hand as big as a ham on her knee. "I thought you'd be used to going with a copper by now, love."

Carol pouted. "I am. It's just . . . oh, drink your pint, you great lummox." She slapped him on the thigh.

Hatchley obliged and they forgot work for the next hour, chatting instead about their plans for the cottage and its small garden. Finally, at about five to eleven, their glasses only half full, Carol said, "There's not a lot of time left, Jim, if you've got that little job to do."

Hatchley looked at his watch. "Plenty of time. Relax, love."

"But it's nearly eleven. You've not even gone up for a refill. That's not like you."

"Trust me."

"Well, you might not want another, though that's a new one on me, but *I* do."

"Fine." Hatchley muttered something about nagging wives and went to the bar. He came back with a pint for himself and a gin and tonic for Carol.

"I hope it's not all going to be like this," she said when he sat down again.

"Like what?"

"Work. Our honeymoon."

"It's a one-off job, I've told you," Hatchley replied. He drained about half his pint in one go. "Hard work, but someone has to do it." He belched and reached for another cigarette.

At about twenty past eleven Carol suggested that if he wasn't going to do anything they should go home. Hatchley told her to look around.

"What do you see?" he asked when she'd looked.

"A pub. What else?"

"Nay, lass, tha'll never make a detective. Look again."

Carol looked again. There were still about a dozen people in the pub, most of them drinking and nobody showing any signs of hurrying.

"What time is it?" Hatchley asked her.

"Nearly half past eleven."

"Any towels over the pumps?"

"What? Oh . . ." She looked. "No. I see what you mean."

"I had a word with young Barraclough, the local lad at Saltby Bay. He's heard about this place and he's told me all about the landlord. Trust me." Hatchley put a sausage finger to the side of his nose and ambled over to the bar.

"Pint of bitter and a gin and tonic, please," he said to the landlord, who refilled the glass without looking up and took Carol's tumbler over to the optic.

"Open late, I see," Hatchley said.

"Aye."

"I do so enjoy a pub with flexible opening hours. Village bobby here?"

The landlord scowled and twitched his head towards the table by the fire.

"That's him?" said Hatchley. "Just the fellow I want to see." He paid the landlord, then went and put the drinks down at their table. "Won't be a minute, love," he said to Carol, and walked over to the table by the fire.

Three men sat there playing cards, all of them in their late forties in varying stages of obesity, baldness or greying hair.

"Police?" Hatchley asked.

One of the men, sturdy, with a broad, flat nose and glassy, fish-like eyes, looked up. "Aye," he said. "What if I am?"

"A minute of your time?" Hatchley gestured to the table where Carol sat nursing her gin and tonic.

The man sighed and shook his head at his mates. "A policeman's lot . . ." he said. They laughed.

"What is it?" he grunted when they'd sat down at Hatchley's table.

"I didn't want to talk in front of your mates," Hatchley began. "Might be a bit embarrassing. Anyways, I take it you're the local bobby?"

"That I am. Constable Kendal, at your service. If you get to the bloody point, that is."

"Aye," said Hatchley, tapping a cigarette on the side of his package. "Well, that's just it. Ciggie?"

"Hmph. Don't mind if I do."

Hatchley gave him a cigarette and lit it for him. "Yon landlord seems a bit of a miserable bugger. I've heard he's a tight-lipped one, too."

"Ollie?" Kendal laughed. "Tight as a Scotsman's sphincter. Why? What's it to you?"

"I'd like to make a little bet with you."

"A bet? I don't get it."

"Let me explain. I'd like to bet you a round of drinks that you can get some information out of him."

Kendal's brow furrowed and his watery eyes seemed to turn into mirrors. He chewed his rubbery lower lip. "Information? What information? What the bloody hell are you talking about?"

Hatchley told him about Ivers and the car. Kendal listened, his expression becoming more and more puzzled. When Hatchley had finished, the constable simply stared at him open-mouthed.

"And by the way," Hatchley added, reaching into his inside pocket for his card. "My name's Hatchley. Detective Sergeant James Hatchley, CID. I've just been posted to your neck of the woods so we'll probably be seeing quite a bit of one another. You might mention to yon Ollie about his licence. Not that I have to remind you, I don't suppose, when it's an offence you've been abetting."

Pale and resigned, Constable Kendal stood up and walked over to the bar. Hatchley sat back, sipped some more beer and grinned.

"What was all that about?" Carol asked.

"Just trying to find out how good the help is around here. Why do a job yourself if you can get someone else to do it for you? There's some blokes, and I've a good idea that landlord is one of them, who'll tell you it's pissing down when the sun's out, just to be contrary."

"And you think he'll talk now?"

"Aye, he'll talk all right. No percentage in not doing, is there?" He ran a hand through his fine, straw-coloured hair. "I've lived in Yorkshire all my life," he said, "and I've still never been able to figure it out. There's some places, some communities, as wide open as a nympho's legs. Friendly. Helpful. And there's others zipped up as tight as a virgin's—sorry, love—and I reckon this is one of them. God help us if anything nasty happens in Redburn."

"Couldn't you just have asked the landlord yourself?"

Hatchley shook his head. "It'll come better from the local bobby, believe me, love. He's got very powerful motivation for doing this. His job. And the landlord's got his licence to think about. Much easier this way. The more highly motivated the seeker, the better the outcome of the search. I read that in a textbook somewhere."

About five minutes later, Kendal plodded back to the table and sat down.

"Well?" said Hatchley.

"He came in to open up at six—they don't go in for that all-day opening here except in season—and he says Ivers's car was gone."

"At six?"

"Thereabouts, aye."

"But he didn't see him go?"

"No. He did see that bird of his drive off, though."

"Oh, aye?"

"Aye. American, she is. Young enough to be his daughter. Has her own car too. Flashy red sportscar. Well, you know these rich folk . . ."

"Tell me about her."

"Ollie says she was getting in her car and driving off just as he came in."

"Which way did she go?"

Kendal looked scornfully at Hatchley and pointed with a callused thumb. "There's only one way out of here, up the bloody hill."

Hatchley scratched his cheek. "Aye, well . . . they haven't issued me my regulation ordnance survey map yet. So let's get this straight. At six o'clock, Ivers's car was already gone and his girl-friend was just getting into hers and driving off. Am I right?"

Kendal nodded.

"Owt else?"

"No." Kendal stood up to leave.

"Just a minute, Constable," Hatchley said. "I won the bet. While you're on your feet I'll have a pint of bitter for myself and a gin and tonic for the missis, if it's no trouble."

SIX

I

"What's Susan up to?" Richmond asked Banks on the way to Harrogate on the afternoon of December 27.

Driving conditions had improved considerably. Most of the main roads had been salted, and for the first time in weeks the sky glowed clear blue and the sun glinted on distant swaths and rolls of snow.

"I've got her chasing down the record," Banks answered. "Some shops might not even bother to reply unless we push them."

"Do you think it'll lead anywhere?"

"It could, but I don't know where. It can't just have been on by accident. It was like some kind of macabre soundtrack. Call it a strong hunch if you like, but there was something bloody odd about it."

"Claude Ivers?"

"Could be. At least we know now he lied to us about being out. We'll talk to him again later. What I want today is a fresh perspective on Caroline Hartley's family background. We've already got Susan's perceptions, now it's time for yours and mine. The old man couldn't have done it, so we'll concentrate on the brother. It sounds like he had plenty of motive, and nobody keeps tabs on his movements. It wouldn't have been hard for him to leave his father to sleep for a couple of hours and slip out. From what Susan said, the old man probably wouldn't have noticed."

"What about transport?"

"Bus. Or train. The services are frequent enough."

They pulled up outside the huge, dark house.

"Bloody hell, it does look spooky, doesn't it?" Richmond said. "He's even got the curtains closed."

They walked up the path through the overgrown garden and knocked at the door. Nobody answered. Banks hammered again, harder. A few seconds later, the door opened slowly and a thin, pale-faced teenager with spiky black hair squinted out at the sharp, cold day. Banks showed his card.

"You can't see Father today," Gary said. "He's ill. The doctor was here."

"It's you we want to talk to," Banks said. "If you don't mind."

Gary Hartley turned his back on them and walked down the hall. He hadn't shut the door, so they exchanged puzzled glances and followed him, closing the door behind them. Not that it made much difference; the place was still freezing.

In the front room, Banks recognized the high ceiling, curlicued corners and old chandelier fixture that Susan had described. He could also see the evidence of what Gary Hartley had done to the place, its ruined grandeur: wainscotting pitted with dart-holes, scratched with obscene graffiti.

Richmond looked stunned. He stood by the door with one hand in his overcoat pocket and the other touching the right side of his moustache, just staring around him. The room was dim, lit only by a standard lamp near the battered green-velvet sofa on which Gary Hartley lay smoking and studiously not looking at his visitors. A small colour television on a table in front of the curtained window was showing the news with the sound turned down. Empty lager cans and wine bottles stood along the front of the stone hearth like rows of soldiers. In places, the carpet had worn through so much that only the crossed threads remained to cover the bare floorboards. The room smelled of stale smoke, beer and unwashed socks.

It must have been beautiful once, Banks thought, but a beauty few could afford. Back in the last century, for every family enjoying the easy life in an elegant Yorkshire mansion like this, there were thousands paying for it, condemned to the misery of starving in cramped hovels packed close to the mills that accounted for their every waking hour.

Banks picked a scuffed, hard-backed chair to sit on and swept a pair of torn jeans to the floor. He managed to light a cigarette with his gloves on. "What did your father do for a living?" he asked Gary.

"He owned a printing business."

"So you're not short of a bob or two?"

Gary laughed and waved his arm in an all-encompassing arc. "As you can see, the fortune dwindles, riches decay."

Where did he get such language? Banks wondered. He had already taken in the remains of an old library in ceiling-high book-cases beside the empty fireplace: beautiful, tooled-leather bindings. Cervantes, Shakespeare, Tolstoy, Dickens. Now he saw a book lying open, face down, beside Gary's sofa. The gold embossed letters on the spine told him it was *Vanity Fair*, something he had always meant to read himself. What looked like a red-wine stain in the shape of South America had ruined the cover. So Gary Hartley drank, smoked, watched television and read the classics. Not much else for him to do, was there? Was he knowledgeable about music, too? Banks saw no signs of a stereo. It was eerie talking to this teenager. He couldn't have been more than a year or so older than Brian, but any other similarity between them ended with the spiky haircut.

"Surely there must be *some* money left?" Banks said.

"Oh, yes. It'll see him to his grave."

"And you?"

He looked surprised. "Me?"

"Yes. When he's gone. Will you have some money left to help you leave here, find a place of your own?"

Gary dropped his cigarette in a lager can. It sizzled. "Never thought about it," he said.

"Is there a will?"

"Not that he's shown me."

"What'll happen to the house?"

"It was for Caroline."

"What do you mean?"

"Dad was going to leave it to Caroline."

Banks leaned forward. "But she deserted him, she left you all. You've been taking care of him by yourself for all these years." At least that was what Susan Gay had told him.

"So what?" Gary got up with curiously jerky movements and took a fresh pack of cigarettes from the mantelpiece. "She was always his favourite, no matter what."

"What now?"

"With her gone, I suppose I'll get it." He looked around the cavernous room, as though the thought horrified him more than anything else, and flopped back down on the sofa.

"Where were you on the evening of December twenty-second?" Richmond asked. He had recovered enough to find himself a chair and take out his notebook.

Gary glanced over at him, a look of scorn on his face. "Just like telly, eh? The old alibi."

"Well?"

"I was here. I'm always here. Or almost always. Sometimes I used to go to school so they didn't get too ratty with me, but it was a waste of time. Since I left, I've got a better education reading those old books. I go to the shops sometimes, just for food and clothes. Then there's haircuts and the bank. That's about it. You'd be surprised how little you have to go out if you don't want to. I can do the whole lot in one morning a week if I'm organized right. Booze is the most important. Get that right and the rest just seems to fall into place."

"What about your friends?" Banks asked. "Don't you ever go out with them?"

"Friends? Those wallies from school? They used to come over sometimes." He pointed to the wainscotting. "As you can see. But they thought I was mad. They just wanted to drink and do damage and when they got bored they didn't come back. Nothing changes much here."

"December twenty-second?" Richmond repeated.

"I told you," Gary said. "I was here."

"Can you prove that?"

"How? You mean witnesses?"

"That would help."

"I probably emptied out the old man's potty. Maybe even changed his sheets if he messed the bed. But he won't remember.

He doesn't know one day from the next. I might even have dropped in at the off-licence for a few cans of lager and some fags, but I can't prove that either."

Every time Gary talked about his father his tone hardened to hatred. Banks could understand that. The kid must be torn in half by his conflicts between duty and desire, responsibility and the need for freedom. He had given in and accepted the yoke, and he must hate both himself for his weakness and his father for making such a demand in the first place. And Caroline, of course. How he must have hated Caroline, though he didn't sound bitter when he spoke of her. Perhaps his hatred had been assuaged by her death and he had allowed himself to feel some simple pity.

"Did you go to Eastvale that evening?" Richmond went on. "Did you call on your sister and lose your temper with her?"

Gary coughed. "You really think I killed her, don't you? That's a laugh. If I was going to I'd have done it a few years ago, when I really found out what she'd lumbered me with, not now."

Five or six years ago, Banks calculated, Gary would have been only twelve or thirteen, perhaps too young for a relatively normal child to commit sororicide—and surely he must have been living a more normal life back then. Also, as Banks had learned over the years, bitterness and resentment could take a long time to reach breaking-point. People nursed grudges and deep-seated animosities for years sometimes before exploding into action. All they needed was the right trigger.

"Did you ever visit Caroline in Eastvale?" Banks asked.

"No. I told you, I hardly go out. Certainly not that far."

"Have you ever met Veronica Shildon?"

"That the lezzie she was shacking up with?"

"Yes."

"No, I haven't."

"But Caroline visited you here?"

He paused. "Sometimes. When she'd come back from London."

"You told the detective constable who visited you a few days ago that you knew nothing of Caroline's life in London. Is that true?"

"Yes."

"So for over five years, when she was between the ages of sixteen and twenty-one, you had no contact."

"Right. Six years, really."

"Did you know she had a baby?"

Gary sniffed. "I knew she was a slut, but I didn't know she had a kid, no."

"She did. Do you know what happened to it? Who the father was?"

"I told you, I didn't even know she'd had one."

He seemed confused by the issue. Banks decided to take his word for the moment.

"Did she ever mention a woman called Ruth to you?"

Gary thought for a moment. "Yeah, some woman who wrote poetry she knew in London."

"Can you remember what she said about her?"

"No. Just that they were friends like, and this Ruth woman had helped her."

"Is that all? Helped her with what?"

"I don't know. Just that she'd helped her."

"What did you think she meant?"

He shrugged. "Maybe took her in off the street or something, helped her with the baby. How should I know?"

"What was her last name?"

"She never mentioned it. Just Ruth."

"Whereabouts in London did she live?"

"I've no idea."

"You're sure there's nothing more you can tell us about her?"

Gary shook his head.

"Do you know anything about music?" Banks asked.

"Can't stand it."

"I mean classical music."

"Any music sounds awful to me."

Another one with a tin ear, Banks thought, just like Superintendent Gristhorpe. But it didn't mean Gary knew nothing about the subject. He read a lot, and could easily have come across the necessary details concerning the Vivaldi piece, perhaps in a biography.

"The last time you saw Caroline," he asked, "did she tell you anything that gave you cause to worry about her, to think she might be in danger, frightened of something?"

Gary appeared to give the question some thought, then he shook his head. "No."

Again, Banks thought he was telling the truth. Just. But there was something on Gary's mind, below the surface, that made his answer seem evasive.

"Is there anything else you want to tell us?"

"Nope."

"Right." Banks nodded to Richmond and they headed for the door. "Don't bother to see us out," Banks said. "We know the way."

Gary didn't reply.

"Jesus Christ," said Richmond when they'd got in the car and turned on the heater. "What a bloody nutcase." He rubbed his hands together.

"You wouldn't think, would you," Banks said, looking at the tall, elegant stone houses, "that behind such a genteel façade you'd find something so twisted."

"Not unless you were a copper," Richmond answered.

Banks laughed. "Time for a pub lunch on the way back," he said, "then you can take a trip to Barnard Castle and I'll see about having a chat with the therapist."

"Rather you than me," Richmond said. "If she's anything like she was when I saw her the other day she'll probably end up convincing you you need therapy yourself—after she's chewed your balls off."

"Who knows, maybe I do need therapy," Banks mused, then turned by the Stray, passed the Royal Baths and headed back towards Eastvale.

II

Ursula Kelly's office was on the second floor of an old building on Castle Hill Road. A back room, it was graced with a superb view over the formal gardens and the river to the eyesore of the East End

Estate and the vale beyond. Not that you could see much today but a uniform shroud of white through which the occasional clump of trees, redbrick street or telegraph pole poked its head.

The waiting room was cramped and chilly, and none of the magazines were to Banks's taste. It wasn't an interview he was looking forward to. He had a great professional resistance to questioning doctors and psychiatrists during a case; much as they were obliged and bound by law, they had never, in his experience, proved useful sources of information. The only one he really trusted was Jenny Fuller, who had helped him out once or twice. As he looked out the window at the snow, he wondered what Jenny would make of Gary Hartley and the whole situation. Pity she was away.

After about ten minutes, Dr Ursula Kelly admitted him to her inner sanctum. She was a severe-looking woman in her early fifties, with grey hair swept back tight and held firm in a bun. The lines of what might once have been a beautiful if harsh face were softened only by the plumpness of middle age. Her eyes, though guarded, couldn't help but twinkle with curiosity and irony. Apart from a few bookcases housing texts and journals, and the desk and couch in the corner, the consulting room was surprisingly bare. Ursula Kelly sat behind the desk with her back to the picture window, and Banks placed himself in front of her. She was wearing a fawn cardigan over her cream blouse, no white coat in evidence.

"What can I do for you, Chief Inspector?" she asked, tapping the eraser of a yellow HB pencil on a sheaf of papers in front of her. She spoke with a faint foreign accent. Austrian, German, Swiss? Banks couldn't quite place it.

"I'm sure you know why I'm here," he said. "My detective sergeant dropped by to see you the other day. Caroline Hartley."

"What about her?"

Banks sighed. It was going to be just as hard as he had expected. Question—answer, question—answer.

"I just wondered if you might be able to tell me a little more than you told him. How long had she been a patient of yours?"

"I had been seeing Caroline for just over three years."

"Is that a long time?"

Ursula Kelly pursed her lips before answering. "It depends. Some people have been coming for ten years or more. I wouldn't call it long, no."

"What was wrong with her?"

The doctor dropped the pencil and leaned back in her chair. She eyed Banks for a long time before answering. "Let's get this clear," she said finally. "I'm not a medical doctor, I'm an analyst, primarily using Jungian methods, if that means anything to you."

"I've heard of Jung."

She raised her eyebrows. "Good. Well, without going into all the ins and outs of it, people don't have to be ill to start seeing me. In the sense that you mean, there was nothing wrong with Caroline Hartley."

"So why did she come? And pay? I'm assuming your services aren't free."

Dr Kelly smiled. "Are yours? She came because she was unhappy and she felt her unhappiness was preventing her from living fully. That is why people come to me."

"And you make them happy?"

She laughed. "Would that it were as easy as that. I do very little, actually, but listen. If the patient makes the connections, they cut so much deeper. The people who consult me generally feel that they are living empty lives, living illusions, if you like. They are aware of what potential they have; they know that life should mean more than it does to them; they know that they are capable of achieving, of feeling more. But they are emotionally numb. So they come for analysis. I'm not a psychiatrist. I don't prescribe drugs. I don't treat schizophrenics or psychotics. I treat people you would perceive as perfectly normal, on the outside."

"And inside?"

"Ah! Aren't we all a mass of contradictions inside? Our parents, whether they mean to or not, bequeath us a lot we'd be better off without."

Banks thought of Gary Hartley and the terrible struggles he had to live with. He also thought of the Philip Larkin poem that Veronica Shildon had quoted.

"Can you tell me anything at all about Caroline Hartley's problems?" he asked. "Anything that might help solve her murder?"

"I understand your concern," Ursula Kelly said, "and believe me, I sympathize with your task, but there is nothing I can tell you."

"Can't or won't?"

"Take it whichever way you wish. But don't think I'm trying to impede your investigation. The things Caroline and I worked on were childhood traumas, often nebulous in the extreme. They could have nothing to do with her death, I assure you. How could the way a child felt about . . . say . . . a lost doll result in her murder twenty years later?"

"Don't you think I'd be the best judge of that, as one professional to another?"

"There is nothing I can tell you. It was her feelings I dealt with. We tried to uncover why she felt the way she did about certain things, what the roots of her fears and insecurities were."

"And what were they?"

She smiled. "Even in ten years, Chief Inspector, we might not have uncovered them all. I can see by the way you're fidgeting you need a cigarette. Please smoke, if you wish. I don't, but it doesn't bother me. Many of my patients feel the need for infantile oral gratification."

Banks ignored the barb and lit up. "I don't suppose I need to remind you," he said, "that the rule of privilege doesn't apply to doctor-patient relationships as it does to those between lawyer and client?"

"It is not a matter of reminding me. I never even thought about it."

"Well, it doesn't. You are, by law, obliged to disclose any information you acquired while practising your profession. If necessary, I could get a court order to make you hand over your files."

"Pah! Do it, then. There is nothing in my files that would interest you very much." She tapped her head. "It is all in here. Look, the women had problems. They came to me. Neither of them hurt anyone. They are not criminals, and they do not have any dangerous psychological disorders. Isn't that what you want to know?"

Banks sighed. "Okay. Can you at least tell me what kind of progress Caroline was making? Was she happy lately? Was anything bothering her?"

"As far as I could tell, she seemed fine. Certainly she wasn't worried about anything. In fact, we'd come to . . ."

"Yes?"

"Let's just say that she'd recently worked through a particularly difficult trauma. They occur from time to time in analysis and they can be painful."

"I don't suppose you'd care to tell me about it?"

"She had confronted one of her demons and won. And people are usually happy when they overcome a major stumbling-block, at least for a while."

"Did she ever talk about her brother, Gary?"

"It's not unusual for patients to talk about their families."

"What did she have to say about him?"

"Nothing of interest to you."

"She treated him very badly. Did she feel no guilt?"

"We all feel guilt, Chief Inspector. Do you not think so?"

"Perhaps *he* should have been your patient. He certainty seems to have his problems, thanks to his sister."

"I don't choose my patients. They choose me."

"Veronica Shildon was a patient of yours, too, wasn't she?"

"Yes. But I can say even less about her. She's still alive."

Judging by how little Ursula Kelly had said about Caroline, Banks knew not to expect very much.

"Was Veronica particularly upset about anything that last session?"

She shook her head. "Your sergeant asked me that, and the answer is the same. No. It was a perfectly normal session as far as I was concerned."

"No sudden traumas?"

"None." She leaned forward and rested her hands on the desk. "Look, Chief Inspector, you might not think I've been very forthcoming. That is your prerogative. In my business you soon become privy to the innermost fears and secrets of the people you deal with, and you get into the habit of keeping them to yourself. You're looking for facts. I don't have any. Even if I did tell you what happened during my sessions with Caroline and Veronica, it wouldn't help you. I deal with a world of shadows, of dreams and nightmares, signs and symbols. What my patients *feel* is the only reality we have to work with. And I have already told you, in all honesty, that as far as I know neither Caroline nor Veronica was in any way especially disturbed of late. If you need to know more, try talking to Veronica herself."

"I already have."

"And?"

"I think she's holding back."

"Well, that is your problem."

Banks pushed his chair back and stood up. "I think you're holding back, too," he said. "Believe me, if I find out that you are and that it's relevant to Caroline's murder, I'll make sure you know about it. You'll need twenty years in analysis to rid yourself of the guilt."

Her jaw muscles clenched and her eyes hardened. "Should that occur, it will be my burden."

Banks walked out and slammed the door behind him. He didn't feel good about his anger and his pathetic threat, but people like Ursula Kelly, with her smug generalizations and pompous, self-righteous air, brought out the worst in him. He took a couple of deep breaths and looked at his watch. Five-thirty. Time to catch the end of rehearsal.

III

Richmond parked his car outside a pub on the main street, got out and sniffed the air. There was no reason, he thought, why it should smell so different up here, but it did have a damper, more acrid quality. Barnard Castle was only twenty or so miles from Eastvale, but it was over the Durham border in Teesdale.

According to his map, the shop should be on his right about half-way down the hill just in front of him. It seemed to be the main tourist street, with an Indian restaurant, coffee-house, bookshop and antique shop all rubbing shoulders with places that sold souvenirs along with walking and camping gear.

The toy shop itself was about half-way down the hill. First,

Richmond looked in the window at the array of goods. Hardly any of them seemed familiar, nothing at all like the toys he had played with as a child. In fact, mostly he had had to use his imagination and pretend that a stick was a sword. It wasn't that his parents had been exceptionally poor, but they had strict priorities, and toys had come very low on the list.

The bell pinged as he entered and a young woman behind the counter looked up from behind a ledger. He guessed her to be in her mid-twenties, and she had a fine head of tangled auburn hair that cascaded over her shoulders and framed an attractive, freckled, oval face. She wore a long, loose cardigan, grey with a maroon pattern, and from what Richmond could see of her above the counter, she seemed to have a slim, shapely figure. A pair of glasses dangled on a chain around her neck, but she didn't put them on as he walked towards her.

"What can I do for you, sir?" she said with a lilting, Geordie accent in a slightly husky voice. "Would it be something for your boy, or your little girl, perhaps?"

Richmond noticed the glint of humour in her eyes. "I'm not married," he said, mentally kicking himself even before he had got the words out. "I mean, I'm not here to buy anything."

She looked at him steadily, fingering the spectacles chain as she did so.

"CID," he said, fumbling for his identification. "I spoke with the manager a couple of days ago, when you were on holiday."

She raised her eyebrows. "Ah, yes. Mr Holbrook told me about you. Tell me, do all policemen dress as well as you do?"

Richmond wondered if she were being sarcastic. He took pride in his dress, certainly. He had the kind of tall, trim, athletic body that clothes looked good on, and he always favoured a suit, white shirt and tie, unlike Banks, who went in for the more casual, rumpled look.

"I'll take that as a compliment," he said finally. "Look, I'm at a bit of a disadvantage. I'm afraid he didn't tell me your name."

She smiled. "It's Rachel, Rachel Pierce. Pleased to meet you." She held out her hand. Richmond shook it. He noticed there was no sign of either a wedding ring or an engagement ring.

She seemed to be laughing at him with her eyes, and it made him feel foolish and disconcerted. How could he question her seriously when she looked at him like that? He remembered his training and aimed for the correct tone.

"Well, Miss Pierce," he opened, "as you may be aware, we are investigating—"

She burst out laughing. Richmond felt himself flush to the tips of his moustache. "What the—?"

She put her hand to her mouth and quietened down. "I'm sorry," she said, seeming more than a little embarrassed herself. "I don't usually giggle. It's just that you seem so stuffy and formal."

"Well, I'm sorry if—"

She waved her hand. "No, no. Don't apologize. It's my fault. I know you have a job to do. It's just that it gets a bit lonely in here after Christmas and I'm afraid that seems to affect my manners. Look," she went on, "it would make this a lot easier for me if you'd let me lock up and make you a cup of tea before we talk. It's near enough closing time already and the only customer I've had all day was a young lad wanting to exchange his Christmas present."

Richmond, encouraged by her friendliness, smiled. "If you're closing anyway," he said, "maybe we could go for a drink and a bite to eat?"

She chewed on her lower lip and looked at him. "All right," she said. "Just give me a minute to make sure everything's secure."

In ten minutes, they were sitting in a cosy pub, Richmond nursing a pint and Rachel sipping rum and coke.

"I'm ready," she said, sitting back and folding her arms. "Grill away, Mr CID."

Richmond smiled. "There's not much to ask, really. You know Charles Cooper?"

"Yes. He's the general manager."

"I understand he's been very busy lately making sure everything was in order for Christmas."

Rachel nodded.

"Do you remember December twenty-second?"

She wrinkled her brow and thought, then said, "Yes. He was here that day sorting out some stock problems. You see, Mr Curtis, the manager, had forgotten to reorder some. . . . But you don't want to hear about that, do you?"

Richmond wasn't too sure. He felt like pinching himself to see if he could escape the way just listening to her voice and watching her animated face made him feel. He tried it—just a little nip at the back of his thigh—but it did no good. He took a deep breath. "How long was he at the shop?" he asked.

"Oh, a couple of hours, perhaps."

"Between what times?"

"He got here about four, or thereabouts, and left at six."

"He left at six o'clock?"

"Yes. You sound surprised. Why?"

"It's nothing." It was, though. Unless he had gone to another branch—and neither Cooper nor his wife had mentioned anything about that—then he had left the shop at six and not got home until eleven. Where the hell had he been, and why had he lied?

"Are you sure he left at six o'clock?" he asked.

"Well, it can't have been much after," Rachel answered. "We closed at seven—extra hours for the holiday period—and he was gone a while before then. He said he'd try to shift some stock over from the Skipton shop before Christmas Eve."

"Did you get the impression he was going to go to Skipton right then?"

"No. They'd be closed, too. Wouldn't be any point, would there?"

"Presumably, if he's general manager, he's got a key?"

"Yes, but he doesn't go carrying boxes of toys around, does he, if he's general manager. He gets some dogsbody to do that."

Richmond fingered his moustache. "Maybe you're right. What was your impression of him? Did you know him well?"

She shook her head. "Not well, no. He'd drop in once in a while. We might have a cup of tea and a chat about how things were going."

"That's all?"

She raised her left eyebrow and squinted her right eye almost shut. "And just what might you mean by that?"

"I'm not sure, really. He didn't make a pass at you or anything?"

"Mr Cooper? Make a pass?" She laughed. "You obviously don't know him."

"So he never did?"

"Never. The thought of it . . ." She laughed again.

"Did he ever talk about things other than business? Personal things."

"No. He kept himself to himself."

"Did you ever hear him mention a woman called Caroline Hartley?"

She shook her head.

"Veronica Shildon?"

"No. He hardly ever even mentioned his own wife, only when I asked after her. I'd met her once or twice at company do's, you see, so it's only polite to ask after her, isn't it?"

"Was there anything odd about him at all?" Richmond asked. "Think. Surely you must have felt or noticed something at some time?"

Rachel frowned. "Look, there *is* something . . . but I don't like to speak out of turn."

"It's not out of turn," Richmond said, leaning forward. "Remember, this is a murder investigation. What is it?"

"Well, I could be wrong. It was just a couple of times, you know."

"What?"

"I think he's a drinker."

"In what way? We're drinking right now."

"I don't know, but not like this. A secret drinker, a problem drinker, whatever you call it."

"What makes you say that?"

"I could smell it on his breath sometimes, early in the day, when he hadn't bothered to take one of those awful breath mints he usually smelled of. And once I saw him take a little flask out of his pocket in the stockroom when he thought I wasn't looking. I can't be sure what it was, of course, but . . ."

Could there be anything in it? Richmond wondered. Rachel Pierce had certainly given him a new perspective on the Coopers, but whether it would lead him to a murderer, he couldn't tell. So the man drank, so he had lied about his alibi—a silly lie, at that, an easy one to check—but it might not mean anything. One thing was certain, though, Banks would want to visit the Coopers again very soon, and he wouldn't be as gentle as he had been on previous occasions.

Richmond looked over at Rachel. Her glass was nearly empty.

"Another?" he asked.

"I shouldn't."

He glanced at his watch. "I think I can say I'm officially off duty now," he said. "Come on, it won't do any harm."

She looked at him a long time. He couldn't fathom the expression on her face. Then she said, "All right, then. Another one."

"Wonderful. There's just one thing I have to do first."

She raised an eyebrow.

"Call my boss," Richmond said. "Don't go away. I won't be a minute."

He glanced back and saw her smiling into her glass as he made for the telephone.

IV

Disguise, I see thou art a wickedness
Wherein the pregnant enemy does much.
How easy it is for the proper false
In women's waxen hearts to set their forms!
Alas, our frailty is the cause, not we,
For such as we are made of such we be.
How will this fadge? My master loves her dearly;
And I (poor monster) fond as much on him;
And she (mistaken) seems to dote on me.
What will become of this? As I am man,
My state is desperate for my master's love.
As I am woman (now alas the day!),
What thriftless sighs shall poor Olivia breathe?
O Time, thou must untangle this, not I;
It is too hard a knot for me t'untie.

"Better, Faith darling, much better! Perhaps just a bit more intro-spection—remember, it *is* a soliloquy—but not too serious." James Conran turned to Banks. "What did you think?"

"I thought she was very good."

"Do you know the play?"

"Yes. Not well. But I know it."

"So you know how it 'fadges' then?"

"They all marry the ones they want and live happily ever after."

Conran stuck a finger in the air. "Ah, not quite, Chief Inspector. Malvolio, remember, ends by vowing revenge on the lot of them for making a fool of him."

All that Banks remembered about the end of *Twelfth Night* was the beautiful song the Clown sang alone when everyone else had walked off to their fates. It was on his Deller Consort tape. "For the rain it raineth every day," the refrain went. It had always seemed a curiously sombre song to end a comedy with. But nothing was black-and-white, especially in Shakespeare's world.

"Perhaps you'd care to see us on opening night," Conran said. "Complimentary tickets, of course."

"Yes, I would. Very much." Accepting free tickets to an amateur production could hardly be called being on the take, Banks thought. "Will you be much longer here?" he asked. "I'd like to talk to some of the cast members. Maybe it would be more comfortable over in the Crooked Billet."

Conran frowned. "What on earth would you want to talk to them about?"

"Police business."

Definitely not pleased, Conran looked at his watch and clapped his hands. The actors walked off stage and went for their coats.

After they had dashed down the alley in the chilly evening, the warmth of the Crooked Billet greeted them like a long lost friend. They unbuttoned their coats and hung them by the door, then pulled two tables together near the fire to accommodate the thirsty thespians. Banks tried to keep track of the introductions and the links between actors and roles. Olivia, played by Teresa Pedmore, and Viola, Faith Green, interested him the most. Marcia Cunningham, the costumes and props manager, was there too. It was a casual and unorthodox method of questioning possible suspects, Banks was aware, but he wanted to get as much of a feel of the troupe as he could before he decided where to go from there.

"I still can't imagine why you want to talk to the cast," Conran complained. "Surely you can't think one of us had anything to do with poor Caroline's death?"

"Don't be so bloody naïve, Mr Conran. There's a chance that anyone who knew her might have done it. Certainly she seemed to know her killer, as there was no sign of forced entry. How long did you stay at the pub the night she died?"

"I don't know. About an hour, I suppose. Maybe a bit longer."

"Until just after seven?"

"About that, yes."

"Then you went home?"

"Yes. I told you."

"There you are, then. You could be lying. You've got no alibi at all."

Conran reddened and his hand tightened on his glass. "Now just wait—"

But Banks ignored Conran completely and went to the bar for another drink. The director certainly seemed jumpy. Banks wondered why. Maybe it was just his artistic temperament.

When he got back to the table, his seat had been taken by a distraught Sir Toby Belch, who seemed to think his part could do with some expansion (perhaps to match his stomach) despite the limitations Shakespeare had imposed.

Banks managed to squeeze himself in between Teresa Pedmore and Faith Green, not a bad place to be at all. Teresa was deep in conversation with the man on her right, so Banks turned to Faith and complimented her on her rendering of Viola's soliloquy. She blushed and replied quickly, her breathy voice pitched quite low.

"Thank you. It's very difficult. I have no formal training. I'm a schoolteacher and I do like to get involved with the plays the department puts on, but . . . It's so difficult doing *Twelfth Night*. I have to remember that I'm really a woman dressed as a man talking about a woman who seems to have fallen in love with me. It's all very strange, a bit perverted really." She put her hand to her mouth and touched Banks's arm. "Oh God, I shouldn't have said that, should I? Not after poor Caroline . . ."

"I'm sure she'd forgive you," Banks said. "Did you have any idea of her sexual inclinations before her death?"

"None at all. None of us did. Not until I read about it in the papers. If you'd asked me, I'd have said she was man-mad."

"Why?"

Faith waved her hand in the air. "Oh, just the way she behaved. She knew how to string a man along. A woman knows about these things. At least, I thought I did."

"But you never actually saw her with a man?"

"Not in the way you mean, no. I'm talking about her general effect, the way she could turn heads."

"Did you notice any personality conflicts among the cast? Especially involving Caroline."

Faith rubbed one of her long blue tear-drop earrings between her finger and thumb. She was probably in her early twenties, Banks thought, with especially beautiful silvery hair hanging in a fringe and straight down to her shoulders. It looked so vibrant and satiny he wanted to reach out and touch it. He was sure sparks would fly out if he did. Her eyes were a little too close together and her lower lip pouted a bit, but the total effect had an interesting kind of unity. Also, as he had noticed on the stage, she was tall and well-formed. It would be difficult, without very good costumes, to conceal the fact that Faith Green was all woman.

She leaned closer to speak to Banks and he smelled her perfume. It was subtle, and probably not cheap. He also smelled the Martini Rossi on her breath.

"I didn't notice anything in particular," she said, flicking her eyes towards the rubicund Sir Toby and Malvolio, who looked like an undertaker's assistant, "but some of the men aren't too keen on Mr Conran."

"Oh? Why's that?"

"I think they're jealous."

"But the women like him?"

"Most of them, yes. And that's partly why the others are jealous. You'd be surprised what shady motives people have for joining in amateur events like this." She widened her eyes and Banks noticed that they were smiling. "S-e-x," she said. "But he's not my type. I like my men dark and handsome." She looked Banks up and down. "Not necessarily tall, mind you. I don't mind being bigger than my boyfriends."

Banks noticed the plural. Surely there had never been school-teachers like this in his time?

"I hear there was something between Mr Conran and Olivia—Teresa, that is."

"You'll have to ask her about that," Faith said. "I'll not tell tales on my friends out of school." She wrinkled her nose.

"Can you tell me anything more about Caroline?"

Faith shrugged. "Not really. I mean, I hardly knew her. She was beautiful in a petite, girlish sort of way, but I can't say she made much of an impression on me. As I said before, I thought she was a bit of a flirt, myself, but I don't suppose she could help the way the men flocked to her."

"Anyone in particular?"

"No, just in general, really. Most of the men seemed to like being with her, including our director."

"Did he make a pass at her?"

"No, he's too subtle for that. He plays the shy and vulnerable one until women approach him, then he reels them in. At least he did with Teresa." She clapped a hand to her mouth. "Look, I *am* telling tales out of school. How do you do it?"

Banks smiled. "Professional secret. So in your opinion, Caroline Hartley was a flirt, but nothing ever came of it?"

"Yes. I suppose that's how she kept them at bay." Faith shook her head and her hair sparked like electricity. "Maybe I was blind, but I'm damned if I could see what she really was."

"What did you think of her as an actress?"

Faith traced a ring around the top of her glass. "She was young, inexperienced. She had a long way to go. And it was only a small part, after all. Young Maggie over there's taken it on now." She nodded towards a serious-looking young woman sitting next to Conran.

"But she was talented?"

"Who am I to say? Perhaps. In time. Look—"

"Did anything odd happen at rehearsal the day Caroline was killed? Does any incident stand out in your mind, however petty it might have seemed at the time?"

"No, not that I remember. Look, will you excuse me for a min? Have to pee."

"Of course."

Banks waited a moment or two, then attracted Teresa Pedmore's attention. Her hair was as dark as Faith's was silver. She had the healthy complexion of a young countrywoman, and it didn't surprise Banks to discover that she was a milkman's daughter from Mortsett, now working in the main Eastvale Post Office and living in town. But that was where her rusticity ended. The haughty tilt of her head when she spoke and her fierce, dark eyes had nothing to do with simple country life. There was an aura of mystery about her; Banks found its source hard to pin down. Something to do with the economy of her body language, perhaps, or the faintly sardonic tone of her voice. And she was ambitious; he could sense that from the start.

"It's about Caroline Hartley, isn't it?" she said before Banks could open his mouth. As she spoke, Banks noticed, she was looking over at James Conran, who was watching her with a frown on his face.

"Yes," Banks answered. "Can you tell me anything about her?"

Teresa shook her head. Coal-black hair danced about her shoulders. "I hardly knew her. Even less so than I thought at the time, according to the papers."

"I understand you were involved with Mr Conran?"

"Who told you that? Faith?"

Banks shook his head. "Faith was subtly evasive. Were you?"

"What if I was? We're both single. James is fun once you get to know him. At least he was."

"And did Caroline Hartley spoil that fun for you?"

"Of course not. How could she?"

"Didn't he switch his attentions from you to her?"

"Look, I don't know who's been telling you all this, but it's rubbish. Or are you just making it up? James and I ended our little fling ages ago."

"So you weren't jealous of Caroline?"

"Not at all."

"How did Caroline behave among the other women in the cast?"

Teresa laughed, showing a set of straight white teeth rarely seen outside America. "I don't know what you're getting at."

"Was she close to anyone?"

"No. I thought she always seemed aloof. You know, friendly but distant. Casual."

"So you didn't like her very much."

"I can't say I cared one way or the other. Not that I'm glad she's . . . you know. This is only the second play the company's done since James took over, but it was Caroline's first. None of us knew her that well."

"How did she get the part?"

Teresa raised her dark, arched eyebrows. "Auditioned, I should think. Like everybody else."

"You didn't notice her form any close attachments to other women in the play?"

"There are only three of us. What are you trying to say, that I'm a lesbian too?"

Banks shifted in his seat. "No. No, I'd say that was very unlikely, wouldn't you?"

Slowly, she relaxed. "Well . . ."

"What about Faith?"

Teresa gave her cigarette a short, sharp flick with her thumbnail. "What did she tell you? I saw you talking to her."

"She told me nothing. That's why I'm asking you."

"There was nothing between them, I can assure you of that. Faith's as straight as I am." She took a breath, sipped some milky Pernod and water, then smiled. "As far as the others go, I don't think you've got much chance of finding a murderer among them, quite frankly. Malvolio's such a puritan prig he probably even whips himself for taking part in such a sinful hobby as acting. Sir Andrew's thick as pigshit—excuse my French—and Orsino's so wrapped up in himself he wouldn't notice if Samantha Fox waggled her boobs in front of his face."

Banks looked over at Orsino. He had muscular shoulders—clearly the fruits of regular weight-training—dark, wavy hair, hollow cheeks, bright eyes and an expression set in a permanent sneer, as if all he saw outside a mirror was unworthy of his regard.

"None of them three had much to do with Caroline anyway, as far as I noticed. They had some scenes together, but I never saw them communicate much off-stage. And you can forget the others, too. I know for a fact that Antonio's queer as a three-pound note, Sebastian's very happily married with a mortgage, a dog and two-point-five kids, and the Clown, well . . . he's very quiet actually, and he never seems to socialize with us."

"Have you ever noticed him talking to Caroline off-stage or between scenes?"

"I've never noticed him talking to anyone. Period. One of the strangest transformations you can imagine. A wonderful Clown, but such a dull, depressing-looking man."

Banks asked her a few more general questions but found out nothing else. Before long, Teresa was asking him about his most exciting cases and it was time to move on. He chatted briefly with some of the others but got no further. Finally, he went back to James Conran, excused himself from the company and walked out into the cold evening, but not before Faith Green managed to catch him at the door and slip him her telephone number.

Outside, Banks caught his breath at the cold. Bright stars stabbed pinpoints of light in the clear sky. Who, Banks wondered, had believed that the sky was just a kind of black-velvet curtain and the light of heaven beyond showed through the holes in it? The Greeks? Anyway, on nights like this it felt exactly that way.

There had been something wrong about his conversations in the Crooked Billet. He couldn't put his finger on it, but everything had seemed too easy, too chummy. Everyone he spoke to had been nervous, worried about something. He hadn't missed the way Faith excused herself before answering one of his questions, nor the way Teresa played with her cigarette when he asked her questions she didn't like. Those two would merit further talking to, definitely. Surely there must have been minor tiffs or conflicts among the cast of a play? According to the people he had talked to, it had all been happy families—much too squeaky clean for his liking. What were they covering up, and when had they decided to do so?

He put his headphones on. In winter they acted as earmuffs, too. The tape he had in was a collection of jazz pieces by the likes of Milhaud, Gershwin and Stravinsky performed by Simon Rattle and the London Sinfonietta. Tracy had bought him it for Christmas, clearly under instructions from Sandra. When Banks switched on the Walkman the erotic clarinet glissando at the opening of Gershwin's *Rhapsody in Blue* almost bowled him over. He turned down the volume and walked on.

The tree was still lit up outside the church in the market square, but there were no carol-singers in evidence this evening. The cobble-stones were icy and he had to step carefully. The blue lamp glowed coldly outside the police station. It was seven o'clock. Just time to drop in and see if any new information had turned up before going home for dinner.

He walked into the bustle of the police station and went straight upstairs to his office. Before he could even shut the door, Susan Gay called after him and entered.

Banks sat down and took his headphones off. "Anything new?"

"I followed up on the record shops," she said breathlessly. "Most of them are open now because they're having Boxing Week sales. Anyway, I've tracked down two copies of that *Luddite poori* thing sold in the past three weeks."

"Good work. Where from?"

"One from a small specialty shop in Skipton and another from the Classical Record Shop in Leeds. But there's more, sir," she went on. "It seemed a long shot, but I asked for a description of the purchaser in both instances?"

"And?"

"The Leeds shop, sir. Before I'd even started he told me who'd bought it. The salesman recognized him."

"Claude Ivers?"

"Yes, sir."

"Well, well, well," Banks said. "So he was lying after all. Why aren't I surprised? You've done a great job, Susan. In fact I think you deserve a day at the seaside tomorrow."

Susan smiled. "Yes, sir. Oh, and DS Richmond phoned from Barnard Castle with a message about Charles Cooper's alibi. It seems things are getting a bit complicated, doesn't it?"

SEVEN

I

A sea-mist clung to the coastline when Banks and Susan arrived in Redburn at eleven o'clock the next morning. Icy roads over the vale and freezing rain on the moors had made driving difficult all the way, and now, as they came down from the land to the sea, the clash of the two elements had produced a fog that reduced visibility to no more than a few yards.

Susan, Banks could tell, was surprised at being chauffeured by a senior officer. But she would soon learn. He preferred his own car because of the stereo and the generous mileage allowance, and he actually enjoyed driving in Yorkshire, even in poor conditions such as these. On the way, he had been listening to *Metamorphosen*, Richard Strauss's haunting string elegy for the bombing of the Munich Hoftheater, and he hadn't spoken much. He didn't know whether Susan liked the music. She had been as silent as he and had spent most of the journey looking out the window, lost in thought.

He parked the car outside the Lobster Inn again, and they made their way up the path to Ivers's cottage. The mist seemed to permeate everything, and by the time they got to the cottage they were glad of the fire blazing in the hearth.

Again it was Patsy Janowski who answered the door. This time, when Banks introduced Detective Constable Gay, her big brown eyes clouded with worry and fixed on the door handle. She was wearing tight jeans and a dark-green turtleneck sweater. Her dark hair, which still fell almost to her eyes in a ragged fringe, was tied back in a pony-tail. Her smooth complexion was tinged with the kind of flush that a brisk walk in fresh weather brings.

"He'll be down in a few minutes," she said. "Sit down and warm yourselves. I'll make some tea."

"Shouldn't we go up, sir?" Susan asked when Patsy had left the room. "It'll give us an edge."

Banks shook his head. "He'll be no trouble. Besides, I want to talk to her alone first." They sat in the creaky wooden chairs near the fire, and Banks rubbed his hands in front of the flames. Although he had been wearing gloves on this trip, the chill seemed to have penetrated right through both leather and flesh. When he felt warm enough, he took off his overcoat and lit a cigarette. Warm air from the fire hooked the smoke and sucked it up the chimney.

Patsy returned with the tea-tray and set it down beside them. There was no fresh-made bread this time.

"What is it?" she asked, joining them by the fire. "Have you found the killer?"

Banks ignored her question and picked up his mug of tea. "Tell me," he asked, "where did you drive to when you left your parking spot behind the Lobster Inn the evening Caroline Hartley was killed?"

Patsy stared at his breast pocket, her eyes wide open and afraid, like a hunted doe's. "I . . . I . . . You can't expect me to remember a particular night just like that. Days are much the same out here."

"I can imagine that, but it was the evening before my last visit. I asked you then, very specifically, where you'd been the night before, and you both told me you'd stayed in. Now I'm asking you again."

Patsy shrugged. "If I said I stayed in, I guess that's what I did."

"But you were seen leaving the car-park."

"It must have been someone else."

"I don't think so. Unless you're in the habit of lending out your car. Where did you go?"

She stirred a spoonful of sugar into her tea and gazed into the steaming mug as she spoke. "I don't remember going anywhere, but I might have gone for a drive early on. I sometimes do that. But I wouldn't have been gone long. There are some beautiful vantage points along the coast, but you have to drive out there, then walk a fair distance to find them."

"Even in this weather?"

"Sure. I'd hardly live here if I minded a bit of rough weather, would I? I like it when the sea gets all churned up."

She seemed to be regaining her composure, but Banks still didn't believe her story. "Why didn't you mention this little drive?" he asked.

She smiled at the fireplace. "It didn't seem important, I guess. I mean, it was nothing to do with what you were asking about."

"Did you go alone?"

She hesitated, then said, "Yes."

"Where was Mr Ivers?"

"Back here, working."

"Then who was using *his* car?"

Her hand went to her mouth. "I . . . I don't understand . . ."

"It's simple, really, Ms Janowski. His car was missing from its usual spot. If he was here working, who was using it?"

Patsy was saved from having to answer by the creak of the stairs as Ivers came down. He was dressed in much the same kind of baggy jeans and loose jersey as he had been on Banks's first visit, but this time he had combed back his longish grey hair. He ducked the low lintel beam and walked into the room, where his height and gaunt features commanded attention. The room had seemed crowded enough with three people in it, but with four it felt cluttered and claustrophobic.

"What's going on?" he asked, looking over at Patsy, who was squeezing her plump lower lip between her fingers and staring out the window.

Banks stood up. "Ah, Mr Ivers. Please join us. Sit down."

"I hardly need to be invited to sit down in my own house," Ivers said, but he sat.

Banks lit another cigarette and leaned against the stone mantelpiece. Not a tall man himself, he wanted the advantage of height. Susan remained where she was, notebook in her lap. Ivers glanced nervously at her, but Banks didn't introduce them.

"We were just talking about memory," he said. "How deceptive it can be."

Ivers frowned. "I don't understand."

"Seems to be a lot of that about," Banks said.

"Mr Ivers," Susan asked, "where did you drive to on the evening of December twenty-second?"

He stared at her but didn't appear to see her, then he turned towards Banks and gripped the arms of his chair. He thrust himself forward in as menacing a manner as possible. "What is this? What are you insinuating?"

Banks flicked a column of ash into the fire. "I'm just asking you a simple question," he said. "Where did you go?"

"I told you I didn't go anywhere."

"I know. But you were lying."

Ivers half rose. "Now look—"

Banks stepped forward and gently pushed him back. "No. You look. Let me save us all a lot of time and effort and tell you what happened."

Ivers settled back and fumbled for his pipe and tobacco in his pants pocket. Patsy poured him some tea and passed it over. Her hand was shaking. The corner of his thin mouth twitched for her in what was meant to be a reassuring smile.

"That evening," Banks began, "you decided to take Veronica her Christmas present. It was a record you bought for her at the Classical Record Shop in the Merrion Centre in Leeds, Vivaldi's *Laudate pueri*, sung by Magda Kalmár, a singer you knew had impressed her. But when you got to the house, just after seven, say, she was out. Caroline Hartley answered the door and let you in. You were simply going to drop off the present, but something happened, something made you angry. Perhaps she said something about your virility, I don't know, or maybe the rage you felt about her stealing Veronica from you finally boiled over. You fought, hit her, then stabbed her with the kitchen knife you found on the table."

"Ingenious," Ivers said. "But not a word of it is true."

Banks knew full well that his theory was full of holes—the two female visitors Caroline Hartley had received *after* Ivers had apparently left, for example—but he went on regardless. He wanted to shake Ivers up a bit, at the very least.

"I don't know why you put the record on, but you did. Perhaps you wanted to make it look like the work of a psychopath. That could also have been why you removed her robe after you hit her. Anyway, when it was done, you washed the knife in the sink. I imagine you must have got blood on your gloves and sleeves, but it would have been easy enough to destroy that evidence when you got home." Banks flicked his cigarette end into the fire. "Right there."

Ivers shook his head and clamped his teeth down on his pipe.

"Well?" Banks said.

"No," he whispered between clenched teeth. "It didn't happen like that at all. I didn't kill her."

"Did you know that Caroline Hartley once had a baby?" Banks asked.

Ivers took his pipe out of his mouth in surprise. "What? No. All I know is that she was the bitch who corrupted my wife and induced her to leave me."

"Which gives you a very good motive for wanting rid of her," Susan said, looking up from her notebook.

Again Ivers looked at her but hardly appeared to see her.

"Perhaps so," he said. "But I'm not a killer. I create, I don't destroy."

Patsy leaned forward and took his hand in hers. With his other hand, he held onto his pipe.

"What happened?" Banks asked.

Ivers sighed and stood up. He stroked Patsy's cheek and went to the fireplace where he knocked out his pipe. He seemed more stooped and frail now, somehow, and his cultured voice no longer held its authoritative tone.

"You're right," he said, "I did go over to Eastvale that evening. I shouldn't have lied. I should have told you the truth. But when you told me what had happened, I was certain I'd be a suspect, and I was right, wasn't I? I couldn't bear the thought of any serious interruption of my work. But I swear, Chief Inspector, that when I left Caroline Hartley the little slut was as alive as you and I. Yes, I went to the house. Yes, Veronica was out shopping. Caroline let me in grudgingly, but she let me in because it was cold and snowing and she didn't want to leave the door open. I wasn't in there more than a few minutes. Out of politeness, I asked how she was and asked about Veronica, then I just handed over the present and left. And that's the truth, whether you believe it or not."

"I'd find it easier to believe if you'd told me the first time I called," Banks said. "You've wasted a lot of our time."

"I've already explained why I couldn't tell you. Good lord, man, what would you have done in my position?"

Banks always hated it when people asked him that. In ninety-nine percent of cases he would have done exactly as they had: the wrong thing.

"How could you even imagine that we wouldn't trace the buyer of the record?"

Ivers shrugged. "I've no idea what you can or can't do. I don't read mystery novels or watch police shows on television. We don't even have a television. Never have had. I knew I hadn't put a gift tag on the record—I remembered I'd forgotten to do that shortly after I left Veronica's—so when you mentioned Vivaldi last time you called I had a good idea you were only guessing it was me. You never asked me outright whether I took her the record or not."

"When you left," Banks said, "was the record still wrapped or had it been opened?"

"Still wrapped, of course. Why should it have been opened?"

"I don't know. But it was. Could Caroline have opened it?"

"She may have done, just to have a laugh at me and my tastes, I suppose. She always said I was an old bore. She once told Veronica she thought my music sounded like the kind of sounds you'd get from a constipated camel."

If Ivers was telling the truth, Banks wondered, then how had the record come to be unwrapped? Unless either Caroline had opened it out of malicious curiosity—"Hello darling, look what the boring old fart's bought you for Christmas!"—or Veronica Shildon herself had returned to the house and opened it? But why would she do that with a Christmas present? Surely she would have put it under the tree with the rest and waited until the morning of the twenty-fifth? And she certainly wouldn't have done anything so mundane if she had walked into the room and found Caroline's body.

"Did you tell her what it was?" Banks asked.

"Not in so many words."

"What did you say?"

"Just that it was something very special for Veronica."

"How did Caroline react?"

"She didn't. She just glanced at it, and I put it down."

"Did you argue with her?"

Ivers shook his head. "Not this time, no. It was cool between us, but civilized. I've told you, I was out again within five minutes."

"What did you do then?"

"I drove over to the shopping centre—I wanted to buy a few last minute things I couldn't get here in the village—then I came home."

"What things?"

Ivers frowned. "Oh, I can't remember. Books, a sweater Patsy wanted, a case of decent claret . . . that kind of thing."

"You didn't by any chance see your wife in the shopping centre, did you?"

"No. I'd have mentioned it if I did. It's a fairly large place, you know, and it was very busy."

"Why did you go to Eastvale that night in particular?"

"Because it was so close to Christmas and Patsy and I . . . well, I always leave things till the last minute, and we just didn't want to have to go anywhere over the next few days. I'm very involved in a complex piece of music right now. It's all to do with the rhythms of the winter sea, so I don't want to spend more time than necessary away from here. I have no other commitments until after the new year, so I thought I'd get the shopping and Veronica's present out of the way, then my time would be my own." He returned to the chair and started to refill his pipe. "Believe me, it's nothing more sinister than that. I haven't killed anyone. I couldn't. Not even someone I hated the way I hated Caroline Hartley. If I'd been stupid enough to believe that killing Caroline would bring back Veronica, I'd have done it two years ago. But I've got a new life now, with Patsy. It's been tough getting here, but I've put Veronica behind me now."

"Yet you still took her a *special* Christmas present. Rather a sentimental gesture, wouldn't you say?"

"I never claimed to have no feelings for her. After so long, you can't help that. She put me through hell, but that's over." He took Patsy's hand. "I'm happier now than I've ever been."

It was the second time Banks had heard someone refer to having a motive for killing Caroline some years ago but not in the present. Ivers's story rang truer than Gary Hartley's, though. In the first place, Ivers obviously did have a comfortable life with an attractive younger woman, a cosy cottage by the sea and his music. Gary Hartley had nothing. On the other hand, Ivers could easily have lost his temper and lashed out at something Caroline said. Sometimes, after all the big things have been endured and overcome, some apparently inconsequential matter sets off an explosion. There was no real evidence pointing either way, though the use of a knife so close to hand indicated a spontaneous act. If he charged Claude Ivers with murder now, he wouldn't have much of a case.

"I'd like you to drop by the Eastvale police station tomorrow morning and sign a statement," Banks said, gesturing for Susan to close her notebook.

"Must I . . . ? My work . . ."

"Much as I love your music, Mr Ivers," Banks said, "I'm afraid you must." He smiled. "Look at it this way, it's a hell of a lot better than being charged with murder and sitting in a cell with the drunks on New Year's Eve."

"You're not charging me?"

"Not yet. But I want you to stay where I can find you. Any unexpected moves on your part will be considered as very suspicious behaviour indeed."

Ivers nodded. "I wasn't going anywhere."

"Good. See you tomorrow then."

Banks and Susan made their way back down the winding path to the car. On their left, only partially obscured by wraiths of mist, the sea lay quiet and the small waves lapped and hissed on the sands. Banks wondered what Ivers's winter sea music would sound like. Something along the lines of Peter Maxwell Davies's Third Symphony perhaps, or the "Sea Interludes" from Britten's *Peter Grimes*? There was certainly a lot of potential in the idea.

They had just reached the road when Banks became aware of a figure running after them. It was Patsy Janowski, and she hadn't even bothered to put an overcoat on. They turned, and she stood facing them, shivering, with her arms wrapped around her chest. "I need to talk to you," she said. "Please. It' really important."

Banks nodded "Go on."

She looked around. "Is there somewhere we can go? I'm freezing."

They were outside the Lobster Inn, and Banks could think of no better place to talk. They went inside and found the lounge almost deserted except for the landlord and a couple of gnarled old men chatting at the bar. The large room was cold and draughty, even by the hearth where they sat. The fire clearly hadn't been lit long and the pub had not yet warmed up.

Banks walked to the bar. The two old men flicked their hooded eyes in his direction and continued talking in low voices, thick with local dialect. The landlord shuffled over and stood in front of Banks drying a glass. He neither spoke nor looked up. Banks found himself marvelling at Jim Hatchley for getting information out of such a taciturn old bugger. One day he'd have to ask Jim how he'd managed it.

He asked for three whiskies and the landlord ambled off without a word. The entire transaction took place in silence. When he got back to the table, Banks found Patsy and Susan Gay huddled around the meagre fire trying to get warm.

"It's not the cold I mind," Patsy was saying, "but the goddamn *chill*. It's so damp it gets right in your bones."

"Where are you from?" Banks asked.

"Huntington Beach, California."

"Warm there?"

Patsy managed a smile. "All year round. They even play beach volley-ball in winter. Don't get me wrong, though. I love England, even the weather. I'm just not dressed right for outdoors today."

Banks passed her the whisky. "Here. This should warm the cockles of your heart, as we say up here."

"Thank you." She took a sip and smacked her lips. Her eyes ranged around the pub and settled briefly, like a butterfly, on various objects: a dented ashtray, the range of wine glasses above the bar, an optic, the old fishing print on the far wall.

Banks lit a cigarette and leaned back in his chair. "What was it you wanted to tell us?"

Patsy frowned. "I know it must seem too late to you, that we've told so many lies, but Claude was telling the truth just now, honest he was. We only lied because we knew he'd be the main suspect."

"You must have known we'd find out the truth sooner or later."

She shook her head. "Claude said it's only on television that things like that happen. Not in real life. Despite what he says, he *has* seen television in his life. He said policemen in real life are just thick." She put her hand to her mouth. "Oh shit, I'm sorry."

Banks smiled. "Where *did* you drive to that night?"

"Well, that's just what I came out to tell you. I know Claude can't have killed Caroline Hartley because I went to see her after he'd left, and I can assure you she was still alive then."

"What do you mean?"

Patsy rubbed her temple and frowned. "What I say. Look, I know it's not very nice, but I was . . . well, checking up on him."

"You suspected he was still involved with Veronica Shildon?"

"Yes. He still loves her, there's no doubt about that. You heard what he said. But I did hope he really had put her behind him . . . and I know he loves me, too. I suppose I'm just jealous, possessive. I've been burned before by people hung up on past relationships."

"Did you know him when he split up with her?"

"No. We met afterwards. He was in real bad shape."

"In what way?"

"In every way. Claude is a naturally confident man, used to getting what he wants and having his own way, but after he split with Veronica his self-esteem was at rock-bottom. He felt betrayed and . . . well . . . sexually, too, he felt worthless and unwanted. He told me he never thought another woman would want him as long as he lived." She smiled and looked into the fire. "I know it sounds like a come-on, but it wasn't. You have to know him. When we got together I helped him build up his confidence again. There was nothing wrong with him, not really. It was all just the psychological mess caused by what that woman did to him."

"Caroline?"

"No, Veronica. He always blamed Caroline, and I never contradicted him. But if anyone's the bitch, Veronica is, the way she treated him. All of a sudden, she comes along and tells him, 'I'm not really the woman you think I am. In fact, I never have been. It's all been an illusion, an act, just to please you. But I can't do it any more. I've seen the light. I've found someone else—a woman, in fact—and I'm leaving you to go and live with her.' I'm sure you can imagine the impact of something like that on a man better than I can. Especially a man as sensitive and vulnerable as Claude. The bitch! Anyway, he never saw it that way. He always saw Caroline as the enemy, the wife-stealer, and Veronica as the victim. He thought she'd end up getting hurt, discarded, when Caroline had finished with her. After all, there was ten years between them." She held up her hand before anyone could say a word. "All right, I know. I know. I'm nobody to talk. There are nearly thirty years between Claude and me. But that's different."

Nobody challenged her. Banks had almost finished his whisky. He felt like another one. A single shouldn't put him over the limit for driving. This time Susan offered to go buy the drinks.

"What are you trying to say, Ms Janowski?" Banks asked, swirling the amber gold in the bottom of the glass. "That you were jealous of Claude Ivers's relationship with his wife and that you followed him that night to find out if he was still seeing her secretly?"

"I didn't exactly follow him," she said. "You've got to understand how difficult all this has been, Claude and me. We've had one or two rows about his seeing Veronica, usually after he's been for dinner with her and got back late. I don't know . . . as I said, I must be a terribly jealous person, but I couldn't just sit back and accept it. Oh, it's not even as if I thought they were having an affair or anything. Sometimes an emotional attachment to another person can seem like just as much of a threat or betrayal as a sexual one— maybe even more so. Can you understand that?" Banks nodded. Susan came back with the drinks. "Anyway," Patsy went on, "he didn't tell me where he was going that evening, and I figured because of the rows we'd had, he was keeping it from me, you know, that he was going to see *her*. That got me all worried. I just couldn't stay in the house alone, so I decided to call at Veronica's to see if I was right."

"And what happened?"

"I couldn't see his car anywhere. You can't park in the street, of course, but it wasn't even anywhere in sight on King Street. Then I finally plucked up my courage and went to the house. I knocked on the door and Caroline Hartley answered. I didn't think she'd recognize me because we'd hardly met, but she did. She must be very good with faces. She asked me in, but I didn't want to go. I asked her if Claude was in the house and she laughed. She told me he had called but Veronica was out and he clearly hadn't wanted to spend a minute longer than he had to with her. He'd left his present and gone. I thanked her and went back to the car. Then I drove home. That's all."

"What time did you arrive at the house?"

"About a quarter after seven, twenty after, maybe. It took about an hour and a quarter to drive from Redburn, then five minutes or so to walk from where I parked the car."

"Did you see anyone else approaching the house as you left?"

Patsy shook her head. "No, I don't think so. The street was quiet. I . . . I can't really remember. There were a few people in King Street, shoppers. I'm so confused about it."

"Think," Banks said. "Try to rerun the scene in your mind. Let us know if you remember anything at all. It could be important. Will you try?"

Patsy nodded. "All right."

"Was Mr Ivers in when you got home?"

"No. He got back later with the shopping."

"Didn't you ask where he'd been?"

"Yes. We had a row. A bad one. But we made up." She blushed and looked into the fireplace.

Banks lit a cigarette and let a few moments pass, then he asked, "How did Caroline Hartley seem when you saw her?"

Patsy shrugged. "Fine, I guess. I never really thought about it. She was obviously being sarcastic about Claude, but that's only to be expected."

"She didn't seem worried or frightened when she answered the door?"

"Not at all."

"What was she wearing?"

"Some sort of kimono-style bathrobe, as if she'd just come out of the shower or something."

"Could you hear music playing?"

"No."

"Can you remember exactly what she said to you?"

Patsy sipped some whisky and frowned. "Just that he'd been and gone and left some boring classical record for Veronica. That's all."

"She knew what the present was?"

"Seemed to, yes. She didn't mention the title, the one you talked about the other day, but she did use the words 'boring classical record.' I remember that because I took it as an insult to Claude."

"She could have been just guessing," Susan said. "After all, Mr Ivers *is* a classical musician, and he knows Veronica's tastes. He'd hardly be likely to bring her the Rolling Stones or something, would he?"

"Possibly not," Banks said. "Either that, or she'd opened it to see what was so special that she didn't know about. Anyway, it doesn't matter for now." He turned back to Patsy. "What happened next?"

"Nothing. I told you. I left and drove home."

Banks stubbed out his cigarette and looked closely at her. She stared back defiantly, lips close together, eyes serious. "Look," she said, "I know what you're thinking. I didn't kill her. Think about it. I'd hardly do that, would I? With her out of the way there was more chance of my losing Claude back to Veronica, wasn't there?"

It made a kind of sense, but Banks knew that murders are rarely so logically committed. Still, he felt inclined to believe her for the moment. For one thing, her story tallied with what the neighbours had seen: one man—Ivers, obviously—and two women. The one who had simply knocked at the door like a salesperson had been Patsy, then, asking after Ivers. And unless she had returned later, she was in the clear.

So if Patsy was the first woman visitor, and she was telling the truth, then who was the next: Faith Green? Teresa Pedmore? Veronica herself? Ruth, the mystery woman from London? Or had someone called even later than the last woman, someone none of the neighbours had seen? A man? It was possible. Gary Hartley? James Conran? Someone else from the Dramatic Society? The father of Caroline's child? A psychopath? Even Ivers himself could have returned. He hadn't been home when Patsy got back to Redburn. Banks made a note to question the neighbours again and see if he could get a better description. It was unlikely, especially after so much time had elapsed, but still worth a try. At least someone might be able to tell them whether the woman who had knocked at the door and gone away was dressed the same as the one who did go in later.

Banks finished his drink. "Thank you, Ms Janowski," he said. "I think you'd better come along tomorrow with Mr Ivers and make a statement, all right?"

She nodded. "Yes, yes, of course." Then she knocked back the rest of her drink and left.

"What do you think?" Banks asked Susan.

"I don't know. I'd want to keep an eye on them."

"Maybe I'll ask Jim Hatchley to drop by once or twice over the next few days and make sure they're not up to anything. Any ideas about what did happen that night?"

Susan paused, took a delicate sip of whisky, then said, "I've been wondering about Veronica Shildon. I know she doesn't seem to have a motive, but I can't help but keep coming back to her. Maybe everything wasn't as wonderful as she made out between her and Caroline Hartley. I mean, what if she was jealous? What if she saw Patsy Janowski leaving the house and thought there was something to it? Maybe there even *was* something to it. Caroline Hartley could have taken her own robe off, and if Veronica had found her naked . . . She could have charged in, had a row with Caroline and killed her. Then she could have changed her clothes, sneaked out and come back later."

They walked out into the cold and sat in the car while it warmed up. "It's possible," Banks said. "But we checked the entire house for blood-stained clothing and found nothing. There were no pieces of charred cloth in the fire either. I'm not saying she couldn't have found a way, just that I haven't figured it out yet. We seem to have too many suspects. Too many motives, opportunities." He slammed the wheel with the flat of his hand. "I still keep coming back to that damn record, though. Why? Why would somebody put a record on and leave it to repeat?"

"Perhaps Caroline herself put it on."

"She hated classical music. She may have opened it, but I doubt she'd have played it."

"But if Veronica had come back . . . ?"

"If it happened the way you suggest, and she'd seen Patsy leaving, she'd have been on the warpath. She'd hardly have stopped to listen to her Christmas present first, especially on December twenty-second. No. It doesn't make sense." He spoke quietly, almost to himself. "But the music is for the burial of a very small child. Caroline's child could be anything up to nine or ten by now. Maybe if I can track the kid down . . ."

"That's if whoever put the record on knew what it was, knew what it meant."

"Oh, the killer knew all right, I'm sure of that."

"Are you sure you're not making too much of it, sir?"

"I might be. But you've got to admit it's a puzzle."

"Talking about records, sir . . ."

"Yes?"

"Do you think you could play something different on the way back? I don't mean to be rude, sir, but that music you were playing on the way over was so boring it nearly put me to sleep."

Banks laughed and drove off. "Your wish is my command."

II

"Well, well, well, if it isn't Mr Banks. It's a rare treat seeing you in here."

"Sorry, vicar. There's something about my job that disinclines me to believe in a benevolent deity."

"You catch your criminals sometimes, don't you?"

"Yes."

"Well, there you are. The Lord works in mysterious ways."

The Reverend Piers Catcott's eyes twinkled. He was a slight man in his late forties, who looked more like an accountant than a minister: thick spectacles, thinning silver hair, slight stoop and an anemic, well-scrubbed complexion. He was also, Banks had discovered from their discussions and arguments over pints in the Queen's Arms, an extraordinarily erudite and intelligent man. Pity, Banks thought, about the superstition he deemed fit to embrace.

"Still," Catcott said, "I don't think you made the supreme sacrifice of entering this hallowed place just to argue theology, did you?"

Banks smiled. "That's right, vicar. We can do that much better in the pub. No, it's just some background information I want. Knowledge, rather. I want to pick your brains."

"Oh dear, I should think that'll be much more comfortable sitting down. That is if you've no objection to taking a pew. Or we could go into the vestry?"

"A pew'll do fine," Banks said, "as long as you don't expect me to kneel."

The small church was dim and cool. Weak evening sunlight filtered through the stained-glass windows. Banks had seen more of it from the outside than in, though he had been in once or twice to look at the Celtic cross and stone font. The pews creaked as they sat down.

"What's the liturgy?" Banks asked.

"Oh, come on, Mr Banks," Catcott said with a thin-lipped smile. "Surely even a heathen like yourself knows that?"

"Humour me."

Catcott put a pale, slender forefinger to his lips. "Very well. The liturgy. The word is often used to refer to the Book of Common Prayer, of course, but the meaning goes back a long time beyond that, a long time. Essentially, it's simply the order of services in the church. As even you probably know, we have different services at different times of the year—Christmas, Easter, Harvest Festival and the like. And, you might remember from your misspent youth, we sing different hymns and have different lessons according to the nature of the service. Do you follow so far?"

Banks nodded.

"There is a liturgical calendar to cover the year's worship. Advent, the fourth Sunday before Christmas, came first, then Christmas itself, ending with Epiphany, the sixth of January, or twelfth night, to you. Then we have the Pre-Lenten season,

followed by Lent, when you're supposed to give up bad habits—"
Here he paused and cast a narrow-eyed look at Banks, "—and the
last three are Eastertide, Pentecost and Trinity. But what on earth
do you want to know all this for? Surely you're not thinking of—"

"No, I'm not. And believe me, vicar, you'd be better off not
knowing. I'm particularly interested in the music that goes along
with these services."

"Liturgical music? Well, that's a slightly different matter. It's very
complicated. Goes back to Gregorian chant. But basically, each
part of the year has its own biblical texts, and early composers set
these to music. People still do it, of course—Vaughan Williams,
Finzi and Britten did quite a bit—but it's rarely part of a normal
church service these days. What you're probably talking about are
biblical texts, or parts of texts, set to music. Actually, most of them
were abolished in 1563."

"What kind of music are you talking about?"

"All kinds, right from early polyphonic motets. A composer
would take a text, perhaps a psalm, and set it to music. In Latin, of
course."

"Like a *Gloria* or a *Magnificat?*"

"Actually, the *Gloria* is part of the Mass, which has its own
liturgy. I told you, it can get quite complicated."

Banks remembered the section titles from his tapes of masses
and requiems: *Kyrie Eleison, Agnus Dei, Credo.* "I think I'm getting the
idea," he said. "What about *Laudate pueri?*"

"Ah, yes, '*Laudate pueri, Dominum . . .*' It means 'Praise the Lord, ye
children.' That was a popular liturgical work. Based on Psalm 112,
if my memory serves me right."

"Do you know Vivaldi's settings?"

"Indeed I do. Magnificent."

"It says in the notes to my tape that the piece may have been
used as part of the burial service for a small child. Is that right?"

Catcott rubbed his smooth chin. "That would make sense, yes."

"Would that be fairly common knowledge?"

"Well, *you* knew it, didn't you? I'd say any reasonably well-
educated person might have a chance of knowing."

"Would someone like Claude Ivers know?"

"Ivers? Of course. I remember reading an article about him in *Gramophone* and he's extremely knowledgeable about sacred music. Pity he doesn't see fit to write any himself instead of that monotonous stuff he churns out."

Banks smiled. Catcott had sown the seeds of another Queen's Arms argument, but there was no time to pursue the point now.

"Thank you, vicar." Banks stood up and shook hands with Catcott, then headed out. His footsteps echoed on the cold stone. Just before he got to the door he heard the vicar call out from behind him, "The collection box for the restoration fund is to your right."

Banks felt in his pocket for a pound, dropped it in the box and left.

III

Fortunately, Charles Cooper was at home when Banks and Richmond called just after tea-time that day. Mrs Cooper flitted about the kitchen offering coffee, but Banks suggested he and Richmond retire with her husband somewhere private. Mrs Cooper seemed worried by that, but she raised no real objection. They settled for the living room, dominated by a huge television screen, and Richmond took out his notebook.

Cooper, Banks noticed, looked a few years older than his wife. He had a weak chin and a veined nose: his sparse grey hair was combed straight back. He was an odd shape, mostly skin and bone with rounded shoulders, but he had a substantial pot-belly bulging through his grey pullover.

"It's a pleasure to meet you at last," said Cooper. "Of course, I've heard all about the business from my wife. Dreadful."

He seemed nervous and fidgety, Banks thought, though his tone seemed calm and genuine enough.

"What did you do on the evening of December twenty-second?" Banks asked.

"I worked." Cooper said with a sigh. "I seemed to do nothing else around that time."

"I understand you're general manager of a chain of toy shops?"

"That's right."

"And on the twenty-second you were dealing with some stock shortages in the Barnard Castle branch?"

Cooper nodded.

"What time did you leave?"

He paused. "Well, let me see . . . I got home about eleven."

"Yes, but what time did you leave the shop?"

"It's about a half-hour drive, a little slower in the snow. I suppose it'd be about ten-fifteen."

"You left the shop at ten-fifteen and came straight home?"

"Why, yes. Look, is—"

"Are you sure, Mr Cooper?"

Cooper looked towards the sideboard and nervously licked his lips. "I ought to know," he said.

Richmond glanced up from his notes. "It's just that the lady who works there told me you left about six, Mr Cooper. Would she have any reason to lie?"

Cooper looked from Richmond to Banks and back. "I . . . I don't understand."

Banks leaned forward. "It's perfectly simple," he said. "You left the shop at six o'clock, not at ten-fifteen, as you led us to believe. What were you doing all that time?"

Cooper pursed his lips and looked down at the liver-spots on the backs of his hands.

"What was your relationship with Caroline Hartley?" Banks asked.

"What do you mean?" he said. "I didn't have a relationship with her."

"Were you fond of her?"

"I suppose so. We were just acquaintances."

"She didn't remind you of your late daughter, Corinne?"

Cooper turned red. "I don't know who told you that, but it's not true. And you've no right to bring my daughter into it. It's exactly as I said. We were neighbours. Yes, I liked the girl, but that's all."

"You didn't attempt to start an affair with her?"

"Don't be ridiculous! She was young enough to be my . . . Besides, you know as well as I do she wasn't interested in men."

"But you did try?"

"I did no such thing." He grasped the chair arms and started to get up. "I think you ought to leave now."

"We'll leave when we're satisfied, Mr Cooper," Banks said. "Please sit down."

Cooper slumped back in his chair and started twisting his hands in his lap.

"Do have a drink if you want," Banks said. "That *is* what's on your mind, isn't it?"

"Damn you!" Cooper jumped up with surprising agility, took a bottle of Scotch from the sideboard and poured himself three fingers. He didn't offer any to Banks or Richmond. He sat down again and drank off half of it in one gulp.

"We're not satisfied yet, Mr Cooper," Banks said. "We're not satisfied at all. You've been lying to us. Now, that's nothing new. In our business we expect it." He jerked his thumb towards the wall. "But a young woman was brutally murdered next door on December twenty-second, a woman you liked, who reminded you of your daughter. Now I'd think that unless you killed her yourself you'd want to help, you'd want to tell us the truth."

"I didn't kill her, for God's sake. Why on earth would I do that?"

"You tell me."

"I told you, I didn't kill her. And whatever I did that night has no bearing whatsoever on what happened next door."

"Let me be the judge of that."

Cooper swirled his drink and took another long sip.

"We'll stay until you tell us," Banks said. "Unless you'd prefer to get your coat and—"

"All right, all right." Cooper waved his free hand. "I did leave the shop at six, but I wasn't anywhere near Eastvale until eleven, I swear it."

"Where were you?"

"Does it really matter?"

"We have to check."

Cooper got up and poured himself another drink. He cocked his ear towards the living-room door, then, satisfied by the sound of washing-up water running in the kitchen, spoke quietly.

"I drink, Mr Banks," he said. "Simple as that. Ever since Corinne . . . well, you don't need to know about that. But Christine doesn't approve." He looked at his glass. "Oh, she's not a teetotaller or anything. She'll allow the occasional glass of Scotch after dinner, but more than one and I can even smell the disapproval. So I drink elsewhere."

"Where were you drinking that night?" Banks asked.

"Tan Hill," said Cooper. "It's an isolated spot. I like it up there."

"Were you alone?"

"No. There's a group of regulars."

"Names?"

Cooper gave the names and Richmond wrote them down.

"What time did you leave?"

"About ten-thirty. I daren't be *too* late. And I keep some breath mints in the car so she can't smell anything."

"Anything else to tell us?"

Cooper shook his head. "No, nothing. That's it. Look, I'm sorry, I . . . I didn't mean to cause any problems. It's really nothing to do with poor Caroline's death at all."

"We'll see," said Banks, and got up to leave with Richmond.

"There is one small thing," Cooper said before they got to the door.

Banks turned. "Yes?"

"The driving. I mean, I'd had a few drinks. I wasn't drunk, honestly. You won't do anything to my licence, will you?"

"I shouldn't worry about that," Banks said. "I think the statute of limitations has just about run out." He made a mental note to find out the licence number of Cooper's car and alert the local police patrols.

"Fancy a trip to Tan Hill?" Banks asked Richmond outside.

"Tonight?"

"Sooner the better, don't you think?"

Richmond looked at his watch and frowned. "Well, I did have a . . . er—"

"Take her with you," Banks said. "It's a routine enquiry. Won't take long."

Richmond touched his moustache. "Not a bad idea," he said. "Not bad at all."

"Off you go then. I'll see if I can get anything more out of the people over the street."

IV

It was a cold night—spiky, needle-sharp cold rather than the damp, numbing chill of the sea-mist—and the crusts of ice over puddles on the pavements cracked as Banks walked over them, hands deep in his fur-lined car-coat pockets. He decided to call first on Patrick Farlowe, who had originally said he was sure he had noticed two women and a man call at the house on separate occasions between about six- and seven-thirty on December 22.

Farlowe was finishing off his meal when Banks arrived, and there was still a little wine left in the bottle. Banks accepted a glass and the invitation to join Farlowe in the den while his wife cleared the table. They certainly lived well in Oakwood Mews, Banks noted: remains of sirloin steaks on the plates, fine cutlery, a cut-glass vase holding two long-stemmed roses. The wine was a decent Crozes-Hermitage.

The den was an upstairs study with two walls of dark book-cases, a deep, leather armchair by a standard lamp and a small teak table beside it for resting cups of coffee, pencils and notepads. The light gleamed on the dark, varnished surfaces of the wood. The Hartley place in Harrogate would have been a larger version of this, Banks thought, before Gary let it fall to ruin.

Farlowe relaxed in his armchair and Banks took the swivel chair in front of the writing-desk. One sniff of the clean, leather-scented air tipped him off that this was a non-smoking room.

"We're very grateful for the information you gave us," Banks began, "but I was just wondering if you remembered anything else about that evening."

Farlowe, a small, roly-poly man with tufts of grey hair over his ears, still wearing a three-piece suit, pressed his damp lips together and scratched the side of his nose. Finally he shook his head. The roll of pink fat around his neck wobbled. "Can't say as I do, no."

"Do you mind if we go over a couple of points?"

"Not at all. Be pleased to."

Banks sipped some wine and asked about the timing.

Farlowe strained to remember for a moment, then answered. "I know the first one, the man, called at about seven o'clock because we'd just had supper and I was in the front room turning the Christmas-tree lights on. Then I caught a glimpse of the woman standing on the doorstep when I went to replace a burned-out bulb a bit later. The door was open and she was talking to the Hartley woman."

"Did you get a clear look at her?"

"No. She had her back to me. Nicely shaped, though."

"So there's no doubt it was a woman?"

"None at all."

"What was she wearing?"

He put a pudgy finger to his lips and whistled while trying to recall the scene. "Let me see . . . It was a winter jacket of some kind, padded or thickly lined. Waist-length, no longer, because I could see the outline of her hips. That's how I knew it was a woman. A youngish one, I'd say. And she wore tight jeans. Lovely long legs she had." He winked.

"What about her hair?"

"It was wrapped in a scarf. I really couldn't see it at all. And she was silhouetted by the hall light of the house, of course, so I couldn't make out any detail. It was only a quick glimpse I got. I already told all this to your constable the other night."

"I know, and I'm sorry to put you through it again, sir. Sometimes, believe it or not, people do remember more when they're given a few days to think about it. What was Caroline Hartley wearing?"

"As far as I could tell, it was some kind of bathrobe. She held it wrapped tight around her while she stood at the door, as if she was feeling the cold. I'm sorry I can't be of any more help. I'd like to see the blighter caught, of course. Don't like the idea of a murderer stalking the neighbourhood."

"The third visitor," Banks asked. "Can you be clearer about the time?"

"I have given the matter some thought," Farlowe said, reaching for a decanter on the table beside him. "Port?"

Banks tossed back the rest of his wine and held his glass out. "Please. And . . . ?"

"I'm trying to recollect why I was at the front window again, but it's slipped my mind. Perhaps I'd heard a noise or something. . . ." He tapped the side of his head. "That's it! I remember. I heard some music and I went out to see if we had carol-singers in the street. Plagued by them we are." He made them sound like an infestation of rodents. "I consider I've handed out my fair share this year. Should be restricted to Christmas Eve, if you ask me. Anyway, it was only the wife, putting the radio on."

"Do you remember the time?"

"No. All I remember, now I come to think about it, is hearing 'Away in a Manger' and heading for the window. But there was no-one at our door. I noticed a woman going into the house over the street, the house where the woman was murdered."

"Can you add anything to your earlier description?"

"I'm sorry. It all happened so fast. I have to admit, I was rather angry at the thought of more singers and I just caught the figure out of the corner of my eye."

"But you're sure it was a woman?"

"Well, this one was wearing a light coat, belted. I think, because it came in at the waist, right down to mid-calves, and she definitely didn't have any trousers on. I thought I could see the bottom of a dress or skirt, too, as if the coat was just a bit too short to cover the dress. And you could see her legs below that."

"What about height? Any idea?"

"A little taller than the woman who answered the door, Caroline Hartley."

"Hair?"

He shook his head. "Again, her head was covered by a scarf of some kind."

"And this woman definitely entered the house?"

"Oh, yes. She was walking in when I saw her."

"So you didn't notice Caroline Hartley's reaction to seeing her?"

"No, not at all. I didn't even see Caroline that time, just this other woman silhouetted as she walked in the door."

"So Caroline might not have let her in?"

"I suppose that's possible. But there didn't seem anything suspicious about it. She didn't seem to be pushing, and I didn't hear any noise of forced entry or anything like that. It all seemed perfectly normal to me. I try to be a responsible neighbour. If I'd thought there was any trouble I would have called the police."

"Did you see her leave?"

"No. But then I didn't look out the window again. Anybody could have arrived or left between seven-thirty and the time when . . . well, you know . . . and I wouldn't have seen them."

Banks finished his port and stood up. "Thank you for being so co-operative, Mr Farlowe. Also for the port. It was very good."

Farlowe smiled. "Yes, it is, rather, isn't it. Sixty-three vintage, you know." He struggled to get out of his armchair, floundering like a seal on a beach.

"Please don't bother showing me out," Banks said. "I'll find my own way."

"Oh, very well. Fine, then. Bye." And Banks saw Mr Farlowe reach for the decanter again as he left the room. A suitable case for gout, that one. A lot of tipplers, it seemed, on Oakwood Mews.

On the way out, he met Mrs Farlowe in the hall. She had seen nothing that night, but she was able to tell him that the radio had been tuned to Radio Three, as always, when she turned it on. No, she couldn't remember what time, but her husband was right. It was a carol service from King's College. "Away in a Manger" had been playing. Lovely tune, that one, isn't it? Banks agreed and left.

From Mrs Eldridge at number eight Banks got no further information. She had seen the man go in first, then the woman knocking on the door at about seven-fifteen. No, she hadn't seen the man leave in the meantime, but the woman in the short coat and tight jeans definitely didn't enter the house. And it wasn't the same woman as the one who called later. This one was a bit taller and dressed differently. Some kind of long dress under her coat instead of jeans. The way it looked, unless Patsy Janowski had dashed off, changed clothes and added a few inches to her height in the interim, the third visitor couldn't possibly have been her.

He needed to know who this third woman was. Unless someone else had come after her, someone nobody had seen arrive, or unless Claude Ivers had been in the house all the time and nobody had seen him leave, then she was the one, almost certainly, who had killed Caroline Hartley. Was it Veronica Shildon, as Susan had suggested? Banks didn't think so—her love and grief seemed genuine—but he needed to talk to her again. There was a lot of ground yet to cover before he could hope to understand the people, and therefore the motives, involved in this case.

There was, however, one small, practical piece of information he carried away with him. Both Mr and Mrs Farlowe had said that the third woman entered the house—bidden or otherwise—when "Away in a Manger" was being played on Radio Three. It should be possible to find out from the local BBC station what time the program started, the order of carols in the concert and the length of each one. Given that information, it would be simple to work out at exactly what time the mysterious third woman had entered Caroline Hartley's house and, in all likelihood, stabbed her to death with a kitchen knife.

EIGHT

I

Banks walked slowly by the river. He wore his fur-lined suede car-coat, collar up, hands thrust deep in his pockets. As he walked, he breathed out plumes of air. The river wasn't entirely frozen over; ducks paddled as usual, apparently oblivious to the cold, in channels between the lumps of grey ice.

As he walked, he thought about the success he had had that morning with the BBC. A keen young researcher in the local studio took the trouble to dig out and listen to the December 22 taped carol broadcast, using a stop-watch. The program had started at seven sharp. "Away in a Manger" began just over midway through the broadcast—7:21, to be exact—and finished two minutes, fourteen seconds later. Banks marvelled at the precision. With such a sense of exact measurement, the young woman perhaps had a future working for the Guinness Book of Records or the Olympic Records Committee. Anyway, they now knew that Caroline's likely killer had been let in between 7:21 and 7:24.

They also knew that it wasn't Charles Cooper. Richmond had talked to the regulars at Tan Hill and confirmed his alibi: Cooper had been drinking there between about six-thirty and ten-thirty on December 22, and on most other evenings leading up to the Christmas period. It would be more difficult for him to explain long absences to his wife at any other time, Banks thought.

Banks started thinking about the victim, Caroline Hartley, again and realized he still didn't know much about her. She had run away from home at sixteen, gone to London, got herself pregnant, picked up a conviction for soliciting, come back up north and shacked up first with Nancy Wood, who was out of the picture now, and then with Veronica Shildon. Attractive to both men and women—but now interested only in the latter—vivacious and enthusiastic, but given to thoughtful, secretive moods, a budding actress, a good mimic. That was about all. It covered ten years of the woman's life, and it didn't add up to a hell of a lot. There had to be more, and the only place to find out—as Caroline's friends and family either wouldn't talk or didn't know—was in London. But where to start?

Banks picked up a flat stone and skimmed it across the water towards The Green. Briefly, he thought of Jenny Fuller, who lived in one of the Georgian semis there. A lecturer in psychology at York, she had helped Banks before. She would be damn useful in this case, too, he thought. But she'd gone away somewhere warm for Christmas. Tough luck.

Up ahead, near the bridge, Banks saw a boy, no older than twelve or thirteen. He had a catapult and was aiming pebbles at the ducks out on the river. Banks approached him. Before saying a word, he took out his identity card and let the boy have a good long look.

The boy read it, then glanced up at Banks and said, "Are you really a copper or just one of those perverts? My dad's warned me about blokes like you."

"Lucky for you, sonny, I'm really a copper," Banks said, and snatched the metal catapult from the boy's hand.

"Hey! What you doing? That's mine."

"That's a dangerous weapon is what that is," Banks said, slipping it in his coat pocket. "Think yourself lucky I don't take you in. What do you want to go aiming at those ducks for anyway? What harm have they ever done you?"

"Dunno," the kid said. "I wasn't meaning to kill them or anything. I just wanted to see if I could hit one. Can I have my catapult back, mister?"

"No."

"Go on. It cost me a quid, that did. I saved up out of my pocket money."

"Well don't bother saving up for another," Banks said, walking away.

"It's bloody daylight robbery," the kid called after him. "You're no better than a thief!"

But Banks ignored him, and soon the shouting died down. There was something in what the boy had said that interested him: "I wasn't meaning to kill them or anything. I just wanted to see if I could hit one."

Could he really divorce the action from its result as cleanly and innocently as that? And if he could, could a murderer, too? There was no doubt that whoever plunged the knife into Caroline Hartley's body had meant her to be dead, but had that been the killer's original intention? The bruise on the cheek indicated that she had been hit, perhaps stunned, first. How had that come about? Was it the kind of thing a woman would do, punch another woman?

Could it have been some kind of sexual encounter gone out of control, with the original object not so much murder but just a desire to see how far things could go? A sado-masochistic fantasy turned reality, perhaps? After all, Caroline Hartley had been naked. But that was absurd. Veronica and Caroline were respectable, middle-class, conservative lesbians; they didn't cruise the gay bars or try to lure innocent schoolgirls back to the house for orgies, like the lesbians one read about in lurid tabloids. Still, when lovers fight, no matter what sex, they can easily become violent towards one another. What happened between the punch and the stabbing? What warped sequence of emotions did the killer feel? Caroline must have been unconscious, or at least momentarily stunned, and the killer must have picked up the knife, which lay so conveniently on the table by the cake.

What made her do it? Would she have done it if the knife hadn't been so close to hand? Would she have gone into the kitchen and taken a knife from the drawer and still had the resolve when she got back to the living room? Impossible questions to answer—the kind that Jenny might have been able to help with—but they had to be answered or he would never find the key to this problem. Banks needed to know what happened in the dark area, what it was that pushed someone beyond argument, past reason, past sex, beyond even simple physical assault, to murder.

He turned his back on the river and started walking up the hill by the formal gardens back around the castle to the market square. Back at the station, as soon as he turned from the stairwell to the corridor that led to his upstairs office, he saw Susan Gay come rushing towards him with a sheet of paper flapping in her hand. She looked like the cat that had got the cream. Her eyes gleamed with success.

"Found her," she announced. "Ruth. It's a small London publishing company. Sappho Press. I faxed them the photo and they said they had it taken for a dust jacket and for general publicity."

"Good work," Banks said. "Tell me, what made you call that particular press out of the dozens we had listed?"

Susan locked puzzled. "I got as far as 'S' in the alphabet. It took me all morning."

"Do you know who Sappho was?"

Susan shook her head.

Gristhorpe would have known, Banks thought, but you could hardly demand a degree in classics of everyone who wanted to join the police. On the other hand, perhaps it wouldn't be a bad idea: an elite squad of literary coppers.

"She was an ancient Greek poet from the isle of Lesbos," he said.

"Is that . . . ?" Susan began.

Banks nodded.

She blushed. "Well I'd like to say I got the literary clue, like in Agatha Christie," she said, "but it was down to pure hard slog."

Banks laughed. "Well done anyway. Tell me the details."

"Her name's Ruth Dunne and apparently she's published a couple of books. Doing very well for herself in the poetry scene. The woman I spoke to said one of the bigger publishers might be after her soon. Faber and Faber perhaps."

"What kind of stuff does she write?"

"Well, that's another thing. They told me she started by writing the kind of thing the Sappho Press people support. I assumed it was feminist stuff, but now you mention it . . . Anyway, she's moved away from that, they said, and it looks like she's shifting into a broader market, whatever that means."

"Did you mention Caroline Hartley?"

"Yes. It's a funny thing. The editor recognized the name. She went to check and then told me Ruth Dunne's second book was dedicated to someone called Caroline. I thought it was odd we didn't find a copy among the victim's things, don't you?"

"She liked to travel light," Banks said. "Still, it would have made it a lot easier for us if we had. Maybe they just lost touch with one another."

Susan passed the paper over. "Anyway, she lives in Kennington. Here's the address. What now?"

"I'm going down there tomorrow. There's a few things I want to talk to Ruth Dunne about. She's the only link we have so far with Caroline Hartley's child and her life down there. I think she might be able to tell us quite a lot."

II

Perhaps I'm pushing too hard, Susan told herself later that evening. She was trying to decide what to wear for her first real date with James Conran, but she couldn't help going over the past two days' events in her mind. Banks had seemed so calm, so sure of himself, with Claude Ivers. Susan, left to her own devices, would have charged into his studio.

She also doubted that she would have left Redburn without bringing both Ivers and the Janowski woman in for a lengthy inter-rogation at the station. After all, they had both been at the Oakwood Mews house around the time of Caroline Hartley's murder, and both had lied about it. She couldn't understand Banks's obsession with the record and the meaning of the music. In her experience, criminals weren't intelligent enough to leave erudite musical clues behind them. Things like that only happened in the detective stories she had read as a teenager. But the music *had* been playing, she had to admit, and that was very odd indeed.

She decided on the blue cotton blouse and navy mid-length skirt. Neither were so close fitting that they would reveal what she thought of as an unacceptably thick waist. And she mustn't over-dress. Mario's was a little up-market, but it wasn't really posh.

The more she thought of the case, the more she thought of Veronica Shildon. Susan had felt intimidated by the woman's reserve and poise; and the mysterious transition from happily married woman to lesbian disturbed her. It just didn't seem possible.

Ivers could be right in blaming Caroline Hartley. Perhaps Veronica knew this too, deep down, and hated herself for allowing herself to fall so low. Then she found Caroline naked after seeing Patsy Janowski leave the house, and she hit out. That seemed as good an explanation as any to her. All they had to do was discover how Veronica had disposed of her bloody clothing. Surely if Banks put his mind to it, instead of dwelling on that damn music, he could come up with something. Gary Hartley, Susan thought, wasn't capable of the crime. He might be bitter, but he was also weak, a captive in his father's cold, decaying mansion.

Banks seemed to suspect everyone except Veronica Shildon—or at least he didn't see her as a serious contender. Perhaps it was to do with his being a man, Susan thought. Men perceived things differently; they were unsuited to spotting subtle nuances. They were basically selfish and saw things only in relation to their own egos, whereas women spun a more general net of consciousness. She knew Banks was astute enough not to get side-tracked by his feelings, at least most of the time, but maybe he was attracted to Veronica Shildon. There was something in that tension between her strait-laced exterior and inner passions that a man might find sexy. And the fact that he couldn't have her would only add to the excitement, make her seem more of a challenge. Didn't men always want unattainable women?

Rubbish, Susan told herself sharply. She was letting her imagination run away with her. Time to apply a bit of lipstick.

When she was ready, she looked again at her small tree and the few trimmings she had hastily put up on Christmas Eve. They made the place look a bit more like a home. As she looked around the room, she couldn't really see what was missing. The wallpaper, red roses on a cream background, was nice enough; the three-piece suite arranged around the gas fireplace looked a little shabby, but nonetheless cosy; and the bookcase added a learned look. There was a beautiful pine table, too, in the corner by the window, where she ate. So what was it?

Looking again at the Christmas trimmings, she realized with a shock what was missing. So simple, really. If she had been on a case looking objectively at a suspect's apartment and had seen one just like this, she would have known immediately. But because it was her own, she hadn't paid it the same attention. The one personal touch, the Christmas decorations, pointed out that there was nothing of *her* there; the room had no personality. The furniture, wallpaper, carpet could all belong to anyone. Where were the knick-knacks that people accumulate over the years? Where were the favourite prints on the walls, the framed photographs of loved ones on the mantelpiece, the ornaments on the windowsill? There were no books, only her textbooks, which she kept in the guest room she used as a study. And where was the music? She had a music centre her parents had bought for her twenty-first birthday, but all she ever listened to was the radio. She had no records or tapes at all.

The doorbell rang. Well, she thought, slipping on her coat, perhaps it's time I started. A nice landscape on the wall, over there, a Constable print or something, a couple of china figurines on the mantelpiece, a few books, and a record of that music Banks played in the car on the way back from Redburn yesterday. She had felt embarrassed and stupid when he had asked what she wanted to listen to, because she had no idea. She heard music on the radio, pop and classical, and enjoyed some of it, but could never remember the names of performers or titles of the pieces.

For some reason, she had asked for some vocal music, and he had played a tape of Kiri Te Kanawa singing highlights from *Madama Butterfly*. Even Susan had heard of Kiri Te Kanawa, the soprano from New Zealand who had sung at Prince Charles's wedding to Lady Di. One song in particular sent shivers all the way up her spine and made the hackles at the back of her neck stand on end. Banks had told her the heroine was imagining the return of her lover in the aria, which translated as "One Fine Day." Susan had taken note of the title, and she would buy it for herself tomorrow, as a start to her collection. Perhaps she would also try to find out what happened in the story: did the lover return, as Butterfly dreamed?

The doorbell rang again. Smiling, Susan went downstairs to the front door to meet James. He told her she looked beautiful. She didn't believe him, but she felt wonderful as they got into his car and drove off into the icy night.

III

"Sorry for the mess," Veronica Shildon said as she let Banks in. He looked around. There was no mess, really. He sat down. Veronica stood by the kitchen door with her arms folded.

"The reason I came," he said, "is to tell you that we've tracked down the woman in the picture."

Veronica shifted her weight from one foot to the other. "Yes?"

"Her name is Ruth Dunne. She's a poet, as you said, published by a small feminist press, and she lives in London."

"You have an address?"

"Yes."

"Thank you for telling me, Chief Inspector. I realize it might have been unethical."

"Ms Shildon, I never do anything unethical." His eyes twinkled when he smiled.

"I—I didn't mean—"

"It's all right."

"Would you like some tea? I was just about to make some."

"Yes, please. It's a bit nippy out there."

"If you'd like something stronger . . . ?"

"No, tea will do fine."

While Veronica made the tea, Banks looked around the room. It was in a state of flux. In the first place, there was hardly anywhere to sit. The suite was gone, leaving only a couple of hard-backed chairs at the table by the window. Also, the sideboard had been moved, and the Christmas tree, along with all the trimmings, was gone, even though it was only December 29. Banks wondered if Veronica could have done it all herself.

"Have you talked to her?" Veronica asked, placing the tray on the table and sitting opposite him.

"No, not yet. I'm going down there tomorrow morning. It wouldn't be wise to phone ahead."

"You don't mean she's a suspect?"

"Until I find out otherwise, she is, and I don't want to give her any reason to run off if she thinks she's sitting pretty."

"It must be an awful job you do," Veronica said.

"Sometimes. But not as awful as what the people we try to catch do."

"Touché."

"Anyway, I just thought I'd let you know."

"And I'm grateful." Veronica put her cup and saucer down. "I'd like to see her," she said. "Ruth Dunne. If it's not too much of an imposition, may I travel down with you?"

Banks scratched the scar by his right eye, then crossed his legs. He knew he should say no. Officially, Veronica Shildon was a major suspect in her lover's murder. He had told her about Ruth Dunne only partly out of goodwill; mainly he had been interested in her reaction to the news. On the other hand, if he got her out of her normal environment, out of this house and out of Eastvale, he might be able to get her to open up a bit more about Caroline's background. Was that worth the risk of her making a break for it? It would be easy for her to disappear in a city as large as London. But why should she? They had no real evidence against her; they couldn't put her under arrest.

"I'm going by train," he said. "I won't be driving down. I never could stand driving in London."

"Are you trying to put me off? I know it's an unusual request to make, Chief Inspector, but I've heard about Ruth often enough from Caroline, though never more than her first name and what a good friend she was. Somehow, now that Caroline's gone, I just feel I'd like to meet her. There's very little else left."

Banks sipped at his tea and let a minute pass. "On two conditions," he said finally. "First of all, I can't allow you to be present at the interview, and second, you'll have to wait until I've talked to her before you see her."

Veronica nodded. "That sounds fair."

"I haven't finished yet."

"But that was two."

"I'll make it three, then. I reserve the right to stop you seeing her at all if for any reason I feel it necessary."

"But why on earth . . . ?"

"It should be obvious. If Ruth Dunne turns out to be even more of a suspect than she is now, I can't allow the two of you to discuss the case together. Do you agree to the terms?"

Veronica nodded slowly. "I suppose I'll have to do."

"And you'll also have to return with me."

"I was thinking of looking up an old friend," Veronica said. "Perhaps staying down for New Year's . . ."

Banks shook his head. "I'm already going out on a limb."

Veronica stood up. "Very well. I understand."

"Right," he said at the door. "Eight-twenty from Eastvale, change at Leeds."

"I'll be there," she said, and closed the door behind him.

IV

Mario's was a cosy restaurant in a narrow cul-de-sac of gift shops off North Market Street. It had a small bar at one end of the long room, stucco walls and small tables with red-and-white-checked cloths and candles in orange pressed-glass jars. A man with a guitar sat on a stool at the far end quietly crooning Italian love songs.

The place was full when James and Susan got there and they had to sit for ten minutes at the bar. James ordered a half-litre of Barolo, which they sipped as they waited.

He looked good, Susan thought. Clearly he had made some sartorial effort, replacing cords and polo-neck with grey slacks, a white shirt and a well-tailored, dark-blue sports jacket. His fair hair, thinning and combed forward flat against his skull, looked newly washed, and he had also shaved, as a couple of nicks under his chin testified. His grey eyes seemed bluer tonight, and they sparkled with life and mischief.

"You'll just love the cannelloni," he said, putting his fingers to his lips and making a kissing gesture.

Susan laughed. How long was it since an attractive man had made her laugh? She had no idea. But very quickly she seemed to be getting over the idea of James Conran as drama teacher and moving towards . . . Well, she didn't quite know and didn't really want to contemplate just yet. At least not tonight. James chatted easily with the barman in fluent Italian and Susan sipped her wine, reading the labels of the liqueur bottles behind the bar. Soon, a white-jacketed waiter ushered them with a flourish to a table for two. Luckily, Susan thought, it wasn't too close to the singer, now lost in the throes of O Sole Mio.

They examined their menus in silence, and Susan finally decided to take James's advice on the cannelloni. He ordered linguine in a white wine and clam sauce for himself. He had recommended that, too, but she was allergic to shellfish.

"I must say again," he said, raising his glass in a toast, "that you look gorgeous tonight."

"Oh, don't be stupid." Susan felt herself blush. She had done the best she could with her appearance, accenting her rather too thin lips and playing down the extra fat on her cheekbones with powder. She knew she wasn't bad looking; her large eyes were a beautiful ultramarine colour and her short, blonde hair, naturally thick and curly, gave her no trouble at all. If she could just lose a couple of inches from her waist and three or four from her hips, she thought, she'd be more inclined to believe compliments and wolf-whistles. Still, it was a long time since she'd gone to such lengths for a date. She smiled and clinked glasses with James.

"All you lack is confidence," he said, as if reading her thoughts. "You have to believe in yourself more."

"I do," Susan answered. "How do you think I've got where I am?"

"I mean your personality, the image you project. Believe you're lovely and people will see you that way."

"Is that what you do?"

James winced in mock agony. "Oh, now you're being cruel."

"I'm sorry."

"It's all right. I'll survive." He leaned forward. "Tell me, I've always wondered, what did you think of me when you were at school? I mean, what did the girls think of me?"

Susan laughed and put her hand to her mouth. "They thought you were gay."

James's face showed no expression, but a sudden chill seemed to emanate from him.

"I'm sorry," Susan said, feeling flustered. "I didn't mean anything by it. *I* didn't think so, if that's any consolation. And it was just because you were in the arts."

"In the arts?"

"Yes, you know how people in the performance arts always seem to be thought gay. If it'll make you feel any better, they thought Mr Curlew was that way, too."

James stared at her, then burst into laughter. "Peter Curlew? The music teacher?"

Susan nodded.

"Well, that's a good one. I do feel better now. Curly was a happily married man with four kids. Devoted family man."

Susan laughed with him. "That just shows you how wrong we were, I suppose. I liked the way he used to conduct to himself whenever he played a record for us. He really got quite worked up, in a world of his own."

"Of course, you lot were all snickering at him behind your hands, weren't you?"

"Yes. Yes, I'm afraid we were." Susan felt strangely ashamed to admit it now, though she hadn't thought of Mr Curlew for years.

"He was a very talented pianist, you know. He could have gone a long way, but those years of dreary teaching broke his spirit."

Susan felt embarrassed. "How are you getting on without Caroline?" she asked, to change the subject.

James paused for a few seconds, as if deep in thought, before answering. "Fine, I suppose. It wasn't a difficult part. It was just that, well, Caroline was special, that's all. Are you any closer?"

Susan shook her head. Not that she would have said even if they were closer to finding Caroline's killer. She frowned. "Do you think anyone in the production could have been involved in her death?"

He cupped his chin in his hand and thought for a moment. "No," he said finally. "No, I can't see it. Nobody knew her that well."

"Her killer didn't need to know her well. She let him or her in, but he or she could have been merely an acquaintance, someone come to talk to her about something."

"I still can't see it."

"There must have been friction with the other women, the leads."

"Why?"

"Competition."

"Over what?"

"Anything. Men. Lines. Parts."

"There wasn't. I'm not saying we were a totally happy family, we had our ups and downs, our off days, but you're grasping at straws. Remember, it's the *Amateur* Dramatic Society. People join for pleasure, not profit. I'd like to think, though, that we're far from amateur in quality."

Susan smiled. "I'm sure you are. Tell me, what was Caroline Hartley really like?"

"I'm sorry, Susan, it's still very upsetting for me, such a loss. I just don't want to—ah, look, here's our food." He rubbed his hands together. "Delightful. And another half-litre of your best Barolo, please, Enzo."

"Do you think we should?" Susan asked. "I've still got half a glass left. I'm not certain I can drink any more."

"Well if you can't, I can. I know I should be drinking white with the linguine, but what the hell, I prefer Barolo. Worry not, not a drop will be wasted. What did you do for Christmas?"

"I—I—"

"Well, what? Did you visit your parents?" He gathered a forkful of food and lifted it to his mouth, his eyes probing her face for an answer all the time.

Susan looked down at her plate. "I . . . not really, no, I didn't. I was busy with the case."

"You don't get on with them, do you?" he said, still looking directly at her, with just a glint of satisfaction in his eyes. She found

his gaze disconcerting and looked down at her plate again to cut off
a bite of cannelloni.

"I don't suppose I do," she admitted when she'd finished
chewing. She shrugged. "It's nothing serious. Just that holidays at
home can be awfully depressing."

"I suppose so," James said. "I'm an orphan myself and I always find
Christmas terribly gloomy. It brings back memories of those awful
orphanage dinners and enforced festivities. But you have a family.
You shouldn't neglect them, you know. One day, it'll be too late."

"Look," Susan said, reaching for her glass, "when I want a lecture
on a daughter's responsibility, I'll ask for one."

James stood up. "I'm sorry, really I am." He patted her arm.
"Excuse me for a moment. Men's room."

Susan held her anger in check and tossed back the last of her
wine. The second half-litre arrived. She refilled her glass and took
a long swig. To hell with caution; she could get as pissed as the next
person if she wanted to. Why couldn't she talk about her parents
without getting so damned emotional? she asked herself. She
picked away at her cannelloni, which was very good, until James
came back. Then she took a deep breath and put down her knife
and fork.

"I'm the one that should apologize," she said. "I didn't mean to
blow up like that. It's just that it's *my* problem, all right?"

"Fine," James said. "Fine. So what *did* you do?"

She sighed. "I stayed at home. I had quite a nice day actually. I'd
dashed out and bought a small tree and a few trimmings the night
before, so the place looked quite seasonal. I watched the Queen's
Message, a variety show, read a book on homicide investigation."

James laughed, a forkful of pasta half-way to his mouth. "You
read a textbook on homicide on Christmas Day?"

Susan blushed. At that moment the manager walked by. He
nodded at James as he passed.

"I don't believe it," James said. "You sitting there by the
Christmas tree listening to carols, reading about dead bodies and
poisons and ballistics."

"Well it's true," Susan said, managing a smile. "Anyway, if my
job dis—"

But she had no time to finish. Before she could even get the word out, a man appeared beside her and began singing into her ear. She didn't know the song, but she could make out words like *bella* and *amore*. She wished she could shrink to nothing and disappear down a crack in the floor. James sat opposite, hands folded on his lap, watching with cool amusement in his eyes. When the singer had gone and Susan had grudgingly thanked him, she turned to James with fury in her eyes.

"You set that up, didn't you, when you went to the gents'? You talked to the manager. Go on, admit it."

"Very well." James turned his hands palms up. "*Mea culpa*. I just thought you might enjoy it, that's all."

"I've never been so embarrassed in my life. I've a good mind—" Susan dropped her napkin on the table and pushed back her chair, but James leaned forward and put his hand gently on her arm. She could see the mild amusement in his eyes turn to concern.

"Don't go, Susan. I just meant I thought it might cheer you up, after a Christmas spent alone. Honest, I didn't mean to embarrass you. I never thought you wouldn't like it. How could I know?"

Looking at his eyes again, she could see he was sincere. Not so much that, but it hadn't even occurred to him that the singer might embarrass her. She eased the chair towards the table again and relaxed.

"All right," she said, forcing a smile. "I'll let you off just this once. But don't you ever—"

"I won't," James said. "I promise. Scout's honour. Cross my heart and hope to die. Come on, eat your cannelloni and drink your wine. Enjoy." And he let his hand rest on hers on the checked tablecloth for a long moment before taking it away.

V

Banks switched off Milhaud's "Creation" as he pulled up outside Faith Green's block of flats. It was a small unit, only three storeys high, with six flats on each floor. He looked at his watch: 8:50.

Plenty of time for Faith to have come home from the Crooked Billet, if she hadn't gone out on a date.

Luckily, she was in. When he knocked, he heard someone cross the room and saw the tiny peep-hole in the door darken.

"Inspector Banks!" Faith said as she pulled the door open with a dramatic flourish. "What a surprise. Do come in. Let me take your coat." She hung up his car-coat, then took his arm and led him into the spacious living room. A number of framed posters from old movies hung on the pastel-green walls: Bogart in *Casablanca*, Garbo in *Camille*, John Garfield and Lana Turner in *The Postman Always Rings Twice*. Faith gestured towards the modular sofa that covered almost two walls, and Banks sat down.

"Drink?"

"Maybe just a small Scotch, if you have it."

"Of course." Faith opened up a glass-fronted cocktail cabinet and poured them both drinks. Banks's was about two fingers taller than he would have liked.

"To what do I owe this pleasure?" Faith asked in her husky voice. "If only you'd told me you were coming, I could have at least put my face on. I must look terrible."

She didn't. With her beautiful eyes and silvery, page-boy hair, it would have been difficult for Faith Green to look terrible. She wore no make-up, but that didn't matter. Her high cheekbones needed no highlights, her full, pink lips no colouring. In skin-tight black slacks and a dark-green silk blouse, her figure, slim at the waist, nicely curved at the hips and well-rounded at the bust, looked terrific. The perfume she wore was the same one Banks remembered from their brief chat at the Crooked Billet—very subtle, with a hint of jasmine.

She settled close to Banks on the sofa and cradled a glass of white wine in her hands. "You should have phoned first," she said. "I gave you my number."

"Maybe you didn't know I was married."

She laughed. "I've never known that to make very much difference to men." Given the way she was sitting and looking at him, he could well believe her. He fiddled for his cigarettes.

"Oh, you're not going to smoke, are you?" She pouted. "Please don't. It's not that I'm so anti, but I just can't bear my flat smelling of smoke. Please?"

Banks removed his hand from his jacket pocket and took a long swig of Scotch. He waited until the pleasant burning sensation had subsided, then said, "Remember the last time we talked? About how things were going between the people in the play?"

"Of course I do." Her eyes twinkled. "I told you I liked my men dark and handsome, and not necessarily tall."

If Banks had been wearing a tie, he would have loosened it at this point. "Miss Green—"

"Faith, please. It's not such a bad name, is it? There are three of us, sisters, but my parents never were that well up on the Bible. The youngest's called Chastity."

Banks laughed. 'Faith it is, then. You told me you had no idea that Caroline Hartley was a lesbian. Are you sure you didn't?"

Faith frowned. "Of course not. What an odd question. She didn't walk around with it written on her forehead. Besides, it's not as obvious in a woman as it sometimes is in a man, is it? I mean, I've known a few homosexuals, and most of them don't mince around and lisp, but you have to admit that some conform to the stereotype. How could you possibly tell with a woman unless she went about dressed like a man or something?"

"Perhaps you would just sense it?"

"Well, I didn't. Not with Caroline. And *she* certainly didn't walk around dressed like a man."

"So she told no-one?"

"Not as far as I know, she didn't. She certainly didn't tell me. I can't vouch for the others. Another drink?"

Banks looked at his glass, amazed to find it empty so soon. "No thanks."

"Oh, come on," Faith said, and took it from him. She brought it back only slightly fuller than the last time and sat about six inches closer. Banks held his ground.

"There's something missing," he said. "Some factor, maybe just a little thing, and I'm trying to find out what it is. I get the feeling that people—you especially—are holding something back, hiding something."

"Little me? Hiding something? Like what?" She spread her hands and looked down as if to indicate that all she had was on display. She wasn't far from the truth.

"I don't know. Do you think there might be a chance that Caroline Hartley was having an affair with someone other than the woman she was living with, perhaps someone in the theatre company?"

Faith stared at him, then backed away a few inches, burst out laughing and pointed at her chest. "Me? You think I'm a lesbian?"

Given the situation, her physical closeness and the heady aura of sex that seemed to emanate from her, it did seem rather a silly thing to think.

"Not you specifically," Banks said. "Anyone."

When Faith had stopped laughing, she moved closer again and said, "Well, I can assure you *I'm* not." She shifted her legs. The material swished as her thighs brushed together. "In fact, if you let me, I can even prove to you I'm not."

Banks held her gaze. "It's quite possible for a person to be bisexual," he said. "Especially if he or she is over-sexed to start with."

Faith seemed to recede several feet into the distance, though she hadn't moved at all. "I ought to be insulted," she said with a pout, "but I'm not. Disappointed in you, yes, but not insulted. Do you really think I'm over-sexed?"

Banks put his thumb and forefinger close together and smiled. "Maybe just a little bit."

All the seductiveness, the heat and smell of sexuality, had gone from her manner, and what sat next to him was a very attractive young woman, perhaps a little shy, a little vulnerable. Perhaps it had all been an act. Could she turn her sexual power on and off at will? Why did he keep forgetting that there were so many actors on the fringes of Caroline Hartley's death?

"I didn't mean it as an insult," Banks went on. "It just seemed the best way to cut the games and get down to business. I really do need information. That's why I'm here."

Faith nodded, then smiled. "All right, I'll play fair. But I'm not just all talk, you know." Just for a moment she upped the voltage again and Banks felt the current.

"Could Caroline have been seeing someone?" he asked quickly.

"She could have been, yes. But I ca' 't help you there. Caroline kept herself to herself. Nobody knew anything about her private life, I'm certain. After a couple of drinks, she'd go off home—"

"By herself?"

"Usually. If it was an especially nasty night James would give her a lift. And before you make too much out of that, he would take Teresa too, and drop her off last." She paused for effect, then added huskily, "At his place, sometimes."

"Teresa told me she didn't care about James's attraction to Caroline. What would you say about that?"

Faith put a slender finger to her lips, then said, "Well, I wouldn't quite put it that way. I don't like to tell tales out of school, but . . ."

"But what? It could be important."

"Teresa's very emotional."

"You mean she fought with Caroline?"

"Not exactly."

"With James Conran?"

Faith swirled her drink and nodded slowly. "I heard them talking once or twice," she said. "Caroline's name came up."

"In what way?"

Faith lowered her voice and leaned closer to Banks. "Usually as that 'prick-teasing little bitch.' Teresa's a good friend," she added, settling back, "but you *did* say it was important."

So Teresa Pedmore had more of a grudge against Caroline Hartley than she had cared to admit. She could have been the woman who visited Caroline's house after Patsy Janowski. On the other hand, so could Faith Green, who was being much more circumspect about her own involvement in the thespian intrigues, if she had any. Both were a little taller than Caroline Hartley. Banks would have to have a word with Teresa later and see what she, in turn, had to say about her friend.

"You say James seemed attracted enough to Caroline to upset Teresa," he said. "How strong would you say his interest was?"

"He flirted with her in the pub. That was all I ever saw."

"How did she react?"

"She gave as good as she got."

"Did they sleep together?"

"Not as far as I know."

"Teresa never referred to them doing that?"

"No, just to the way James fussed about her. It wasn't Caroline who manoeuvred the seating in the pub. If anyone, Teresa should have blamed James, not Caroline."

"People aren't very logical when it comes to blame," Banks said, thinking of what Claude Ivers and Patsy Janowski had said about Caroline and Veronica.

"Where did you all go after the rehearsal on the day of Caroline's death?"

"I came home. Honestly. I was tired. I didn't even have a date."

"Why didn't you all go for a drink as usual?"

Faith shrugged. "No special reason. Sometimes we just didn't, that's all. People just wandered off home. There's nothing more to it than that. It was close to Christmas. There was shopping to do, family to visit."

Banks didn't believe her. She fiddled with her pearl necklace as she spoke and looked away from him. She also spoke as if there was nobody listening to her.

"Did something happen at that rehearsal, Faith?" he asked. "Was there a row between Caroline and Teresa?"

Faith shifted in her seat. She turned her eyes on him again. They gave away nothing. A waft of perfume drifted over.

"Another drink?"

"No. Tell me what happened."

"Leave me alone. Nothing happened."

Banks put his glass down on the St Ives coaster and stood up.

Faith scratched the inside of her elbow. "Are you going now?" she asked. All of a sudden she seemed like a frightened girl whose parents were about to turn the lights out.

"Yes. Thanks very much for the drinks. You've been a great help."

She touched his arm. "Nothing happened. Really. Believe me. We just finished our rehearsal and we all went home. Don't you believe me?"

Banks moved towards the door. Faith walked beside him, still holding on. "You must catch him soon, you know," she said.

"Him?"

"Whoever killed Caroline. Was it a woman? I suppose it could have been. But you must."

"Don't worry. We will. With or without your help. Why are you so concerned?"

Faith let go of his arm. "The rest of us are in danger, aren't we? It stands to reason."

"What do you mean?"

"Whoever killed Caroline. He might be stalking the cast. A serial killer."

"A psychopathic killer? It's possible, but I don't think so. You've been reading too many books, Faith."

"So you really don't think the rest of us are in danger?"

"No. But you might as well keep your door locked anyway. And always look and see who's there." He paused, half out the door.

"What is it?" Faith asked.

"Some of you *could* be in danger," he added slowly, "if you know more about the crime than you're telling, and if the killer knows you know, or suspects that you do."

Faith shook her head. "I know nothing more than I told you."

"Then you've nothing to worry about, have you?"

Banks smiled and left. He wanted to get Teresa's version of that final night, but she would have to wait. It was going on for ten o'clock, he was tired, and he was going to London early in the morning. If he still needed to talk to her when he got back, he could do it then.

As he walked over the brittle ice listening to the rest of the Milhaud piece, he recalled Faith Green's expression at the door. She had told him that she knew nothing, but had looked distinctly worried when he had hinted she might be in danger. Of course, knowing her, it could have been just another act, but perhaps, he thought, it wouldn't be a bad idea to have Richmond and Susan Gay keep an eye on the thespians while he was in London.

NINE

I

It wasn't until the Intercity train pulled out of Leeds City Station
that Veronica Shildon seemed to relax.

Banks had met her at Eastvale Station early that morning and
they had paced the platform, shivering and breathing plumes of
mist, until the overheated old diesel rattled in and carried them off.
Silent but for small talk, they'd watched the shrouded landscape
roll by. South of Ripon, the dales and moors to the west gave way
to rolling farmland, where patches of frozen brown earth and
clumps of bare trees showed through the gauze of snow, and,
finally, to the suburbs and industrial estates of the city itself. They
had endured a half-hour wait on the cold, grimy platform at Leeds,
breathing in the diesel smell of warm engines and listening to the
crackly voice over the loudspeaker.

Now, well past the sign at the station's entrance in honour of the
local beer magnate—"Joshua Tetley Welcomes You to Leeds"—
Banks looked over his shoulder and watched the city recede into
the distance. First it filled the horizon, an urban sprawl under a
heavy sky. Tall chimneys and church spires poked through the
grey-brown snow; the Town Hall dome and the white university
library tower dominated the distance. Then the city was gone and
only bare fields stretched east and west.

Veronica took off her heavy blue winter coat and, folding it
carefully, placed it in the luggage rack. Then she smoothed her
tweed skirt and sat back down opposite Banks, resting her hands on
the table between them.

"I'm sorry," she said with an embarrassed smile. "I know I must be a burden, but I didn't like the idea of travelling down by myself. It's a while since I've been anywhere alone."

"That's all right," said Banks, who had been uncharitably wishing he could spend the journey with the *Guardian* crossword and some Poulenc chamber music on his Walkman. "Coffee?"

"Yes, please."

The buffet car hadn't opened yet, but a British Rail steward was making his way slowly along the corridor with an urn and a selection of biscuits. Banks headed him off, bought two coffees and pushed one over the smooth table to Veronica. Automatically, he reached for his cigarettes, then remembered he was in a non-smoking carriage.

It wasn't Veronica's fault; she would have been happy to sit anywhere with him since he had allowed her to come along. The problem was that there was only one smokers' car on the entire train and, as usual, it was almost full and completely unventilated. Even Banks refused to sit in it. He could do without a cigarette for a couple of hours, easily. It might even do him good. As an alternative, he caught up with the steward and bought a Penguin biscuit.

After Wakefield, they sped along past dreary fields and embankments trying to sip the hot, weak coffee without spilling any. Their carriage was unusually quiet and empty. Perhaps, Banks guessed, this was because they were in that limbo between Christmas and New Year's. Everyone was both broke and in need of a brief hibernation or period of recovery between the two festive occasions.

Deep into South Yorkshire, Banks noticed Veronica looking out at the desolate landscape of pit-wheels and slag-heaps and asked her what she was thinking about.

"It's funny," she said, "but I was thinking how I still feel only half here. Do you know what I mean? I can accept that Caroline is gone, that she's dead and I'll never see her again, but I can't believe that my life is whole, or even real, without her." She nodded towards the window. "Even the world out there doesn't seem real, somehow. Not any more."

"That's understandable," Banks said. "It takes time. How did you meet her?"

Veronica gave him a long, appraising look and then leaned forward and rested her arms on the table, clasping her slim, freckled hands.

"It must seem very odd to you. Perverted, even. But it's not. There was nothing sordid about it."

Banks said nothing.

Veronica sighed and went on. "I first met Caroline at the café where she worked. I used to go for long walks by the river . . . oh, just thinking about my life and how empty it felt . . . somehow, the moving water seemed to help soothe me. We got on speaking terms, then once I saw her in the market square and we went for a coffee. We discovered we were both in therapy. After that . . . well, it didn't happen quickly."

"What attracted you to her?"

"I didn't even know I *was* attracted to her at first. Could you imagine someone like me admitting I'd fallen in love with a woman? But Caroline was so alive, so childlike in her enthusiasm for life. It was infectious. I'd felt half dead for years. I'd been shutting the world out. It's possible to do that, you know. So many people accept what life dishes out to them. Apart from the occasional daydream, they never imagine it could be any different, any better. Even the half-life I have now is preferable to what my life was like before Caroline. There's no going back. I was living like a zombie, denying everything that counts, until Caroline came along. She showed me how good it was to *feel* again. She made me feel alive for the first time. She got me interested in things because she was so passionate about them herself."

"Like what?"

"Oh, theatre, books, film. So many neat things. And music. Claude was always trying to get me interested in music, and it really frustrated him that I didn't seem to care as much as he did, or notice as much about it as he did. I suppose I loved opera most of all, but he never had much time for it. Most seasons I went to Leeds to see Opera North by myself. I liked to listen—I still do like classical music—but I never actually bought records for myself. There always seemed something stuffy about the music we listened to, perhaps because Claude hated anything popular, anything outside the classical field. But with Caroline it was jazz and blues and folk music. Somehow it just seemed more alive. We even went to clubs to see folk groups perform. I'd never done that before. Ever."

"But your husband's a musician himself. He loves music. Didn't he mean anything to you? Why couldn't you respond to his enthusiasm?"

Veronica lowered her head and scratched the table surface with her thumb-nail. The train hit a bumpy stretch of track and rocked.

"I don't know. Somehow I just felt completely stifled by his existence. That's the only way I can put it. Like it didn't matter what I thought or felt or did because he was the one our lives revolved around. I depended on him for everything, even for my tastes in music and books. I was suffocated by his presence. Anything I did would have been insignificant beside what he did. He was the great Claude Ivers, after all, always the teacher, the master. One dismissive comment from him on anything that mattered to me and I was reduced to silence, or tears, so I learned not to let things matter. I was the great man's wife, not a person in my own right."

She sat up straight, her brow furrowed. "How can I explain it to you? Claude wasn't cruel, he didn't do any of it on purpose. It's just the way he is, and the way I am, or was. I still have my problems, more than ever now Caroline's gone, I suppose, but when I look back I can't believe I'm the same person I was then. She worked an act of magic—she breathed life into dust. And I know I can carry on somehow, no matter how hard, just because of her, just because I had her in my life, even for such a short time." She paused and glanced out the window. Banks could read the intense feeling in the set of her jaw, the way the small muscles below her cheekbones seemed drawn tight.

"Do you see?" she went on, turning her clear, grey-green eyes on Banks. "It wasn't black-and-white. He wasn't a bad husband. Neglectful, maybe. Certainly the last few years he was far too wrapped up in his work to notice me. And I was dying, drying up inside. If Caroline hadn't come along I don't know what would have become of me."

"But you started seeing the therapist before you met Caroline," Banks said. "What made you do that?"

"Desperation, despair. I'd read an article about Jungian therapy in a women's magazine. It sounded interesting, but not for me. Time passed and I became so miserable I had to do something or I was frightened I would try to kill myself. I suppose I told myself therapy was a sort of intellectual fun, not anything deep and personal. More like going to an evening class—you know, pottery, basket-weaving or creative writing. It wasn't like going to the real doctor or to a psychiatrist, and somehow I could handle that. It still took a lot of nerve, more than I believed I ever had. But I was so unhappy. And it helped. It can be a painful process, you know. You keep circling things without ever really zooming in on them, and sometimes you feel it's a waste of time, it's going nowhere. Then you do focus on things and you find you were circling them for good reason. Occasionally you get some kind of insight, and that sustains you for a while. Then I met Caroline."

"Had you ever experienced feelings like that before?" Banks asked.

"Towards another woman?"

"Yes."

Veronica shook her head. "I hadn't experienced feelings like that for *anyone* before, male or female. Somehow or other, her being a woman just wasn't an issue. Not after a while, anyway. Everything began to feel so natural I didn't even have to think."

"What about your past, your upbringing?"

Veronica smiled. "Yes, isn't it tempting to try and put everything down to that? I don't mean to be dismissive, but I don't think it's so. I had no horrible experiences with men in my past. I'd never been abused, raped or beaten." She paused. "At least not physically."

"What was your family background like?"

"Solid, suburban, upper middle class. Very repressed. Utterly cold. We never spoke about feelings and nobody told me about the facts of life. My mother was well-bred, very Victorian, and my father was kind and gentle but rather distant, aloof. And he was away a lot. I never had much contact with boys while I was growing up. I went to convent school, and even at university I didn't mix very much. I was in an all-girls residence and I tended to stay home and study a lot. I was shy. Men frightened me with their deep voices and their aggressive mannerisms. I don't know why. When I met Claude he was a guest lecturer for a music appreciation course. It was the kind of thing genteel young ladies did, appreciate music, so I took the course. I was fascinated by his knowledge and his obvious passion for his subject—the very things I came to hate later. For some reason he noticed me. He was an older man, much safer than the randy boys in the campus pub. I was twenty-one when I married him."

"So you never had any other boyfriends?"

"Never. I was reclusive, frightened as a mouse. Believe it or not, when Claude seemed to lose interest in sex, that suited me fine. Now, when I look back, I can't remember what I did from day to day. How I got through. I was a housewife. I had no outside job. I suppose I cleaned and cooked and watched daytime television in a kind of trance. Then there was the Valium, of course."

"How long were you married?"

"We were together for fifteen years. I never complained. I never took an interest in life outside his circle of friends and acquaintances. I had no passions of my own. I don't blame Claude for that. He had his own life, and music was more important to him even than marriage. I think it has to be like that with a great artist, don't you? And I believe Claude *is* a great artist. But great artists make lousy husbands."

"Did you ever think of having children?"

"I did. But Claude thought they would interfere with his peace and quiet. He never really liked children. And I suppose I was, am, afraid of childbirth. Terrified, to be honest. Anyway, he just went ahead and had a vasectomy. He never even told me until it was done. What do you think of childless marriages, Mr Banks?"

Banks shrugged. "I wouldn't know. Never had one."

"Some people say there's no love in them, but I don't agree. Sometimes I think it would be best if we were all childless. Childless and parentless." She caught the paradox and smiled. "Impossible, I realize. There'd be no one here to feel anything. I know I feel alone and it hurts because Caroline isn't here. But at the same time I seem to be saying we'd all be better off without any feelings or any attachments. I want it both ways, don't I?"

"Don't we all? Look, this philosophy's made me thirsty. I know it's early, but how about a drink?"

Veronica laughed. "Have I driven you to drink already? All right, I'll have a gin and tonic."

Banks made his way down to the buffet car, holding onto the tops of seats to keep his balance in the rocking train. Most of the other passengers seemed to be business people with their heads buried deep in the *Financial Times* or briefcases full of papers open in front of them. One man even tapped away at the keys of a laptop computer. After a short queue, Banks got Veronica's drink and a miniature Bell's for himself. Going back one-handed was a little more difficult, but he made it without falling or dropping anything.

Back in his seat, he poured the drinks. They passed a small town: smoking chimneys; grimy factory yards stacked with pallets; a new redbrick school with hardly any windows; a roundabout; snow-covered playing fields as white as the rugby posts. The train's rhythm was soothing, even if it wasn't the same as the steam-train journeys Banks remembered taking with his father when he was young. The sound was different, and he missed the tangy smell of the smoke, the sight of it curling over trees by a wooded embankment where the track curved and he could see the engine through the window.

Veronica seemed content to sip her drink in silence. There was so much more he wanted to ask her, to understand about her relationship with Caroline Hartley, but he didn't feel he could justify his questions. He thought of what she had said about a childless and parentless life and remembered the Philip Larkin poem, which he had recently reread. It was certainly depressing—the ending as much as the beginning—but he found something in the wit and gusto of Larkin's colloquial style that brought a smile to the lips, too. Perhaps that was the secret of great art, it could engender more than one feeling in the spectator at the same time: tragedy and comedy, laughter and tears, irony and passion, hope and despair.

"What's your wife like?"

The suddenness of the question surprised Banks, and he guessed he must have shown it.

"I'm sorry," Veronica went on quickly, blushing, "I hope I'm not being presumptuous."

"No. I was just thinking about something else, that's all. My wife? Well, she's just an inch or so shorter than I am. She's slim, with an oval face, blonde hair and dark eyebrows, what I'd call a no-nonsense personality and . . . let me think . . ."

Veronica laughed and held up her hand. "No, no. That'll do. I didn't want a *policeman's* description. I suppose I hadn't thought how difficult it is to answer off the cuff like that. If anyone had asked me to describe Caroline I wouldn't have known where to start."

"You did well enough earlier."

"But that was just scratching the surface."

She drank some more gin and tonic and looked at her reflection in the window, as if she couldn't believe what she was seeing.

"I suppose my wife and I are still together," Banks said, "because she has always been determined and independent. She'd hate to be a housewife worrying about meals and three-pence-off coupons in the papers. Some people might see that as a fault, but I don't. It's what she is and I wouldn't want to turn her into some sort of chattel or slave. And she wouldn't want to depend on me to entertain her or keep her happy. Oh, we've had some dull patches and a few close shaves on both sides, but I think we do pretty well."

"And you put it down to her independence?"

"Mostly, yes. More an independent spirit, really. And intelligence. It's very hard being a policeman's wife. We're a high-divorce profession. It's not so much the worry, though that's there, but the long absences and the unpredictability. I've seen plenty of marriages go down the tubes because the wife hasn't been able to take it any more. But Sandra has always had a mind of her own. And a life of her own—photography, the gallery, friends, books. She doesn't let herself get bored—she loves life too much—so I don't feel I have to be around to entertain her or pay attention to her all the time."

"That sounds like Caroline and me. Though I suppose I depended on her quite a lot, especially at first. But she helped me become more independent, she and Ursula."

Banks wondered why on earth he had opened up that way to Veronica. There was something about the woman he couldn't quite put his finger on. A terrible honesty, a visible effort she made to communicate, to be open. She was working at living, not simply coasting through life like so many. She didn't shirk experience, and Banks found it was impossible not to be as frank in return with someone like that. Was he letting his feelings overrun his judgment? After all, this woman *could* be a murderess.

"How long had you known Caroline before you left your husband?" Banks asked.

"Known her? A few months, but mostly just casually."

"But how did you know how you felt, what you wanted to do?"

"I just knew. Do you mean sexually?"

"Well . . ."

"I don't know," she went on, cutting through his embarrassment. "Certainly it wasn't anything I'd experienced or even thought about before. I suppose I must have, but I don't remember. Of course, there were crushes and a little petting at school, but I imagine everyone indulges in that. I don't know. It was awkward. We were at her flat and she just . . . took me. After that, I knew. I knew what had been missing in my life, what I had been repressing, if you like. And I knew I had to change things. I was buoyant with love and I suppose I expected Claude to understand when I told him."

"But he didn't?"

"It was the closest he ever came to hitting me."

Banks remembered the ex-husband's anger, his humiliation. "What happened?"

"Oh, I know what I did wrong now. At least I think I do." She laughed at herself. "I was crazy with joy then. I expected him to feel happy for me. Can you believe that? Anyway, I moved out the next day and went to live with Caroline in her flat. Then he sold the house and left Eastvale. Later we got the little place on Oakwood Mews. The rest you know."

"And you never looked back."

"Never. I'd found what I was looking for."

"And now?"

Veronica's face darkened. "Now I don't know."

"But you wouldn't go back to him?"

"To Claude? I couldn't do that. Even if he wanted to." She shook her head slowly. "No, whatever the future holds for me, it's certainly not more of my miserable mistake of a past."

In the silence that followed, Banks glanced out the window and was surprised to find the train was passing Peterborough. The landmarks were so familiar: the tall kiln chimneys of the brick factory growing straight from the ground; the white sign of the Great Northern Hotel against its charcoal-grey stone; the truncated cathedral tower.

"What is it?" Veronica asked. "You look so engrossed. Have you seen something?"

"My home town," Banks explained. "Not much of a place, but mine own."

Veronica laughed.

"Where do you come from?" Banks asked.

"Crosby. Near Liverpool, but light-years away, really. It's a horribly stuck-up suburb, at least it was then."

"I'd hardly say Peterborough was stuck-up," Banks said. "Doesn't your poet, Larkin, have something to say about childhood places?"

"You've been doing your research, I see. Yes, he does. And he set it on a train journey like this. It's very funny and very sad. It ends, 'Nothing, like something, can happen anywhere.'"

"Do you read a lot of poetry?"

"Yes. Quite a bit."

"Do you read any journals?"

"Some. The *Poetry Review* occasionally. Mostly I read old stuff. I prefer rhyme and metre, so I tend to stay away from contemporary work, except Larkin, Seamus Heaney and a couple of others, of course. That's one area Caroline and I disagreed on. She liked free verse and I never could see the point of it. What was it Robert Frost said: Like playing tennis without a net?"

"But you've never noticed Ruth Dunne's name in print, never come across her work?"

Veronica tightened her lips and looked out the window. She seemed irritated that Banks had broken the spell and plunged into what must have felt like an interrogation.

"I don't remember it, no. Why?"

"I just wondered what kind of stuff she writes, and why Caroline didn't tell you about her."

"Because she tended to be secretive about her past. Sketchy, anyway. I also suspect that maybe she didn't want to make me jealous."

"Were they still seeing one another?"

"As far as I know, Caroline made no trips to London while we were together. I haven't even been myself for at least three years. No, I mean jealous of a past lover. It can happen, you know—people have even been jealous over *dead* lovers—and I was especially vulnerable, being in such a new and frightening relationship."

"Frightening?"

"Well, yes. Of course. Especially at first. Do you imagine it was easy for me, with my background and my sheltered existence, to go to bed with a woman, to give up my marriage and live with one?"

"Was there anyone else who might have been jealous enough of Caroline's relationship with you?"

Veronica raised her eyebrows. "You're never very far away from your job, are you? It makes it hard to trust you, to open up to you. I can never tell what you're thinking from your expression."

Banks laughed. "That's because I'm a good poker player. But seriously, despite all evidence to the contrary, I *am* a human being. And I'd be a liar if I didn't admit that the foremost thing on my mind is catching Caroline's killer right now. The work is never far away. That's because somebody took something they had no right to."

"And do you think catching and punishing the criminal will do any good?"

"I don't know. It becomes too abstract for me at that point. I told you, I like concrete things. Put it this way, I wouldn't like to think that the person who stabbed Caroline is going to be walking around Eastvale, or anywhere else for that matter, whistling 'Oh, What a Beautiful Mornin' for the rest of his or her life. Do you know what I mean?"

"Revenge?"

"Perhaps. But I don't think so. Something more subtle, more *right* than mere revenge."

"But why do you take it so personally?"

"Somebody has to. Caroline isn't around to take it so personally herself."

Veronica stared at Banks. Her eyes narrowed, then she shook her head.

"What?" Banks asked.

"Nothing. Just trying to understand, thinking what a strange job you do, what a strange man you are. Do all policemen get as involved in their cases?"

Banks shrugged. "I don't know. For some it's just a day's work. Like anyone else, they'll skive off as much as they can. Some get very cynical, some are lazy, some are cruel, vicious bastards with brains the size of a pea. Just people."

"You probably think I don't care about revenge or justice or whatever it is."

"No. I think you're confused and you're too shaken by Caroline's death to think about whoever did it. You're also probably too civilized to feel the blood-lust of revenge."

"Repressed?"

"Maybe."

"Then perhaps a little repression is a good thing. I'll have to tell Ursula that before she releases the raging beast inside me."

Banks smiled. "I hope we've got the killer safely behind bars long before that."

The train passed a patch of waste ground scattered with bright yellow oil drums and old tires, then a factory yard, a housing estate and a graffiti-scarred embankment. Soon, Banks could see Alexander Palace through the window.

"Better get ready," he said, standing up and reaching for his camel-hair overcoat. "We'll be at King's Cross in a few minutes."

II

Half an hour later, Banks looked across the street at the Gothic extravaganza of St Pancras, complete with its chimneys, crocketed towers and crenellated gables. So, here he was, back in London for the first time in almost three years. Black taxis and red double-decker buses clogged the roads and poisoned the streets with exhaust fumes. Horns honked, drivers yelled at one another and pedestrians took their lives into their hands crossing the street.

Veronica had taken a taxi to her friend's house. For Banks, the first priority was lunch, which meant a pint and a sandwich. He walked down Euston Road for a while, taking in the atmosphere, loving it almost as much as he hated it. There didn't appear to have been much snow down here. Apart from occasional lumps of grey slush in the gutters, the streets were mostly clear. The sky was leaden, though, and seemed to promise at least a cold drizzle before the end of the day.

He turned down Tottenham Court Road, found a cosy pub and managed to elbow himself a place at the bar. It was lunchtime, so the place was crowded with hungry and thirsty clerks come to slag the boss and gird up their loins for another session at the grindstone. Banks had forgotten how much he liked London pubs. The Yorkshire people were so proud of their beer and their pubs, it had been easy to forget that a London boozer could be as much fun as any up north. Banks drank a pint of draught Guinness and ate a thick ham-and-cheese sandwich. As always in London, such gourmet treats cost an arm and a leg; even the pint cost a good deal more than it would in Eastvale. Luckily, he was on expenses.

The raised voices all around him, with their London accents, brought it all back, the good and the bad. For years he had loved the city's streets, their energy. Even some of the villains he'd nicked had a bit of class, and those that lacked class at least had a sense of humour.

He pushed his plate aside and lit a cigarette. The bottles ranged at the back of the bar were reflected in the gilt-edged mirror. The barmaid had broken into a sweat trying to keep up with the customers—her upper lip and brow were moist with it—but she managed to maintain her smile. Banks ordered another pint.

He couldn't put his finger on when it had all started to go wrong for him in London. It had been a series of events, most likely, over a long period. But somehow it all merged into one big mess when he looked back: Brian getting into fights at school; his own marriage on the rocks; anxiety attacks that had convinced him he was dying.

But the worst thing of all had been the job. Slowly, subtly, it had changed. And Banks had found himself changing with it. He was becoming more like the vicious criminals he dealt with day in, day out, less able to see good in people and hope for the world. He ran on pure anger and cynicism, occasionally thumped suspects in interrogation and trampled over everyone's rights. And the damnedest thing was, it was all getting him good results, gaining him a reputation as a good copper. He sacrificed his humanity for his job, and he grew to hate himself, what he had become. He had been no better than Dirty Dick Burgess, a superintendent from the Met with whom he had recently done battle in Eastvale.

Life had dragged on without joy, without love. He was losing Sandra and he couldn't even talk to her about it. He was living in a sewer crowded with rats fighting for food and space: no air, no light, no escape. The move up north, if he admitted it, had been his way of escape. Put simply, he had run away before it got too late.

And just in time. While everything in Eastvale hadn't been roses, it had been a damn sight better than those last months in London, during which he seemed to do nothing but stand over corpses in stinking, run-down slums: a woman ripped open from pubes to breastbone, intestines spilling on the carpet; the decaying body of a man with his head hacked off and placed between his legs. He had seen those things, dreamed about them, and knew he could never forget. Even in Eastvale, he sometimes awoke in a cold sweat as the head tried to speak to him.

He finished his pint quickly and walked outside, pulling up his overcoat collar against the chill. So, he was back, but not to stay. Never to stay. So enjoy it. The city seemed noisier, busier and dirtier than ever, but a fresh breeze brought the smell of roast chestnuts from a street vendor on Oxford Street. Banks thought of the good days, the good years: searching for old, leather-bound editions of Dickens on autumn afternoons along Charing Cross Road; Portobello Road market on a crisp, windy spring morning; playing darts with Barney Merritt and his other mates in the Magpie and Stump after a hard day in the witness box; family

outings to Epping Forest on Sunday afternoons; drinks in the street
on warm summer nights at the back of Leicester Square after going
to the pictures with Sandra, the kids safe with a sitter. No, it hadn't
all been bad. Not even Soho. Even that had its comic moments, its
heart. At least it had seemed so before everything went wrong.
Still, he felt human again. He was out of the sewer, and a brief visit
like this one wasn't going to suck him back into it.

First he made a phone call to Barney Merritt, an old friend from
the Yard, to confirm his bed for the night. That done, he caught the
Tube to the Oval. As he sat in the small compartment and read the
ads above the windows, he remembered the countless other
Underground journeys he had made because he always tried to
avoid driving in London. He remembered standing in the smoking
car, crushed together with a hundred or more other commuters, all
hanging on their straps, trying to read the paper and puffing away.
It had been awful, but part of the ritual. How he'd managed to
breathe, he had no idea. Now you couldn't even smoke on the plat-
forms and escalators, let alone on the trains.

He walked down Kennington Road and found the turn-off, a
narrow street of three-storey terrace houses divided into flats, each
floor with its own bay window. At number twenty-three, a huge
cactus stood in the window of the middle flat, and in the top oriel
he could see what looked a stuffed toy animal of some kind. Her
name was printed above the top bell: R. Dunne. No first name, to
discourage weirdos, but all the weirdos knew that only women left
out their first names. There was no intercom. Banks pushed the
bell and waited. Would she be in? What did poets do all day? Stare
at the sky with their eyes in a "fine frenzy rolling"?

Just when he was beginning to think she wasn't home, he heard
footsteps inside the hall and the door opened on a chain. A face—
the face—peered round at him.

"Yes?"

Banks showed his identification card and told her the purpose
of his visit. She shut the door, slid off the chain and let him in.

Banks followed the slender, boyish figure in turquoise slacks
and baggy orange sweatshirt all the way up the carpeted stairs to
the top. The place was clean and brightly decorated, with none of

the smells and graffiti he had encountered in such places so often
in the past. In fact, he told himself, flats like this must cost a fortune
these days. How much did poets make? Surely not that much. It
would be rude to ask.

The flat itself was small. The door opened on a narrow corridor,
and Banks followed Ruth Dunne to the right into the living-room.
He hadn't known what to expect, had no preconceived idea of
what a poet's dwelling should look like, but whatever he might
have imagined, it wasn't this. There was a divan in front of the gas
fire covered with a gaudy, crocheted quilt and flanked on both
sides by sagging armchairs, similarly draped. He was surprised to
find no bookshelves in evidence and assumed her study was elsewhere in the flat, but what was there surprised him as much as what
wasn't: several stuffed toys—a green elephant, a pink frog, a
magenta giraffe—lay around in alcoves and on the ledge by the bay
window, and on three of the four walls elaborate cuckoo clocks
ticked, all set at different times.

"It must be noisy," Banks said, nodding at the clocks.

Ruth Dunne smiled. "You get used to it."

"Why the different times?"

"I'm not interested in time, just clocks. In fact my friends tell me
I'm a chronically late person."

On the low table between the divan and the fire lay a coffee-
table book on watch-making, a couple of bills, an ashtray and a
pack of unfiltered Gauloises.

"Make yourself comfortable," Ruth said. "I've never been
interrogated by the police before. At least not by a detective
chief inspector. Would you like some coffee?"

"Please."

"It's instant, I'm afraid."

"That'll do fine. Black."

Ruth nodded and left the room. If Banks had expected a hostile
welcome, for whatever reason, he was certainly disarmed by Ruth
Dunne's charm and hospitality. And by her appearance. Her shiny
brown hair, medium length, was combed casually back, parted at
one side, and the forelock almost covered her left eye. Her face was
unlined and without make-up. Strong-featured, handsome rather

than pretty, but with a great deal of character in the eyes. They'd seen a lot, Banks reckoned, those hazel eyes. Felt a lot, too. In life, she looked far more natural and approachable than the arrogant, knowing woman in the photograph, yet there was certainly something regal in her bearing.

"How did you find me?" she asked, bringing back two mugs of steaming black coffee and sitting with her legs curled under her on the divan. She held her mug with both hands and sniffed the aroma. The gas fire hissed quietly in the background. Banks sat in one of the armchairs, the kind that seem to embrace you like an old friend, and lit a cigarette. Then he showed her the photograph, which she laughed at, and told her.

"So easy," she said when he'd finished.

"A lot of police work is. Easy and boring. Time-consuming, too."

"I hope that's not a subtle way of hinting I should have come forward earlier?"

"No reason to, had you? Did you know about Caroline's death?"

Ruth reached for the blue paper packet of Gauloises, tapped one out and nodded. "Read about it in the paper. Not much of a report, really. Can you tell me what happened?"

Banks wished he could, but knew he couldn't. If he told her, then he'd have no way of checking what she already knew.

She noticed his hesitation and waved her hand. "All right. I suppose I should think myself lucky to be spared the gory details. Look, I imagine I'm a suspect, if you've come all this way. Can we get that out of the way first? I might have an alibi, you never know, and it'll make for a hell of a more pleasant afternoon if you don't keep thinking of me as a crazed, butch dyke killer." She finally lit the cigarette she'd been toying with, and the acrid tang of French tobacco infused the air.

Banks asked her where she had been and what she had been doing on December 22. Ruth sucked on her Gauloise, thought for a moment, then got up and disappeared down the corridor. When she reappeared, she held an open appointment calendar and carried it over to him.

"I was giving a poetry reading in Leamington Spa, of all places," she said. "Very supportive of the arts they are up there."

"What time did it start?"

"About eight."

"How did you get there?"

"I drove. I've got a Fiesta. It's life in the fast lane all the way for us poets, you know. I was a bit early, too, for a change, so the organizers should remember me."

"Good audience?"

"Pretty good. Adrian Henri and Wendy Cope were reading there, too, if you want to check with them."

Banks noted down the details. If Ruth Dunne had indeed been in Leamington Spa at eight o'clock that evening, there was no conceivable way she could have been in Eastvale at seven-twenty or later. If she was telling the truth about the reading, which could be easily checked, then she was in the clear.

"One thing puzzles me," Banks said. "Caroline had your picture but we couldn't find a copy of your book among her things. Can you think why that might be?"

"Plenty of reasons. She wasn't much of a one for material possessions, wasn't Caroline. She never did seem to hang onto things like the rest of us, acquire possessions. I always envied her that. I did give her a copy of the first book, but I've no idea what happened to it. I sent the second one, too, the one I dedicated to her, but I wasn't sure what her address was then. The odds are it went to an old address and got lost in the system."

Either that or Nancy Wood had run off with both of them, Banks thought, nodding.

"But she hung onto the photograph."

"Maybe she liked my looks better than my poetry."

"What kind of poetry do you write, if you don't mind me asking?"

"I don't mind, but it's a hard one to answer." She tapped the fingers holding the cigarette against her cheek. The short blonde hairs on the back of her hand caught the light. "Let me see, I don't write confessional lesbian poetry, nor do I go in for feminist diatribes. A little wit, I like to think, a good sense of structure, landscape, emotion, myth. . . . Will that do to be going on with?"

"Do you like Larkin?"

Ruth laughed. "I shouldn't, but I do. It's hard not to. I never much admired his conservative, middle class 'little Englandism,' but the bugger certainly had a way with a stanza." She cocked her head. "Do we have a literary copper here? Another Adam Dalgliesh?"

Banks smiled. He didn't know who Adam Dalgliesh was. Some television detective, no doubt, who went around quoting Shakespeare.

"Just curious, that's all," he answered. "Who's your favourite?"

"H.D. A woman called Hilda Dolittle, friend of Ezra Pound's."

Banks shook his head. "Never heard of her."

"Ah. Clearly *not* a literary copper then. Give her a try."

"Maybe I will." Banks took another sip of his coffee and fiddled for a cigarette. "Back to Caroline. When did you last see her?"

"Let me see . . . It was years ago, five or six at least. I think she was about twenty or twenty-one at the time. Twenty going on sixty."

"Why do you say that?" Banks remembered Caroline as beautiful and youthful even in death.

"The kind of life she was leading ages a woman fast—especially on the inside."

"What life?"

"You mean you don't know?"

"Tell me."

Ruth shifted into the cross-legged position. "Oh, I get it. You ask the questions, I answer them. Right?"

Banks allowed himself a smile. "I'm not meaning to be rude," he said, "but that's basically how it goes. I need all the information I can get on Caroline. So far I don't have a hell of a lot, especially about the time she spent in London. If it'll make talking easier for you, I can tell you that we already know she had a conviction for soliciting and gave birth to a child. That's all."

Ruth looked down into her coffee and Banks was surprised to see tears rolling over her cheeks.

"I'm sorry," she said, putting the mug down and wiping her face with the back of her hand. "It just sounds so sad, so pathetic. You mustn't think I'm being flippant, the way I talk. I don't get many visitors so I try to enjoy everyone I meet. I was very upset when I read about Caroline, but I hadn't seen her for a long time. I'll tell you anything I can." A marmalade cat slipped into the room, looked once at Banks, then jumped on the divan next to Ruth and purred. "Meet T.S. Eliot," Ruth said. "He named so many cats, so I thought at least one should be named after him. I call him T.S. for short."

Banks said hello to T.S., who seemed more interested in nestling into the hollow formed by Ruth's crossed legs. She picked up her coffee again with both hands and blew gently on the surface before drinking.

"Caroline started as a dancer," she said. "An exotic dancer, I believe they're called. Well, it's not too much of a leap from that to pleasing the odd, and I do mean *odd*, punter or two for extra pocket-money. I'm sure you know much more about vice here than I do, but before long she was doing the lot: dancing, peep-shows, turning tricks. She was a beautiful child, and she looked even younger than she was. A lot of men around that scene have a taste for fourteen- or fifteen-year-olds, or even younger, and Caroline could fulfil that fantasy when she was eighteen."

"Was she on drugs?"

Ruth frowned and shook her head. "Not as far as I know. Not like some of them. She might have had the odd joint, maybe an upper or a downer now and then—who doesn't?—but nothing really heavy or habitual. She wasn't hooked on anything."

"What about her pimp?"

"Bloke called Reggie. Charming character. One of his women did for him with a Woolworth's sheath-knife shortly before Caroline broke away. You can check your records, I'm sure they'll have all the details. Caroline wasn't involved, but it was a godsend for her in a way."

"How?"

"Surely it's obvious. She was scared stiff of Reggie. He used to bash her about regularly. With him out of the way, she had a chance to slip between the cracks before the next snake came along."

"When did she break away?"

Ruth leaned forward and stubbed out her cigarette. "About a year before she went back up north."

"And you knew her during that period?"

"We lived together. Here. I got this place before the prices rocketed. You wouldn't believe how cheap it was. I knew her before for a little while, too. I'd like to think I played a small part in getting her out of the life."

"Who played the largest part?"

"She did that herself. She was a bright kid and she saw where she was heading. Not many you can say that about. She'd been wanting out for a while, but Reggie wouldn't let go and she didn't know where to run."

"How did you come to meet her?"

"After a poetry reading. Funny, I can remember it like it was yesterday. Out in Camden Town. All we had in the audience was a prostitute and a drunk who wanted to grab the mike and sing 'Your Cheating Heart.' He did, too, right in the middle of my best poem. Afterwards we drove down to Soho—not the drunk, just me and my fellow readers—to the Pillars of Hercules. Know it?"

Banks nodded. He'd enjoyed many a pint of draught Beck's there.

"We just happened to be jammed in a corner next to Caroline and another girl. We got talking, and one thing led to another. Right from the start Caroline struck me as intelligent and wise, wasted on that scummy life. She knew it too, but she didn't know what else she could do. We soon became close friends. We went to the theatre a lot and she loved it. Cinema, art exhibitions." She gave a small laugh. "Anything but classical music or opera. She didn't mind ballet, though. It was all a world she'd never known."

"Was that all there was to your relationship?"

Ruth paused to light another Gauloise before answering. "Of course not. We were lovers. But don't look at me as if I was some kind of corrupter of youth. Caroline knew exactly what she was doing."

"Were you the first woman she'd had such a relationship with?"

"Yes. That was obvious right from the start. She was shy about things at first, but she soon learned." Ruth inhaled the smoke deeply and blew it out. "God, did she learn."

One of the cuckoo clocks went through its motions. They waited until it stopped.

"What do you think turned her into a lesbian?" Banks asked.

Ruth shifted on the sofa and T.S. scampered off. "It doesn't happen like that. Women don't suddenly, quote, turn into lesbians, unquote. They discover that's what they are, what they always were but were afraid to admit because there was too much working against them—social morality, male domination, you name it."

"Do you think there are a lot of women in that situation?"

"More than you imagine."

"What about the men in her life?"

"Work it out for yourself. What do you think it does to a woman to have gross old men sticking their willies in her and meek suburban husbands asking if they can pee in her mouth? You've got the pimp at one end and the perverts at the other. No quarter."

"So Caroline discovered her lesbianism under your guidance?"

Ruth flicked a column of ash into the tray. "You could put it like that, yes. I seduced her. It didn't take her long to figure out that she loathed and feared sex with men. The only difficult thing was overcoming the taboos and learning how to respond to a woman's body, a woman's way of making love. And I'm not talking about dildos and vibrators."

"Why did you split up?"

"Why does anybody split up? I think we'd done what we could for each other. Caroline was restless. She wanted to go back up north. There were no great rows or anything, just a mutual agreement, and off she went."

"Did you know she had a baby?"

"Yes. Colm's. But that was before I met her. She told me she'd just arrived in London and was lucky enough to meet Colm in a pub. Apparently he was a decent enough bloke, just broke all the time. Some of his mates weren't so decent and that's partly what got Caroline involved in the game to start with. You know, just a temporary dancing job at this club, no harm in it, is there? Bit of extra cash, no questions asked. Creeps. In all fairness, I don't think Colm knew. At least not for a while. Then she had his baby and they put it up for adoption."

"Do you remember the name of the club?"

"Yes. It was the Hole-in-the-Wall, just off Greek Street. Dingy looking place."

"This Colm," Banks asked. "Do you know his second name?"

"No. It's funny, but come to think of it, Caroline never used last names when she spoke about people."

"Seen him lately?"

"Me? I've never seen him."

"How come you know so much about him?"

"Because Caroline told me about him when we were first getting to know each other"

"Where did he live?"

"Notting Hill somewhere. Or it could have been Muswell Hill. I'm not sure. Honestly. I can't help you on that one. She never was much of a one for details, just the broad gesture."

"Are you sure Caroline wasn't already pregnant when she arrived in London?"

Ruth frowned and paused, as if she had suddenly remembered something. She turned her eyes away, and when she spoke there was an odd, distant tone to her voice. "What do you mean?"

"I'm just asking."

"As far as I know she wasn't. Unless she was lying to me. I suppose Colm will be able to confirm it if you can find him."

"Why did that question upset you so much?"

She put her hand to her chest. "I don't know what you're talking about."

"You're more defensive than you were earlier."

Ruth shrugged. "It just reminded me of something, that's all."

"Reminded you of what?"

Ruth reached for her coffee cup, but it was empty. Banks waited. He noticed her hand was shaking a little.

"Something that was bothering Caroline. It's not important," Ruth said. "Probably not even true."

"Let me decide."

"Well, it was those dreams she'd been having, and the things she'd been remembering. At least she thought she had. She didn't really know if they were memories or fantasies."

"What about?"

Ruth looked him in the eye, her cheeks flushed. "Oh hell," she said. "Caroline was beginning to think she'd been molested as a child. She felt she'd repressed the incident, but it was making its way back up from her subconscious, perhaps because of all the weird johns she was servicing."

"Molested? When? Where? Who by?"

"I've told you, she wasn't sure she believed it herself."

"Do you know?"

"Shit, yes. When she was a kid. At home. By her father."

TEN

I

"You knew, didn't you?" Banks challenged Veronica Shildon later
that evening. They were eating in an Indonesian restaurant in
Soho. The view out the window was hardly romantic—a peep-
show offering "NAKED GIRLS IN BED" for 50 p—but the food
was excellent and the bar served Tiger beer. Veronica played with
her *nasi goreng*, mixing the shrimp in with the rice. "Knew what?"

"About Caroline's past."

"No. Not the way you think."

"You could have saved me a lot of time and effort."

Veronica shook her head. Her eyes looked watery, on the verge
of tears. Banks couldn't be sure whether it was emotion or the hot
chili peppers. His own scalp was prickling with the heat and his
nose was starting to run. He took another swig of cold Tiger.

"Some things I knew," she said finally. "I knew Caroline had
been on the streets, but I didn't know any of the names or places
involved. When she talked about Ruth she always spoke with affection, but she never mentioned her second name or where they'd
lived."

"You knew they were lovers, though?"

"Yes."

"But weren't you jealous? Didn't you question Caroline about it?"

Veronica snorted. "I had little right to be jealous, did I?
Remember where I was coming from. Caroline told me there'd
been others. She was even living with Nancy Wood when I first
met her. And I was with Claude. You must be very naïve, Mr Banks,
if you think we walked into our relationship like a couple of virgins

with no emotional baggage. And, somehow, I don't honestly believe you are naïve."

"No matter what the rules are," Banks said, "no matter what people try to convince themselves about what they accept and understand, about how open-minded they are, they still can't stop feeling things like jealousy, hatred and fear. Those are powerful, primitive emotions—instincts, if you like—and you can't convince me that you were both so bloody civilized you calmly decided not to feel anything about one another's pasts."

Veronica put down her fork and poured some more beer into her half empty glass. "Quite a speech. And not so long ago you were telling me I was too civilized to feel the need to revenge Caroline's murder."

"Perhaps you are. But that's another matter. Can you answer my question?"

"Yes. I didn't feel jealous about Ruth Dunne. For one thing, it was years ago, and for another, from what I could gather she'd done Caroline a big favour, perhaps the same kind of favour Caroline later did for me. As I said, I didn't know all the details, but I know the gist. And when I talked to Ruth this afternoon after you'd been to see her, I liked her. I was *glad* to think Caroline had met and loved someone like her. That's my answer. Believe it or not, as you choose. Or do you think people like us are just so perverted that all we do is rip each other's clothes off and jump into bed together?"

Banks said nothing. He ate a mouthful of pork *satay* and washed it down with beer. Attracting the waiter's attention, he then ordered two more Tigers. He did believe Veronica. After all, she had felt secure in her relationship with Caroline, and Ruth Dunne had certainly posed no threat.

"So why didn't you tell me what you did know about Caroline's past?" he asked after the beers had arrived.

"I've already told you. I hardly knew anything."

"Maybe not, but if you'd told us what you *did* know, it would have made it easier for us to find out the rest."

Veronica slammed her knife and fork down. Her cheeks flushed and her eyes narrowed to glaring slits. "All right, damn you! So I'm sorry. What more do you want me to say?"

Some of the other diners looked around and frowned, whispering comments to one another. Veronica held Banks's gaze for a few seconds, then picked up her fork again and speared a spicy shrimp far too violently. A few grains of rice skipped off the edge of her plate onto the napkin on her knee.

"What I want to know," Banks said, "is why you didn't tell me what you knew, and whether there's anything else you've been keeping to yourself. See, it's simple really."

Veronica sighed. "You're an exasperating man," she said. "Do you know that?"

Banks smiled.

"All right. I didn't tell you because I didn't want to . . . to soil Caroline's memory. She wasn't that kind of person any more. I couldn't see how it would do any good to drag all that up and let the newspapers get hold of it. Is that good enough?"

"It's a start. But I'll bet there's more to it than that."

Veronica said nothing. Her mouth was pressed shut so tight the edges of her lips turned white.

Banks went on. "You didn't want me or anyone else to think you were the kind of woman to be living with someone with such a lurid past. Am I right?"

"You're a bastard, is what you are," said Veronica through gritted teeth. "What you don't understand is that it takes more than a couple of years of therapy to undo a lifetime's damage. Christ, all the time I keep hearing my mother's voice in my mind, calling me dirty, calling me perverted. Maybe you're right and I didn't want that guilt by association. But I still don't see what good knowing that does you."

"The reason for Caroline's murder could lie in her past. She was running with a pretty rough crowd. I know some of them. I worked the vice squad in Soho for eighteen months, and it's not as glamorous as "Miami Vice," you can be sure of that. Drugs. Prostitution. Gambling. Big criminal business. Very profitable and very dangerous. If Caroline maintained any kind of involvement with these people it could explain a lot."

"But she didn't," Veronica insisted, pressing her hands together and leaning across the table. "She didn't. I lived with her for two

years. In all that time we never went to London and she never
mentioned much about her life there. Don't you see? It was the
future we wanted, not the past. Both of us had had enough of the
past."

Banks pushed his empty plate aside, asked Veronica's permission
to smoke and reached for his cigarettes. When he'd lit one and
inhaled, he took a sip of beer. Veronica folded her napkin in a
perfect square and laid it on the coral tablecloth beside her plate. A
small mound of rice dotted with chunks of garlic, onion and diced
pork remained, but the shrimp were all gone.

Banks glanced out the window and watched a punter in a cloth
cap and donkey jacket hesitate outside the peep-show. He was
probably having a hard time making up his mind with so much to
choose from: "NUDE NAUGHTY AND NASTY" down the street,
"LIVE EROTIC NUDE BED SHOW" next door, and now
"NAKED GIRLS IN BED" opposite. Shoving his hands in his
pockets, he hunched his shoulders and carried on towards Leicester
Square. Either lost his bottle or come to his senses, Banks thought.

Veronica had been watching him, and when Banks turned back
to face her she gave him a small smile. "What were you looking at?"

"Nothing."

"But you were watching so intently."

Banks shrugged. "Coffee? Liqueur?"

"I'd love a Cointreau, if they've got any."

"They'll have it." Banks called the waiter. He ordered a
Drambuie for himself.

"What did you see out there?" Veronica asked again.

"I told you, it was nothing. Just a man, likely down from the
provinces for a soccer match or something. He was checking out
Soho. Probably surprised it was so cheap."

"What do you get for 50 p?"

"Brief glance at a naked tart, if you're lucky. It's a loss leader,
really," Banks said. "Supposed to give you a taste for the real action.
You sit in a booth, put your coin in the slot and a shutter slides
aside so you can see the girl. As soon as your meter's up, so to
speak, the shutter closes. Of course, Soho's been cleaned up a lot
lately, but you can't really keep its spirit down." Already, Banks

noticed, his accent and his patterns of speech had reverted to those of his London days. He had never lost them in almost three years up north, but they had been modified quite a bit. Now here he was, to all intents and purposes a London copper again.

"Do you approve?" Veronica asked.

"It's not a matter of approval. I don't visit the booths or the clubs myself, if that's what you mean."

"But would you like to see it all stamped out of existence?"

"It'd just spring up somewhere else, wouldn't it? That's what I mean about the spirit. Every big city has its vice area: the Red Light district in Amsterdam, the Reeperbahn, Times Square, the Tenderloin, the Yonge Street strip in Toronto. . . . They're all much the same except for what local laws do and don't allow. Prostitution is legal in Amsterdam, for example, and they even have licensed brothels in parts of Nevada. Then there's Las Vegas and Atlantic City for gambling. You can't really stamp it out. For better or for worse, it seems to be part of the human condition. I admire its energy, its vitality, but I despise what it does to people. I recognize its humour, too. In my job, you get to see the funny side from time to time. Maybe it actually makes policing easier, so much vice concentrated in one small area. We can keep closer tabs on it. But we'll never stamp it out."

"I feel so sheltered," Veronica said, looking out the window again. "I never knew any of this existed when I was growing up. Even later, it never seemed to have anything to do with my life. I couldn't even imagine what people did together except for . . . you know." She shook her head.

"And now you're worldly wise?"

"I don't think so, no. But after Caroline, after she brought me to life, at least I was able to see what all the fuss was about. If that's what it felt like, then no wonder everyone went crazy over it. Do you know that Shakespeare sonnet, the one that starts 'The expense of spirit in a waste of shame'? I never understood it until a couple of years ago."

"It's about lust, isn't it?" Banks said. "'Had, having, and in quest to have, extreme.'" Christ, he thought, I'm getting just like that Dalgliesh fellow Ruth Dunne mentioned. Better watch it. He nodded towards the window. "Suits that lot out there more than it suits you."

Veronica smiled. "No, you don't know what I mean. At last I could understand. Even *lust* I could finally understand. Do you see?"

"Yes." Banks lit another cigarette and Veronica held the glass of Cointreau in her hand. "About Caroline's child," he said.

"She never told me."

"Okay. But did she ever make any references to a person called Colm?"

"No. And I'm sure I'd remember a name like that."

"She had no contact with anyone you didn't know, no mysterious letters or phone calls?"

"Not that I ever found out about. I'm not saying she couldn't have had. She could be very secretive when she wanted. What are you getting at?"

Banks sighed and swirled his Drambuie in its glass. "I don't know. I thought she might have kept in touch with the foster parents, adopters, whatever."

"Surely that would have been just too painful for her?"

"Maybe so. Forgive me, I'm grasping at straws." And he was. The child must be about nine or ten now. Far too young to hunt out his mother and stab her with a kitchen knife for abandoning him, or her. Far too young to see the irony in leaving a requiem for himself on the stereo. "There is one thing you might be able to help me with, though," he said.

"Yes?"

"Ruth mentioned that Caroline had begun to suspect she'd been sexually abused as a child. Do you know anything about that?"

Veronica blushed and turned her face to the window. Her profile looked stern against the gaudy neon outside, and the muscle at the corner of her jaw twitched.

"Well?"

"I . . . I can't see what it's got to do with—"

"We've already been through that. Let me be the judge."

"Poor Caroline." Veronica looked directly at Banks again and her expression seemed to relax into sadness. "Melancholy" was a better word, Banks decided, a good Romantic word. Veronica looked melancholy as she fingered her glass and tilted her head before she spoke. "I suppose I didn't tell you for the same reason I didn't tell you anything else about her past. I didn't think it mattered and it would only look bad. Now I feel foolish, but I'm not afraid."

"Did she talk to you about it?"

"Yes. At first it was like Ruth said. She had dreams, terrible dreams. Do you know what sexual abuse does to a child, Mr Banks?"

Banks nodded. Jenny Fuller, the psychologist who occasionally helped with cases, had explained it to him once.

"Then you know they begin to hate themselves. They lose all self-respect, they get depressed, they feel suicidal, and they often seek reckless, self-destructive ways of life. All those things happened to Caroline. And more."

"Is that why she left home?"

"Yes. But she'd had to wait a long time to get out. Till she was sixteen."

"What do you mean? When did this start happening?"

"When she was eight."

"Eight? Jesus Christ! Go on. I take it this is fact, not fantasy?"

"I can't offer you irrefutable proof, especially now Caroline's dead, but you can take my word for it if you're willing. As I said, at first it was just dreams, fears, suspicions, then when she started working on it with Ursula, more memories began to surface. She'd buried the events, of course, which is perfectly natural under the circumstances. Just imagine a child's confusion when the father she loves starts to do strange and frightening things with her body and tells her she must never tell anybody or terrible things will happen to her. It ties her in knots emotionally. It must be good, because Daddy is doing it. Perhaps she even enjoys the attention. But it doesn't *feel* good, it hurts. And why will she go to hell if she ever tells anyone?"

"What happened?"

"As far as she could piece it together, it occurred first when she was eight. Her mother was having a difficult pregnancy and spent the last two weeks of her term in hospital under close observation. Something to do with her blood pressure and the possibility of toxaemia. Caroline was left alone in the big house with her father, and he started coming to her bedroom at nights, asking her to be a good girl and play with him. Before long he was having intercrural sex with her. It's not very clear how far he went. She remembered pain, but not extreme agony or bleeding. Obviously, he was careful. He didn't want anyone to find out."

"What does 'intercrural' mean?" Banks asked. "I've never heard the word before."

Veronica blushed. "I suppose it is a bit technical. It was Ursula who used it first. It means between the thighs, rather than true penetration."

Banks nodded. "What happened when the mother came home?"

"It continued, but with even more caution. It didn't stop until she was twelve and had her first period."

"He wasn't interested after that?"

"No. She'd become a woman. That terrified him, or so Ursula reckoned."

Banks drew on his cigarette and looked out at the peep-show. Two swaying teenagers in studded leather jackets stood in the foyer now, arguing with the cashier. A girl slipped out past them. She couldn't have been more than seventeen or eighteen from what Banks could see of her pale drawn face in the street light. She clutched a short, black, shiny plastic coat tightly around her skinny frame and held her handbag close to her side. She looked hungry, cold and tired. As far as he could make out, she wasn't wearing stockings or tights—in fact she looked naked but for the coat—which probably meant she was on her way to do the same job in another club nearby, after she'd stopped off somewhere for her fix.

"Gary Hartley told DC Gay that his sister had always hated him," Banks said, almost to himself. "He said she even tried to drown him in his bath once when he was a baby. Apparently, she made his life a misery. Her mother's, too. Gary blamed her for sending his mother to an early grave. I've met him myself, and he's a very disturbed young man."

Veronica said nothing. She had finished her drink and had only the dregs of her coffee left to distract her. The waiter sidled up with the bill.

"What I'd like to know is," Banks said, picking it up, "did Gary know why she'd treated him that way right from the start? Just imagine the psychological effect. There he was, someone new and strange, the root and cause of all her suffering at her father's hands. Her mother had deserted her, and now when she came back she was more interested in this whining, crying little brat than in Caroline herself. My sister was born when I was six and I clearly remember feeling jealous. It must have been countless times worse for Caroline, after what had happened with her father. Of course, Gary couldn't have known at the time, not for years perhaps, but did she ever tell him that her father had abused her sexually?"

Veronica started to speak, then stopped herself. She glanced at Banks's cigarette as if she wanted one. Finally, when she could find nowhere to hide, she breathed, "Yes."

"When?"

"As soon as she felt certain it was true."

"Which was?"

"A couple of weeks before she died."

II

Banks walked Veronica to Charing Cross Road and got her a taxi to Holland Park, where she was staying with her friend. After she'd gone, he paused to breathe the night air and feel the cool needles of rain on his face, then went back down Old Compton Street to club-land. It was Friday night, about ten-thirty, and the punters were already deserting the Leicester Square boozers for the lure of more drink and a whiff of sex.

In a seedy alley off Greek Street, notable mostly for the rubbish on its pavements, Banks found the Hole-in-the-Wall. Remarkable. It had been there in his days on the vice squad, and it was still there, looking just the same. Not many places had such staying power—except the old landmarks, almost traditions by now, like the Raymond Revue Bar.

He kicked off a sheet of wet newspaper that had stuck to his sole and walked down the steps. The narrow entrance on the street was ringed with low-watt bulbs, and photos in a glass display case showed healthy, smiling, busty young women, some in leather, some in lacy underwear. The sign promised a topless bar and "LIVE GIRLS TOTALLY NUDE."

The place was dim and smoky inside, noisy with customers trying to talk above the blaring music. It took Banks a minute or so to get his bearings. During that time, a greasy-haired lad with a sloth-like manner had relieved him of his admittance fee and indicated in slow-motion that there were any number of seats available. Banks chose to sit at the bar.

He ordered a half of lager and tried not to have a heart attack when he heard the price. The woman who served him had a nice smile and tired blue eyes. Her curly blonde hair framed a pale, moon-shaped face with too much red lipstick and blue eye-shadow. Her breasts stood firmly and proudly to attention, evidence, Banks was sure, of a recent silicone job.

Other waitresses out on the dim floor weaving among the smoky spotlights didn't boast the barmaid's dimensions. Still, they came, like fruit, in all shapes and sizes—melons, apples, pears, mangoes—and, as is the way of all flesh, some were slack and some were firm. The girls themselves looked blank and only seemed to react if some over-eager punter tweaked a nipple, strictly against house rules. Then they would either scold him and walk off in a huff, call one of the bouncers or make arrangements for tweaking the other nipple in private later.

On the stage, gyrating and chewing gum at the same time to a song that seemed to be called "I Want Your Sex," was a young black woman dressed only in a white G-string. She looked in good shape: strong thighs, flat, taut stomach and firm breasts. Perhaps she really wanted to be a dancer. Some girls on the circuit did. When she wasn't dancing like this to earn a living, Banks thought, she was probably working out on a Nautilus machine or doing ballet exercises in a pink tutu in a studio in Bloomsbury.

Watching the action and thinking his thoughts in the hot and smoky club, Banks felt a surge of the old excitement, the adrenaline. It was good to be back, to be here, where anything could happen. Most of the time his job was routine, but he had to admit to himself that part of its appeal lay in those rare moments out on the edge, never far from trouble or danger, where you could smell evil getting closer and closer.

The lager tasted like piss. Cat's piss, at that. Banks shoved it aside and lit a cigarette. That helped.

"Can I get you anything more, sir?" the barmaid asked. He was sitting and she was standing, which somehow put her exquisitely manufactured breasts at Banks's eye-level. He shifted his gaze from the goose-bumps around her chocolate-coloured nipples to her eyes. He felt his cheek burn and, if he cared to admit it, more than just that.

"No," he said, his mouth dry. "I haven't finished this one yet."

She smiled. Her teeth were good. "I know. But people often don't. They tell me it tastes like cat's piss and ask for a real drink."

"How much does a real drink cost?"

She told him.

"Forget it. I'm here on business. Tuffy in?"

Her eyes narrowed. "Who are you? You ain't law, are you?"

Banks shook his head. "Not down here, no. Just tell him Mr Banks wants to see him, will you, love?"

Banks watched her pick up a phone at the back of the bar. It took no more than a few seconds.

"He said to go through." She seemed surprised by the instruction and looked at Banks in a new light. Clearly, anyone who got in to see the boss that easily had to be a somebody. "It's down past the—"

"I know where it is, love." Banks slid off the bar stool and threaded his way past tables of drooling punters to the fire-door at the back of the club. Beyond the door was a brightly lit corridor, and at the end was an office door. In front stood two giants. Banks didn't recognize either of them. Turnover in hired muscle was about as fast as that in young female flesh. Both looked in their late twenties, and both had clearly boxed. Judging by the state of their noses, neither had won many bouts; still, they could make mince-meat of Banks with their hands tied behind their backs, unless his speed and slipperiness gave him an edge. He felt a tremor of fear as he neared them, but nothing happened. They stood back like hotel doormen and opened the door for him. One smiled and showed the empty spaces of his failed vocation.

In the office, with its scratched desk, threadbare carpet, telephone, pin-ups on the wall and institutional green filing cabinets, sat Tuffy Telfer himself. About sixty now, he was fat, bald and rubicund, with a birthmark the shape of a teardrop at one side of his fleshy red nose. His eyes were hooded and wary, lizard-like, and they were the one feature that didn't seem to fit the rest of him. They looked more as if they belonged to some sexy Hollywood star of the forties or fifties—Victor Mature, perhaps, or Leslie Howard—rather than an ugly, aging gangster.

Tuffy was one of the few remaining old-fashioned British gangsters. He had worked his way up from vandalism and burglary as a juvenile, through fencing, refitting stolen cars and pimping to get to the dizzy heights he occupied today. The only good things Banks knew about him were that he loved his wife, a peroxide ex-stripper called Mirabelle, and that he never had anything to do with drugs. As a pimp, he had been one of the few *not* to get his girls hooked. Still, it was no reason to get sentimental over the bastard. He'd had one of his girls splashed with acid for trying to turn him in, though nobody could prove it, and there were plenty of women old before their time thanks to Tuffy Telfer. Banks had been the bane of his existence for about three months many years ago. The evil old sod hadn't been able to make a move without Banks getting there first. The police had never got enough evidence to arrest Tuffy himself, though Banks had managed to put one or two of his minions away for long stretches.

"Well, well, well," said Tuffy in the East-end accent he usually put on for the punters. He had actually been raised by a meek middle-class family in Wood Green, but few people other than the police knew that. "If it ain't Inspector Banks."

"*Chief* Inspector now, Tuffy."

"I always thought you'd go far, son. Sit down, sit down. A drink?" The only classy piece of furniture in the entire room was a well-stocked cocktail cabinet.

"A real drink?"

"Wha'? Oh, I get it." Telfer laughed. "Been sampling the lager downstairs, eh? Yeah, a real drink."

"I'll have a Scotch then. Mind if I smoke?"

Telfer laughed again. "Go ahead. Can't indulge no more myself." He tapped his chest. "Quack says it's bad for the ticker. But I'll get enough second-hand smoke running this place to see me to my grave. A bit more won't do any harm."

Tuffy was hamming it up, as usual. He didn't have to be here to run the Hole-in-the-Wall; he had underlings who could do that for him. Nor was he so poor he had to sit in such a poky office night after night. The club was just a minor outpost of Tuffy's empire, and nobody, not even vice, knew where all its colonies were. He had a house in Belgravia and owned property all over the city. He also mixed with the rich and famous. But every Friday and Saturday night he chose to come and sit here, just like in the old days, to run his club. It was part of his image, part of the sentimentality of organized crime.

"Making ends meet?" Banks asked.

"Just. Times is hard, very hard." One of the musclemen put Banks's drink—a generous helping—on the desk in front of him. "But what can I say?" Tuffy went on. "I get by. What you been up to?"

"Moved up north. Yorkshire."

Tuffy raised his eyebrows. "Bit drastic, in'it?"

"I like it fine."

"Whatever suits."

"Not having a glass yourself?"

Tuffy sniffed. "Doctor's orders. I'm a sick man, Mr Banks. Old Tuffy's not long for this world, and there'll not be many to mourn his passing, I can tell you that. Except for the nearest and dearest, bless her heart."

"How is Mirabelle?"

"She's hale and hearty. Thank you for asking, Mr Banks. Remembers you fondly, does my Mirabelle. Wish I could say the same myself." There was humour in his voice, but hardness in his hooded eyes. Banks heard one of the bruisers shift from foot to foot behind him and a shiver went up his spine. "What can I do you for?" Tuffy asked.

"Information."

Tuffy said nothing, just sat staring. Banks sipped some Scotch and cast around for an ashtray. Suddenly, one appeared from behind his shoulder, as if by magic. He set it in front of him.

"A few years ago you had a dancer working the club, name of Caroline Hartley. Remember her?"

"What if I do?" Telfer's expression betrayed no emotion.

"She's dead. Murdered."

"What's it got to do with me?"

"You tell me, Tuffy."

Telfer stared at Banks for a moment, then laughed. "Know how many girls we get passing through here?" he said.

"A fair number, I'll bet."

"A fair number indeed. The punters are constantly demanding fresh meat. See the same dancer twice they think they've been had. And you're talking how many years ago?"

"Six or seven."

Telfer rested his pale, pudgy hands on the blotter. "Well, you can see my point then, can't you?"

"What about your records?"

"Records? What you talking about?"

Banks nodded towards the filing cabinets. "You must keep clear and accurate records, Tuffy—cash flow, wages, rent, bar take. For the taxman, remember?"

Telfer cleared his throat. "Yeah, well, what if I do?"

"You could look her up. Come on, Tuffy, we've been through all this before, years ago. I know you keep a few notes on every girl who passes through here in case you might want to use her again, maybe for a video, a stag party, some special—"

Telfer held up a hand. "All right, all right, I get your drift. It's all above-board. You know that. Cedric, see if you can find the file, will you?"

One of the bruisers opened a filing cabinet. "Cedric?" Banks whispered, eyebrows raised.

Telfer shrugged. His chins wobbled. They sat silently, Telfer tapping his short fat fingers on the desk while Cedric rummaged through the files, muttering the alphabet to himself as he did so.

"Ain't here," Cedric announced finally.

"You sure?" Telfer asked. "It begins with a 'aitch—Hartley. That comes after 'gee' and before 'eye.'"

Cedric grunted. "Ain't here. Got a Carrie 'Eart, but no Caroline 'Artley."

"Let's have a look," Banks said. "She might have used a stage name."

Telfer nodded and Cedric handed over the file. Pinned to the top-left corner was a four-by-five black-and-white picture of a younger Caroline Hartley, topless and smiling, her small breasts pushed together by her arms. She could easily have passed for a fourteen-year-old, even a mature twelve-year-old. Below the photo, in Telfer's surprisingly neat and elegant hand, were the meagre details that had interested him about Caroline Hartley: "Vital statistics: 34-22-34. Colour of hair: jet-black. Eyes: blue. Skin: olive and satiny" (Banks hadn't suspected Tuffy had such a poetic streak). And so it went on. Telfer obviously gave his applicants quite an interview.

The one piece of information that Banks hoped he might find was at the end, an address under her real name: "Caroline Hartley, c/o Colm Grey." It was old now, of course, and might no longer be of any use. But if it was Colm Grey's address, and he was poor, he might well have hung onto his flat, unless he'd left the city altogether. Also, now Banks had his last name, Colm Grey would be easier to track down. He recognized the street name. It was somewhere between Notting Hill and Westbourne Park. He had lived not far from there himself twenty years ago.

"Got what you want?" asked Telfer.

"Maybe." Banks handed the file back to Cedric, who replaced it, then finished his Scotch.

"Well, then," said Tuffy with a smile. "Nice of you to drop in. But you mustn't let me keep you." He stood up and shook hands. His grip was firm but his palm was sweaty. "Not staying long, are you? Around here, I mean."

Banks smiled. "No."

"Not thinking of coming back to stay?"

"No."

"Good. Good. Just wanted to be sure. Well, do pop in again the next time you're down, won't you, and we'll have another good old natter."

"Sure, Tuffy. And give my love to Mirabelle."

"I will. I will, Mr Banks."

The bruisers stood aside and Banks walked out of the office and down the corridor unscathed. When he got back to the noisy smoky club, he breathed a sigh of relief. Tuffy obviously remembered what a pain in the arse he'd been, but working on the edge of the law, as he did, he had to play it careful. True, plenty of his operations *were* above-board. It was a game—give and take, live and let live—and both sides knew it. Banks had come close to breaking the rules once or twice, and Tuffy wanted to be sure he wouldn't be around to do that again. Questions that sounded like friendly curiosity were often, in fact, thinly veiled threats.

"Another drink, dear?" the mammarially magnificent barmaid said as Banks passed by.

"No, love. Sorry, have to be off now. Maybe another time."

"Story of my life," she said, and her breasts swung as she turned away.

Outside, Banks fastened his overcoat, shoved his hands deep in his pockets and walked along Greek Street towards the Tottenham Court Road Tube station. He had thought of taking a taxi, but it was only midnight, and Barney lived a stone's throw from the Central line. At Soho Square he saw a drunk in a tweed overcoat and trilby vomiting in the gutter. A tart, inadequately dressed for the cold, stood behind him and leaned against the wall, arms folded across her chest, looking disgusted.

How did that poem end? Banks wondered. The one Veronica had quoted earlier that evening. Then he remembered. After its haunting summary of the horrors of lust, it finished, "All this the world well knows; yet none knows well / To shun the heaven that leads men to this hell." Certainly knew his stuff, did old Willie. They didn't call him "the Bard" for nothing, Banks reflected, as he turned up Sutton Row towards the bright lights of Charing Cross Road.

III

The next morning, after a chat with Barney over bacon and eggs, Banks set out to find Colm Grey. He had arranged to have lunch with Veronica and had asked Barney to check Ruth Dunne's alibi and to see what he could find on the stabbing of Caroline's pimp, Reggie, just to cover all the angles.

The rush-hour crowd had dwindled by the time he got a train, and he was even able to grab a seat and read the *Guardian*, the way he used to do.

He got off at Westbourne Park and walked towards Notting Hill until he found the address on St Luke's Road. Five names matched the bells beside the front door, and he was in luck: C. Grey was one of them, flat four.

Banks pushed the bell and stood by the intercom. No response. He tried again and waited a couple of minutes. It looked like Grey was out. The way things stood at the moment, Grey was hardly a prime suspect, but he was a loose end that had to be tied up. He was the only one who knew the full story about Caroline Hartley's child. Just as Banks started to walk away, he thought he heard a movement behind the door. Sure enough, it opened and a young man stood there, hair standing on end, eyes bleary, stuffing a white shirt in the waist of his jeans.

He frowned when he saw Banks. "Wharrisit? What time is it?"

"Half past nine. Sorry to disturb you." Banks introduced himself and showed his identification. "It's about Caroline Hartley."

The name didn't register at first, then Grey suddenly gaped and said, "Bloody hell! You'd better come in."

Banks followed him upstairs to a two-room flat best described as cosy. The furniture needed reupholstering and the place needed dusting and a damn good tidying up.

"I was sleeping," Grey said as he bent to turn on the gas fire. "Excuse me a minute." When he came back he had washed his face and combed his hair and he carried a cup of instant coffee. "Want some?" he asked Banks.

"No. This shouldn't take long. Mind if I smoke?"

"Be my guest."

Grey sat opposite him, leaning forward as if hunched over his steaming coffee cup. He was lanky with a long pale face, pitted from ancient acne or chicken-pox. He heeded a shave and a trim, and his slightly protruding eyes were watery blue.

"Is it bad news?" he asked, as if he were used to life being one long round of bad news.

"You mean you don't know?"

"Obviously, or I wouldn't be asking. Well?"

Banks took a deep breath. He had assumed Grey would have read about the murder in the papers. "Caroline Hartley was murdered in Eastvale on December twenty-second," he said finally.

At first, Grey didn't seem to react. He couldn't have been much paler, so losing colour would have been no indication, and his eyes were already watery enough to look like they were on the verge on tears. All he did was sit silent and still for about a minute, completely still, and so silent Banks wondered if he were even breathing. Banks tried to imagine Grey and Caroline Hartley as a couple, but he couldn't.

"Are you all right?" he asked.

"Can I have one?" Grey indicated the cigarettes. "Supposed to have chucked it in, but . . ."

Banks gave him a cigarette, which he lit and puffed on like a dying man on oxygen. "I don't suppose this is a social call, either?" he said.

Banks shook his head.

Grey sighed. "I haven't seen Caroline for about eight years. Ever since she started running with the wrong crowd."

"Tuffy Telfer?"

"That's the bastard. Just like a father to her, he was, to hear her speak."

Banks hoped not. "Did you ever meet him?"

"No. I wouldn't have trusted myself with him for ten seconds. I'd have swung for the bastard."

Not a chance, Banks thought. Colm Grey couldn't have got within a hundred yards of Tuffy Telfer without getting at least both arms and legs broken. "What caused you and Caroline to split up?" he asked.

"Just about everything." Grey flicked some ash onto the hearth by the gas fire and reached for his coffee again. "I suppose it really started going downhill when she got pregnant."

"What happened? Did you try to give her the push?"

Grey stared at Banks. "Couldn't be further from it. We were in love. I was, anyway. When she got pregnant she just turned crazy. I wanted to have it, the kid, even though we were poor, and she didn't want rid of it at first. At least I don't think she did. Maybe I pushed her too hard, I don't know. Maybe she was just doing it to please me. Anyway, she was miserable all the time she was carrying, but she wouldn't have an abortion either. There was time, if she'd wanted, but she kept putting it off until it was too late. Then she was up and down like a yo-yo, one day wishing she could have a miscarriage, taking risks walking out in icy weather, maybe hoping she'd just slip and fall, the next day feeling guilty and hating herself for being so cruel. Then, as soon as the child was born, she couldn't wait to get shut of the blighter."

"Where is the child now?"

"No idea. Caroline never even wanted to see it. As soon as it was born it was whisked off to its new parents. She didn't even want to know whether it was a girl or a boy. Then things started getting worse for us, fast. Caroline worked at getting her figure back, like nothing had ever happened. As soon as she got introduced to Telfer's crowd, that was it. She seemed hell-bent on self-destruction, don't ask me why."

"Who introduced her to Telfer?"

Colm bit his lower lip, then said, "I blamed myself, after I found out. You know what it's like, a man doesn't always choose his friends well. The crowd we went about with, Caroline and me, it was a pretty mixed bunch. Some of them liked to go up west on a weekend and do the clubs. We went along too a few times. Caroline seemed fascinated by it all. Or horrified, I never could make out which. She was well into the scene before I even found out, and there was nothing I could do to stop her. She was a good-looking kid, a real beauty, and she must have caught someone's eye. I should think they're always on the look-out for new talent at those places.

"One night she came home really late. I was beside myself with worry and it came out as anger—you know, like when your mother always yelled at you if you were late. We had a blazing row and I called her all the names under the sun. It was then she told me. In detail. And she rubbed my face in it, laughed at me for not catching on sooner. Where did I think her new clothes were coming from? How did I think we could afford to go out so often? I was humiliated. I should have walked out there and then, but I was a fool. Maybe it was just a wild phase, maybe it would go away. That's what I tried to convince myself. But it didn't go away. The trouble was, I still loved her." Colm rested his chin in his hand and stared at the floor. "A couple of months later we split up. She left. Just walked out one evening and never came back. Didn't even take her belongings with her, what little she had." He smiled sadly. "Never much of a one for possessions, wasn't Caroline. Said they only tied her down."

"Had you been fighting all that time?"

"No. There was only the one big row, then everything was sort of cold. I was trying to accept what she was up to, but I couldn't. It just wasn't working with her coming in at all hours—or not at all—and me knowing what she'd been up to, imagining her in bed with fat, greasy punters and dancing naked in front of slobbering businessmen."

"Where did she go?"

"Dunno. Never saw or heard from her again. She was a great kid and I loved her, but I couldn't stand it. I was heading for a breakdown. She was living life in the fast lane, heading for self-destruct. I tried to stop her but she just laughed at me and told me not to be such a bore."

"Did she ever tell you anything about her past?"

"Not a lot, no. Didn't get on with her mum and dad so she ran off to the big city. Usual story."

"Ever mention her brother?"

"No. Didn't know she had one."

"Did she ever tell you about her dreams?"

"Dreams?" he frowned. "No, why?"

"It doesn't matter. What about you? What did you do after she'd gone?"

"Me? Well, I didn't exactly join the Foreign Legion, but I did run away and try to forget. I sublet the flat for a year and drifted around Europe. France mostly, grape-picking and all that. Came back, got a job as a bicycle courier, and now I'm doing 'the Knowledge.' Nearly there, too With a bit of luck I'll 'Get Out' and have my 'Bill and Badge' inside a year."

"Good luck." Banks had heard how difficult it was riding around on a moped day after day in the traffic fumes, memorizing over eighteen thousand street names and the numerous permutations of routes between them. But that was what one had to do to qualify as a London taxi driver. "Did you forget her?" he asked.

"You never do, do you, really? What did she do after she left me? Do you know?"

Banks gave him a potted history of Caroline's life up to her death, and again Grey sat still after he'd finished.

"She always was funny about sex," he said. "Not that I'd have guessed, like, that she was a lezzie. I've nothing against them—live and let live, I say—but sex always seemed like some kind of trial or test with her, you know, as if she was trying to find out whether she really liked it or not. I suppose not liking it made it easier for her to live on the game, in a way. It was just a job. She didn't have to like it."

Banks nodded. It was common knowledge that a lot of prostitutes were lesbians

There was nothing more to say. He stood up and held out his hand. Grey leaned forward and shook it.

"Were you working on the twenty-second?" Banks asked. Grey smiled. "My alibi? Yes, yes I was. You can check. And I've got to get started today, too. When you're doing 'the Knowledge' you eat, breathe and sleep it."

"I know."

"Besides, I don't even know where Eastvale is."

On his way out Banks offered Grey another cigarette, but he declined. "It didn't taste all that good, and I couldn't justify starting again. Thanks for telling me . . . you know . . . about her life. At least someone seemed to make her happy. She deserved that." He shook his head. "She was just one fucked-up kid when I knew her. We never had a chance."

Outside, Banks turned up his collar and walked through the squares and side-streets towards Notting Hill Gate. This area had been his first home in London when he had come as a student. Back then, the tall houses with their white façades had been in poor repair, and small flats were just about affordable. Banks had paid seven pounds a week for an L-shaped room, with free mice, in a house that included one out-of-work jazz trumpeter, an earnest social worker, a morose and anorexic-looking woman on the second floor who wore beads and a kaftan and never spoke to anyone, and Jimmy, the cheerful and charming bus driver who Banks suspected of selling marijuana on the side.

He passed the house, on Powis Terrace, and felt a twinge of nostalgia. That small room, now with lace curtains in the window, was where he and Sandra had first made love in those carefree days when he had been unhappy with his business studies courses but still hadn't quite known what to do with his life.

Back then the area had been very much a swinging sixties enclave with its requisite mixture of musicians, poets, artists, dopers, revolutionaries and general drop-outs. It had suited Banks at the time. He enjoyed the music, the animated discussions and the aura of spontaneity, but he could never wholeheartedly turn on, tune in and drop out. He had wanted to get away from home, from the dull routine of Peterborough, and the Notting Hill flat had been both a cheap and exciting way of finding out what life was all about. Ah, to be eighteen again . . .

He walked up to the main intersection and took the Underground at Notting Hill Gate. He was on the Central line, and he still had some time to kill, so he got off at Tottenham Court Road, in the same general area he'd been in the previous evening. He was feeling vaguely depressed after his talk with Colm Grey, which had reduced a couple of his favourite theories to shreds, and thought a city walk in the bracing air might help blow away the blues.

Soho was another world in the daytime. The clubs and love shops and peep-shows were still there, but somehow the glitz and sleaze only managed to look anaemic in daylight. The gaudy lights held no allure; they were washed out, paled by even the grey winter

light. In the daytime, the siren-song of sex for hire was muted to a
distant, nagging whine; there was no hiding the cheap, shabby
reality of the product.

But another kind of vital street life took the ascendant—the
world of markets, of business. Banks wandered among the stalls on
Berwick Street, which seemed to sell everything from pineapples
and melons to cotton panties, cups and saucers, watches, mixed
nuts and egg-cutters. Under one stall, a big brown dog lay sheltered watching the passers-by with mournful eyes.

Feeling better, he found a phone booth on Great Marlborough
Street and called Barney Merritt at Scotland Yard. As Banks had
expected, and hoped, Ruth Dunne's alibi checked out.

The stabbing of Reggie Becker was also as clear-cut as could be.
The killer, a seventeen-year-old prostitute called Brenda Meers, had
stabbed Becker five times in broad daylight on Greek Street. At least
two of the wounds had nicked major arteries and he had bled to
death before the ambulance got there. Eyewitnesses abounded,
though fewer came forward later than were present at the time.
When asked why she had done it, Brenda Meers said it was because
Reggie was trying to make her go with a man who wanted her to
drink his urine and eat his faeces. She had been with him before and
didn't think she could stand it again. She had begged Reggie all
morning not to make her go, but he wouldn't relent, so she walked
into Woolworth's, bought a cheap sheath-knife and stabbed him. As
far as the police were concerned, Reggie Becker was no great loss,
and Brenda would at least get the benefit of psychiatric counselling.

So that was that: the London connection ruled out. But maybe
he hadn't wasted his time entirely. He now had a much fuller
picture of Caroline Hartley, even if he did have to throw out that
neat theory of a connection between the Vivaldi *Laudate pueri* and
the child she had given birth to. He still believed the music was
important, but he could no longer tell how or where it fit.

He looked at his watch. Just time to buy Sandra and Tracy presents in Liberty's, and maybe something for Brian from Virgin
Records on Oxford Street. Then it would be time to meet Veronica
for lunch and set off. He wondered what, if any, developments
would be waiting for him back in Eastvale.

ELEVEN

I

"You don't think he did it, do you?" Susan Gay asked Banks over coffee and toasted teacakes in the Golden Grill. It was two, largely frustrating days after his return from London.

"Gary Hartley?" Banks shrugged. "I don't know. I don't suppose it makes much sense. Gary finds out Caroline was abused as a child so he kills her? All I know is that she told him about it a couple of weeks before she was killed. But you're right, we've no real motive at all. On the other hand, she *did* make his life a misery. Then she ran off and left him stuck with the old man. A thing like that can fester into hatred. The timing is interesting, too."

"Does he know anything about classical music?"

"We'll have to find out. He's certainly well-read. Look at all those books around the place, and the way he speaks, his vocabulary. He's way beyond the range of most teenagers. He could easily have come across the information about *Laudate pueri* somewhere, then seen the record at Caroline's."

"So you're going to see him?"

"Yes. And I'd like you to come along if you can spare the time. Anything happening with the break-ins?"

"Nothing that can't wait."

"Good. Remember, Gary's lied to us before. I want to see the old man, too. Who knows, we might be able to get something out of him."

"He was pretty useless last time," Susan said. "I'm not convinced he's all there." She shivered.

"Cold?"

She shook her head. "Just the thought of that house."

"I know what you mean. Let Phil know, will you? I want the three of us in on this. I'll be with the super, filling him in." Banks looked at his watch. "Say half an hour?"

Susan nodded and left.

Thirty minutes later they sat in an unmarked police Rover with Susan at the wheel and Banks hunched rather glumly in the back, missing his music. Sandra was using the Cortina to buy photographic supplies in York, so they had had to sign a car out of the pool. Susan's driving was assured, though not as good as Richmond's, Banks noted. Sergeant Hatchley had been the worst, he remembered, a bloody maniac on the road.

Despite more snow, road conditions were clear enough. It was, in fact, much brighter in the north, for once, than it had been in London, and a weak winter sun shone on the distant snow-covered fells, spreading a pastel coral glow.

In under an hour they pulled into the familiar Harrogate street and rang Hartley's doorbell. As expected, Gary answered. Giving nothing but a "you again" look, he wandered back into the front room, leaving them to follow.

The room hadn't been cleaned or tidied since their last visit, and a few more beer cans and tab ends had joined the wreckage on the hearth. The air smelled stale, like a pub after closing-time. Banks longed to open the window to let in some air. Before he could get there, Richmond beat him to it, yanking back the heavy curtains and raising the window. Gary squinted at the burst of sunlight but said nothing.

"We've got a few more questions to ask you," Banks said, "but first I'd like a word with your father."

"You can't. He's sick, he's resting." Gary gripped the chair arm and sat up. He reached for a cigarette and lit it. "Doctor's orders."

"I'm sorry, Gary. I already know most of it. I just need him to fill me in on a few details."

"What do you know? What are you talking about?"

"Caroline . . . your father."

Gary sagged back into his chair. "Oh God," he whispered. "You know?"

"Yes."

"Then you can hardly imagine he's going to tell you anything, can you? He's asleep, anyway. Practically in a bloody coma."

Banks stood up. "Stay with him, will you, Phil? Susan, come with me."

Susan followed Banks upstairs. They both heard Gary cry "No!" as they went.

"This way, sir." Susan pointed to Mr Hartley's door and Banks pushed it open.

If only Gary had turned off the electric fire, Banks thought later, the smell wouldn't have been so bad. As it was, Susan put her hand over nose and mouth and staggered back, while Banks reached for a handkerchief. Neither advanced any further into the room. The old man lay back on his pillows, emaciated almost beyond recognition. Judging by the reddish discoloration of the veins in his scrawny neck, Banks guessed he had been dead at least two days. It would take an expert to fix the time more exactly than that, though, as there were many factors to take into consideration, not least among them his age, the state of his health and the warm temperature of the room.

"Call the local CID," Banks told Susan, "and tell them to arrange for a police surgeon and a scene-of-crime team. You know the drill."

Susan hurried downstairs and went to phone while Banks gently closed the door and returned to the front room. Gary looked at him as he entered. The boy seemed drained of all emotion, tired beyond belief. Banks motioned for Richmond to stand by the window, where Gary couldn't see him, then sat down close to Gary and leaned forward.

"Want to tell me about it, son?" he asked.

"What's to tell?" Gary lit a new cigarette from the stub of his old one. His long fingers were stained yellow with nicotine around the nails.

"You know." Banks pointed at the ceiling. "What happened?"

Gary shrugged. "Is he dead?"

"Yes."

"I told you he was sick."

"How did he die, Gary?"

"He had cancer."

"How long has he been dead?"

"How should I know?"

"Why didn't you call a doctor?"

"No point, was there?"

"When did you last look in on him, take him some food?"

Gary sucked on his cigarette and looked away into the cold hearth, littered with butts and empty beer cans. Sweat formed on his pale brow.

"When did you last go up and see him, Gary?" Banks asked again.

"I don't know."

"Yesterday? The day before?"

"I don't know."

"I'm no expert, Gary, but I'd say you haven't been up there for at least three days, have you?"

"If you say so."

"Did you kill him?"

"He was sick, getting worse."

"But did you kill him?"

"I never touched him, if that's what you mean. Never laid a finger on the old bastard. I couldn't bear . . ."

Banks noticed the boy was crying. He had turned his head aside but it was shaking, and strange snuffling sounds came from between the fingers he had placed over his mouth and nose.

"You deserted him. You left him up there to die. Is that what you did?"

Banks couldn't be sure, but he thought Gary was nodding.

"Why? For God's sake why?"

"You know," he said, wiping his nose with the back of his hand and turning to face Banks angrily. "You told me. You know all about it. What he did . . ."

"For what he did to Caroline?"

"You know it is."

"What about Caroline? Did you kill her too?"

"Why should I do that?"

"I'm asking. She tried to kill *you* once. Did you?"

Gary sighed and tossed his half-smoked cigarette into the grate. "I suppose so," he said wearily. "I don't know. I think *he* did, but maybe we all did. Maybe this miserable bloody family killed her."

II

By mid-afternoon the sun had disappeared behind smoke-coloured clouds and Banks had turned his desk lamp on. They sat in his office—Banks, Gary Hartley and Susan Gay—taking notes and waiting for a pot of coffee before getting started on the interrogation.

Gary, sitting in a hard-backed chair opposite Banks, looked frightened now. He wasn't fidgeting or squirming, but his eyes were filled with a kind of resigned, mournful fear. Banks, still not completely sure what had gone on in that large, cold house, wanted him to relax and talk. Fresh, hot coffee might help.

While he waited, Banks glanced over the brief notes the forensic pathologist had made after his preliminary investigation of the scene. He'd estimated time of death at not less than two days and not more than three. For three days then, perhaps—since shortly after Banks's and Richmond's visit—the poor, frightened kid in front of them had sat in the cold ruin of a room, smoking and drinking, knowing the corpse of his father lay rotting upstairs in the heat of an electric fire. The doctor hadn't called; he had no reason to as long as Mr Hartley had a full prescription of pain-killers and someone to take care of his basic needs.

"Rigor mortis disappeared . . . greenish discoloration of the abdomen," the report read, "reddish veins in neck, shoulders and thighs . . . no mattling as yet." The temperature would have speeded the process of decomposition considerably, Banks realized. Also, the air was dry, and some degree of mummification might have occurred if the old man had lain there much longer. Banks suspected that cause of death was starvation—Gary had simply left him to die—but it would be a while before more exact information about cause and time could be known. Older persons decompose more slowly than younger ones, and thin ones more slowly than fat ones. Bodies of diseased persons break down quickly. Stomach contents would have to be examined and inner organs checked for the degree of putrefaction.

All very interesting, Banks thought, but none of it really mattered if Gary Hartley confessed.

Finally, PC Tolliver arrived with the coffee and styrofoam cups. Susan poured Gary a cup and pushed the milk and sugar towards him. He didn't acknowledge her. Banks walked over to the window and glanced out at the grey market square, then sat down to begin. He spoke quietly, intimately almost, to put the boy at ease.

"Earlier, Gary, you seemed confused. You said you supposed that you had killed Caroline, then you told me you think your father killed her. Can you be a bit clearer about that?"

"I'm not sure. I . . . I . . ."

"Why not tell me about it, the night you killed her? Start at the beginning."

"I don't remember."

"Try. It's important."

Gary screwed up his eyes in concentration, but when he opened them, he shook his head. "It's all dark. All dark inside. And it hurts."

"Where does it hurt, Gary?"

"My head. My eyes. Everywhere." He covered his face with his hands and shuddered.

Banks let a few seconds pass, then asked, "How did you get to Eastvale?"

"What?"

"To Eastvale? Did you go by bus or train? Did you borrow a car?"

Gary shook his head. "I didn't go to Eastvale. I wasn't in Eastvale."

"Then how did you kill Caroline?"

"I've told you, I don't know." He hung his head in his hands. "I just don't know."

"What happened to your father, Gary?"

"He's dead."

"How did he die? Did you kill him?"

"No. I didn't go near him."

"Did you stop going up to his room? Did you stop feeding him?"

"I couldn't go. Not after Caroline, not after I knew. I thought about it and I carried on for a while, but I couldn't." He looked at Banks, his eyes pleading. "You must understand. I couldn't. Not after she was dead."

"So you stopped tending to him?"

"He killed her."

"But he couldn't have, Gary. He was an invalid, bed-ridden. He couldn't have gone to Eastvale and killed her."

Suddenly, Gary banged the metal desk with his fist. Susan moved forward but Banks motioned her back.

"I've told you it wasn't in Eastvale!" Gary yelled. "How many times do I have to tell you? Caroline didn't die in Eastvale."

"But she did, Gary. Come on, you know that."

He shook his head. "He killed her. And I killed her too."

Susan looked up from her notes and frowned. "Tell me how he killed her," Banks asked.

"I don't know. I wasn't there. But he did it like . . . like. . . . Oh Christ, she was just a child . . . just a little child!" And he put his head in his hands and sobbed, shaking all over.

Banks stood up and put a comforting arm over his shoulder. At first, Gary didn't react, but then he yielded and buried his head in Banks's chest. Banks held on to him tightly and stroked his hair, then when Gary's grasp loosened, he extricated himself and returned to his chair. Now he thought he understood why Gary was talking the way he was. Now he knew what had happened. Now he understood the Hartley family. But he still had no idea who had killed Caroline Hartley, and why.

III

When Susan Gay got to the Crooked Billet at six o'clock, James Conran wasn't there. Casting around for a suitable place to sit, she caught the eye of Marcia Cunningham, the costumes manager, who beckoned her over. Marcia seemed to be sitting with someone, but a group of drinkers blocked Susan's view.

Susan elbowed her way through the after-work crowd, loosening her overcoat as she went. It was cold outside, and enough snow had fallen to speckle her shoulders, but in the pub it was warm. She took off her green woolly gloves and slipped them in her pocket, then, when she reached Marcia, removed her coat and hung it on a peg by the bar. She noted that the buttons of the pink cardigan Marcia was wearing were incorrectly fastened, making the thing look askew.

"They've not finished yet," Marcia said. "What with it being so close to first night, or should I say *twelfth* night, James thought an extra half hour might be in order. Especially with the new Maria. They didn't need me, so he asked me to pass on his apologies if I saw you. He'll be in a little later."

"Thank you." Susan smoothed her skirt and sat down.

"How rude of me," Marcia said, indicating the woman beside her. "Susan Gay, this is Sandra Banks." Then she put her hand to her mouth. "Silly me, I'm forgetting you probably know each other already."

Susan certainly recognized Sandra. With her looks, she would be hard to miss—that determined mouth, lively blue eyes, long blonde hair and dark eyebrows. She possessed a natural elegance. Susan had always envied her and felt awkward and dowdy when she was around.

"Yes," Susan said, "we've met once or twice. Good evening, Mrs Banks."

"Please, call me Sandra."

"Sandra was just finishing up some work in the gallery so I popped in and asked if she'd like a drink."

Susan noticed that their glasses were empty and offered to get a round. When she came back, there was still no sign of James or the others. She didn't know how she was going to maintain small talk with Sandra Banks for the next twenty minutes or so, especially after the emotional scene she had just witnessed between Banks and Gary Hartley. She felt embarrassed. Strong emotion always made her feel that way, and when Banks had hugged the boy close she had had to avert her gaze. But she had seen her boss's expression over the back of the boy's head. It hadn't given much away, but she had noticed compassion in his eyes and she knew from the set of his lips that he shared the boy's pain.

Luckily, Marcia saved her. In appearance rather like one of those plump, ruddy-cheeked characters one sees in illustrations of Dickens novels, she had an ebullient manner to match.

"Any closer to catching those vandals?" she asked.

Conscious of Sandra watching her, Susan said, "Not yet, I'm afraid. A couple of kids did some damage to a youth club in the north end and we think it's the same ones. We've got our eye on them."

"Do you think you'll ever catch them?"

Susan caught Sandra smiling at the question and could hardly keep herself from doing the same. Her discomfort waned slightly. Instead of feeling resentful, under scrutiny, she was beginning to feel more as if she had an ally. Sandra had been through it all, knew what it was like to be police in the public eye. But Susan knew she would still have to be cautious. Sandra was, after all, the detective chief inspector's wife, and if Susan made any blunders they would certainly be passed on to Banks.

"Hard to say," she replied. "We've got a couple of leads and several likely candidates. That's about all."

What she hadn't said was that they had at least found a pattern to the kind of places the kids liked to wreck. Most of them were community centres of some kind, never private establishments like cinemas or pubs. As there was a limited number of such social clubs in Eastvale, extra men had been posted on guard. Their instructions were to lie low, blend in and catch the kids in the act, rather than stand as sentries and scare them off. Soon they might put a stop to the trail of vandalism that had cost the town a fortune over the past few months.

"It was such a mess," Marcia said, shaking her head. "All those costumes, ruined. I almost sat down and cried. Anyway, I took them home and now I've a bit of time I'm sorting through the remnants to see if I can't resurrect some. I've put a couple together already. I hate waste."

"That sounds a hell of a job," said Sandra. "I don't think I could face it."

"Oh, I love sewing, fixing things, making things. It makes me feel useful. And I see what I've done at the end. Job satisfaction, I suppose, though it's a pity there's no pay to match."

Sandra laughed. "I'd offer to help but I've got two left thumbs when it comes to sewing. I can't even get the bloody thread through the needle. Poor Alan has to sew his own buttons on."

Susan tried to imagine Detective Chief Inspector Alan Banks sewing buttons on a shirt, but she couldn't.

"It's all right," Marcia said. "Keeps me out of mischief these cold winter evenings. Since Frank's been gone I find I need to do more and more to occupy myself."

"Marcia's husband died six months ago," Sandra explained to Susan.

"Aye," said Marcia. "Just like that, he went. Good as new one moment, then, bang, curtains. And never had a day's illness in his life. Didn't drink and gave up his pipe years ago. Only sixty, he was."

Susan shook her head. "It does seem unfair."

"Whoever told us life would be fair, love? Nobody did, that's who. Anyway, enough of that. Walking out with Mr Conran are you?"

Susan felt herself blushing. "Well I . . . I . . ."

"I know," Marcia went on. "It's none of my business. Tell me to shut up if you want. I'm just an old busybody, that's all."

Now Susan couldn't help laughing. "We've been out to dinner a couple of times, and to the pictures. That's all."

Marcia nodded. "I wasn't probing into your sex life, lass, just curious, that's all. What's he like when he's out of his director's hat?"

"He makes me laugh."

"There's a few in that theatre over there could do with a laugh or two."

Susan leaned forward. "Marcia, you know that girl who was killed, Caroline Hartley? Was there really anything between her and James?"

"Not that I know of, love," Marcia answered. "Just larked around, that's all. Besides, she was one of *them*, wasn't she? Not that I . . . well, you know what I mean."

"Yes, but James didn't know that. None of you did."

"Still," Marcia insisted. "Nothing to it as far as I could see. Oh, he had his eye on her all right. What man wouldn't? Maybe not your *Playboy* material, but dangerous as dynamite nonetheless."

"What makes you say that?" Sandra chipped in.

"I don't really know. Maybe it's hindsight. I just get feelings about people sometimes, and I knew from the start that one was trouble. Still, it looks as if she meant trouble for herself mostly, doesn't it?"

"Is James Conran a suspect?" Sandra asked.

"Your husband seems to think so," Susan said. "But everyone who had anything to do with Caroline Hartley is a suspect."

"Aren't you worried about getting involved with him?" Sandra asked.

"A bit, I suppose. I mean, not that I think James is guilty of anything, just that being involved might blur my objectivity. It's an awkward position to be in, that's all. Besides," she laughed, "he's my old teacher. It feels strange to be having dinner with him. I like him, but I'm keeping him at arm's length. At least until this business is over."

"Good for you," Sandra said.

"Anyway, I don't see as it should matter. The chief inspector went off to London with Veronica Shildon, and I'd say she's a prime suspect." Susan realized too late what she had implied, and wondered if an attempt to backtrack and make her meaning clear would only make things worse.

All Sandra said was, "I'm sure Alan knows what he's doing." And Susan could have sworn she noticed a ghost of a smile on her face. "I know. I'm sorry. I didn't mean to imply . . . just . . ."

"It's all right," Sandra said. "I just wanted to point out that what he's doing isn't the same. I'm not criticizing you."

"I don't suppose I understand his methods yet."

"I'm not sure I do, either." Sandra laughed.

Suddenly, Susan's world turned pitch-black. She felt a light pressure on her brow and cheeks and she could no longer see Sandra and Marcia. The bustling pub seemed to fall silent, then a voice whispered in her ear, "Guess who?"

"James," she said, and her vision was restored.

IV

Banks felt unusually tired when he got home about eight o'clock that evening. The paperwork was done, and Gary Hartley had been sent back to Harrogate to face whatever charges could be made.

Sandra had just got home herself, and both children were out. Over a dinner of left-over chicken casserole, Sandra told him about her evening with Susan and Marcia. In turn, Banks tried to explain Gary Hartley to her.

"He'd always hated Caroline, all his life. She was the bane of his existence. She used to tease him, torment him, torture him, and he never had any idea why. She even tried to drown him once. To cap it all, she left home and he got lumbered with looking after his invalid father, who made it perfectly clear that he still preferred Caroline. When you look at it like that, it's not a bad motive for murder, wouldn't you say?"

"Did he do it?" Sandra asked.

Banks shook his head. "No. Not literally. When she told him what had happened when her mother had been in hospital having him, he suddenly realized why she hated him. She wanted to apologize, make up even, if she could. But Gary's sensitive. It's not something you can really work out in your mind. Christ, most people don't even talk about it. And Caroline had blanked out the memory for years. It was always there, though, under the surface, shoving and cracking the crust. Gary just reacted emotionally. He was overwhelmed by what she said, and suddenly his whole world was turned upside-down. All his anger had been pointed in the wrong direction—at her—for so long."

"He killed his father?"

"He sat in his room downstairs and let the old man starve to death."

Sandra shivered. "Good God!"

She was right to be so appalled, Banks thought. It was an act of utmost cruelty, the kind for which a public ignorant of the facts might demand a return of the noose. But still, he couldn't forget Gary's pain and confusion; he couldn't help but feel pity for the boy, no matter what atrocity he had committed. He gave Sandra the gist of their discussion.

"I can see what he meant when he said her father had killed her," she said, "but why implicate himself too? You said he didn't do it."

"But he blamed himself—for being born, if you like. After all, that's when it started. That's when Caroline was left alone with her father. He couldn't give us any concrete details of the crime because he hadn't done it. But in his mind he was responsible. All he could say was that it was all dark to him. Dark and painful."

"I don't understand," Sandra said, frowning.

"I think he was describing being born," Banks said. "Dark. Dark and painful."

"My God. And you said Caroline tried to drown him, too?"

"Yes. He was about four and she was twelve. He can't remember the details clearly, of course, and there's no-one else alive to tell what happened, but he thinks his mother left him for a moment to fetch some clean towels. She left the bathroom door open and Caroline walked in. He said he remembers how she pulled his feet and his head went under the water. The next thing he knew, he was up again in his mother's arms gasping for air and Caroline was gone. Nobody ever spoke about it afterwards."

"He must have been terrified of her."

"He was. And he didn't know why she was treating him that way. She didn't know, either. He turned in on himself to shut it all out."

"Is he insane?" Sandra asked.

"Not for me to say. He's in need of help, certainly. Just imagine the hatred of all those years boiling over, finding its true object at last. All the humiliation. His own life ruined, knowing he was only second-best to his sister. The only wonder is he didn't do it sooner. It took Caroline's murder and the truth about her childhood to set him free."

Banks remembered the slouching figure that had shuffled out of his office after telling everything. He would be under care in Harrogate now, perhaps going through the whole story again at the hands of less sympathetic interrogators. After all, look at what he'd done. But Gary Hartley wouldn't be hanged. He wouldn't even be sent to jail. He would first be bound over for psychiatric evaluation, then he might well spend a good part of his life in mental institutions. Which was better? It was impossible for Banks to decide. Gary's life was blighted, just as his sister's had been, though, unlike Caroline, Gary hadn't even managed to snatch his few moments of happiness.

"Then who *did* kill Caroline Hartley?" Sandra asked.

Banks scratched his head. "I'm buggered if I know. I'm pretty sure we can rule out Gary now, and her friends in London. When Caroline moved on, she always seemed to burn her bridges."

"Which leaves?"

"Well, unless we're dealing with a psycho, we're back to the locals. Ivers and his girlfriend aren't home-free yet, whatever they told us. They lied to us at the start, and Patsy Janowski has a good motive for corroborating everything Ivers might claim. She loves the man and wants to hang onto him. And then there's the amateur theatre crowd. I've been intending to have another talk with Teresa Pedmore."

"And Veronica Shildon?" Sandra asked. "Susan Gay seems to think you've been overlooking her."

"Susan's prejudiced."

"Are you sure you're not?"

Banks stared at her. "Don't you know me better than that?"

"Just asking."

He shook his head. "Officially she's a suspect, of course, but Veronica Shildon didn't do it. I must be overlooking something."

"Any idea what?"

Banks brought his fist up slowly to his temple. "Damned if I know." Then he stood up. "Hell, it's been a rough day. I'm having a stiff Scotch then I'm off to bed." He poured the drink and went into the hall to his jacket. When he came back he said, "And I'm having a bloody cigarette as well, house rule or no house rule."

TWELVE

I

The wind numbed Banks to the marrow when he got out of his car near the Lobster Inn the following afternoon. It was January 3—only three days to twelfth night. The sky was a pale eggshell blue, with a few wispy grey clouds twisting over the horizon like strips of gauze. But the sun had no warmth in it. The wind kicked up little whitecaps as it danced over the ruffled water and slid up the rough sea-wall right onto the front. Banks dashed into the pub.

There already, ensconced in front of the meagre fire, sat Detective Sergeant Jim Hatchley, pint in one ham-like hand and a huge, foul-smelling cigar smouldering between two sausage-shaped fingers of the other. Banks thought he had put on weight; his bulk seemed to loom larger than ever. The sergeant shifted in his seat when Banks came over and sat opposite him.

"Miserable old bugger saves all his coal till evening," he said, by way of greeting, gesturing over at the landlord who sat on a high stool behind the bar reading a tabloid. "Bigger crowd then, you see."

Banks nodded. "How's married life treating you?"

"Can't complain. She's a good lass. I could do without being at the bloody seaside in winter, though. Plays havoc with my rheumatism."

"Didn't know you had it."

"Nor did I."

"Never mind. Just wait till spring. You'll be the envy of us all then. Everyone will want to come out and visit you on their week-ends off."

"Aye, maybe. We'll have to see about renting out the spare room for bed and breakfast. Carol's got some fancy ideas about starting a garden, too. Sounds like a lot of back-breaking work to me."

And Banks knew what Hatchley felt about work, the dreaded four-letter word, back-breaking or not. "I'm sorry to lumber you with this, Jim," he said. "Especially on your honeymoon."

"That's all right. Gets me out of the house. We're not spring chickens, you know. Can't expect to be at it all the time." He winked. "Besides, a man needs time alone with his pint and his paper."

Banks noticed a copy of the *Sun* folded in Hatchley's pocket. From the little he could see, it looked to be open at page three. An attractive new wife, and he still ogled the naked page-three girl. Old habits die hard.

The landlord stirred; his newspaper began to rustle with impatience. Clearly it was all very well for him to be rude to customers, but customers were not expected to be rude to him by warming themselves in front of the sparse flames for too long without buying a drink. Banks walked over and the paper rose up again, covering the man's beady eyes.

"Two pints of bitter, please," Banks said, and slowly the paper came to rest on the bar. With a why-can't-everyone-leave-me-alone sigh, the man pulled the pints and plonked them down in front of Banks, holding his other hand out for the money as soon as he had done so. Banks paid and walked back to Sergeant Hatchley.

"Anything come up?" Banks asked, reaching for a cigarette.

Hatchley pulled a cigar tube from his inside pocket. "Have one of these. Christmas present from the in-laws. Havana. Nice and mild."

Banks remembered the last cigar he had smoked, one of Dirty Dick Burgess's Tom Thumbs, and declined. "Best stick with the devil you know," he said, lighting the cigarette.

"As you like. Well," Hatchley said, "there's nowt been happening around here. I've been up with Carol a couple of evenings, for a drink, like, and noticed that Ivers and his fancy woman in here once or twice. Tall chap in need of a haircut. Looks a bit like that Irish bloke from *Camelot*, Richard Harris, after a bad night. And that lass of his, young enough to be his granddaughter I'd say. Still, it takes all sorts. Lovely pair of thighs under them tight jeans, and a bum like two peaches in a wet paper bag. Anyroad, they'd come in about nine-ish, nod hello to a few locals, knock back a couple of drinks and leave about ten."

"Ever talk to them?"

"No. They don't know who I am. They keep themselves to themselves, too. The local constable's a very obliging chap. I've had him keeping an eye open and he says they've done nothing out of the ordinary. Hardly been out of the house. Are they still in the running?"

Banks nodded. "There's a couple of problems with the timing, but nothing they couldn't have worked out between them."

"Between them?"

"Yes. If they killed Caroline Hartley, they must have been in it together. It's the only way they could have done it."

"But you're not sure they did?"

"No. I'm just not satisfied with their stories."

"What about motive?"

"That I don't know. The husband had one, clearly enough, but the girl didn't share it. It'd have to be something we don't know about."

"Money?"

"I don't think so. Caroline Hartley didn't have much. It would have to be something more obscure than that."

"Perhaps she's the kind who'd do anything for him, just to hang onto him?"

"Maybe."

"Or they didn't do it?"

"Could be that, too."

"Or maybe you're over-complicating things as usual?"

Banks grinned. "Maybe I am."

"So what now?" Hatchley asked.

"A quick visit, just to let them know we haven't forgotten them."

"Me too?"

"Yes."

"But they'll recognize me. They'll know me in future."

"It won't do them any harm to know we're keeping an eye on them. Come on, sup up."

Grudgingly, Sergeant Hatchley drained his pint and stubbed out his cigar. "Still another ten minutes left in that," he complained.

"Take it with you."

"Never mind."

Hatchley followed Banks out into the sharp wind. Thin ice splintered as they made their way up the footpath to Ivers's cottage, from which a welcoming plume of smoke curled and drifted west. Hatchley groaned and panted as they walked. Banks knocked. This time, Ivers himself answered the door.

"Come in. Sit down. Sit down," he said. Hatchley took the bulky armchair by the mullioned window and Banks lowered himself into a wooden rocker by the fire. "Have you caught him?" Ivers asked. "The man who killed Caroline?"

Banks shook his head. "Afraid not."

Ivers frowned. "Oh . . . well. Patsy! Patsy! Some tea, if you've got a minute."

Patsy Janowski came in from her study, glared at Banks's right shoe-lace and went into the kitchen.

"How do you think I can help you again?" Ivers asked.

"I'm not sure," Banks said. "First, I'd just like to go over one or two details."

"Shall we wait for Patsy with the tea?"

They waited. Banks passed the time talking music with Ivers, who was excited about the harmonic breakthroughs he had made over the past two days. Hatchley, hands folded in his lap, looked bored.

Finally, Patsy emerged with a tray and put it down on the table in front of the fire. She wore jeans with a plain white shirt, the top two buttons undone. Banks noticed Hatchley take a discreet look down the front as she bent to put the tray down. She didn't seem pleased to see Banks, and if either of them recognized Sergeant Hatchley, they didn't show it. This time, Patsy was surly and evasive and Ivers seemed open and helpful. Luckily, Banks had learned never to take anything at face value. When tea was poured, he began with the questions.

"It's the timing that's important, you see," he opened. "Can you be any clearer about what time you delivered the Christmas present, Mr Ivers?"

"I'm sorry, I can't. Sometime around seven, I'm sure of that."

"And you stayed how long?"

"No more than five minutes."

"That's rather a long time, isn't it?"

"What do you mean?"

"People have funny ideas about time, about how short or long various periods are. I'd say five minutes was a bit long to spend with someone you didn't like on an errand like that. Why not just hand over the present and leave?"

"Maybe it wasn't that long," Ivers said. "I just went in, handed it over, exchanged a few insincere pleasantries and left. Maybe two minutes, I don't know."

Banks sipped some tea, then lit a cigarette. Patsy, legs curled under her on the rug in front of the fire, passed him an ashtray from the hearth.

"What pleasantries?" he asked. "What did you say to each other?"

"As I said before, I asked how she was, how Veronica was, made a remark about the weather. And she answered me politely. I handed over the record, told her it was something special for Veronica for Christmas, then I left. We'd at least reached a stage where we could behave in a civilized manner towards one another."

"You said it was something special?"

"Something like that."

"How did she react?"

Ivers closed his eyes for a moment and frowned. "She didn't, really. I mean, she didn't say anything. She looked interested, though. Curious."

"That may be why she opened it, if she did," Banks said, almost to himself. "Did she seem at all strange to you? Did she say anything odd?"

Ivers shook his head. "No."

"Did she seem to be expecting someone?"

"How would I know? She certainly didn't say anything if she was."

"Was she on edge? Did she keep glancing towards the door? Did she give the impression she wanted you out of the way as soon as possible?"

"I'd say yes to the latter," Ivers answered, "but no to the others. She seemed perfectly all right to me."

"What was she doing?"

"Doing?"

"Yes. When you called. You went into the front room, didn't you? Was she listening to music, polishing the silver, watching television, reading?"

"I don't know. Nothing . . . I . . . eating, perhaps. There was some cake on the table. I remember that."

"What was she wearing?"

"I can't remember."

"Claude's hopeless about things like that," Patsy cut in. "Half the time he doesn't even notice what *I'm* wearing."

Taking in the stooped, lanky figure of the composer in his usual baggy clothes, Banks was inclined to believe her. Here was the genius so wrapped up in his music that he didn't notice such mundane things as what other people said, did or wore.

On the other hand, Ivers obviously had a taste for attractive women. In different ways, both Veronica and Patsy were evidence enough of that. And what red-blooded male would forget a woman as beautiful as Caroline Hartley answering the door in her bathrobe? Surely a man with a taste for so seductive a woman as Patsy Janowski couldn't fail to remember, or to react? But then Ivers knew Caroline; he knew she was a lesbian. Perhaps it was all a matter of perspective. Banks pressed on.

"What about you, Ms Janowski? Can you remember what she was wearing?"

"I didn't even go into the house. I only saw her standing in the doorway."

"Can you remember?"

"It looked like some kind of bathrobe to me, a kimono-style thing. Dark green I think the colour was. She was hugging it tight around her because of the cold."

"What time did you arrive?"

"After seven. I left here about twenty minutes after Claude."

"How long after seven?"

"I'm not sure. I told you before. Maybe about a quarter after, twenty past."

"What were you wearing?"

"Wearing?" Patsy frowned. "I don't see what that's—"

"Just answer, please."

She shot his right lapel a baleful glance. "Jeans, boots and my fur-lined jacket."

"How long is the jacket?"

"It comes down to my waist," Patsy said, looking puzzled. "Look, I don't—"

"Would you say that Caroline was expecting someone else? Someone other than you?"

"I couldn't say, really."

"Did she react as if she had been expecting someone else when she saw you standing there at the door? Did she show any disappointment?"

"No, not especially." Patsy thought for a moment. "She was real nice, given who I am. I'm sorry, but it all happened so quickly and I was too concerned about Claude to pay much attention."

"Did she seem nervous or surprised to see you, anxious for you to leave quickly?"

"No, not at all. She was surprised to see me, of course, but that's only natural. And she wanted to shut the door because of the cold."

"Why didn't she ask you in?"

Patsy looked at the hearth. "She hardly knew me. Besides, all I had to ask her was whether Claude was there."

"And she said he wasn't."

"Yes."

"And you believed her?"

Patsy's tone hardened. She spoke between clenched teeth. "Of course I did."

"Are you *sure* he wasn't still in the house?"

Ivers leaned forward. "Now wait—"

"Let her answer Mr Ivers," Sergeant Hatchley said.

"Caroline said he'd gone. She said he'd just left the record and gone. I hadn't any reason to believe she was lying."

"Was she in a hurry to get rid of you?"

"I've told you, no. Everything was normal as far as I could tell."

"But she didn't invite you inside. Doesn't that seem odd to you, Ms Janowski? You've already said it was so cold on the doorstep that Caroline Hartley had to hold her robe tight around her. Wouldn't it have made more sense to invite you in, even if just for a few minutes? After all, Mr Ivers here says he only stayed for five minutes."

"Are you trying to suggest that I *did* go inside?" Patsy exploded. "Just what's going on in that policeman's mind of yours? Are you accusing me of killing her? Because if you are you'd better damn well arrest me right now and let me call my lawyer!"

"There's no reason to be melodramatic, Ms Janowski," Banks said. "I'm not suggesting anything of the kind. I happen to know already that you didn't enter the house."

Patsy's brow furrowed and some of the angry red colour drained from her cheeks. "Then I . . . I don't understand."

"Did you hear music playing?"

"No. I can't remember any."

"And you didn't ask to go inside, to look around?"

"No. Why would I? I knew he wouldn't still be there if Veronica wasn't home."

"The point is," Banks said, "that Mr Ivers *could* have been in the house, couldn't he? You've just confirmed to me that you didn't go in and look."

"I've told you, he wouldn't—"

"Could he have been inside?"

She looked at Ivers, then back to Banks. "That's an unfair question. The goddamn Duke of Edinburgh *could* have been inside for all I know, but I don't think he was."

"The thing is," Banks said, "that nobody saw Mr Ivers leave. Caroline Hartley didn't invite you in, even though it was cold, and you didn't insist on seeing for yourself."

"That doesn't mean anything," Ivers burst out, "and you know it. It was pure bloody luck on your part that anyone noticed me arrive, or Patsy. You can't expect them to be watching for me to leave, too."

"Maybe not, but it would have made everything a lot tidier."

"And if you're suggesting that Caroline didn't let Patsy in because *I* was there, have you considered that she might have been hiding someone else? Have you thought about that?"

"Yes, Mr Ivers, I've thought about that. The problem is, no-one else was seen near the house between your visit and Ms Janowski's." He turned to Patsy. "When you left, did you notice anyone hanging around the area?"

"I don't think so."

"Concentrate. It could be important. I've asked you before to try to visualize the scene. Did you see anyone behaving strangely, or anyone who looked furtive, suspicious, out of place?"

Patsy closed her eyes. "No, I'm sure I didn't . . . Except—"

"What?"

"I'm not very clear. There was a woman."

"Where?"

"The end of the street. It was very dark there . . . snowing. And she was some distance away from me. But I remember thinking there was something odd about her, I don't know what. I'm damned if I can think what it was."

"Think," Banks encouraged her. The timing was certainly right. Patsy had called at about twenty past seven, and the killer—if indeed the last observed visitor was the killer—only two or three minutes later. There was a good chance that they had passed in the street.

Patsy opened her eyes. "It's no good. It was ages ago now and I hardly paid any attention at the time. It's just one of those odd little things, like a *déjà vu.*"

"Did you think you knew this woman, recognized her?"

"No. It wasn't anything like that. I'd remember that. It was when I got to King Street. She was crossing over, as if she was heading for the mews. We were on opposite sides and I didn't get a very close look. It was something else, just a little thing. I'm sorry, Chief Inspector, really I am. Especially," she added sharply, "as any information I might give could get us off the hook. I simply can't remember."

"If you do remember anything at all about the woman," Banks said, "no matter how minor a detail it might seem to you, call me immediately, is that clear?"

Patsy nodded.

"And you're not off the hook yet. Not by a long chalk."

Banks gestured for Hatchley to get up, a lengthy task that involved quite a bit of heaving and puffing, then they left. Banks almost slipped on the icy pathway, but Hatchley caught his arm and steadied him just in time.

"Well," said the sergeant, stamping and rubbing his hands outside the Lobster Inn, "that's that then. I don't mind doing a bit of extra work, you know," he said, glancing longingly at the pub, "even when I'm supposed to be on my honeymoon. I know it's not my case, but I wish you'd fill me in on a few more details."

Banks caught his glance and interpreted the signals. "Fine," he said. "Over a pint?"

Hatchley beamed. "Well, if you insist . . ."

II

"Susan, love, could I have a word?"

"Of course."

Susan and Marcia were sitting in the Crooked Billet with the entire cast of *Twelfth Night* after rehearsal. It had gone badly, and those who weren't busy arguing were drowning their depression in drink. James didn't seem too concerned, Susan thought, watching him listen patiently to Malvolio's complaints about the final scene. But he was used to it: he'd directed plays before. She shifted along the bench to let Marcia Cunningham sit beside her. "What is it?"

Marcia looked puzzled. "I'm not sure. It's nothing really. At least I don't think it is. But it's very odd."

"Police business?"

"Well, it might have something to do with the break-in. You did say to mention anything that came up."

"Go on."

"But that's just it, you see, love. It doesn't make sense."

"Marcia," Susan said, "why don't you just tell me? Get it off your chest."

Marcia frowned. "It's hard to explain. You'd probably think I was just being silly if I told you. Can't you pop around and have a look for yourself? I don't live far away."

"What, now?"

"Whenever you can spare the time, love." Marcia looked at her watch. "I'll have to be off in a few minutes, anyway."

Susan recognized a deadline when she heard one. Now she was with CID she was never really off duty. She wouldn't get anywhere if she put personal pleasure before the job, however fruitless the trek to Marcia's might seem. And the vandalism was *her* case. A success so early in her CID career would look good. What could she do but agree? As Marcia couldn't be induced to say any more, Susan would have to put James off and go with her. It wouldn't take long, Marcia had assured her, so she wouldn't have to cancel their dinner date, just postpone it for half an hour or so. James would understand. He certainly had plenty to occupy himself with in her absence.

"All right," Susan said. "I'll come with you."

"Thanks, love. It might be a waste of time but well, wait till you see."

Susan told James she had to nip out for a while and would be back in half an hour or so, then she buttoned up her winter coat and left with Marcia. They walked north-east along York Road, past the excavated pre-Roman site, where the little burial mounds and hut foundations looked eerie under their carapace of moonlit ice.

"It's just down here." Marcia led Susan down a sloping street of pre-war semis opposite the site. Though the house itself was small, it had gardens at both front and back and a fine view of the river and The Green from the kitchen window. The furniture looked dated and worn, and swaths of material lay scattered here and there, along with stacks of patterns and magazines, in the untidy living-room. Marcia didn't apologize for the mess. Her sense of disorder, Susan realized, didn't stop at the way she dressed.

On the mantelpiece above the electric fire stood a framed photograph of Marcia's late husband, a handsome man, posing on the seafront at some holiday resort with a pipe in his mouth. Marcia switched on the fire. Susan took off her coat and knelt by the reddening element, rubbing her hands. She could smell dust burning as it heated up.

"Sorry it's so cold," Marcia said. "We wanted central heating, but since my Frank died I just haven't been able to afford it."

"I don't have it either," Susan said. "I always do this when I get home." She stood up and turned. "What is it you've got to show me?"

Marcia dragged a large box into the centre of the room. "It's this. Remember I told you yesterday I was patching up some of the damage those hooligans did to the costumes?"

Susan nodded.

"Well, I have. Look." She held up a long pearl gown with shoulder straps and plunging neckline.

Susan looked closely. "But surely . . . ?"

"Cut to shreds, it was," Marcia said. "Look." She pointed out the faint lines of stitching. "Of course, you'd never get away with wearing it for a banquet at the Ritz, but it'll do for a stage performance. Even the nobs in the front row wouldn't be able to see how it had been sewn back together."

"You're a genius, Marcia," Susan exclaimed, touching the fabric. "You should have been a surgeon."

Marcia shrugged. "Can't stand the sight of blood. Anyway, it was just like doing a jigsaw puzzle really." And she showed Susan more dresses and gowns she had resurrected from the box of snipped-up originals. That so untidy a person should be able to bring such order out of chaos astonished Susan.

"You didn't bring me here just to praise you, did you?" she said finally. "I don't mean to be rude, but I told James I'd be back in half an hour."

"Sorry, love," Marcia said. "Just got carried away, that's all. Forgot how impatient young love is."

Susan blushed. "Marcia! The point."

"Yes, well." Marcia reached into the box and took out a simple burgundy dress. "This is the point. I worked on this one all afternoon." She held it up, and Susan could see that the sleeves had been cut off up to elbow-level and a large patch of the front, around the breasts, was also missing.

"I don't understand," she said. "Haven't you finished?"

"I've done all I could, love. That's the point. This is it. All there was."

"I still don't understand."

"And you a copper, too. It's simple. I managed to sort out the bits and pieces of the other dresses here and patch them together, as you've seen."

Susan nodded.

"But when it came to this one, I couldn't find all the pieces. Some of them've plain disappeared."

"Disappeared?"

"Wake up, lass. Yes, disappeared. I've looked everywhere. Even back at the centre to see if they'd fallen on the floor or something. Not a trace."

"But it doesn't make any sense," Susan said slowly. "Who on earth would want to steal pieces of a ruined dress?"

"My point exactly," Marcia said. "That's why I asked you to come here and see it for yourself. Who would do such a thing? And why?"

"There has to be a simple explanation."

Marcia nodded. "Yes. But what is it? Your lot didn't take any for analysis or whatever, did they?"

Susan shook her head. "No. They must have dropped out somewhere. Maybe when you were bringing the box home."

"I looked everywhere. I'm telling you, love, if there'd been pieces I would've found them."

Susan couldn't help but feel disappointed. It was hardly an important discovery—certainly not one that would lead to the identity of the vandals—but Marcia was right in that it was mystifying. It was slightly disturbing, too. When Susan picked up the dress and held it in front of her, she shivered as if someone had just walked over her grave. It looked as if the arms had been deliberately cut off rather than torn, and two circles of fabric around the breasts had been snipped out in a similar way. Shaking her head, Susan folded the dress and handed it back to Marcia.

III

"Chief Inspector Banks! Have you any news?"

"No news," Banks said. "Maybe a few questions."

"Come in." Veronica Shildon led him into her front room. It looked larger and colder than it had before, as if even all the heat from the fiercely burning fire in the hearth couldn't penetrate every shadowy corner. Two small, threadbare armchairs stood in front of the fire.

"Christine Cooper let me have them until I get around to buying a new suite," Veronica said, noticing Banks looking at them. "She was going to throw them out."

Banks nodded. After Veronica had taken his coat, he sat in one of the armchairs and warmed himself by the flames. "It's certainly more comfortable than a hard-backed chair," he said.

"Can I offer you a drink?" she asked.

"Tea would do nicely."

Veronica brewed the tea and came to sit in the other armchair, placed so they didn't face each other directly but at an angle that required a slight turning of the head to make eye-contact. The fire danced in the hollows of Veronica's cheeks and reflected like tiny orange candle flames in her eyes.

"I don't feel I thanked you enough for letting me come to London with you," she said, crossing her legs and sitting back in the chair. "It can't have been an easy decision for you to make. Anyway, I'm grateful. Somehow, seeing Ruth Dunne gave me more of Caroline than I'd had, if you can understand that."

Banks, who had more than once spent hours with colleagues extolling the virtues and playfully noting the faults of deceased friends, knew exactly what Veronica meant. Somehow, sharing memories of the dead seemed to make them live larger in one's mind and heart, and Veronica had had nobody in Eastvale to talk to about Caroline because nobody here had really known her.

Banks nodded. "I don't really know why I *am* here, to tell the truth," he said finally. "Nothing I learned in London really helped. Now it's early evening on a cold January day and I'm still no closer to the solution than I was last week. Maybe I'm just the cop who came in from the cold."

Veronica raised an eyebrow. "Frustration?"

"Certainly. More than that."

"Tell me," she said slowly, "am I . . . I mean, do you still believe that *I* might have murdered Caroline?"

Banks lit a cigarette and shifted his legs. The fire was burning his shins. "Ms Shildon," he said, "we've no evidence at all to link you to the crime. We never have had. Everything you told us checks out, and we found no traces of blood-stained clothing in the house. Nor did there appear to be any blood on your person. Unless you're an especially clever and cold-blooded killer, which I don't think you are then I don't see how you could have murdered Caroline. You also appear to lack a motive. At least I haven't been able to find one I'm comfortable with."

"But surely you don't take things at face value?"

"No, I don't. It's a simple statistic that most murders are committed by people who are close to the victim, often family members or lovers Given that, you're obviously a prime suspect. There could have been a way, certainly, if you'd been planning the act. There could also be a motive we don't know about. Caroline *could* have been having an affair and you *could* have found out about t "

"So you still think I might have done it?"

Banks shrugged. "It's not so much a matter of what I think. It's maybe not probable, but it certainly is possible. Until I find out exactly who did do it, I can't count anybody from Caroline's circle out."

"Including me?"

"Including you."

"God, what a terrible job it must be, having to see people that way all the time, as potential criminals. How can you ever get close to anyone?"

"You're exaggerating. It's my job, not my life. Do you think doctors go around all the time seeing everyone as potential patients, for example, or lawyers as potential clients?"

"Of the latter I'm quite certain," Veronica said with a quiet laugh, "but as for doctors, the only ones I've known get very irritated when guests ask their advice about aches and pains at cocktail parties."

"Anyway," Banks went on, "people create their own problems."

"What do you mean?"

"Everyone lies, evades or holds back the full truth. Oh, you all have your own perfectly good reasons for doing it—protecting Caroline's memory, covering up a petty crime, unwillingness to reveal an unattractive aspect of your own personality, inability to face up to things or simply not wanting to get involved. But can't you see where that leaves us? If we're faced with several people all closely connected to the victim, and they all lie to us, one of them could conceivably be lying to cover up murder."

"But surely you must have instincts? You must trust some people."

"Yes, I do. My instincts tell me that you didn't kill Caroline, but I'd be a proper fool if I let my heart rule my head and overlooked an important piece of evidence. That's the trouble, trusting your instincts can sometimes blind you to the obvious. Already I've told you too much."

"Does your instinct tell you who did kill her?"

Banks shook his head and flicked a column of ash into the fire. "Unfortunately, no. Gary Hartley confessed, in a way, but . . ." He told her what had happened in Harrogate. Veronica sat forward and clasped her hands on her lap as he spoke.

"The poor boy," she said when he'd finished. "Is there anything I can do?"

"I don't think so. He's undergoing psychiatric tests right now. But the point is, whatever he did do, he didn't kill Caroline. If anything, towards the end, when he knew the full story, he felt pity for her. It was his father he turned on, with years of pent-up hatred. I still can't imagine what torture it must have been for both of them. The old man unable to help himself, unable to get out of bed, starving and lying in his own waste; and Gary downstairs getting drunk and listening to the feeble cries and taps growing fainter, knowing he was slowly killing his own father." Banks shuddered. "There are some things it doesn't do to dwell on, perhaps. But none of this gets us any closer to Caroline's killer."

"It's the 'why' I can't understand," Veronica said. "Who could possibly have had a reason for killing Caroline?"

"That we don't know." Banks sipped some tea. "I thought it might have had something to do with her past, but neither Ruth Dunne nor Colm Grey, the father of her child, had anything to do with it. Unless there's a very obscure connection, such as a dissatisfied customer come back to wreak revenge, which hardly seems likely, all we can surmise is that it was someone she knew, and someone who hadn't planned to kill her."

"How do you know that?"

"There was no sign of forced entry, and the weapon, it just came to hand."

"But she didn't know many people," Veronica said. "Surely that would be a help."

"It is and it isn't. If she didn't know many people very well, then how could she offend someone so much they'd want to kill her?"

"Why do you say offend? Maybe you're wrong. Perhaps she found out something that someone didn't want known, or she saw something she shouldn't have."

"But according to what everyone tells me—yourself included— she wasn't acting at all strangely prior to her death. Surely if something along those lines was bothering her she would have been."

Veronica shook her head. "I don't know . . . she could have been holding back, pretending . . . for my sake."

"But you didn't get that impression? Your instinct didn't tell you so?"

"No. Then, I never know whether to trust my instincts or not. I've made mistakes."

"We all have," Banks said. "But you're right to consider other motives. We shouldn't overlook the possibility that someone had a very practical reason for wanting her out of the way. The problem is, it just makes the motive harder to get at, because it's less personal. Let's say, to be absurd, that she saw two spies exchanging documents. In the first place, how would she know they were doing anything illegal, and in the second, how would they know she was a threat?" He shook his head. "That kind of thing only happens in books. Real murders are much simpler, in a way—at least as far as motive is concerned—but not necessarily easier to solve. Gary Hartley might have had a deep-seated reason to kill his sister, but he didn't do it. Your estranged husband had a motive, too. He blamed Caroline for the separation. But he seems happy enough in his new life with Patsy. Why would he do anything to ruin that? On the other hand, who knows what people really feel?"

"What do you mean?"

"He could have done it, if Patsy Janowski is in it with him or is lying to protect him. He delivered the record, we know that for a fact. As to who put it on the turntable . . ."

Veronica shook her head slowly. "Claude couldn't murder anyone. Oh, he has his moods and his rages, but he's not a killer. Anyway, do you really think the music is important?"

"It's a clue of some kind, but it didn't mean what I thought it did. I believe Caroline opened it out of curiosity. She wanted to know what Claude thought was so special to you. Beyond that, your guess is as good as mine. Maybe she would even play a little of it, again to satisfy her curiosity, but I can't believe she'd leave the arm up so it would repeat forever."

Veronica smiled. "That's just like Caroline," she said quietly. "Such curiosity. You know, she always wanted to shake all her Christmas presents. It was well nigh impossible to stop her opening them on Christmas Eve."

Banks laughed. "I know, my daughter's the same."

Veronica shook her head. "Such a child . . . in some ways."

Banks leaned forward. "What did you say?"

"About Caroline. I said she was such a child in so many ways."

"Yes," Banks whispered. "Yes, she was." He remembered something Ruth Dunne had said to him in London. He tossed his cigarette end into the fire and finished his tea.

"Does it mean something?" Veronica asked.

"It might do." He stood up. "If it does, I've been a bit slow on the uptake. Look, I'd better go now. Much as I'd like to stay here and keep warm, I've got more work to do. I'm sorry."

"It's all right. You don't have to apologize. I don't expect you to keep me company. That's not part of your job."

Banks put the empty teacup on the table. "It's not a task I despise," he said. "But there are a few points I have to review back at the station."

"When you find out," Veronica said, twisting the silver ring around her middle finger, "will you let m٠ know?"

"You'd find out soon enough."

"No. I don't want to find it out from the papers. I want *you* to let me know. As soon as you find out. No matter what the time, day or night. Will you do that for me?"

"Is this some sort of desire for revenge? Do you need an object to hate?"

"No. You once told me I was far too civilized for such feelings. I just want to understand. I want to know why Caroline had to die, what the killer was feeling."

"We might never know that."

She put her hand on his sleeve. "But you will tell me, won't you, when you know? Promise?"

"I'll do my best," Banks said.

Veronica sighed. "Good."

"What about the record?" Banks said at the door. "Technically, it's yours, you know."

Veronica leaned against the doorjamb and wrapped her arms around her to keep warm. "I can live in this house," she said, "especially when I get it redecorated and bring new furniture in. But do you know something? I think that if I ever heard that music again I'd go insane."

Banks said goodnight and Veronica closed the door. It was a shame, he thought, that such a glorious and transcendent piece of music should be associated with such a bloody deed, but at least he thought he now knew why the record had been left playing, if not who had put it on

IV

Susan systematically picked the strips of glittering silver tinsel from her tiny artificial Christmas tree. Carefully, she replaced each flimsy strand on the card from which it came, to put away for next year. She did the same with the single string of lights and the red and green coloured balls, the only decorations she had bought.

When she had finished with the tree, she stood on a chair and untaped the intricate concertinas of coloured crêpe paper she had draped across the ceiling and folded them together. Apart from the Father Christmas above the mantelpiece, a three-dimensional figure that closed like a book when you folded it in half, that was it.

When she had put all traces of Christmas in the cupboard, Susan stood in the centre of her living-room and gazed around. Somehow, even without all the festive decorations she had dashed out and bought at the last moment, the place was beginning to feel a little more like a home. There was still a lot to do—framed prints to buy, perhaps a few ornaments—but she was getting there. Already she had found time to buy three records: highlights from *Madama Butterfly*, *The Four Seasons* and a recording of traditional folk music, the kind she had heard a few times at university many years ago. The opening chords of "Autumn" were playing as she walked into the kitchen to make some cocoa.

James hadn't seen the inside of her flat yet. She would have to invite him soon if he was going to keep on taking her to dinner— not that he paid, Susan always insisted on going Dutch—but something held her back. Perhaps it was the same thing that had held her back so far from stopping in at his place for a nightcap. Damn it all, the man had been her teacher at school, and that was a difficult image to throw out. Still, at least she would make sure she had a few more books and records when she did invite him. She wouldn't want him to think she lived in such a cultural vacuum.

She poured out her cup of cocoa and sat down to listen to the music, curling her feet under her in the small armchair. If she was honest with herself, she decided, her resistance to James had little to do with the fact that he had been her teacher, and was only partly related to his involvement in the case. As far as Susan was concerned, Veronica Shildon was guilty, and it was simply a matter of proving it, of finding evidence that she had returned earlier than she said and murdered her lover—such a distasteful word, Susan thought, when applied to a relationship like theirs—out of jealousy, self-disgust or some other powerful, negative emotion. Either that or the estranged husband had done it because Caroline had corrupted and stolen his wife. So, although James and the theatre crowd were officially suspects, Susan couldn't believe that any of them were really guilty. No, it was something else that kept her at arm's length from James.

She had for some reason stayed away from sexual relationships over the past few years. And, again if she was honest, it wasn't only because of her career. That was important to her, yes, but many women could manage both a lover and a career. Some of her colleagues, and, stranger still, a couple of the more charming villains she had nixed, had asked her out, but she had always said no. Somehow they had all been too close to home. She didn't want to be talked about around the station. She had dated occasionally, but had never been able to commit herself to anything. She supposed that, as far as the men were concerned, there always seemed to be a million things she would rather be doing than being with them, and they were right. Because of that, she had spent too many evenings alone in her soulless flat. But also, because of that, she had passed all her examinations and her career was flourishing.

She certainly found James attractive, as well as charming and lively company. He was a great ham, had a fine sense of the dramatic. But there was more to him than that; an intensity and a kind of masculine self-assurance. He would probably make a fine lover. So why was she avoiding the inevitable? Her excuse was the case, but her real reason was fear. Fear of what? she asked herself. He hadn't even tried to touch her yet, though she was sure she had seen the desire in his eyes. Was she afraid of enjoying herself? Of losing control? Of feeling nothing? She didn't know, but if she was to change her life in any way at all, she would have to find out. And that meant confronting it. So, when the case was over . . .

A skin had formed on the top of her cocoa. She had never liked that, ever since childhood. That sweet and sticky skin made her shudder when, inadvertently, she had sipped without looking and it had stuck like a warm spider's web to her lips. Carefully, using her spoon, she pushed it to the edge of the cup, dredged it out and laid it in the saucer.

For some reason, that photo of Marcia Cunningham's handsome husband with his pipe at a rakish angle came into her mind. He reminded her of James just a little. Not his looks, but his expression. She found herself looking at the mantelpiece. Now that the Father Christmas was gone, it seemed so empty. She would like to have a photo or two there, but of whom? Not her family, that was for certain. James? Much too early for that yet. Herself, the graduation picture from police college? It would do, for a start.

Then she remembered the dress Marcia had dragged her all that way to look at. There was a puzzle, to be sure. No doubt the vandals would have an explanation, when and if they were caught. Still, it was a strange thing for someone to do. Maybe they had taken strips of material to fasten around their foreheads as Rambo headbands or something. There was no telling what weird fantasies went on in the adolescent mind these days.

Susan put her cup down. The record had finished, and even though it wasn't late she decided to go to bed and have an early night. There was still that American tome on homicide investigation for bedtime reading. Or should she do a little advance reading of Shakespeare from the cut-price *Complete Works* she had picked up at W.H. Smith's?

In a couple of days it would be twelfth night, the first night of the play. She just hoped that no police business came up to stop her from attending. James seemed so much to want her there, even though her knowledge of Shakespeare left a lot to be desired. And she was looking forward to the evening. She couldn't see how any of the present cases would get in her way. There wasn't much else they could do on the Caroline Hartley murder until they got new evidence, or until Banks took his head out of the sand and gave Veronica Shildon a long, hard, objective interrogation. Besides, Susan was only a helper, a note-taker on that one. And as for the vandals, until they were caught red-handed there wasn't much to be done about them, either. Picking up the heavy *Complete Works* from her bookshelf, she wandered off to bed.

V

"A message for you, sir," Sergeant Rowe called out as Banks walked into the police station after his visit to Veronica Shildon. He handed over a piece of paper. "It was a woman called Patty Jarouchki, I think. Sounded American. Anyway, she left her number. Said for you to call her as soon as you can."

Banks thanked him and hurried upstairs to his office, grabbing a black coffee on the way. The CID offices were quiet, the tapping of a keyboard from Richmond's office the only sign of life. He picked up the phone and dialled the number Sergeant Rowe had given him. Patsy Janowski answered on the third ring.

"You had a message for me?" Banks said.

"Yes. Remember you asked me to try and recall if I'd noticed anything unusual in the area?"

"Yes."

"Well, it's not really . . . I mean, it's not clear at all, but you know I said there was a woman?"

"The one crossing King Street?"

"Yes. What about her?"

"I didn't get a good look or anything—I'm sure it wasn't anyone I knew—but I do remember she was walking funny."

"In what way?"

"Just . . . funny."

"Did she have a limp, a wooden leg?"

"No, no, it was nothing like that. At least I don't think so."

"A strange kind of walk? Some people have them. Bowlegged? Knock-kneed?"

"Not even that. She was just struggling a bit. There was snow on the ground. Oh, I know I shouldn't have called you. It's still not clear, and it's probably nothing. I feel stupid."

Banks could imagine her eyes ranging about the room, resting on the tongs by the fire, the old snuff-box on the mantelpiece. "You did right," he assured her.

"But I've told you nothing, really."

"It might mean something. If you think of anything else, will you stop accusing yourself of idiocy and call me?"

He could almost hear her smile at the other end of the line. "All right," she said. "But I don't think it'll get any clearer."

Banks said goodnight and broke the connection. For a moment he just sat on the edge of his desk, coffee in hand, staring at the calendar. It showed a wintry scene in Aysgarth, Wensleydale. Finally, he lit a cigarette and went over to the window. Outside, beyond the venetian blinds, the market square was deserted. The Christmas-tree lights still twinkled, but nobody passed to see them. It was that time of year when everyone had spent too much and drunk too much and seen too many people; now most Eastvalers were holed up in their houses keeping warm and watching repeats on television.

The day's depression was still with him, and the mystery of Caroline Hartley's death was still shrouded in fog. There had to be some way of making sense of it all, Banks told himself. He must have overlooked something. The only solution to his bleak mood was mental activity. As he stood at the window looking down on the forlorn Christmas lights, he tried to recreate the sequence of events in his mind.

First of all, he discounted the arrival of yet another visitor after the mysterious woman at seven-twenty. He also accepted that by the time Patsy Janowski had called and talked to Caroline Hartley briefly at her door, Claude Ivers was busy doing his last-minute shopping in the centre and getting ready to head back to Redburn, and Veronica Shildon was shopping too.

A woman, perhaps the same one Patsy said walked strangely, knocked at Caroline's door and was admitted to the house. What had happened inside? Had the woman been an ex-lover or a jilted suitor? Had she called to remonstrate and ended up losing her temper and killing Caroline? Presumably there could have been sex involved. After all, Caroline had been naked, and the kind of sex she was interested in wouldn't oblige by leaving semen traces for the forensic boys to track down.

There was just no way of knowing. Caroline's life had been full of mysteries, a breeding ground for motives. As a working hypothesis, Banks accepted that the crime was spur-of-the-moment rather than a planned murder. The use of the handy knife and the lack of precaution about being seen, or caught by Veronica, who had been likely to arrive home at any moment, seemed to point that way. And unless Caroline had been involved in some unknown criminal activity, the odds were that passion of one kind or another lay at the root of her death.

After the murder came the clearing up. The killer had washed the knife, removed any possible fingerprints she might have left, and either put the Vivaldi record on the turntable or lifted up the arm. Given the savage nature of the wounds, the killer must also have got blood on her own clothing. If she had removed her coat before the deed, she could easily have covered her blood-spattered clothing with it and destroyed all evidence as soon as she got home.

Banks went to refill his coffee mug and returned to his office.

Something in Patsy Janowski's sketchy description of the woman bothered him, but he couldn't think what it was. He walked to the filing cabinet and dug out the reports on interviews with Caroline Hartley's neighbours. Nothing much there helped, either. The details were vague, as the evening had been dark and snowy. Again, he read through the descriptions of the mystery woman: Mr Farlowe had said she was wearing a mid-length, light trenchcoat with the belt fastened. He had seen her legs beneath it, and perhaps the bottom of a dress. She had been wearing a head-scarf, so he had been able to say nothing about her hair. Mrs Eldridge had little to add, but what she remembered agreed with Farlowe's account.

Despite the coffee, Banks was getting tired. It really was time to go home. There was nothing to be gained by pacing the office. He slipped on his camel-hair overcoat and put the Walkman in his pocket. After he'd walked down the stairs and said goodnight to Sergeant Rowe at the front desk, he hesitated outside the station under the blue lamp and looked at the Queen's Arms. A rosy glow shone warmly from its smoky windows. But no, he decided, best go home and spend some time with Sandra. It was a clear, quiet night. He would leave the car in the station car-park and walk the mile or so home.

He put the headphones on, pressed the button and the opening of Poulenc's "Gloria" came on. As he walked on the crisp snow down Market Street, he looked at the patterns frost had made on the shop windows and wished that the odd bits and pieces of knowledge he had about the Hartley case could make similar symmetrical shapes. They didn't. He began to walk faster. Christ, his feet were cold. He should have worn sheepskin-lined boots, or at least galoshes. But he had never really thought about walking home until the impulse struck him. Then something leaped into his mind as he turned into his cul-de-sac and saw the welcome lights of home ahead, something that made him forget his cold feet for the last hundred yards.

Patsy Janowski had said the woman walked strangely. She couldn't explain it any better than that. But Mr Farlowe said he was sure the visitor was a woman because he had seen her legs below her long coat. If that was the case, then her legs were bare; she either wasn't wearing boots at all, or she was wearing very short ones. It had been snowing quite heavily that evening since about five o'clock, and the snow had been forecast as early as the previous evening, so even a woman going to work that morning would have known to take her boots. Even before the snow, the weather had been grey and cold. Most of December had been lined-boots and overcoat weather.

Now why would a woman be trudging around in the snow without boots at seven-twenty that night? Banks wondered. She could have been in a hurry and simply slipped on the first pair of shoes that caught her eye. She could have come from somewhere she hadn't needed boots. But that didn't make sense. In such weather, most people wear boots to work, then change into more comfortable shoes when they get there. When it's time to leave, they slip back into their boots for the journey home.

The woman might have arrived by car and parked close by. The nearest space, where Patsy said she and Ivers parked, was a fair distance to walk in the snow without boots. The woman might have driven to Caroline's, found she couldn't park any closer and ended up having to walk farther than she'd bargained for. Which meant it could have been someone who didn't know the area well.

Given what Patsy had said about the walk, it sounded as if the woman had probably been wearing pumps or high-heels—most likely the latter. That would explain her odd walk; trying to make one's way through four or five inches of snow in high-heels would be difficult indeed. And wet.

Was it, then, someone who had nipped out of a local function, committed the murder and dashed back before she was missed?

There had probably been a lot of parties going on that night, Hatchley's wedding reception among them. It couldn't have been anyone from there, of course, as Banks knew most of the guests. But it was an interesting avenue to explore. If he could find someone who had been at such a function that night, someone who had a connection with Caroline Hartley, then maybe he'd get somewhere. Feeling a little more positive about things, he turned off the tape and went into the house.

THIRTEEN

I

Teresa Pedmore rented a two-bedroom terrace house on Nelson Grove, in a pleasant enough area of town south of the castle, close to the river. The houses were old but in good repair, and their inhabitants, though only renting, took pride in adding individual touches to the outside trim. A low blue gate led to Teresa's house, where her matching door was edged in white. Lace curtains hung in the windows.

Teresa professed to be surprised to see Banks, though he was never sure what to believe when dealing with actors. Faith could have told Teresa about the visit Banks had paid her earlier, though he thought it unlikely. That would have meant confessing what she had said about Teresa.

The front door led straight into the living-room. Cream-and-red-striped wallpaper covered the walls, where a number of framed prints hung. Banks, who had learned what little he knew about art from Sandra, recognized a Constable landscape, a Stubbs horse and a Lowry. Perhaps the most striking thing about the room, though, was that it was furnished with antiques: a Welsh dresser, Queen Anne writing-desk, Regency table and chairs. The only contemporary items were the tan three-piece suite arranged in a semicircle around the hearth and a small television set. Remembering the importance of the music, Banks looked around for evidence of a stereo but could find none.

Teresa gestured towards one of the armchairs and Banks sat down. He was surprised by her taste and impressed with her farm-girl looks, the blushes of red in her creamy cheeks. Her wavy chestnut hair framed a rather chubby, heart-shaped face with a wide, full mouth, an oddly delicate nose that didn't quite seem to belong and thick brows over large almond eyes. She certainly wasn't good-looking in the overtly sexual way Faith Green was, but the fierce confidence and determination in her simplest movements and gestures more than compensated. She was as tall and well-shaped as Faith, and wore a white silky blouse and knee-length navy skirt.

She picked up an engraved silver box from the low table and offered him a cigarette, lighting it with an old lighter as big as a paperweight. It was years since Banks had been offered a cigarette from a box, and he would certainly never have expected it in a small rented terrace house in Eastvale.

The cigarette was too strong, but he persevered. His lungs soon remembered the old days of Capstan Full Strength and rallied to the task. Almost before he had a chance to say yes or no, Teresa was pouring amber liquid from a cut-glass decanter into a crystal snifter. As she handed Banks the glass, the edges of her wide mouth twitched up in a smile.

"I suppose you're wondering where I get my money from," she said. "Policemen are always suspicious about people living above their means, aren't they?" She sat down and crossed her long legs.

Banks swirled the glass in his hand and breathed in the fumes: cognac. "*Are* you living above your means?" he asked.

She laughed, a low, murmuring sound. "How clever of you. Not at all. It only looks that way. The furniture isn't original, of course. I just like the designs, the look and feel of it. And one day, believe me, I'll have real antiques. I think the only valuable objects in the room are the decanter and the cigarette box, and they belonged to my grandfather. Family heirlooms. The Lowry is genuine, too, a present from a distant, wealthy relative. As for the rest, cognac and what have you . . . What can I say? I like to live well. I don't drink a lot, but I drink the best. I make decent money, I don't run a car, I have no children and my rent is reasonable."

Banks, who wondered why she was telling him all this, nodded as if he were suitably impressed. Perhaps she was trying to paint a picture of herself as someone who had far too much class and refined sensibility to commit so tasteless an act as murder. He sipped the cognac. Courvoisier VSOP, he guessed. Maybe she was right.

"I suppose you think I should have stayed on the farm," she went on. "Married a local farmer and started having babies." She made a dismissive gesture with her cigarette.

For Christ's sake, Banks thought, do I look so old that people immediately assume I'm a fuddy-duddy? Still, Teresa couldn't have been more than twenty-two, twenty-three; there were sixteen or seventeen years between them, which made it technically possible for him to be her father. He just didn't feel that old, and he could certainly understand young people wanting to escape what they felt to be claustrophobic social backgrounds.

"What do you want to do?" he asked.

"Act, of course."

She reminded Banks of Sally Lumb, another, albeit younger, Dales hopeful he had met during the Steadman case eighteen months ago. The memory made him feel sad. Such dreams often turn to pain. But what are we if we don't dream? Banks asked himself. And at least try to make them come true.

"James is trying to fix things so I get a part in *Weymouth Sands*. He's doing the script for the BBC, you know. He knows all the casting people. It's terribly exciting." The Dales accent was still there, despite the evidence of elocution lessons, and it made the upper class phrase "terribly exciting" sound very funny indeed. "More cognac?"

Banks noticed his snifter was empty. He shook his head. "No, no thanks. It's very good, but I'd better not."

Teresa shrugged. She didn't press him. Fine cognac is, after all, very expensive.

"You're still on good terms with James Conran, then?" Banks asked.

Her eyebrows rose. "Why shouldn't I be?"

"I heard rumours you'd had a falling out."

"Who told you that?"

"Are they true?"

"It's that common little tramp, Faith, isn't it?"

"Was James Conran paying too much attention to Caroline Hartley?"

The name stopped Teresa in her tracks. She reached for another cigarette from the box but didn't offer Banks one this time. "It's easy to exaggerate things," she continued quietly. "Everyone argues now and then. I'll bet even you argue with your wife, don't you? But it doesn't mean anything."

"Did you argue with James Conran over Caroline?"

Her eyes flashed briefly, then she drew on her cigarette, tilted her head back and blew out a long stream of smoke through narrow nostrils. "What has Faith been saying about me?" she asked. "I've got a right to know."

"Look," Banks said, "I haven't told you who passed on the information. Nor am I going to. It's not important. What counts is that you answer my questions. And if you won't do it here, you can come down to the police station and answer them."

"You can't make me do that." Teresa leaned forward and flicked off a column of ash. "Surely?"

"What did you do after the rehearsal on December twenty-second?"

"What? I . . . I came home."

"Straight home?"

"No. I did some Christmas shopping first. Look—"

"What time did you get home?"

"—what is this? Are you trying to imply I might have had something to do with Caroline Hartley's death?"

"I'm not implying anything, I'm asking questions." Banks pulled out one of his own Silk Cuts and lit up. "What time did you get home?"

"I don't know. How can I remember? It was ages ago."

"Did you go out again?"

"No. I stayed home and worked on my role."

"You didn't have a date with Mr Conran?"

"No. We . . . I . . ."

"Were you still seeing him at that time?"

"Of course I was."

"As a lover?"

"That's none of your damn business." She mashed her cigarette out and clasped her hands in her lap.

"When did you and Mr Conran stop being lovers?"

"I'm not answering that."

"But you did stop."

There was a pause, then she hissed, "Yes."

"Before Caroline Hartley's murder?"

"Yes."

"And did Caroline have anything to do with this parting?"

"No. It was completely amicable on both sides. Things just didn't work out that way. We'd never been very deeply involved, anyway, if you know what I mean."

"A casual affair?"

"You could call it that, though neither of us is married."

"And Caroline Hartley came between you?"

Teresa scratched her palm and looked down.

"Am I right?" Banks persisted.

"Look," Teresa answered. "What if I say you are? It doesn't mean anything, does it? It doesn't mean I'd kill her. I'm not a fanatically jealous woman, but every woman has her pride. Anyway, it wasn't Caroline I blamed."

"Was Conran having an affair with Caroline?"

She shook her head. "I don't think so. We didn't know she was gay, but even so there was something about her, something different. Elusive. She could keep the men at bay while seeming to draw them to her. It's difficult to explain. No, I don't think he even saw her outside rehearsals and the pub."

That seemed to square with what Veronica Shildon had said.

"But he was attracted to her?"

"A bit smitten, you might say," said Teresa. "That was what annoyed me, him chatting her up in public like that when everyone could see, the way he looked at her. That kind of thing. But then James is like that. He goes after anything in a skirt."

"Am I to take it you don't much care for him any longer?"

"Not as a man, no. As a professional, I respect him a great deal."

"That's a very neat distinction."

"Surely you sometimes have to work with people you respect but don't like?"

"Did you argue over his attentions to Caroline?"

"I told him to stop drooling over her in public. I found it embarrassing. But that was only a part of it. What I said before was true. It wasn't much of a relationship to begin with. It had run its course."

"Do you think you'll get this part in *Weymouth Sands*?"

"James still appreciates me as an actress," she said, "which is more than he does that gossipy bitch who told you all about my personal life."

"Who's that?"

"Faith bloody Green, obviously. There's no need to be coy. You know damn well it was her who told you. And I can guess why."

"Why?"

"Why do you think? Because she couldn't get him herself."

"Did she try?"

Teresa gave Banks a disdainful look. "You've met Faith, Chief Inspector. What do you think the answer is?"

"But Conran wasn't interested?"

"It appears not."

"Any reason?"

"Not that I know of. Not his type, perhaps. Too much woman, too aggressive . . . I don't know. I'm just guessing."

"What did he think of her? Did they have any arguments?"

"If she's been trying to imply I had a good reason for killing Caroline Hartley, it's probably because she had an even better one."

Banks sat up. "Why? Over her interest in Conran?"

Teresa sniffed. "No. It wasn't that. I think she soon realized that her tastes run to rougher trade than James. It was just that she had to try, like she does with every man. No, it was something else that happened."

"Tell me."

Teresa leaned forward and lowered her voice dramatically. "It was after rehearsal that night, the night Caroline was killed."

"What happened?"

"Most people left early because it was close to Christmas, but James wanted to spend half an hour or so with Faith and myself, just getting the blocking right. Our parts are large and very important, you see. Anyway, James wanted Faith to stay behind, so I left first. But I forgot my scarf, and it was cold outside, so I came back.

I don't think they heard me. I was in the props room, you know, where we leave our coats and bags, and I heard voices out in the auditorium. I'm not a naturally nosy person, but I wondered what was going on. Anyway, to cut a long story short, I walked a little closer and listened. And guess what?"

"What?"

Teresa smiled. "They were arguing. I bet she didn't tell you about *that*, did she?"

"What were they arguing about?"

"Caroline Hartley. As far as I could gather, James was telling Faith that if she didn't do a better job of learning her lines, he'd give her part to Caroline."

"What was Faith's reaction?"

"She walked out in a huff. I had to be quick to hide behind a door without being seen."

"Can you remember their exact words?"

"I can remember what Faith said to James before she left. She said, 'You'd do anything to get into that little slut's pants, wouldn't you?' I wish I'd been there to see his face. Of course, he can't have meant it about giving her part away. James would know quite well there wasn't enough time for Caroline to take over Faith's role. He was just trying to get her to try a bit harder."

"What happened after that?"

"I don't know. As soon as Faith left, I got out of there pretty quickly. I didn't want to be caught snooping."

"Where was Conran?"

"Still in the auditorium, as far as I know."

"Could he have left by the front door?"

Teresa shook her head. "No, we always use the back during rehearsals. The front's kept locked after the gallery closes, unless there's some sort of an event on."

"Who has a key to the back door?"

"Only Marcia and James from the Dramatic Society, as far as I know. Usually one or the other would be last to leave. James, more often than not, as Marcia was always first to arrive, and she tended to disappear to the pub early if she knew she wasn't needed."

"What time did this argument occur?"

"Six. Maybe a little after."

"What were you wearing?"

Teresa frowned and sat back in her chair. "What do you mean?"

"What clothes were you wearing?"

"Me? Jeans, a leather coat, my wool scarf. Same as usual for rehearsals."

"What about footwear?"

"I had my boots on. It *is* winter, after all. I don't see what—"

"And Faith?"

"I can't remember. I doubt I paid much attention."

"What did she usually wear? Jeans? Skirt and blouse? Dress?"

"She usually wore a skirt and blouse. She is a teacher, believe it or not. She came straight from school. But I don't know for sure what she was wearing that day."

"What about her overcoat?"

"What she always wore, I suppose."

"Which is?"

"A long coat, like a light raincoat with epaulettes, but lined."

"Belted?"

"Yes."

"And her footwear?"

"How should I know?"

"Was she wearing boots or shoes?"

"Boots, I should think. Because of the weather."

"But you can't be sure?"

"No. I can't say I pay Faith's feet much attention."

"Why didn't you tell me all this earlier?" Banks asked.

Teresa sighed and shifted in her chair. "I don't know. It didn't seem all that important. And I didn't want any trouble, anything spoiling the play. It was bad enough with Caroline getting murdered. When I heard about her being gay, I was sure her death must have had something to do with her private life, that it didn't involve any of us. I know I sound hard, but this play is important to me, believe it or not. If I do well, the TV people will hear about me . . ."

Banks stood up. "I see."

"And as for Faith," Teresa went on. "I know I sounded bitchy right now, but it was only because I was annoyed at what she'd said to you.

She'd no right to go talking about my personal life. But she's not a killer. Not Faith. And certainly not over a petty incident like that."

Banks buttoned his overcoat and headed for the door. "Thanks very much," he said. "You've been a great help." And he left her reaching for another cigarette from the engraved silver box.

Damn them all! he cursed as he walked out into the cold night. Of course Faith could have killed Caroline. Perhaps not over a petty matter, such as the argument Teresa had described, but there could have been another reason. A woman like Caroline Hartley, whether intentionally or not, causes violent emotion in all who come into contact with her. Even Veronica Shildon had admitted to Banks that she'd never understood lust until she met Caroline.

Faith could have simmered for a while after the row—it would certainly have been a blow to her pride—and then, if she had something else against Caroline, too, she could have gone to visit her and remonstrate. Faith certainly worked hard at her Mae West role, but what if it was just an act? What if her true inclination lay elsewhere, or she leaned both ways?

It didn't seem likely that James Conran would kill the goose he hoped would lay a golden egg. He had high hopes for Caroline as an actress and he was sexually attracted to her as a woman. He didn't know she was gay. Given his masculine pride and confidence, he probably assumed that she would come around eventually; it was just a matter of time and persistence. Still, there might have been something else in the relationship that Banks didn't know about.

Caroline had seemed to bring out the worst in both Faith and Teresa. How could he be sure either of them was telling him the truth? Instead of feeling that he had cleverly played one off against the other, he was beginning to feel that he might be the one who had been played. Cursing actors, he pulled up in front of his house feeling nothing but frustration.

II

The bell was ringing in the distance. All around lay dark jungle: snakes slithered along branches, phosphorescent insects hummed in the air and squat, furry creatures lurked in the lush foliage. But the bell was ringing in the dark and she had to find her way through the jungle to discover why. There were probably booby traps, too—holes lightly covered with grass matting that would give way under her weight to a thirty-foot drop onto sharpened bamboo shoots. And . . .

She was at least half-awake now. The jungle was gone, a figment of the night. The ringing was coming from her telephone, in the living-room. Hardly a dangerous journey, after all, though one she was loath to make, being so comfortably snuggled up under the warm blankets.

She looked at the bedside clock. Two twenty-three in the morning. Bloody hell. And she hadn't got to bed until midnight. Slowly, without turning on the light, she made her way through to the living-room by touch. She fumbled the receiver and put it to her ear.

"Susan?"

"Mmm."

"Sergeant Rowe here. Sorry to disturb you, lass, but it's important. At least it might be."

"What's happened?"

"We've caught the vandals."

"How? No, wait. I'm coming in. Give me fifteen minutes."

"Right you are, lass. They'll still be here."

Susan replaced the receiver and shook her head to clear the cobwebs. Luckily, she hadn't drunk too much at dinner. She put on the living-room light, squinting in the brightness, then went into the bathroom and splashed cold water on her face. There was no time for make-up and grooming, just a quick wash, a brush through the hair and out into the cold quiet night. With luck, there would be fresh coffee at the station.

Holding her coat around her she shivered as she got into the car. It started on the third try. Driving slowly because of the ice, she took nearly ten minutes to get to the car-park behind the station. She nipped in through the back door and walked to the front desk.

"They're upstairs," Sergeant Rowe said.

"Any background information?"

"Aye. Tolliver and Wilson caught them trying to jemmy their way into the Darby and Joan Club on Heughton Drive. Our lads had enough sense to let them jemmy open the lock and step over the threshold before pouncing. A slight altercation ensued"— Sergeant Rowe stopped and smiled at his use of jargon—"in which said officers managed to apprehend the suspects. In other words, they put up a bit of a fight but came off worst."

"Do we know who they are?"

"Rob Chalmers and Billy Morley. Both spent time in remand homes."

"How old are they?"

"We're in luck. One's eighteen, the other seventeen."

Susan smiled. "Not a case for the juvenile court, then. Have they been cautioned?"

"Charged and cautioned. We've got the jemmy and the gloves they were wearing bagged and ready for testing."

"And?"

"They're not saying owt. Been watching American cop shows like the rest. Refuse to talk till they've seen their lawyers. Lawyers! I ask you."

"And I assume said lawyers are on their way?"

Rowe scratched his bulbous nose. "Bit of trouble tracking them down. I think we might manage it by morning."

"Good. Where are they?"

"Interview rooms upstairs. Tolliver's with one, Wilson's with the other."

"Right."

Susan poured herself a mug of coffee and went upstairs, still feeling the same thrill as she had on her first day in CID. She took a few sips of the strong black liquid, hung her coat up in the office, then took a quick glance in her compact mirror and applied a little make-up. At least now she didn't look as if she had got straight out of bed. Satisfied, she smoothed her skirt, ran her hand through her curls, took a deep breath and walked into the first interview room.

PC Tolliver stood by the door, a bruise by the side of his left eye and a crust of blood under his right nostril. Sitting, or rather slouching, behind the table, legs stretched out, arms behind his head, was a youth with dark, oily, slicked-back hair, as if he had used half a jar of Brylcreem. He was wearing a green parka, open over a torn T-shirt, and faded, grubby jeans. Susan could smell beer on his breath even at the door. When he saw her walk in, he didn't move. She ignored him and looked over at Tolliver.

"All right, Mike?"

"I'll mend."

"Who've we got?"

"Robert S. Chalmers, age eighteen. Unemployed. Previous form for assault, damage to property, theft—all as a juvenile. A real charmer." Susan winced in acknowledgment of his joke. Bad puns were a thing with PC Tolliver.

Susan sat down. Tolliver went to the chair by the small window in the corner and took out his notebook.

"Hello, Robert," she said, forcing a smile.

"Fuck off."

The animosity that came from him was almost overwhelming. Susan tensed up inside, determined not to react. On the outside she remained calm and cool. He had acted in this hostile way partly because she was a woman, she was sure. A thug like Chalmers would take it as an insult that they sent a small woman rather than a burly man to interrogate him. He would also expect to be able to deal with her easily. To him, women were probably creatures to be used and discarded. There wouldn't be any short-age of them in his life. He was good-looking in a surly, James Dean, early Elvis Presley way, his upper lip permanently curved in a sneer.

"I hear you've been attempting to gain unlawful entry to the Darby and Joan Club," she said. "What's the problem, can't you wait till you're sixty-five?"

"Very funny."

"It's not funny, Robert. It's aggravated burglary. Do you know how much time you can get for that?"

Chalmers glared at her. "I'm not saying anything till my lawyer gets here."

"It might help you if you did. Co-operation. We'd mention that in court."

"I told you, I ain't saying nothing. I know you bastards. You'd fit me up with a verbal." He moved in his chair and Susan saw him wince slightly with pain.

"What's wrong, Robert?"

"Bastard over there beat me up." He grinned. "Don't worry, love, he only bruised a rib or two—he didn't damage my tackle."

Susan bit her tongue. "Be sensible, Robert, like your friend William."

Susan saw a flicker of apprehension in the boy's eyes, but they quickly regained their hard-bitten look and he laughed. "I'm not stupid, you know, love," he said. "Pull the other one."

Susan stared at him, long and hard, and made her assessment. Was it worth pushing at him? She decided not. He'd been through this kind of thing too many times before to fall for the usual tricks or to scare easily. Maybe his accomplice would be softer.

She stood up. "Right, I'll just go and have another word with your mate, then. He'll be able to fill in all the details. That should give us enough."

Though hardly anything perceptible changed in Chalmers's expression, Susan somehow knew that what she had said worried him. Not that the other had talked already; he wouldn't fall for that. But that Billy Morley was less tough, more nervous, more likely to crack. Chalmers just shrugged and resumed his slouch, gritting his teeth for a second as he shifted. He put his hands in his pockets and pretended to whistle at the ceiling.

Susan went to the next room, stopping to lean against the wall on the way to take a few deep breaths. No matter how often she came across them, people like Chalmers frightened her. They frightened her more than the people who committed crimes out of passion or greed. She could hear her father's voice going on about the younger generation. In his day, the story went, people were frightened of coppers, they respected the law. Now, though, they didn't give a damn; they'd as soon thump a policeman and run. She had to admit there was a lot of truth in what he said. There had always been gangs, youngsters had always been full of mischief and sometimes gone too far, but they certainly used to run when the police arrived. Now they didn't seem to care. Why had it

happened? Was television to blame? Partly, perhaps. But it was
more than that. Maybe they had become cynical about those in
authority after reading about too many corrupt politicians,
perverted judges and bent coppers. Everyone was on the fiddle;
nothing really mattered any more. But it wasn't Susan's job to
analyse society, just to get the truth out of the bastards. Taking a
final deep breath, she walked into the next office to confront Billy
Morley.

This lad, guarded by PC Wilson, who sported a small cut over
his left eye, seemed a little more nervous than his friend. Skinny to
the point of emaciation, he had a spotty, weasly face and dark,
beady eyes that darted all over the place. He was sitting straight up
in his chair rubbing his upper arm and licking his thin lips.

"You the lawyer?" he asked hopefully. "This bastard here nearly
broke my arm. Hit me with his stick."

"You were resisting arrest," PC Wilson said.

"I wasn't doing nothing of the kind. I was minding my own business."

"Aye," said Wilson, "you and your jemmy."

"It's not mine. It's—"

"Well?" asked Wilson.

He folded his arms. "I'm not saying anything."

By this time Susan had sat down and arranged herself as
comfortably as she could in the stiff, bolted-down chair. First she
gave PC Wilson the signal to fade into the background and take
notes, then she took a good look at Morley. He didn't frighten her
nearly as much as Chalmers. Basically, she thought, he was weak—
especially alone. He was also the younger of the two. Chalmers,
she suspected, was a true hard case, but Morley was just a follower
and probably a coward at heart. Chalmers had known that, and the
knowledge had flitted across his face for a moment. Being a woman
would put Susan at an advantage with someone like Morley, who
probably jumped each time his mother yelled.

"I'm not your solicitor, William," Susan said. "I'm a detective
constable. I've come to ask you a few questions. It's a serious charge
you're facing. Do you understand that?"

"What do you mean?"

"Aggravated burglary. Under section ten of the Theft Act, you could do life. Add to that resisting arrest, assaulting a police officer, and I'm pretty sure any judge would come down hard on you."

"Bollocks! That's crap! You can't get life." He shook his head. "Not just for . . . I don't believe you."

"It's true, William. You're not a juvenile now, you're an adult. No more fun and games."

"But—"

"But nothing. I'm telling you, William, it doesn't look good. Do you know what *aggravated* burglary means?"

Morley shook his head.

Susan clasped her hands on the table in front of her. "It means committing a burglary while carrying an offensive weapon."

"What offensive weapon?"

"The jemmy."

Susan was interpreting the law with a certain amount of licence. "Aggravated burglary" usually involved firearms or explosives.

She shook her head. "The best we could do for you is drop the charge to going equipped for stealing. That's thirteen years. Then there's malicious damage to property. . . . Whichever way it cuts, William, you're in a lot of trouble. You can only help yourself by talking to me."

Morley pinched his long, sharp nose and sniffed. "I want my lawyer."

"What were you after?" Susan asked. "Did someone tell you there was money there?"

"We weren't after no money. We—I'm not saying anything till my law—"

"Your solicitor may be some time, William. Solicitors like a good night's sleep. They don't enjoy getting up at two-thirty in the morning just to help a pathetic little creep like you. It'll be better if you co-operate."

Morley gaped at her, as if her insulting words, delivered in such a matter-of-fact, even tone, had pricked him like darts. "I told you," he stammered. "I war—"

Susan rested her hands on the table, palms down, and spoke softly. "William, be sensible for once in your life. Look at the facts.

We already know the two of you broke into the Darby and Joan Club. You used a jemmy. It'll have your fingerprints on it. You must have handled it at some time. It's being tested right now. And there'll be fibres we can match with the gloves you were wearing, too. We also have two very reliable witnesses. PC Wilson here and his colleague caught you red-handed. There's no getting around that, solicitor or no solicitor. We've followed correct procedure so far. You've been warned and charged. Right now we're reviewing your options, so to speak."

"He hit me," Morley whined. "He's broke my arm. I need a doctor."

For a moment Susan thought that might be true. Morley was pale and his sharp, narrow brow looked clammy. Then she realized it was fear.

"Look at his eye, William," she said. "Nobody's going to believe he attacked you for no reason."

Morley fell silent for a while. Susan could almost hear him thinking, trying to decide what to do.

"It'll go easier for you if you tell us what you were up to," she said gently. "Perhaps you were only trespassing." That would never wash, she knew. Trespassing, in itself, wasn't an offence except in certain special circumstances, such as poaching and espionage, and breaking the lock of a club with a jemmy was a long way from simple trespass. Still, it wouldn't do Morley any harm to let him look on the bright side.

He remained silent, chewing at the edge of his thumb.

"What's wrong, William? Are you frightened of Robert? Is that what it is?" She was about to tell him Chalmers had already talked, tried to put the blame on him, but realized just in time that such a ploy could ruin any advantage she had. He might suspect a trick then, no doubt having seen such tactics used on television, and her carefully constructed house of cards would fall down.

"There's nothing to be afraid of. You'll be helping him too."

Ten tense seconds later, Morley took his thumb from his mouth and said, "We weren't burgling anything. That wasn't it at all."

"What were you doing there, then?" Susan asked.

"Just having fun."

"What do you mean, fun?"

"You know, it was something to do. Smashing things and stuff. It wasn't no aggravated burglary, or whatever you call it. You can't charge us with that."

"It looks like burglary to us, William. Are you trying to tell me you were going to vandalize the place?"

"We weren't going to take anything or hurt anyone. Nothing like that."

"Were you going to cause damage?"

"Just a bit of fun."

"Why?"

"What do you mean, why?"

"Why would you want to do such a thing?"

"I dunno." Morley squirmed in his chair and grasped his arm again. "Fucking hurts, that."

"Will you please not use language like that in front of me, William," Susan said. "I find it offensive. Answer my question. Why did you do it?"

"No reason. Do you have to have a fucking reason for everything? I told you, it was just fun, that's all."

"I've told you once," Susan said, mustering as much quiet authority as she could, "I don't like that kind of language. Learn some manners."

Morley tried hard to glare at her, but he looked more ashamed and defeated than defiant.

"Was it the same kind of fun you had in those other places?" Susan asked.

"What other places?"

"Come on, William. You know what I mean. This isn't the first time, is it?"

Morley remained silent for a while, then said quietly, still rubbing his arm. "I suppose not."

"Suppose?"

"All right. No, its not. But we never hurt anyone or anything."

Susan could taste success. Her first real case. She was only assisting on the Hartley murder, but this one was all hers. If she could wrap up a four-month problem of vandalism with a neat confession, it would look very good on her record. As she listed the dates and places vandalized over the past few months—mostly youth clubs and recreation centres—Morley nodded glumly at each one, until she mentioned the Community Centre.

"Come again?" he said.

"Eastvale Community Centre, night of December twenty-second."

Morley shook his head. "You can't do us for that one."

"What are you saying?"

"I'm saying we didn't do it, that's what."

"Come on, William. What's the point in denying it? It'll all be taken into account. You're doing yourself no good."

He leaned forward. Spittle collected at the corners of his mouth. "Because we didn't f—. . . . Because we didn't do it, that's why. I wasn't even in Eastvale that night. I spent Christmas with my mother down in Coventry. I can prove it. Call her. Go on."

Susan took the number. "What about Robert?"

"How should I know. But *I* didn't do it. He wouldn't do it by himself, would he? Stands to reason. Rob—now, wait a minute, wait a minute! He was out of town, too. He was down in Bristol with his brother over Christmas. We didn't do it, I'm telling you."

Susan tapped her pen on the desk and sighed. True, it didn't make sense for the lad to lie at this point, when he had confessed to everything else. Damn! Just when she thought she had got it all wrapped up. That meant there must be two sets of vandals. One down, one to go. She stood up. "Take his statement, will you, John? I'll go and make out a report for the chief inspector. We'll check the alibis for the Community Centre job tomorrow morning." As she passed the room where Robert Chalmers was being held, she almost went in for another try. But there was nothing more to learn. Instead, she carried on down the corridor to her office.

III

"Of all the times to come pestering me! It's opening night tonight. Don't you know that? How did you even know I'd be here? Normally I'd be at school at this time."

"I know," Banks said. "I phoned. They told me you'd taken the day off."

"You did what?" Faith Green was really pacing now, arms folded under her breasts. She wore purple tights and a baggy, hip-length sweater with red and blue hoops around it. Her silver hair and matching hoop earrings flashed in the morning sunlight that shone through her large picture window.

"How dare you?" she went on. "Do you realize what damage that could do my career? It doesn't matter that I'm guilty of nothing. Just a hint of police around that place and the smell sticks."

"Why don't you sit down?" Banks perched at the edge of his armchair, faintly amused by Faith's performance. It certainly differed from his last visit. His amusement, however, was over-shadowed by irritation.

She stopped and glared at him. "Am I making you nervous? Good."

Banks leaned back in the chair and crossed his legs. "Remember last time I called, I asked if you'd noticed anything odd about the rehearsal on December twenty-second?"

Faith resumed pacing again, stopped in front of the Greta Garbo poster, as if seeking inspiration, and said, with her back to Banks, "So?"

"Were you telling me the truth?"

"I'm not in the habit of lying."

"It'd be easier if you sat down," Banks said.

"Oh, all right, damn you!" Faith flounced towards the sofa and flung herself onto it. "There," she said with a pout. "Does that suit you?"

"Fine. I must say you're not quite as welcoming as you were last time."

Faith looked at him for a moment, trying to gauge his meaning. "That was different," she said finally. "I didn't see why we had to have such a boring time just because you were asking silly questions."

"And this time?"

"I should be rehearsing, going through my lines. I'm tense enough as it is. You're upsetting me."

"How?"

"Asking questions again."

Banks sighed. "All right. How about if I stop asking and start telling?" And he relayed what Teresa had told him about the argument between Faith and James Conran. The further he got, the paler Faith's face turned and the more angry her eyes became.

"Who told you this?" she demanded when he'd finished.

"That doesn't matter."

"It does to me. It couldn't have been James, surely. The last thing *he'd* do is make himself look bad." She paused, then slapped the arm of the sofa. "Of course! How stupid of me. It was Teresa, wasn't it? She must have stayed behind and eavesdropped. I thought she'd been behaving oddly towards me lately. Did you tell her what I told you?"

"Look, it really doesn't—"

"The snooping bitch! She's no right, no right at all. And neither had—"

"Is it true?" Banks asked.

"It's none of her—"

"But is it true?"

"—business to listen to my private—"

"So it *is* true?"

Faith hesitated, looked over to Garbo again and sighed deeply. "All right, so we had a row. I've got nothing to hide. It's nothing new. Happens all the time in the theatre."

"It's the timing that interests me most," Banks said. "You could conceivably have been angry enough at Caroline Hartley to stew over it for a couple of drinks, then go pay her a visit. You didn't know she lived with anyone."

Faith's jaw dropped. When she finally spoke, it was in a squeaky, uncontrolled voice, far different from her stage speech.

"Are you suggesting that I killed the damn woman over some stupid argument with the director of a small-town play?"

"You did call her a 'little slut.' I think that suggests a bit more than a tiff over a part in an amateur production, don't you?"

"It's just a figure of speech, a . . ."

"Why did you call her a slut, Faith? Was it because Conran fancied her but he didn't fancy you? Is that why you told me about him and Teresa, too? Out of jealous spite?"

For the first time, Faith seemed speechless. But it didn't last long. Finally, red-faced, she stretched out her arm dramatically and pointed at the door.

"Out!" she yelled. "Out, you wretched, insulting little man! Out!"

"Calm down, Faith," Banks said. "I need answers. Is that why?"

Faith let her arm fall slowly and sat in silence for a few moments contemplating the upholstery of the sofa. "What if I did call her a slut?" she said finally. "Heat of the moment, that's all. And I'll tell you something, the way I felt at the time, if I'd killed anybody it would have been our bloody philandering director. It's unprofessional, letting your prick rule your judgment like that. It happened with Teresa, it was happening with Caroline . . ."

"But it didn't happen with you?"

"Huh! Do you think I really cared about that? I've no trouble finding a man when I want one. A *real* man, too, not some artsy-fartsy wimp like James Conran."

"But maybe he hurt your pride? Some people don't handle rejection well. Or perhaps it wasn't Conran that really bothered you. Was it Caroline herself?"

Faith stared at him, then spoke slowly. "Look, you asked me about that the last time you were here. I told you I'm not a lesbian. I told you I could prove it to you. Do you want me to prove it now?"

She sat up, crossed her arms and reached for the bottom of her sweater.

Banks held his hand up. "No," he said, "I'm not asking you to prove it. And quite honestly, it's not really the kind of thing you *can* prove, is it?"

Faith let her hands drop but remained sitting cross-legged on the sofa. "You mean you think I'm bi?"

Banks shrugged.

"Well, you can't prove that either, can you?"

"We might be able to, if we talk to the right people."

Faith laughed. "My ex-lovers? Well, good luck to you, darling. You'll need it."

"What did you do after the argument?" Banks asked.

"Came home, like I said." She put her hand to her brow. "Quite honestly, I was shagged out, dear."

Faith seemed to have regained her composure since her outburst, or at least her poise. She pushed her fringe back from her eyes and managed a brief smile as she went on. "Look, Chief Inspector, I know you have to catch your criminal and all that, but it's not me. And I've got a lot of work to do before curtain tonight. Besides, I need to be calm, relaxed. You're making me all flustered. I'll blow my lines. Be a darling and bugger off. You can come back some other time, if you want."

Banks smiled. "I shouldn't worry about being nervous. I've heard a bit of anxiety adds an edge to a performance."

Faith narrowed her eyes at him for a moment, as if wondering whether she was being had. "Well . . ." she went on. "If that's all . . . ?"

"Far from it. You argued with James Conran in the auditorium, am I right?"

"Yes."

"What happened next?"

"I left, of course. I don't put up with that kind of treatment—not from anyone."

"And you went straight home?"

"I did."

"Was anyone else in the centre at the time?"

"Well, obviously Teresa bloody Pedmore was, but I didn't see her."

"Anyone else?"

Faith shook her head.

"Are you sure?"

"I told you, I didn't see anyone. But then I didn't see them all leave, either. There are plenty of cubby-holes behind the stage there, as you know quite well. The whole bloody cast could have been hiding there and listening, for all I know."

"But as far as you know, the only person there was James Conran, and you left him in the auditorium."

Faith nodded, a puzzled expression on her face. "And Teresa, I suppose, if she saw me leave."

"Yes," Banks said. "And Teresa. What were you wearing that evening?"

"To rehearsal?"

"Yes."

Faith shrugged. "Same as I usually wear, I suppose, when I come from school."

"Which is?"

"They're very conservative, you know. Blouse, skirt and cardigan is required uniform."

"How long was the skirt?"

She arched her eyebrows. "Why, Chief Inspector, I didn't know you cared." She stood up with exaggerated slowness and put the edge of her hand just below her knee. "About that long," she said, then she shifted her weight to her left leg, dropping her right hip in a half-comic, half-seductive pose. "As I said, they're very conservative."

"What about your overcoat?"

"What is this?"

"Can you tell me?"

"I can do better if it'll get you out of here quicker." She walked to the hall cupboard and pulled out a long, heavily-lined gabardine. "It's not quite warm enough for the weather we've been having lately," she said, "but it'll do until someone buys me a mink."

"What about footwear?"

She raised one eyebrow. "You *are* getting intimate, aren't you? Whatever will it be next, I wonder?"

"Footwear?"

"Boots, of course. What do you think I'd be wearing in that weather? Bloody high-heels?" She laughed. "Tell me, have you a shoe fetish or something?"

Banks smiled and got to his feet. "No. Sorry to disappoint you. Thank you very much for your time. I'll see myself out."

But Faith followed him to the door and leaned against the frame, arms loosely folded. "You know, Chief Inspector," she said, "I *am* very disappointed in you. I might be persuaded to change my mind, but it would take a lot of doing. I've never been so insulted and abused by a man as I've been by you. But the funny thing is, I still like you." She took him by the elbow and steered him out the open door. "And now you really must go."

Banks headed down the corridor and turned when he heard Faith calling after him.

"Chief Inspector! Will you be there tonight? Will you be watching the play?"

"I'll be there," Banks said. "I wouldn't miss it for anything." And he went on his way.

FOURTEEN

I

The community hall was surprisingly full for the first night of an amateur production, Banks thought. There they all sat, chattering and coughing nervously before the play started: a party of fourth-formers from Eastvale Comprehensive, present under sufferance; friends and relatives of the cast; a group of pensioners; members of the local Literary Institute. The old boiler groaned away in the cellar, but it didn't seem to be doing much good. There was a chill in the hall and most people kept their scarves on and their coats draped over their shoulders.

Banks sat beside Sandra. Their seats, compliments of James Conran, were front and centre, about ten rows back. Further ahead, Banks could make out Susan's blonde curls. The director himself sat beside her, occasionally leaning over to whisper in her ear. He could also see Marcia talking animatedly to a grey-haired man beside her.

It was almost seven-thirty. Banks eyed the moth-eaten curtains for signs of movement. Much as he enjoyed Shakespeare, he hoped the performance would not last too long. He remembered an actor telling him once in London that he didn't like doing *Hamlet* because the pubs had always closed by the time it was over. Banks didn't think *Twelfth Night* was that long, but a bad performance could make it seem so.

Finally, the lights went off abruptly, there being no dimmer-switch in the Eastvale Community Centre, and the curtains began to jerk open. Rusted rings creaked on the rail. The audience clapped, then made themselves as comfortable as they could in the moulded-plastic chairs.

If music be the food of love, play on.
Give me excess of it, that, surfeiting,
The appetite may sicken, and so die. . . .

So spoke the Duke, and the play was underway. The set was simple, Banks noticed. A few well-placed columns, drapes and portraits gave the impression of a palace. Banks recognized the music, played on a lute, as a Dowland melody, fitting enough for the period.

Though he was no Shakespeare expert, Banks had seen two other performances of *Twelfth Night*, one at school and one in Stratford. He remembered the general plot but not the fine details. This time, he noticed, too many cast members shouted or rushed their lines and mauled the poetry of Shakespeare's language in the process. On the other hand, the groupings and movements on stage constantly held the attention. The way people faced one another or paced about as they talked kept everything in motion. From what little he knew of directing, Banks assumed that Conran himself was responsible for this. Occasionally, a member of the audience would shift in his or her seat, and there were quite a few present suffering from coughs and colds, but on the whole most people were attentive. When an actor or actress hesitated over lines, waiting for a prompt, nobody laughed or walked out.

Faith and Teresa were good. They had the poise and the skill to bring off their roles, even if it was difficult to believe in Faith's masquerade as a man. In their scenes together, though, there was an obvious tension, perhaps because Faith knew who had told Banks about her row with Conran, and Teresa knew who had told him about her jealousy over Caroline Hartley. Ironically, this seemed to give an edge to the performances, especially to Viola's initial rudeness on their first meeting. The ambiguity of their relationship—Viola, dressed as a man, courting Olivia on her brother's behalf—soon absorbed Banks. To hear Faith complimenting Teresa's beauty was an odd thing indeed, but to watch their love blossom was even stranger.

For Banks, this had a dark side, too. He couldn't help but think of Caroline and Veronica, knowing, as the characters themselves did not, that both Viola and Olivia were female. Maria, the role that Caroline would have played, was an added reminder of the recent tragedy.

During the intermission, Banks felt distracted. He left Sandra chatting with some acquaintances and nipped out onto North Market Street for a cigarette in the icy cold. The dim gaslights glinted on the snow and ice, and even as he stood, a gentle snowfall began, flakes drifting down like feathers. He shuddered, flicked his half-smoked cigarette end into a grate and went back inside.

The vague connection between the play and reality was beginning to make Banks feel very uneasy. By the fourth act, his attention began to wander—to thoughts of his recent interviews with Faith and Teresa and the file of unread paperwork in his in-tray, including a report on the arrest of the vandals that Susan had stayed up half the night to prepare. Then his attention would return to the play in time to hear the Clown and Malvolio chatting about Pythagoras's opinion of wild fowl, or Sebastian in raptures about the pearl Olivia had given him. He couldn't maintain lasting concentration. There was something in his mind, a glimmer of an idea, disparate facts coming together, but he couldn't grasp it, couldn't see the complete picture yet. There was an element still missing.

By the final act, Banks's back and buttocks hurt, and he found it difficult to keep still in the hard chair. Surreptitiously, he glanced at his watch. Almost ten. Surely not long to go. Even before he expected it, true identities were revealed, everybody was married off, except for Malvolio, and the Clown began to sing:

When that I was and a little tiny boy,
     With hey, ho, the wind and the rain,
A foolish thing was but a toy,
     For the rain it raineth every day.

Then the music ended and the curtains closed. The audience applauded; the cast appeared to take bows. Soon the formalities were all over and everyone shuffled out of the hall, relieved to be leaving the hard seats

"Time for a drink?" Banks said to Sandra as they fastened their coats on the front steps.

Sandra took his arm. "Of course. Champagne. It's the only civilized thing to do after an evening at the theatre. Except go for dinner."

"There aren't any restaurants open this late. Maybe Gibson's Fish and—"

Sandra pulled a face and tugged his arm. "I'll settle for a lager and lime and a packet of cheese-and-onion crisps."

"A cheap date," Banks said. "Now I know why I married you."

They set off down North Market Street to the Queen's Arms, which was much closer to the front exit of the Community Centre than was the usual cast watering-hole out back, the Crooked Billet.

It was only twenty past ten when they got there, enough time for a couple of pints at least. The pub was quiet at first, but many of the theatre-goers following Banks and Sandra seemed to have the same idea about a drink, and it soon got crowded. By then, Banks and Sandra had a small, dimpled, copper-topped table near the fireplace, where they warmed their hands before drinking.

They discussed the play against a background buzz of conversation, but Banks still felt uneasy and found it hard to concentrate. Instead, he couldn't help but put together what he knew about the Caroline Hartley murder, trying different patterns to see if he could at least discover the shape of the missing piece.

"Alan?"

"What? Oh, sorry."

"What the hell's up with you? I asked you twice what you thought about Malvolio."

Banks sipped some beer and shook his head. "Sorry, love. I feel a bit distracted."

"There's something bothering you, isn't there?"

"Yes."

She put her hand on his arm. "About the case? It's only natural, after seeing the play, isn't it? After all, Caroline Hartley was supposed to be in it."

"It's not just that." Banks couldn't put his thoughts into words. All he could think of was the woman who walked strangely in the snow and Vivaldi's burial music for a small child. And there was something about the play that snagged on his mind. Not the production details or any particular line, but something else, something obvious that he just couldn't bring into focus. Faith and Teresa? He didn't know. All he knew was that he felt not only puzzled but tense, too, the kind of edginess one has before a storm breaks. Often, he knew, that feeling signalled that he was close to solving the case, but there was even more this time, a sense of danger, of evil he had overlooked.

Suddenly he became aware of someone tapping him on the shoulder. It was Marcia Cunningham.

"Hello, Mr Banks," she said. "Wondered if I'd find you here."

"I'd have thought you'd be at the Crooked Billet with the rest," Banks said.

Marcia shook her head. "It was all right during rehearsals, but I don't know if I can handle the first-night post-mortems. Besides, I'm with a friend."

She introduced Banks to the trim, middle-aged man standing behind her. Albert. There was one more chair at the table, and Banks offered his as well to the two newcomers. They demurred at first, then sat. Banks leaned against the stone fireplace.

"Last orders!" called Cyril, the landlord. "Last orders, please!"

In the scramble for the bar, Banks managed to get in another round. When he got back to the table Marcia Cunningham was chatting to Sandra.

"I was just saying to Sandra," she repeated, "that I was wondering if you'd solved the little mystery of the dress?"

"Pardon?"

"The dress, the one with the pieces missing."

"I'm sorry, Marcia," Banks said, "I've no idea what you're talking about."

Marcia frowned. "But surely young Susan must have told you?"

"Whatever it is, I can assure you she didn't. It was her case, anyway. I've been far too preoccupied with the Caroline Hartley murder."

Marcia shrugged and smiled at Albert. "Well, I don't suppose it's very important, really."

"Why don't you tell me anyway?" Banks asked, realizing he might have been a little abrupt. He remembered what Veronica Shildon had said about people asking doctors for medical advice at cocktail parties. Sometimes being a policeman was much the same; you were never off duty. "We've caught the vandals, you know," he added.

Marcia raised her eyebrows. "You have? Have they told you why they did it?"

"I haven't had time to read Susan's report yet. But don't expect too much. People like that don't have reasons you and I can fathom."

"Oh, I know that, Mr Banks. I was just wondering what they did with the pieces, that's all."

Banks frowned. "I'm sorry. I don't follow."

Marcia took a sip of mild and launched into her story. Albert sat beside her, still and silent as a faithful retainer. His thin face showed an intricate pattern of pinkish blood vessels just below the skin. He nodded from time to time, as if in support of what Marcia was saying.

"What do you make of it, then?" Marcia asked when she'd finished.

Banks looked at Sandra, who shook her head.

"It's odd behaviour for vandals, I'll give you that," he said. "I can't think of any reason—" Then he suddenly fell silent, and the other images that had been haunting him formed into some kind of order—vague and shadowy as yet, without real substance, but still something resembling a pattern. "That's if . . ." he went on after a pause. "Look, Marcia, do you still have it, the dress?"

"Of course. It's at home."

"Could I see it?"

"Any time you want. There's nothing more I can do with it."

"How about now?"

"Now? Well, I don't know . . . I . . ." she looked at Albert, who smiled.

"Is it really so important, Alan?" Sandra asked, putting a hand on his arm.

"It might be," he said. "I can't explain yet, but it might be."

"All right," Marcia said. "We were going home in a minute anyway. It's not far."

"My car's parked behind the station. I'll give you a lift," Banks said. He turned to Sandra. "I'll see you—"

"No you won't. I'm coming with you. I'm damned if I'm walking home alone."

"All right."

They grabbed their coats and made for the door.

II

"What did you think of it?" James asked Susan after they had carried their drinks to a table for two in the Crooked Billet. His eyes were shining and he seemed to exude a special kind of energy. Susan thought that if she touched him now, she would feel an electric shock like the ones she sometimes got from static.

"I enjoyed it," she said. "I thought the cast did a terrific job." As soon as she'd spoken she knew she had said the wrong thing, even before James's eyes lost a little of their sparkle. It wasn't that she hadn't mentioned his direction, but that her comment had been hopelessly pedestrian. The trouble was, she knew nothing about Shakespeare beyond what James himself had tried to teach her at school. What a confession! And she had forgotten all that. She hadn't got far reading *Twelfth Night* at home, either; the language was too difficult for her to grasp much of what was going on. Next to James, with all his knowledge and enthusiasm, she felt inadequate.

James patted her arm. "It could have been better," he said. "Especially the pacing of the third act, that scene . . ."

And Susan sat back with relief to listen. He hadn't wanted intelligent comments after all, just someone to sound out his theories on. That she could do, and for the next twenty minutes she listened and gave her opinion whenever he asked for it. It wasn't so difficult when he got technical. She found she could easily remember scenes that had seemed dull, awkward or over-long, and James confirmed that there were good reasons for this, things he hoped to put right before the next performance tomorrow night.

Occasionally, she drifted off into thoughts of work: her interviews with Chalmers and Morley, the torn dress she hadn't yet told Banks about, the damn nuisance of having even more vandals to chase. But she put her lack of concentration down to tiredness. After all, she had been up most of the night before, and all day.

At eleven-twenty, glasses empty and no prospect of another drink, James asked if Susan fancied a nightcap back at his house. A drink and a talk with a friend, perhaps some music . . . what could be wrong with that? She couldn't put him off forever. Besides, she needed to relax. She still felt nervous about being alone with him, but she reached for her coat and followed him out into the night anyway. It was just for a drink, after all; she wasn't going to let him seduce her.

They pulled up in the alley at the back of the house, where James parked his car, and entered through the back door. Susan made herself comfortable in the armchair by the fire, while James busied himself with drinks in the kitchen. Before he settled, he put a compact disc of Beethoven's "Pastorale" Symphony on.

"Makes me think of spring," he said, sitting down. "Somehow, if I close my curtains and relax, I can almost believe winter's over."

"It soon will be," Susan said. She felt herself relaxing, becoming warm and heavy-limbed.

"Perhaps when the good weather comes we could take a ride out into the dale now and then?" James suggested. "Or even venture a little farther afield? A short hike and a pub lunch?"

"Sounds marvellous," Susan murmured. "Believe it or not, I've hardly ever made time to take advantage of the countryside."

"You know what they say, 'All work and no play . . .'"

Susan laughed. James sat on the floor by her knees, his shoulder resting against the armchair so he could look at her when they talked. It was closer than she would have liked just yet, but not uncomfortably so.

"How's business, anyway?" he asked. "Caught any big criminals lately?"

Susan shook her head. Then she told him about the previous evening. "So we're still hot on the trail of your vandals," she said, cupping the large glass of brandy in both hands. "They're a strange lot. Can you imagine why any young yob would snip up a dress and then run away with some of the pieces?"

"What?"

Susan explained what Marcia had told her and what she had seen.

"So Marcia still has the dress, then?" he said.

"What's left of it."

"What's she going to do with it?"

"I don't know," Susan answered. She was feeling drowsy and vulnerable from the heat and the brandy. "I suppose I should take it in for analysis. You never know . . ."

"Never know what?"

"What you might find." She looked down at the top of his head. "Why are you so interested, anyway, James?"

"Just curiosity, that's all. I suppose they must have had some reason for doing it. Maybe one of them cut himself and used it as a bandage. Another drink?"

Susan looked at her glass. "No thanks, I'd better not." Already she felt that warmth, tiredness and alcohol were making her let her guard down more than she cared to, and she certainly didn't want to lose control.

"Busy day at the nick tomorrow?"

Susan laughed. "Who knows?"

"Excuse me while I get one."

"Of course."

While he was gone, Susan listened to the music. She could have sworn she heard a cuckoo in one section, but doubted that anyone as serious as Beethoven would use such a frivolous gimmick.

"Perhaps one of them was a fetishist," James suggested, after he had sat down at her feet again.

"And liked to wear only little bits of women's clothes? Don't be silly, James. I don't see why you have to keep harping on about it. It's nothing."

"You'd be surprised the things people like to dress up in."

"Like you in that policeman's uniform that day?"

"That's different. That was just a joke."

"I didn't mean to suggest you were kinky or anything," Susan said. "But didn't you tell me you were just a little bit shy of making a direct approach to a woman?"

"Yes, well. . . . Acting's in my blood, I suppose. Hamming it up. Maybe there are deep-rooted psychological reasons. I don't really know." He shrugged.

Susan laughed. "You're always doing melodramatic things like that. Dressing up, arranging for that singer in Mario's. A real practical joker, aren't you?"

"I told you," James said, a little irritably. "I'm just a bit insecure. It helps."

"Especially with women?"

"Yes."

As soon as Susan realized what she had said, a tiny shiver went up her spine. She could feel the chill, as palpable as the winter night outside, fall between them. James fell silent and Susan sipped at her brandy, thinking, and not liking what she thought: James's penchant for play-acting and dressing up, the vandals' denial of breaking into the Community Centre, James's attraction to Caroline, the burgundy dress. No, it couldn't be. Not possibly. It was too absurd. But her thoughts suddenly spanned two cases. It was like hot-wiring a car; the engine jumped to life. Now she could think of at least one good reason why the dress had been cut up the way it had.

Before long, she became aware of a slight tickle up the side of her leg. She looked down and saw that James was touching her, very gently. She shifted in her seat—not too abruptly, she hoped—and he stopped.

The music ended and Susan finished what little she had left in her glass. "I'd better be going," she said, sitting forward in her chair.

"Don't go just yet," James said. "It's been such a wonderful evening. I don't want it to end."

Susan laughed. Didn't he feel the same unease she did? Maybe not. Better for her that he didn't. She must act naturally, then investigate her vague fears later from a more secure position. Surely, she would then discover how absurd they were. No doubt the beer and brandy had caused her imagination to run wild. It was most important now, though, that she make an early exit without letting James see that she entertained any suspicions at all.

"Don't be such a romantic," she laughed. "There'll be plenty of other evenings."

She tried to sit up, but he was on his knees, blocking her way. "James!"

"What's the harm in it?" he said, leaning forward towards her.

He put his hands on her shoulders and she pushed them off. "If this is what first night does to you . . ." she said, trying for a light tone. But she couldn't think of a way to end her sentence.

Finally, he moved aside and she managed to get to her feet. She felt as if she were treading on thin ice. Did he know what she was beginning to suspect? How could he? Was it obvious that she was humouring him and trying to get out fast? All she knew was that she had to stay cool and get out of there. Maybe then she would be able to dismiss her fears. But she couldn't stay, not after the frightening images had started in her mind. Crazy or not, she had to talk seriously to Banks about James, no matter how difficult it might be to swallow her pride and her feelings.

"Don't sulk," she said, tousling his hair. "It doesn't suit you."

"Damn you!" he said, jerking away from her touch. Anger flashed in his eyes. "What's wrong with you? Don't you think I'm man enough for you? You're just like her, aren't you?"

Susan felt as if she had been thrust under a cold shower. Every nerve-end tingled. She edged closer to the door. "Like who, James?" she asked quietly.

He turned to face her, and she could see that he knew. It was too late. "You know damn well who I'm talking about, don't you?"

"I don't even know what you're talking about," Susan lied. Somehow, she thought, if she didn't say the name, there was still a chance.

"Don't lie. You can't fool me. I can tell. I can tell what you're thinking. You've been toying with me, leading me on all this time, trying to get me to confess. It's all been a game, hasn't it?" He moved quickly so that he was standing between Susan and the door.

"Don't be stupid," she said. "I don't know what you mean. And move out of the way, please. I want to leave."

Conran shook his head slowly. "You're thinking about me and Caroline, aren't you?"

There was no point pretending any longer. Susan looked at him and said, "You went to her, didn't you? That night."

"It was an accident," Conran pleaded. "It was a ghastly accident."

"James, you've got to—"

"No! That's where you're wrong. No, I don't. It was all an accident. All that stupid bitch's fault." And suddenly, he didn't look like the James she knew any longer. Not at all like the James she knew and thought she trusted.

III

The four of them stood in Marcia Cunningham's front room and looked at the remains of the dress.

"Who would do something like that?" Sandra asked.

"That's the point," Banks said. "No casual vandal would go to such trouble, at least not for any reason we can think of."

"But it must have happened then," Marcia said. "I'd have noticed if it had been done before. And certainly no-one from the cast would have done it."

"I'm not saying it was done before," Banks said. "What I'm saying is that it's possible vandals didn't do this."

"Then who?"

"Look at this." Banks passed the dress to Sandra, who studied the remains of its front. "Look at those spots."

"What are they? Paint?"

"Could be. But I don't think so. They're hard to see because the dress is so dark. And we can't be sure, not without forensic examination, but if I'm right . . ."

"What are you getting at, Alan?" Sandra asked. "You're not making much sense, you know."

"The last person seen entering Caroline Hartley's house was a woman, according to all our witnesses. And Patsy Janowski said she saw a woman who walked funny at the end of the street. I thought it was because she might have been wearing high-heels."

"But that's stupid," Sandra said. "In that weather?"

"Exactly."

"Are you suggesting that the killer wore this dress?" Marcia asked. "I can't believe it." She pointed at the dress. "And that's . . . that's blood!"

"The way Caroline Hartley was stabbed," Banks said, "there was no way the murderer could have avoided blood stains. If she was wearing this dress, it would have been easy enough to put her raincoat on again and get away from the scene, get time to think. I don't think the murder was planned, not right from the start. But then there was still a blood-stained dress to explain. Why not simply cut off the sleeves and the stained front, then stage a break-in and cut up the other dresses? That would raise much less suspicion than just doing away with the dress altogether. If our killer had done that, Marcia would have missed it and started to wonder what might have happened. But how could the killer know that Marcia would be so diligent as to try and sew them back together again?"

"But that means," Marcia said slowly, "that the killer was someone who knew about our costumes, someone who had access to them. It means—'

"Yes," said Banks. "And if she was wearing shoes, not boots, what does that suggest?"

"We don't have any boots," Marcia said. "Not that I know of. Shoes, yes, but not boots."

"The killer couldn't find any suitable boots to complete the disguise, so had to make do with women's shoes."

"I still don't understand," Marcia said.

"It was the play gave me the idea, that and what Patsy said. All that stuff about a woman walking funny, and a play about confused identity. Couldn't it have been a man dressed as a woman? Would any of the shoes have been big enough?"

"Well . . . yes, of course," Marcia said. "We have all kinds of sizes. But why? Why would anybody dress up and do that?"

"We don't know," Banks said. "A sick joke? Maybe someone knew Caroline was a lesbian, someone who wanted her badly. Do you have a plastic bag?"

"I think so . . . somewhere." Marcia gestured vaguely, her brows knit together.

"There's one in the larder, by the newspapers, love," said Albert, who had remained silent until now. "I'll go and get it."

Albert brought the bag and Banks put the dress in it.

"What about the break-in?" Marcia asked.

"It could have been staged later, when the killer discovered what he'd done." Banks looked at his watch. "It's after eleven-thirty," he said. "Let's try the Crooked Billet and see if they're still there."

"Who?" asked Marcia.

"Susan and Conran," Banks said. "I assume they *are* together." He turned to Marcia. "When did you tell Susan about this dress?"

"The other day. She couldn't make anything of it."

"That's hardly surprising. Does James Conran know?"

"I haven't told him," Marcia said.

"Has Susan?"

"I don't know. I mean, she's seeing him. She might have mentioned it. Why?"

Banks looked at Sandra. "I don't want to alarm anyone," he said, "but if I'm right, we'd better try to find Susan right away. Excuse us, Marcia, Albert." And he took Sandra by the arm and led her to the door.

"But why?" Sandra asked.

"Because I think James Conran's the killer," Banks said on their way down the path. "I think he wanted Caroline Hartley so badly he went over to the house to see her. I don't know why he dressed up, or what happened in there, but he's the only one in the society apart from Marcia who had access to the prop room."

They got in the car and Banks cursed the ignition until it started on his fourth attempt. "Don't you see?" he said as he skidded off. "According to Faith and Teresa, Conran was the last one to leave the centre. And even if he did go to the pub, he had a key. He could have easily gone back there and changed. Why do you think he was paying so much attention to Susan? He wanted to know how the investigation was going, how close we were."

"My God," said Sandra. "Poor Susan."

IV

James blocked Susan's way. "She asked for it, you know," he said. "She was nothing but a prick-teaser, then she . . ."

"Then she what?" Susan felt real fear now, like ice in her spine. Her mind was racing in search of a way out. If only she had told Banks about the dress, then maybe he would have been able to put two and two together before she had. If only she could keep Conran talking. If only . . .

"You know what?" he said. "It turned out she didn't like men, she was just playing, leading me on, just like you were, playing me for a fool."

"That's not true."

"Stop lying. It's too late now. What are you going to do?" James asked.

"What do you think?"

"Turn me in? Can't you let it go?"

"Don't be an idiot."

"What is it with you, Susan? Just what makes you tick? Professional all the way?"

"Something like that," Susan muttered, "but it doesn't really matter any more, does it?"

"You could forget this ever happened," James said, moving forward and reaching for her hand. She noticed a sheen of sweat on his forehead and upper lip.

She snatched her hand away. "No, I couldn't. Don't be a bloody fool, James. Let me go. Don't make things worse." He was still rational, she thought; James was no madman, just troubled. She could talk sense to him, and he might listen. The main problem was that he was highly-strung and, at the moment, in a state of near panic. She would have to be very careful how she handled him.

"Where do you want to go?" he asked.

"To the phone," she said calmly.

Conran stood aside and let her pass. But no sooner had she picked up the receiver than he grabbed it from her and pulled her back into the front room.

"No!" he said. "I can't let you. I'm not going to jail. Not just because of that perverted slut. Don't you see? It wasn't my fault."

"Don't be a fool, James. What's the alternative?"

Conran licked his lips and looked around the room like a caged animal. "I could get out of here. Go away. You'd never have to see me again. Just don't try to stop me."

"I have to. You know that."

"I mean it. I don't want to hurt you. Look, we could go together. I've got some money saved up. Wherever you want. We could go somewhere warm."

"James," Susan said softly, "you've got a problem. You don't necessarily have to go to jail. Maybe you can get help. A doctor—"

"What do you mean, problems? I don't have any problems." Conran pointed at his chest. "Me? You tell me I've got problems? She was the one with the problem. Not me. I'm not queer. I'm not a homosexual. I'm normal."

His face was flushed and sweaty now and he was breathing fast. Susan wasn't sure if she could talk him down and persuade him to give himself up. Not if he didn't want to.

"Nobody says you're not normal," she said cautiously. "But you're obviously upset. You need help. Let me help you, James."

"I'm not going with you," he said. "And if you phone, I won't be here when your friends arrive."

"You're making it worse," Susan said. "At least if you come in with me, it'll look good. It's no use running. We'll get you in the end. You know we will."

"I don't care. I'm not going to jail. You don't understand. I couldn't live in jail. The things they do in there . . . I've heard about them." He shuddered.

"I told you, James. It might not mean prison. Perhaps you can get help in a hospital."

"No! There's nothing wrong with me. I'm perfectly normal. I'll not have doctors poking about in my head."

Susan got up and walked towards the front door. She held her breath as she turned her back on him. Before she even got to the hallway, she felt his hands around her neck. They were strong and she couldn't pry them apart. Because he was standing behind her, all she could do was wriggle, and it didn't help. She flailed back with her hands but met only empty air. She tried to swing her hips back into his groin, but she couldn't reach him. Her throat hurt and she couldn't breathe. She lashed back with one foot, felt it connect and heard him gasp. But his grip never slackened. She felt all the life and sensation going out of her body, like water down the drain. Her knees buckled and he let her sink forward to the floor, his hands still locked tight around her throat. The blackness had seeped in everywhere now. She thought she could hear someone hammering on the door, then she heard nothing at all.

V

"I'll call an ambulance and stay with her," Sandra said, kneeling over Susan.

Banks nodded and dashed back to the Cortina. He had heard Conran's car start up as they broke in. There was only one way his back lane led, and that was to the main Swainsdale road. Once there, he could turn back towards Eastvale or head out into the dale. As Banks negotiated the turns, he radioed for help from Eastvale and from Helmthorpe, which had one patrol car. If Conran didn't turn off on one of the side-roads, at least they could make sure the main road was blocked and he could get no further than the dale's largest village. At the junction, Conran turned left into Swainsdale.

The Cortina skidded on a patch of ice. Banks steadied it. He knew the road like the back of his hand. Narrow for the most part, with drystone walls on either side, it dipped and meandered, treacherous in the icy darkness. He kept Conran's tail-lights in view, about a couple of hundred yards ahead.

When he got closer, he put his foot down. Conran did the same. It was almost like racing through a dark tunnel, or doing a slalom run. Snow was piled almost as high as the walls at the road-sides. Beyond, the fields stretched up the daleside, an endless swath of dull pearl in the moonlight.

Conran screeched through Fortford, almost losing control as he took the bend by the pub. The car's side scraped against the jutting stones in the wall and sent a shower of sparks out into the night. Banks slowed and the Cortina took the turn easily. He knew there was a long stretch of straight road before the next bend.

Conran had gained a hundred yards or so, but once around the corner, Banks put his foot down and set about catching up. The red tail-lights drew closer. Banks glanced ahead for landmarks and saw the drumlin with the six leaning trees silhouetted by the moon about a mile in front of them. Just before that, there would be another kink in the road.

He was right behind Conran's car now, but there was no easy way to stop him. He couldn't pull in front in such conditions on a narrow road. If he tried, Conran would easily be able to nudge him into the wall. All he could do was ride his tail and push, hoping Conran would panic and make a mistake.

A few moments later, it happened. Either through ignorance, or just plain panic, Conran missed the bend. Banks had already slowed enough to take it, but instead he eased on the brake as he watched Conran's car slide up the heaped snow in slow motion, take off the top of the drystone wall, spraying sparks again as it went, and land with a loud thud in the field.

Banks turned off his engine. The silence after the accident was so deep he could hear the blood ring in his ears. On a distant hill-side, a sheep bleated—an eerie sound on a winter's night.

Banks got out of the car and climbed the wall to see what had happened. There was very little damage as far as he could tell by the moonlight. Conran's car lay on its side, the two free wheels still spin-ning. Conran himself had managed to get the passenger door open and was now struggling up the hillside, thigh-deep in snow. The farther he went, the deeper the snow became, until he could move no more. Banks walked in his wake and found him curled up and shiver-ing in a cot of snow. He looked up as Banks came towards him.

"Please let me go," he said. "Please! I don't want to go to jail. I couldn't stand being in jail."

Banks thought of Caroline Hartley's body, and of Susan Gay laid out on the floor, her face purple. "Think yourself bloody lucky we don't still have hanging," he said, and dragged Conran up out of the snow.

FIFTEEN

I

Only the sound of thin ice splintering underfoot accompanied Banks on his way to Oakwood Mews later that night. Eastvale was asleep, tucked up warm and safe in bed, and not even the faint sound of a distant car disturbed its tranquillity. But the town didn't know what had gone on between Caroline Hartley and James Conran in that cosy firelit room with the stately music playing. It didn't know what folly, irony and pride had finally erupted in blood. Banks did. Sometimes, as he walked, he thought that his next step would break the crust over a great darkness and he would fall. He told himself not to be ridiculous, to keep going.

Apart from the dim, amber light shed by its widely-spaced, black-leaded gas-lamps, Oakwood Mews was as dark as the rest of the side-streets at that time of night. Not one light showed in a window. Easy, Banks thought, for a murderer to creep in and out unseen now.

For a moment, he stood by the iron gate and looked at number eleven. Should he? It was two-thirty in the morning. He was tired, and Veronica Shildon was no doubt fast asleep. She wouldn't be able to get back to sleep after what he had to tell her. Sighing, he opened the gate. He had a promise to keep.

He pressed the bell and heard the chimes ring faintly in the hall. Nothing happened, so he rang again and stood back. A few seconds later a light came on in the front upstairs window. Banks heard the soft footsteps and the turning of the key in the lock. The door opened an inch or two, on its chain. When Veronica saw who it was, she immediately took off the chain and let him in.

"I had an idea it was you," Veronica said. "Will you give me a few moments?" She pointed him towards the living-room and went back upstairs.

Banks turned on a shaded wall-light and sat down. Embers glowed in the grate. It was cool in the room, but the memory of heat, at least, remained. Banks unfastened his heavy car-coat but didn't take it off.

In a few minutes, Veronica returned in a blue-and-white track-suit. She had combed her hair and washed the sleep out of her eyes.

"Sorry," she said, "but I can't stand sitting around in a dressing-gown. It always makes me think I'm ill. Let me put this on." And she switched on a small electric heater. Its bar shone bright red in no time. "Can I offer you a cup of tea or something?"

"Given the night I've had," Banks said, "a drop of whisky would be more welcome. That is, if you have any?"

"Of course. Please forgive me if I don't join you. I'd prefer cocoa."

While Veronica made her cocoa, Banks sipped the Scotch and stared into the embers. It had all been so easy once they had got back to the station: wet clothes drying over the heater in the cramped office; steam rising; Conran spilling his guts in the hope of some consideration at sentencing. Now came the hard part.

Veronica sat in the armchair near the electric fire and folded her legs under her. She cradled the cocoa mug in both hands and blew on the surface. Banks noticed that her hands were shaking.

"I always used to have cocoa before bed when I was young," she said. "It's funny, they say it helps you sleep when it's got caffeine in it. Do you understand that?" Suddenly she looked directly at Banks. He could see the pain and fear in her eyes. "I'm prattling on, aren't I?" she said. "I assume you've got something important to tell me, or you wouldn't be here at this time." She looked away.

Banks lit a cigarette and sucked the smoke in deeply. "Are you sure you want to know?" he asked.

"No, I'm not sure. I'm frightened. I'd rather forget everything that happened. But I never got anywhere by denying things, refusing to face the truth."

"All right." Now he was here, he didn't know where to start. The name, just the bald name, seemed inadequate, but the *why* was even more meaningless.

Veronica helped him out. "Will you tell me who first?" she asked. "Who killed Caroline?"

Banks flicked some ash into the grate. "It was James Conran."

Veronica said nothing at first. Only the nerve twitching at the side of her jaw showed that she reacted in any way. "How did you find out?" she asked finally.

"I was slow," Banks replied. "Almost too slow. Given Caroline's life, her past, I was sure there was a complex reason for her death. There were too many puzzles—Gary Hartley, Ruth Dunne, Colm Grey . . ."

"Me."

Banks shrugged. 'I didn't look close enough to home."

"Was there a complicated motive?"

Banks shook his head. "No, I was wrong. Some crimes are just plain . . . I was going to say accidents, but that's not really the case. Stupid, perhaps, certainly pointless and often just sheer bad luck."

"Go on."

"As far as the evidence was concerned, we knew that Conran was attracted to Caroline, but there's nothing unusual about that. She was a very beautiful woman. We also found out he tended to prefer her over other actresses in the cast, which gave rise to a certain amount of jealousy. Caroline dealt with normal male attention by doing what she knew best, what she'd learned on the game—teasing, flirting, stringing them along. It was an ideal way for her because it deflected suspicion away from her true sexual inclinations," he looked at Veronica, who was staring down into the murky cocoa, "and it kept them at a distance. Many flirts are afraid of real contact. It's just a game.

"But as I said, I was looking for deep, complex motives—something to do with her family, her time in London, her way of life. As it turns out, her death was to do with all those things, but not directly concerned with any of them."

"Another drink?" Veronica had noticed his glass was empty and went to refill it. Banks didn't object. Embers shifted with a sigh in the fireplace. It was much warmer now the electric fire had heated the room. Banks took his coat off.

"What happened?" Veronica asked, handing him the tumbler.

"On December twenty-second, after rehearsal, everyone went their separate ways. Caroline came straight home, took a shower and made herself comfortable in the living-room with a cup of tea and some chocolate cake. Your husband called with the present, which Caroline opened because he had said it was something special and she wanted to know what could be so special to you. I'm sure she intended to rewrap it before you found out. I'm speculating, of course. No one but Caroline was in the house at this time, so we'll never know all the details. But I think I'm right. It couldn't have happened any other way. Anyway, shortly after Claude Ivers left, Patsy Janowski arrived, checking up on him. She thought he was still involved with you." Veronica sniffed and shifted position. Banks went on. "She spoke to Caroline briefly at the door—very briefly, because it was cold and Caroline was only wearing her bathrobe—then she left. On her way down the street, she saw a woman who appeared to be walking oddly, heading across King Street, but thought nothing of it. By then it was dark and the air was filled with snow. It was difficult to look up and keep your eyes open without getting them full of cold snow."

"What about James Conran?" Veronica asked. "How does he fit in?"

"I was getting to that. It had been a particularly difficult rehearsal. He had insulted Faith Green by telling her that Caroline could play her part better, and Teresa Pedmore was probably still angry at him for being so obvious about his lust for Caroline in public. By this time, he was pretty well besotted with her, and he's one of those types who's like a little boy who breaks things when he doesn't get his own way. Because of the bad atmosphere, everyone went their separate ways, including Caroline. After he locked up, Conran went to the Crooked Billet and drank several double Scotches very quickly. His row with Faith made him want Caroline all the more. After all he thought he was doing for her, he was getting very impatient that she didn't seem to be keeping up her end of what he thought was the bargain.

"Then he had an idea. He was always a bit of a theatrical type, the kind who got dressed up and recited 'The Boy Stood on the Burning Deck' at parties when he was a kid, so he thought that, as a joke, he'd dress up as a woman and go see Caroline. *Twelfth Night*, as you know, is about a woman who passes herself off as a man, you see, and that's where he got the idea. It would make her laugh, he thought, if he passed himself off as a woman, and when you make women laugh you soften them and break down their reserve. Also, he'd had enough drinks to make it seem a good idea and to make him feel brave enough. He knew where she lived, but he didn't know that she lived with anyone.

"He went back to the Community Centre—only he and Marcia Cunningham from the Dramatic Society had keys to the back door—chose a dress, a wig, and found some women's shoes that fit him. But it must have been an uncomfortable walk for him. The shoes were a little too tight and pinched his toes, and it's very hard to walk in high-heels in the snow, I should imagine. Especially if you're a man. That's what Patsy Janowski noticed, but she didn't realize what it meant.

"He said Caroline seemed to recognize him, laughed and let him in. She had no reason not to. Apparently he'd done things like that in rehearsal—dressed up, played practical jokes, clowned around—so as far as she was concerned it wasn't out of character for him. She may have been puzzled by his visit, even worried that you would come back and wonder what was going on, but as far as she knew, she had no reason to fear him."

Veronica grimaced and massaged her right calf. Banks took a sip of fiery Scotch. "Are you sure you want me to go on?" he asked. "It isn't very pleasant."

"I didn't expect it to be," Veronica said. "I've got a touch of cramp, that's all. It's not what you're saying that's making me grit my teeth. I want to know everything. But I think I've changed my mind about that drink." She limped to the cocktail cabinet, poured herself a glass of sherry and sat down again carefully. "Please go on. I'll be fine."

"Conran was a little drunk and feeling his oats. Caroline must have seemed especially inviting dressed in only her bathrobe.

Eventually, it happened. Conran made a pass and Caroline ducked it. According to him, she made some reference to the way he was dressed and told him she preferred real women. She accused him of playing some kind of sick joke. He was stunned. He had no idea. When he started to protest, she laughed at him and told him the clothes suited him, maybe he ought to consider going after some of the men in the cast. Then he hit her. She fell back on the sofa, stunned by the blow, and her robe fell open. He said he couldn't help himself. He wanted her. And if rape was the only way he could get what he wanted, then so be it. He had to have her right there."

Veronica was gripping the sherry glass tightly, her face pale. Banks paused and asked if she was all right.

"Yes," she whispered. "Go on." She closed her eyes.

"He couldn't do it," Banks said. "There she was, a beautiful, naked woman, just what he'd dreamed about ever since he'd met her, and he couldn't function. He says he doesn't remember the next part very well. He just remembers blind rage, the colour red. Everything was red inside his eyes, he said. And then it was done. He saw what had happened. He'd picked up the knife from the table and stabbed Caroline. When the rage passed and the realization dawned, he didn't panic, he started thinking clearly again. He knew he had to find some way of covering his tracks. First he washed the knife and rinsed the blood off his hands. When he went back into the room he was horrified by what he'd done. He said he sat down and just stared at Caroline, crying like a baby. That's when he saw the record she'd opened. He knew the piece because he'd had a lot to do with church choral music ever since he was young. He knew that the *Laudate pueri* was played at the burial services of small children. That's another reason I should have thought of him sooner, but then almost anyone could have known the significance of the music, or someone might simply have thought it sounded right."

"But I don't understand," Veronica said. "Why did he play it?"

"He said he put it on as a genuine gesture, that Caroline had always seemed childlike in her ways and in her enthusiasms, and she seemed to him especially like a child now as she lay there."

"So the music was for Caroline?" Veronica asked.

"Yes. A kind of requiem. It was right there in front of him. He was hardly going to search through the whole collection for something else, especially as it seemed so fitting."

Veronica looked down into her sherry glass and said quietly, "Then maybe I *can* listen to it again. Go on."

"You have to remember, too, Veronica, that Conran's a theatre director. He has a sense of the dramatic, a feel for arrangement. He told me that when he had stopped crying for what he'd done, he began to see the whole thing as a scene or a tableau of some kind, and the music seemed right. What he'd done wasn't real to him any more, it was a part of a drama, and it needed the appropriate sound-track.

"Next he made sure he'd tidied everything up, then he left. He noticed the stains on the dress but could do nothing about them. At least his coat would cover him up until he got home and formed a clear plan. He was just about to burn the dress when he had a better idea. He knew it would be missed if he simply destroyed it. Marcia was in charge of costumes and he knew she was careful and diligent. That was when he came up with the idea of a break-in. There'd been a lot of vandalism in the area lately, and he saw it would make a perfect cover for getting rid of the evidence. Remember, he had no idea he would end up killing anyone and ruining the dress when he first put it on and went out, but now he had a serious problem. He went back later that night, careful not to be seen this time, broke in, scrawled a little of the usual graffiti and snipped up the dresses. He also replaced the wig and the shoes, which he'd cleaned carefully. When he got home, he snipped his coat into small pieces and burned them in a metal wastebin, a bit at a time; after that, he cut the sleeves and part of the front off the dress he'd worn and burned them too. He missed a few tiny spots, but the dress was a dark burgundy colour so they were very difficult to see. And that was it. All he had to do was try to stay cool when the questions started. That was easy enough for someone with actor's training, especially as he seemed so able most of the time to divorce himself from the reality of what he'd done. It had been an act, a role, like any other. And there was no reason why we should connect the break-in with the murder."

"How did you catch him?" Veronica asked.

"It was partly the play. At least that started me thinking about the possibility of someone dressing up. And there were a few other clues. That report about the woman visitor wearing high-heels on such a snowy night. The vandals denying that they had wrecked the Community Centre. Marcia being unable to find the missing pieces of that particular dress. Not to mention that I was running out of other suspects." But he didn't tell Veronica that Susan Gay had known about the cut-up dress for two days and hadn't thought it important enough to mention, nor that he hadn't read her report on the vandals until Conran had already been caught. He had been too concerned about Susan to stop in at the station and check, and as it turned out, his instinct had been right.

"How is she?" Veronica asked, when Banks had told her about the scene at Conran's house.

"She'll be all right. Sandra acted quickly and got her breathing. She won't be talking or eating real food for a while."

"How does she feel?"

"I don't know. Sandra's still with her at the hospital, along with Superintendent Gristhorpe. She's sedated right now, but when she comes round she'll probably be very hard on herself." He shrugged. "I don't know how she'll deal with it."

And he didn't. Susan had made mistakes, yes, but mistakes that could be easily understood. Everyone new to the job made them. After all, why on earth should she link a partially destroyed dress to a murder? And no matter what anyone said, she would go on believing that she should have linked them, should have known. But she should at least have passed on the information, and verbally, too, not only in a routine report that might get stuck at the bottom of the chief inspector's in-tray for days, especially when he was busy on a murder investigation. And Banks should have read the report. In a perfect world, he would have done. But police, perhaps more than anyone else, get notoriously behind in their paperwork. And so mistakes are made. Susan's career hung in the balance, and Banks couldn't guess which way it would go. Certainly he would support her as far as he could, but it would be her own decisions and actions that counted in the long run, her own strength.

"It all seems so . . . pointless," Veronica said, "so absolutely bloody senseless."

"It was," Bank agreed. "Murder often is." He put down his glass and reached for his coat.

"I'm glad you told me," she said. "I mean, I'm glad you came right away like you said you would."

"What are you going to do now?"

"I'll go back to bed. Don't worry about me. I probably won't be able to sleep but . . . your job's over, you don't have to take care of me."

"I mean in the future. Have you any plans?"

Veronica uncurled her legs and got to her feet, rubbing her calves to restore the circulation. "I don't know," she said. "Maybe a holiday. Or maybe I'll just struggle on with work and life. I'll manage," she said, attempting a smile. "I'm a survivor."

Banks fastened his coat and headed for the door. Veronica held it open for him. "Once again," she said, "thank you for coming."

On impulse, Banks leaned forward and kissed her cool forehead. She gave him a puzzled look, then smiled. He hesitated on the path and looked back at her. He could think of nothing else to say. If Conran were mad, his actions might have been easier to explain, or to dismiss. Madmen did strange and evil things, and nobody knew why; it just happened that way. But he wasn't mad. He was highly-strung, egotistical, with a deep-rooted fear of his own latent homosexuality, but he wasn't mad. He had sat at that desk in Banks's office and spilled his heart out for over an hour before Banks, disgusted with the man's whining self-pity, had left the task for Phil Richmond to finish.

Veronica's face, shadowed by the hall's soft light, looked drawn but determined. She held herself stiffly, arms crossed, yet there seemed a supple strength in her limbs to match the strength in her spirit. Perhaps that was why he liked her: she tried; she wasn't afraid to face things; she made an effort at life.

At the end of Oakwood Mews, Banks remembered the Walkman in his pocket. He needed music, not so much as the food of love but as something to soothe the savage breast. The tape he had in was at the last movement of Messiaen's "Quartet for the End

of Time." That eerie, fractured and haunting music would do just
fine for the walk home. In his other pocket he felt the catapult he
had confiscated from the kid on the riverbank and forgotten about.

He walked up to the market square listening to the music. Piano
chords sounded like icicles falling and the violin notes stretched so
tight they felt as if they would snap any second. As he walked, he
thought about Veronica Shildon, who had tried to face some difficult truths and start a new life. He thought about how that life had
been shattered, just like the ice under his feet, by a stupid, drunken,
pointless act—lust beyond reason—and about how she would go
about putting it together again. Veronica was right, she was a
survivor. And Shakespeare was right, too; lust often *is* "murderous,
bloody, full of blame, / Savage, extreme, rude, cruel, not to trust."

Banks passed the police station with hardly a glance.
Sometimes, the formality of the job and its cold, calculated procedures just didn't reflect what really happened, the pain people felt,
the pain Banks felt. Perhaps the rites and rituals of the job—the
forms to be filled in, the legal procedures to be followed—were
intended to keep the pain at a distance. If so, they didn't always
succeed.

About twenty yards beyond the station, on Market Street, he
stopped and turned. That damn blue light was still shining above
the door like a beacon proclaiming benign, paternal innocence and
simplicity. Almost without thinking, he took the catapult from his
pocket, scraped up a couple of fair-sized stones from the icy gutter,
put one in the sling and took aim. The stone clattered on the pavement somewhere along North Market Street. He took a deep
breath, sighed out a plume of air, then aimed again carefully, trying
to recreate his childhood accuracy. This time the lamp disinte-
grated in a burst of powder-blue glass and Banks took off down a
side-street, the back way home, feeling afraid and guilty and oddly
elated, like a naughty schoolboy.

WEDNESDAY'S CHILD

For Sheila

"Lost in the desart wild
Is your little child.
How can Lyca sleep
If her mother weep?"

.   .   .

Sleeping Lyca lay
While the beasts of prey,
Come from caverns deep,
View'd the maid asleep.

William Blake
"The Little Girl Lost"

ONE

I

The room was a tip the woman a slattern. On the floor, near the door to the kitchen, a child's doll with one eye missing lay naked on its back, right arm raised above its head. The carpet around it was so stained with ground-in mud and food, it was hard to tell what shade of brown it had been originally. High in one corner, by the front window, pale flowered wallpaper had peeled away from a damp patch. The windows were streaked with grime, and the flimsy orange curtains needed washing.

When Detective Chief Inspector Alan Banks perched at the edge of the scuffed olive-green armchair, he felt a spring dig into the back of his left thigh. He noticed Detective Constable Susan Gay turn up her nose as she looked at a garish oil-painting of Elvis Presley above the mantelpiece. "The King" was wearing a jewelled white cape with a high collar and held a microphone in his ringed hand.

In contrast to the shabby decor, a compact music centre in mint condition stood against one wall, a green-and-yellow budgie in a cage nonchalantly sharpened its bill on a cuttlefish, and an enormous matte black colour television blared out from one corner. "Blockbusters" was on, and Banks heard Bob Holness ask, "What 'B' is the name of an African country bordering on South Africa?"

"Could you turn the sound down, please, Mrs Scupham?" Banks asked the woman.

She looked at him blankly at first, as if she didn't understand his request, then she walked over and turned off the TV altogether. "You can call me Brenda," she said when she sat down again.

Banks took a closer look at her. In her late twenties, with long dirty-blonde hair showing dark roots, she possessed a kind of blowzy sexuality that hinted at concupiscent pleasure in bed. It was evident in the languor of her movements, the way she walked as if she were in a hot and humid climate.

She was a few pounds overweight, and her pink polo-neck sweater and black mini-skirt looked a size too small. Her full, pouty lips were liberally coated in scarlet lipstick, which matched her long, painted fingernails, and her vacuous, pale blue eyes, surrounded by matching eye-shadow, made Banks feel he had to repeat every question he asked.

Seeing the ashtray on the scratched coffee-table in front of him, Banks took out his cigarettes and offered the woman one. She accepted, leaning forward and holding back her hair with one hand as he lit it for her. She blew the smoke out through her nose, emulating some star she had seen in a film. He lit a cigarette himself, mostly to mask the peculiar smell, redolent of boiled cabbage and nail-polish remover, that permeated the room.

"When did you first get the feeling something was wrong?" he asked her.

She paused and frowned, then answered in a low voice, husky from too many cigarettes. "Just this afternoon. I phoned them, and they said they'd never heard of Mr Brown and Miss Peterson."

"And you got worried?"

"Yes."

"Why did you wait so long before checking up?"

Brenda paused to draw on her cigarette. "I don't know," she said. "I thought she'd be all right, you know. . . ."

"But you could have called this morning. That's when they said they'd bring her back, isn't it?"

"Yes. I don't know. I suppose so. I just . . . besides, I'd got things to do."

"Did the visitors show you any identification?"

"They had cards, like, all official."

"What did the cards say?"

Mrs Scupham turned her head to one side, showing only her profile. "I didn't really get a good look. It all happened so fast."

"Did the cards have photographs on them?"

"No, I don't think so. I'm sure I would have noticed."

"What exactly did they say to you?" Banks asked.

"They told me their names and said they was from the social, like, and then they showed their cards . . ."

"This was at the door, before you let them in?"

"Yes. And ther they said they'd come to see me about my Gemma. Well, I had to let them in, didn't I? They were from the authorities."

Her voice cracked a little when she mentioned her daughter's name, and she sucked her lower lip. Banks nodded. "What happened next?"

"When I let them in, they said they'd had reports of Gemma being . . . well, being abused . . ."

"Did they say where they'd heard this?"

She shook her head.

"Didn't you ask them?"

"I didn't think to. They seemed so . . . I mean, he was wearing a nice suit and his hair was all short and neatly brushed down, and she was dressed proper smart, too. They just seemed so sure of themselves. I didn't think to ask anything."

"Was there any truth in what they said?"

Mrs Scupham flushed. "Of course not. I love my Gemma. I wouldn't harm her."

"Go on," Banks said. "What did they say next?"

"That's about it really. They said they had to take her in, just overnight, for some tests and examinations, and if everything was all right they'd bring her back this morning, just like I told you on the phone. When they didn't come, I got so worried . . . I . . . How could anyone do something like that, steal someone else's child?"

Banks could see the tears forming in her eyes. He knew there was nothing he could say to console her. In fact, the best thing he could do was keep quiet about how bloody stupid she'd been, and not ask her if she hadn't heard about the cases, just a few years ago, when bogus social workers had visited homes all around England with stories just like the one they'd given her. No, best keep quiet.

She had a fear of authority, probably bred into her, that meant she would believe just about anything that someone in a suit with a card, a nice haircut and an educated accent told her. She wasn't unique in that. Most often, the phoney social workers had simply asked to examine the children in the home, not to remove them. For all the mothers who had sent them packing, Banks wondered how many had allowed the examination and had then been too afraid or ashamed to admit it.

"How old is Gemma?" Banks asked.

"Seven. Just seven."

"Where's your husband?"

Mrs Scupham crossed her legs and folded her hands on her lap. "I'm not married," she said. "You might as well know. Well, there's no shame in it these days, is there, what with so much divorce about."

"What about Gemma's father?"

"Terry?" She curled her upper lip in disgust. "He's long gone."

"Do you know where he is?"

Mrs Scupham shook her head. "He left when Gemma was three. I haven't seen or heard from him since. And good riddance."

"We need to contact him," Banks pressed. "Can you give us any information at all that might help?"

"Why? You don't . . . surely you don't think Terry could have had anything to do with it?"

"We don't think anything yet. At the very least he deserves to know what's happened to his daughter."

"I don't see why. He never cared when he was around. Why should he care now?"

"Where is he, Brenda?"

"I've told you, I don't know."

"What's his full name?"

"Garswood. Terry Garswood. Terence, I suppose, but everyone called him Terry."

"What was his job?"

"He was in the army. Hardly ever around."

"Is there anyone else? A man, I mean."

"There's Les. We've been together nearly a year now."

"Where is he?"

She jerked her head. "Where he always is, The Barleycorn round the corner."

"Does he know what's happened?"

"Oh, aye, he knows. We had a row."

Banks saw Susan Gay look up from her notebook and shake her head slowly in disbelief.

"Can I have another fag?" Brenda Scupham asked. "I meant to get some more, but it just slipped my mind."

"Of course." Banks gave her a Silk Cut. "Where do you work, Brenda?"

"I don't . . . I . . . I stay home." He lit the cigarette for her, and she coughed when she took her first drag. Patting her chest, she said, "Must stop."

Banks nodded. "Me, too. Look, Brenda, do you think you could give us a description of this Mr Brown and Miss Peterson?"

She frowned. "I'll try. I'm not very good with faces, though. Like I said, he had a nice suit on, Mr Brown, navy blue it was, with narrow white stripes. And he had a white shirt and a plain tie. I'm not sure what colour that was, dark anyways."

"How tall was he?"

"About average."

"What's that?" Banks stood up. "Taller or shorter than me?" At around five foot nine, Banks was small for a policeman, hardly above regulation height.

"About the same."

"Hair?"

"Black, sort of like yours, but longer, and combed straight back. And he was going a bit thin at the sides."

"How old would you say he was?"

"I don't know. He had a boyish look about him, but he was probably around thirty, I'd say."

"Is there anything else you can tell us about him? His voice, mannerisms?"

"Not really." Brenda flicked some ash at the ashtray and missed. "Like I said, he had a posh accent. Oh, there was one thing, though I don't suppose it'd be any help."

"What's that?"

"He had a nice smile."

And so it went. When they had finished, Banks had a description of Mr Brown that would match at least half the young businessmen in Eastvale, or in the entire country, for that matter, and one of Miss Peterson—brunette, hair coiled up at the back, well-spoken, nice figure, expensive clothes—that would fit a good number of young professional women.

"Did you recognize either of them?" he asked. "Had you seen them around before?" Banks didn't expect much to come from this—Eastvale was a fair-sized town—but it was worth a try.

She shook her head.

"Did they touch anything while they were here?"

"I don't think so."

"Did you offer them tea or anything?"

"No. Of course I didn't."

Banks was thinking of fingerprints. There was a slight chance that if they had drunk tea or coffee, Mrs Scupham might not have washed the cups yet. Certainly any prints on the door handles, if they hadn't been too blurred in the first place, would have been obscured by now.

Banks asked for, and got, a fairly recent school photograph of Gemma Scupham. She was a pretty child, with the same long hair as her mother—her blonde colouring was natural, though—and a sad, pensive expression on her face that belied her seven years.

"Where could she be?" Brenda Scupham asked. "What have they done to her?"

"Don't worry. We'll find her." Banks knew how empty the words sounded as soon as he had spoken them. "Is there anything else you can tell us?"

"No, I don't think so."

"What was Gemma wearing?"

"Wearing? Oh, those yellow overall things, what do you call them?"

"Dungarees?"

"Yes, that's right. Yellow dungarees over a white T-shirt. It had some cartoon animal on the front. Donald Duck, I think. She loved cartoons."

"Did the visitors mention any name other than Brown or Peterson?"

"No."

"Did you see their car?"

"No, I didn't look. You don't, do you? I just let them in and we talked, then they went off with Gemma. They were so nice, I . . . I just can't believe it.' Her lower lip trembled and she started to cry, but it turned into another coughing fit.

Banks stood up and gestured for Susan to follow him out into the hall. "You'd better stay with her," he whispered.

"But, sir—"

Banks held his hand up. "It's procedure, Susan. And she might remember something else, something important. I'd also like you to get something with Gemma's fingerprints on it. But first I want you to radio in and tell Sergeant Rowe to phone Superintendent Gristhorpe and let him know what's going on. You'd better get someone to contact all the Yorkshire social services, too. You never know, someone might have made a cock-up of the paperwork and we'd look right wallies if we didn't check. Ask Phil to organize a house-to-house of the neighbourhood." He handed her the photograph. "And arrange to get some copies of this made."

Susan went out to the unmarked police Rover, and Banks turned back into the living-room, where Brenda Scupham seemed lost in her own world of grief. He touched her lightly on the shoulder. "I have to go," he said "DC Gay will be back in a moment. She'll stay with you. And don't worry. We're doing all we can."

He walked down the short path to the patrol car and tapped on the window. "You told me you searched the place, right?" he said to the constable behind the wheel, pointing back up the path with his thumb.

"Yes, sir, first thing."

"Well, do it again, just to be certain. And send someone to get Mrs Scupham a packet of fags, too. Silk Cut'll do. I'm off to the pub." He headed down the street leaving a puzzled young PC behind him.

II

Detective Superintendent Gristhorpe squatted by his dry-stone wall in the back garden of his house above the village of Lyndgarth and contemplated retirement. He would be sixty in November, and while retirement was not mandatory, surely after more than forty years on the job it was time to move aside and devote himself to his books and his garden, as the wise old Roman, Virgil, had recommended.

He placed a stone, then stood up, acutely aware of the creak in his knees and the ache in his lower back as he did so. He had been working at the wall for too long. Why he bothered, the Lord only knew. After all, it went nowhere and closed in nothing. His grand-father had been a master waller in the dale, but the skill had not been passed down the generations. He supposed he liked it for the same reason he liked fishing: mindless relaxation. In an age of tech-nocratic utilitarianism, Gristhorpe thought, a man needs as much purposeless activity as he can find.

The sun had set a short while ago, and the sharp line of Aldington Edge cut high on the horizon to the north, underlining a dark mauve and purple sky. As Gristhorpe walked towards the back door, he felt the chill in the light breeze that ruffled his thatch of unruly grey hair. Mid-September, and autumn was coming to the dale.

Inside the house, he brewed a pot of strong black tea, threw together a Wensleydale cheese-and-pickle sandwich, then went into his living-room. The eighteenth-century farmhouse was stur-dily built, with walls thick enough to withstand the worst a Yorkshire winter could throw at them, and since his wife's death Gristhorpe had transformed the living-room into a library. He had placed his favourite armchair close to the stone hearth and spent so many an off-duty hour reading there that the heat from the fire had cracked the leather upholstery on one side.

Gristhorpe had given the television his wife had enjoyed so much to Mrs Hawkins, the lady who "did" for him, but he kept the old walnut-cabinet wireless so he could listen to the news, "My Word," cricket and the plays that sometimes came on in the evenings. Two walls were lined with floor-to-ceiling bookshelves, and a series of framed prints from Hogarth's "The Rake's Progress" hung over the fireplace.

Gristhorpe set his tea and sandwich beside the books on the small round table, within easy reach, and settled back with a sigh into his chair. The only sounds that broke the silence were the wind soughing through the elms and the ticking of the grandfather clock in the hall.

To retire or not to retire, that was the question that kept him from immediately picking up *The Way of All Flesh*. Over the past few years he had delegated most of the investigative work to his team and spent his time on administrative and co-ordinating duties. He had absolute trust in Alan Banks, his protégé, and both DS Richmond and the recently appointed DC Gay were coming along well. Should he move aside and clear the space for Banks's promotion? Certainly Alan showed an enthusiasm for work and learning that reminded Gristhorpe of himself as a young lad. Both lacked formal education beyond the local grammar school, but neither let it hold him back. Banks was a good detective, despite his anti-authoritarian tendencies, occasional rashness and a loathing for the politics that were now becoming so much a part of the job. But Gristhorpe admired him for that. He, himself, hated police politics. Banks, though twenty years younger, was a real copper, a man who had come from the street. He also had imagination and curiosity, two qualities that Gristhorpe thought essential.

And what would he do with his time if he did retire? There was the dry-stone wall, of course, but that was hardly a full-time occupation. Nor was reading, especially with the way his eyesight had been declining of late. He was at an age when every odd ache or pain brought a little more fear than it had before, when colds lingered and settled on the chest. But he was no hypochondriac. The Gristhorpes were robust, always had been.

He would like to travel, he decided, to revisit Venice, Florence, Paris, Madrid, and go somewhere he had never been before—the Far East, perhaps, or Russia. But travel cost money, and a policeman's pension wouldn't stretch that far. Gristhorpe sighed and picked up Samuel Butler. He didn't have to make his decision tonight; best wait for a while.

He had hardly got through the first paragraph when the phone rang. Marking the page with a leather strip and putting the book aside, he got up and walked into the hall. It was Sergeant Rowe from the station. He had received a message from Susan Gay about a child gone missing from the East Side Estate. Could the superintendent come in as soon as possible? Gristhorpe could get few more details over the phone, except that the child had been taken by a man and a woman pretending to be social workers and that she had been gone over a day. As he listened to Sergeant Rowe deliver the message in his flat, emotionless voice, Gristhorpe felt a shiver go up his spine.

Grimly, he put on his tweed jacket and went outside to the car. It was completely dark now, and the lights of Lyndgarth twinkled below on the daleside. Gristhorpe drove through the village, past the squat St Mary's, and onto the main Eastvale road. It was a journey he had made hundreds of times, and he drove automatically, without even having to think about the dips and turns. Normally, even in the dark, he would glance at certain landmarks— the lights of the old Lister house way up on the opposite slopes of the valley; the six trees bent over by the wind on the drumlin to the west—but this time he was too distracted to notice the landscape.

As he drove towards the lights of Eastvale, he remembered that long Saturday in October, 1965, when he and dozens of other young policemen had stood in the drizzle and the biting wind 1,600 feet up the Pennines listening to their orders. There they all stood, in anoraks and wellington boots, shivering in the late autumn cold on the top of Saddleworth Moor, complaining about the Saturday afternoon football they were missing. It was eerie enough just being up there in the banshee wind, the rain and inky light, with those outcrops of rocks like decayed teeth on the skyline. All day they had searched, dragging their feet through the mud and peat, from 9:30 a.m. until well after three o'clock. The rain had stopped by then, and the weather was a little warmer, the moor shrouded in a slight mist.

Suddenly Gristhorpe had heard the shout from a searcher in the distance: a young lad, he remembered, just out of training college, who had taken a break to answer a call of nature. Those nearby,

Gristhorpe included, hurried towards him, and watched in horror as Detective Sergeant Eckersley came and scraped away the clinging peat from a child's arm bone. A little more digging revealed a head. Eckersley stopped at that. He sent for the scene-of-crime officers, and soon they all arrived, out of nowhere, the Assistant Chief Constable, police surgeons, photographers, Joe Mounsey, the lot.

They put up canvas screens and everyone but the brass and the SOCOs had to stand back. As the doctor scraped off the dirt and the flash camera popped, the whole gruesome discovery finally lay revealed. Gristhorpe caught only a glimpse of the body through a gap in the canvas, but it was enough.

They had been looking for a boy called John Kilbride, but what they had found was the near-skeletal body of a girl lying on her side with her right arm raised above her head. Close to her feet, her clothes lay bundled—a blue coat, a pink cardigan, a red-and-green tartan skirt. Instead of John Kilbride, they had found the body of Lesley Ann Downey, aged ten, another victim of the couple who came to be called the "Moors Murderers," Ian Brady and Myra Hindley.

Somehow, that day stood engraved in Gristhorpe's memory more than any other day in his life. Months, even years, might go by and he wouldn't even think of that October day in 1965, but when something like this happened, there it was, every bit as real and as horrifying as if he were back there on the moor seeing that arm sticking up through the quagmire as if it were waving or pointing.

He had thought of it only once in the past few years, and that was when a sixteen-year-old girl had gone missing from one of the Swainsdale villages. And now two people, a man and a woman— just as Brady and Hindley had been—had walked bold as brass into a house on the East Side Estate and abducted a seven-year-old girl.

As Gristhorpe drove down narrow North Market Street past the Town Hall, the lit window displays of the tourist shops and the community centre, he gripped the wheel so hard his knuckles turned white as he once again heard the girl's voice in his head from the tape Brady and Hindley recorded before they murdered her:

Lesley Ann whimpering and begging for her mummy and daddy to help her; Brady telling her to put something in her mouth and saying he wants to photograph her. And that damn music, that damn music, "The Little Drummer Boy." Gristhorpe had never been able to listen comfortably to any music since then without hearing the girl screaming and begging for mercy in his head, and he let everyone believe he was tone deaf to avoid awkward explanations.

He turned his car into the parking area at the back of the station, an old Tudor-fronted building, the front of which faced Eastvale's market square, and sat for a few moments to calm himself down and rid himself of the memory. And before he went inside, he delivered a silent prayer—not without some embarrassment, for he wasn't a religious man—that there should be nothing, *nothing* to compare between this affair and the Moors Murders. No time for thoughts of retirement now.

III

As Banks walked down the street towards The Barleycorn, he glanced at the rows of identical red brick houses. There was no doubt about it, the East Side Estate was a disaster. True, some tenants had bought the houses when the Thatcher government sold them off, and many had added a white fence here, a lick of paint there, or even a dormer window. But it was a shabby area, with junk-littered lawns, children's tricycles left in the street, and mangy dogs running free, fouling the pavements, barking and snapping at passers-by.

And The Barleycorn was a typical estate pub, right from its unimaginative name and its squat flat-roofed exterior to its jukebox, video games and poorly kept keg beer.

Banks pushed open the door and glanced around. Little Richard's "Good Golly Miss Molly" was playing too loudly on the jukebox. The cash register rang up another sale. Most of the tables were empty, and only a few diehard drinkers stood at the bar.

As the door shut behind him, Banks noticed the people look in his direction, and suddenly one man took off towards the back. Banks dashed after him, bumping his knee on a chair and knocking it over as he went. He caught the man by the shoulder just before he had reached the exit. The man tried to pull free, but Banks kept his grip, spun him around and hit him hard, just once, in the solar plexus. The man groaned and doubled up. Banks took him by the elbow and helped him to a table the way one escorts an elderly relative.

As soon as they had sat down, the barman rushed over.

"Look, mister, I don't want no trouble," he said.

"Good," Banks answered. "Neither do I. But I'd like a small brandy for my friend here, just to settle his stomach."

"What do you think I am, a bloody waitress?"

Banks looked at the man. He was about six feet tall and gone to fat. His nose looked as if it had been broken a few times, and old scar tissue hooded his left eye.

"Just bring the drink," Banks said. "I won't have anything myself. Not while I'm on duty."

The barman stared at Banks, then his jaw dropped. He shrugged and turned back to the bar. In a few seconds he came back with the brandy. "It's on the house," he mumbled.

Banks thanked him and passed the glass over to his companion, who sat rubbing his stomach and gasping for breath. "Here's to your health, Les."

The man glared at him through teary eyes, knocked back the brandy in one and banged the glass down hard on the table. "You didn't need to have done that," he said. "I was only off for a piss."

"Bollocks, Les,' said Banks. 'The only time I've seen anyone run as fast as that to the bog they had dysentery. Why were you running?"

"I told you."

"I know, but I want you to tell me the truth."

Les Poole was well known to the Eastvale police and had been a frequent guest at the station. He had congenitally sticky fingers and couldn't stand the idea of anything belonging to anyone else but him. Consequently, he had been in and out of jail since Borstal, mostly for burglary. No doubt, Banks thought, had he the intelligence, he might also have risen to the dizzy heights of fraud and blackmail. Les had never held a job, though rumour had it that he had, in fact, once worked as a dustbin man for six weeks but got the sack for wasting too much time rummaging through people's rubbish looking for things he could keep or sell. In short, Banks thought, Les Poole was little more than a doodle in the margin of life. At least until now.

Les was an odd-looking character, too, like someone who had fallen through a time warp from the 1950s. He had greased-back hair, complete with quiff, sideboards and duck's arse, a triangular face with a Kirk Douglas dimple on his chin, a long, thin nose, and eyes as flat and grey as slate. About Banks's height, he was wearing a black leather jacket, red T-shirt and jeans. His beer-belly bulged over the belt. He looked as if he should be playing stand-up bass in a rockabilly band. Why he had always been so attractive to women, Banks couldn't fathom. Maybe it was his long dark eyelashes.

"Well?" prompted Banks.

"Well what?"

Banks sighed. "Let's start this again, Les. What we'll do is we'll back up and lead nice and slowly to the question. Maybe that way you'll be able to understand it, all right?"

Les Poole just glared at him.

Banks lit a cigarette and went on. "I came down here to ask if you know anything about young Gemma's disappearance. Do you?"

"She was taken away, that's all I know. Brenda told me."

"Where were you when it happened?"

"Eh?"

"Where were you yesterday afternoon?"

"Out and about."

"Doing what?"

"Oh, this and that."

"Right. So while you were out and about doing this and that, a man and a woman, both well-dressed and official-looking, called at your house, said they were child-care workers, talked their way inside and persuaded Brenda to hand over her daughter for tests and further examination. Now what I want to know, Les, is do you know anything about that?"

Les shrugged. "It's not my kid, is it? I can't help it if she's so fucking daft she'll give her kid away."

The barman appeared at Banks's shoulder and asked if they wanted anything else.

"I'll have a pint, Sid," Les said.

"Bring me one too, this time," Banks added. "I feel like I bloody well need it."

After the barman had brought the beer, which tasted more like cold dishwater than real ale, Banks carried on.

"Right," he said, "so we've established you don't give a damn about the child one way or another. That still doesn't answer my questions. Where were you, and do you know anything about it?"

"Now come on, Mr Banks. I know I've been in a bit of bother now and then, but surely even you can't suspect me of doing a thing like that? This is what they call persecution, this is. Just because I've got a record you think you can pin everything on me."

"Don't be a silly bugger, Les. I'm not trying to pin anything on you yet. For a start, I couldn't picture you in a suit, and even if you'd managed to nick one from somewhere, I think Brenda might still have recognized you, don't you?"

"You don't have to take the piss, you know."

"Let's make it simple, then. Do you know *anything* about what happened?"

"No."

"Right. Another one: what were you doing?"

"What's that got to do with anything? I don't see what that's got to do with anything. I mean, if you don't suspect me, why does it matter where I was?"

"Got a job, Les?"

"Me? Nah."

"I don't suppose you'd want me to know if you did have, would you? I might tell the social and they'd cut off your benefits, wouldn't they?"

"I don't have a job, Mr Banks. You know what it's like these days, all that unemployment and all."

"Join the rest of us in the nineties, Les. Maggie's gone. The three million unemployed are a thing of the past."

"Still . . ."

"Okay. So you don't have a job. What were you doing?"

"Just helping a mate move some junk, that's all."

"That's better. His name?"

"John."

"And where does he live, this John?"

"He's got a shop, second-hand stuff, down Rampart Street, over by The Oak . . ."

"I know it. So you spent the afternoon with this bloke John, helping him in his shop?"

"Yeah."

"I suppose he'd confirm that?"

"Come again?"

"If I asked him, he'd tell me you were with him."

"Course he would."

"Where'd you get the nice new television and stereo, Les?"

"What do you mean? They're Brenda's. She had them before she met me. Ask her."

"Oh, I'm sure she'll back you up. The thing is, they don't look that old. And Fletcher's electronics warehouse got broken into last Friday night. Someone took off with a van full of stereos and televisions. Did you know that?"

"Can't say as I did. Anyway, what's all this in aid of? I thought you were after the kid?"

"I cast a wide net, Les. A wide net. Why did Brenda wait so long before calling us?"

"How should I know? Because she's a stupid cow, I suppose."

"Sure it was nothing to do with you?"

"What do you mean?"

"She said you had a row. Maybe you didn't want the police coming to the house and seeing that television, or the new music centre."

"Look, I told you—"

"I know what you told me, Les. Why don't you answer the question? Was it you persuaded Brenda to wait so long before calling us?"

Poole looked away and said nothing.

"Do you know Gemma could be dead?"

Poole shrugged.

"For Christ's sake, don't you care?"

"I told you, she's not my kid. Bloody nuisance, if you ask me."

"You ever hit her, Les?"

"Me? Course I c dn't. That's not my style."

"Ever see Brenda do it?"

Poole shook his head. Banks stood up, glanced at the beer in his glass and decided to leave it.

"I'm off now, Les," he said, "but I'll be around. You'll be seeing so much of the police in the next few days you'll think you've died and gone to hell. And I want you to stick around, too. Know what I mean? Be seeing you."

Banks left The Barleycorn for the dark autumn evening. He was wearing only his sports jacket over his shirt, and he felt the chill in the air as he walked back to Brenda Scupham's with a terrier yapping at his heels. Television screens flickered behind curtains, some pulled back just an inch or two so the neighbours could watch all the excitement at number twenty-four.

As he turned up the path, he thought of Brenda and the enormity of what she had allowed. He could have told her about the recent Children's Act, designed to protect parents from over-zealous social workers but he knew he would only get a blank stare in return. Besides, telling her that was as clear an example as you can get of bolting the stable door after the horse has gone.

He thought again about Les Poole and wondered what he was hiding. Maybe it had just been the criminal's typical nervousness at an encounter with the police. Whatever it was, it had been evident in his clipped answers, his evasions, his nervous body language, and most of all in the guilty thoughts Banks could see skittering about like tiny insects behind the slate eyes.

IV

Gristhorpe tried to recall whether he had left anything undone. He had informed the ACC, made sure the press had all the information they needed, set up a mobile unit on a patch of waste ground at the end of Brenda Scupham's street, drawn up a search plan, arranged to draft in extra personnel and got someone working on a list of all known local child-molesters. Also, he had faxed the bare details and a copy of Gemma's photograph to the paedophile squad, which operated out of Vine Street police station, in London. Soon, every policeman in the county would be on the alert. In the morning, the searchers would begin. For now, though, there was nothing more he could do until he had discussed developments with Banks.

His stomach rumbled, and he remembered the cheese-and-pickle sandwich left uneaten on the table at home, the tea going cold. Leaving a message for Banks, he went across the street to the Queen's Arms and persuaded Cyril, the landlord, to make him a ham sandwich, which he washed down with a half-pint of bitter.

He had been sitting hunched over his beer at a dimpled, copper-topped table for about ten minutes, oblivious to the buzz of conversation around him, when a voice startled him out of his dark thoughts.

"Sir?"

Gristhorpe looked up and saw Banks standing over him. "Everything all right, Alan?" Gristhorpe asked. "You look knackered."

"I am," said Banks, sitting down and reaching for his cigarettes. "This Gemma Scupham business . . ."

"Aye," said Gristhorpe. "Get yourself a drink and we'll see what we can come up with."

Banks bought a packet of cheese-and-onion crisps and a pint, then told Gristhorpe about his suspicions of Les Poole.

Gristhorpe rubbed his chin and frowned. "We'll keep an eye on him, then," he said. "Give him a bit of slack. If we bring him in over that Fletcher's warehouse job it'll do us no good. Besides, we can hardly cart off the poor woman's telly when someone's just abducted her child, can we?"

"Agreed," said Banks. "OK. So far we've got six men working on the house-to-house, questioning the neighbours. Phil and Susan are with them. At least there's a chance someone might have seen the car."

"What about the mother? Who's with her?"

"Susan stayed for a while, then she offered to get a WPC to come in, but Mrs Scupham didn't want one. I don't think either she or Les feels comfortable with the police around. Anyway, she's got a friend in."

"I suppose we'd better start with the obvious, hadn't we?" Gristhorpe said. "Do you believe the mother's story?"

Banks took a sip of beer. "I think so. She seemed genuinely shocked, and I don't think she's bright enough to make up a story like that."

"Oh, come on, Alan. It doesn't take much imagination. She could have hurt the child, gone too far and killed her—or Poole could have—then they dumped the body and made up this cock-and-bull story."

"Yes, she could have. All I'm saying is the story seems a bit over-elaborate. It would have been a hell of a lot easier just to say that Gemma had been snatched while she was out playing, wouldn't it, rather than having to make up descriptions of two people and risk us finding it odd that no one in the street saw them. They're a nosy lot down on the East Side Estate. Anyway, I had the officers on the scene search the house thoroughly twice and they didn't come up with anything. We've got a SOCO team there now doing their bit. If there's any chance Gemma was harmed in the house then taken somewhere else, they'll find it."

Gristhorpe sighed. "I suppose we can rule out kidnapping?"

"Brenda Scupham's got no money. She might be fiddling the social, making a bit on the side, but that hardly makes her Mrs Rothschild."

"What about the father? Custody battle? Maybe he hired someone to snatch Gemma for him?"

Banks shook his head. "According to Brenda, he's not interested, hasn't been for years. We're tracking him down anyway."

Gristhorpe waved a plume of smoke aside. "I don't like the alternatives," he said.

"Me neither, but we've got to face them. Remember those stories a while back? Paedophiles posing as social workers and asking to examine people's kids for evidence of abuse?"

Gristhorpe nodded.

"Luckily, most parents sent them away," Banks went on. "But suppose this time they succeeded?"

"I've checked on the descriptions with the divisions involved," Gristhorpe said, "and they don't match. But you're right. It's something we have to consider. Someone else could have got the idea from reading the papers. Then there's the ritual stuff to consider, too."

Not long ago, the press had been rife with stories of children used for ritual abuse, often with satanic overtones. In Cleveland, Nottingham, Rochdale and the Orkneys, children were taken into care after allegations of just such abuse involving torture, starvation, humiliation and sexual molestation. Nobody had come up with any hard evidence—in fact, most people thought it was more likely that the children needed to be protected from the social workers—but the rumours were disturbing enough. And Gristhorpe didn't fool himself that such a thing couldn't happen in Eastvale. It could.

That Satanists now existed out in the dale was beyond doubt. There had been trouble with them recently, when local farmers had complained of finding sheep ritually slaughtered in copses and hollows. There was a big difference between sheep and children, of course, as there was between Satanism and witchcraft. Gristhorpe had been aware of local witch covens for years. They consisted mostly of meek husbands and bored housewives in search of an evening's naughtiness dancing naked in the woods. But the Satanists were a different breed. If they could go as far as killing sheep and draining their blood, what would they stop at?

"But you know what I'm thinking about most of all, don't you, Alan?" Banks was one of the few people Gristhorpe had talked to about his small role in the Moors Murders and the lasting effect it had on him.

Banks nodded.

"Different way of operating, of course. Brady and Hindley snatched their victims. But there could be reasons for that. It's the couple aspect that bothers me. A man *and* a woman. I know there's been a lot of argument about Myra Hindley's degree of involvement, but there's no doubt they acted together. Call it what you will—maybe some kind of psychotic symbiosis—but without the other, it's a good bet neither would have committed those crimes. Alone, they were nothing, nobodies living in fantasy worlds, but together they progressed from Hitler-worship and pornography to murder. Hindley acted as a catalyst to turn Brady's fantasies into reality, and he acted them out to impress her and exercise his power over her. Christ, Alan, if a couple like that's got hold of little Gemma Scupham, God have mercy on her soul." Again, Gristhorpe remembered the tape, Lesley Ann begging, "Please don't undress me!" Brady telling her, "If you don't keep that hand down I'll slit your neck." And that other gruesome touch, the children's choir singing carols in the background.

"We don't know," said Banks. "We know bugger-all so far."

Gristhorpe rubbed his brow. "Aye, you're right. No sense jumping to conclusions. On the bright side, let's hope it was some poor young childless couple who just went too far to get themselves a kiddie." He shook his head. "It doesn't make sense, though, does it? If they took the child out of love, how could they reconcile themselves to the mother's pain? There'd be too much guilt to allow them any happiness. And I doubt they'd be able to keep a secret like that for very long."

"I've asked Phil if he can tie in with HOLMES on this," Banks said. "Remember that course he went on?"

Gristhorpe nodded. HOLMES stood for Home Office Large Major Enquiry System. Developed during the hunt for the Yorkshire Ripper, HOLMES basically allows all reports coming out of an investigation to be entered and organized into a relational database. That way, a key word or phrase can be tracked more accurately through previously unrelated data than before.

And that was as far as Gristhorpe could follow. The rest, like most computer talk, was gobbledegook to him. In fact, the mere mention of megabytes and DOS brought out the latent Luddite in him. Still, he didn't underestimate their value. An enquiry like this would generate a lot of paperwork, and every statement, every report, no matter how minor or negative, would be entered, and cross-checks would be made. He wanted no cock-ups along the lines of the Yorkshire Ripper investigation, where the left hand hadn't seemed to know what the right hand was doing.

"Phil says he'd like computers in the mobile unit," Banks added. "That way the officers can put everything on disk and pass it on to him without any retyping."

"I'll see what I can do. Any more ideas?"

"Just a couple. I'd like a chat with the girl's teacher, see what I can find out about her. I'm damn sure there's been some abuse involved. Both Poole and Brenda Scupham deny it, but not convincingly enough."

Gristhorpe nodded. "Go on."

"And I think we should consider bringing Jenny Fuller in. She might at least be able to give us some idea of what kind of people we're looking for."

"I couldn't agree more," Gristhorpe said. He liked Jenny Fuller. Not only was she a competent psychologist who had helped them before in unusual cases, but she was a pleasure to have around. A right bonny lass, as Gristhorpe's father would have said.

"Should we bring Jim Hatchley back from the seaside?" Banks asked.

Gristhorpe scowled. "I suppose there might come a time we'll need him. Leave it for now, though." Detective Sergeant Jim Hatchley had been transferred to a CID outpost on the Yorkshire coast, largely to make way for Philip Richmond's promotion. Gristhorpe had never much liked Hatchley, but grudgingly admitted he had his uses. As far as Gristhorpe was concerned, he was an idle, foul-mouthed, prejudiced slob, but his brain worked well enough when he took the trouble to use it, and he had a list of dirty tricks as long as your arm that often got results without compromising procedure.

Banks drained his glass. "Anything else?"

"Not tonight. We'll have a meeting first thing in the morning, see what's turned up. You'd better get home and get some sleep."

Banks grunted. "I might as well have another pint first. There never seems to be anyone in these days."

"Where's Sandra?"

"Community Centre, still organizing that local artists' exhibition. I'll swear she spends more time there than she does at home. And Tracy's out at the pictures with that boyfriend of hers."

Gristhorpe caught the anxiety in Banks's tone. "Don't worry about her, Alan," he said. "Tracy's a sensible lass. She can take care of herself."

Banks sighed. "I hope so." He gestured towards Gristhorpe's empty glass. "What about you?"

"Aye, why not? It might help me sleep."

While Banks went to the bar, Gristhorpe considered the night ahead. He knew he wouldn't be going home. For years, he had kept a camp-bed in the station storeroom for emergencies like this. Tonight, and perhaps for the next two or three nights, he would stay in his office. But he doubted that he would get much sleep. Not until he found out what had happened to Gemma Scupham, one way or the other.

TWO

I

Early the next morning, Banks stood on his doorstep holding the milk bottles and breathed in the clear air. It was a magnificent day: not a cloud in the light blue sky, and hardly any wind. He could smell peat-smoke in the air, and it seemed to accentuate the chill autumn edge, the advancing touch of winter. More than anything, it was a day for walking out in the dale, and it would bring dozens of tourists to the Eastvale area.

He went inside and put the milk in the fridge. He could hear Tracy taking her morning shower and Sandra moving about in the bedroom, getting dressed. It had been a good night when he got back from the Queen's Arms. Sandra had got home before him, and before bed they enjoyed a nightcap and some Ella Fitzgerald on the CD player she had bought him for his fortieth birthday. Tracy came home on time, cheerful enough, and Banks couldn't detect any change for the worse in her that he could attribute to her boyfriend, Keith Harrison. Still, he thought as he poured himself a cup of coffee, domestic life had changed a lot over the summer.

For one thing, Brian had left home for Portsmouth Polytechnic, where he intended to study architecture. Much as they had locked horns the past few years—especially over music and staying out too late—Banks missed him. He was left with Tracy, now so grown-up he hardly knew her: blonde hair chopped short and layered raggedly, mad about boys, make-up, clothes, pop music.

They never seemed to talk any more, and he missed those chats about history—her former passion—especially when he had been able to educate her on a point or two. Banks had always felt insecure about his lack of a good formal education, so Tracy's questions had often made him feel useful. But he knew nothing about the latest pop groups, fashion or cosmetics.

And Sandra had become absorbed in her work. He told himself, as he buttered his toast, not to be so damned selfish and to stop feeling sorry for himself. She was doing what she wanted—getting involved in the arts—after so many years of sacrifice for the sake of the family and for his career. And if he hadn't wanted an independent, spirited, creative woman, then he shouldn't have married her. Still, he worried. She was late so often, and some of these local artists were handsome young devils with the reputation of being ladies' men. They were more free-spirited than he was, too, with Bohemian attitudes about sex, no doubt.

Perhaps Sandra found him boring now and was looking for excitement elsewhere. At thirty-eight, she was a fine-looking woman, with an unusual mix of long blonde hair and dark eyebrows over intelligent blue eyes. The slim, shapely figure she had worked hard to maintain always turned heads. Again he told himself not to be such a fool. It was the work that was taking up her time, not another man.

Sandra and Tracy were still upstairs when he had finished his coffee and toast. He called out goodbye, put on his charcoal sports jacket, patting the side pocket for cigarettes and lighter, and set off. It was such a fine morning—and he knew how quickly the day could turn to misery—that he decided to walk the mile or so to Eastvale Regional Headquarters rather than drive. He could always sign a car out of the pool if he needed one.

He stuck the Walkman in his pocket and turned it on. Ivor Gurney's setting of "In Flanders" started: "I'm homesick for my hills again—My hills again!" Banks had come to Gurney first through some of his poems in an anthology of First World War poetry, then, learning he had been a composer too, went in search of the music. There wasn't much available, just a handful of songs—settings of other people's poems—and some piano music, but Banks found the spareness and simplicity intensely moving.

As he walked along Market Street, he said hello to the shopkeepers winding out their awnings and called in at the newsagent's for his copy of *The Independent*. Glancing at the front page as he walked, he spotted Gemma Scupham's photograph and a brief request for information. Good, they'd been quick off the mark.

When he got to the market square, the first car was disgorging its family of tourists, dad with a camera slung around his neck, and the children in orange and yellow cagoules. It was hard to believe on such a day that a seven-year-old girl probably lay dead somewhere in the dale.

Banks went straight to the conference room upstairs in the station. It was their largest room, with a well-polished oval table at its centre, around which stood ten stiff-backed chairs. It was rare that ten people actually sat there, though, and this morning, in addition to Banks, only Superintendent Gristhorpe, Susan Gay and Phil Richmond occupied chairs. Banks helped himself to a black coffee from the urn by the window and sat down. He was a few minutes early, and the others were chatting informally, pads and pencils in front of them.

First, Gristhorpe tossed a pile of newspapers onto the table and bade everyone have a look. Gemma Scupham's disappearance had made it in all the national dailies as well as in the *Yorkshire Post*. In some of the tabloids, she even made the headline: the photo of the melancholy-looking little girl with the straggly blonde hair appeared under captions such as HAVE YOU SEEN THIS GIRL? in "Jesus type." The stories gave few details, which hardly surprised Banks as there were scant few to give. A couple of pieces implied criticism of Brenda Scupham, but nothing libellous. Most were sympathetic to the mother.

"That might help us a bit," Gristhorpe said. "But I wouldn't count on it. And remember, the press boys will be around here in droves as soon as the London trains come in this morning. Let's be careful what we say, eh, or before we know it we'll be up to our necks in tales of satanic rituals." Gristhorpe stood up, grimaced and put his hand to the small of his back. "Anyway, let's get on. We've circulated Gemma's picture, and Susan managed to lift a set of her prints from a paint-box. so we've got them on file for comparison. Nothing new came up during the night. We did about as well as can be expected on the house-to-house. Four people say they remembered seeing a car parked outside Brenda Scupham's house on Tuesday afternoon. Of these, two say it was black, one dark brown and one dark blue." Gristhorpe paused. "I think, therefore, that we can be certain it was a dark car." He refilled his coffee cup and sat down again. "As far as the make is concerned we got even less. They all agreed it was a pretty small car, but not as small as a Mini, and it looked quite new. It wasn't an estate car or a van of any kind, so we're looking at a compact. One said it reminded him of those Japanese jobbies he's seen advertised on television, so it may be an import. Needless to say, no one got the number."

"Did anyone see the couple?" Banks asked.

"Yes." Gristhorpe looked at the file in front of him. "The woman at number eleven said she was washing her windows and she saw a well-dressed couple going up the path. Said they looked official, that's all. She thought maybe Mrs Scupham or her friend had got in trouble with DHSS."

"Hmm," said Banks. "Hardly surprising. I don't suppose anybody saw them leaving with the child?"

Gristhorpe shook his head.

"Well," Banks said, "at least it helps confirm Brenda Scupham's story."

"Aye." Gristhorpe looked over at Susan Gay, who had done most of the questioning. "Who would you say was our most reliable witness?"

"Mr Carter at number sixteen, sir. It wasn't so much that he'd seen more than the others, but he seemed to be thinking very seri-ously about what he *had* seen, and he told me he had a strong visual memory—not quite photographic, but he could close his eyes and picture scenes. He seemed careful not to make anything up. You know, sir, how a lot of them embroider on the truth."

"What colour did he say the car was?" Banks asked.

"Dark blue, and he thought it was a Japanese design, too. But he didn't see this Peterson and Brown couple, just the car."

"Shame," said Gristhorpe. "Had he seen it around before?"

"No, sir."

"Think it would do any good talking to him again?"

"It might," said Susan. "I'll drop by sometime today. He's a pensioner and I get the impression he's lonely. He seemed pleased to have a bit of company. It took me a while to get him round to what he'd seen."

Gristhorpe smiled. "Let him ramble a while, if it helps. Indulge him. And we'd better organize a house-to-house of the entire estate. I want to know if anything like this has happened there before, people posing as social workers after children. No one's likely to admit to it, but if you get the feeling that anyone's being particularly evasive, for whatever reason, make a note and we'll get back to them. Can you handle that, Susan?"

Susan Gay nodded.

"Take as many PCs as you can find, and make sure you give them a damn good briefing first. Most of the lads are out on the search, but we've been promised extra manpower on this." He turned to Richmond. "We've got to check with all the garages in the area and see if they remember anyone matching the description stopping for petrol. And I want to see all the police traffic reports— parking or speeding tickets—for Tuesday. In fact, make it for the past week. I want to know if anyone remembers a smartly dressed couple with a little girl in a dark blue compact. Better check with the car-rental agencies, too. Phil, can you handle all that?"

Richmond nodded. "Yes, sir. I've already got a computer print-out of locals with any kind of history of child molestation. None of the descriptions match. Do you want me to start on that too?"

"How many?"

"Six, sir—that's four in the Swainsdale area and two in Sergeant Hatchley's patch. But we've no way of telling where our couple started out from."

"I know," said Gristhorpe. "I'll get onto DS Hatchley, and you just do the best you can. We'll see if we can't pay a couple of visits ourselves. But I want priority on tracking down that car. Someone must have noticed it. By the way, those computers you wanted have been delivered to the mobile unit. Do you think you can take a trip out there and give the lads a quick lesson?"

"No problem."

"Any questions?" Gristhorpe asked.

"Did forensics find anything at the house?" Banks asked.

Gristhorpe shook his head. "Not a sausage. The SOCO team did a thorough job, and they couldn't find any traces of a struggle—no blood, nothing—or any indications that Gemma had been harmed on the premises. I think we can assume that Mrs Scupham is telling the truth and this couple really did abduct the lass."

"Anything new on Les Poole?" Banks asked.

"Nothing," Gristhorpe answered. "According to the PCs on the night shift, he got back from the pub about ten o'clock and hasn't been out since. Anything else?"

"What about Gemma's father?" Susan asked.

"As far as we know, he's serving with the army in Belfast, poor sod. We'll arrange to get the locals to interview him today, if possible, just to make sure he's got nothing to do with it." Gristhorpe clapped his hands. "Right. If there's nothing else, we'd better get cracking." As they left, he touched Banks on the shoulder. "Alan, a moment?"

"Of course."

Gristhorpe poured more coffee for himself and Banks. He didn't look too bad for someone who hadn't had much sleep, Banks thought. Perhaps the bags under his eyes were heavier than usual, but he seemed alert and full of drive.

"I'm getting involved in this one, Alan," he said. "At every level. I'll not be content just to sit in my office and co-ordinate, though I'll be doing that, of course. I'll be spending a fair amount of time at the mobile unit and I'll be conducting some interviews myself. I want you to know that, and I want you to know so you don't let it interfere with your usual way of working. I've always given you a pretty free hand, and it's usually got results. I don't want to change that. What I *do* want is to be present when we get the breaks. Know what I mean?"

Banks nodded.

"And there's something else," Gristhorpe said. "Something the ACC made very clear as a priority concern."

Banks thought he could guess what was coming, but kept silent while Gristhorpe went on.

"Gemma Scupham might be the first," he said, "but she might not be the last. Let's bear that in mind."

Banks carried his coffee through to his office, where he lit a cigarette, then stood by the venetian blind and looked down on the market square. The façade of the Norman church and the cobbles of the market square shone pale gold in the pure light. Two more cars had arrived, and yet another was just pulling in. Banks watched the young couple get out and stand hand in hand gazing around them at the ancient square with its weathered stone cross. Honeymooners, by the look of them. The church clock rang nine.

He thought about Brenda Scupham, with her aura of sexuality, and of the sly, weasy Les Poole, and he tried to imagine what kind of parents they must have made. They can't have had much time for Gemma, with Les always at the pub or the bookie's and Brenda at home doing God knows what. Watching television, most likely. Did they talk to her? Play with her? And did they abuse her?

Then he thought of Gemma herself: that haunted face, those eyes that had seen much more and much worse than her young mind could comprehend, possibly lying dead out there right now in some ditch, or buried in a makeshift grave. And he thought of what Gristhorpe had just said. He stubbed out his cigarette and reached for the telephone. No time for brooding. Time to get to work.

II

A desolate, stunned air pervaded the East Side Estate that morning, Banks sensed, as he walked from the mobile unit to the school. Even the dogs seemed to be indoors, and those people he did see going on errands or pushing babies in prams had their heads bowed and seemed drawn in on themselves. He passed the maisonettes with their obscene messages scrawled on the cracked paintwork, and the two blocks of flats—each fourteen storeys high—where he knew the lifts, when they worked, smelled of urine and glue. Hardly anyone was out on the street.

The school itself was a square red brick building with only a few small windows. A high chain-link fence bordered the asphalt playground. Banks looked at his watch. Eleven o'clock. Gemma's teacher should be waiting for him in the staff-room.

He walked through the front doors, noting that one of the glass panes was cracked in a spider-web pattern, and asked the first adult he saw the way to the staff-room. As he walked along the corridor, he was struck by the brightness of the place, so much in contrast with its ugly exterior. Most of it, he thought, was due to the children's paintings tacked along the walls. These weren't skilled, professional efforts, but the gaudy outbursts of untrained minds—yellow sunbursts with rays shooting in all directions, bright golden angels, red and green stick figures of mummy and daddy and cats and dogs.

There was a funny smell about the place, too, that transported him back to his own infants' school, but it took him some moments to identify it. When he did, he smiled to himself, remembering for the first time in ages those blissful, carefree days before school became a matter of learning facts and studying for exams. It was Plasticine, that coloured putty-like stuff he had tried in vain to mould into the shapes of hippos and crocodiles.

He walked straight into the staff-room, and a woman, who looked hardly older than a schoolgirl herself, came forward to greet him. "Chief Inspector Banks?" she asked, holding out her hand. "I'm Peggy Graham."

It was a big room with well-spaced tables and chairs, a notice-board full of mimeographed memos, handwritten notes and printed flyers for concerts, courses and package holidays. A couple of other teachers, sitting over newspapers, glanced up at his entry, then looked down again. One corner of the room had been converted into a mini-kitchen, complete with a fridge, microwave and coffee-maker. Here and there on the rough, orange-painted walls hung more examples of untrammelled art.

"A bit overwhelming, isn't it?" Peggy Graham asked, noticing him looking around. "I could do without the orange walls myself, but it was a playroom before we got it, so . . . Sit down. Can I get you some coffee or something?"

"If it's no trouble," Banks said.

She went to get it. Peggy Graham, Banks noticed, was a small, bird-like woman, perhaps fresh out of teachers' training school. Her grey pleated skirt covered her knees, and a dark blue cardigan hung over her white cotton blouse. She wore her mousy hair in a pony tail, and large glasses made her nose look tiny. Her eyes, behind them, were big, pale and milky blue, and they seemed charged with worry and sincerity. Her lips were thin and curved slightly downwards at the corners. She wore no make-up.

"Well," she said, sitting down beside him with the coffee. It came in a mug with a picture of Big Bird on it. "This is just dreadful about Gemma, isn't it? Just dreadful."

She spoke, he thought, as if she were talking to a class of five-year-olds, and her mouth was so mobile she looked as if she were miming. Banks nodded.

"What could have happened?" she asked. "Have you got *any* idea?"

"I'm afraid not," Banks said.

"I don't suppose you could say anything even if you did have, could you?"

"We have to be very careful."

"Of course." She sat back in her chair, crossed her legs and rested her hands on her lap. Banks noticed the thin gold wedding band. "How can I help you?" she asked.

"I'm not really sure. In cases like this it helps to find out as much as you can about the child. What was Gemma like?"

Peggy Graham pursed her lips. "Well, that's a hard one. Gemma's a very quiet child. She always seems a bit withdrawn."

"In what way?"

"Just . . . quiet. Oh, she's bright, very bright. She's an excellent reader, and I think, given the opportunity, she could be very creative. That's one of hers on the wall."

Banks walked over to the crayon sketch Peggy had pointed at. It showed a girl with pigtails standing beside a tree on a carpet of grass under a bright sun. The leaves were individually defined in bright green, and the grass was dotted with yellow flowers— buttercups, perhaps, or dandelions. The girl, a stick-figure, just stood there with her arms stretched out. Banks found something disturbing about it, and he realized that the girl's round face had no features. He went back to his chair.

"Very good," he said. "Did you ever get the feeling that there was something bothering her?"

"She always seems . . . well, preoccupied." Peggy gave a nervous laugh. "I call her Wednesday's child. You know, 'Wednesday's child is full of woe.' She seemed woeful. Of course, I tried to talk to her, but she never said much. Mostly she was attentive in class. Once or twice I noticed she was weeping, just quietly, to herself."

"What did you do?"

"I didn't want to embarrass her in front of the others. I asked her afterwards what was wrong, but she wouldn't say. Gemma's always been a very secretive child. What goes on in that imagination of hers I've no idea. Half the time she seems to be in another world."

"A better one?"

Peggy Graham twisted her ring. "I don't know. I like to think so."

"What was your impression?"

"I think she was lonely and she felt unloved."

Her first use of the past tense in reference to Gemma wasn't lost on Banks. "Lonely? Didn't she have any friends?"

"Oh yes. She was quite popular here, even though she was quiet. Don't get the wrong impression. She liked playing games with the other girls. Sometimes she seemed quite gay—oops, I shouldn't have said that, should I, now they've censored it from all the Noddy books—cheerful, I suppose. It's just that she was moody. She had these woeful, silent moods when you just couldn't reach her. Sometimes they'd last for days."

"And you don't know why?"

"I can only guess. And you mustn't tell anyone I said this. I think it was her home life."

"What about it?"

"I think she was neglected. I don't mean she wasn't well fed or clothed, or abused in any way. Though she did look a bit . . . well, shabby . . . sometimes. You know, she was wearing the same dress and socks day after day. And sometimes I just felt like picking her up and dumping her in a bath. It wasn't that she smelled or anything. She was just a bit grubby. I don't think her parents spent enough time with her, encouraging her, that sort of thing. I think that was the root of her loneliness. It happens a lot, and there isn't much you can do about it. A supportive home environment is

perhaps even more important than school for a child's development, but we can't be parents as well as teachers, can we? And we
can't tell parents how to bring up their children."

"You mentioned abuse," Banks said. "Did you ever notice any
signs of physical abuse?"

"Oh, no. I couldn't . . . I mean, if I had I would certainly have
reported it. We did have a case here a year or so ago. It was dreadful, just dreadful what some parents can sink to."

"But you saw no signs with Gemma? No bruises, cuts, anything
like that?"

"No. Well, there was one time. About a week or so ago, I think
it was. It was quite warm, like now. Gemma was wearing a short-
sleeved dress and I noticed a bruise on her upper arm, the left one,
I think. Naturally, I asked her about it, but she said she'd got it
playing games."

"Did you believe her?"

"Yes. I had no reason to doubt her word."

"So you didn't report it?"

"No. I mean, one wouldn't want to be alarmist. Not after that
business with the Cleveland social workers and everything. Look,
maybe I should have done something. Lord knows, if I'm in any
way responsible . . . But if you brought in the authorities every
time a child had a bruise there'd be no time for anything else,
would there?"

"It's all right," Banks said. "Nobody's blaming you. Everybody's
a bit sensitive about things like that these days. I picked up plenty
of bruises when I was a lad, believe me, and my mum and dad
wouldn't have appreciated being accused of abusing me. And I got
a good hiding when I deserved it, too."

Peggy smiled at him over her glasses. "As I said," she went on,
"Gemma's explanation seemed perfectly reasonable to me. Children
can play pretty rough sometimes. They're a lot more resilient than
we give them credit for."

"Was that the only mark you ever saw on her?"

"Oh, yes. I mean if it had been a regular occurrence I'd have
said something for certain. We do have to keep an eye open for
these things."

"And she never seemed in pain of any kind?"

"Not physical pain, no. She just sometimes seemed withdrawn, lost in her own world. But children often create their own imaginary worlds. They can be very complex beings, Chief Inspector. They're not all the same. Just because a child is quiet, it doesn't mean there's anything wrong with her."

"I understand. Please believe me, I'm not criticizing. I'm just trying to find out something about her."

"How could it help?"

"I honestly don't know."

"You think she's dead, don't you?"

"I wouldn't say that."

"She's been gone nearly two days now. That's what the papers say. Not in so many words, perhaps, but . . ."

"She could still be alive."

"Then she might be better off dead," Peggy Graham whispered. She felt up the sleeve of her cardigan for a tissue, lifted her glasses and wiped her moist eyes. They looked small and shy without the lenses to magnify them. "I'm sorry. It's just . . . we're all so upset."

"Did you, or anyone else on staff, notice any strangers hanging around the school recently?"

"No. And I'm sure anything like that would have been reported. We have very strict guidelines to follow."

"Nobody saw a dark blue car? Are you sure?"

She shook her head. "I'm sure."

"Did you ever see Gemma talking to any strangers nearby? Male or female?"

"No. She always came and left with her friends, the ones from the same street. She didn't live far away."

Banks stood up. "Thank you very much," he said. "If you do remember anything, here's my card. Please call."

Peggy Graham took the card. "Of course. But I don't see how there could be anything else."

"Just in case."

"All right." She got to her feet. "I'll walk to the door with you."

As they walked, a host of children came out of one of the classrooms. Some were laughing and scrapping, but many of them seemed subdued. Perhaps they were too young to understand the enormity of what had happened, Banks thought, but they were old enough to sense the mood of tension and fear. One little girl with glossy dark curls and brown spaniel eyes tugged at Banks's sleeve.

"Are you the policeman?" she asked.

"Yes," he answered, wondering how on earth she knew.

"Are you looking for Gemma?"

"Yes, I am."

"Please find her" the little girl said, clutching his sleeve tighter. "Bring her back. She's my friend."

"I'll do my best," said Banks. He turned to Peggy Graham. She blushed.

"I'm afraid I told them a policeman was coming," she said. "Sorry."

"It's all right. Look, can I talk to this girl?"

"Elizabeth? Well . . . I suppose so. Though I don't know what. . . . Come this way." And she led both Banks and Elizabeth into the empty classroom.

"Now, Elizabeth," she said. "The nice policeman wants to talk to you about Gemma, to help him to find her. Just answer his questions. I'll stay here with you." She glanced at Banks to ask if he minded, and he nodded his agreement. Elizabeth took hold of Peggy Graham's hand and stood beside her.

Banks crouched, hearing his knees crack as he did so, and rested his elbows on his thighs. "You know we're trying to find Gemma," he said. "Did she ever say anything to you about going away?"

Elizabeth shook her head.

"Or about anyone wanting to take her away?"

Another shake.

"Did she have any older friends, big girls or big boys?"

"No."

"Did she ever talk about her mummy and daddy?"

"It wasn't her daddy."

"Mr Poole?"

Elizabeth nodded. "She wouldn't call him Daddy."

"What did she say about him?"

"I don't know."

"Did she like him?"

"No."

"Did he ever hurt Gemma?"

"She cried."

"Why did she cry?"

"Don't know."

"Did he ever hurt her, Elizabeth?"

"I don't know. She didn't like him. She said he smelled and he always told her to go away."

"When did he tell her to go away?"

"He said she was a sp . . . sp . . . a spilled cat."

"A spilled cat? Do you mean 'spoiled brat'?"

"Yes."

"When did he say this?"

"He wouldn't let her have the book."

"What book?"

"She wanted a book and he wouldn't let her have it. He threw her other books away."

"Why?"

"She spilled some paint on his newspaper. It too dirty. He was angry. He threw her books away and he wouldn't let her have any more."

"What was too dirty, Elizabeth?"

"No. It too dirty."

Banks looked at Peggy Graham. "I think she's trying to say 'at two-thirty,'" she said, frowning.

"Is that right?" Banks asked Elizabeth. "She spilled paint on his newspaper at two-thirty, so he threw her books away?"

She nodded.

"What were the books?"

"Story books. With pictures. Gemma likes reading. She reads to me. I'm not very good. Please find her." Elizabeth started crying. Peggy Graham put an arm around her. "It's all right, dear. The nice policeman will find Gemma. Don't cry."

Elizabeth sniffled a few moments longer, then wiped her nose on her sleeve and left the room. Banks sighed.

"What was all that about?" Peggy asked.

"I wish I knew. Thanks for letting me talk to her anyway. I hope she doesn't stay upset."

"Don't worry. Elizabeth's tough enough."

Banks walked through the playground full of children. They were skipping, playing hopscotch, running around as usual, but like the ones coming out of the classroom they seemed much quieter, more subdued than children usually are.

He looked at his watch. Close to noon. Time to write up his notes before lunch with Jenny. Not that he had learned much from the teacher that he hadn't known or suspected already. Gemma kept herself to herself, perhaps suffered neglect at home, but was probably not physically abused. Still, there was the business of the bruise. How had she got it? And what had Elizabeth meant about "at two-thirty" and Gemma's books? Banks walked past the tower block with JESUS SAVES written in red on the wall and back to the unmarked car he had parked by the mobile unit.

III

Damn it, cursed Jenny Fuller. She had pulled up at the lights just in time and all the essays on the back seat had slid off onto the floor. So few of the students bothered with paper-clips or staples; it would be a hell of a job reshuffling them. If she hadn't been in such a hurry to meet Banks it would never have happened. She was on the south-eastern edge of Eastvale, coming up to the roundabout by the Red Lion, and she only had five minutes to park and get to Le Bistro. Still, Alan would wait.

The lights changed and the car lurched off again. To hell with the papers. She shouldn't be teaching until October anyway, and if it hadn't been for those American students—those American students with odd ideas of academic timetables and thousands of dollars to spend on an English education—then she could have been relaxing on a beach somewhere.

She smiled to herself, imagining Alan Banks sitting at one of Le Bistro's wobbly little tables, no doubt feeling out of place among the yuppie lunch crowd with their Perriers and portable telephones. He would be far more comfortable in the Queen's Arms with a pie and a pint in front of him, not at a table covered in a coral cloth with a long-stemmed rose in a vase at its centre. But Jenny had been lecturing to the Americans all morning, and she was damned if she was going to be done out of the shrimp *provençale* and the glass of white wine she had promised to treat herself.

Jenny remembered her surprise the first time the Eastvale CID had brought her into a case, involving a peeping Tom, three years ago. She had guessed (correctly) that they wanted a visible female presence as a sop to Dorothy Wycombe and the Eastvale feminist contingent, WEEF, Women of Eastvale for Emancipation and Freedom. Still, she had done a good job, and since then her professional field of interests had broadened to include a certain amount of criminal and deviant psychology. She had even attended a series of fascinating lectures on the psychological profiling of serial killers, given by a visiting American from the FBI Behavioral Sciences section.

She had also had a brief fling with the visitor, but she didn't care to remember that too clearly. Like most of her affairs, it was best forgotten. Still, that was eighteen months ago, when she had been still hurting over her split with Dennis Osmond. Since then she had not been involved with anyone. Instead, she had done a lot of thinking about her lousy relationships, and the reasons for them. She hadn't come up with any answers yet. Most often she ended up wondering why the hell her professional insights seemed to shed no light at all on her personal life.

The tires screeched as she turned right at the market square and drove down by Castle Hill between the terraced river gardens and the formal gardens. People sat on the terraces and ate packed lunches on one side of the road, while on the other, mothers dragged bored children around the displays of fading flowers.

At last, she crossed the small bridge over the River Swain, turned right and pulled up outside the café.

Le Bistro was one of Eastvale's newest cafés. Tourism, the dale's main industry, had increased, and the many Americans drawn to do the "James Herriot" tour wanted a little more than fish and chips and warm beer, quaint as they found such things. In addition, a more sophisticated, cosmopolitan crowd had moved up from London while property in the north was still a good deal cheaper than down south. Many of them commuted from Eastvale to York, Darlington, and even as far as Tyneside, Leeds and Bradford, and they naturally demanded a little more diversity in matters of dining.

Best of all, as far as Jenny was concerned, was that Le Bistro was actually situated in a converted Georgian semi only four houses south of her own. The new owners had, somehow, received planning permission to knock down the wall between the two houses and turn them into a café. For Jenny it was a godsend, as she often couldn't be bothered to cook after a hard day. The food was good and the prices were relatively reasonable.

She dashed through the door. The place was fairly busy, but she saw Banks immediately. There he was in a dark grey sports jacket, white shirt and tie. As usual, his top button was open and the tie loose and askew. Under close-cropped black hair, his dark blue eyes sparkled as he looked over at her. He was working on a crossword and holding what looked like a glass of mineral water. Jenny couldn't suppress a giggle as she sat down in a flurry of apologies. Le Bistro didn't serve pints.

"It's all right," said Banks rather glumly, putting his newspaper away in his briefcase. "I'm supposed to be cutting down on the ale anyway."

"Since when?"

Banks patted his stomach. "Since I turned forty and noticed this beginning to swell."

"Nonsense. You're as lean as ever. You're just suffering from male menopause. Next you'll be having an affair with a twenty-one-year-old rookie policewoman."

Banks laughed. "Chance would be a fine thing. But don't joke about it. You never know. Anyway, how are you?"

Jenny shrugged and tossed back the thick mane of red hair that cascaded over her shoulders. "Okay, I suppose. I'm not sure I like teaching summer school though."

"Working in summer?" mocked Banks. "Tut-tut, what a terrible thing. What is the world coming to?"

Jenny thumped him on the arm. "It's supposed to be one of the perks of the job, remember? Teachers get summers off. Not this year, though."

"Never mind. You're looking well for it."

"Why, thank you, kind sir." Jenny inclined her head graciously. "And you haven't changed. Honestly, Alan. You still don't look a day over thirty-nine. How's Sandra?"

"Busy."

"Oh-oh. Feeling all neglected, are we?"

Banks grinned. "Something like that. But we're not here to talk about me."

"And how's Susan Gay?" Jenny had spent some time helping Susan adjust to her CID posting, on a semi-professional basis, and the two had become fairly close. They were different personalities, but Jenny saw something in Susan—a sense of determination, a single-mindedness—that both appealed to her and disturbed her. If she could persuade Susan to relax a little, she felt, then a more balanced and attractive personality might be permitted to emerge.

Banks told her Susan was doing well, though she still seemed a little tense and prickly, and the two chatted about family and mutual friends. "Have you studied the menu yet?" Jenny asked him after a short silence.

"Mm. No sausage and chips, I noticed. How's the croque monsieur?"

"Good."

"Then I'll have that. And by the way, I like the music."

Jenny cocked an ear. Singing quietly in the background was the unmistakable voice of Edith Piaf. Typical of him to notice that, she thought. Left to herself she would have ignored it as wallpaper music.

"Wine?" she asked.

"Not for me. It makes me sleepy and I've a lot of paperwork to do this afternoon."

"So, it's about little Gemma Scupham, is it?" Jenny said, unfolding a coral napkin and spreading it over her lap. "That's why you've called me in?"

Banks nodded. "Superintendent Gristhorpe thought you might be able to help."

"At least I'm not the token feminist this time."

"No. Seriously, Jenny, can you help?"

"Maybe. What do you want from me?"

"For the moment I'd just like grounding in a few basics. I can understand a lot about things most people don't even want to think about—robbery, murder, even rape—but I can't seem to grasp the motivation for something like this."

Jenny took a deep breath and held it a moment. "All right. I'll do what I can. Shall we order first, though?" She called over the waitress and gave their orders, asking for a glass of white wine for herself right now, and a coffee for Banks, then she sat back in her chair. "First you'd better tell me the details so far," she said.

Banks told her. Before he finished, the food arrived, and they both tucked in.

Jenny pushed her plate away and set the half-full wineglass in front of her. Banks ordered another coffee.

"I don't really know where to start," she said. "I mean, it's not really my field."

"You do know something about sexual deviance, though."

"Honestly, Alan, you make me sound like a real pervert. Basically, nobody really knows what causes someone to be a paedophile or a rapist or a sadist. They don't necessarily realize they're doing anything wrong."

"Are you telling me that a man who sexually assaults little children doesn't think he's doing anything wrong?'

"Depends what you mean by wrong. He would know he's breaking the law, of course, but . . . He's only satisfying desires he can't help feeling. He never *asked* to feel them in the first place. And many also feel tremendous guilt and remorse."

"For doing something they don't even think is wrong? You make it sound almost legitimate."

"You asked. I'm just telling you what little I know."

"I'm sorry. Go on."

"Look, you might think a person is simply born the way he or she is, but sexual behaviour isn't fixed from the start. There are theories that almost everything is biologically based, caused by chemicals, or by genes. For what it's worth, most studies indicate that sexual behaviour is mostly a matter of learning. At first, everything is diffuse, in a kind of flux—polymorphous perverse, I believe Freud called infant sexuality. It depends on a number of factors what preferences come to the fore."

"Like what?"

"Experience. Learning. Family. They're probably the most important. You try something, and if you like it, you do it again. That's experience. Many people are given no information about sex, or such wrong-headed information that they become very confused. That's learning, or lack of it. Even what we call normal sexuality is a dark, murky thing at best. Look at the extremes of sexual jealousy, of how sex and desire can so easily turn to violence. There's loss of control. Then there's the association of orgasm with death. Did you know it used to be called the 'little death'?"

"You don't make it sound like much fun."

"That's the point," Jenny said. "For a lot of people, it isn't. Desire is a ball and chain they can't get rid of, or a ringmaster they don't dare disobey. Sexuality has lots of possible outcomes other than what we label 'normal' or socially acceptable. It's *learned* behaviour. When you're prepubescent or adolescent, any object or situation *could* become stimulating. Remember the thrill you used to get looking at pictures of naked women? It's easy as an adolescent to get fixated on things like underwear, big breasts, the image rather than the real thing. Remember our peeping Tom? That was his particular fixation, a visual stimulation.

"It doesn't take long before most of us start to prefer certain stimuli to others. Pretty soon sexual excitement and satisfaction become limited to a certain, fairly narrow range. That's what we call normal. Your good old, socially approved, heterosexual sex. The problem with most sexual deviants, though, is that they can't handle what we regard as normal personal relationships. Many try, but they fail. It's a lot more complicated than that, of course. It may not be apparent on the surface that they've failed, for example. They may become very good at faking it in order to cover up their real needs and actions."

"So what kind of person are we talking about? You said it's someone who can't handle ordinary relationships."

"I'll have to do some research and see what I can come up with, but your basic deviant is probably pretty much the chap-next-door type, with some very notable exceptions, of course. By the way, you don't have to look around so nervously, you can smoke if you want. Giselle will fetch an ashtray. Remember, it's a *French* restaurant. Everyone smokes over there."

Banks lit up and Giselle duly brought the ashtray along with their bill. "Go on," he said. "You were telling me about the chap next door."

"It's just that most sex offenders become skilled at leading quite normal lives on the surface. They learn to play the game. They can hold down a job, keep a marriage going, even raise children—"

"Paedophiles?"

"Yes."

"I must admit that's a surprise," said Banks. "I've come across psychopaths and deviants of various kinds before—I mean, I'm not entirely ignorant on the subject—and it *has* often amazed me how they keep their secrets. Look at Dennis Nilsen, for Christ's sake, chopping up kids and putting their heads on the ring to boil while he takes his dog for a walk, saying hello to the neighbours. Such a nice, quiet man." Banks shook his head. "I know the Boston Strangler was married, and Sutcliffe, the Yorkshire Ripper. But how the hell can a paedophile keep a thing like that hidden from his wife and kids?"

"People can become very adept at keeping secrets if they have to, Alan. You don't spend all your life in someone else's company, under someone's scrutiny, do you? Surely you managed to find time alone to masturbate when you were a kid? And you probably thought about it a fair bit, too, anticipated the picture you'd look at or the girl you'd imagine undressing. The whole thing takes on a kind of magical intensity, a ritualistic element, if you like. A sex offender will simply spend all his free time anticipating and planning his deviant acts."

Banks loosened his tie a little more. Jenny noticed him look around the restaurant and smile at the three businessmen at the

next table, who seemed to have been listening with growing fascination and horror to the conversation. "You seem to know a lot
about adolescent male behaviour," he said.

Jenny laughed. "Alan, I've embarrassed you. Oh, don't look so
uncomfortable. It *is* part of my field, after all. The things little boys
and little girls get up to."

"What's your prognosis?" Banks asked.

Jenny sighed. "For you? I'm afraid there's no hope. No, really, I
honestly haven't done enough research for anything like that yet."
She frowned, the lines crinkling her smooth forehead. "You know
what really puzzles me, though? Again, it's probably something
you've already considered from your point of view, but psychologically it's interesting, too."

"What's that?"

"The woman."

"You mean why she was there?"

"Yes. What's her part in the whole business?"

"Well, her presence would certainly give credibility to the social
worker story. I doubt that even someone as thick as Brenda
Scupham would have trusted a man alone."

"No. I realize that. But think about it, Alan." Jenny leaned
forward, her hands clasped on the table. "She's a woman. Surely
you're not telling me she didn't know what they were doing, taking
the child?"

"They acted together, yes. But he may have conned her into it
somehow, for the sake of credibility. She might not have known
what his motives were, especially if, as you say, paedophiles are
good at keeping secrets."

"Except from themselves. But I still think it's a strange thing for
a woman to do—help abduct another woman's child. It's an even
stranger thing for a couple to do. What on earth would she want
with Gemma?"

"Now don't tell me you're going to give me all that sisterhood
crap, because I just don't accept it. Women are just as—"

Jenny held her hand up. "All right. I won't. But there's no need
to start getting all shirty. It's not sisterhood I'm talking about, it's a
very practical thing. As far as I know, sexual deviants can be fat or

thin, big or little, young or old, rich or poor, but they almost always act *alone*. To put it technically, we're talking about people who exhibit primary characteristics of social aversion."

"Hmm. I'm not saying we haven't considered they might have simply wanted a child so badly that they took someone else's, that they're not paedophiles. We just don't know. But think of the risk involved."

Jenny ran her fingers around the stem of her wineglass. "Maybe it does seem far-fetched. But women have snatched babies from prams. It's not my job to evaluate that kind of information. All I'm saying is that the couple element is curious, in psychological terms. And the method is unusual. As you say, think of the risk involved. Maybe the risk was part of the thrill."

A short silence followed. Banks lit another cigarette. Jenny pulled a face and waved the smoke away. She noticed that Edith Piaf had finished now, replaced by some innocuous accordion music meant to evoke the Gauloise atmosphere of Parisian cafés.

"The superintendent mentioned the Moors Murderers, Brady and Hindley," said Banks. "I know he's got a bee in his bonnet about that case, but you have to admit there are parallels."

"Hmm."

"What I'm saying," Banks went on, "is it may be one way of explaining the couple aspect. Brady thought human beings were contemptible creatures and pleasure the only end worth pursuing. And Hindley was besotted with him. She was witnessing it all as a demonstration of some form of love for him. I know it sounds weird, but . . ."

"I've heard the theory," said Jenny. "It's all to do with dominance. And I've heard a lot weirder theories, too. Christ, Alan, you know as well as I do that most psychology is guesswork. We don't really *know* anything. But Superintendent Gristhorpe may be right. It *could* be something like that. I'll look into it."

"So you'll help?"

"Of course I'll help, idiot. Did you think I'd say no?"

"Quickly, Jenny," said Banks, taking money from his wallet and placing it on the bill. "Especially if there's even the slightest chance that Gemma Scupham might still be alive."

IV

"Have you found her yet?"

Nothing much had changed in Brenda Scupham's front room by Thursday afternoon. The doll still lay in the same position on the floor, and the peculiar smell remained. But Brenda looked more tired. Her eyes were red-rimmed and her hair hung limp and lifeless beside her pale cheeks. She was wearing a grubby pink track-suit bottom and a loose green sweatshirt. Les Poole slouched in the armchair, feet up, smoking.

"What's wrong, Les?" Banks asked. "Is The Barleycorn not on all-day opening?"

"Very funny. I don't *live* there, you know."

Brenda Scupham shot him a mean look, then turned to Banks. "Leave him alone. He's not done anything. He might not be much, but he's all I've got. I asked you, have you found my Gemma yet?"

"No," said Banks, turning from Poole. "No, we haven't."

"Well, what do you want? More questions?"

"I'm afraid so."

Brenda Scupham sighed and sat down. "I don't know where this is going to get us."

"I need to know more about Gemma's habits, for a start."

"What do you mean, habits?"

"Her routines. How did she get to school?"

"She walked. It's not far."

"Alone?"

"No, she met up with the Ferris girl from over the street and the Bramhope kid from two houses down."

"Did she come home with them, too?"

"Yes."

Banks made a note of the names. "What about lunch-time?"

"School dinners."

"Why?"

"What do you mean, why?"

"The school's not far away. Surely it'd have saved you a penny or two if she came home for lunch?"

Brenda Scupham shrugged. "She said she liked school dinners."

"Did she ever say anything about anyone following her or stopping her in the street?"

"Never."

"And she wasn't out on her own?"

"No. She was always with her friends, whether she was off to school or playing out. Why are you asking all these questions?"

"Brenda, I'm trying to figure out why Gemma's abductors came to the house rather than snatching her in the street. Surely she must have been alone out there at some time?"

"I dare say. She'd nip to the shop now and then. You can't keep your eyes on them every minute of the day. She is seven, you know. She knows to look right before left when she's crossing the street, and not to take sweets from strangers." When she realized what she'd said, she put her hand to her mouth and her eyes filled with tears.

"I'm sorry if this is painful for you," Banks said, "but it is important."

"I know."

"Was Gemma a happy child, would you say?"

"I suppose so. They live in their own worlds, don't they?"

"Would she be given to exaggeration, to lying?"

"Not that I know of, no."

"It's just that I heard a story about Les here throwing some of Gemma's books out. Does that mean anything to you?"

Les Poole sat up and turned to Banks. "What?"

"You heard, Les. What's so important about her spilling paint on your paper at two-thirty?"

Poole looked puzzled for a few seconds, then he laughed out loud. "Who told you that?"

"Never mind. What's it all about?"

He laughed again. "It was *the* two-thirty. The two-thirty from Cheltenham. Silly little bugger spilled coloured water all over my racing form. You know, the jar she'd been dipping her bloody paintbrush in."

"And for that you threw her books out?"

"Don't be daft. They were just some old colouring books. She was painting in them on the other side of the table and she knocked her paint jar over and ruined my bloody paper. So I grabbed the books and tore them up."

"How did she react?"

"Oh, she whined and sulked for a while."

"Did you ever grab her hard by the arm?"

"No, I never touched her. Just the books. Look, what's all this—"

"Why wouldn't you get her the new book she wanted?"

Poole sat back in the chair and crossed his legs. "Couldn't afford it, could we? You can't give kids everything they ask for. You ought to know that if you've got kids of your own. Look, get to the point, Mr Banks. I might not have had much time for the little beggar but I didn't run off with her, did I? We're the victims, not the criminals. I think it's about time you realized that."

Banks looked at him, and Poole quickly averted his gaze. It made Banks think of his first lesson in police thinking. He had been involved in interviewing a petty thief about a burglary in Belsize Park, and he came away convinced that the man hadn't committed it. Surprised to see the charges being laid and the evidence gathered, he had mentioned his doubts to his commanding officer. The man, a twenty-year veteran called Bill Carstairs, had looked at Banks and shaken his head, then he said, "He might not have done this job, but he sure as hell has done something he ought to be put away for." Looking at Poole made Banks feel the same way. The man was guilty of something. If he had nothing to do with Gemma's disappearance, or even with the Fletcher's warehouse job, he was still guilty of *something*.

Banks turned back to Brenda Scupham.

"You think we abused Gemma, don't you?" she said.

"I don't know."

"You've been listening to gossip. Probably gossip from kids, at that. Look, I'll admit I didn't want her. I was twenty-one, the last thing I wanted was to be lumbered with a kid, but I was brought up Catholic, and I couldn't get rid of her. I might not be the best mother on earth. I might be selfish, I might not be up to encouraging her in school and paying as much attention to her as I should. I'm not even a very good house-keeper. But all that . . . I mean, what I'm saying is I never abused her."

It was an impassioned speech, but Banks got the feeling that she was protesting too much. "What about Les?" he asked.

She glanced over at him. "If he ever touched her he knows he'd be out of here before his feet could touch the floor."

"So why did you give her up so easily?"

Brenda Scupham chewed on her lip and fought back the tears. "Do you think I haven't had it on my mind night and day since? Do you think there's a moment goes by I don't ask myself the same question?" She shook her head. "It all happened so fast."

"But if you hadn't abused Gemma in any way, why didn't you just tell Mr Brown and Miss Peterson that and send them away?"

"Because they were the authorities. I mean, they looked like they were and everything. I suppose I thought if they'd had some information then they had to look into it, you know, like the police. And then when they found there was nothing in it, they'd bring Gemma back."

"Did Gemma go willingly?"

"What?"

"When she left with them, did she cry, struggle?"

"No, she just seemed to accept it. She didn't say anything."

Banks stood up. "That's it for now," he said. "We'll keep you informed. If you remember anything, you can report it at the mobile unit at the end of the street."

Brenda folded her arms and nodded. "You make *me* feel like a criminal, Mr Banks," she said. "It's not right. I've tried to be a good mother. I'm not perfect, but who is?"

Banks paused at the door. "Mrs Scupham," he said, "I'm not trying to prove any kind of case against you. Believe it or not, all the questions I ask you are to do with trying to find Gemma. I know it seems cruel, but I need to know the answers. And if you think about it for a while, considering how many other children there are on this estate, and all over Swainsdale, and how many of them really *are* abused, there's a very important question needs answering."

Brenda Scupham's brow furrowed, and even Poole glanced over from his fireside seat.

"What's that?" she asked.

"Why Gemma?" Banks said, and left.

THREE

I

Marjorie Bingham lingered behind the others on the narrow track and kicked at small stones as she walked. She could hear her husband's muffled voice, carried back on the breeze, as he explained the history of Dales lead mining to Andrew and Jane:

"Most people think that lead mining here only goes back as far as Roman times. It doesn't, you know. It goes back much further than that. It might even go back as far as the Bronze Age—though there's no hard evidence for that, of course—but certainly the Brigantes . . ."

God, she thought, what a bloody bore Roger has become. Only six months up from Coventry after the company move and here he is, playing the country squire and rabbiting on about spalling hammers, knockstones, buckers and hotching tubs. And just look at him: pants tucked into the expensive hiking boots, walking-stick, orange Gore-Tex anorak. All for a quarter-mile track from the Range Rover to the old mine.

Knowing Andrew, Marjorie thought, he was probably thinking about opening time, and Jane was absorbed with her new baby, which she carried in a kind of makeshift sack on her back. Little Annette was asleep, one leg poking out each side of the central strap, her head lolling, oblivious to them all, and especially oblivious to the bloody lead mines.

"Of course, the Romans used lead in great quantities. You know how advanced their plumbing systems were for their time. I know you've been to the Roman Baths in Bath, Andrew, and I'm sure you'll agree . . ."

Young Megan capered ahead picking flowers, reciting, "He loves me, he loves me not . . ." as she pulled off the petals and tossed them in the air. Then she spread her arms out and pretended to walk a tightrope. She didn't have a care in the world, either, Marjorie thought. Why do we lose that sense of wonder in nature? she asked herself. How does it happen? Where does it go? It wasn't that she didn't appreciate the countryside—there was no denying it was beautiful, not to mention healthy, especially on a lovely autumn morning like this—but she couldn't feel ecstatic about it. To be honest, she loved the shops and the busy hum of city life much more. Even Eastvale would have been preferable. But no: Roger said they had to seize their opportunity for a newer, better lifestyle when it came along. And so they had ended up in dull, sleepy Lyndgarth.

A weekend in the country now and again suited Marjorie perfectly—that was what it was there for, after all, unless you were a farmer, a painter or a poet—but this felt more like incarceration. She hadn't been able to find a job, and the new neighbours weren't particularly friendly, either. Someone told her you have to winter out two years before you are accepted, but she didn't think she could stand it that long. And the fact that Roger was in his element didn't help much either. She was bored stiff. She didn't have children to fill her days like Jane. Still, at least their visit had brought a welcome break to the routine. She should be grateful for that. She would have been if it hadn't been for Roger seizing his chance to pontificate.

"The Pennine mines are the only ones in Yorkshire. Know why? It's because the lead ore occurs in Carboniferous rocks—the Yoredale Series and Millstone Grit. The ores aren't exactly *part* of the rocks, you understand, but . . ."

At last they reached the old smelting mill, not much more than a pile of stones, really, and not much bigger than a detached house. Most of the roof had collapsed, leaving only the weatherworn beams. Inside, sunlight shone through the roof and through the gaps between the stones onto the ruined ore hearths and furnaces, and picked out the motes of dust they kicked up. Marjorie had never liked the old mill. It was a dry, smelly, spidery sort of place.

Over in one corner, the dusty ground was darkened, as if some wandering drunk had been sick there.

"In the earlier mills," Roger went on, "they used to burn off the sulphur first, changing the lead to oxide. Of course, for that you need places to roast then reduce the ore. But by the time this mill was built, they'd invented vertical furnaces that used bellows . . ."

They all obediently followed his pointing stick and oohed and aahed. He should have been a bloody tour guide, Marjorie thought.

Suddenly, Jane looked nervously around the mill. "Where's Megan?" she asked.

"Probably playing outside," Marjorie said, noting the anxiety in her voice. "Don't worry, I'll find her. I've heard this bit before, anyway." Roger glared at her as she left.

Thankful to be out of the gloomy smelting mill and away from the droning echo of Roger's voice, Marjorie shielded her eyes and looked around. Megan was clambering over a pile of scree towards the opening of the flue. Marjorie knew all about the flue, because she'd heard Roger read her the relevant sections from the book several times out loud. "Listen to this, darling . . ." But the only thing she needed to know right now was that it could be dangerous.

Built originally to extract and condense the fumes of the smelting process and carry them far away from the immediate area, the flue was a bricked hump about two hundred yards long. It looked very much like a tall factory chimney that had fallen on its side and half buried itself in the gentle slope of the hillside. Because it was old, sections of the arched roof had collapsed here and there, and more were liable to follow suit at any moment. It had originally ended at a vertical chimney on the hilltop, designed to carry the lead fumes away, but that had long since fallen down.

Megan was happily scrambling along over the scree to the dark entrance. Marjorie set off after her. "Megan!" she shouted. "Come away!" Behind, she noticed that the others had come out of the smelting mill and stood watching a few yards away. "It's all right," Marjorie said over her shoulder. "I'll catch up with her before she gets inside. It's quite safe out here."

Maybe she had underestimated the six-year-old's speed and nimbleness, she thought, as she struggled over the rocks, trying not to trip up. But she made it. Megan got to the verge of the flue just as Marjorie managed to grab her shoulder.

"It's not safe, Megan," she said, sitting down to catch her breath. "You mustn't go in there." As she looked into the black hole, she shivered. Far up ahead, she could see the tiny coin of light where the flue ended. Its floor was scattered with bits of stone, most likely fallen from the arched roof. A few yards or so in, she noticed a large, oddly-shaped hump. It was probably a collapsed section, but something about it made her curious. It looked somehow deliberate, not quite as random as the other scatterings. She packed Megan off down the rise to join her parents and crawled into the opening.

"Where do you think you're going?" she heard Roger calling. "Marjorie! Come back!" But she ignored him. Just for a moment, the sunlight had flashed on something ahead.

It was dark inside the flue, despite the light from behind her, and she hurt her knees as she crawled over the bed of flinty stones. She tried to stand, back bent low. The place smelled dank and foisty, and she tried to keep her breathing to an absolute minimum. She remembered Roger saying that the poisonous fumes of the volatilized lead condensed on the flue walls, which boys were employed to scrape at regular intervals. What a job that would be, she thought, crawling through here day after day and scraping lead off the stone.

When she arrived about six feet away from the hump, she could still make out nothing clearly. If she edged to one side and moulded her back against the curve of the wall, some light passed her and provided a faint outline. Then Roger blocked the entrance and yelled for her to come back.

"Get out of the way," she shouted. "I can't see a bloody thing!"

Oddly enough, Roger did as she asked. A faint wash of light picked out some of the details in the heap of stones, and as soon as Marjorie saw the small hand sticking out of the pile, she screamed and started to turn. As she did so, she stumbled and kicked some small stones near the body. A cloud of flies rose out of the heap and buzzed angrily up the flue.

II

"We've had three confessions already," said Gristhorpe, as Banks took the Helmthorpe road out of Eastvale. Roger Bingham's message had been vague, and both avoided speculating whether the body of Gemma Scupham had been discovered. "One of them told us at great length exactly what he'd done with Gemma and how much he enjoyed it. I tell you, Alan, sometimes it's a bloody shame you can't lock a man up for his thoughts." He ran a hand through his unruly grey hair. "Good God, did I really say that? Shows how much this business is getting to me. Anyway, we got him for wasting police time instead. He'll do six months with any luck."

"The searchers turn up anything yet?" Banks asked.

Gristhorpe shook his head. "They're doing the area east of the estate now, past the railway tracks. We've taken on a few civilian volunteers. And we've interviewed all the known local child-molesters. Nothing there."

At Fortford, Banks turned left by the pub and passed between the Roman fort and the village green.

"Anything on the car?" Gristhorpe asked.

After his visit to Brenda Scupham the previous afternoon, Banks had caught up with his paperwork on the case, helped Susan with the house-to-house and Richmond check the garages and car-rental agencies.

"Not so far. We've got through most of the garages and agencies. Phil's still at it."

"Well, maybe it was their own car, after all," said Gristhorpe. "They've vanished into thin air, Alan. How can they do that?"

"Either very clever or very lucky, I suppose. No one on the estate was very communicative, either," he went on. "I only did a couple of streets with Susan, but she said the others were no different. And she had another chat with that Mr Carter at number sixteen. Waste of time, she said. He just wanted to talk about Dunkirk. People are scared, you know, even when we show them our warrant cards."

"I don't blame them," said Gristhorpe.

"But I reckon if it *had* happened to someone else around there, they'd speak up now."

"You never know with people, Alan. Remember the old Yorkshire saying, 'There's nowt so queer as folk.'"

Banks laughed. At the junction in Relton, he turned right. A slow-moving tractor in front pulled over to the side and gave him just enough space to squeeze by. "I've been on the phone to Belfast, too," he added. "The lads over there spent most of yesterday with Terry Garswood, Gemma's father, and they're certain he had nothing to do with it. For a start, he was on duty that day and couldn't have got away without someone noticing, and apparently he had neither the inclination nor the money to hire someone else to steal her for him."

"Well, look on the bright side," said Gristhorpe. "At least that's one less lead to follow. There it is." He pointed out of the car window. "Pull in here."

They were on Mortsett Lane, about halfway between Relton and Gratly, below the looming bulk of Tetchley Fell. Banks pulled up on the gravelled lay-by next to a Range Rover and looked at the narrow track. There was no way you could get a car up there, he thought. The stony path was only about three feet wide, and it was bordered by small boulders and chips of flint that would play havoc with tires. Ahead, he could just make out the partially collapsed roof of the smelting mill over the rise.

He had seen the place before, but from a different perspective. Looking down from the Roman road that cut diagonally across the fell, he had been impressed by the range of colour, from pale yellow to dark green, purple and grey, and by the flue hugging the hillside like a long stone tunnel. Now, as they neared the mill, all he could see was the murky opening to his left and the group of people huddled together by the mill to his right.

"Which one of you is Mr Bingham?" Gristhorpe asked, after he had introduced Banks and himself.

"I am," said a countryish type, in gear far too expensive and inappropriate for the short walk. "My wife, Marjorie, found the . . . er . . . Well, I remembered there was a phonebox back down on the road."

Gristhorpe nodded and turned to the woman. "Did you disturb anything?"

She shook her head. "No. I never touched . . . I . . . When I saw the hand I ran back. And the flies . . . Oh, my God . . . the flies . . ."

Her husband took her hand and she buried her face in his shoulder. The other couple looked on sadly, the man with a grim set to his mouth and the woman stroking her child's golden hair. Banks noticed a head over her shoulder, a sleeping baby in a backpack.

Gristhorpe turned to Banks. "Shall we?"

Banks nodded and followed him over the scree. They had to walk carefully, as many of the stones wobbled under them. Finally, they managed to scrabble to the gloomy semi-circle and peer inside. Gristhorpe brought the torch out of his pocket and shone it ahead. They could easily see the heap that Marjorie Bingham had mentioned, but couldn't pick out any details from so far away. Gristhorpe had to bend almost double to walk, which made it very difficult to negotiate a path through the rubble that littered the flue's floor. Banks, being a little shorter, found it easier. But he felt uncomfortable.

He had never liked caves; they always seemed to bring out a latent sense of claustrophobia. Once he and Sandra had visited Ingleton and gone in the caves there. When he had to stoop and almost crawl on his belly to get under a low overhang, he had felt the weight of the mountain pressing on his back and had to struggle to keep his breathing regular. The flue wasn't as bad as that, but he could still feel the heavy darkness pushing at him from all sides.

Gristhorpe walked a few feet behind him with the torch. Its beam danced over lead-stained stones, which glistened here and there as if snails had left their slimy tracks. They went as cautiously as they could in order not to destroy any forensic evidence, but it was impossible to pick a narrow path through the rubble of the flue. Finally, they stood close enough, and Gristhorpe's torch lit on a small hand raised from a heap of rocks. They could see nothing else of the body, as it had been entirely covered by stones.

As they stood and looked at the hand, a gust of wind blew and made a low moaning sound in the flue like someone blowing over the lip of a bottle. Gristhorpe turned off the torch and they headed back for the entrance. They had probably disturbed too much already, but they had to verify that there was indeed a body on the site. So often people simply *thought* they had found a corpse, and the truth turned out to be different. Now they had to follow procedure.

First they would call the police surgeon to ascertain that the body was indeed dead. No matter how obvious it might appear, no matter even if the body is decapitated or chopped into a dozen pieces, it is not dead until a qualified doctor says it is.

Then the SOCO team would arrive and mark off the area with their white plastic tape. It might not seem necessary in such an isolated place, but the searching of a crime scene was a very serious business, and there were guidelines to follow. With Vic Manson in charge, they would take photographs and search the area around the body, looking for hairs, fibres, anything that the killer may have left behind. And then, when the photographs had been taken, the doctor would take a closer look at the body. In this case, he might move aside a few stones and look for obvious causes of death. There was nothing more that Banks and Gristhorpe could do until they at least had some information on the identity of the victim.

Banks gulped in the fresh, bright air as they emerged into daylight. He felt as if he had just made an ascent from the bottom of a deep, dark ocean with only seconds to spare before his oxygen ran out. Gristhorpe stood beside him and stretched, rubbing his lower back and grimacing.

"I'll call it in," said Banks.

Gristhorpe nodded. "Aye. And I'll have another word with this lot over here." He shook his head slowly. "Looks like we've found her."

There was nothing to do but wait after Banks had made the call over the police radio. Gristhorpe got Marjorie Bingham's story, then let the shocked group go home.

Banks leaned against the rough stone of the smelting mill and lit a cigarette as Gristhorpe walked carefully around the flue entrance looking down at the ground. It was quiet up there except for the occasional mournful call of a curlew gliding over the moorland, a cry that harmonized strangely with the deep sigh of the breeze blowing down the flue and ruffling the blades of grass on the hill-side. The sky was the whitish blue of skim milk, and it set off the browns, greens and yellows of the desolate landscape. Beyond the mill, Banks could see the purple-grey cleft of a dried-up stream-bed cutting across the moorland.

Gristhorpe, kneeling to peer at the grass a few yards to the right of the flue entrance, beckoned Banks over. Banks knelt beside him and looked at the rusty smear on the grass.

"Blood?" he said.

"Looks like it. If so, maybe she was killed out here and they dragged her into the flue to hide the body."

Banks looked at the blood again. "It doesn't look like much, though, does it?" he said. "And I'd say it's smeared rather than spilled."

"Aye," said Gristhorpe, standing. "Like someone wiped off a knife or something. We'll leave it to the SOCOs."

The first to arrive was Peter Darby, the photographer. He came bounding up the track, fresh-faced, two cameras slung around his neck and a square metal case at his side. If it's Gemma Scupham in there, Banks thought, he won't look so bloody cheerful when he comes out.

Darby went to take some preliminary photographs, starting with the stained grass, on Gristhorpe's suggestion, then the flue entrance, then carefully making his way inside. Banks could see the bulbs flash in the black hole as Darby took his pictures. When he'd finished in the flue, he took more photographs in and around the smelting mill.

About half an hour after Peter Darby, Dr Glendenning came huffing and puffing up the path.

"At least I didn't need a bloody truss to get here this time," he said, referring to the occasion when they had all been winched up the side of Rawley Force to get to a body in a hanging valley. He pointed towards the flue. "In there, you said?"

Gristhorpe nodded.

"Hmphh. Why the bloody hell do you keep on finding bodies in awkward places, eh? I'm not getting any younger, you know. It's not even my job. You could get a bloody GP to pronounce the body dead at the scene."

Banks shrugged. "Sorry." Glendenning was a Home Office pathologist, one of the best in the country, and both Banks and Gristhorpe knew he would be offended if they didn't call him to the scene first.

"Aye, well . . ." He turned towards the entrance.

They accompanied Glendenning as he picked his way over the scree, complaining all the way, and ducked to enter the flue. Banks held the torch this time. It didn't provide much light, but the SOCOs had been instructed to bring bottled-gas lamps as it would be impossible to get a van with a generator up the narrow track.

Glendenning knelt for a while, sniffing the air and glancing around the inside of the flue, then he touched the small hand and moved it, muttering to himself. Next he took out a mercury thermometer and held it close to the body, measuring the air temperature.

The entrance of the flue darkened and someone called out. It was Vic Manson, fingerprint expert and leader of the SOCO team. He came up the passage with a gas-lamp and soon the place was full of light. It cast eerie shadows on the slimy stone walls and gave an unreal sheen to the heap of stones on the ground. Manson called back to one of his assistants and asked him to bring up some large plastic bags.

Then everyone stood silent, breath held, as the men started to lift the stones and place them in the bags for later forensic investigation. A few spiders scurried away and a couple of obstinate flies buzzed the men angrily then zigzagged off.

Banks leaned against the wall, his back bent into its curve. One stone, two, three . . . Then a whole arm became visible.

Banks and Gristhorpe moved forward. They crouched over and looked at the small hand, then both saw the man's wristwatch and frayed sleeve of a grey bomber-jacket. "It's not her," Gristhorpe whispered. "Jesus Christ, it's not Gemma Scupham."

Banks felt the relief, too. He had always clung to a vague hope that Gemma might still be alive, but the discovery of the body had seemed to wreck all that. Nobody else in the dale had been reported missing. And now, as Manson and his men picked stone after stone away, they looked down at what was obviously the body of a young man, complete with moustache. A young man with unusually small hands. But, Banks asked himself, if it isn't Gemma Scupham, then who the hell is it?

III

Jenny darted into the Eastvale Regional Headquarters at two o'clock, just in time for her appointment with Banks. She always seemed to be rushing these days, she thought, as if she were a watch a few minutes slow always trying to catch up. She wasn't even really late this time.

"Miss Fuller?"

Jenny walked over to the front desk. "Yes?"

"Message from Detective Superintendent Gristhorpe, miss. Says he's on his way. You can wait in his office if you wish."

Jenny frowned. "But I thought I was to see Alan—Chief Inspector Banks?"

"He's at the scene."

"What scene?"

"It looks like a murder scene. I'm sorry I can't say any more, miss. We don't really know anything yet."

"That's all right," Jenny said. "I'll wait."

"Very well. The superintendent's office—"

"I know where it is, thanks."

Jenny poured herself some coffee from the machine at the bottom of the stairs then went up to Gristhorpe's office. She had been there before, but never alone. It was larger than Alan's, and much better appointed. She had heard that rank determines the level of luxury in policemen's offices, but she also knew that the department itself was hardly likely to supply such things as the large teak desk, or the matching bookcases that covered one wall. The cream and burgundy patterned carpet, perhaps—it was hardly an expensive one, Jenny noticed—but not the shaded desk lamp and the books that lined the shelves.

She glanced over the titles. They were mostly works of criminology and law—the essential *Archbold's Criminal Pleading, Evidence &*

Practice and Glaister's *Medical Jurisprudence and Toxicology* in addition to several other technical and forensic texts—but there were also books on history, fishing, cricket, a few novels and Sir Arthur Quiller-Couch's edition of *The Oxford Book of English Verse*. What surprised Jenny most was the number of mystery paperbacks: about four feet of them, mostly Margery Allingham, Ngaio Marsh, Edmund Crispin and Michael Innes.

"That's just the overflow," a voice said behind her, making her jump. "The rest are at home."

"I didn't hear you come in," Jenny said, putting her hand to her chest. "You startled me."

"We coppers are a light-footed lot," Gristhorpe said, with a twinkle in his baby-blue eyes. "Have to be to catch the villains. Sit down."

Jenny sat. "This murder, I couldn't help thinking . . . It's not . . . ?"

"No, it's not, thank God. It's bad enough, though. We don't know who the victim is yet. I left Alan at the scene. I decided to stick with the Gemma Scupham case and let him handle the murder."

Jenny had never felt entirely at ease with Superintendent Gristhorpe, but she didn't know why. He seemed very much his own man—self-contained, strong, determined—and he projected a solid, comforting presence. But something made her feel awkward. Perhaps, she speculated, it was the underlying sense of isolation she sensed, the fortress he seemed to have built around his feelings. She knew about his wife's death from cancer several years ago, and guessed that perhaps a part of him had died with her. Susan Gay, she remembered, had said that she also felt uncomfortable with him, yet he had a reputation as a kind and compassionate man.

His physical presence was difficult to ignore, too. He was a big man—bulky, but not fat—with bushy eyebrows and an unruly thatch of grey hair. With his reddish, pock-marked complexion and the slightly hooked nose, he was very much the dalesman, she thought, if indeed there was such a creature, weathered and moulded by the landscape.

"I did a bit of preliminary research last night," Jenny began. "I *can* probably give you a capsule version of the paedophile types."

Gristhorpe nodded. As she spoke, Jenny somehow felt that he probably knew more than she did about the subject. After all, some of his books dealt with criminal psychology and forensic psychiatry, and he was reputed to be well read. But she didn't feel he was simply being polite when he let her speak. No, he was listening all right, listening for something he might not have come across or thought of himself. Watching her carefully with those deceptively innocent eyes.

She balanced her black-rimmed reading-glasses on her nose and took her notes out of her briefcase. "Basically, there are four types of paedophile," she began. "And so far it doesn't seem like your couple fits any. The first kind is someone who hasn't really been able to establish satisfactory relationships with his peers. It's the most common type, and he only feels sexually comfortable with children. He usually *knows* his victim, maybe a family friend, or even a relation."

Gristhorpe nodded. "What about age, roughly?"

"Average age is about forty."

"Hmm. Go on."

"The second type is someone who seems to develop normally but finds it increasingly difficult to adjust to adult life—work, marriage, et cetera. Feels inadequate, often turns to drink. Usually the marriage, if there is one, breaks down. With this type, something sets things in motion. He reaches a kind of breaking-point. Maybe his wife or girlfriend is having an affair, intensifying his feelings of inadequacy. This kind doesn't usually know his victim. It may be someone he sees passing by in a car or something. Again, not much like the situation you described at Brenda Scupham's."

"No," agreed Gristhorpe. "But we've got to keep an open mind at this point."

"And I think we can dismiss the third type, too," Jenny went on. "This is someone who generally had his formative sexual experiences with young boys in an institution of some kind."

"Ah," said Gristhorpe. "Public school?"

Jenny looked up at him and smiled. "I suppose that would qualify." She turned back to her notes. "Anyway, this type is generally a homosexual paedophile, the type that cruises the streets for victims or uses male prostitutes."

"And the last?"

"The wild card," Jenny said. "The psychopathic paedophile. It's hard to pin this type down. He's in search of new sexual thrills, and pain and fear are generally involved. He'll hurt his victims, introduce sharp objects into the sexual organs, that kind of thing. The more aggressive he gets, the more excited he becomes. A person like this usually has a history of anti-social behaviour."

Gristhorpe held the bridge of his nose and grunted.

"I'm sorry I can't really be of any more help yet," Jenny said, "but I'm working on it. The really odd thing, as I told Alan, is that there were two of them, a man and a woman. I want to look a bit further into that aspect."

Gristhorpe nodded. "Go ahead. And please don't underestimate your usefulness."

Jenny smiled at him and shuffled her notes back into the briefcase.

"This stuff the newspapers were on about," Gristhorpe went on, "organized gangs of paedophiles, what do you think of that?"

Jenny shook her head. "It doesn't figure. Paedophiles are like other sexual deviants, essentially loners, solo operators. And most of the allegations of ritual abuse turned out to be social workers' fantasies. Of course, when you get abuse in families, people close ranks. They might look like organized gangs, but they're not really. Paedophiles simply aren't the types to form clubs, except . . ."

"Except what?"

"I was thinking of kiddie porn, child prostitution and the like. It's around, it happens, there's no denying it, and that takes a bit of organization."

"Videos, magazines?"

"Yes. Even snuff films."

"We're doing our best," Gristhorpe said. "I've been in touch with the paedophile squad. Those rings are hard to penetrate, but if anything concerning Gemma turns up, believe me, we'll know about it."

Jenny stood up. "I'll do a bit more research."

"Thanks." Gristhorpe walked over to open the door for her.

Jenny dashed back to her car, got in and turned her key in the ignition. Suddenly she paused. She couldn't remember where she was supposed to go or why she was in such a hurry. She checked her appointment book and then racked her brains to see if she had forgotten anything. No. The truth was, she had nowhere to go and no reason at all to hurry.

IV

Banks breathed deeply, grateful for the fresh air outside the flue. Claustrophobia was bad enough, but what he had just seen made it even worse.

After Gristhorpe had gone to meet Jenny, the SOCOs had slowly and carefully removed all the stones from the body of a man in his mid- to late-twenties. When they had finished, Dr Glendenning bent forward to see what he could find out. First, he opened the bomber-jacket and cursed when he had to stop the tangle of greyish intestines from spilling out of the man's shirt. A couple more flies finally gave up the ghost and crawled out from under the tubing and took off indignantly. The wind moaned down the flue. Quickly, Banks had searched the dead man's pockets: all empty.

Banks lit a cigarette; fresh air wasn't enough to get the taste of the flue and of death out of his mouth. The smell was difficult to pin down. Sickly, sweet, with a slight metallic edge, it always seemed to linger around him like an aura for days after attending the scene of a murder.

Glendenning had been crouched in the flue alone for over half an hour now, and the SOCOs were still going over the ground inside the taped-off area: every blade of glass, every stone.

Banks wandered into the smelting mill and looked at the ruins of the furnace and the ore hearth while he waited, trying to put the first shocking glimpse of those spilled intestines out of his mind. He had seen the same thing once before, back in London, and it wasn't something even the most hardened policeman forgot easily.

He stared at the dullish brown patch in the corner, marked off by the SOCOs as blood. The murder, they said, had probably taken place in the mill.

At last, Glendenning emerged from the flue, red in the face. He stood upright and dusted his jacket where it had come into contact with the stones. A cigarette dangled from his mouth.

"I suppose you want to know it all right away, don't you?" he said to Banks, sitting on a boulder outside the smelting mill. "Time of death, cause of death, what he had for breakfast?"

Banks grinned. "As much as you can tell me."

"Aye, well, that might be a bit more than usual in this case. Given the temperature, I'd say rigor mortis went basically according to the norm. It was just after two o'clock when I got the chance to have a really good look at him. Allowing, say, two to three hours for rigor to start, then about ten or twelve to spread, I'd say he was killed sometime after dark last night, but not much later than ten o'clock. His body temperature confirms it, too. Is that good enough for you?"

Banks said it was, thank you very much, doctor, and mentioned the blood in the smelting mill.

"You're probably right about that," Glendenning said. "I'll check post-mortem lividity later when I get him on the table, but as far as I could tell there was no blood around the body, and there would be, given a wound like that."

"What about cause of death?"

"That's not difficult. Looks like he was gutted. You saw that for yourself." Glendenning lit a new cigarette from the stub of his old one. "It's an especially vicious crime," he went on. "In the first place, to do something like that you have to get very close."

"Would it take a lot of strength?"

"Aye, a fair bit to drag the knife up when it's stuck so deeply in. But not a superman. Given a sharp enough knife. What are you getting at? Man or woman?"

"Something like that."

"You know how I hate guesswork, laddie, but I'd go for a moderately strong man or an exceptionally strong woman."

"Thanks. First we'll check all the female bodybuilders in Yorkshire. Left-handed or right?"

"I should be able to tell you later when I get a good look at the entry point and the direction of the slit."

"What about the weapon?"

"Again, you'll have to wait. All I can say now is it looks like a typical upthrust knife wound. Have you made arrangements for the removal?"

Banks nodded.

"Good. I'll get to it as soon as I can." Glendenning stood up and headed down the track to his car. Banks looked at his watch: almost three o'clock and he hadn't had lunch yet. Maybe an hour or so more up here and he'd be able to leave the scene for a local constable to guard. He called Vic Manson over.

"Any sign of the murder weapon?"

"Not so far. I don't think it's around here. The lads have almost finished the third grid search, and they'd have found it by now."

Banks walked back over to the smelting mill and leaned against the wall watching the men examine the scree outside the flue entrance. "A particularly vicious crime," Dr Glendenning had said. Indeed it was. It was hard to believe, thought Banks, that in such beautiful countryside on such a fine autumn evening, one human being had got so close to another that he could watch, and perhaps even savour the look in his victim's eyes as he thrust a sharp knife in his groin and slowly dragged it up through the stomach to the chest.

V

Brenda Scupham lay alone in bed that night. Les was out at the pub. Not that she really cared. These days he was practically worse than useless. He mostly kept out of her way, and that suited her fine. The only thing was she didn't really want to be alone tonight. A nice warm body to love her and hold her would help take her mind off the bad things she couldn't seem to stop herself from feeling.

She hadn't wanted Gemma, it was true. But things like that happened. She had done her best. At first, there always seemed to be so much to do: changing nappies, feeding, scraping and saving for new clothes. And the sleepless nights she had listened to Gemma cry from her cot, leaving her till she cried herself to sleep because her own mother had said you shouldn't make a habit of being at a baby's beck and call. Well, she should know all about that, Brenda thought.

Even as she got older, Gemma had got in the way, too. Every time Brenda had a man over, she had to explain the child. Nobody stayed with her when they found out she had a kid. One night was the best she could expect from most, then a hasty exit, usually well before dawn, and Gemma there wailing away.

Brenda understood women who had beaten or killed their children. It happened all the time. They could drive you to that. One night, she remembered with shame, she had wrapped three-month-old Gemma in blankets and left her on the steps of the Catholic church. She hadn't been home five minutes before guilt sent her racing back to reclaim the bundle. Luckily, nobody else had got there first.

But no matter what those policemen tried to say, she had never abused Gemma. Some mothers sat their children on the elements of electric cookers, poured boiling water on them, locked them in the cellar without food or drink until they died of dehydration. Brenda would never have done anything like that. She put up with Gemma and took her pleasure when she could. True, she had left the child alone for visits to the pub. But nothing had ever happened to her. Also true, she never had much time to spend with her, what with the odd bit of waitressing she did on the sly to eke out her social. Meals had occasionally been forgotten, old clothes left unwashed too long. Gemma herself, like most kids, was not over-fond of bath-time, and she had never complained about going without a bath for a couple of weeks.

What upset Brenda most as she lay there alone in the dark was accepting that she had never really *liked* her child. Oh, she had got used to her, all right, but there was something secretive and isolated about Gemma, something alien that Brenda felt she could never reach. And there was something creepy about the way she skulked around the place. Many a time Brenda had felt Gemma's accusing, woebegone eyes on her. Even now, alone in the dark, she could feel

Gemma's eyes looking at her in that way. Still, you didn't *choose* your child, no more than she chose to be born. She wasn't made to order.

But now Gemma was gone, Brenda felt guilty for feeling relieved when Miss Peterson and Mr Brown took her away. Why did it have to be so complicated? Why couldn't they have been real social workers like they said they were? Then she wouldn't have to feel so guilty for being relieved. Now she couldn't even bear to think about what they might have done to Gemma. She shivered. Gemma must be dead. Brenda only hoped it had happened quickly and painlessly and that soon the police would find out everything and leave her alone to get her grieving done.

Again she replayed what she could remember of the social workers' visit. Maybe she had been a fool for believing them, but they *had* looked so real, and they *had* been so convincing. She knew she had neglected Gemma and that she was wrong to do so, however much she couldn't help herself. She knew she was guilty, especially after what happened the week before. But they surely couldn't have known about that? No, they were right. She had to let them take the child. She found herself hoping, after the door closed, that they would decide to keep her or find her a good home. It would be best for everyone that way.

And then there was Les. She remembered defending him to the police that morning, saying he wasn't much but he was better than nothing. She wasn't even sure that was true any longer. Mostly, she'd been thinking of sex. He used to do it three, four times a night, if he hadn't had a skinful of ale, and she couldn't get enough of him. He had made her laugh, too. But lately all the passion had gone. It happened, she knew, and you became nothing more than a maid, your home no more than a hotel room.

She turned on her side and put her hand between her legs, then began gently stroking herself with her fingers. It would help her forget, she thought, rubbing harder. Forget her foolishness, forget her guilt, forget Gemma. Gemma, precious stone, name stolen from an old schoolfriend whose serene beauty she had always envied.

Just before the climax flooded her, an image of Gemma going out of the door with Mr Brown and Miss Peterson appeared in her mind's eye. As she came, it receded, like someone waving goodbye from a train window.

FOUR

I

At ten past eleven on Saturday morning, Banks stood at his office
window, coffee in hand, and looked down on the market square. It
was another beautiful day—the fifth in a row—with a pale blue sky
and high wispy clouds. It was also four days since Gemma
Scupham's abduction.

Down in the cobbled square, the market was in full swing.
Tourists and locals browsed the stalls, where vendors dealt in
everything from clothes and used books to car accessories and
small electrical gadgets. As Banks watched them unload new
stock from the vans, he speculated how much of the goods were
stolen, fallen off the back of a lorry. Most of the things for sale
were legitimate, of course—over-production or sub-standard
stuff rejected by a company's quality control and sold at slightly
above cost—but a busy market was an ideal place for getting rid
of hot property.

There would be nothing from the Fletcher's warehouse job,
though; televisions and stereos attracted too much attention at
outdoor markets. Mostly, they would be sold by word of mouth,
through pubs and video retailers.

Banks thought again about how smooth the operation had
been. The burglars had cut through a chain-link fence, drugged a
guard dog, and disabled the alarm system. They had then loaded a
van up with electrical goods, taken off into the night and never
been seen since. It would have taken at least three men, he speculated, and Les Poole was probably one of them. But there were far
more serious things to think about now. At least Poole was under

surveillance, and any step he made out of line would soon come to Banks's attention.

The traffic along Market Street slowed almost to a standstill as yet more tourists poured into town. Because it was market day, parking was a problem. Drivers would spend an extra half-hour cruising around the narrow streets looking for a parking space. It would be a busy day for the traffic police.

Banks opened the window a couple of inches. He could hear the honking horns and the babble of voices down in the square, and the smell of fresh bread drifted up from the bakery on Market Street, mingled with exhaust fumes.

At their morning conference, Gristhorpe had assigned Banks and DC Susan Gay to the lead-mine murder; Gristhorpe himself, along with DS Richmond, would pursue the Gemma Scupham investigation, with Jenny Fuller acting as consultant. With each day that went by, the pressure increased. Parents were scared; they were keeping their children home from school. Ever since Gemma had disappeared, police forces county-wide had been knocking on doors and conducting searches of wasteland and out-of-the-way areas. The surprising thing was that nothing had come to light so far. The way it seemed, Gemma had disappeared from the face of the earth. Despite his reassignment, Banks knew he would have to keep up to date on the case. He couldn't forget Gemma Scupham that easily.

For a moment, he found himself wondering if the two cases could be connected in some way. It was rare that two serious crimes should happen in Swainsdale at about the same time. Could it be more than mere coincidence? He didn't see how, but it was something worth bearing in mind.

His first task was to identify the body they had found. Certainly a photograph could be published; clothing labels sometimes helped; then there were medical features—an operation scar, birthmark—and dental charts. It would be easy enough to track down such information if the man were local, but practically impossible if he were a stranger to the area. Banks had already sent DC Gay to make enquiries in Gratly and Relton, the nearest villages to the mine, but he didn't expect much to come of that. At best, someone might have seen a car heading towards the mine.

A red van had got itself wedged into the junction of Market Street and the square, just in front of the Queen's Arms, and irate motorists started honking. The van's owner kept on unloading boxes of tights and women's underwear, oblivious to the angry tourists. One man got out and headed towards him.

Banks turned away from the window and went over the lead-mine scene in his mind. The victim had probably been murdered in the smelting mill, an out-of-the-way place. His pockets had been emptied and his body had been hidden in the flue, which few people ever entered due to the danger of falling stones. Safe to assume, Banks thought, that the killer didn't want the body found for a while. That made sense, as most leads in an investigation occur in the first twenty-four hours. But the body *had* been found much sooner than the killer expected, and that might just give Banks an edge.

Just as Banks was about to leave his office in search of more coffee, the phone rang. It was Vic Manson from the forensic lab near Wetherby.

"You've been quick," Banks said. "What have you got?"

"Lucky. You want to know who he is?"

"You're sure?"

"Uh-huh. I'd like to claim brilliant deduction, but it was routine."

"Fingerprints?" Banks guessed. It was the first thing they would check, and while most people's prints weren't on file anywhere, a lot were. Another break.

"Got it. Seems he did a stretch in Armley Jail. Tried to con an old lady out of her life's savings, but she turned out to be smarter than him. Name's Carl Johnson. He's from Bradford, but he's been living in your neck of the woods for a year or so. Flat 6, 59 Calvin Street."

Banks knew the street. It was in the north-eastern part of Eastvale, where a few of the large old houses had been converted into cheap flats.

"You can get your man to pull his file from the computer," Manson said.

"Thanks, Vic. I'll do that. Keep at it."

"Have I any bloody choice? We're snowed under. Anyway, I'll get back to you soon as we find out any more."

Banks hurried over to Richmond's office. Richmond sat over his keyboard, tapping away, and Banks waited until he reached a point when he could pause. Then he explained what Vic Manson had said.

"No problem," said Richmond. "Just let me finish entering this report in the database and I'll get you a printout."

"Thanks, Phil."

Banks grabbed a coffee and went back to his office to wait. The market square was teeming with people now, lingering at stalls, feeling the goods, listening to the vendors' pitches, watching the man who juggled plates as if he were a circus performer.

Carl Johnson. The name didn't ring a bell. If he had been in London, Banks would have got out on the street to question informers and meet with undercover officers. Someone would have heard a whisper, a boast, a rumour. But in Eastvale no real criminal underbelly existed. And he certainly knew of no one capable of killing in the way Carl Johnson had been killed. There were low-lifes like Les Poole, of course, but Poole was a coward at heart, and whatever he was, he wasn't a murderer. Still, it might be worth mentioning Johnson's name to him, just to see the reaction.

Had the killer not known about Johnson's record, that he would be easy to identify? Certainly whoever it was had gone to great lengths to hide the body, but he hadn't tried to destroy the finger-prints, as some killers did. Perhaps he was squeamish—unlikely, given the way he'd killed Johnson—or he was careless. Careless or cocky. Whatever the reason, Banks at least had something to go on: Flat 6, 59 Calvin Street. That was the place to start.

II

If Gristhorpe had expected inverted crosses, black candles, penta-grams and ceremonial robes, he couldn't have been more mistaken. Melville Westman's Helmthorpe cottage was as ordinary as could be: teal wallpaper with white curlicue patterns, beige three-piece suite, television, music centre. Sunlight poured through the windows past the white lace curtains and gave the place a bright, airy feel. The only clues to Westman's interests were to be found in the bookcase: Eliphas Levi's *Le Dogme et le Rituel de la Haute Magic*, Mathers's translation of *The Key of Solomon*, Crowley's *Magick in Theory and Practice*, *Malleus Maleficarum* and a few other books on astrology, Cabbala, the tarot, witchcraft and ritual magic. In addition, a sampler over the fireplace bore the motto, "Do what thou wilt shall be the whole of the law," in the same kind of embroidery one would expect to find such ancient saws as, "A house is built of bricks; a home is built on love."

Similarly, if Gristhorpe had expected a bedraggled, wild-eyed Charles Manson look-alike, he would have been disappointed. Westman was a dapper, middle-aged man with sparse mousy hair, dressed in a grey V-neck pullover over a white shirt, wearing equally grey pants with sharp creases. He was a short, portly man, but he had presence. It was partly in the slightly flared nostrils that gave his face a constant expression of arrogant sneering, and partly in the controlled intensity of his cold eyes.

"It took you long enough," he said to Gristhorpe, gesturing towards an armchair.

Gristhorpe sat down. "What do you mean?"

"Oh, come on, Superintendent! Let's not play games. The girl, the missing girl. I read about it in the paper."

"What's that got to do with you?"

Westman sat opposite Gristhorpe and leaned forward in his chair, linking his hands on his lap. "Nothing, of course. But you have to ask, don't you?"

"And?"

Westman smiled and shook his head slowly. "And nothing."

"Mr Westman," Gristhorpe said. "In cases like this we have to consider every possibility. If you know anything about the child's disappearance, it'd be best if you told me."

"I told you. I know nothing. Why should I?"

"We both know about your involvement in witchcraft and Satanism. Don't be naïve."

"Involvement? Witchcraft? Satanism? Superintendent, just because I practise a different religion from you, don't assume I'm some kind of monster. I'm not a Satanist, and I'm not a witch, either. Most people you would call witches are silly dabblers who appropriate the old ways and practices as an excuse for sexual excess. Ex-hippies and New Agers."

"Whatever you call yourself," Gristhorpe said, "there's a history of people like you being involved in sacrifice."

"Sacrificial virgins? Really! Again, you're confusing me with the psychopathic Satanists who use the ancient ways as an excuse. People who read too much Aleister Crowley—he *did* exaggerate, you know—and found he appealed to their sick fantasies. You find a few bloody pentagrams daubed on a wall and a bit of gibberish in Latin and you think you're dealing with the real thing. You're not."

Gristhorpe pointed towards the bookcase. "I notice you have a few Aleister Crowley books yourself. Does that make you a psychopathic Satanist?"

Westman's lips curled at the edges like an old sandwich. "Crowley has things to teach to those who understand. Do you know the purpose of magic, Superintendent?"

"Power," said Gristhorpe.

Westman sniffed. "Typical. It comes from the same root as 'magi,' wise man. The purpose of the 'Great Work' is to become God, and you dismiss it as mere human hunger for power."

Gristhorpe sighed and tried to hold onto his temper. The man's sanctimonious tone was grating on his nerves. "Mr Westman, I don't really give a damn what illusions you cling to. That's not the purpose—"

"Illusions! Superintendent, believe me, the work of the magician is far from an illusion. It's a matter of will, courage, intense study of—"

"I don't want a lecture, Mr Westman. I know enough about the subject already. I know, for example, that sacrifice is important because you regard living creatures as storehouses of energy. When you kill them, when you spill their blood, you release this energy and concentrate it. I also know it's as much a matter of blood-lust, of murderous frenzy, as it is of any practical purpose. The incense, incantations, and finally the gushing of blood. It's orgasmic, a sexual kick."

Westman waved his hand. "I can see you know nothing, Superintendent. Again, you're talking about the deviants, the charlatans."

"And," Gristhorpe went on, "a human sacrifice is the most effective of all, gives you the biggest kick. Especially the sacrifice of a pure child."

Westman pursed his lips and put his forefinger to them. He stared at Gristhorpe for a few moments, then shrugged and sat back in the chair. "Human sacrifice is rare in true magic," he said. "It's difficult enough for those who practise such arts to simply exist in such a narrow-minded world as the one we inhabit; we are hardly likely to make things worse by kidnapping children and slaughtering them."

"So you know nothing at all about Gemma Scupham?"

"Only what I read in the newspapers. And though I expected a visit, given my notoriety, as far as I can gather, I bear no resemblance to either of the suspects."

"True, but that doesn't mean you're not associated with them in some way. A lot of people don't do their own dirty work."

"Insults, is it now? Well, maybe you're right. Maybe I prepared a couple of zombies to do the job. Do you remember the Rochdale scandal, Superintendent? Ten children were taken from their parents and put into care by child-workers who believed a few wild tales about ritualistic, satanic abuse. And what happened? They were sent home. There was no evidence. Children have overactive imaginations. If some six-year-old tells you he's eaten a cat, the odds are it was a chocolate one, or some kind of animal-shaped breakfast cereal."

"I know about the Rochdale affair," Gristhorpe said, "and about what happened in Nottingham. It didn't come out at the trial, but we found out later there *was* ritual abuse involved. These kids were tortured, starved, humiliated and used as sex objects."

"But they weren't sacrificed to the devil, or any such nonsense. All these tales about organized satanic abuse were discredited. Most such abuse takes place in extended families, between family members."

"That's not the issue." Gristhorpe leaned forward. "Gemma Scupham was abducted from her home and we can't find hide nor hair of her. If she'd been killed and dumped somewhere in the dale, we'd most likely have found her now. We haven't. What does that imply to you?"

"I don't know. You're supposed to be the detective. You tell me."

"One of two things. Either she's dead and her body has been very well hidden, perhaps somewhere other than Swainsdale, or someone is keeping her alive somewhere, maybe for a part she's due to play in some ritual. That's why I'm here talking to you. And, believe me, I'd rather be elsewhere."

"I applaud your deductive abilities, Superintendent, but you'd be making better use of your time if you *were* somewhere else. I know nothing."

Gristhorpe looked around the room. "What if I were to arrange for a search warrant?"

Westman stood up. "You don't need to do that. Be my guest."

Gristhorpe did. It was a small cottage, and it didn't take him long. Upstairs was a bedroom and an office, where a computer hummed on a messy desk and a printer pushed out sheets of paper.

"I'm a systems consultant," Westman said. "It means I get to do most of my work at home. It also means I have to work weekends sometimes, too."

Gristhorpe nodded. They went downstairs and looked at the kitchen, then into the cellar, a dark, chill place with whitewashed walls, mostly used for storing coal and the various bits and pieces of an old Vincent motorcycle.

"A hobby," Westman explained. "Are you satisfied now?"

They climbed back up to the living-room. "Do you know of anyone who might be involved?" Gristhorpe asked. "For any reason?"

Westman raised his eyebrows. "Asking for help now, are you? I'd be happy to oblige, but I told you, I've no idea. I do not, have not, and never will sacrifice children, or any other human beings for that matter. I told you, I'm not a dabbler. It would take too long to explain to you about my beliefs, and you'd probably be too preju- diced to understand anyway. It's certainly not tabloid Satanism."

"But you must know people who do know about these things. These dabblers you mentioned—these Satanists, thrill-seekers—any of them around these parts?"

"Not that I know of. There are a couple of witches' covens, but they're pretty tame, and you probably know about them, anyway. Amateurs. You'd never find them sacrificing a fly, let alone a child. Their get-togethers are a bit like a church social. No, Superintendent, I think you're on the wrong track."

Gristhorpe stood up. "Maybe, Mr Westman, but I like to keep an open mind. Don't trouble yourself, I'll see myself out."

In the street, Gristhorpe breathed in the fresh air. He didn't know why he felt such distaste for Westman and his kind. After all, he had read a fair bit about the black arts and he knew there was nothing necessarily *evil* about an interest in magic. Perhaps it was his Methodist background. He had given up going to chapel years ago, but there was still an innate sense that such desire for Godlike power, whether mumbo-jumbo or not, was a sacrilege, a blasphemy against reason and common sense as much as against God.

The limestone face of Crow Scar towered over the village to the north. Today it was bright in the autumn sun, and the higher pastures were already turning pale brown. The dry-stone walls that criss-crossed the daleside shone like the ribs and vertebrae of a giant poking through the earth.

Gristhorpe walked along High Street, busy with tourists window-shopping for walking-gear and local crafts, or ramblers sitting at the wooden picnic-tables outside The Dog and Gun and The Hare and Hounds, sipping pints of Theakston's and nibbling at sandwiches. It was tempting to join them, but Gristhorpe decided to wait until he got back to Eastvale before eating a late lunch.

He turned at the fork and headed for the Helmthorpe station. It was a converted terrace house, built of local greyish limestone, and was staffed by a sergeant and two constables. Constable Weaver sat pecking away at an old manual typewriter when Gristhorpe entered. Gristhorpe remembered him from the Steadman case, the first murder they'd had in Helmthorpe in a hundred years.

Weaver looked up, blushed and walked over. "I can't seem to get used to the computer, sir," he said. "Keep giving the wrong commands."

Gristhorpe smiled. "I know what you mean. I can't help but feel like an incompetent idiot when I have to deal with the things. Still, they have their uses. Look lad, do you know Melville Westman?"

"Yes."

"Anything on him? I'm not asking for anything that might be on record, you understand, just rumours, suspicions?"

Weaver shook his head. "Not really, sir. I mean, we know he's one of those black magicians, but he's not stepped out of line in any real way. Can't say I believe in it myself, curses and whatnot."

"What about the sheep?"

"Aye, well we suspected him, all right—still do, for that matter—but there was nowt we could prove. Why, sir?"

"It might be nothing, but I'd like you to keep a discreet eye on him, if you can. And keep your ears open for gossip."

"Is this about the young lass, sir?"

"Yes. But for Christ's sake don't spread it around."

Weaver looked hurt. "Of course not, sir."

"Good. Let me know if you see or hear anything out of the ordinary, and try not to let him know you're watching. He's a canny bugger, that one is."

"Yes, sir."

Gristhorpe walked outside and headed for his car. Westman was probably telling the truth, he thought, but there had been so many revelations about the links between child abuse and satanic rituals in the past few years that he had to check out the possibility. It couldn't happen here, everyone said. But it did. His stomach rumbled. Definitely time to head back to Eastvale.

III

Banks believed you could tell a lot about people from their homes. It wasn't infallible. For example, a normally fastidious person might let things go under pressure. On the whole, though, it had always worked well for him.

When he stood in the tiny living-room of Flat 6, 59 Calvin Street and tried to figure out Carl Johnson, he found very little to go on. First, he sniffed the air: stale, dusty, with an underlying hint of rotting vegetables. It was just what one would expect of a place unoccupied for a couple of days. Then he listened. He didn't expect to hear ghosts or echoes of the dead man's thoughts, but homes had their voices, too, that sometimes whispered of past evils or remembered laughter. Nothing. His immediate impression was of a temporary resting-place, somewhere to eat and sleep. What furniture there was looked second-hand, OXFAM or jumble-sale stuff. The carpet was worn so thin he could hardly make out its pattern. There were no photos or prints on the cream painted walls; nor was there any evidence of books, not even a tattered bestseller.

The kitchen was simply a curtained-off portion of the room, with a hotplate, toaster and a little storage space. Banks found a couple of dirty pans and plates in the sink. The cupboards offered nothing more than tea-bags, instant coffee, sugar, margarine and a few cans of baked beans. There was no refrigerator, and a curdled bottle of milk stood by the sink next to some mouldy white bread and three cans of McEwan's lager.

The bedroom, painted the same drab cream as the living-room, was furnished with a single bed, the covers in disarray, pillow greasy and stained with sweat or hair-cream. Discarded clothes lay in an untidy heap on the floor. The dresser held socks and under-wear, and apart from a couple of checked shirts, sneakers, one pair of Hush Puppies, jeans and a blouson jacket, there was little else in the closet. Banks could spot no evidence of Johnson having shared his flat or bed with anyone.

Banks had never seen a place that told so little about its occu-pier. Of course, that in itself indicated a number of things: Johnson clearly didn't care about a neat, clean, permanent home; he wasn't sentimental about possessions or interested in art and literature. But these were all negatives. What *did* he care about? There was no indication. He didn't even seem to own a television or a radio. What did a man do, coming home to such surroundings? What did he think about as he sat in the creaky winged armchair with the threadbare arms and guzzled his baked beans on toast? Did he spend every evening out? At the pub? With a girlfriend?

From what Banks knew of his criminal record, Carl Johnson was thirty years old and, after a bit of trouble over "Paki-bashing" and soccer hooliganism in Bradford as a lad, he had spent three years of his adult life in prison for attempted fraud. It wasn't a distinguished life, and it seemed to have left nothing of distinction to posterity.

Banks felt oppressed by the place. He levered open a window and let some fresh air in. He could hear a baby crying in a room across the Street.

Next, he had to do a more thorough search. He had found no letters, no passport, no bills, not even a birth certificate. Surely nobody could live a life so free of bureaucracy in this day and age? Banks searched under the sofa cushions, under the mattress, over the tops of the doors, deep in the back of the kitchen and bedroom cupboards. Nothing. There aren't many hiding places in a flat, as he had discovered in his days on the drug squad, and most of them are well known to the police.

Carl Johnson's flat was no exception. Banks found the thick legal-sized envelope taped to the underside of the cistern lid—a fairly obvious place—and took it into the front room. He had been careful to handle only the edges. Now he placed it on the card table by the window and slit a corner with his penknife to see what was inside. Twenty-pound notes. A lot of them, by the looks of it. Using the knife, he tried to peel each one at a time back and add it up. It was too awkward, and he kept losing his place. Patience. He took an evidence bag from his pocket, dropped the money in and took one last look around the room.

The whole place had a smell of petty greed about it, but petty criminals of Johnson's kind didn't usually end up gutted like a fish in old lead mines. What was different about Johnson? What had he been up to? Blackmail? Banks could read nothing more from the flat, so he locked up and left.

Across the hallway, he noticed a head peeping out of Flat 4 and walked over. The head retreated and its owner tried to close the door, but Banks got a foot in.

"I didn't see anything, honest, mister," the woman said. She was about twenty-five, with straight red hair and a pasty, freckled complexion.

"What do you mean?"

"I didn't see you. You weren't here. I've got nothing. Please—"

Banks took out his warrant card. The woman put her hand to her heart. "Thank God," she said. "You just never know what might happen these days, the things you read in the papers."

"True," Banks agreed. "Why were you watching?"

"I heard you in there, that's all. It's been quiet for a while."

"How long?"

"I'm not sure. Two or three days, anyway."

"Do you know Carl Johnson?" Johnson's identity hadn't been revealed in the press yet, so the woman couldn't know he was dead.

"No, I wouldn't say I knew him. We chatted on the stairs now and then if we bumped into each other. He seemed a pleasant enough type, always a smile and a hello. What are you after, anyway? What were you doing up there? Has he done a moonlight flit?"

"Something like that."

"He didn't look like a criminal type to me." She hugged herself and shuddered. "You just can't tell, can you?"

"What did you talk about, when you met on the stairs?"

"Oh, this and that. How expensive things are getting, the weather . . . you know, just ordinary stuff."

"Did you ever meet any of his friends?"

"No. I don't really think he had any. He was a bit of a loner. I did hear voices a couple of times, but that's all."

"When? Recently?"

"Last couple of weeks, anyway."

"How many people do you think were talking?"

"Only two, I'd say."

"Could you describe the other voice?"

"I'm sorry, I wasn't really listening. I mean, it's muffled anyway, you couldn't actually hear what anyone was saying. And I had the telly on. I could only hear them in the quiet bits."

"Was it a man?"

"Oh, yes, it was another man. I'm certain about that. At least, he had a sort of deep voice."

"Thank you, Mrs . . . ?"

"Gerrard. Miss."

"Thank you, Miss Gerrard. Do you know if Mr Johnson owned a car?"

"I don't think he did. I never saw him in one, anyway."

"Do you have any idea what he did for a living?"

She looked away. "Well, he . . ."

"Look, Miss Gerrard, I don't care if he was cheating on the social or the taxman. That's not what I'm interested in."

She chewed her lower lip a few seconds, then smiled. "Well, we all do it a bit don't we? I suppose even coppers cheat on their income tax, don't they?"

Bank smiled back and put a finger to the side of his nose.

"And an important detective like yourself wouldn't be interested in something as petty as that, would he?"

Banks shook his head.

"Right," she said. "I only know because he mentioned the weather once, how nice it was to have outdoor work."

"Outdoor work?"

"Yes."

"Like what? Road work, construction?"

"Oh, no, he weren't no ditch-digger. He was a gardener, Mr Johnson was, had real green fingers."

It was amazing the skills one could learn in prison these days, Banks thought. "Where did he work?"

"Like I say, I only know because we got talking about it, how some people are so filthy rich and the rest of us just manage to scrape by. He wasn't no communist, mind you, he—"

"Miss Gerrard, do you know who he worked for?"

"Oh, yes. I do go on a bit, don't I? It was Mr Harkness, lives in that nice old house out Fortford way. Paid quite well, Mr Johnson said. But then, he could afford to, couldn't he?"

The name rang a bell. There had been a feature about him in the local rag a year or two ago. Adam Harkness, Banks remembered, had come from a local family that had emigrated to South Africa and made a fortune in diamonds. Harkness had followed in his father's footsteps, and after living for a while in Amsterdam had come back to Swainsdale in semi-retirement.

"Thank you," Banks said. "You've been very helpful."

"Have I?" She shrugged. "Oh well, always a pleasure to oblige."

Banks walked out into the street and mulled over what he had learned from Miss Gerrard. Johnson had been working for Adam Harkness, probably for cash in hand, no questions asked. That might explain the thousand or so pounds in the envelope. On the other hand, surely gardening didn't pay *that* much? And why did he hide the money? To guard against thieves, perhaps? Having sticky fingers himself, Johnson would probably be all too aware of the danger of leaving large sums of money lying around the place. Maybe he didn't have a bank account, was the kind who hid his fortune in a mattress or, in this case, under the cistern lid. But it still didn't ring true. Banks looked at his watch. Almost four in the afternoon. Time to pay Adam Harkness a visit before dinner.

IV

Detective Sergeant Philip Richmond's eyes were beginning to ache. He saved his data, then stood up and stretched, rubbing the small of his back. He'd been at it for four hours, much too long to sit staring at a screen. Probably get cancer of the eyeballs from all the radiation it emitted. They were all very well, these computers, he mused, but you had to be careful not to get carried away with them. These days, though, the more courses he took, the more he learned about computers, the better his chances of promotion were.

He walked over to the window. Luckily, the new computer room faced the market square, like Banks's office, but the window was tiny, as the place was nothing but a converted storage room for cleaners' materials. Anyway, the doctor had told him to look away from the screen into the distance occasionally to exercise his eye muscles, so he did.

Already many of the tourists were walking back to their cars—no doubt jamming up many of Eastvale's side streets and collecting a healthy amount in tickets—and some of the market stalls were closing.

He'd knock off soon, and then get himself ready for his date with Rachel Pierce. He had met her last Christmas in Barnard Castle, at the toy shop where she worked, while checking an alibi on a murder case, and they had been going steady ever since. There was still no talk of wedding bells, but if things continued going as well as they had been for much longer, Richmond knew he would seriously consider tying the knot. He had never met anyone quite as warm and as funny as Rachel before. They even shared a taste for science fiction; they both loved Philip K. Dick and Roger Zelazny. Tonight they would go and see that new horror film at the Crown—new for Eastvale, anyway, which was usually a good few months behind the rest of the country. Rachel loved scary films, and Richmond loved the way they made her cling to him. He looked at his watch. Barring emergencies, he would be with her in a couple of hours.

The phone rang.

Richmond cursed and answered it. The switchboard operator told him it was someone calling for Superintendent Gristhorpe, who was out, so she had put the call through to Richmond.

"Hello?" a woman's voice came on the line.

Richmond introduced himself. "What can I do for you?"

"Well," she said hesitantly, "I really wanted the man in charge. I called that temporary number, you know, the one you mentioned in the paper, and the constable there told me to call this number if I wanted to talk to Superintendent Gristhorpe."

Richmond explained the situation. "I'm sure I can help you," he added. "What's it about?"

"All right," she said. "The reason I'm calling you so late is that I've only just heard it from the woman who does the cleaning. She does it once a week, you see, on Saturday mornings."

"Heard what?"

"They've gone. Lock, stock and barrel. Both of them. Oh, don't get me wrong, it's not as if they aren't fully paid up or anything, and I wouldn't say they looked exactly like the couple the papers described, but it is funny, isn't it? People don't usually just take off like that without so much as a by-your-leave, not when they've paid cash in advance."

Richmond held the receiver away from his ear for a moment and frowned. Why didn't this make any sense? Was he going insane? Had the computer radiation finally eaten its way into his frontal lobes?

"Where are you calling from?" he asked.

She sounded surprised. "Eastvale, of course. My office. I'm working late."

"Your name?"

"Patricia. Patricia Cummings. But—"

"One thing at a time. You said your office. What kind of office?"

"I'm an estate agent. Randall and Palmer's, just across the square from the police station. Now—"

"All right," Richmond said. "I know the place. What are you calling about?"

"I thought I'd made myself perfectly clear, but apparently you need it spelled out."

Richmond grinned. "Yes, please. Spell it out."

"It's about that girl who disappeared, Gemma Scupham. At least it might be. That's why I wanted to speak to the man in charge. I think I might know something about the couple you're looking for, the ones who did it."

"I'll be right over," Richmond said, and hung up. He left a message at the front desk for Gristhorpe and dashed out into the market square.

FIVE

I

As Banks drove west towards Fortford again, the low sun silhouetted the trees ahead. Some of them, stripped bare by Dutch elm
disease, looked like skeletal hands clawing their way out of the
earth. An evening haze hung over Fortford and softened the edges
of the hills beyond the village. It muted the vibrant greens of the
ryegrass on the lower dalesides and washed out the browns and
greys of the upper pastures.

Banks drove into the village and passed the green, to his left,
where a group of elderly locals sat gossiping and passing the time
on a bench below the partially excavated Roman fort on the round
hillock opposite. Smoke from their pipes drifted slowly on the hazy
evening air.

It felt like a summer evening, Banks thought, and wondered just
how long the fine weather would last; not long, if you believed the
forecasters. Still, at least for now he could drive with his window
down and enjoy the fresh air, except when it was permeated by the
overripe tang of manure. Sometimes, though, a different smell
would drift in, a garden bonfire, burning vegetation acrid on the air.
He listened to Gurney's "Preludes" and felt that the piano music
possessed the same starkly beautiful quality as the songs, unmistakably Gurney, heart-rending in the way it snatched moments of
order from chaos.

At the corner, by the whitewashed sixteenth-century pub, he
turned right onto the Lyndgarth road. Way ahead, about half-way
up the daleside, he could see Lyndgarth itself, limestone cottages
clustered around a small green, and the stubby, square tower of St

Mary's. About half a mile north of the village, he could make out Gristhorpe's old grey farmhouse. Just to the left of Lyndgarth, a little lower down the hillside, stood the dark ruin of Devraulx Abbey, partially hidden by trees, looking eerie and haunted in the smoky evening light.

Banks drove only as far as the small stone bridge over the River Swain and turned left into a gravelled drive. Sheltered on all sides but the water by poplars, "Leasholme" was an ideal, secluded spot for a reclusive millionaire to retire to. Banks had phoned Adam Harkness earlier and been invited that very evening. He doubted he would find out much from Carl Johnson's employer, but he had to try.

He parked at the end of the drive beside Harkness's Jaguar. The house itself was a mix of Elizabethan and seventeenth-century styles, built mostly of limestone, with grit-stone lintels and corner-stones and a flagged roof. It was, however, larger than most, and had clearly belonged to a wealthy landowner. Over the door, the date read 1617, but Banks guessed the original structure had been there earlier. The large garden had little to show but roses that time of year, but it looked well designed and cared for. Carl Johnson's green fingers, no doubt.

Finally, irritated by the cloud of gnats that hung over him, Banks rang the bell.

Harkness opened the door a few moments later and beckoned him inside, then led him along a cavernous hallway into a room at the back of the house, which turned out to be the library. Bookcases, made of dark wood, covered three walls, flanking a heavy door in one and a stone hearth in another. A white wicker armchair faced the fourth wall, where french windows opened into the garden. The well-kept lawn sloped down to the riverbank, fringed with rushes, and just to the left, a large copper beech framed a view of the Leas, with Lyndgarth and Aldington Edge beyond, just obscuring Devraulx Abbey behind its thick foliage. The river possessed a magical quality in the fading light; slow-moving, mirror-like, it presented a perfect reflection of the reeds that grew by its banks.

"It is spectacular, isn't it?" Harkness said. "It's one of the reasons I bought the place. It's much too big for me, of course. I don't even use half the rooms."

Banks had noticed the dust in the hall and a certain mustiness to the atmosphere. Even the library was untidy, with a large desk littered with papers, pens, rubber bands and a few books placed in small piles on the floor beneath the shelves.

"How long have you been here?" Banks asked.

"Two years. I still travel a fair bit. I'm not retired yet, you know, still got a lot of life in me. But I thought it was time I deserved to take things easy, put in a bit more golf."

Harkness looked about fifty-five. He was Banks's height, with silver hair and that brick-red, lined complexion peculiar to the Englishmen who have spent years in warmer climates. He wore a white short-sleeved shirt and navy-blue trousers. The pot-belly and sagging breasts showed he wasn't a man who took much exercise off the golf course.

"Drink?"

"A small Scotch, please," Banks said.

"Sit down." Harkness offered Banks the wicker chair and pulled a swivel chair for himself from behind the desk.

Banks sat. Music played softly in the background: the Radio Three Dvorak concert, by the sound of it. He glanced at the books on the shelves and, for some reason, got the impression they were more for show than use, bought by the yard. A full set of the *Encyclopaedia Britannica*, some Book Club editions of Jane Austen and Dickens, a mail-order "Great Writers" series.

Harkness passed Banks the drink in a heavy crystal glass then joined him, carefully tugging up the creases of his trousers before he sat. "You didn't tell me very much on the telephone," he said. "How can I help you?"

"I'd just like to ask you a few questions about Carl Johnson."

Harkness shook his head slowly. "I still find it hard to believe such a thing could happen. We live in dangerous times." His accent was an odd mix of South African and public-school English, his manner relaxed. A man used to being in charge, Banks guessed.

"Did you know much about Mr Johnson? About his life, his background?"

Harkness shook his head. "I rarely saw him. He would come and put in his hours whether I was here or not. That was our arrangement. I'm afraid I know nothing at all about his personal life."

"Did you know he had a criminal record?"

Harkness raised an eyebrow and looked at Banks over the top of his glass. "I know he'd been in jail, if that's what you mean."

"How did you find out?"

"He told me when he came for the interview." Harkness allowed a brief smile. "In fact, he told me that's where he learned the job."

"And that didn't bother you?"

"The man had served his time. He was obviously honest enough to let me know about his past right from the start. Besides, I believe in giving everyone another chance. Everyone's capable of change, given the right conditions. Carl was a good, hard worker. And he was always very open and honest in his dealings with me. Anyway, I'm not an easy man to defraud."

"I thought you hardly ever talked to him."

"We had to discuss his work occasionally."

"How much did you pay him?"

"Five pounds an hour. I know that's not very much for a skilled worker, but he seemed grateful enough. And it was . . . how shall I say? . . . cash in hand."

"How long had he been working for you?"

"Since March."

"How did you make contact with him?"

"My previous gardener left. I placed an advertisement in the local paper and Carl Johnson replied. He seemed to know his stuff, and I was impressed with his frankness, so I took him on. I never regretted it." He pointed towards the windows. "As you can see, he did a fine job."

Banks put his glass down. Harkness offered him another, but he refused. The light had almost gone now, and the river seemed to hoard its last rays and glow from deep within. Harkness turned on the desk lamp.

"Do you know any reason," Banks asked, "why someone might want to kill him?"

"None. But as I said, I knew nothing about his personal life."

"When did you last see him?"

"Monday."

"Did he seem worried about anything?"

"Not that I could tell. We had a brief conversation about the lawn and the roses, as far as I can remember, and that's all. As I said, he didn't confide in me."

"He didn't seem different in any way?"

"No."

"Did he ever mention any of his friends or acquaintances, a girl-friend, perhaps?"

"No. I assumed he acted like any normal young man on his own time."

"Ever heard of a bloke called Les Poole?"

"No."

Banks scratched the scar by his right eye and crossed his legs. "Mr Harkness," he said, "can you think of any reason why Johnson had over a thousand pounds hidden in his flat?"

"A thousand pounds, you say? Well . . . no. I certainly didn't pay him that much. Perhaps he saved up."

"Perhaps."

"He may have worked for others, too. We didn't have an exclusive contract."

"You never asked?"

"Why should I? He was always available when I needed him."

"Where were you on Thursday evening?"

"Really, Chief Inspector! You can't believe I had anything to do with the man's death?"

"Just a matter of elimination, sir."

"Oh, very well." Harkness rubbed his chin. "Let me see . . . Well, Thursday, I'd have been at the Golf Club. I played that afternoon with Martin Lambert, and after the game we had dinner at the club."

"What time did you leave?"

"Not until well after eleven. The others will vouch for me."

Banks nodded. He felt that Harkness was enjoying the game, one he knew he could win. There was a kind of smugness and arro-gance about him that irked Banks. He had come across it before in powerful and wealthy people and had never been able accept it.

"I understand you were born around these parts?" he asked.

"Yes. Lyndgarth, as a matter of fact. We emigrated when I was four."

"South Africa?"

"Yes. Johannesburg. My father saw opportunities there. He liked to take risks, and this one paid off. Why do you ask?"

"Out of interest. You took over the business?"

"When he died. And, I might add, I succeeded him out of ability, not nepotism. I worked with him for years. He taught me all he knew."

"Is the company still in existence?"

"Very much so. And our mines are still productive. But I've had very little to do with that part of the operation of late. I moved to Amsterdam over ten years ago to handle the sales end of the business." He looked down, swirled the amber liquid in his crystal snifter, then looked Banks in the eye. "Quite frankly, I couldn't stomach the politics over there. Apartheid disgusted me, and I lacked the courage to become a revolutionary. Who wants another white liberal, anyway?"

"So you moved to Amsterdam?"

"Yes."

"But you kept your business interests in South Africa?"

"I said I couldn't stand living with the politics, Chief Inspector. I didn't say I was a fool. I also don't believe in sanctions. But that's not what you came to hear about."

"Still, it is fascinating. Are you married?"

"Divorced, back in Amsterdam." He shifted in his chair. "If you don't mind—"

"I'm sorry." Banks put down his empty glass and stood up. "It's just a copper's instinct. Curiosity."

"It's also what killed the cat."

Harkness said it with a smile, but Banks could hardly miss the cutting edge. He ignored it and walked to the library door.

As they walked down the gloomy hall with its waist-high wainscoting, Banks turned to one of the doors. "What's in here?" he asked.

Harkness opened the door and turned on a light. "Living-room."

It was a spacious high-ceilinged room with wall-to-wall thick pile carpeting and a burgundy three-piece suite. Next to the fireplace stood a tall bookcase stacked with old *National Geographic* magazines. A couple of landscapes hung on the walls: original oils, by the look of them. Banks couldn't tell who the artists were, but Sandra would probably know. Again, Banks noticed how untidy the room was and how dusty the fixtures. Beside the sofa was a long, low table, and at its centre stood a tarnished silver goblet encrusted with dirt. Banks picked it up. "What's this?" he asked.

Harkness shrugged. "Carl found it when he was digging the garden one day and he brought it to me. It looks old. I keep meaning to get it cleaned up and valued. He thought it might be worth something. I suppose," he went on, "you could take that as another example of his honesty. He could have kept it."

Banks examined the goblet. It had some kind of design engraved on it, but he couldn't make out what it was through the grime. It looked like a coat of arms. He put it back down on the table. It was something Tracy would be interested in, he thought. Would have been, he corrected himself.

Harkness noticed him looking around. "It's a bit of a mess, I'm afraid. But as I said, the house is too big and I don't use all of it anyway."

"Don't you have a cleaning lady?"

"Can't abide maids. Ever since I was a child in South Africa we had them, and I never could stand them. Always fussing around you. And I suppose as much as anything I couldn't stand the idea of anyone having to clean up after anyone else. It seemed so undignified, somehow."

Banks, whose mother had charred at a Peterborough office block to bring in a bit of extra money, said, "Yet you employed a gardener?"

Harkness led the way to the front door. "That's different, don't you think? A gardener is a kind of artist in a way, and I've no objection to being a patron of the arts. I always thought of the grounds as very much Carl's creation."

"I suppose you're right," Banks said at the door. "Just one more question: Did he ever mention the old lead mine near Relton?"

"No. Why?"

"I just wondered if it was special to him for some reason. Can you think of any reason he might have been there?"

Harkness shook his head. "None at all. Digging for hidden treasure, perhaps?" His eyes twinkled.

"Perhaps," Banks said. "Thank you for your time."

"My pleasure."

Harkness closed the door slowly but firmly and Banks got into his car. As he drove back to Eastvale in the blue-grey twilight with the haunting piano music playing, he wondered about Harkness. Many business dealings don't bear close scrutiny, of course, and you don't get as rich as Harkness without skirting the law and stepping on a few toes here and there. Is that what Harkness was getting at with his remark about curiosity killing the cat? If that was so, where did Johnson fit in? It might be useful having a criminal for a gardener if you wanted other kinds of dirty business done. On the other hand, it might also, after a while, turn out to be very inconvenient, too. At least, Banks concluded, it might be worthwhile asking a few questions about Mr Adam Harkness.

II

"This must be it, sir," said DS Richmond as he pulled in behind Patricia Cummings outside the last cottage in a terrace of four, right on the north-western edge of Eastvale, where the road curved by the side of River Swain into the dale. It was a pleasant spot, handy for both the town life, with its cinemas, shops and pubs, and for getting out into the more rural reaches of the dale itself. The holiday cottages were small—just right for a couple—and the view of the entry into the dale proper was magnificent. Of course, the slopes there were not as dramatic as they became beyond Fortford and Helmthorpe, but looking down the valley even in the fading light one could make out the grey, looming shapes of the higher fells and peaks massed in the distance, and the nearer, gentler slopes with their dry-stone walls and grazing sheep showed a promise of what was to come.

Patricia Cummings opened the door, and Richmond entered the living-room with Gristhorpe, who had returned to the station just a few minutes after Richmond had been to see Patricia. She turned on the light, and they looked around the small room that the estate agent would probably describe as cosy, with its two little armchairs arranged by the fireplace. Gristhorpe felt he had to stoop under the low ceiling, even though a few inches remained. He felt like Alice must have done before she took the shrinking potion.

What struck Gristhorpe immediately was the absolute cleanliness of the place. It reminded him of his grandmother's cottage, a similarly tiny place in Lyndgarth, in which he had never seen a speck of dust nor a thing out of place. The dominant smell was pine-scented furniture polish, and the gleaming dark surfaces of wood stood testament to its thorough application. They glanced in the kitchen. There, too, everything shone: the sink, the small fridge, the mini-washer and dryer unit under the counter.

"Did the cleaner do the place?" Gristhorpe asked.

Patricia Cummings shook her head. "No. It was like this when she found it. Spotless. She phoned me because she was sure they were supposed to be staying another two weeks."

"And were they?"

"Yes."

"They'd already paid the rent?"

"For a month, altogether. Cash in advance."

"I see."

Mrs Cummings shifted from one foot to the other. She was a middle-aged woman, neatly dressed in a grey suit with a pearl blouse and ruff. She had a small lipsticked mouth and pouchy rouged cheeks that wobbled as she spoke. Gristhorpe noticed a gold band with a big diamond cluster biting into the flesh of her plump ring finger.

"They said they were responding to an advertisement we placed in *The Dalesman*," she said.

"What names did they give?"

"Manley. Mr and Mrs Manley."

"Did you see any identification?"

"Well, no . . . I mean, they paid cash."

"Is that unusual?"

"Not really. Not normal, but it happens."

"I see." Gristhorpe looked over towards Richmond, who seemed similarly constrained by the tininess of the place. "Let's have a look around, shall we, Phil?"

Richmond nodded.

"I'll show you," Patricia Cummings said.

"If you don't mind," Gristhorpe told her, "it would be best if you waited here. It would give forensics one less person to eliminate, if it comes to that."

"Very well. Is it all right if I sit down?"

"By all means."

The stone staircase was narrow and its whitewashed ceiling low. Both men had to stoop as they went up. Upstairs were two small bedrooms and a bathroom-toilet. Everywhere was just as spotless as the living-room, ceramic surfaces gleaming.

"Someone's really done a job on this, sir," Richmond said as they entered the first bedroom. "Look, they've even washed the sheets and folded them." It was true; a small pile of neatly folded sheets lay on the mattress, and the oak chest of drawers shone with recent polish. The same pine scent hung in the air. The second bedroom was a little shabbier, but it was easy to see why. From the neatly made bed and the thin patina of dust that covered the wardrobe, it was clear the room hadn't been used by the cottage's most recent occupants.

"I can't imagine why there'd even *be* two bedrooms," Richmond said. "I mean, it'd feel crowded enough in this place with two people, let alone children as well."

"Aye," said Gristhorpe. "It's old-world rustic charm all right."

Both the sink and the bathtub had been thoroughly cleaned out, and shelves and medicine cabinet emptied.

"Come on," said Gristhorpe. "There's nothing for us here."

They went back downstairs and found Patricia Cummings painting her nails. The sickly smell of the polish pervaded the small room. She raised her eyebrows when they entered.

"Are all the cottages rented out?" Gristhorpe asked.

"All four," she said.

They went outside. The row reminded Gristhorpe of Gallows View, a similar terrace not too far away, where he and Banks had investigated a case some years ago. The light of the cottage next door was on, and Gristhorpe thought he saw the curtains twitch as they walked towards it. Gristhorpe knocked, and a few moments later a skinny young man with long, greasy hair answered.

Gristhorpe introduced himself and Richmond, and the young man let them in. The place was furnished exactly the same as next door: sideboard along one wall, a small television on a stand, two armchairs, an open fireplace, wall-to-wall dark carpets and wallpaper patterned with grapevines against an off-white background. Job lot, no doubt. The young man had made his mark by arranging a row of books along the sideboard, using wine bottles as bookends. They were mostly poetry, Gristhorpe noticed, and a couple of local wildlife guides.

"This won't take long," he said to the youth, who had introduced himself as Tony Roper. "I'd just like to know if you can tell me anything about your neighbours."

"Not really," said Tony, leaning against the sideboard. "I mean, I came here mostly for the isolation, so I didn't do much mixing." He had a Scottish accent, Gristhorpe noticed, leaning more towards Glasgow than Edinburgh.

"Did you meet them?"

"Just in passing."

"Did they introduce themselves?"

"The Manleys. Chris and Connie. That's what they said. They seemed pleasant enough. Always had a smile and a hello whenever we bumped into one another. Look, what's wrong? Nothing's happened to them, has it?"

"When did you last see them?"

Tony frowned. "Let me see . . . It was a couple of days ago. Thursday, I think. Thursday morning. They were going off in the car."

"Did they say where?"

"No. I didn't ask."

"Had they packed all their stuff, as if they were leaving?"

"I'm afraid I didn't notice. Sorry. I was out walking most of the time."

"It's all right," Gristhorpe said. "Just try and remember what you can. Did you see or hear them after that time?"

"Come to think of it, I don't reckon I did. But they never made much noise anyway. Maybe a bit of telly in the evenings. That's about all."

"Did they ever have any visitors?"

"Not that I know of."

"You never heard them arguing or talking with anyone?"

"No."

"Were they out a lot?"

"A fair bit, I'd say. But so was I. I've been doing a lot of walking, meditating, writing. I'm really sorry, but I honestly didn't pay them a lot of attention. I've been pretty much lost in my own world."

"That's all right," Gristhorpe said. "You're doing fine. What did they look like?"

"Well, he . . . Chris . . . was about medium height, with light, sandy-coloured hair brushed back. Receding a bit. He looked quite fit, wiry, you know, and he had a pleasant, open kind of smile. The kind you could trust."

"Any distinctive features?"

"You mean scars, tattoos, that kind of thing?"

"Anything."

Tony shook his head. "No. He was quite ordinary looking, really. I just noticed the smile, that's all."

"How old would you say he was?"

"Hard to say. I'd guess he was in his late twenties."

"What about the woman?"

"Connie?" Tony blushed a little. "Well, Connie's a blonde. I don't know if it's real or not. Maybe a year or two younger than him. Very pretty. A real looker. She's got lovely blue eyes, a really smooth complexion, a bit pale . . ."

"How tall?"

"An inch or two shorter than him."

"What about her figure?"

Tony blushed again. "Nice. I mean, nice so's you'd notice in the street, especially in those tight jeans she wore, and the white T-shirt."

Gristhorpe smiled and nodded. "Did you notice what kind of car they drove?"

"Yes. It was parked outside often enough. It was a Fiesta."

"What colour?"

"White."

"Did they always dress casually?"

"I suppose so. I never paid much attention, except to her, of course. Now I think of it, Chris was a bit more formal. He usually wore a jacket and a tie. You don't think anything's happened to them, do you?"

"Don't worry, Tony," Gristhorpe said. "I'm sure they're fine. Just one more thing. Did you ever hear sounds of a child there at all?"

Tony frowned. "No."

"Are you sure?"

"I'd have noticed. Yes, I'm sure. They didn't have any children."

"Fine. Thanks very much, Tony," Gristhorpe said. "We'll leave you to enjoy the rest of your holiday in peace."

Tony nodded and accompanied them to the door.

"You'll let me know, will you, if they're all right? I mean, I didn't really know them, but they *were* neighbours, in a way."

"We'll let you know," said Gristhorpe, and followed Richmond to the car.

"Will you be needing me any more?" asked Patricia Cummings.

Gristhorpe smiled at her. "No, thanks very much, Mrs Cummings. You can go home now. Just one thing, could you leave that set of keys with us?"

"Why?"

"So we can let the scene-of-crime team in."

"But—"

"This *is* important, Mrs Cummings, believe me. I wouldn't ask it otherwise. And don't rent the place out again until we give the OK."

Her cheeks quivered a bit, then she dropped the keys into Gristhorpe's outstretched hand, climbed into her car and drove off with a screech of rubber. Gristhorpe got into the police Rover beside Richmond. "Well, Phil," he said, "what do you think?"

"I'm not sure, sir. The description doesn't fit."

"But it would if they dyed their hair and got dressed up in business clothes, wouldn't it? Both descriptions were vague enough—Brenda Scupham's *and* Tony Roper's."

"That's true. But what about the car?"

"They could have stolen one for the abduction, or rented one."

"A bit risky, isn't it? And we've checked all the rental agencies."

"But we used the descriptions Brenda Scupham gave us." Gristhorpe scratched his ear. "Better get back to the rental agencies and find out about *any* couples their general age and appearance. Mention the man's smile. That seems to be a common factor. And the woman is clearly attractive. Someone might remember them."

Richmond nodded. "You think it was this Manley couple, sir?"

"I'm not saying that, but I think we'd better treat them as serious contenders for the moment."

"It certainly seems odd the way they left the place in such a hurry."

"Yes," Gristhorpe muttered. "And that cleaning job. Why?"

"Just a fastidious couple, maybe?"

"Maybe. But *why* did they leave in a hurry?"

"Could be any number of reasons," Richmond said. "A family emergency, maybe?"

"Did you notice a phone in the cottage?"

"No. I suppose that's part of the rustic peace."

"Mm. There is one thing."

"Sir?"

"Let's say, for the sake of argument, that they did have to leave because of a family emergency. Nobody could have phoned them, but they could have used the nearest phonebox if they had to keep checking on someone who was ill."

"You mean they wouldn't have stayed behind to clean up the place, sir?"

"There's that, aye. But there's something odder. The money. They paid cash in advance. How much do these places go for?"

"I don't know, sir. I forgot to ask."

"It doesn't matter, but it must be a fair whack. Say a hundred and fifty a week."

"Something like that. And probably a deposit, too."

"Then why didn't they ask for some of their money back?"

"They might have had a hard time getting it."

"Perhaps. But they didn't even try. That's three hundred quid we're talking about, Phil. Plus deposit."

"Maybe they were loaded."

Gristhorpe fixed Richmond with the closest his benign features could get to a look of contempt. "Phil, if they were loaded, the *first* thing they would do is ask for their money back. That's how the rich get that way, and that's how they stay that way."

"I suppose so," Richmond mumbled. "What do we do now?"

"We get the forensic team in, that's what we do," Gristhorpe said, and reached for the radio.

III

The house was in darkness when Banks got home from the station around ten o'clock that Saturday evening. Tracy, he remembered, was at a dance in Relton with her friends. Banks had grilled her thoroughly about who was going and who was driving. He had been undecided, loath to let her go, but Sandra had tipped the balance. She was probably right, Banks admitted. Barring a punch-up between the Eastvale lads and the Relton lads, a fairly regular feature of these local dances, it ought to be a harmless enough affair. And Tracy was a big girl now.

So where was Sandra? Banks turned the lights on, then went into the kitchen thinking he might find a note. Nothing. Feeling anxious and irritated, he sat down, turned on the television and started switching channels: an American cop show, a documentary on Africa, a pirate film, a quiz show. He turned it off. The silence in the house closed in on him. This was absurd. Normally he would change into jeans and a sports shirt, pour a drink, put some music on, perhaps even smoke a cigarette if both Sandra and Tracy were out. Now all he could do was sit down and tap his fingers on the chair arm. It was no good. He couldn't stay home.

Grabbing his jacket against the evening chill, he walked along Market Street past the closed shops and the Golden Grill and the

Queen's Arms. The light through the red and amber coloured windows beckoned, and he could see people at tables through the small clear panes, but instead of dropping in, he continued along North Market Street, quiet under its old-fashioned gas-lamps, window displays of gourmet teas, expensive hiking gear, imported shoes and special blends of tobacco.

The front doors of the community centre stood open. From the hall, Banks could hear a soprano struggling through Schubert's "Die Junge Nonne" to a hesitant piano accompaniment. It was Saturday, amateur recital night. He took the broad staircase to his left and walked up to the first floor. He could hear voices from some of the rooms, mostly used for the meetings of local hobby clubs or for committees of various kinds. The double glass doors of the gallery were closed, but a faint light shone from behind the partition at the far end of the room.

Banks walked softly down the carpeted gallery, its walls bare of pictures at the moment, and stopped outside the cramped office at the end. He had already heard Sandra's voice, but she was unaware of his presence.

"But you can't *do* that," she was pleading. "You've already agreed—"

"What? You don't give a . . . Now look—" She moved the receiver away from her ear and swore before slamming it down in its cradle. Then she took two deep breaths, tucked loose strands of blonde hair behind her ears, and picked up the phone again.

"Sandra," Banks said as gently as he could.

She turned round and put her hand to her chest. Banks could see the angry tears burning in her eyes. "Alan, it's you. What are you doing here? You scared me."

"Sorry."

"Look, it's not a good time. I've got so damn much to do."

"Let's go for a drink."

She started dialling. "I'd love to, but I—"

Banks broke the connection.

Sandra stood up and faced him, eyes blazing. "What the hell do you think you're doing?"

He took her arm. "Come on. Let's go."

She shook him off. "What are you playing at?"

Banks sighed and sat on the edge of the desk. "Look at you," he said. "You're frustrated as hell." He smiled. "You look pretty close to murder, too. I think it's time you took a break, that's all. God knows, you've helped take my mind off my problems often enough when you've watched me beating my head against a brick wall. I'm just trying to return the favour."

Sandra bit her lower lip. Some of the anger left her eyes, but the tears still burned there. "It's just that bloody Morton Ganning," she said. "He's only pulled out of the show, that's all."

"Well, bugger him," Banks said.

"But you don't understand."

Banks took her coat from the rack by the office door. "Come on. You can tell me over a drink."

Sandra glared at him for a moment, then smoothed her skirt and walked over. Before she could put her coat on, Banks put his arms around her and held her close. At first she stood limp, then slowly, she raised her arms and linked them behind him. She buried her head in his shoulder then broke free, gave him a playful thump on the arm and that cheeky smile he loved so much. "All right, then," she said. "But you're buying."

Ten minutes later they managed to squeeze into a small corner table in the Queen's Arms. The place was busy and loud with the jokes and laughter of the Saturday night crowd, so they had to put their heads close together to talk. Soon, though, the noise became a background buzz and they no longer had to strain to hear one another.

"He's the most famous of the lot," Sandra was saying. "He's got paintings in galleries all over the country. It was going to be a hell of a coup to get him, but now he's backed out. He's a real bastard."

"I thought the idea was to give locals a chance, the lesser-known ones?"

"It is. But Ganning would have drawn a damn good crowd. Indirectly, he'd have got them all more publicity, given them more chance of making a sale."

"For the right reasons?"

"That doesn't matter. So what if they come to see *his* work? They'd see the others too."

"I suppose so."

Sandra sipped her gin and tonic. "I'm sorry to go on about it, Alan, really I am. It's just that I've been so involved. I've put in so much bloody work it makes me boil."

"I know."

"What's that supposed to mean?"

"Nothing."

Her blue eyes hardened. "Yes it is. I can tell by your tone. You're not complaining, are you? That I haven't been doing my little wifely duties—cooking your meals, washing your clothes?"

Banks laughed. "I didn't marry you for your 'little wifely duties' as you call them. I can look after myself. No. If I am complaining at all, it's about hardly seeing you over these past few weeks."

"Like I hardly see you when you're on a case?"

"Touché."

"So what do you mean? You expect me to be there whenever you decide to come home?"

"No, it's not that."

"What is it then?"

Banks lit a cigarette, playing for time. "It's . . . well, just that the house seems so empty. You're never there, Tracy's never there. I feel like I'm living alone."

Sandra leaned back in her chair. She reached out and grabbed one of Banks's cigarettes. "Hey," he said, putting his hand over hers. "You've stopped."

She broke free. "And I'll stop again tomorrow. What's really bothering you, Alan?"

"What I said. The empty house."

"So it's not just me, what I'm doing?"

"No, I don't suppose it is."

"But you take it out on me?"

"I'm not taking anything out on you. I'm trying to explain what the problem is. For Christ's sake, you asked me."

"Okay, okay. Keep your shirt on. Maybe you need another pint."

"Wouldn't mind."

Sandra held out her hand. "Money, then."

Banks looked gloomily into the last quarter-inch of deep gold liquid in his glass while Sandra threaded her way to the bar. She was right. It wasn't just her at all. It was the whole damn situation at home. He felt as if his children had suddenly become different people overnight, and his wife hadn't even noticed. He watched her coming back. She walked slowly, concentrating on not spilling the drinks. It was absurd, he felt, but even after all these years just seeing her made his heart speed up.

Sandra placed the glass carefully on the beer-mat in front of him and he thanked her.

"Look," she said, "I know what you mean, but you have to accept things. Brian's gone. He's got his own life to lead. When did you leave home?"

"But that's not the same."

"Yes it is."

"It was stifling in Peterborough, with Dad always on at me and Mum just taking it all. It wasn't the same at all."

"Perhaps the circumstances weren't," Sandra allowed. "But the impulse certainly is."

"He's got a perfectly good home with us. I don't see why he'd want to go as far as bloody Portsmouth. I mean, he could have gone to Leeds, or York, or Bradford and come home on weekends."

Sandra sighed. "Sometimes you can be damned obtuse, Alan Banks, do you know that?"

"What do you mean?"

"He's left the nest, flown the coop. For him it's a matter of the farther the better. It doesn't mean he doesn't love us any more. It's just a part of growing up. You did it yourself. That's what I mean."

"But I told you, that was different."

"Not all that much. Didn't you use to get on at him all the time about his music?"

"I never interfered with what he wanted. I even bought him a guitar."

"Yes. In the hope he'd start playing classical or jazz or something other than what he did."

"Don't tell me you liked that bloody racket any more than I did?"

"That doesn't matter. Oh, what's the use. What I'm trying to say is that we didn't drive him away, no more than your parents drove you away, not really. He wants to be independent like you did. He wants his own life."

"I know that, but . . ."

"But nothing. We still have Tracy. Enjoy her while you can."

"But she's never home. She's always out with that Harrison boy, getting up to God knows what."

"She's not getting up to anything. She's sensible."

"She doesn't seem interested in anything else any more. Her schoolwork's slipping."

"Not much," Sandra said. "And I'll bet yours slipped a bit when you got your first girlfriend."

Banks said nothing.

"Alan, you're jealous, that's all."

"Jealous? Of my own daughter?"

"Oh, come on. You know she was the apple of your eye. You never were as close to Brian as you were to her. Now she seems to have no time for you, you resent it."

Banks rubbed his cheek. "Do I?"

"Of course you do. If only you could bring as much perception to your own family as you do to your cases you wouldn't have these problems."

"Knowing is one thing, feeling all right about it is quite another."

"I realize that. But you have to start with knowing."

"How do you cope?" Banks asked. "You've been like a stranger to me these past few months."

"I didn't say I'd been coping very well either, only that I've been doing a lot of thinking about things."

"And?"

"It's not easy, but we've reached that time where our children are no longer children. They can no longer keep us together."

Banks felt a chill run through him. "What do you mean they can't keep us together?"

"What I say. Oh, for God's sake don't look so worried. I didn't mean it *that* way. Maybe I didn't choose the best words. The kids gave us a lot in common, shared pleasures, anxieties. They'll still do that, of course, though I'm sure more on the anxieties side, but we can't relate to them the same way. They're not just children to be seen and not heard. You can't just order them not to do things. They'll only rebel and do worse. Remember your own childhood? You were a bit of a shit-disturber even when I met you. Still are, if truth be known. See Brian and Tracy for what they are, for what they're becoming."

"But what did you mean about them keeping us together? It sounded ominous to me."

"Only that we won't have them to gather around for much longer. We'll have to find other things, discover one another in other ways."

"It could be fun."

Sandra nodded. "It could be. But we've both been avoiding it so far."

"You too?"

"Of course. How many times have we spent an evening in the house alone together these past eighteen years?"

"There's been times."

"Oh yes, but you can count them on the fingers of one hand. Besides, we knew Brian would be back from Boys' Brigade or Tracy from the Guides, or they were up in their rooms. We're not old, Alan. We married young and we've got a lot ahead of us."

Banks looked at Sandra. Not old, certainly. The earnest face, her eyes shining with emotion, black eyebrows contrasting the blonde hair that hung down over her shoulders. A lump came to his throat. If I walked into the pub right this moment, he thought, and saw her sitting there, I'd be over like a shot.

"Where do we start?" he asked.

Sandra tossed back her head and laughed. People turned to look at her but she paid them no attention. "Well, I've got this bloody show to organize still, and it's not all been a matter of staying late at the gallery to avoid facing things. I *do* have a lot of hours to put in."

"I know that," Banks said. "And so do I."

Sandra frowned. "There's still nothing on that missing child, is there?"

Banks shook his head. "No. It's been five days now since she was abducted."

"Just imagine what her poor mother must be going through. Have you given up hope?"

"We don't expect miracles." He paused. "You know something? She reminds me of Tracy when she was that age. The blonde hair, the serious expression. Tracy always did take after you."

"You're being sentimental, Alan. From the photo I saw in the paper she didn't look a bit like Tracy."

Banks smiled. "Maybe not. But I'm on another case now. That reminds me. Have you ever heard of a bloke called Adam Harkness?"

"Harkness? Of course I have. He's pretty well known locally as a patron of the arts."

"Yes, he mentioned something like that. Has he given your lot any money?"

"We weren't as needy as some. Remember that bumper grant we got?"

"The oversight?"

"They still haven't asked for it back. Anyway, he's given money to the Amateur Operatic Society and a couple of other groups." She frowned.

"What is it?"

"Well, some of the arts groups are a bit, you know, leftish. They tend to get blinkered. It's the old package deal: if you're against this, you have to be against that too. You know, you have to be pro-abortion, anti-apartheid and green to boot."

"Well?"

"Some of them wouldn't take Harkness's money because of the way he makes it."

"South Africa?"

"Yes."

"But he's anti-apartheid. He just told me. That's partly why he left. Besides, things have changed over there. Apartheid's fallen to pieces."

Sandra shrugged. "Maybe. And I wouldn't know about his personal beliefs. All I know is that Linda Fish—you know, that woman who runs the Writers' Circle—wouldn't take any money towards engaging visiting speakers and readers."

"Linda Fish, the Champagne socialist?"

"Well, yes."

"What does she know about him?"

"Oh, she's got contacts among South African writers, or so she claims. All this anti-apartheid stuff is a load of bunk, she thinks. She's got a point. I mean, after all, whatever he professes to believe he's *still* earning his fortune by exploiting the system, isn't he?"

"I'd better have a talk with her."

"Well," Sandra said, "you don't make his kind of money by being square and above-board, do you? Let's drop it anyway. I'm sure Linda will be delighted to see you. I think she's secretly fancied you ever since she found out you'd read Thomas Hardy."

Banks gave a mock shudder. "Look," he said, "I've just had an idea."

Sandra raised her eyebrows.

"Not that kind of idea. Well . . . Anyway, when all this is over—the show, the case—let's go on holiday, just you and me. Somewhere exotic."

"Can we afford it?"

"No. But we'll manage somehow. Tracy can stay with your mum and dad. I'm sure they won't mind."

"No. They're always glad to see her. I bet she'll mind this time, though. To be separated from the first boyfriend for even a day is a pretty traumatic experience, you know."

"We'll deal with that problem when we get to it. What about the holiday?"

"You're on. I'll start thinking of suitably exotic places."

"And . . . er . . . about that other idea . . ."

"What other idea?"

"You know. *Erotic* places."

"Oh, *that* one."

"Yes. Well?"

Sandra looked at her watch. "It's ten past eleven. Tracy said she'll be home at twelve."

"When has she ever been on time?"

"Still," Sandra said, finishing her drink and grabbing Banks's arm. "I think we'd better hurry."

IV

The tea was cold. Wearily, Brenda Scupham picked up her cup and carried it to the microwave. When she had reheated it, she went back into the living-room, flopped down on the sofa and lit a cigarette.

She had been watching television. That was how she had let the tea get cold. Not even watching it really, just sitting there and letting the images and sounds tumble over her and deaden the thoughts that she couldn't keep at bay. It had been a documentary about some obscure African tribe. That much she remembered. Now the news was on and someone had blown up a jumbo jet over a jungle somewhere. Images of the strewn wreckage taken from a helicopter washed over her.

Brenda sipped her tea. Too hot now. It wasn't tea she needed, anyway, it was a drink. The pill she had taken had some effect, but it would work better with a gin and tonic. Getting up, she went and poured herself a stiff one, then sat down again.

It was that man from the newspaper who had got her thinking such terrible thoughts. Mostly the police did a good job of keeping the press away from her, but this one she had agreed to talk to. For one thing, he was from the *Yorkshire Post*, and for another, she liked the look of him. He had been kind and gentle in his questioning, too, sensitive to her feelings, but had nevertheless probed areas Brenda hadn't even known existed. And somehow, talking about her grief over the loss of her "poor Gemma" had actually made her feel it more, just as speculating about what might have happened to the child had made her imagine awful things happening, fears she couldn't shut out even now, long after the man had gone, after she had taken the tranquillizer, and after the images of Africa had numbed her. It was like being at the dentist's when the anaesthetic numbs your gums but you can still feel a shadow of pain in the background when he probes with his drill.

Now she found herself drifting way back to when she first got pregnant. Right from the start she knew instinctively that she didn't want the child growing inside her. Some days, she hoped to fall and induce a miscarriage, and other, worse days, she wished she would get run over by a bus. The odd thing was, though, that she couldn't actually bring herself to do any of these things— throw herself down the stairs, get rid of the foetus, jump out of a window. Maybe it was because she had been brought up Catholic and believed in a sort of elemental way that both suicide and abortion were sins. She couldn't even sit in a bathtub and drink gin like that dateless June Williams had done when Billy Jackson had got her in the family way (not that it had worked anyway; all June had got out of it was wrinkled skin and a nasty hangover). No, whatever happened just had to happen; it had to be God's will, even though Brenda didn't think now that she really believed in God.

Later, still stunned by the pain of childbirth, when she saw Gemma for the first time, she remembered wondering even back then how such a strange child could possibly be hers. And she turned her back. Oh, she had done the necessaries, of course. She could no more neglect to feed the child and keep her warm than she could have thrown herself under a bus. But that was where it stopped. She had been unable to feel love for Gemma, which is why it felt so strange, after talking about her loss to the reporter, that she should actually *feel* it now. And she felt guilty, too, guilty for the way she had neglected and abandoned Gemma. She knew she might never get a chance to make it up to her.

She poured another gin. Maybe this would do the trick. The thing was, it had been guilt made her hand Gemma over in the first place. Guilt and fear. The social workers, real or not, had been right when they talked about abuse; it was their timing that seemed uncanny, for though Brenda might have neglected her daughter, she had never, *ever* hit her until a few days before they called. Even then, she hadn't really hit Gemma, but when the man and the woman with their posh accents and their well-cut clothes called at her door, she somehow felt they had arrived in answer to a call; they were her retribution or her salvation, she didn't really know which.

Gemma had angered Les. When she spilled the paint on the racing page of his paper, he retaliated, as he usually did, not by violence, but by hitting her where it hurt, tearing up and throwing out some of her colouring books. Afterwards, he had been in a terrible mood all through tea-time, needling Brenda, complaining, arguing. And to cap it all, Gemma had been sitting there giving them the evil eye. She hadn't said a word, nor shed a tear, but the accusation and the hurt in those eyes had been too much. Finally, Brenda grabbed her by the arm and shook her until she did start to cry, then let go of her and watched her run up to her room, no doubt to throw herself on her bed and cry herself to sleep. She had shaken Gemma so hard there were bruises on her arm. And when the social workers came, it was as if they knew not only how Brenda had lost her temper that day, but that if it happened again she might keep on shaking Gemma until she killed her. It was silly, she knew that—of course they couldn't *know*—but that had been how she felt.

And that was why she had given up Gemma so easily, to save her. Or was it to get rid of her? Brenda still couldn't be sure; the complexity of her feelings about the whole business knotted deep in her breast and she couldn't, try as she might, sort it all out and analyze it like she assumed most people did. She couldn't help not being smart, and most of the time it never really bothered her that other people knew more about the world than she did, or that they were able to talk about things she couldn't understand, or look at a situation and break it down into all its parts. It never really bothered her, but sometimes she thought it was bloody unfair.

She finished her gin and lit another cigarette. Now she had talked to the reporter she thought she might like to go on television. They had asked her on the second day, but she had been too scared. Maybe, though, in her best outfit, with the right make-up, she might not look too bad. She could make an appeal to the kidnapper, and if Gemma was still alive. . . . Still alive . . . no, she couldn't think about that again. But it might help.

She heard a key in the door. Les back from the pub. Her expression hardened. Over these past few days, she realized, she had come to hate him. The door opened. She went and poured herself another gin and tonic. She would have to do something about Les soon. She couldn't go on like this.

V

Later that Saturday night, after closing-time, a car weaved its way over a desolate stretch of the North York Moors some thirty miles east of Eastvale. Its occupants—Mark Hudson and Mandy Vernon—could hardly keep their hands off one another. They had been for a slap-up dinner and drinks at the White Horse Farm Hotel, in Rosedale, and were now on their way back to Helmsley.

As Mark tried to concentrate on the narrow, unfenced road, the rabbits running away from the headlights' beam, his hand kept straying to Mandy's thigh, where her short skirt exposed a long stretch of delectable nylon-encased warm flesh. Finally, he pulled into a lay-by. All around them lay darkness, not even a farmhouse light in sight.

First they kissed, but the gear-stick and steering wheel got in the way. Metros weren't built for passion. Then Mark suggested they get in the back. They did so, but when he got his hand up her skirt and started tugging at her tights, she banged her knee on the back of the seat and cursed.

"There's not enough room," she said. "I'll break my bloody leg."

"Let's get out, then," Mark suggested.

"What? Do it in the open air?"

"Yes. Why not?"

"But it's cold."

"It's not that cold. Don't worry, I'll keep you warm. I've got a blanket in the back."

Mandy considered it for a moment. His hand found her left breast inside her blouse and he started rubbing her nipple between his thumb and forefinger.

"All right," she said. "We've not got much choice, have we?"

And indeed they hadn't. They couldn't take a room at the hotel because Mark was married, supposed to be at a company do, and Mandy still lived with her mother and brother, who expected her home from her girlfriend's by midnight. He had bought her an expensive five-course dinner, and they had drunk Châteauneuf-du-Pape. Going home, he had even negotiated the winding one-in-three hill that led over the open moors because it was more isolated up there than on the valley road. This might be one of the last warm evenings of the year; he might never get another chance.

Using the torch, they made their way over the heather and found a shaded knoll surrounded by rocks and boulders about fifty yards from the road. Mark spread the blanket and Mandy lay down. Open moorland stretched for miles all around, and a half-moon frosted the heather and gave the place the eerie look of a moonscape. It *was* cold, but they soon ceased to notice as they warmed each other with caresses. Finally, Mark got Mandy's tights and knickers down around her ankles, pushed her knees apart and lay on top of her.

Mandy stretched out her arms and snatched at the heather as the waves of pleasure swept through her. Soon, Mark speeded up and began to make grunting sounds deep in his throat. Mandy knew the end was close. She could smell the port and Stilton on his breath and feel his stubble against her shoulder. The more he groaned, the more she snatched at the heather by the nearest rock, but even as he came and she encouraged him with cries of ecstasy, she was aware that what she clutched in her right hand wasn't grass or heather, but something softer, some kind of material, more like an article of clothing.

SIX

I

That Sunday morning in Eastvale passed as most Sundays did. The locals read the papers, washed their cars, put the roast in, went to church, messed about in the garden. Some took walks in the dale or went to visit nearby relatives. The fine weather held, and tourists came, of course, jamming the market square with their cars, posing by the ancient cross or the façade of the Norman church for photographs, perhaps enjoying a pub lunch at the Queen's Arms or tea and sandwiches at the Golden Grill, then driving on to the craft show at Helmthorpe, the sheep fair at Relton, or the big car-boot sale in Hoggett's field near Fortford. And out in the dale, around massive Witch Fell between Skield and Swainshead, the search for seven-year-old Gemma Scupham went into its fourth full day.

Back in Eastvale, at eleven-thirty that morning, a very nervous and hungover Mark Hudson walked into the police station carrying a Marks and Spencer's bag. He quickly placed it on the front desk, mumbling. "You might be interested in this," then tried to make a casual exit.

It was not to be. The desk sergeant caught a glimpse of yellow cotton in the bag, and before he knew it Mark Hudson was whisked politely upstairs to the CID.

Gristhorpe, aware that his office was far too comfortable for the interrogation of suspects, had Hudson taken to an interview room with a metal desk and chairs bolted to the floor and a small window covered by a metal grille. It smelled of Dettol and stale cigarette smoke.

With Richmond along to take notes, Gristhorpe planted himself firmly opposite a sweating Mark Hudson and began.

"Where did you find the clothes?"

"On the moors."

"More precisely?"

"On the road between Rosedale Abbey and Hutton-le-Hole. I don't remember exactly where."

"When?"

"Last night. Look, I just—"

"What were you doing out there?"

Hudson paused and licked his lips. He looked around the room and Gristhorpe could tell he didn't like what he saw. "I . . . well, I'd been to a company do at the White Horse. I was on my way home."

"Where do you live?"

"Helmsley."

"What company do you work for?"

Hudson looked surprised at the question. "Burton's. You know, the rag trade. I'm a sales rep."

"And this do you were at, what was it in honour of?"

"Well, it wasn't really . . . I mean, it was just an informal affair, some of the lads getting together for a meal and a chat."

"I see." Gristhorpe eased back in his chair. "And what made you stop in such a godforsaken place?"

"I needed to . . . you know, call of nature."

"Were you by yourself?"

"Yes."

Gristhorpe sniffed a lie, but he left it alone.

"Why did you wait so long before coming here? You must have known what you'd found. It's been in all the papers."

"I know. I just thought . . . It was very late. And I didn't want to get involved." He leaned forward. "And I was right, wasn't I? I decide to help, and here I am being interrogated like a suspect."

"Mr Hudson," said Gristhorpe, "in the first place, you're not being interrogated, you're simply being questioned, and in the second place, a child is missing, perhaps dead. How would you treat someone who walks in here, drops a bundle of what looks like the child's clothes and then tries to scarper?"

"I didn't try to scarper. I just wanted you to have the clothes, in case there was a clue. As I said, I didn't want to get involved. I thought of putting them in the post, but I knew that would take too long. I know how important time is in things like this, so I finally decided to come forward."

"Well, thank you very much, Mr Hudson."

"Look, if I really had done anything to that child, I'd hardly have come in here at all, would I?"

Gristhorpe fixed Hudson with his baby-blue eyes. "Psychopaths are unpredictable, Mark," he said. "We never know what they'll do next, or why they do it."

"For God's sake!"

"Where's the girl, Mark?"

Hudson hesitated, looked away. "What girl?"

"Come on, Mark. You know who I mean. The girl who was with you. Your accomplice."

"Accomplice?"

"Miss Peterson. Where is she?"

"I've never heard of anyone called Peterson."

Gristhorpe gave that one a "maybe." "Where's Gemma Scupham?"

"Please, you've got to believe me. I don't know anything. I had nothing to do with it. I'm just trying to do my civic duty."

Gristhorpe let the staring match continue until Hudson looked down at the stained metal desk, then he asked, "Can you remember exactly where you found the bundle of clothing?"

Hudson rubbed his damp forehead. "I was thinking about that on my way here," he said. "That you might want to know."

"It could be useful. We still haven't found the girl's body."

"Yes, well . . . I could try. I mean, I think I might remember if I saw the spot again. But it was dark and it's pretty bleak up there. I must admit after I found the clothes I didn't want to hang around."

"And you were no doubt under the influence of Bacchus?"

"What?"

"You'd been drinking."

"I'd had a little wine, yes. But I wasn't over the limit, if that's what you mean."

"I don't care how much you had to drink," said Gristhorpe, standing up. "Although judging by your eyes this morning I'd say you're a bloody liar. It's your memory I'm concerned about. What I want you to do is to take me to the spot where you found the clothes. I'll go with you in your car and DS Richmond here will follow. All right?"

"I don't have much choice, do I?"

"No," said Gristhorpe. "No, you don't."

II

Gristhorpe said nothing during the journey. They crawled up Sutton Bank into the Hambleton Hills, passed through Helmsley, then turned off the main road into Hutton-le-Hole. On the broad village green, split by Hutton Beck, the sides connected by a small white bridge, tourists ate picnics. Several sheep also picnicked from the grass itself, keeping their distance from the humans. It was a marvel of work-saving, Gristhorpe thought, letting the sheep wander the village and keep the green well cropped.

Beyond Hutton, they turned north onto a narrow, unfenced road over the desolate moors.

"I'd have more chance if we were going the other way," Hudson said. "I mean, that was the way I was driving, and it was very dark."

"Don't worry," said Gristhorpe, "you'll get your chance."

They had no luck on the way to Rosedale, so Gristhorpe turned in the car park and set off back again, up the one-in-three hill, with Richmond still behind. The moorland stretched for miles on all sides, a dark sea of purple heather, just past its prime. Hudson seemed to be concentrating as they drove, screwing up his eyes and looking into the distance, trying to remember how long he had been driving before he stopped. Finally, he pointed to a small outcrop of rocks among the heather about fifty yards from the roadside. "This is it!" he shouted. "This is the place."

Gristhorpe turned into the lay-by and waited for Richmond to pull in behind. "Are you sure?" he asked.

"Well, I can't be a hundred percent, but I'd been driving about this long, and I remember those rocks over there. There aren't many spots like that around here."

Gristhorpe opened the door. "By the roadside here, then? Let's take a look."

"Well, actually," Hudson said, "it was further from the road, closer to the rocks."

Richmond had joined them, and Gristhorpe gave him a puzzled look before he said, "Phil. If you stopped for a piss on this road at half past twelve at night, would you walk fifty yards or so away from your car to do it?"

Richmond shook his head. "No way, sir."

"I thought not." He fixed Hudson with his innocent gaze again. "But you did, right?"

"Yes."

"Why?"

"I don't know. I wasn't really thinking about it. I suppose I didn't want to be seen."

Gristhorpe looked around the desolate landscape in disbelief. "Didn't want to be seen?"

"That's right."

"You had a torch, I assume?"

"Yes."

Gristhorpe raised his bushy eyebrows and shook his head. "Come on, then, show us where."

Hudson led them over the rough, springy heather towards the outcrop, a natural shelter, and pointed. Gristhorpe didn't want to ruin any more evidence there might be, so he stood at the entrance and looked. It was a small area, maybe three or four yards square, surrounded on all sides but one with rocks, some as high as Gristhorpe's chest, but most of them no more than knee-high stones. In the centre, a small area of heather looked as if it had been flattened recently. There had been some blood on the yellow dungarees, he recalled. In all likelihood, there would be more blood around here, and perhaps other valuable trace evidence.

"Where exactly did you find the bundle of clothes?" Gristhorpe asked.

Hudson thought for a moment, then pointed towards one of the smaller rocks near a corner of the flattened heather. "There. Stuffed under there. I think."

"What made you look there?"

He shrugged. "I don't know. Maybe I saw something out the corner of my eye."

Gristhorpe stood for a few moments taking in the scene, then turned to go back to the car.

"Can I go home now?" Hudson asked when they arrived. "My wife. She'll be wondering where I am."

"You can phone her when we get back to the station."

"Station?"

"Yes. Phil?" Gristhorpe ignored Hudson's protests. "Radio in and get the SOCO team, if you can raise any of them on a Sunday afternoon."

"Will do, sir." Richmond went to his car.

"But I don't understand," Hudson went on as Gristhorpe took him by the arm and gently guided him into the passenger seat.

"Don't you? It's simple really. I don't believe you. First off, I don't believe anyone would walk this far for a piss on a dark night in a place like this, and second I don't like the fact that you didn't show up at the station till nearly noon and then tried to leave as soon as you'd dumped the bag."

"But I've explained all that."

Gristhorpe started the car. "Not to my satisfaction, you haven't. Not by a long chalk. I don't like it at all. Besides, there's another thing."

"What?"

"I don't like *you*."

III

When Jenny Fuller pulled up outside Superintendent Gristhorpe's house above Lyndgarth at about seven o'clock that evening, lights shone a welcome from the lower windows. She hadn't phoned to say she was coming, but Phil Richmond had told her at the station that the superintendent had finally abandoned his camp-bed and gone home.

She knocked at the heavy door and waited. When Gristhorpe opened it, he was clearly surprised to see her there but didn't hesitate to invite her in.

"I've just finished doing a bit of work on the wall," he said as they stood in the hall. "Until it got too dark. Fancy a cup of tea?"

"Mm, yes please," Jenny said.

"I can offer you something stronger if you'd like?"

"No. No, tea will be fine. I was just on my way to visit a colleague in Lyndgarth and I thought I'd drop by. I don't have much, I'm afraid, but I can give you a sketch of what I've dug up so far. It might be some help."

Gristhorpe directed her to the study while he went to the kitchen. Jenny stood and gazed at the books, the clearly divided sections on military and naval history, general history, Yorkshire, then the novels, philosophy, poetry. On the small table by the armchair lay a paperback copy of *The Way of All Flesh*. Jenny had always loved the title but had never read it. Her background in English was distinctly weak, she realized.

Somehow the house and this room in particular spoke of a solitary, meditative, serious man, perhaps ill at ease in company. All that was missing was a pipe lying in an ashtray on the table, and perhaps a pipe-rack over the hearth. But Gristhorpe had a gregarious side to his character, too, she knew. He enjoyed telling tales with his mates and colleagues over a pint; he wasn't at all uneasy in groups. A man's man, perhaps?

Gristhorpe came back bearing a tray with a teapot and two mugs, a little jug of milk and a bowl of sugar. Jenny moved the book from the table and he set the tray down. He bade her sit in the leather armchair that she knew instinctively was "his" and pulled up a smaller chair for himself.

"That camp-bed was beginning to make me feel like an old man," he said. "Besides, they know where I am if anything breaks."

"No progress?"

"I wouldn't say that. We've talked to the neighbours again, and to Gemma's schoolfriends, the kids she played with, and none of

them saw anyone hanging about or heard Gemma mention anyone
they didn't know. So that's a blank. But . . ." Gristhorpe went on to
tell her about the Manleys' deserted cottage and his outing to the
moors with Mark Hudson.

"What's happened to him?" she asked.

"I sent him home when I finally got the truth out of him. He led
us on a merry dance, but he's got nothing to do with Gemma. He
was out for a bit of extramarital activity. He'd settled on the spot in
advance because it was some distance from the road and the rocks
offered protection. He just stumbled across the clothing. We've
got the woman's name. Of course, we'll talk to her and have
another chat with him, just for procedure's sake."

"So the clothing *is* Gemma Scupham's?"

"Yes. The mother identified it. And there's a bit of blood on it—
at least, it looks like blood. But we won't know much more till
tomorrow, when the forensic team gets its job done."

"Still . . ." Jenny shivered.

"Cold?"

"Oh, no. I'm fine, really." Jenny was wearing jeans and a fuzzy
russet jumper that matched the colour of her hair, a warm enough
outfit for a mild night. "Someone walked over my grave, that's all."
She sipped some soothing tea. "I've been looking at instances of
pairs of sexual deviants, and quite frankly there's hardly any. Often
you'll find a couple who might commit crimes for gain, like Bonnie
and Clyde, I suppose, but deviants usually act solo."

"What about the ones who don't?" Gristhorpe asked.

"There are *some* case studies. Usually you get a dominant leader
and an accomplice, and usually they're both male. Leopold and
Loeb, for example."

Gristhorpe nodded.

"Have you read *Compulsion?*" Jenny asked.

"Yes. It was one of Ian Brady's favourite books, you know."

"There are some parallels. The way your couple seem to have
coldly planned and executed the crime, for a start," Jenny said. "But
there's another thing: mixed pairs are very rare. Brady and Hindley
come to mind, of course."

"Aye," said Gristhorpe. "Maybe Alan's told you I've got what you might call an unhealthy preoccupation with that case. But I was involved in the search. And I heard the tape of young Lesley Ann Downey pleading for her life." He shook his head and let the silence hang.

"Is that why you're getting so actively involved in this case? I mean, you don't usually."

Gristhorpe smiled. "Partly, I suppose. And maybe I'm trying to prove there's life in the old dog yet. I'm getting near retiring age, you know. But mostly I want to stop them before they do it again. We spend most of our time making cases against people we think have broken the law. Oh, we talk about prevention—we have coppers on the beat, keeping their eyes open—but mostly we come on the scene after the fact. That's also true this time, I realize. Gemma Scupham may be lost to us, but I'm damned if I'm going to let it happen to another child on my patch. Make sense?"

Jenny nodded.

"So what do you think?" he asked.

"From what little I know so far," Jenny said, "I'd say it's certainly possible we could be dealing with a Brady-Hindley pair. And they may not be paedophiles, as such. Paedophiles have a genuine sexual attraction to children, and they don't usually go in for murder unless they panic, but children also make good victims just because they're very vulnerable, like women. Brady's last victim was a seventeen-year-old male homosexual, I gather. Hardly a child."

"You've obviously done your research," Gristhorpe said. "Owt else?"

"I'd look more closely at why they did it the way they did, and why they chose Gemma Scupham. It's also come out from a few studies lately that more women are involved in paedophilia than we'd ever thought before, so I wouldn't discount that possibility altogether. Maybe she wasn't along just for the ride."

"Could *he* have been the one along for the ride?" Gristhorpe asked.

"I doubt it. Not according to the statistics, at least."

"Any good news?"

Jenny shook her head. "What it comes down to," she said, leaning forward, "is that in my opinion—and remember it's still all basically guesswork—you're probably dealing with a psychopath, most likely the male, and a woman who's become fixated on him, who'll do anything he says. There's something odd about them, though, something odd about the whole business. The psychology doesn't quite add up." She frowned. "Anyway, I'd concentrate on him. He might not be a paedophile in particular, so I wouldn't depend on criminal records. I think it's more likely that he just likes to act out sadistic fantasies in front of an adoring audience. I—Oh, God, what am I saying? That poor damn kid." Jenny flopped back in the chair and put her hand to her forehead. "I'm sorry," she said. "I'm behaving like a silly girl."

"Nay, lass," said Gristhorpe. "When they played that tape there wasn't a dry eye in the courtroom—and they were hardened coppers all."

"Still," said Jenny, "if I'm to be any help I have to try to remain calm and objective."

"Aye," said Gristhorpe, sitting down again. "Aye, you can try. But I don't imagine it's easy for any of us with a possible psychopath on the loose, is it? Another cup of tea?"

Jenny looked at her watch. No, she didn't have to hurry; she had plenty of time. "Yes," she said. "That'd be very nice. I think I will."

SEVEN

I

"Don't tell me you've been burning the midnight oil?" Gristhorpe said, when Vic Manson phoned at nine o'clock Monday morning.

Manson laughed. "Afraid so."

"Anything?"

"Where do you want me to start?"

"Start with the search of the moorland."

"The lads haven't finished yet. They're still out there. No sign of a body so far."

"What about the clothes?"

"I've got Frank's report in front of me. He's our blood expert. It was a dry stain, so we can't tell as much as we'd like—the presence of certain drugs, for example—but it *is* blood, it's human, and it's group A, one of the most common, unfortunately, and the same as Gemma's, according to our files. We're doing more tests."

"Anything else?"

"Well, we can tell a fair bit about how it came to be there and—this is the interesting part—first, there wasn't very much, nowhere near enough to cause loss of life. It was restricted to the bib area of the T-shirt and the dungarees, which might make you think on first sight that someone cut her throat, but no way, according to Frank. At least not while she was wearing them."

"Then how did it get to be there?"

"It didn't drip. It was smeared, as if you cut your finger and wiped it on your shirt."

"But you surely wouldn't wipe it on a white T-shirt and yellow dungarees?"

"I wouldn't, no. That'd be grounds for divorce. But Gemma was only seven, remember. How careful were you about getting your clothes dirty when you were seven? Someone else washed them for you."

"Still . . . And less of your cheek, Vic. What kind of injury could have caused it?"

"We can't say for certain, but most likely a scratch, a small cut, something like that."

"Any idea how long the clothes had been out there?"

"Sorry."

"Anything else at all?"

"Yes. In addition to the items I've mentioned, we received a pair of white cotton socks and child's sneakers. There was no underwear. You might care to consider that."

"I will."

"And there was some whitish powder or dust on the dungarees. It's being analyzed."

"What about the cottage?"

"Very interesting. Whoever cleaned that place up really did a good job. They even took the vacuum bag with them and combed out all the fibres from the brushes."

"As if they had something to hide?"

"Either that or they were a right pair of oddballs. Maybe house-cleaning in the nude got them all excited."

"Aye, and maybe pigs can fly. But we've got nothing to tie them in to the missing lass?"

"No prints, no bloodstains, no bodily fluids. Just hair. It's practically impossible to get rid of every hair from a scene."

"And it's also practically impossible to pin it down to any one person," said Gristhorpe.

"There's still the DNA typing. It takes a bloody long time, though, and it's not as reliable as people think."

"Was there anything that might have indicated the child's presence?"

"No. The hairs were definitely adult. Some sandy coloured, fairly short, probably a man's, and the others we found were long and blonde. A woman's, I'd say. A child's hairs are usually finer in pigment, with a much more rudimentary character. We found some fibres, too, mostly from clothes you can buy anywhere—lamb's-wool, rayon, that kind of thing. No white or yellow cotton. There was something else, though, and I think this will interest you."

"Yes."

"Well, you know we took the drains apart?"

"Will Patricia Cummings ever let me forget?"

"There's a fair bit of dark sludge in there."

"Could it be blood?"

"Let me finish. No, it's not blood. We haven't run the final tests yet, but we think it's hair-dye, the kind you can wash out easily."

"Well, well, well," said Gristhorpe. "That *is* interesting. Just one more thing, Vic."

"Yes."

"I think you'd better get the lads digging up the cottage gardens, front and back. I know it's a long shot—most likely somebody would have seen them burying anything out there—but we can't overlook it."

"I suppose not," Manson sighed. "Your estate agent's going to love us for this."

"Can't be helped, Vic."

"Okay. I'll be in touch later."

Gristhorpe sat at his desk for a moment running his palm over his chin and frowning. This was the first positive link between Mr Brown and Miss Peterson, who had abducted Gemma Scupham on Tuesday afternoon, and Chris and Connie Manley, who had abandoned a prepaid holiday cottage in spotless condition on the Thursday of that same week. Coincidence wasn't enough; nor was the fact that Manson's men had found traces of hair-dye in the drains, but it was a bloody good start. His phone buzzed.

"Gristhorpe," he grunted.

"Sir," said Sergeant Rowe, "I think there's someone here you'd better see."

"Yes? Who is it?"

"A Mr Bruce Parkinson, sir. From what he tells me, I think he might know something about the car. You know, the one they used to take that young lass away."

Christ, it was coming in thick and fast now, the way it usually did after days of hard slog leading nowhere. "Hang onto him, Geoff," said Gristhorpe. "I'll be right down."

II

Dark satanic mills, indeed, thought DC Susan Gay as she approached Bradford. Even on a fine autumn day like this, even with most of the mills closed down or turned into craft shops or business centres, the tall, dark chimneys down in the valley still had a gloomy aspect.

Bradford had been cleaned up. It now advertised itself as the gateway to Brontë country and boasted such tourist attractions as Bolling Hall, the National Museum of Photography and even Undercliffe Cemetery. But as Susan navigated her way through the one-way streets of the city centre, past the gothic Victorian Wool Exchange and the Town Hall, with its huge campanile tower, Bradford still felt to her like a nineteenth-century city in fancy dress.

After driving around in circles for what seemed like ages, she finally turned past St George's Hall and drove by the enormous Metro Travel Interchange onto Wakefield Road. The next time she had to stop for a red light, she consulted her street map again and found Hawthorne Terrace. It didn't seem too far away: a right, a left and a right again. Soon she found herself in an area of terrace back-to-backs, with washing hanging across rundown tarmac streets. The car bumped in potholes as she looked for the street name. There it was.

An old man in a turban and a long white beard hobbled across the street on his walking-stick. Despite the chill that had crept into the air that morning, people sat out on their doorsteps. Children played hand-cricket against wickets chalked on walls and she had to drive very slowly in case one of the less cautious players ran out in front of her chasing a catch. Some of the corner shops had posters in Hindi in their windows. One showed a golden-skinned woman apparently swooning in a rajah's arms—a new video release, by the look of it. She noticed the smells in the air, too: cumin, coriander, cardamom.

At last she bumped to a halt outside number six, watched by a group of children over the street. There were no gardens, just a cracked pavement beyond the kerb, then the houses themselves in an unbroken row. The red bricks had darkened over the years, and these places hadn't been sandblasted clean like the Town Hall. Like any other northern city, Bradford had its share of new housing, both council and private, but the Johnsons' part of town was pre-war, and here, old didn't mean charming, as it often did out in the country. Still, it was no real slum, no indication of abject poverty. As she locked her car door and looked around, Susan noticed the individualizing touches to some of the houses: an ornate brass door-knocker on one bright red door; a dormer window atop one house; double-glazing in another.

Taking a deep breath, Susan knocked. She knew that, even though the Johnsons had agreed to her coming, she would be intruding on their grief. No matter what the late Carl's police record said, to them he was a son who had been brutally murdered. At least she wasn't the one to break the news. The Bradford police had already done that. The upstairs curtains, she noticed, were drawn, a sign that there had been a death in the family.

A woman opened the door. In her late fifties, Susan guessed, she looked well preserved, with a trim figure, dyed red hair nicely permed and just the right amount of make-up to hide a few wrinkles. She was wearing a black skirt and a white blouse tucked in the waistband. A pair of glasses dangled on a cord around her neck.

"Come in, dearie," she said, after Susan had introduced herself. "Make yourself at home."

The front door led straight into a small living-room. The furniture was old and worn, but everything was clean and well cared for. A framed print of a white flower in a jar standing in front of a range of mountains in varying shades of blue brightened the wall opposite the window, which admitted enough sunlight to make the wooden surfaces of the sideboard gleam. Mrs Johnson noticed Susan looking at it.

"It's a Hockney print," she said proudly. "We bought it at the photography museum when we went to see his exhibition. It brightens up the place a bit, doesn't it? He's a local lad, you know, Hockney." Her accent sounded vaguely posh and wholly put-on.

"Yes," said Susan. She remembered Sandra Banks telling her about David Hockney once. A local lad he might be, but he lived near the sea now in southern California, a far cry from Bradford. "It's very nice," she added.

"I think so," said Mrs Johnson. "I've always had an eye for a good painting, you know. Sometimes I think if I'd stuck at it and not . . . " She looked around. "Well . . . it's too late for that now, isn't it? Cup of tea?"

"Yes, please."

"Sit down, dearie, there you go. Won't be a minute. Mr Johnson's just gone to the corner shop. He won't be long."

Susan sat in one of the dark blue armchairs. It was upholstered in some velvety kind of material, and she didn't like the feel of it against her fingertips, so she folded her hands in her lap. A clock ticked on the mantelpiece. Beside it stood a couple of postcards from sunny beaches, and three cards of condolence, from neighbours no doubt. Below was a brown tiled hearth and fireplace, its grate covered by a gas-fire with fake glowing coals. Even though it was still warm enough indoors, Susan could make out a faint glow and hear the hiss of the gas supply. The Johnsons obviously didn't want her to think they were stingy.

Before Mrs Johnson returned with the tea, the front door opened and a tall, thin man in baggy jeans and a red short-sleeved jumper over a white shirt walked in. When he saw Susan, he smiled and held out his hand. He had a narrow, lined face, a long nose, and a few fluffy grey hairs around the edges of his predominantly bald head. The corners of his thin lips were perpetually upturned as if on the verge of a conspiratorial smile.

"You must be from the police?" he said. "Pleased to see you."

It was an odd greeting, certainly not the kind Susan was used to, but she shook his hand and mumbled her condolences.

"Fox's Custard Creams," he said.

"Pardon?"

"That's what Mother sent me out for. Fox's Custard Creams." He shook his head. "She thought they'd go nice with a cup of tea." Unlike his wife's, Mr Johnson's accent was clearly and unashamedly West Riding. "You think I could get any, though? Could I hell-as-like."

At that moment, Mrs Johnson came in with a tray bearing cups and saucers, her best china, by the look of it, delicate pieces with rose patterns and gold around the rims, and a teapot covered by a quilted pink cosy. She set this down on the low polished-wood table in front of the settee.

"What's wrong?" she asked her husband.

He glanced at Susan. "Everything's changed, that's what. Oh, it's been going on for years, I know, but I just can't seem to get used to it, especially as I'm home most of the time now."

"He got made redundant," said Mrs Johnson, whispering as if she were telling someone a neighbour had cancer. "Had a good job as a clerk in the accounts department at British Home Stores, but they had staff cutbacks. I ask you, after nearly thirty years' loyal service. And how's a man to get a job at his age? It's young 'uns they want these days." Her accent slipped as she expressed her disgust.

"Now that's enough of that, Edie," he said, then looked at Susan again. "I'm as tolerant as the next man—I don't want you to think I'm not—but I'd say things have come to a pretty pass when you can buy all the poppadoms and samosas you want at the corner shop but you can't get a packet of Fox's blooming Custard Creams. What'll it be next? that's what I ask myself. Baked beans? Milk? Butter? *Tea*?"

"Well, you'll have to go to Taylor's in future won't you?"

"Taylor's! Taylor's was bought out by Gandhi's or some such lot months back, woman. Shows how much shopping you do."

"I go to the supermarket down on the main road." She looked at Susan. "It's a Sainsbury's, you know, very nice."

"Anyway," said Mr Johnson, "the lass doesn't want to hear about our problems, does she? She's got a job to do." He sat down and they all waited quietly as Mrs Johnson poured the tea.

"We do have some ginger biscuits," she said to Susan, "if you'd like one."

"No thanks. Tea'll be fine, Mrs Johnson, honest."

"Where do you come from, lass?" asked Mr Johnson.

"Sheffield."

"I thought it were Yorkshire, but I couldn't quite place it. Sheffield, eh." He nodded, and kept on nodding, as if he couldn't think of anything else to say.

"I'm sorry to be calling at a time like this," Susan said, accepting her cup and saucer from Mrs Johnson, "but it's important we get as much information as we can as soon as possible." She placed the tea carefully at the edge of the low table and took out her notebook. In a crucial interrogation, either she would have someone along to do that, or she would be taking the notes while Banks asked the questions, but the Johnsons were hardly suspects, and all she hoped to get was a few names of their son's friends and acquaintances. "When did you last see Carl?" she asked first.

"Now then, when was it, love?" Mr Johnson asked his wife. "Seven years? Eight?"

"More like nine or ten, I'd say."

"Nine years?" Susan grasped at a number. "You hadn't seen him in all that time?"

"Broke his mother's heart, Carl did," said Mr Johnson, with the incongruous smile hovering as he spoke. "He never had no time for us."

"Now that's not true," said Mrs Johnson. "He fell in with bad company, that's what happened. He was always too easily led, our Carl."

"Aye, and look where it got him."

"Stop it, Bert, don't talk like that. You know I don't like it when you talk like that."

Susan coughed and they both looked at her shamefacedly. "Sorry," said Mrs Johnson. "I know we weren't close, but he *was* our son."

"Yes," said Susan. "What I was wondering was if you could tell me anything about him, his friends, what he liked to do."

"We don't really know," said Mrs Johnson, "do we, Bert?" Her husband shook his head. "It was nine years ago, I remember now. His twenty-first birthday. That was the last time we saw him."

"What happened?"

"There was a local lass," Mr Johnson explained. "Our Carl got her . . . well, you know. Anyway, instead of doing the honourable thing, he said it was her problem. She came round, right at his birthday party, and told us. We had a barney and Carl stormed out. We never saw him again. He sent us a postcard about a year later, just to let us know he was all right."

"Where was it from?"

"London. It was a picture of Tower Bridge."

"Always did have a temper, did Carl," Mrs Johnson said.

"What was the girl's name?" Susan asked.

Mr Johnson frowned. "Beryl, if I remember correctly," he said. "I think she moved away years back, though."

"Her mum and dad still live round the corner," said Mrs Johnson. Susan got their address and made a note to call on them later.

"Did Carl keep in touch at all?"

"No. He wasn't even in much after he turned sixteen, but there's not been a dicky-bird since that postcard. He'd be thirty when he . . . when he . . . wouldn't he?"

"Yes," Susan said.

"It's awful young to die," Mrs Johnson muttered. "I blame bad company. Even when he was at school, whenever he got in trouble it was because somebody put him up to it, got him to do the dirty work. When he got caught shoplifting that time, it was that what's-his-name, you know, Bert, the lad with the spotty face."

"They all had spotty faces," said Mr Johnson, grinning at Susan.

"You know who I mean. Robert Naylor, that's the one. He was behind it all. He always looked up to the wrong people did our Carl. Always trusted the wrong ones. I'm sure he wasn't *bad* in himself, just too easily led. He always seemed to have this . . . this *fascination* for bad 'uns. He liked to watch those old James Cagney films on telly. Just loved them, he did. What was his favourite, Bert? You know, that one where James Cagney keeps getting these headaches, the one where he loves his mother."

"*White Heat.*" Mr Johnson looked at Susan. "You know the one. 'Top of the world, Ma!'"

Susan didn't, but she nodded anyway.

"That's the one," said Mrs Johnson. "Loved that film, our Carl did. I blame the telly myself for a lot of the violence that goes on these days, I really do. They can get away with anything now."

"Did you know any of his other friends?" Susan asked her.

"Only when he was at school. He just wasn't home much after he left school."

"You don't know the names of anyone else he went around with?"

"Sorry, dearie, no. It's so long ago I just can't remember. It's a miracle Robert Naylor came back to me, and that's only because of the shoplifting. Had the police round then, we did."

"What about this Robert Naylor? Where does he live?"

Mrs Johnson shook her head. Susan made a note of the name anyway. It might be worth trying to track him down. If he was such a "bad 'un" he might even have a record by now. There didn't seem anything else to be gained from talking to the Johnsons, Susan thought. Best nip round the corner and find out about the girl Carl got pregnant, then head back to Eastvale. She finished her tea and stood up to leave.

"Nay, lass," said Mr Johnson. "Have another cup."

"No, I really must be going. Thank you very much."

"Well," he said, "I suppose you've got your job to do."

"Thank you for your time," Susan said, and opened the door.

"You can be sure of one thing, you mark my words," said Mrs Johnson.

Susan paused in the doorway. "Yes?"

"There'll be someone behind this had an influence on our Carl. Put him up to things. A bad 'un. A *real* bad 'un, with no conscience." And she nodded, as if to emphasize her words.

"I'll remember that," said Susan, then walked out into the cobbled street where bed-sheets, shirts and underclothes flapped on a breeze that carried the fragrances of the east.

III

The man sitting under a graphic poster about the perils of drunken driving had the irritated, pursed-lipped look of an accountant whose figures won't add up right. When he saw Gristhorpe coming, he got to his feet sharply.

"What are you going to do about it, then?" he asked.

Gristhorpe looked over to Sergeant Rowe, who raised his eyebrows and shook his head, then he led the man to one of the downstairs interview rooms. He was in his mid-thirties, Gristhorpe guessed, dressed neatly in a grey suit, white shirt and blue and red striped tie, fair hair combed back, wire-framed glasses, and his chin thrust out. His complexion had a scrubbed and faintly ruddy complexion that Gristhorpe always, rightly or wrongly, associated with the churchy crowd, and he smelled of Pears soap. When they sat down, Gristhorpe asked him what the problem was.

"My car's been stolen, that's what. Didn't the sergeant tell you?"

"You're here about a stolen car?"

"That's right. It's outside."

Gristhorpe rubbed his brow. "I'm afraid I don't understand. Can you explain it from the beginning?"

The man sighed and looked at his watch. "Look," he said, "I've been here twenty-two minutes already, first waiting to see the sergeant back there, then explaining everything to him. Are you telling me I have to go through it all again? Because if you are, you've got a nerve. I had trouble enough getting this time off from the office in the first place. Why don't you ask the other policeman what happened?"

Gristhorpe kept his silence throughout the tirade. He was used to impatient, precise and fastidious people like Mr Parkinson and found it best to let them carry on until they ran out of steam. "I'd rather hear it from you, sir," he replied.

"Oh, very well. I've been away for a while. When I—"

"Since when?"

"When what?"

"When did you go away?"

"Last Monday morning, a week ago. As I was saying, I left my car in the garage as usual, then I—"

"What do you mean, 'as usual'?"

"Exactly what I say. Now if—"

"You mean you were in the habit of doing this?"

"I think that's what 'as usual' means, don't you, Inspector?"

"Carry on." Gristhorpe didn't bother to correct him over rank. If the car turned out to be a useful lead, it would be important to find out how many people knew about Parkinson's habit of leaving his car for days at a time, and why he did so, but for now it was best to let him finish.

"When I returned this morning, it was exactly as I had left it, except for one thing."

"Yes?"

"The mileage. I always keep a careful record of how many miles I've done on each journey. I find it's important these days, with the price of petrol the way it is. Anyway, when I left, the mileometer stood at 7655. I know this for a fact because I wrote it down in the log I keep. When I got back it read 7782. Now, that's a difference of one hundred and twenty-seven miles, Inspector. Someone has driven my car one hundred and twenty-seven miles in my absence. How do you explain that?"

Gristhorpe scratched his bristly chin. "It certainly sounds as if someone borrowed it. If you—"

"Borrowed?" echoed Parkinson. "That implies I gave someone permission. I did no such thing. Someone stole my car, Inspector. *Stole* it. The fact that they returned it is irrelevant."

"Mm, you've got a point," said Gristhorpe. "Were there any signs of forced entry? Scratches around the door, that kind of thing?"

"There were scratches at the bottom of the chassis I'm positive weren't there before, but none at all around the door or windows. I imagine that today's criminal has more sophisticated means of entry than the wire coat-hanger some fools are reduced to when they lock themselves out of their cars?"

"You imagine right," said Gristhorpe. "Keys aren't hard to come by. And garages are easy to get into. What make is the car?"

"Make. I don't see—"

"For our records."

"Very well. It's a Toyota. I find the Japanese perfectly reliable when it comes to cars."

"Of course. And what colour?"

"Dark blue. Look, you can save us both a lot of time if you come and have a look yourself. It's parked right outside."

"Fine." Gristhorpe stood up. "Let's go."

Parkinson led. As he walked, he stuck his hands in his pockets and jingled keys and loose change. Outside the station, opposite the market square, Gristhorpe sniffed the air. His experienced dalesman's nose smelled rain. Already, clouds were blowing in from the northwest. He also smelled pub grub from the Queen's Arms, steak-and-kidney pie if he was right, and he realized he was getting hungry.

Parkinson's car was, indeed, a dark blue Toyota, illegally parked right in front of the police station.

"Look at that," Parkinson said, pointing to scratched paintwork on the bottom of the chassis, just behind the left front wheel. "Careless driving that is. Must have caught against a stone or something. Well? Aren't you going to have a look inside?"

"The fewer people do that, the better, sir," said Gristhorpe, looking to see what stones and dirt were trapped in the tread of the tires.

Parkinson frowned. "What on earth do you mean by that?"

Gristhorpe turned to face him. "You say you left last Monday?"

"Yes."

"What time?"

"I took the eight-thirty flight from Leeds and Bradford."

"To where?"

"I don't see as it's any of your business, but Brussels. EEC business."

Gristhorpe nodded. They were standing in the middle of the pavement and passers-by had to get around them somehow. A woman with a pram asked Parkinson to step out of the way so she could get by. A teenager with cropped hair and a tattoo on his cheek swore at him. Parkinson was clearly uncomfortable talking in the street. A mark of his middle-class background, Gristhorpe thought. The working classes—both urban and rural—had always felt quite comfortable standing and chatting in the street. But Parkinson hopped from foot to foot, glancing irritably from the corners of his eyes as people brushed and jostled past them to get by. His glasses had slipped down his nose, and a stray lock of hair fell over his right eye.

"How did you get to the airport?" Gristhorpe pressed on.

"A friend drove me. A business colleague. It's no mystery, Inspector, believe me. Long-term parking at the airport is expensive. My colleague drives a company car, and the company pays. It's as simple as that." He pushed his glasses back up to the bridge of his nose. "It's not that I'm overly concerned about saving money, of course. But why pay when you don't have to?"

"Indeed. Do you always do it that way?"

"What way?"

"Don't you ever take it in turns?"

"I told you. He has a company car. Look, I don't see—"

"Please bear with me. Did nobody notice the car was gone?"

"How could they? It was in the garage, and the garage door was locked."

"Have you asked if anyone heard anything?"

"That's your job. That's why—"

"Where do you live, sir?"

"Bartlett Drive. Just off the Helmthorpe road."

"I know it." If Gristhorpe remembered correctly, Bartlett Drive was close to the holiday cottage the Manleys had so suddenly deserted. "And the car was replaced as if it had never been gone?"

"That's right. Only they didn't bargain for my record-keeping."

"Quite. Look, I'll get someone to drive you home and take a full statement, then—"

"What? You'll do what?" A couple walking by stopped and stared. Parkinson blushed and lowered his voice. "I've already told you I've given up enough time already. Now why don't you—"

Gristhorpe held his hand up, palm out, and his innocent gaze silenced Parkinson just as it had put the fear of God into many a villain. "I can understand your feelings," Gristhorpe said, "but please listen to me for a minute. There's a chance, a very good chance, that your car was used to abduct a little girl from her home last Tuesday afternoon. If that's the case, it's essential that we get a forensic team to go over the car thoroughly. Do you understand?"

Parkinson nodded, mouth open.

"Now, this may mean some inconvenience to you. You'll get your car back in the same condition it's in now, but I can't say exactly when. Of course, we'll try to help you in any way we can, but basically, you're acting like the true public-spirited citizen that you are. You're generously helping us try to get to the bottom of a particularly nasty bit of business, right?"

"Well," said Parkinson. "Seeing as you put it *that* way." And the first drops of rain fell on their heads.

IV

Banks and Susan stood at the bar in the Queen's Arms that Monday lunch-time, wedged between two farmers and a family of tourists, and munched cheese-and-onion sandwiches with their drinks. Banks had a pint of Theakston's bitter, Susan a Slimline Tonic Water. A song about a broken love affair was playing on the jukebox in the background, and somewhere by the door to the toilets, a video game beeped as aliens went down in flames. From what he could overhear, Banks gathered that the farmers were talking about money and the tourists were arguing about whether to go home because of the rain or carry on to the Bowes Museum.

"So you found the girl's parents?" Banks asked.

"Uh-uh." Susan put her hand to her mouth and wiped away some crumbs, then swallowed. "Sorry, sir. Yes, they were home. Seems like everyone except the Pakistanis around there is unemployed or retired."

"Get anything?"

Susan shook her head. Tight blonde curls danced over her ears. Banks noticed the dangling earrings, stylized, elongated Egyptian cats in light gold. Susan had certainly brightened up her appearance a bit lately. "Dead end," she said. "Oh, it happened all right. Right charmer Carl Johnson was, from what I can gather. But the girl, Beryl's her name, she's been living in America for the past five years."

"What happened?"

"Just what his folks said. He got her in the family way, then dumped her. She came around to make a fuss, embarrass him like, at his twenty-first birthday party. He was still living at home then, off and on, and his parents invited a few close relatives over. There was a big row and he stormed out. Didn't even take any of his clothes with him. They never saw him again."

Banks sipped at his pint and thought for a moment. "So they've no idea who he hung around with, or where he went?"

"No." Susan frowned. "They know he went to London, but that's all. There was a chap called Robert Naylor. Mrs Johnson saw him as bad influence."

"Has he got form?"

"Yes, sir. I checked. Just minor vandalism, drunk and disorderly. But he's dead. Nothing suspicious. He was riding his motorbike too fast. He lost control and skidded into a lorry on the M1."

"So that's that."

"I'm afraid so, sir. From what I can gather, Johnson was the type to fall in with bad company."

"That's obvious enough."

"What I mean, sir, is that both his parents and Beryl's mother said he looked up to tough guys. He wasn't much in himself, they said, but he liked to be around dangerous people."

Banks took another sip of beer. One of the tourists bumped his elbow and he spilled a little on the bar. The woman apologized. "Sounds like the kind that hero-worships psychos and terrorists," Banks said. "He'd probably have been happy working for the Krays or someone like that back in the old days."

"That's it, sir. He was a weakling himself, but he liked to boast about the rough company he kept."

"It fits. Small-time con-man, wants to be in with the big boys. So you're thinking that might give us somewhere to look for his killer?"

"Well, there *could* be a connection, couldn't there?" Susan said, pushing her empty plate away.

Banks lit a cigarette, taking care that the smoke didn't drift directly into Susan's face. "You mean he might have been playing out of his league, tried a double-cross or something?"

"It's possible," said Susan.

"True. At least it's an angle to work on, and there don't seem very many. I dropped by The Barleycorn last night and found Les

Poole. I just thought I'd mention Johnson to him, seeing as they're both in the same business, so to speak."

"And?"

"Nothing. Poole denied knowing him—well, of course he would—and he's not a bad liar. No signs in his voice or his body language that he wasn't telling the truth. But . . ." Banks shook his head. "I don't know. There was something there. The only way I can describe it is as a whiff of fear. It came and went in a second, and I'm not sure even Les was aware of it, but it was there. Anyway, no good chasing will-o'-the-wisps. Adam Harkness's Golf Club alibi checks out. I still think we might bring South Africa up whenever we question someone, though. Johnson *could* have been blackmailing Harkness, and Harkness could afford to pay someone to get rid of him. Have you had time to ask around the other flats?"

"Last night, sir. I meant to tell you, but I set off for Bradford so early. There's a student on the ground floor called Edwina Whixley. She heard male voices occasionally from Johnson's room. And she saw someone coming down the stairs one day she thought *might* have been visiting him."

"Did you get a description?"

"Yes." Susan fished for her notebook and found the page. "About five foot five, mid-thirties, cropped black hair and squarish head. He was wearing a suede zip-up jacket and jeans."

"That's all?"

"Yes, sir."

"Ring a bell?"

Susan shook her head.

"Me, neither. Maybe you can get her to come and look at some mug-shots. And you might as well check into Johnson's form, his prison mates, that kind of thing. See if you can come up with any local names, anyone fitting the description."

"Yes, sir." Susan picked up her bag and left.

She had a very purposeful, no-nonsense walk, Banks noticed. He remembered the trouble she had had not so long ago and decided it had actually done her good. Susan Gay wasn't the kind to throw her hands up in the air and surrender. Adversity strengthened her; she learned from her mistakes. Maybe that hardened her a bit, made her more cynical and less trusting, but perhaps they weren't such bad qualities for a detective. It was hard not to be cynical when you saw so much villainy and human misery, but in many cases the cynicism was just a shell, as the sick jokes at crime scenes and post-mortems were ways of coping with the horror and the gruesomeness of death, and perhaps, too, with the fact that it comes to us all at one time. The best coppers, Banks thought, are the ones who hang onto their humanity against all odds. He hoped he had managed to do that; he knew Gristhorpe had; and he hoped that Susan would. She was young yet.

The tourists decided to go home, partly because their youngest child was making a fearful racket, and the farmers had moved on to discuss the prospects for the three-forty at Newmarket. Banks drained his pint, then headed back to the office. There was paper-work to be done. And he would make an appointment to meet with Linda Fish, from the Writers' Circle, tomorrow, much as the thought made him wince, and see what light she could shed on Mr Adam Harkness.

V

The strange woman called on Brenda Scupham shortly after Les had left for the pub that Monday evening. She was washing the dishes and lip-synching to a Patsy Cline record when the doorbell rang. Drying her hands with the tea towel, she walked through and opened the door.

"Mrs Scupham? Brenda Scupham?"

The woman stood there in the rain, a navy-blue raincoat buttoned up to her neck and a dark scarf fastened over her head. Wind tugged at the black umbrella she held. Beyond her, Brenda could see the nosy woman from number eleven across the street peeking through her curtains.

Brenda hugged herself against the cold and frowned. "Yes. What do you want?"

"I'm Lenora Carlyle," the woman said. "You might have heard of me?"

"Are you a reporter?"

"No. Can I come in?"

Brenda stood back, and the woman let down her umbrella and entered. Brenda noticed immediately in the hall light her intense dark eyes and Romany complexion. She unfastened her scarf and shook out her head of luxuriant, coal-black hair.

"I don't want anything," Brenda went on, suddenly nervous.

"I'm not a reporter, Brenda, and I'm not selling anything," the woman said in soft, hypnotic tones. "I'm a psychic. I'm here because of your daughter, Gemma. I want to help you."

Brenda just gaped and stood back as the woman unbuttoned her raincoat. Numbly, she took the umbrella and stood it on the rubber mat with the shoes, then she took the woman's coat and hung it up.

Lenora Carlyle was heavy-set, wearing a chunky-knit black cardigan covered with red and yellow roses, black slacks, and a religious symbol of some kind on a chain around her neck. Or so the odd-looking cross with the loop at the top seemed to Brenda. Lenora straightened her cardigan and smiled, revealing stained and crooked teeth.

Brenda led her into the living-room and turned off the music. She still felt a little frightened. The supernatural always made her feel that way. She wasn't sure if she believed in it or not, but she'd heard of enough strange things happening to people to make her wonder—like the time her old friend Laurie Burton dreamed about her father for the first time in years the very night he died.

After they had sat down, Brenda lit a cigarette and asked, "What do you mean, help? How can you help?"

"I don't know yet," Lenora said, "but I'm sure I can. If you'll let me."

"How much do you want?"

"I don't want anything."

Brenda felt suspicious, but you couldn't argue with that. "What do you want me to do?" she asked.

Lenora put a friendly hand on her knee. "Nothing, dear, except relax and be open. Are you a believer?"

"I . . . I don't know."

"It's all right. The Lord knows His own. Do you have something of Gemma's? Something personal."

"Like what?"

"Well, hair would be best, but perhaps an article of clothing, a favourite toy. Something she felt strongly about, touched a lot."

Brenda thought of the teddy bear one of her ex-boyfriends— Bob? Ken?—had bought Gemma some years ago. Even now she was older, Gemma never slept without it. Brenda felt a pang of guilt as she thought about it. If there were any chance that Gemma was alive, she would miss her teddy bear terribly. Being without it would make her so miserable. But no. Gemma was dead; she had to be.

She went upstairs to Gemma's room and Lenora Carlyle followed her. While Brenda walked to the tiny bed to pick up the bear, Lenora stood on the threshold and seemed to take several deep breaths.

"What is it?" Brenda asked.

Lenora didn't answer. Instead, she walked forward, reached out for the bear, and sat down on the bed with it. The bedspread had Walt Disney characters printed all over it: Mickey Mouse, Donald Duck, Bambi, Dumbo. How Gemma loved cartoons. They were the only things that made her smile, Brenda remembered. But it was an odd, inward smile, not one to be shared.

Lenora clutched the bear to her breast and rocked slowly, eyes closed. Brenda felt a shiver go up her spine. It was as if the atmosphere of the room had subtly changed, somehow become thicker, deeper and colder. For what seemed like ages, Lenora hung onto the bear and rocked silently. Brenda clutched her blouse at her throat. Then finally, Lenora opened her eyes. They were glazed and unfocused. She began to speak.

"Gemma is alive," she said. "Alive. But, oh, she's so alone, so frightened. So much suffering. She wants you. She wants her mother. She *needs* you Brenda. You must find her."

Brenda felt light-headed. "She can't be," she whispered. "They've found her clothes. . . . I've seen them."

"She's alive, Brenda." Lenora turned and grasped Brenda's wrist. Her grip was tight.

Brenda steadied herself on the back of the small chair by Gemma's desk. She felt dizzy, her skin cold and clammy, as if she had had too much to drink and the world was spinning fast. "Where can I find her?" she asked. "Where do I look? Tell me, where do I look?"

EIGHT

I

By Tuesday morning, the searchers had turned up nothing buried in the garden of the holiday cottage; nor had anything of interest been discovered on the moors where Gemma's clothing had been found. Gristhorpe sat in his office going over the paperwork, waiting to hear from forensics about Parkinson's car. Outside, mucky clouds, like balls of black wool, started to attack from the west.

It was close to twelve when Vic Manson called.

"What did you find?" Gristhorpe asked.

"Plenty. The girl was in there all right. We found her prints. Windows, back of the front seat, all over. I checked them with the ones on file, and they match."

"Good work, Vic."

"And we found yellow fibres."

"The dungarees?"

"Looks like it. I'm still waiting for the confirmation."

"Anything else?"

"A bit of black hair-dye smeared on the driver's headrest. Soil and gravel in the wheels, could have come from just about anywhere locally. Lay-by, track, drive, quarry."

"No particular kind of limestone deposit you only find on Aldington Edge, or anything like that?"

Manson laughed. "Sorry, no. Look, remember that whitish powder I told you about on the kid's dungarees? It's a lime solution, most likely whitewash."

"Where from?"

"Same as the soil and gravel, it could have come from anywhere, really. A pub wall, a cellar, outhouse."

"You can't be more specific?"

"Whitewash is whitewash. Now if you'll kindly get off the bloody phone and let me get on with the confirmations, we'll have a pile of stuff that just might stand up in court when you catch the bastards."

"All right, all right. And Vic?"

"Yes."

"I'm eternally grateful."

"I'll remember that."

Gristhorpe hung up. He no longer had to sit around waiting for the phone to ring. There were things to do: question Parkinson again, and his neighbours; get in touch with the press and television. They could run this on "Crimewatch." And where had he seen whitewash recently? Calling for Richmond on his way, he swept down the corridor towards the stairs.

II

Why was it, Banks thought, as he sat in Corrigan's Bar and Grill on York Road near the bus station, that so many people gravitated towards these trendy, renovated pubs? What on earth was wrong with a down-to-earth, honest-to-goodness old pub? Just look at Le Bistro, that place he had met Jenny last week. All coral pink tablecloths, long-stemmed wine glasses and stiff napkins.

And now this: eighteenth-century Yorkshire translated almost overnight into twentieth-century New York, complete with booths, brass rails, square Formica-top tables and waitresses who might bustle in New York, but in Yorkshire moved at their normal couldn't-care-less pace. At least some things didn't change.

And then there was the menu: a large, thin laminated card of bold, handwritten items with outrageous prices. Burgers, of course, club sandwiches, corned beef on rye (and they didn't mean Fray Bentos), and such delights for dessert as raspberry cheesecake, pecan pie and frozen yoghurt. All to the accompaniment (not *too* loud, thank the Lord) of Euro-pop.

Maybe he was getting conservative since the move to Yorkshire, he wondered. Certainly in London, Sandra and he had happily embraced the changes that seemed to happen so fast from the sixties on, delighted in the varieties of food and ambience available. But somehow here, in a town with a cobbled market square, ancient cross, Norman church and excavated pre-Roman ruins, so close to the timeless, glacier-carved dales and towering fells with their jagged limestone edges and criss-cross dry-stone walls, the phoney American theme and fashionable food seemed an affront.

The beer was a problem, too, just as it was in Le Bistro. Here was no Theakston's bitter, no Old Peculier, no Tetley's, Marston's or Sam Smith's, just a choice of gassy keg beer and imported bottled lagers from Germany. Holland, Mexico and Spain, all ice cold, of course. Funnily enough, he sat over a glass (they didn't serve pints, only tall heavy glasses that tapered towards their thick bases) of Labatt's, one of the less interesting lagers he remembered from his trip to Toronto.

Such were his thoughts as he puzzled over the menu waiting for Linda Fish, the Champagne socialist, to show. Corrigan's had been *her* choice, and as he wanted information, he had thought it best to comply. The sacrifices a copper makes in the course of duty, he thought to himself, shaking his head. At least there was an ashtray on the table. He looked out of the window at the lunch-time shoppers darting in and out of the shopping centre opposite in the rain. Raincoats, waxed-jackets, a chill in the air: it looked as if autumn had arrived at last.

Linda walked in after he had been musing gloomily for ten minutes or so. She packed up her telescope umbrella and looked around, then waved and came over to join him. She had always reminded Banks of an overgrown child. It was partly the way she dressed—today blue sweatpants and a matching sweatshirt with a pink teddy bear on its front—and partly the slightly unformed face, a kind of freckled, doughy blob on which had been stuck two watery eyes accentuated by blue shadow, a button nose and thin lips made fuller by lipstick. Her straw-coloured hair looked as if she had just cut it herself with blunt scissors in front of a funfair mirror. As always, she carried her oversized and scuffed leather shoulder-bag, something she had picked up in Florence, she had once told him, and with great sentimental value. Whether it was stuffed with bricks and toiletries or unpublished manuscripts, he had no idea, but it certainly looked heavy.

Linda squeezed her bulk into the booth opposite Banks. "I hope you don't mind meeting here," she said conspiratorially, "but I'm afraid I've become quite addicted to the chili-burgers."

"It's fine," Banks lied. She wasn't from Yorkshire, and her slight lisp seemed to make the Home Counties accent sound even posher. Whatever you might say or think about Linda, though, Banks reminded himself, she was far from stupid. Not only did she run the local Writers' Circle with such energy and enthusiasm that left most bystanders gasping, but she was indeed a *published* writer, not a mere hopeful or dilettante. She had, in fact, published a short novel with a large firm only a year ago. Banks had read it, and admitted it was good. Very good, in fact. No, Linda Fish was no fool. If she wanted to look ridiculous, then that was her business.

"I'm afraid I won't be able to tell you very much, you know," she said.

"Even a little will help." Banks flapped the menu. "Anything you'd recommend?"

Her blue eyes narrowed in a smile. "I can see you're uncomfortable," she said. "I'm sorry I suggested we meet here. Men are obviously much happier in pubs."

Banks laughed. "You're right about that. But let's see what I can salvage from the situation. Who knows, I might even find something I like."

"Good," said Linda. "Well, you know what I'm having. Are you not familiar with this kind of food?"

"American? Yes. I've never been to the States but I was in Toronto a couple of years ago. I think I can find my way around. I always found it was best to stick with the burgers."

"I think you're right."

A waitress ambled along, playing with her hair as she approached. "Yes?" She stood beside the booth, weight balanced on her left hip, order pad in one hand and pencil in the other. She didn't even look at them. Linda ordered her chili-burger and a bottle of San Miguel, and Banks went for the mushroom-and-cheese burger and another glass of Labatt's. He leaned back on the red vinyl banquette and lit a Silk Cut. The grill had filled up a bit since Linda arrived, mostly truant sixth-formers buzzing with conversation and laughter, and the Euro-pop droned on.

"Do you want to interrogate me before lunch or after?" Linda asked.

Banks smiled. "I always find a full stomach helps. But if you're—"

She waved her hand. "Oh no, I'm not in a hurry or anything. I'm just interested." She stuck her hand deep in her bag and frowned, leaning slightly to the side, as she rummaged around in there like a kid at a fairground lucky-dip. "Ah, got them." She pulled out a packet of menthol cigarettes.

"You know," she said, lighting up, "I'd never really thought about it before, but you could be useful to me."

"Me? How?"

"I'm thinking of writing a detective story."

"Good lord," said Banks, whose knowledge of detective fiction stopped at Sherlock Holmes.

"From what I've read," Linda went on, "it's clear that one can get away without knowing much police procedure, but a little realism does no harm. What I was thinking was—"

The waitress appeared with their food and drinks at that moment, and Linda's attention was diverted towards her chili-burger. Feeling relieved at the interruption, Banks bit into his burger. It was good. But his reprieve was only temporary.

"What I was thinking," Linda went on, wiping the chili sauce from her chin with a paper napkin, "was perhaps that you could advise me. You know, on police procedure. And maybe tell me a bit about some of your cases. Give me an insight into the criminal mind, so to speak."

"Well," said Banks, "I'd be glad to help if you have any specific questions. But I don't really think I can just sit down and tell you all about it."

Her eyes narrowed again, and she bit into her burger. When she had finished that mouthful, she went on. "I suppose that's a compromise of sorts. I'm sure your time is too valuable to waste on writers of fiction. Though I *did* get the impression that you are fairly well read."

Banks laughed. "I like a good book, yes."

"Well, then. Even Hardy and Dickens had to do their research, you know. They had to ask people about things."

Banks held up his hands. "All right, you've convinced me. Just give me specific questions and I'll do my best to answer them, okay?"

"Okay. I haven't got that far yet, but when I do I'll take you up on it."

"Now, what can you tell me about Adam Harkness?"

"Ah-hah, the interrogation at last. As I said, I can't tell you very much, really. But I don't believe all that phoney anti-apartheid rubbish, for a start."

"Why not?"

"Because it doesn't square with what I've heard. Oh, I'm sure he probably even believes it himself now, and it's a trendy enough position for white South African expatriates to take. But how do you think his father made his money? You can't tell me he didn't exploit the blacks. Everybody did. And you won't see Adam Harkness giving his money away to support the ANC."

"He told me he left South Africa because he didn't agree with the politics."

"That's not what I heard."

"What did you hear?"

"It's just rumours, but I've a friend lives there, a writer, and she said there was some kind of scandal about to break but the Harknesses hushed it up."

"What kind of scandal?"

"Nobody really knows. My friend suspects he killed someone, a black mine-worker, but there's no proof."

It was possible, Banks supposed, ten or more years ago to cover up the murder of a black by a rich and powerful white man in South Africa. For all he knew, despite the scrapping of racial classification, it probably still was. Attitudes don't change overnight, whatever politicians might decree.

"Have you ever heard of a man called Carl Johnson?" Banks asked.

"Only from the papers. He was the one killed, wasn't he, at the old lead mine?"

"That's right. He worked as a gardener for Harkness."

"Did he now?" She leaned forward. "And you think there might be some connection?"

"There might be."

"You surely don't think Adam Harkness murdered him?"

"Harkness has an alibi. But a man like him can afford to have things done."

Her eyes opened wide. They looked like oysters on a half-shell. "Do you mean that kind of thing really goes on? In England? Hit men and contracts and all that."

Banks smiled. "It has been known."

"Well . . . there's obviously more to this crime business than I realized. But I'm afraid I can't help you any further."

"Could you get in touch with your friend? Ask her for more information?"

"I could try, but I got the impression they put a lid on it pretty securely. Still, if it might help . . ."

"It might."

"I've just had a thought."

"Yes?"

"If the rumour's true, about Harkness and the black miner, and if that Johnson person was killed at an old mine, there's a sort of symmetry to that, isn't there?"

"I suppose there is," Banks agreed. Symmetry, for Christ's sake, he thought. Plenty of it in books, but not in real life. "It's just a very isolated spot," he said.

"So why would anyone go there to meet a killer?"

"Obviously it was someone he trusted. He didn't have a car, so someone must have picked him up, or met him somewhere, and taken him there. Perhaps he thought he was going to get money."

"Oh, yes," said Linda. "I see. Well, I'd better leave the police work to you, hadn't I? But, you know, that's exactly the kind of thinking I'm interested in. Now, I'm going to have a chocolate sundae and you can tell me all about your most interesting case."

III

Gristhorpe and Richmond stood in the rain outside Parkinson's house. Semi-detached, with a frosted-glass door and a pebble-dash façade, it was more modern than the row of tiny limestone cottages that faced it across the lopsided square of unkempt grass. Gristhorpe hadn't realized that Parkinson's house was so close to the abandoned cottage. This was the extreme north-western edge of Eastvale, and both the new and the old houses shared a superb view west along the valley bottom. Not today, though; everything was lost in the grey haze of rain.

Richmond wore a belted navy-blue Aquascutum over his suit, and Gristhorpe a rumpled fawn raincoat with the collar turned up. Neither wore a hat. It was the kind of rain that you felt inside rather than out, Gristhorpe thought, already registering the aches in his joints. Outside you merely got beaded in moisture, but inside you were damp and chilled to the marrow.

They had already tried the semis to the west, the last pair, with only the Helmthorpe Road and a dry-stone wall between them and the open country, but found nobody home. In fact, as Gristhorpe stood there looking around, he noticed how quiet and secluded the area was. Given that Parkinson had kept his car in the garage at the back of his house, it wouldn't have been at all difficult for someone to "borrow" it without being seen. Apart from a few cars and delivery vans on the main road, there was nothing else around.

They walked up the path and rang the bell of the semi adjoining Parkinson's. A few moments later a man answered and, after they had showed their identification, he invited them in.

"Come in out of the rain," he said, taking their coats. "I'll put the kettle on."

He was about forty, small and thick-set, with sparse fair hair and lively grey eyes. His right arm, encased in plaster, hung in a sling over the lower part of his chest.

They settled down in the cheerful living-room, where the element of an electric fire took some of the chill out of their bones, and their host, Mr David Ackroyd, came in with mugs of tea and joined them. Two women were talking on the radio about menopause. He turned it off and sat down. Richmond installed himself in the armchair opposite, long legs crossed, notebook and pen in hand.

"What happened?" Gristhorpe asked, indicating the arm.

"Broke it on Sunday. Doing a bit of climbing out Swainshead way." He shook his head. "Silly bugger I am. I ought to know I'm too old for that sort of thing."

"So you're not usually home weekdays?"

"Good lord, no. I'm a civil servant . . . well, civil as I can be to some of the riff-raff we get in the job centre these days." His eyes twinkled. "And servant to the devil, according to some. I'll be back at work again in a couple of days. The doctor says I just need a bit of a rest to get over the shock."

"Are you married?"

He frowned. "Yes. Why do you ask?"

"Does your wife work?"

"She's an auditor with the tax office."

"So she's usually out all day, too?"

"Yes. Most people around here are. Have to be to pay the mortgages, prices being the way they are. What's going on?"

"Just trying to feel out the lie of the land, so to speak," Gristhorpe said. "Did you know Mr Parkinson's car was stolen while he was away?"

"Yes. He came dashing in to tell me as soon as he checked the mileage. I told him to go to the police."

"Did you notice anything at all?"

"No. Of course, I was out at work all the time until the weekend. Everything seemed quite normal."

"Did he often make these trips?"

"Yes. Quite proud of himself he was about it too. He got a promotion in the company a short while ago. Exports. They do a bit of business with the Common Market countries. You know how it is, everything's Euro-this and Euro-that these days."

"And he always left his car in the garage?"

"Yes. Look, between you and me, Bruce is a bit tight. Short arms and deep pockets, if you know what I mean. He hasn't quite got to the company-car level yet but his boss, the bloke who usually goes with him, has. He lives a few miles north of here, so it's easy for him to pick Bruce up."

"How many people do you think knew about this arrangement?"

"I couldn't say."

"But Mr Parkinson was the sort to talk about such things in public?"

"Well, I suppose so. I mean, it's nothing, is it, really? Just idle chatter, pub talk. He liked to let people know how important he was, how he got to travel to Europe on business and all that. I don't think he was worried that someone might overhear him and take off with his car."

"Could that have happened?"

"Easily enough, I suppose." He rubbed the plaster on his arm. Gristhorpe noticed that a couple of people had signed it in ball-point just below the elbow. "We ought to be more careful, oughtn't we?" Ackroyd went on. "Lord knows, we hear enough about crime prevention on telly, we should know better than to go blabbing all our holiday and business plans in a pub. You just don't think, do you?"

"Which pub is this, Mr Ackroyd?"

"Pub? Well, I was speaking figuratively, really, but there's a local in the next street. It's called The Drayman's Rest. Nothing special really, but they do a decent pint and the company's all right."

"Do you and Mr Parkinson go there regularly?"

"I suppose you could say that. Not that we're big drinkers, mind you." He laughed. "Bruce always drinks halves and makes them last. It's just the social thing, the local, isn't it? A chat and a few laughs with the lads after work, that sort of thing."

"Do you know most of the regulars?"

"Oh, aye. Except we get a few strangers in from the holiday cottages over the road. They never cause any trouble, though, and we make them welcome enough."

"Get friendly with them, do you?"

"Well, some are easier than others, if you know what I mean. Some just like to keep to themselves, grab a sandwich and a pint and sit in the corner reading the paper. But there's outgoing ones. I like talking to people. That's how you learn, isn't it?"

"Have you met any interesting strangers in there recently?"

"What?"

"The past couple of weeks. Anyone been especially friendly?"

Ackroyd rubbed his chin. "Aye, well now you mention it, there was Chris and Connie."

Gristhorpe looked over at Richmond. "The Manleys?"

"That's it. I always thought it a bit odd that they liked to stand at the bar and talk to the locals."

"Why?"

"Well, with a bird like her I wouldn't be in the pub in the first place," Ackroyd said, and winked. "But usually it's the couples tend to keep to themselves."

"They didn't?"

"No. Oh, they weren't pushy or anything. Just always there with a hello and a chat. Nowt special. It might be the weather, the news . . . that kind of thing."

"And Mr Parkinson's European business trips?"

"Well, he did go on a bit. . . . Now wait a minute, you can't be suggesting that Chris and Connie . . . ? No, I don't believe it. Besides, they had a car of their own. I saw them in it."

"A white Fiesta?"

"That's right."

"What kind of impression did they give you, Mr Ackroyd?"

"They just seemed like regular folk. I mean, Chris liked to talk about cars. Bit of a know-it-all, maybe. You know, the kind that likes to dominate conversations. And she seemed happy enough to be there."

"Did she say much?"

"No, but she didn't need to. I mean most of the men in that place would've given their right arms—" He stopped, looked at his cast and laughed. "No, that wasn't how I got it, honest. But what I'm trying to say is that it wasn't just that she was a looker, though she was that all right. The long blonde hair, those lovely red lips and the blue eyes. And from what I could tell she had all her curves in the right places, too. No, it wasn't just that. She was sexy. She had a presence. Like she didn't have to do anything. Just walk in, smile, stand there leaning on the bar. There was something about her you could feel, like an electric charge. I am rambling on, aren't I? Do you know what I mean?"

"I think so, Mr Ackroyd." Some women just gave out an aura of sex, Gristhorpe knew. That kind of sex appeal was common enough on screen—the way Marilyn Monroe's clothes always seemed to want to slip off her body, for example—but it also happened in real life. It was nothing to do with looks, though a combination of beauty and sex appeal could be deadly when it occurred, and some women didn't even realize they had it.

"How did Mr Manley act towards her?" he asked.

"No special way in particular. I mean, he wasn't much to look at himself. I got the impression he was sort of pleased that so many men obviously fancied her. You knew she was *his* and you could look but you couldn't touch. Now I think about it, he definitely seemed to be showing her off, like."

"Nobody tried to chat her up?"

"No." He scratched his cheek. "And that's a funny thing, you know. Now you've got me talking I'm thinking things that never really entered my head at the time. They were just an interesting couple of holidaymakers, but the more I think about them . . ."

"Yes?"

"Well, the thing that really struck you about Chris was his smile. When he smiled at you, you immediately wanted to trust him. I suppose it worked with the women too. But there was something . . . I mean, I can't put my finger on it, but you just sort of *knew* that if you really did try it on with Connie, outside a bit of mild flirting, that is, then he'd be something to reckon with. That's the only way I can express it. I suppose everyone picked up on that because nobody tried it on. Not even Andy Lumsden, and he goes after anything in a skirt as a rule."

"Where were they from?"

"Chris and Connie? Do you know, I couldn't tell you. He didn't have a Yorkshire accent, that's for certain. But it was hard to place.

South, maybe. It was sort of characterless, like those television newsreaders."

"They didn't say where they were from?"

"Come to think of it, no. Just said they were taking some time off and travelling around for a while, having a rest from the fast lane. They never really said anything about themselves. Funny that, isn't it?"

"They didn't even say what they were taking time off from?"

"No."

Gristhorpe stood up and nodded to Richmond. He shook Mr Ackroyd's good hand and wished him well, then they walked back out into the drizzle.

"What now?" Richmond asked.

Gristhorpe looked at his watch. "It's half past two," he said. "I reckon we've just got time for a pint and a sandwich at The Drayman's Rest, don't you?"

IV

Susan Gay parked her red Golf outside and went up to her flat. She had had a busy day going over mug-shots with Edwina Whixley—to no avail—and questioning the other occupants of 59 Calvin Street again. She had also made an appointment to see the governor of Armley Jail, where Johnson had served his time, at four-thirty the following afternoon. She knew she could probably have asked him questions over the phone, but phone calls, she always felt, were too open to interruptions, and too limiting. If the governor needed to consult a warden for additional information, for example, that might prove difficult over the phone. Besides, she was old-fashioned; she liked to be able to watch people's eyes when she talked to them.

She put her briefcase by the door and dropped her keys on the hall table. She had made a lot of changes to the place since her promotion to CID. It had once been little more than a hotel suite, somewhere to sleep. But now she had plants and a growing collection of books and records.

Susan favoured the more traditional, romantic kind of classical music, the ones you remember bits from and find yourself humming along with now and then: Beethoven, Tchaikovsky, Chopin, bits of opera from films and TV adverts. Most of her records were "greatest hits," so she didn't have their complete symphonies or anything, just the movements everyone remembered.

Her reading was still limited mostly to technical stuff, like forensics and criminology, but she made space on her shelves for the occasional Jeffrey Archer, Dick Francis and Robert Ludlum. Banks wouldn't approve of her tastes, she was sure, but at least now she knew she *had* tastes.

As usual, if she was in, she had "Calendar" on the television as she fussed around in the kitchen throwing together a salad. Normally, she would just be listening, as the TV set was in the living-room, but this evening, an item caught her attention and she walked through, salad bowl in hand and stood and watched open-mouthed.

It was Brenda Scupham and a gypsyish looking woman on the couch being interviewed. She hadn't caught the introduction, but they were talking about clairvoyance. Brenda, in a tight lemon chiffon blouse tucked into a black mini-skirt much too short for a worried mother, sat staring blankly into the camera, while the other woman explained how objects dear to people bear psychic traces of them and act as conduits into the extrasensory world.

Brenda nodded in agreement occasionally. When Richard Whiteley turned to her and asked her what she thought, she said, "I don't know. I really don't know," then she looked over at the other woman. "But I'm convinced my Gemma is still alive and I want to beg whoever knows where she is to let her come back to her mother, please. You won't be punished, I promise."

"What about the police?" he asked. "What do they think?"

Brenda shook her head. "I don't know," she said. "I think they believe she's dead. Ever since they found her clothes, I think they've given up on her."

Susan flopped into her armchair, salad forgotten for the moment. Bloody hell, she thought, Superintendent Gristhorpe's going to *love* this.

NINE

I

Gristhorpe was indeed furious when he heard about Brenda Scupham's television appearance. As he had no TV set of his own, though, he didn't find out until Wednesday morning.

"It's been over a week now since Gemma Scupham disappeared," he said, shaking his head over coffee and toasted teacakes with Banks at the Golden Grill. "I can't say I hold out much hope. Especially since we found the clothes."

"I can't, either," Banks agreed. "But Brenda Scupham's got some bloody psychic to convince her that Gemma's alive. Who would you rather listen to, if you were her?"

"I suppose you're right. Anyway, it all connects: the abandoned cottage, the borrowed car, the hair-dye. We've got descriptions of the Manleys out—both as themselves and as Peterson and Brown. Somebody, somewhere must know them. How about you?"

Banks sipped some hot black coffee. "Not much. The lab finally came through with the scene analysis. The blood in the mill matched Johnson's, so we can be pretty certain that's where he was killed. Glendenning says it was a right-handed upthrust wound. Six-inch blade, single-edged. Probably some kind of sheath-knife, and you know how common those are. No handy footprints or tire tracks, and no sign of the weapon. I'm off to see Harkness again, though I don't suppose it'll do much good."

"You think he did it?"

"Apart from the mysterious stranger seen leaving Johnson's building, he's the only lead I've got. I keep telling myself that just because I didn't take to the man it doesn't mean he's a killer. But nobody gets that rich without making a few enemies. And Johnson was a crook. He *could* have been involved somewhere along the line."

"Aye, maybe you're right. Be careful, though, the last thing I need right now is the ACC on my back."

Banks laughed. "You know me. Diplomacy personified."

"Aye, well . . . I'd better be off to see Mrs Scupham. See if I can't talk some sense into her. I want a word with that bloody psychic, too. I've got Phil out looking for her." He looked outside. A fine mist nuzzled the window.

"Hang on a minute, sir," Banks said. "You know, Brenda Scupham might be right."

"What?"

"If Gemma *is* alive, a television appeal won't do any harm. It might even do some good."

"I realize that. We can't have any idea what the woman's going through. All I want to do is reassure her that we *are* doing the best we can. If Gemma is alive, we've more chance of finding her than some bloody tea-leaf reader. There's a trail to follow somewhere in all this, and I think we're picking it up. But these people, the Manleys or whatever they call themselves now, they talked to enough people, got on well enough with the locals, but they gave nothing away. We don't even know where they come from, and we can't be sure what they look like, either. They're still two-dimensional."

"What about the notes they used to pay for the cottage?"

"Patricia Cummings, the estate agent, said she paid the cash directly into the bank. Right now it's mixed up with all the rest of the money they've got in their vaults."

"How did they hear about the cottage? Did they say?"

"Told her they'd read about it in *The Dalesman*."

"You could get—"

"I know, I know—the list of subscribers. We're checking on it. But you can buy *The Dalesman* at almost any newsagent's, in this part of the country, anyway."

"Just a thought."

Gristhorpe finished his teacake and wiped his mouth with the paper serviette. "At the moment it looks like our best bet lies with the descriptions—if that's what they really look like. Christ knows, maybe they're Hollywood special-effects people underneath it all. We've got the artist working with Parkinson and the crowd in The Drayman's Rest. Should be ready for tomorrow's papers. And I was thinking about the whitewash they found on Gemma's clothes, too. I've seen it in two places recently: Melville Westman's, the Satanist, or whatever he calls himself, and the holiday cottage."

"I suppose the Manleys could have kept Gemma there," Banks said. "Perhaps they drugged her. She's not very big. It wouldn't be difficult to get her out of the cottage after dark."

"Aye, that's true enough. Still, I'm getting a warrant and sending a few lads to give Westman's place a good going-over."

"You don't like him any better than I like Harkness, do you?"

Gristhorpe grinned. "No," he said. "No, I don't." He pushed his chair back. "Must be off. See you later, Alan." And he walked out into Market Street.

II

Adam Harkness's house clearly hadn't been vacuumed or tidied since Banks's last visit. At least a crackling fire took the chill out of the damp air in the library. The french windows were firmly closed. Beyond the streaked glass, drops of rain pitted the river's surface. Lyndgarth and Aldington Edge were shrouded in a veil of low grey cloud.

"Please, sit down," Harkness said. "Now what can I do for you, Chief Inspector? Have you found Carl's killer?"

Banks rubbed his hands in front of the fire, then sat. "Not yet," he said. "There's a couple of points you might be able to help me clear up, though."

Harkness raised a challenging eyebrow and sat in the chair opposite Banks. "Yes?"

"We've learned that Johnson might have met with a certain individual on a couple of occasions shortly before his murder. Did he talk to you about any of his friends?"

"I've already told you. He was my gardener. He came a couple of times a week and kept the garden in trim. That's all."

"Is it? Please think about it, Mr Harkness. Even if Johnson was only the hired help, it would be perfectly natural to have a bit of a chat now and then about innocuous stuff, wouldn't it?" He felt that he was giving Harkness a fair chance to come up with something he may have forgotten or chosen not to admit earlier, but it did no good.

Harkness folded his hands in his lap. "I knew nothing whatso- ever about Carl Johnson's private life. The moment he left my prop- erty, his life was his own, and I neither know nor care what he did."

"Even if it was of a criminal nature?"

"You might believe he was irredeemably branded as a criminal. I do not. Besides, as I keep telling you, I have no knowledge of his activities, criminal or otherwise."

Banks described the man Edwina Whixley had seen coming down the stairs of Johnson's building: thick-set, medium height, short dark hair, squarish head. "Ever see or hear about him?"

Harkness shook his head. "Carl always came here alone. He never introduced me to any of his colleagues."

"So you never saw this man?"

"No."

"How did Johnson get here?"

"What?"

"Carl Johnson? How did he get here? He didn't have a car."

"There are still buses, Chief Inspector, including a fairly regular service from Eastvale to Lyndgarth. There's a bus-stop just by the bridge."

"Of course. Did Johnson ever mention any of his old prison friends?"

"What? Not to me. It would hardly have been appropriate, would it?" Harkness picked up the poker and jabbed at the fire. "Look, why don't you save us both a lot of wasted time and energy and accept that I'm telling the truth when I say I knew *nothing* about Carl's private life?"

"I don't know what gives you the impression I don't believe you."

"Your attitude, for a start, and the questions you keep on asking over and over again."

"Sir," said Banks, "you have to understand that this is a murder investigation. People forget things. Sometimes they don't realize the importance of what they know. All I'm doing is trying to jog your memory into giving up *something* that Johnson might have let slip in a moment of idle chatter. Anything. It might mean nothing at all to you—a name, a date, an opinion, whatever—but it might be vital to us."

Harkness paused. "Well . . . of course, yes . . . I suppose I see what you mean. The thing is, though, there really *is* nothing. I'm sure if he'd said anything I would have remembered it by now. The fact is we just didn't talk beyond discussing the garden and the weather. Basically, we had nothing else in common. He seemed a reticent sort of fellow, anyway, kept himself to himself, and that suited me fine. Also, remember, I'm often away on business."

"Was there ever any evidence that Johnson had used the house in your absence?"

"What do you mean, 'used the house'? For what purpose?"

"I don't know. I assume he had a key?"

"Yes. But . . ."

"Nothing was ever out of place?"

"No. Are you suggesting he might have been stealing things?"

"No. I don't think even Carl Johnson would have been that stupid. To be honest, I don't know what I'm getting at." Banks scratched his head and glanced at the river and the copper beech, leaves dripping, beyond the french windows. "This is a fairly out-of-the-way place. It could be suitable for criminal activities in any number of ways."

"I noticed nothing," Harkness said, with a thin smile. "Not even a muddy footprint on my carpet."

"You see," Banks went on, "Johnson's life is a bit of a mystery to us. We've got his record, the bald facts. But how did he think? We don't seem to be able to find anyone who was close to him. And there are years missing. He may have been to Europe, Amsterdam perhaps. He may even have had friends from South Africa."

Harkness sat bolt upright and gripped the arms of the chair. "What are you insinuating?"

"I've heard rumours of some sort of a scandal. Something involving you back in South Africa. There was some sort of cover-up. Do you know what I'm talking about?"

Harkness snorted. "There are always scandals surrounding the wealthy, Chief Inspector. You ought to know that. Usually they derive from envy. No, I can't say I do know what you're talking about."

"But was there any such scandal involving you or your family out there?"

"No, nothing that stands out."

Banks got that almost-infallible tingle that told him Harkness was holding back. He gave his man-of-the-world shrug. "Of course, I'm not suggesting there was any truth in it, but we have to investigate everything that comes up."

Harkness stood up. "It seems to me that you are spending an unusual amount of time investigating *me* when you should be looking for Carl Johnson's killer. I suggest you look among his criminal cronies for your killer."

"You've got a point, there. And, believe me, we're trying to track them down. Just out of interest, did Johnson ever mention South Africa to you?"

"No, he did not. And don't think I don't know what you're getting at. You're suggesting he was blackmailing me over some secret or other, aren't you, and that I killed him to silence him? Come on, is that what you're getting at?"

Banks stood up and spoke slowly. "But you couldn't have killed him, could you, sir? You were dining at the Golf Club at the time of the murder. A number of very influential people saw you there." He regarded Harkness, who maintained an expression of outraged dignity, then said, "Thank you very much for your time," and left.

As he drove down to the main road with the windscreen-wipers tapping time to Gurney's "Sleep," he smiled to himself. He had got at least some of what he had wanted: a sure sense that Harkness was holding something back; and the satisfying knowledge that the man, rich, confident and powerful notwithstanding, could be rattled. Time now to make a few overseas phone calls, then perhaps have another chat with Mr Adam Harkness.

III

"You think I acted dishonestly, is that what you're saying?"

"Irresponsibly is the word I had in mind," Gristhorpe replied. He was sitting opposite Lenora Carlyle in a small interview room at the station. A WPC sat by the window to take notes. With her wild black hair, her high, prominent cheekbones and blazing dark eyes, Lenora certainly looked dramatic. She seemed composed as she sat there, he noticed, arms folded across her jumper, a slightly superior smile revealing stained teeth. It was the kind of smile, Gristhorpe thought, that she probably reserved for the poor, lost disbelievers with whom she no doubt had to deal now and then.

"I do my job, Superintendent," she said, "and you do yours."

"And just what is your job? In this case it seems to consist of giving a poor woman false hope." Gristhorpe had just been to see Brenda Scupham, and he had noticed the fervour in her eyes when she spoke of what Lenora had told her.

"I can tell there's no convincing you, but I don't happen to believe it's false. Look, are you upset because Brenda criticized you on television? Is that why you've got me in here?"

"What was the source of your information about Gemma Scupham?"

"I'm a psychic. You know that already."

"So the 'other side' is the source?"

"If you want to put it like that, yes."

"Are you sure?"

"What are you getting at?"

Gristhorpe leaned back and rested his forearms on the table. "Ms Carlyle, we're investigating the abduction of a child, a very serious crime, and one that happens to be especially odious to me. All of a sudden, you walk into Brenda Scupham's house and tell her you know the child is still alive. I'd be a bloody idiot if I didn't ask you *how* you know."

"I've told you."

"Aye. And, as you well know, I don't happen to believe in convenient messages from the other side."

She smiled. "It's stalemate, isn't it, then?"

"No, it isn't. Are you aware that I could hold you if I wanted?"

"What do you mean?"

"You profess to have information about a missing child, but you won't reveal your source. As far as I know, you could have something to do with Gemma Scupham's disappearance."

"Now look here—"

"No. *You* look here. If that child *is* alive and you know something that could help us find her, you'd better tell me, because I'm getting tired of this."

"I only know what I told Brenda—that Gemma is alive, she's scared and she wants her mother. You know, you'd do much better with an open mind. The police *have* used psychics to help them in the past."

And a fat lot of good it's done, thought Gristhorpe, feeling himself being manipulated into the position of doing exactly that. The woman might know something, after all, and he couldn't dismiss that possibility, even if it meant playing her game. "All right," he sighed. "Did you get any impressions about where she is?"

Lenora shook her head.

"Any images, sounds, smells?"

"Nothing like that. Just an overwhelming emotional sense of her presence somewhere. Alive. And her fear."

"Near or far?"

"I can't say."

Gristhorpe scratched his chin. "Not much to go on, is it?"

"I can't help that. I'm merely a medium for the messages. Do you want to consult me professionally? Do you want me to try and help you?"

Gristhorpe noticed the smile of triumph. "Ms Carlyle," he shot back, "if you *fail* to help us, I'll make sure you're thrown in jail. Do you know Melville Westman?"

It was only fleeting, but he saw it, a split-second sign of recognition. It was second nature for him to notice the signs, the body language, the way eye-contact broke off. He could see her trying to decide how much to admit. "Well?" he prodded.

"The name sounds vaguely familiar," she said with a toss of her head. "I might have come across him."

"Let me fill you in. Melville Westman calls himself a magician. There have been incidents in the past few years of such groups using children in their rituals. Now, I don't know what you're up to, but if you and Westman have any involvement in Gemma's disappearance, direct or indirect, I'll find out about it."

"This is ridiculous!" Lenora said. "I've had enough of your accusations and insinuations." She tried to push the chair back to get to her feet, but forgot it was bolted to the floor and she got stuck, half-standing, between it and the table.

"Sit down." Gristhorpe waved his hand. "I haven't finished yet. What's your connection with Westman?"

She sat down, chewed on her lower lip for a moment, and answered, "I know him, that's all. We're acquaintances."

"Met at the magician's circle, did you?"

"You don't have to be sarcastic. It's a small community for anyone interested in the occult. We've had discussions, loaned one another books, that's all."

"I'm asking you if Westman has told you anything about Gemma Scupham's whereabouts. Are you some kind of messenger, some salve to the conscience come to spare the mother a little pain until you've finished with the child? Or are you just tormenting her?"

"Don't be absurd. What would Melville want with the child?"

"You tell me."

"He wouldn't. He's not that kind."

"What kind?"

"The kind that performs elaborate rituals, sacrifices animals and . . ."

"Children?"

"Look, I'm not denying there are lunatic fringes around, but Melville Westman doesn't belong to one."

"Is there anyone in the area you would associate with a lunatic fringe?"

"No."

"Ever heard of the Manleys? Chris and Connie. Or Miss Peterson and Mr Brown?"

"No."

"Did Melville Westman send you?"

"No, he bloody well didn't. I came forward to help the mother of my own free will," Lenora said through clenched teeth. "And this is how you treat me. I thought the police would—"

"You know nothing about the way we work, or you'd hardly have had Brenda Scupham shooting her mouth off on television."

"That wasn't my doing."

"It doesn't matter whose doing it was. It happened. And if that child *is* dead, I want you to think of how much harm you've done her mother."

Lenora put her fist to her heart. "The child is alive, Superintendent. I'm convinced of it."

For a moment, Gristhorpe was taken aback by the passion in her voice. After everything he had accused her of, she was still clinging to her original story. He let the silence stretch for a while longer, holding her intense gaze. He could feel something pass across the air between them. He couldn't put his finger on what it was, a tingling sensation, the hackles on his neck rising, and he certainly had no idea whether or not she was right about Gemma. He did know, though, that she was telling the truth as far as she knew it. The damn woman was genuine in her beliefs. He could see, now, how Brenda Scupham had been convinced.

"I want you to know," he said slowly, "that I'll check and double-check on everything you've told me." Then he broke off the staring match and looked towards the bare wall. "Now get out. Go on, get out before I change my mind." And he didn't even turn to watch her go. He knew exactly the kind of smile he would see on her face.

IV

Armley Jail was built in 1847 by Perkin and Backhouse. Standing on a low hill to the west of the city centre, it looks like a structure from the Middle Ages, with its keep and battlements all in dark, solid stone—especially in the iron-grey sky and the rain that swept across the scene. Eastvale Castle seemed welcoming in comparison, Susan thought. Even the modern addition to the prison couldn't quite overcome the sense of dank medieval dungeons she felt as she approached the gates. The architects could hardly have come up with a place more likely to terrify the criminals and reassure the good citizens, she thought, giving a shiver as she got out of the car and felt the rain sting her cheek.

She showed her warrant card, and at four-thirty on that dreary September afternoon, the prison gates admitted her, and a uniformed attendant led her to a small office in the administrative block to meet Gerald Mackenzie. She had found herself wondering on her way what kind of person felt drawn to prison work. It must be a strange world, she thought, locked in with the malcontents. Like the police, the prison service probably attracted its share of bullies, but it also had an appeal, she guessed, for the reformers, for people who believed in rehabilitation. For many, perhaps, it was just a job, a source of income to pay the mortgage and help feed the wife and kids.

Mackenzie turned out to be a surprisingly young man with thin brown hair, matching suit, a crisp white shirt and what she took to be a regimental or club tie of some kind. The black-framed glasses he wore gave him the look of a middle-management man. He was polite, offered coffee, and seemed happy enough to give her the time and information she wanted.

"From what I can remember," he said, placing a finger at the corner of his small mouth, "Johnson was a fairly unassuming sort of fellow. Never caused any trouble. Never drew attention to himself." He shook his head. "In fact, I find it very hard to believe he ended up the way he did. Unless he was the victim of some random crime?"

"We don't think so," Susan said. "How did he spend his time?"

"He was a keen gardener, I remember. Never went in much for the more intellectual pursuits or the team games."

"Was he much of a socializer in any way?"

"No. As I said, I got the impression he kept very much to himself. I must confess, it's hard to keep abreast of everyone we have in here—unless they're troublemakers of course. The well-behaved ones you tend to leave to themselves. It's like teaching, I suppose. I've done a bit of that, you know. You spend most of your energy on the difficult students and leave the good ones to fend for themselves. I mean, there's always far more to say about a wrong answer than a right one, isn't there?"

"I suppose so," said Susan. The memory of an essay she wrote at police college came to mind. When the professor had handed it back to her, it had been covered in red ink. "So Johnson was an exemplary prisoner?"

"Inmate. Well, yes. Yes, he was."

"And you don't know a lot more about him, his routine, his contacts here?"

"No. I don't actually spend much time on the shop floor, so to speak. Administration, paperwork . . . it all seems to take up so much time these days. But look, I'll see if I can get Ollie Watson to come in. He worked Johnson's wing."

"Would you?"

"No trouble."

Mackenzie ducked out of the office for a moment and Susan examined a framed picture of a pretty dark-skinned woman, Indian perhaps, with three small children. Mackenzie's family, she assumed, judging by the way the children shared both his and the woman's features a certain slant to the nose here, a dimple there.

A few minutes later, Mackenzie returned with Ollie Watson. As soon as she saw the fat, uniformed man with the small black moustache, Susan wondered if the "Ollie" was a nickname because the man looked so much like Oliver Hardy. He pulled at the creases of his pants and sat down on a chair, which creaked under him.

"Mr Watson," Susan said after the introductions, "Mr Mackenzie tells me you're in the best position to give me some information about Carl Johnson's time in here."

Watson nodded. "Yes ma'm." He shifted in his seat. It creaked again. "No trouble, Carl wasn't. But you never felt you ever got to *know* him, like you do with some. Never seemed much interested in anything, 'cept the garden, I suppose."

"Did he have friends?"

"Not close ones, no. He didn't mix much. And people left him alone. Not because they were scared of him or anything. Just . . . there was something remote about him. It was as if they hardly even noticed him most of the time."

"What about his cell-mates? Did he share?"

"Most of the time, yes." He smiled. "As you probably know, it gets a bit overcrowded in here. Must be because you lot are doing such a good job."

Susan laughed. "Us or the courts. Was there anyone in particular?"

"Let me see . . ." Watson held out his hand and counted them off on his fingers. "There was Addison, that's one. Basically harmless, I'd say. Business fraud. Then there was Rodgers. No real problems there, either. Just possession . . ."

"Johnson was brutally murdered," Susan butted in on Watson's leisurely thought process. "Did he meet anyone you think capable of doing that?"

"Good lord, no. Not in here," said Watson, as if prison were the last place on earth where one would expect to find real evil-doers. "He was never in with any of the really hard, serious lags. We keep them separate as best we can."

"But someone could have involved him in a criminal scheme, something that went wrong? Drugs, perhaps?"

"I suppose it's possible. But Rodgers was only in for possession of marijuana. He wasn't a dealer."

"What about the business fraud?"

"Like I said, he was harmless enough. Just the old purchasing scam."

Susan nodded. She had come across that before. A purchasing officer for a large company simply rents some office space, a phone and headed stationery, then he "supplies" his company with goods or services that don't exist and pockets the payment. He has to be careful to charge only small amounts, so the purchase orders don't have to go to higher management for signing. If it can be worked carefully and slowly over a number of years, the purchasing scam can prove extremely lucrative, but most practitioners get greedy and make mistakes.

"Could he have got Johnson involved in something more ambitious? After all, Johnson was a bit of a con-man himself."

Watson shook his head. "Prison took the life out of Addison. It does that to some people. You're on the job long enough you get to recognize the signs, who'll be back and who won't. Addison won't. He'll be straight as a die from now on. He was just a mild-mannered clerk fancied a crack at the high life."

Susan nodded, but she had already noted Addison's name in her book. "What about the others?"

"Aye." Watson lifted his hand again. "Who did we say . . . Addison, then the possession fellow, Rodgers. Then there was Poole. I wouldn't worry about him, either."

"Poole?" said Susan, suddenly alert. "What was his first name?"

"Leslie. But everyone called him Les. Funny-looking bloke, too. One of those old-fashioned Elvis Presley haircuts." Watson laughed. "Until the prison barber got to him, that is. From what he said, though, the women seemed—"

But Susan was no longer listening. She couldn't help but feel a sudden surge of joy. She had one-upped Richmond. With all his courses, caches and megabytes, he hadn't discovered what she had by sheer old-fashioned legwork. He was working on the Gemma Scupham case, of course, not the Johnson murder, but still . . .

"Sorry for interrupting," she apologized to Watson, then looked at Mackenzie. "May I use your phone, sir?"

TEN

I

In the evening beyond the venetian blinds in Banks's office, puddles gleamed between the cobbles, and water dripped from the cross-bars of lamp-posts, from eaves and awnings. Muted light glowed behind the red and amber windows of the Queen's Arms, and he could hear the buzz of laughter and conversation from inside. The square itself was quiet except for the occasional click of high-heels on cobbles as someone walked home from work late or went out on a date. An occasional gust of cool evening air wafted through his partly open window, bringing with it that peculiar fresh and sharp after-the-rain smell. It made him think of an old John Coltrane tune that captured in music just such a sense of an evening after rain. He could make out the gold hands against the blue face of the church clock: almost eight. He lit a cigarette. The gaslights around the square—an affectation for tourists—came on, dim at first, then brighter, reflecting in twisted sheets of incandescent light among the puddles. It was the time of day Banks loved most, not being much of a morning-person, but his epiphany was interrupted by a knock at the office door, shortly followed by PC Tolliver and DC Susan Gay leading in an agitated Les Poole.

"Found him at the Crown and Anchor, sir," explained Tolliver. "Sorry it took so long. It's not one of his usual haunts."

"Bit up-market for you, isn't it, Les?" Banks said. "Come into some money lately?"

Poole just grunted and worked at his Elvis Presley sneer. Tolliver left and Susan Gay sat down in the chair beside the door, getting out her notebook and pen. Banks gestured for Poole to sit opposite him at the desk. Poole was wearing jeans and a leather jacket over a turquoise T-shirt, taut over his bulging stomach. Even from across the desk, Banks could smell the beer on his breath.

"Now then, Les," he said, "you might be wondering why we've dragged you away from the pub this evening?"

Les Poole shifted in his chair and said nothing; his features settled in a sullen and hard-done-by expression.

"Dunno."

"Have a guess."

"You found out something about Gemma?"

"Wrong. I'm working on another case now, Les. The super's taken that one over."

Poole shrugged. "Dunno then. Look, shouldn't I have a brief?"

"Up to you. We haven't charged you with anything yet. You're just helping us with our enquiries."

"Still . . . what do you want?"

"Information."

"About what?"

"Can you read, Les?"

"Course I can."

"Read the papers?"

"Now and then. Sporting pages mostly. I mean, most of your actual news is bad, isn't it? Why bother depressing yourself, I always say."

Banks scratched the thin scar beside his right eye. "Quite. How about the telly? That nice new one you've got."

Poole half rose. "Now look, if this is about that—"

"Relax, Les. Sit down. It's not about the Fletcher's warehouse job, the one you were going to tell me you know nothing about. Though we might get back to that a bit later. No, this is much more serious."

Poole sat down and folded his arms. "I don't know what you're on about."

"Then let me make it clear. I can do it in two words, Les: Carl Johnson. Remember, the bloke I asked you about a couple of days ago, the one you said you'd never heard of?"

"Who?"

"You heard."

"So what. I still don't know no Ben Johnson."

"It's Carl, Les. As in Carl Lewis. Better pay more attention to those sporting pages, hadn't you? And I think it was a bit too much of a slip to be convincing. Don't you, Susan?"

Banks looked over Poole's shoulder at Susan Gay, who sat by the door. She nodded. Poole glanced around and glared at her, then turned back, tilted his head to one side and pretended to examine the calendar on the office wall, a scene of the waterfalls at Aysgarth in full spate.

"According to the governor of Armley Jail," Susan said, reading from her notes to give the statement authority, "a Mr Leslie Poole shared a cell with a Mr Carl Johnson for six months about four years ago."

"Bit of a coincidence, isn't it, Les?" Banks said.

Poole looked up defiantly. "What if it is? I can't be expected to remember everyone I meet, can I?"

"Have we refreshed your memory?"

"Yeah, well . . . now you mention it. But it was a different bloke. Same name, all right, but a different bloke."

"Different from whom?"

"The one you mean."

"How do you know which one I mean?"

"Stands to reason, dunnit? The bloke who got killed."

"Ah. That's better, Les. And here was me thinking you weren't up on current affairs. How did you hear about it?"

"Saw it on the telly, didn't I? On the news. Someone gets croaked around these parts you can't help but hear about it somewhere."

"Good. Now seeing as this Carl Johnson you heard about on the news is the same Carl Johnson you shared a cell with in Armley Jail—"

"I told you, it was a different bloke!"

Banks sighed. "Les, don't give me this crap. I'm tired and I'm hungry. I haven't eaten since elevenses, and here I am sticking around out of the goodness of my heart just to talk to you. I'm trying to be very civilized about this. That's why we're in my nice comfortable office just having a friendly chat instead of in some smelly interview room. Listen, Les, we've got prison records, we've got fingerprints, we've got warders who remember. Believe me, it was the same person."

"Well, bugger me!" Les said, sitting up sharply. "What a turn-up for the book. Poor old Carl, eh? And here was me hoping it must have been someone else."

Banks sighed. "Very touching, Les. When did you last see him?"

"Oh, years ago. How long was it you said? Four years."

"You haven't seen him since you came out?"

"No. Why should I?"

"No reason, I suppose. Except maybe that you both live in the same town?"

"Eastvale ain't that small."

"Still," said Banks, "it's a bit of a coincidence, isn't it? He's been in Eastvale a few months now. It strikes me that, given your records, the two of you might have got together to do a little creative thievery. Like the Fletcher's warehouse job, for example. I'm sure Carl was versatile enough for that."

"Now there you go again, accusing me of that. I ain't done nothing."

"Les, we could drive down to your house right now, pick up the television and the compact music centre, maybe even the video, too, and likely as not *prove* they came from that job."

"Brenda bought those in good faith!"

"Bollocks, Les. What's it to be?"

Poole licked his lips. "You wouldn't," he said. "You wouldn't dare go and take them away, not after what's happened to poor Brenda." A sly smile came to his face. "Think how bad it would look in the papers."

"Don't push me, Les." Banks spoke quietly, but the menace in his voice came through clearly. "What we're dealing with here is a man who was gutted. Ever been fishing, Les? Ever cleaned a fish? You take one of those sharp knives and slit its gullet open to empty the entrails. Well, someone took a knife like that, someone who must have known Carl Johnson pretty well to get so close to him in such a remote spot, and stuck the knife in just above his balls and dragged it slowly up his guts, sliced his belly button in two, until it got stuck on the chest bone. And Carl's insides opened up and spilled like a bag of offal, Les. If his jacket hadn't been zipped up afterwards they'd have spilled all over the bloody dale." He pointed at Poole's beer-belly. "Do you know how many yards of intestine you've got in there? Are you seriously telling me that I'll let a few stolen electrical goods get in the way of my finding out who did that?"

Poole held his stomach and paled. "It wasn't me, Mr Banks. Honest, it wasn't. I've got to go to the toilet. I need a piss."

Banks turned away. "Go."

Poole opened the door, and Banks asked the uniformed PC standing there to escort him to the gents.

Banks turned to Susan. "What do you think?"

"I think he's close, sir," she said.

"To what?"

"To telling us what he knows."

"Mm," said Banks. "Some of it, maybe. He's a slippery bugger is Les."

He lit a cigarette. A short while later, Poole returned and resumed his seat.

"You were saying, Les?"

"That I'd nothing to do with it."

"No," said Banks. "I don't believe you had. For one thing, you haven't got the bottle. Just for the record, though, where were you last Thursday evening?"

"Thursday? . . . Let me see. I was helping my mate in his shop on Rampart Street."

"You seem to spend a lot of time at this place, Les. I never took you for a hard worker before, maybe I was wrong. What do you do there?"

"This and that."

"Be more specific, Les."

"I help out, don't I? Make deliveries, serve customers, lug stuff around."

"What's your mate's name again?"

"John."

"John what."

"John Fairley. It's just a junk shop. You know, old 78s, second-hand furniture, the odd antique. Nothing really valuable. We empty out old people's houses, when they snuff it, like."

"Nothing new? No televisions, stereos, videos?"

"You're at it again. I told you I had nothing to do with that. Let it drop."

"What's he look like, this John Fairley?"

"Pretty ordinary."

"You can do better than that."

"I'm not very good at this sort of thing. He's strong, you know, stocky, muscular. He's a nice bloke, John, decent as they come."

"What colour's his hair?"

"Black. Like yours."

But Banks could see the guilt and anxiety in Poole's eyes. John's shop was where they fenced the stuff, all right, and John Fairley's description matched that of the man Edwina Whixley had seen coming down from Carl Johnson's flat, vague as it was.

"Do we know him, Les?"

"Shouldn't think so. I told you, he's straight."

"If I went to see this mate of yours, this John, he'd tell me you were in the shop all evening Thursday, would he?"

"Well, not *all* evening. We worked a bit late, unloading a van full of stuff from some old codger from the Leaview Estate who croaked a few weeks back."

"What time did you finish?"

"About seven o'clock."

"And where did you go after that?"

"Pub."

"Of course. Which one?"

"Well, first we went to The Oak. That's the nearest to Rampart Street. Had a couple there, just to rinse the dust out of my mouth, like, then later we went down the local, The Barleycorn."

"I assume you were seen at these places?"

"I suppose so. That's what I did. Cross my heart and hope to die."

"I wouldn't do that, Les."

"What?"

"Hope to die. Look what happened to Carl Johnson."

Poole swallowed. "That's got nothing to do with me."

"But we don't know why he was killed, do we? Let's just take a hypothetical scenario, all right? A sort of falling out among thieves. Say Carl was involved in the Fletcher's warehouse job, and say there were two or three others in on it as well. Now, maybe Carl got too greedy, or maybe he tried to stick away a few pieces of merchandise for himself—like one of his accomplices might have done, too—you know, a nice new telly, and maybe a stereo. Follow my drift so far?"

Poole nodded.

"Good. So let's say one of these thieves doesn't have much regard for human life. He gets mad at Carl, arranges to meet him to discuss the problem, persuades him to go for a ride, then guts him. Now, what do you think this bloke, who's already killed once, might do if he gets wind there's a problem with *another* of his accomplices?"

Poole's jaw dropped.

"What's wrong, Les? Cat got your tongue?"

Poole shook his head. "Nothing. I ain't done nothing."

"So you keep saying. Say it often enough and *you* might believe it, but I won't. Are you sure there's nothing you want to tell me, Les? Maybe you met this bloke, or maybe Carl talked about him. I'd hate to have to hang around some filthy old lead mine while the doc tried to stuff you into a body sack without spilling your guts all over the dirt."

Poole put his hands over his ears. "Stop it!" he yelled. "It's not bloody fair. You can't do this to me!"

Banks slammed the desk. "Yes, I bloody well can," he said. "And I'll go on doing it until I find out the truth. If I have to, I'll lock you up. More likely I'll just let you go and tell the press you were kind enough to give us a few tips on the warehouse job. What's it to be, Les? Your choice."

Poole looked around the office like a caged animal. Seeing no way out, he sagged in his chair and muttered, "All right. You're a bastard, you know."

Banks glanced over at Susan Gay. She turned a page in her notebook.

"Look, about this 'ypo-whatsit story of yours," Poole said.

"Hypothetical."

"That's right. I mean, you can't pin owt on anyone for just telling an 'ypothetical story, can you?"

Banks grabbed his coffee mug, pushed his chair back, put his feet on the desk and lit a cigarette. "Maybe, maybe not," he said. "Just tell us about the bloke, Les. Talk to me. I'm listening."

"Yeah, well, I did bump into Carl a couple of times, accidental like. We had a jar or two now and then, talked about old times. There was this mate he mentioned. I didn't want to say before because I didn't want to get involved, not now that I'm going straight and all—What's up with you?"

"Sorry, Les," Banks said. "Just a bit of coffee went down the wrong way. Carry on. Tell me about this mate of Carl's."

Poole scowled. "Anyway, I remembered from the time inside, like, this bloke he used to talk about sometimes, like it was his hero or something. I never met him myself, but just hearing about him gave me the creeps. Funny that, like Carl seemed to get some kind of kick out of telling me about this bloke and what he did and all that, but to me it was a bit over the top. I mean, I'm no fucking angel, I'll admit that, but I've got my limits. I never hurt anyone. Remember, this is all 'ypothetical."

"The man, Les."

"Hold on, I'm getting to him. Anyways, as I was saying Carl said he was here in Eastvale. Well, that's when I cut out. I didn't want nothing to do with them. I didn't want to get mixed up in anything."

"What didn't you want to get mixed up in, Les?"

"You know, anything, like, criminal."

"I see. Were they in on the Fletcher's warehouse job? Johnson and this other bloke."

"I think so. But like I said, I stayed well away after I heard this bloke was in town."

"Tell me about him."

"Not much to tell. Like I said, I never met him. According to Carl, he's never been inside, yet he's been up to more evil than many as have."

"What kind of evil?"

"You name it. If what Carl says is right, this bloke worked with some of the London mobs, you know, peddling porn and hurting people who wouldn't pay up, but now he's gone freelance. Bit of a rover. Never stays in one place very long. Got lots of contacts."

"And he's never been inside?"

"Not as anyone knows of." Poole leaned forward. "Look, Mr Banks," he said, licking his lips. "This bloke's really nasty, know what I mean? Carl told me he was in a fish-and-chip shop once and got arguing with the woman in front. She was carrying a dog with her, like, one of those little Pekinese things, and this bloke just plucked it out of her arms and flung it in the frier then walked out cool as a cucumber. He's a nutter. I didn't want nothing to do with him."

"Can't say I blame you," said Banks. "What's his name?"

"Dunno. Carl never said."

"Les!"

"Look, I don't want anyone knowing I—"

"Just between you and me, Les. Off the record."

"You promise?"

"I'm in the business of preventing crime, remember? It'd hardly be in my interests to have another murder on my patch, would it? And you've no idea how much I'd miss you."

"Huh. Even so . . ."

"Les."

Poole paused. "All right, all right. I'll trust you—still 'ypothetical, like. All I know is his name is Chivers. It's pronounced with a 'sh', like in shivers. I don't know if it's his real name or a nickname."

"What does he look like?"

"I don't know. I told you, I never met him."

Banks wasn't convinced. For a start, he was certain that Poole *had* been connected with the Fletcher's warehouse job, and now it seemed a good bet that Johnson and this Chivers person had been involved, too, along with John Fairley, the junk-shop owner. He could understand Poole's not wishing to implicate himself, of course, especially as it was now a matter of murder.

The thing to remember about Les Poole was that he had spent time inside; he knew the value of information and of silence. He knew how to get as much slack as he could while giving as little as possible in return. Maybe he was a small-time crook, a coward and a bully, not too bright, but he knew the ropes; he knew how to duck and dodge to save his own neck, how to measure out exactly enough co-operation to get himself out of trouble. Banks sensed that he was holding back, that he *had* met this Chivers, but there was no percentage in pushing him yet. They needed more leverage, and Poole was right about one thing: impounding Brenda Scupham's television would look very bad indeed.

"Is he still in Eastvale?"

"Dunno. Don't think so."

"Is there anything else you can tell me about him?"

"No. 'Cept I'd stay out of his way if I were you. Carl said he had this bird and—"

"What bird's this, Les?"

"This bird Chivers had with him. Some blonde bint. Apparently, he always has a bit of spare with him. The lasses like him. Must be his unpredictable, violent nature."

They liked Les, too, Banks remembered, and wondered if there had been a spot of bother about this blonde. Maybe Les had made a pass and Chivers put a scare in him. Or maybe Carl Johnson had. It wasn't so difficult, he thought, to fill in the rest from the scraps Poole dished out.

"What did Carl say about Chivers's girlfriend?" he asked.

"Just that Chivers knifed a bloke once for looking at her the wrong way. Didn't kill him, like, just cut him up a bit. Anyway, like I said, he never had any shortage of birds. Not scrubbers either, according to Carl. Quality goods. Maybe it was his smile," Les added.

"What smile?"

"Nothing. Just that Carl said he had this really nice smile, like. Said his mates called him 'Smiler' Chivers."

When Banks heard Poole's last comment, the warning bells began to ring. "Susan," he said, looking over Poole's shoulder. "Do you know if the super's still here?"

II

Brenda Scupham couldn't concentrate on the television programme. For a moment she thought of going out, maybe to the pub, but decided she couldn't stand the questions and the looks people would give her. She hadn't enjoyed going out much at all since Gemma had gone. For one thing, people had given her dirty looks when they saw her, as if they blamed her or she wasn't obeying the proper rules of mourning or something. Instead, she took another tranquillizer and poured herself a small measure of gin. Again she wondered what the hell was going on.

All she knew was that the police had called at her house earlier that evening looking for Les. He'd been out of course, and she hadn't known where, though she was sure the policeman hadn't believed her. When she asked what they wanted, they wouldn't tell her anything. Surely, she thought, if it had anything to do with Gemma, they should tell her?

She looked over at the television and video. Maybe that's what it was all about? She knew they were stolen. She wasn't *that* stupid. Les hadn't said so, of course, but then he wouldn't; he never gave away anything. He had dropped them off in John's van one afternoon and said they were bankrupt stock. All the time the police had been coming and going because of Gemma, Brenda had been worried they would spot the stolen goods and arrest her. But they hadn't. Perhaps now they had some more evidence and had decided to arrest Les after all.

How her life could have changed so much in just one week was beyond her. But it had, and even the tranquillizers did no real good. She had enjoyed going on television with Lenora Carlyle—that had been the high spot of her week—but nothing had come of it. Just as nothing had come of the police search, the "Crimewatch" reconstruction, or her appeals through the newspapers. And now, as she sat and thought about the police visit, she wondered if Les might have been involved in some way with Gemma's disappearance. She couldn't imagine how or why—except he hadn't got on very well with Gemma—but he *had* been acting strangely of late.

And the more she thought about it, the more she lost faith in Lenora's conviction that Gemma was still alive. She couldn't be. Not after all this time, not after the bloodstained clothing they had brought for her to identify. And apart from that one statement, Lenora had come up with nothing else, had she? Surely she ought to be able to picture where Gemma was if she was any good as a psychic? But no, nothing. And what if Gemma was alive somewhere? It didn't bear thinking about. She felt closer to her daughter now she was gone than she ever had while Gemma had been around.

Time after time her thoughts circled back to Mr Brown and Miss Peterson. Should she have known they weren't who they said they were? And if she hadn't felt so guilty about not loving Gemma the way a good mother should and about shaking her the week before, would she have let her go so easily? They had been so convincing, kind and understanding rather than accusing in their approach. They had looked so young, so official, so competent, but how was she to know what child-care workers were supposed to look like?

Again she thought of the police officers who had come to her house earlier. Maybe they had found Gemma and some clue had led them to Les. But still she couldn't imagine what he could possibly have to do with it. He had been out when the child-care workers called. Still, there was no denying the police were after him. If he had anything to do with Gemma's abduction, Brenda thought, she would kill him. Damn the consequences. It was all his fault anyway. Yes, she thought, reaching for the gin bottle again. She would kill the bastard. For now, though, she was sick of thinking and worrying.

The only thing that worked, that took away the pain, even though it lasted such a short time, was the video. Slowly, she got up and went over to the player. The cassette was still in. All she had to do was rewind and watch herself on television again. She had been nervous, but she was surprised when she watched the playback that it didn't show so much. And she had looked so pretty.

Brenda poured herself another generous measure, turned on one element of the fire and reclined on the sofa with her dressing-gown wrapped around her. She had watched the video once and was rewinding for a second viewing when she heard Les's key in the door.

III

"You don't believe for a moment he told you everything, do you?" Gristhorpe asked Banks later in the Queen's Arms. It was a quiet Wednesday evening, a week since the first news of Gemma Scupham's disappearance—and despite the helicopters and search tactics learned from the North American Association of Search and Rescue, she still hadn't been found. Banks and Gristhorpe sat at a table near the window eating the roast beef sandwiches that they had persuaded Cyril, the landlord, to make for them.

Banks chewed and swallowed his mouthful, then said, "No. For a start, I'm sure he's seen this Chivers bloke, but he couldn't really admit to it without implicating himself in the warehouse job. We let him walk. For now. Les won't stray far. He's got nowhere to go."

"And then?"

Banks grinned. 'Just an idea, but I'd like to find out if Les really does know anything about Gemma's abduction. I had a phone call just after I'd finished with Poole. Jim Hatchley's coming into town. Seems his mother-in-law's commissioned him to install a shower—"

Gristhorpe slapped the table. One of the customers at the bar turned and looked. "No, Alan. I'm not having any of Hatchley's interrogation methods in this one. If Gemma's abductors get off because we've bent the rules I'd never bloody forgive myself. Or Sergeant Hatchley, for that matter."

"No," said Banks, "that's not what I had in mind." He outlined his plan and both of them ended up laughing.

"Aye," said Gristhorpe, nodding slowly. "Aye, he'd be the best man for *that* job, all right. And it might work, at that. Either way, we've nothing to lose."

Banks washed his sandwich down with a swig of Theakston's bitter and lit a cigarette. "So where do we go now?" he asked.

Gristhorpe leaned back in his chair and folded his hands in his lap. "Let's start with a summary. I find it helps to get everything as clear as possible. In the first place, we know that a couple who called themselves Chris and Connie Manley rented a cottage and changed their appearance. Then they 'borrowed' a dark blue Toyota from Bruce Parkinson, passed themselves off as social workers called Mr Brown and Miss Peterson, and conned Brenda Scupham into handing over her daughter on Tuesday afternoon. After that, they drove a hundred and twenty-seven miles before returning the car to its owner.

"As far as we know, they left the cottage on Thursday in a white Fiesta. We don't have the number, and Phil's already checked and re-checked with the rental outlets. Nothing. And it hasn't been reported stolen. We could check the ownership of every white Fiesta in the country, and we bloody well will if we have to, but that'll take us till doomsday. They might not be registered as owners, anyway. Nobody saw them with the child in Eastvale, and there was no evidence of a child's presence in the cottage, but she could have been there—the whitewash supports that—and we found her prints in Parkinson's car. Why they took her, we don't know. Or where. All we know is they most likely didn't bring her back, which to me indicates that she could well be lying dead and buried somewhere in a hundred-and-twenty-mile radius. And that includes the area of the North York Moors where we found the bloodstained clothes. Vic says there wasn't enough blood on them to cause death, but that doesn't mean the rest didn't spill elsewhere, or that she might not have died in some other way. Poole told you that this Chivers person was involved in the porn trade in London, so that's another ugly possibility to consider. I've been onto the paedophile squad again, but they've got nothing on anyone of that name or description.

"Anyway. Next we find Carl Johnson's body in the old lead mine on Friday morning. Dr Glendenning says he was probably killed sometime after dark on Thursday. You follow all the leads you can think of in the Johnson murder, and we arrive at this same man called Chivers with a smile that people notice, a blonde girlfriend and a nasty disposition. You think Poole knows a bit more. Maybe he does. There are too many coincidences for my liking. Chivers and the girl are the ones who took Gemma.

Maybe one or both of them also killed Carl Johnson. Chivers, most likely, as it took a fair bit of strength to rip his guts open. But why? What's the connection?"

"Johnson could have double-crossed them on the warehouse job, or maybe he knew about Gemma and threatened to tell. Whatever Johnson was, he wasn't a paedophile."

"Assuming he found out they'd taken her?"

"Yes."

"That's probably our best bet. Makes more sense than killing over a bloody TV set, though stranger things have happened."

"Or it could have been over the girlfriend," Banks added. "Especially after what Poole told me about the knifing."

"Aye," said Gristhorpe. "That's another strong possibility. But let's imagine that Carl Johnson found out Chivers and his girlfriend had taken Gemma and . . . well, done whatever they did to her. Now Johnson's no angel, and he seems to have an unhealthy fascination with bad 'uns, from what you tell me, but somehow, they've gone too far for him. He doesn't like child-molesters. He becomes a threat. They lure him out to the mine. Maybe the girl does it with promises of sex, or Chivers with money, I don't know. But somehow they get him there and . . ." Gristhorpe paused. "The mine might be a connection. I know the area's been thoroughly searched already, but I think we should go over it again tomorrow. There's plenty of spots around there a body could be hidden away. Maybe the clothes on the moors were just a decoy. What do you think, Alan?"

Banks frowned "It's all *possible*, but there are still too many uncertainties for my liking. I'd like to know more about the girl's part in all this, for a start. Who is she? What's in it for her? And we've no evidence that Chivers killed Johnson."

"You're right, we don't have enough information to come to conclusions yet. But we're getting there. I thought you fancied Adam Harkness for the Johnson murder?"

"I did, though I'd no real reason to. Looks like I might have been wrong, doesn't it?"

Gristhorpe smiled. "Happens to us all, Alan. You always did have a chip on your shoulder when it came to the rich and influential, didn't you?"

"What?"

"Nay, Alan, I'm not criticizing. You're a working-class lad. You got where you are through brains, ability and sheer hard slog. I'm not much different myself, just a poor farm-boy at heart. I've no great love for them as were born with silver spoons in their mouths. And I don't mind sticking up for you when Harkness complains to the ACC about police harassment. All I'm saying is be careful it doesn't blur your objectivity."

Banks grinned. "Fair enough," he said. "But I haven't finished with Mr Harkness yet. I called the Johannesburg police and set a few enquiries in motion. You never know, there might be something to that scandal yet. And I called Piet in Amsterdam to see if he can track down Harkness's ex-wife. There's still a chance Harkness might have been involved somewhere along the line. What about your black magician, Melville Westman?"

"Nothing," said Gristhorpe. "The lads did a thorough job. He looks clean. It's my bet that Gemma was in the Manleys' cottage at some point, and that's where the whitewash on her clothes came from. That's not to say I won't be having another word with Mr Westman, though." Gristhorpe smiled. His own feelings about people like Melville Westman and Lenora Carlyle were not so different from Banks's feelings about the rich and powerful, he realized: different chip, different shoulder, but a prejudice, nonetheless.

"I'm going to call my old mate Barney Merritt at the Yard first thing in the morning," Banks said. "He ought to be able to get something out of Criminal Intelligence about Chivers a damn sight quicker than the formal channels. The more we know about him, the more likely we are to be able to guess at the way he thinks. The bastard might never have been nicked but I'll bet a pound to a penny he's on the books somewhere."

Gristhorpe nodded. "Oh, aye. No doubt about it. And it looks as if we're all working on the same case now. You'd better get up to date on the Gemma files, and we'd better let Phil know so he can access his databases or whatever he does. I want this bloke, Alan. I want him bad. I mean I want him in front of me. I want to see him sweat. Do you know what I mean?"

Banks nodded and finished his drink. From the bar, they heard Cyril call time. "'t's late," he said quietly. "Time we were off home."

"Aye. Everything all right?"

"Fine," said Banks. "Just think yourself lucky you don't have daughters."

Banks walked in the rain, coat buttoned tight, and listened to his Walkman. It was after eleven-thirty when he got home, and the house was in darkness. Sandra was already in bed, he assumed; Tracy, too. He knew he wouldn't be able to sleep just yet, after the conversation with Gristhorpe had got his mind working, and as he had drunk only two pints in the pub, he felt he could allow himself a small Scotch. What was it the medics said, three drinks a day is moderate? Some kind soul had brought him a bottle of Glen Garioch from a holiday in Scotland, so he poured himself a finger and sat down. Though he wasn't supposed to smoke in the house, he lit a cigarette anyway and put on a CD of Barenboim playing Chopin's Nocturnes. Even at low volume, the clarity of the sound was astonishing. He had hardly begun to let his mind roam freely over the image of Chivers he had created so far when he heard the front door open and close softly, then the creak of a stair.

He opened the living-room door and saw Tracy tiptoeing upstairs.

"Come down here a moment," he whispered, careful not to wake Sandra.

Tracy hesitated, halfway up, then shrugged and followed him into the living-room.

Banks held out his wristwatch towards her. "Know what time it is?"

"Of course I do."

"Where've you been?"

"Out with Keith."

"Where to?"

"Oh, Dad! We went to the pictures, then after that we were hungry so we went for a burger."

"A burger? At this time of night?"

"You know, that new McDonald's that's opened in the shopping centre. It's open till midnight."

"How did you get home?"

"Keith walked me."

"It's too late to be out on a weeknight. You've got school in the morning."

"It's only midnight. I'll get plenty of sleep." There she stood, about seven stones of teenage rebellion, weight balanced on one hip, once long and beautiful blonde hair chopped short, wearing black leggings and a long, fawn cable-knit jumper, pale translucent skin glowing from the chill.

"You're too young to be out so late," he said.

"Oh, don't be so old-fashioned. *Everyone* stays out until midnight these days."

"I don't care what everyone else does. It's you I'm talking about."

"It would be different if it was Brian, wouldn't it? He could always stay out as late as he wanted, couldn't he?"

"He had to live with the same rules as you."

"Rules! I bet you've no idea what he's up to now, have you? Or what he got up to when he was still at home. It's all right for him. Honestly, it's not fair. Just because I'm a girl."

"Tracy, love, it's not a safe world."

Her cheeks blazed red and her eyes flashed dangerously, just like Sandra's did when she was angry. "I'm fed up of it," she said. "Living here, being interrogated every time I come in. Sometimes it's just absolutely fucking awful having a policeman for a father!"

And with that, she stormed out of the room and up the stairs without giving Banks a chance to respond. He stood there a moment, stunned by her language—not that she knew such words, even five-year-olds knew them, but that she would use them that way in front of him—then he felt himself relax a little and he began to shake his head slowly. By the time he had sat down again and picked up his drink, he had started to smile. "Kids . . ." he mused aloud. "What can you do?" But even as he said it, he knew that Sandra had been right: the problem was that Tracy wasn't a kid any more.

IV

Brenda had locked the door earlier, and slid the bolt and put the chain on, too. When the key wouldn't work, she could hear Les fumble around for a while, rattling it and mumbling. Brenda could see his silhouette through the frosted-glass panes in the door as she sat on the stairs and listened. He tried the key again, then she heard him swear in frustration and start knocking. She didn't answer.

"Brenda," he said, "I know you're in there. Come on, love, and open up. There's something wrong with my key."

She could tell by the way he slurred his words that he'd been drinking. The police either hadn't found him, then, or had let him go before closing time.

He rattled the door. "Brenda! It's fucking cold out here. Let me in."

Still she ignored him, sitting on the staircase, arms wrapped around herself.

The letter-box opened. "I know you're in there," he said. "Have a heart, Brenda."

She stood up and walked down the stairs to the door. "Go away," she said. "I don't want you here any more. Go away."

"Brenda!" He was still on his knees by the letter-box. "Don't be daft, love. Let me in. We'll talk about it."

"There's nothing to talk about. Go away."

"Where? This is my home. It's all I've got."

"Go back to the police. I'm sure they'll give you a bed for the night."

He was silent for a few moments. Then she heard shuffling outside. The letter-box snapped shut, then opened again. "It wasn't nothing, love," he said. "A mistake. It was some other bloke they were after."

"Liar."

"It was. Honest it was."

"What have you done with my Gemma?"

Another pause, even longer this time, then, "How could you think such a thing? It wasn't nothing to do with that. Look, let me in. It's raining. I'll catch cold. I'm freezing my goolies off out here."

"Good."

"Brenda! The neighbours are watching."

"I couldn't care less."

"What about my things?"

Brenda dashed up to the bedroom. Les's "things," such as they were, shouldn't take up much space. She was a bit unsteady on her feet, but she managed to stand on a chair and get an old suitcase down from the top of the wardrobe. First, she emptied out his underwear drawer. Shirts and trousers followed, then she tossed in his old denim jacket. He was wearing the leather one, she remembered. She dropped a couple of pairs of shoes on the top, then went into the bathroom and picked up his razor, shaving cream, toothbrush. For some reason, she didn't know why, she also picked up a package of tampons and put them in the suitcase, too, smiling as she did so. And on further thought, she took his condoms from the bedside drawer and put them in as well.

Enjoying herself more than she had since her TV appearance, Brenda searched around for anything else that belonged to him. A comb. Brylcreem. Half a packet of cigarettes. No, she would keep them for herself. Nothing else.

As she struggled to fasten the suitcase, she could hear him outside in the street yelling up at her: "Brenda! Come on, Brenda, let me in. Please. I'm freezing to death out here."

She walked over to the window. Les stood by the gate at the bottom of the path, partly lit by a nearby street-lamp. Across the street, lights came on as people opened their doors or peered through curtains to see what was going on. This would give the neighbours something to talk about, Brenda thought, as she opened the window.

Les looked up at her. For a moment, she remembered a scene in a play they'd taken her to see with the school years ago, where some wally in tights down on the ground had been chatting up a bird on a balcony. She giggled and swayed, then got a hold on herself. After all, she had an audience. "Bugger off, Les," she yelled. "I've had enough of you and your filthy ways. If it wasn't for you I'd still have my Gemma."

"Open the fucking door, cow," said Les, "or I'll kick it down. You never liked the little bitch anyway."

"I loved my daughter," said Brenda. "It was you used to upset her. Where is she, Les? What have you done with her?"

Another door opened down the street. "Be quiet," a woman shouted. "My husband's got to get up to go to work at five o'clock in the morning."

"Shut up, you stuck-up old bag," shouted someone else. "Your husband's never done a day's work in his life. This is the best show we've had in ages." Bursts of laughter echoed down the street.

A window slid open. "Give him hell, love!" a woman's voice encouraged Brenda.

"What's going on?" someone else asked. "Has anyone called the police yet?"

"See what you've started," Les said, looking around at the gathering of neighbours and trying to keep his voice down. "Come on, love, let me in. We'll have a cuddle and talk about it. I've done nowt wrong."

"And what about that telly?" Brenda taunted him. "Where did that come from, eh? Have you noticed the way the police look at it every time they come here?"

"Must be fans of 'The Bill,'" someone joked, and the neighbours laughed. "Anyone got a bottle," the joker continued. "I could do with a wee nip."

"Buy your own you tight-fisted old bugger," came the reply.

"Open the door," Les pleaded. "Brenda, come on, love, have mercy."

"I'll not show no mercy for you, you snake. Where's my Gemma?"

"I'll do you for bloody slander, I will," yelled Les. "Making accusations like that in front of witnesses." He turned to the nearest neighbour, an old woman in a dressing-gown. "You heard her, didn't you?"

"Maybe she's right," said the woman.

"Aye," said the man next door.

"Hey," said Les, "Now, come on." He looked up at the window again. "Brenda, let me in. I don't like the look of this lot."

"Too bad." Brenda swung the suitcase behind her as far as she could, then let it fly out the window. It hit the gatepost and burst open, showering its contents over the garden and street. Les put his hands up to try and stop it from hitting him, but all he managed to catch was the packet of tampons. It spilled its contents on him as he grasped it too tightly. One of the neighbours noticed and started laughing. Les stood there in the rain, half in shadow, surrounded by the flotsam and jetsam of his life and a packet of tampons spilled like cigarettes at his feet. He looked up at Brenda and shouted one last appeal. Brenda closed the window. Before she pulled the curtains on him, she noticed some of the neighbours edging forward in a semi-circle towards Les, who was backing down the street, looking behind him for a clear escape route.

ELEVEN

I

"Les Poole's done a bunk, sir."

"Has he, now?" Banks looked up from his morning coffee at Susan Gay standing in his office door. She was wearing a cream skirt and jacket over a powder-blue blouse fastened at the neck with an antique jet brooch. Matching jet teardrops hung from her small ears. Her complexion looked fresh-scrubbed under the tight blonde curls that still glistened from her morning shower. Her eyes were lit with excitement.

"Come in and tell me about it," Banks said.

Susan sat down opposite him. He noticed her glance at the morning papers spread out on his desk. There, on the front pages of all of them, the police artist's impression of Smiler Chivers and his blonde girlfriend stared out.

"There was a bit of a barney last night on the East Side Estate," Susan began. "According to PC Evans, who walks the beat down there, Les Poole was out in the street yelling at Brenda to let him in."

"She locked him out?"

"Seems like it."

"Why?"

"Well, that's where it gets interesting. PC Evans talked to some of the neighbours. Most of them were a bit tight-lipped, but he found one chap who'd been watching it all from his bedroom window down the street. He said it looked like the others had turned into a mob and were about to attack Poole. That's why he ran off."

"Any idea why, apart from his sparkling personality?"

"While they were yelling at each other, Brenda apparently made some comment about Poole being responsible for Gemma's disappearance."

"What?"

"That's all he heard, sir, the neighbour. Brenda kept asking Poole what he'd done with Gemma."

Banks reached for a cigarette, his first of the day. "What do you think?" he asked.

"About Poole?"

"Yes."

"I don't know. I mean it could just have been something Brenda thought up on the spur of the moment to hit out at him, couldn't it?"

"I know Poole's been holding something back," Banks said. "That's just his nature. But I never really thought . . ." He stubbed out his unfinished cigarette and stood up. "Come on. First, let's send some of the lads out looking for him. And then we'd better have another word with Brenda." He picked up one of the newspapers. "We'll see if she recognizes the artist's impression, too."

They drove in silence to East Side Estate. It was a blustery morning, with occasional shafts of sunlight piercing the clouds and illuminating a bridge, a clump of trees or a block of maisonettes for a few seconds then disappearing. There ought to be a shimmering dramatic soundtrack, Banks thought, something to harmonize with the odd sense of revelation the fleeting rays of light conveyed.

Banks knocked on the frosted pane of Brenda's door, but no one answered. He knocked harder. Across the street, a curtain twitched. Discarded cellophane wrapping and newspaper blew across the road, scraping against the tarmac.

"They'll be having the time of their lives," Susan said, nodding towards the houses opposite. "Twice in two days. A real bonanza."

Banks renewed his efforts. Eventually he was rewarded by the sight of a blurry figure walking down the stairs.

"Who is it?" Brenda asked.

"Police."

She fiddled with the bolts and chain and let them in.

"Sorry," she said, rubbing the back of her hand over her eyes. "I was fast asleep. Must have been those pills the doctor gave me."

She looked dreadful, Banks thought: knotted and straggly hair in need of a good wash, puffy complexion, mottled skin, red eyes. She wore a white terry-cloth robe, and when she sat down in the living-room under the gaze of Elvis, it was clear she wore nothing under-neath. As she leaned forward to pick up a cigarette from the table, the bathrobe hung loose at the front, revealing her plump, round breasts. Unembarrassed, she pulled the lapels together and slouched back in the chair Banks and Susan sat on the sofa opposite her.

"What is it?" Brenda asked after she had exhaled a lungful of smoke. "Have you found Gemma?"

"No," said Banks. "It's about Les."

She snorted. "Oh, him. Well, he's gone, and good riddance, too."

"So I heard. Any idea *where* he's gone?"

She shook her head.

"Why did you throw him out, Brenda?"

"You should know. It was you lot had him at the station last night, wasn't it?"

"Did you know the neighbours nearly lynched him?"

"So what?"

"Brenda, it's dangerous to make accusations like the one you did, especially in front of a crowd. You know from experience how people feel whenever children are involved. They can turn very nasty. There's records of people being torn apart by angry mobs."

"Yes, I know. I know all about what people do to child-moles-ters. They deserve it."

"Did Les molest Gemma? Is that it?"

Brenda blew out more smoke and sighed. "No," she said. "No, he never did anything like that."

"Maybe when you weren't around?"

"No. I'd have known. Gemma would have . . ." She paused and stared at the end of her cigarette.

"Perhaps Gemma wouldn't have mentioned it to you," Banks suggested. "You told us yourself she's a quiet, secretive child. And children are almost always afraid to speak out when things like that happen."

"No," Brenda said again. "I would have known. Believe me."

Whether he believed her or not, Banks felt that line of questioning had come to a dead end. "What reason do you have to think Les was involved in her disappearance, then?" he asked.

Brenda frowned. "You had him in for questioning, didn't you?"

"What made you think that had anything to do with Gemma?"

"What else would it be about?"

"So you just assumed. Is that it?"

"Of course. Unless . . ."

"Unless what?"

Brenda reddened, and Banks noticed her glance towards the television set.

"Did you think it was about the Fletcher's warehouse job?"

Brenda shook her head. "I . . . I don't know."

"Did Les ever mention an acquaintance named Carl Johnson to you?"

"No. He never talked about his pub mates. If I ever asked him where he'd been or who he'd been with, he just told me to mind my own business."

"Look, this is important," Banks said slowly. "Think about it. When you accused Les out in the street, did you have any other basis for doing so other than the fact that we'd taken him in for questioning?"

"What?"

Banks explained. Brenda leaned forward to put out her cigarette. She held her robe closed this time. "That and the way he's been acting," she said.

"What do you mean?"

"It's hard to put into words. Ever since Gemma . . . well, things haven't been the same between us. Do you know what I mean?"

Banks nodded.

"I don't know why, but they haven't. And he just looks so sheepish, the way he creeps around all the time, giving me guilty smiles. Mostly, though, he's been keeping out of my way."

"In what way could he have been involved, Brenda?" Susan asked.

Brenda looked sideways towards her, as if seeing her for the first time. "How should I know?" she said. "I'm not the detective, am

I?" She spoke more harshly than she had to Banks. Woman to woman, he thought, Brenda Scupham was uncomfortable.

Banks gently took the focus away from Susan. "Brenda, have you any proof at all that Les had something to do with Gemma's disappearance?"

"No. Just a feeling."

"Okay. I'm not dismissing that. What you told us, about this Mr Brown and Miss Peterson, that was all true, wasn't it?"

"Yes. That's how it happened."

Banks showed her the newspaper pictures of Chivers and the blonde. "Do you recognize these people?"

She squinted at the pictures. "It could be him. The hair's sort of the same, but a different colour. I don't know about her, though. People look so different with their hair up. Him, though . . . I think . . . yes . . . I think it might be."

Banks put the paper aside. "You told us Les wasn't in when they came."

"That's right. He was at the pub."

"How did he react when you told him?"

"I don't know what you mean."

"Did he seem shocked, upset, what?"

Tears came to Brenda's eyes. "He said I was a stupid cow for letting them take her . . . but . . ."

"But what?"

She rubbed the backs of her hands across her eyes. "I need a cup of tea. I can't really get started without my cup of tea in a morning. Do you want some?"

"All right," said Banks. It wouldn't be a bad idea to give her a couple of minutes to mull over his question.

He and Susan waited silently while Brenda went into the kitchen and made tea. Outside, a car went by, a dog barked, and two laughing children kicked a tin can down the street. The wind shrilled at the ill-fitting windows, stirring the curtains in its draught. Banks studied the portrait of Elvis. It really was grotesque: a piece of kitsch dedicated to a bloated and gaudy idol.

As a teenager, he had been a keen Elvis fan. He had seen all those dreadful movies of the early sixties, where Elvis usually played a slightly podgy beach-bum, and he had bought all the new singles as soon as they came out. Somehow, though, after The Beatles, Bob Dylan, The Rolling Stones and the rest, Elvis had never seemed important again.

Still, he remembered how he had listened to "They Remind Me Too Much of You" over and over again the night June Higgins chucked him for John Hill. He had been assembling a model Messerschmitt at the time, so maybe it was the glue fumes that had made his eyes water. Glue-sniffing hadn't been invented back then. He had been thirteen; now Elvis was dead but lived on in garish oils on walls like this.

The whistle blew. When it stopped, Banks heard Brenda go upstairs. A few moments later she came in with the teapot and three mugs. She had taken the opportunity to get dressed, run a brush through her hair and put on a bit of make-up.

"Where were we?" she asked, pouring the tea. "There's milk and sugar if you want it." Susan helped herself to a splash of milk and two teaspoons of sugar. Both Banks and Brenda took theirs as it came.

"Les's reaction when you told him about Gemma."

"Yes. I've been thinking about it while the tea was mashing," Brenda said. "He didn't believe me at first. I'd say more than anything he was surprised. It's just that . . . well, he turned away from me, and I couldn't see his face, but it was like he knew something or he suspected something, like he was frowning and he didn't want me to see his expression. Do you know what I mean?"

"I think so."

"I could just feel it. I know I've not got any proof or anything, but sometimes you can sense things about people, can't you? Lenora says she thinks I'm a bit psychic, too, so maybe that's it. But I never thought for a moment he had anything to do with it. I mean, how could I? What could Les have had to do with those two well-dressed people who came to the door? And we lived together. I know he didn't care for Gemma much, she got on his nerves, but he wouldn't hurt her. I mean he *was* surprised, shocked, I'm sure of that, but when it sank in, he seemed to be *thinking*, puzzling over something. I put it out of my mind, but it nagged. After that we never really got on well. I'm glad he's gone." She paused, as if surprised at herself for saying so much, then reached for a second cigarette.

"What made you accuse him last night?" Banks asked.

"It's just something that had been at the back of my mind, that's all. Like I said, I never really believed he had anything to do with it. I just had this nagging feeling something wasn't right. I suppose I lashed out, just for the sake of it. I couldn't help myself."

"What about now?"

"What?"

"You said you didn't think Les had anything to do with Gemma's disappearance at first. What do you think now?"

Brenda paused to blow on her hot tea, cradling the mug in her palms, then she turned her eyes up to Banks and shook her head. "I don't know," she whispered. "I just don't know."

II

Banks and Jenny dashed across the cobbles in the rain to the Queen's Arms. Once through the door, they shook their coats and hung them up.

"Double brandy, then?" Banks asked.

"No. No, really, Alan. I didn't mean it," Jenny said. "Just a small Scotch and water, please."

Now she was embarrassed. She put her briefcase on the chair beside her and sat down at a table near the window. She had been in Banks's office going over all the material on the Carl Johnson murder—statements, forensic reports, the lot—and when she got to the photographs of his body, she had turned pale and said she needed a drink. She didn't know why they should affect her that way—she had seen similar images in textbooks—but suddenly she had felt dizzy and nauseated. Something about the way the belly gaped open like a huge fish-mouth . . . no, she wouldn't think about it any more.

Banks returned with their drinks and reached for his cigarettes.

"I'm sorry," she said. "You must think I'm a real idiot."

"Not at all. I just wasn't thinking. I should have prepared you."

"Anyway, I'm fine now." She raised her glass. "Cheers."

"Cheers."

She could see Market Street through a clear, rain-streaked pane. Young mothers walked by pushing prams, plastic rainhats tied over their heads, and delivery vans blocked the traffic while men in white smocks carried boxes in and out of the shops, oblivious to the downpour. All the hurly and burly of commerce so essential to a thriving English market town. So normal. She shivered.

"I take it you're assuming the crimes are related now?" she asked.

Banks nodded. "We are for the moment. I've read over the paperwork on the Gemma Scupham case, and I've filled the super in on Johnson. How are you getting on with him, by the way?"

Jenny smiled. "Fine. He doesn't seem like such an ogre when you get to know him a bit."

"True, he's not. Anyway, we know that the Manleys abducted Gemma, and that in all likelihood the man's real name is Chivers. We still don't know who the woman is."

"But you don't know for sure that this Chivers killed Carl Johnson?"

"No. I realize it's a bit thin, but when you get connections like this between two major crimes you can't overlook them. Maybe in a big city you could, but not in Eastvale."

"And even if he did it, you don't know if the woman was present?"

"No."

"Then what do you want from me?"

"For a start, I want to know if you think it could be the same person, or same people, psychologically speaking."

Jenny took a deep breath. "The two crimes are so different. I can't really find a pattern."

"Are there no elements in common?"

Jenny thought for a moment, and the images of Johnson's body came back. She sipped at her drink. "From all I've seen and heard," she said, "I'd say that the two crimes at least demonstrate a complete lack of empathy on the criminal's part, which leans towards the theory of the psychopath. If that's the case, he probably wasn't sexually interested in Gemma, only in his power over her, which he may have been demonstrating to the woman, as I said to the superintendent last time we met." She ran her hand through her hair. "I just don't have anything more to go on."

"Think about the Johnson murder."

Jenny leaned forward and rested her hands on the table. "All right. The couple who took Gemma showed no feeling for the mother at all. Whoever killed Johnson didn't feel his pain, or if he did, he enjoyed it. You know even better than I do that murder can take many forms—there's the heat of the moment, and there's at least some distancing, as when a gun's used. Even the classic poisoner often prefers to be far away when the poison takes effect. But here we have someone who, according to all the evidence you've shown me, must have stood very close indeed to his victim, looked him in the eye as he killed slowly. Could you do that? Could I? I don't think so. Most of us have at least some sensitivity to another's pain—we imagine what it would feel like if we suffered it ourselves. But one class of person doesn't—the psychopath. He can't relate to anyone else's pain, can't imagine it happening to him. He's so self-centred that he lacks empathy completely."

"You keep saying 'he.'"

Jenny slapped his wrist playfully. "You know as well as I do that, statistically speaking, most psychopaths are men. And it might be pretty interesting to try to find out why. But that's beside the point. That's what the two crimes, what I know of them, have in common. There are other elements that fit the psychopath profile, too: the apparent coolness and bravado with which Gemma was abducted; the charm Chivers must have exhibited to her mother; the clever deceit he must have played to get Johnson out to the mill, if that's what he did. And you can add that he's also likely to be manipulative, impulsive, egocentric and irresponsible. You're nursing your pint, Alan. Anything wrong?"

"What? Oh, no. I'm just preserving my liver. I have to meet Jim Hatchley for dinner in a couple of hours."

"So he's in town again, is he?"

"Just for a little job."

Jenny held her hand up. "Say no more. I don't want to know anything about it. I can't understand why you like that man."

Banks shrugged. "Jim's all right. Anyway, back to Chivers. What if he committed the Carl Johnson murder out of self-preservation?"

"The method was still his choice."

"Yes." Banks lit another cigarette. "Look, I'll tell you what I'm getting at. Just before you arrived, I talked to my old friend Barney Merritt at the Yard, and he told me that Criminal Intelligence has got quite a file on Chivers. They've never been able to put him away for anything, but they've had reports of his suspected activities from time to time, and they've usually had some connection with organized crime. The closest they came to nabbing him was four years ago. An outsider trying to muscle in on a protection racket in Birmingham was found on a building site with a bullet in his brain. The police knew Chivers was connected with the local mob up there, and a couple of witnesses placed him with the victim in a pub near the site. Soon as things got serious, though, the witnesses started to lose their memories."

"What are you telling me, Alan, that he's a hit man or something?"

Banks waved his hand. "No, hold on, let me finish. Most of the information in the CI files concerns his suspected connection with criminal gangs in London and in Birmingham, doing hits, nobbling witnesses, enforcing debt-collection and the like. But word has it that when business is slack, Chivers is not averse to a bit of murder and mayhem on the side, just for the fun of it. And according to Barney, his employers started to get bad feelings about him about a year ago. They're keeping their distance. Again, there's nothing proven, just hearsay."

"Interesting," said Jenny. "Is there any more?"

"Just a few details. He's prime suspect—without a scrap of proof—in three murders down south, one involving a fair amount of torture before death, and there are rumours of one or two fourteen-year-old girls he's treated roughly in bed."

Jenny shook her head. "If you're getting at some kind of connection between that and Gemma, I'd say it's highly unlikely."

"But why? He likes his sex rough and strange. He likes them young. What happens when fourteen isn't enough of a kick any more?"

"The fact that he likes having sex with fourteen-year-old girls in no way indicates, psychologically, that he could be interested in seven-year-olds. Quite the opposite, really."

Banks frowned. "I don't understand."

"It was something else I discovered in my research. According to statistics, the younger the child, the older the paedophile is likely to be. Your Chivers sounds about the right age for an unhealthy interest in fourteen-year-olds, but, you know, if you'd given me no information at all about Gemma's abduction, I'd say you should be looking for someone over forty, most likely someone who knew Gemma—a family friend, neighbour or even a relative— who lives in the area, or not far away, and probably lives alone. I certainly wouldn't be looking for a young couple from Birmingham, or wherever."

Banks shook his head. "Okay, let's get back on track. Tell me what you think of this scenario. We know that plenty of psychopaths have found gainful employment in organized crime. They're good at frightening people, they're clever, and they make good killers. The problem is that they're hard to control. Now, what do you do with a psychopath when you find him more of a business liability than an asset? You try to cut him loose and hope to hell he doesn't bear a grudge. Or you have him killed, and so the cycle continues. His old bosses don't trust Chivers any more, Jenny. He's *persona non grata*. They're scared of him. He has to provide his own entertainment now."

"Hmm." Jenny swirled her glass and took another sip. "It makes some sense, but I doubt that it's quite like that. In the first place, if he's hard to control, it's more likely to mean that he's losing control of himself. From what you told me, Chivers must have been a highly organized personality type at one time, exhibiting a great deal of control. But psychopaths are also highly unstable. They're prone to deterioration. His personality could be disintegrating towards the disorganized type, and right now he might be in the middle, the mixed type. Most serial killers, for example, keep on killing until they're caught or until they lose touch completely with reality. That's why you don't find many of them over forty. They've either been caught by then, or they're hopelessly insane."

Banks stubbed out his cigarette. "Are you suggesting that Chivers could be turning into a serial killer?"

Jenny shrugged. "Not necessarily a serial killer, but it's possible, isn't it? He doesn't fit the general profile of a paedophile, and he's certainly changing into *something*. Yes, it makes sense, Alan. I'm not saying it's true, but it's certainly consistent with the information you've got."

"So what next?"

Jenny shuddered. "Your guess is as good as mine. Whatever it is, you can be sure it won't be very pleasant. If he is experiencing loss of control, then he's probably at a very volatile and unpredictable stage." She finished her drink. "I'll give you one piece of advice, though."

"What's that?"

"If it is true, be very careful. This man's a loose cannon on the deck. He's very dangerous. Maybe even more so than you realize."

III

"Congratulations," said Banks. "I really mean it, Jim. I'm happy for you. Why the hell didn't you tell me before?"

"Aye, well . . . weren't sure." Sergeant Hatchley blushed. A typical Yorkshireman, he wasn't comfortable with expressions of sentiment.

The two of them sat in the large oak-panelled dining-room of the Red Lion Hotel, an enormous Victorian structure by the roundabout on the southern edge of Eastvale. Hatchley was looking a bit healthier than he had on his arrival that afternoon. Then the ravages of a hangover had still been apparent around his eyes and in his skin, but now he had regained his normal ruddy complexion and that tell-me-another-one look in his pale blue eyes. Just for a few moments, though, his colour deepened even more and his eyes filled with pride. Banks was congratulating him on his wife's pregnancy. Their first.

"When's it due?" Banks asked.

"I don't know. Don't they usually take nine months?"

"I just wondered if the doctor had given you a date."

"Mebbe Carol knows. She didn't say owt to me, though. This is a good bit of beef." He cut into his prime-rib roast and washed it down with a draught of Theakston's bitter. "Ah, it's good to be home again."

Banks was eating lamb and drinking red wine. Not that he had become averse to Theakston's, but the Red Lion had a decent house claret and it seemed a shame to ignore it. "You still think of Eastvale as home?" he asked.

"Grew up here," replied Hatchley around a mouthful of Yorkshire pudding. "Place gets in your blood."

"How are you liking the coast?"

"It's all right. Been a good summer." Sergeant Hatchley had been transferred to Saltby Bay, between Scarborough and Whitby, mostly in order to make way for Phil Richmond's boost up the promotion ladder. Hatchley was a good sergeant and always would be; Richmond, Banks suspected, would probably make at least Chief Inspector, his own rank, and might go even further if he kept on top of the latest computer technology and showed a bit more initiative and leadership quality. Susan Gay, their most recent DC, was certainly demonstrating plenty of initiative, though it didn't always lead where it should.

"Do I detect a note of nostalgia?" Banks asked.

Hatchley grinned. "Let me put it this way. It's a bit like a holiday. Trouble is—and I never thought I'd be complaining about *this*—it's a holiday that never bloody ends. There's not much goes on for CID to deal with out there, save for a bit of organized pickpocketing in season, a few B-and-Es, or a spot of trouble with the bookies now and then. It's mostly paperwork, a desk job." Hatchley uttered those last two words with flat-vowelled Yorkshire contempt.

"Thought you'd be enjoying the rest."

"I might be a bit of a lazy sod, but I'm not bloody retiring age yet. You know me, I like a bit of action now and then. Out there, half the time I think I've died and gone to Harrogate, only by the sea."

"What are you getting at, Jim?"

Hatchley hesitated for a moment, then put his knife and fork down. "I'll be blunt. We're all right for now, Carol and me, but after the baby's born, do you think there's any chance of us getting back to Eastvale?"

Banks sipped some wine and thought for a moment.

"Look," Hatchley said, "I know the super doesn't like me. Never has. I knew that even before you came on the scene."

Three and a half years ago, Banks thought. Was that all? So much had happened. He raised his eyebrows. ·

"But we get on all right, don't we?" Hatchley went on. "I mean, it took us a while, we didn't have the best of starts. But I know my faults. I've got strengths, too, is all I'm saying."

"I know that," Banks said. "And you're right." He remembered that it had taken him two years to call Sergeant Hatchley by his first name. By then he had developed a grudging respect for the man's tenacity. Hatchley might take the easy way out, act in unorthodox ways, cut corners, take risks, but he generally got what he set out to get. In other words, he was a bit of a maverick, like Banks himself, and he was neither as thick nor as thuggish as Banks had first thought.

Apart from Gristhorpe, Banks felt most comfortable with Hatchley. Phil Richmond was all right, pleasant enough, but he always seemed a bit remote and self-absorbed. For God's sake, Banks thought, what could you expect from a man who read science fiction, listened to New Age music and spent half his time playing computer games? Susan Gay was too prickly, too over-sensitive to feel really at ease with, though he admired her spunk and her common sense.

"It's not up to me," Banks said finally. "You know that. But the way Phil's going it wouldn't surprise me if he went in for a transfer to the Yard before long."

"Aye, well, he always was an ambitious lad, was Phil."

It was said without rancour, but Banks knew it must have hurt Hatchley to be shunted to a backwater so as not to impede a younger man's progress up the ranks. Transfer to CID was no more a "promotion" *per se* than transfer to Traffic and Communications—

a sergeant was a sergeant, whether he or she had the prefix "detective" or not—though some, like Susan Gay, actually saw it that way, as a mark of recognition of special abilities. Some detectives were transferred back to uniform; some returned from choice. But Banks knew that Hatchley had no desire to walk the beat or drive the patrol cars again. What he wanted was to come back to Eastvale as a Detective Sergeant, and there simply wasn't room for him with Richmond at the same rank.

Banks shrugged. "What can I say, Jim? Be patient."

"Can I count on your support, if the situation arises?"

Banks nodded. "You can." He smiled to himself as the unbidden image of Jim Hatchley and Susan Gay working together came to mind. Oh, there would be fun and games ahead if Sergeant Hatchley came back to Eastvale.

Hatchley finished his pint and looked Banks in the eye. "Aye, well that's all right then. How about a sweet?"

"Not for me."

Hatchley caught the waiter's attention and ordered Black Forest gateau, a cup of coffee and another pint of Theakston's. Banks stayed with his glass of red wine, which was still half-full.

"Down to business, then," Hatchley said, as he tucked into the dessert.

Banks gave him a summary of the case and its twists and turns so far, then explained what he wanted him to do.

"A pleasure," said Hatchley, smiling.

"And in the meantime, you can concentrate on installing that shower or whatever it is. I can't say how long we'll be. It depends."

Hatchley pulled a face. "I hope it's sooner rather than later."

"Problem?"

"Oh, not really. As you know, I've got a few days leave. There's not a lot on in Saltby at the moment, anyway, and Carol will be all right. She's built up quite a gaggle of mates out there, and there'll be no keeping them away since we heard about the baby. You know how women get all gooey-eyed about things like that. You can almost hear the bloody knitting needles clacking from here. No, it's just that it might mean staying on longer than I have to at the in-laws, that's all."

"You don't get on?"

"It's not that. We had them for two weeks in July. It's just . . . well, you know how it is with in-laws."

Banks remembered Mr and Mrs Ellis from Hatchley's wedding the previous Christmas. Mrs Ellis in particular had seemed angry that Hatchley stayed at the reception too long and drank too much. But then, he thought, she had every right to be annoyed. "They don't approve of your drinking?" he guessed.

"You make it sound as if I'm an alcoholic or something," Hatchley said indignantly. "Just because a bloke enjoys a pint or two of ale now and then. . . . No, they're religious, Four Square Gospel," he sighed, as if that explained it all. "You know, Chapel on Sundays, the whole kit and caboodle. Never mind." He sat up straight and puffed out his chest. "A man's got to do what a man's got to do. Just hurry up and find the bugger. What about this Chivers bloke? Any leads?"

"According to Phil, we've already had sightings from St Austell, King's Lynn, Clitheroe and the Kyle of Lochalsh."

Hatchley laughed. "It was ever thus. Tell me about him. He sounds interesting."

Banks told him what Barney Merritt had said and what he and Jenny had discussed late afternoon.

"Reckon he's done her, the kid?"

Banks nodded. "It's been over a week, Jim. I just don't like to think about what probably happened *before* he killed her."

Hatchley's eyes narrowed to slits. "Know who the tart is? The blonde?"

"No idea. He picks them up and casts them off. They're fascinated by him, like flies to shit. According to what Barney could dig up, his full name's Jeremy Chivers, called Jem for short. He grew up in a nice middle-class home in Sevenoaks. No record of any trouble as a kid. No one can figure out how he got hooked up with the gangs. He had a good education, moved to work for an insurance company in London, then it all started."

"It's not hard for rats to find the local sewer," said Hatchley.

"No. Anyway, he's twenty-eight now, apparently looks even younger. And he's no fool. You've got to be pretty smart to keep on doing what he does and get away with it. It all satisfies whatever weird appetites he's developing."

"If you ask me," said Hatchley, "we'd all be best off if he found himself at the end of a noose."

Banks remembered his early feelings about Hatchley. That comment, so typical of him and so typical of the burned-out, cynical London coppers Banks had been trying to get away from at the time, brought them all back.

Once, Banks would have cheerfully echoed the sentiment. Sometimes, even now, he felt it. It was impossible to contemplate someone like Chivers and what he had done to Carl Johnson—if he had done it—and, perhaps, to Gemma Scupham, without wanting to see him dangling at the end of a rope, or worse, to make it personal, to squeeze the life out of him with one's own hands. Like everyone who had read about the case in the newspapers, like everyone who had children of his own, Banks could easily give voice to the outraged cliché that hanging was too good for the likes of Chivers. What was even worse was that Banks didn't know, could not predict for certain, what he would do if he ever did get Chivers within hurting distance.

The conflict was always there: on the one hand, pure atavistic rage for revenge, the gut feeling that someone who did what Chivers did no longer deserved to be a member of the human race, had somehow, through his monstrous acts, forfeited his humanity; and on the other hand, the feeling that such a reaction makes us no better than him, however we sugar-coat our socially sanctioned murders, and with it the idea that perhaps more insight is to be gained from the study of such a mind than from its destruction, and that knowledge like that may help prevent Chiverses of the future. There was no easy solution for him. The two sides of the argument struggled for ascendancy; some days sheer outrage won out, others a kind of noble humanism took supremacy.

Instead of responding to Hatchley's comment, Banks gestured for the bill and lit a cigarette. It was time to go home, perhaps listen to Mitsuko Uchida playing some Mozart piano sonatas and snuggle up to Sandra, if she was in.

"Ah well," sighed Hatchley. "Back to the in-laws, I suppose." He reached into his pocket, pulled out a packet of extra-strong Trebor mints and popped one in his mouth. "Once more unto the breach, dear friends. . . ."

IV

The piece of luck that Banks had been hoping for came at about six-thirty in the morning. Like most police luck, it was more a result of hard slog and keen observation than any magnanimous gesture on the part of some almighty deity.

The telephone woke Banks from a disjointed dream full of anger and frustration. He groped for the receiver in the dark. Beside him, Sandra stirred and muttered in her sleep.

"Sir?" It was Susan Gay.

"Mmm," Banks mumbled.

"Sorry to wake you, sir, but they've found him. Poole."

"Where is he?"

"At the station."

"What time is it?"

"Half past six."

"All right. Phone Jim Hatchley at Carol's parents' place and get him down there, but keep him out of sight. And—"

"I've already phoned the super, sir. He's on his way in."

"Good. I'll be there as soon as I can."

Sandra turned over and sighed. Banks crept out of bed as quietly as he could, grabbed the clothes he had left folded on a chair and went into the bathroom. He still couldn't shake the feeling the dream had left him with. Probably something to do with the row he had with Tracy after he got back from dinner with Jim Hatchley. Not even a row, really. Trying to be more under-standing towards her, he had simply made some comment about how nice it was to have her home with the family, and she had burst into tears and dashed up to her room. Sandra had shot him a nasty look and hurried up after her. It turned out her boyfriend had chucked her for someone else. Well, how was he supposed to know? It all changed so quickly. She never told him about anything these days.

As soon as he had showered and dressed, he went out to the car. The wind had dropped, but the pre-dawn sky was overcast, a dreary iron grey, except to the east where it was flushed deep red close to the horizon. For the first time that year, Banks could see his breath. Already, lights were on in some of the houses, and the woman in the newsagent's at the corner of Banks's street and Market Street was sorting the papers for the delivery kids.

Inside the station, an outsider would have had no idea it was so early in the morning. Activity went on under the fluorescent lights as usual, as it did twenty-four hours a day. Only a copper would sense that end-of-the-night-shift feel as constables changed back into civvies to go home and the day shift came in bright-eyed and bushy-tailed, shaved faces shining, or make-up freshly applied.

Upstairs, where the CID had their offices, was quieter. They hardly had a need for shift work, and their hours varied depending on what was going on. This past week, with a murder and a missing child, long hours had been taking their toll on everyone. Richmond was there, looking red-eyed from too much staring at the computer screen, and Susan Gay had dark blue smears under her eyes.

"What happened?" Banks asked her.

"I'd just come in," she said. "Couldn't sleep so I came in at six and thought I'd have another look at the forensic reports, then they brought him in. Found him sleeping in a ditch a mile or so down the Helmthorpe Road."

"Jesus Christ," said Banks. "It must have been cold. Where is he?"

"Interview room. PC Evans is with him."

"Sergeant Hatchley?"

"Got here just before you. He's in position."

Banks nodded. "Let's wait for the super."

Gristhorpe arrived fifteen minutes later, looking brighter than the rest of them. His hair was a mess, as usual, but his innocent blue eyes shone every bit as alert and probing as ever.

"Let's have at him, then," he said, rubbing his hands. "Alan, would you like to lead, seeing as you know him so well? Let me play monster in reserve."

"All right."

They headed for the small interview room. Before they went in, Banks asked Richmond if he would get them a large pot of tea.

The drab room seemed overcrowded with four of them, and the heat was turned too high. PC Evans went and sat in the corner by the window, ready to take notes, Banks sat opposite Poole, and Gristhorpe at right angles.

Poole licked his lips and looked around the room.

"You look like you've been dragged through a hedge backwards, Les," Banks said. "What happened?"

"Sleeping rough. Nowhere to go, had I?"

He was unshaven, his leather jacket was scuffed and stained with mud, his greasy hair bedraggled and matted. He also had a black eye and a split lip. The tea arrived. Banks played mother and passed a large steaming mug over to Les. "Here, have a cuppa," he said. "You don't look like you've had your breakfast yet."

"Thanks." Poole grasped the mug with both hands.

"How'd you get the war wounds?"

"Bloody mob, wasn't it? I need protection, I do."

"From your neighbours?"

"Bloody right." He pointed to his face. "They did this to me before I managed to run off. I'm a victim. I should press charges." Poole slurped some tea.

"Be our guest," said Banks. "But later. There's a few other things to deal with first."

Poole frowned. "Oh? Like what?"

"Like why did you run?"

"That's a daft question. You'd bloody run if you had a mob like that after you."

"Where were you heading?"

"Dunno. Anywhere. I'd got no money so I could hardly stay in a bleeding hotel, could I?"

"What about your mate at the shop?"

"Wasn't in."

"What did the mob want with you, Les?"

"It was all that silly bitch Brenda's fault. Put on a right show, she did, chucking my stuff at me like that. And that's another thing. I'll bloody sue her for damage to property."

"You do that, Les. She'd probably have to sell the telly and that nice little stereo system to pay her costs. Why did they turn on you?"

Les glanced nervously at Gristhorpe, then said to Banks, "Is he going to stay here all the time?"

Banks nodded. "If I can't get the truth out of you, he takes over. Believe me, you'll be a lot happier if that never happens. We were talking about your neighbours. Look at me."

Poole turned back. "Yeah, well, Brenda yelled some stupid things out the window. It was her fault. She could have got me killed."

"What did she yell?"

Banks could see Poole weighing him up, gauging what he knew already. Finally, he said, "Seeing as she's probably already told you, it doesn't matter, does it?" He kept glancing at Gristhorpe out of the corner of his eye.

"It matters a lot," Banks said. "It's a very serious allegation, that is, saying you were mixed up with Gemma's disappearance. They don't take kindly to child-molesters in prison, Les. This time it won't be as easy as your other stretches inside. Why don't you tell us what you know?"

Poole finished his tea and reached for the pot. Banks let him pour another large mug. "Because I don't know anything," he said. "I told you, Brenda was out of line."

"No smoke without fire, Les."

"Come on, Mr Banks, you know me. Do I look like a child-molester?"

"How would I know? What do you think they look like? Ogres with hairs growing out of their noses and warts on their bald heads? Do you think they go around carrying signs?"

"She was trying to stir it, to wind me up. Honest. Ask her. Ask her if she *really* thinks I had anything to do with it."

"I have, Les."

"Yeah? And what did she say?"

"How did you feel when she told you Gemma had been abducted?"

"Feel?"

"Yes, Les. It's something people do. Part of what makes them human."

"I know what it means. Don't think I don't have feelings." He paused, and gulped down more tea. "How did I feel? I dunno."

"Were you upset?"

"Well, I was worried."

"Were you surprised?"

"Course I was."

"Did anything spring to mind, anything to make you wonder maybe about what had happened?"

"I don't know what you mean."

"I think you do, Les."

Banks looked over at Gristhorpe, who nodded grimly. Poole licked his lips again. "Look, what's going on here? You trying to fit me up?"

Banks let the silence stretch. Poole squirmed in his hard chair. "I need a piss," he said finally.

Banks stood up. "Come on, then."

They walked down the corridor to the gents and Banks stood by the inside of the door while Poole went to the urinal.

"Tell us where Gemma is, Les," Banks said, as Poole relieved himself. "It'll save us all a lot of trouble."

All of a sudden, the stall door burst open. Poole turned. A red-faced giant in a rumpled grey suit with short fair hair and hands like hams stood in front of him. Poole pissed all over his shoes and cursed, cringing back against the urinal, holding his arms out to ward off an attack.

"Is that him?" the giant said. "Is that the fucking pervert who—"

Banks dashed over and held him back. "Jim, don't. We're still questioning—"

"Is that the fucking pervert or isn't it?"

Hatchley strained to get past Banks, who was backing towards the door with Poole scrabbling behind him. "Get out, Les," Banks said. "While you can. I'll keep him back. Go on. Hurry!"

They backed into the corridor and two uniformed constables came to hold Hatchley, still shouting obscenities. Banks put a protective arm around Poole and led him back to the interview room. On the way, they passed Susan Gay, who looked at Poole and blushed. Banks followed her gaze. "Better zip it up, Les," he said, "or we'll have you for indecent exposure as well."

Poole did as he was told and Banks ushered him back into the room, Hatchley cursing and shouting behind them, held back by the two men.

"What the hell's going on?" Gristhorpe asked.

"It's Jim," Banks explained, sitting Poole down again. "You know what he's been like since that bloke interfered with his little girl."

"Aye," said Gristhorpe, "but can't we keep a leash on him?"

"Not easy, sir. He's a good man. Just a bit unhinged at the moment."

Poole followed the exchange, paling.

"Look," he said, "I ain't no pervert. Tell him. Keep him away from me."

"We'll try," Banks said, "but we might have a hard time getting him to believe us."

Poole ran a hand through his greasy hair. "All right," he said. "All right. I'll tell you all I know. Okay? Just keep him off me."

Banks stared at him.

"Then you can tell them all I'm not a pervert and I had nothing to do with it, all right?"

"If that's the way it turns out. If I believe you. And it's a big if, Les, after the bollocks you've been feeding us this past week."

"I know, I know." Poole licked his lips. "Look, first off, you've got to believe me, I had nothing to do with what happened to Gemma. Nothing."

"Convince me."

Outside, they could hear Hatchley bellowing about what he would do to perverts if he had his way: "I'd cut your balls off with a blunt penknife, I bloody would! And I'd feed them down your fucking throat!" He got close enough to thump at the door and rattle the handle before they could hear him being dragged off still yelling down the corridor. Banks could hardly keep from laughing. Jim and the uniforms sounded like they were having the time of their lives.

"Christ," said Les, with a shudder. "Just keep him off me, that's all."

"So you had nothing to do with Gemma's disappearance?" Banks said.

"No. See, I used to talk about the kid down the pub, over a jar, like. I admit I wasn't very flattering, but she was a strange one was Gemma. She could irritate you just by looking at you that way she had, accusing like. Make you feel like dirt."

"So you complained about your girlfriend's kid. Nothing odd in that, is there, Les?"

"Well, that's just it, isn't it? What I've been saying. It was just pub talk, that's all. Now, I never touched her, Mr Banks. Never. Not a word of a lie. But Brenda got pissed off that time after Gemma spilled her paints on my racing form and gave her a bloody good shaking. First time I seen her do it, and it scared me, honest it did. Left big bruises on the kid's arm. I felt sorry for her, but I'm not her fucking father, what am I supposed to do?"

"Get to the point, Les. Those lads out there can't hold Sergeant Hatchley down forever."

"Aye, well, I didn't exactly tell you the truth before. You see, I did meet this Chivers and his bird a couple of times, with Carl at the pub. Never took to him. She wasn't a bad-looking bint, mind you. A bit weird, but not bad. He thought I was coming on to her once and warned me, all quiet and civilized, like, that if I went so much as within a yard of her he'd cut off my balls and shove them up my arse." Poole paused and swallowed. No doubt he was realizing, Banks thought, that threats to his privates were coming thick and fast from all sides. "He gave me the creeps, Mr Banks. There was something not right about him. About the pair of them, if you ask me."

"Did this Chivers seem interested when you talked about Gemma?"

"Well, yeah, about as interested as he seemed in anything. He was a cool one. Cold. Like a fucking reptile. There was just no reading him. He'd ask about her, yeah, just over a few drinks, like, but I thought nothing of it. And once he told me about a case he'd read in the papers where some couple had pretended to be child-care workers and asked to examine a child. Thought that was funny, he did. Thought it showed bottle. I put it out of my mind. To be honest, soon as we'd done the Fl—soon as we'd finished our bit of business, I wouldn't go near him or her. I can't explain it. They seemed nice and normal enough on the surface, all charm and that nice smile of his, but inside he was hard and cold, and you never knew what he was going to do next. I suppose that's the kind of thing she liked. There's no figuring out some women's taste."

"So Chivers showed some interest in Gemma and he told you about the newspaper story, right?"

"Right. And that's as far as it went."

"Did Chivers give you any reason to believe he was interested in little children?"

"Well, no, not directly. I mean, Carl told me a few stories about him, how he'd been involved in the porn trade down The Smoke and how he wasn't averse to a bit of bondage and that. Just titillating stories, that's all. And when you saw him and his bird together, they were weird, like they had something going that no one could get in on. She hung on his every word and when he told her to do something, she did. I mean . . . it was . . . Once, we was in the car, like, plann—, just talking, with them two in the front and me and Carl in the back, and he told her to suck him off. She got right down there and did it, and all the time he kept talking, just stopping once, like, to give a little sigh when he shot his load. Then she sat back up again as if nothing had happened."

"But they never made any direct reference to children?"

"No. But you see what I mean, don't you, Mr Banks? I mean, as far as I'm concerned, them two was capable of anything."

"I see what you mean. What did you do?"

"Well, I kept quiet, didn't I? I mean, there was no way of knowing it was them took Gemma. The descriptions weren't the same. And then when Carl turned up dead, I had a good idea who might have liked killing someone that way and . . . I was scared. I mean, wouldn't you be? Maybe Carl had made the same connection, too, and Chivers had offed him while the bint looked on and laughed. That's the kind of feeling they gave you."

"Do you have any evidence that Chivers killed Carl?"

"Evidence? That's down to you lot, isn't it? No, I told you. I kept away from him. It just seemed like something he would do."

"Where are they now, Les?"

"I've no idea, honest I don't. And you can turn your gorilla on me and I can't tell you any different. I haven't seen nor heard of them since last week. And I don't want to."

"Do you think they're still in Eastvale, Les?"

"Be daft if they were, wouldn't they? But I don't mind saying I was scared shitless those two nights sleeping out. I kept thinking there was someone creeping up on me to cut my throat. You know what it's like out in the country, all those animal noises and the wind blowing barn doors." He shuddered.

"Is that everything, Les?"

"Cross my heart."

Banks noticed he didn't say "hope to die" this time. "It'd better be," said Banks, standing and stretching. He walked over to the door and peered outside, then turned to Gristhorpe. "Looks like they've got Jim away somewhere. What shall we do now?"

Gristhorpe assessed Poole with a steady gaze. "I think he's told us all he knows," he said finally. "We'd better take him to the charge room then lock him up."

"Good idea," Banks said. "Give him a nice warm cell for the day. For his own safety."

"Aye," said Gristhorpe. "What'll we charge him with?"

"We could start with indecent exposure."

They spent another hour or so going over Poole's statement with him, and Poole made no objections as the constable finally led him down to the charge room. He just looked anxiously right and left to make sure Hatchley wasn't around. Banks wandered to his office for a cigarette and another cup of coffee. Gristhorpe joined him there, and a few minutes later Jim Hatchley walked in with a big grin on his face.

"Haven't had as much fun since the last rugby club trip," he said. "How did you know he'd be going for a piss anyway? I was getting a bit fed up stuck in there. I'd read the *Sport* twice already."

"People want to urinate a lot when they're anxious," Banks said. "He did before. Besides, tea's a diuretic, didn't you know that?"

Hatchley shook his head.

"Anyway, he'd have wanted to go eventually. We'd just have kept him as long as necessary."

"Aye," said Hatchley, "and me in the fucking shithouse."

Banks smiled. "Effective, though, wasn't it? More dramatic that way."

"Very dramatic. Thinking of doing a bit of local theatre, are you?"

Banks laughed. "Sometimes that's what I think I am doing already." He walked over to the window and stretched. "Christ, it's been a long morning," he muttered.

The gold hands against the blue face of the church clock stood at ten-twenty. Susan Gay walked in and out with the latest developments. Not much. There had been more reports of Chivers, from Welshpool, Ramsgate and Llaneilian, and all had to be checked out by the locals. So far, they didn't have one clear lead. Just after eleven, the phone rang, and Banks picked it up.

"Detective Inspector Loder here. Dorset CID."

Banks sighed. "Not another report of Chivers?"

"More than that," said Loder. "In fact, I think you'd better get down to Weymouth if you can."

Banks sat upright. "You've got him?"

"Not exactly, but we've got a dead blonde in a hotel room, and she matches the description you put out."

TWELVE

I

Gristhorpe sat in the passenger seat of the unmarked police car with a road map spread out on his knees. Banks drove. He would have preferred his own Cortina, mostly because of the stereo system, but Sandra needed it for all her gallery work. Besides, Gristhorpe was tone deaf; for all his learning, he couldn't appreciate music. Banks had packed his Walkman and a couple of tapes in his overnight bag; he knew it wouldn't be easy getting to sleep in a strange hotel room, especially after what awaited them in Weymouth, and music would help.

They were heading down the M1 past Sheffield with its huge cooling towers, shaped like giant whalebone corsets, and its wasteland of disused steel factories. It was almost one-thirty in the afternoon, and despite the intermittent rain they were making good time.

Gristhorpe, after much muttering to himself, decided it would be best to turn off the motorway just south of Northampton and go via Oxford, Swindon and Salisbury. Banks drove as fast as he could, and just over an hour later they reached the junction with the A43. They skirted Oxford in the late afternoon and didn't get held up until they hit Swindon at rush-hour.

After Blandford Forum, they passed the time reading signposts and testing one another on Hardy's names for the places. They managed to keep abreast until Gristhorpe went ahead with Middleton Abbey for Milton Abbas.

After a traffic snarl-up in the centre of Dorchester, they approached Weymouth in the early evening. Loder had given clear directions to the hotel, and luckily it was easy to spot, one of the Georgian terraces on the Dorchester Road close to the point where it merged with The Esplanade.

A plump, curly-haired woman called Maureen greeted them in the small lobby and told them that Inspector Loder and his men had been gone for some time but had left a guard outside the room and requested she call them at the station as soon as Banks and Gristhorpe arrived. Their booking for the night had already been made: two singles on the third floor, one floor down from where the body had been discovered.

Out of courtesy, Banks and Gristhorpe waited for Loder to arrive before going up to the room. They had requested that, as far as possible, things should be left as they were when the chambermaid discovered the body that morning. Of course, Loder's scene-of-crime men had done their business, and the Home Office pathologist had examined the body *in situ*, but the corpse was still there, waiting for them, in the position she been found.

Loder walked in fifteen minutes later. He was a painfully thin man with a hatchet face and a sparse fuzz of grey hair. Close to retirement, Banks guessed, and tired. His worn navy blue suit hung on him, and his wire-rimmed glasses seemed precariously balanced near the end of his long, thin nose. As he spoke, his grey-green eyes peered over the tops of the lenses.

After the formalities were over, the three men headed up the thickly carpeted stairs to room 403.

"We tried to do as you asked," Loder said as they climbed. "You might see some traces of the SOCO team's presence, but otherwise . . ." He had a local accent, a kind of deep burr like a mist around his vowels, and he spoke slowly, pausing between thoughts.

The uniformed constable stepped aside at Loder's gesture, and they entered the room and turned on the light. They had no need to wear surgical gloves, as the forensic scientists had already been over the scene. What they were getting was part preservation, part re-creation.

First, Banks studied the room in general. It was unusually spacious for a seaside hotel room, with a high ceiling, ornate moulding and an oriel window overlooking the sea, now only a dim presence beyond the Esplanade lights. The window was open a fraction and Banks felt the pleasant chill of the breeze and heard the distant wash of waves on the beach. Gristhorpe stood beside him, similarly watchful. The wallpaper, a bright flower pattern, gave a cheerful aura, and a framed watercolour of Weymouth's seafront hung over the writing-desk. There was little other furniture: armchair, television, dressing-table, wardrobe and bedside tables—and the large bed itself. Banks left that until last.

The shape of a woman's body was clearly defined by the twisted white sheet that covered it. At first glance, it looked like someone sprawled on her back in the morning just before stretching and getting up. But instead of her head resting on the pillow, the pillow was resting on her head.

"Is this how you found her?" Banks asked Loder.

He nodded. "The doc did his stuff, of course, but he tried not to disturb her too much. We put the body back much as it was, as you requested."

There was an implied criticism in his tone. Why on earth, Loder seemed to be asking, did you want us to leave the body? But Banks ignored him. He always liked to get the feel of a scene; somehow it told him much more than photographs, drawings and reports. There was nothing morbid in his need to *see* the body where it lay; in fact, in many instances, this included, he would far rather not. But it did make a difference. Not only did it give him some sort of contact with the victim, the symbolism of having *touched* the corpse, something he needed to fuel him through a murder investigation, but it also sometimes enabled him to enter the criminal's and the victim's minds. He didn't think there was anything particularly psychic about this; it was more a Holmesian manner of working back from the little things one observed to the circumstances that created them. There was no denying, though, that sometimes he did get a true *feel* for the way the killer thought and what his next moves might be.

From the disapproval in his tone, Banks formed the impression that Loder was a highly moral man, outraged not only by the murder but by the delay in getting the corpse to its proper place. It was a woman's body, too, and that seemed to embarrass him.

Slowly, Banks walked over to the bed and picked up the pillow. Gristhorpe stood beside him. The woman's long blonde hair lay spread out on the undersheet. She had been beautiful, no doubt about that: fine bone structure, a clear complexion, full lips. Apart from her head, only her neck and shoulders were exposed, alabaster skin clouded with the bluish tinge of cyanosis.

Her left hand grasped the top of the sheet and bunched it up. She wore red nail polish, but Banks thought he could also detect traces of blood around the tips of her fingers and smeared on the white sheet. He lifted the sheet. She was naked underneath. Carefully, he replaced it, as if to avoid causing her further embarrassment. Loder wasn't the only sensitive one, no matter what he thought.

Gristhorpe opened one of her eyelids. "See that," he said pointing to the red pinpricks of blood in the once-blue eye.

Banks nodded. It was a petechial haemorrhage, one sign of asphyxiation, most likely in this case caused by the pillow.

Banks touched her right hand and shivered; it was cold and stiff with rigor.

"We've got the skin and blood samples, of course," said Loder, when he saw Banks examining the nails. "Looks like she put up a bit of a struggle. We should be able to type the killer, maybe even do a DNA profile."

"We don't have time for that," Gristhorpe said. "This one's got to be stopped fast."

"We-ell," said Loder, in his slow burr, "at least it'll come in useful in court. Is it her, the one you're looking for?"

"We didn't have a very good description," Gristhorpe answered. "Alan?"

"Couldn't say." Banks turned to Loder. "She was with the man, though, you said?"

"Yes. The one with the nice smile. You mentioned it specifically in the papers. That's why we called you boys in."

"Any identification?" Gristhorpe asked.

Loder shook his head. "Nothing. Whoever did it took everything. Clothes, handbag, the lot. We tried her fingerprints but they're not on file." He paused. "It looks as if she was killed here, and the doc says she certainly hasn't been moved since she died.

He's anxious to get to the PM, of course, but ruling out drugs, his findings so far are consistent with asphyxiation."

"Any idea of the time?"

"Doc puts it between six and nine in the morning."

"Anything else we should know?"

Loder glanced towards the body and paused for a moment before speaking. "Nothing else unusual about the body," he said, "unless you count the fact that she'd had sex around the time she was killed."

"Forced?"

"Not so far as the doc could make out." Loder walked towards the window, leaned on the sill and looked out over the Esplanade lights. "But it probably wouldn't be, would it, if she was sleeping with the bloke. Now, if you gentlemen are through, could we possibly get out of here? I seem to have spent far too much time with her already today." He sounded weary, and Banks wondered if he were not only tired but ill; he certainly seemed unusually thin and pale.

"Of course," said Gristhorpe, looking over at Banks. "Just a couple more questions first, while they're fresh in my mind."

Loder sighed. "All right."

"I don't suppose the chambermaid actually cleaned the room, did she, given what she found here?"

"No," said Loder, a thin smile on his lips. "No, she didn't. I'm sure you'll want to talk to her yourselves, but the one odd thing—and I noticed it, too—was that the room looked as if it *had* just been cleaned. The SOCO team tried to disturb things as little as possible. They took their samples, dusted for prints and so on, but you can see what it was like."

Indeed they could. The room looked spotless, clean and tidy. Under the thin patina of fingerprint powder, wood surfaces gleamed with recent polishing. Gristhorpe glanced in the small bathroom toilet, and it was the same, as if the fixtures and fittings had been scrubbed with Ajax, the towels hung neatly on the racks. There wasn't a smear of toothpaste or a trace of stubble stuck to the sides of the sink.

"The cottage the Manleys left in Eastvale was just the same," Gristhorpe said. "What do you make of it, Alan?"

Banks shrugged. "Partly getting rid of evidence, I suppose," he said. "Though he kindly left us semen samples, not to mention blood and skin under her fingernails. Maybe he's got a pathological obsession with cleanliness and neatness. I've heard it's not uncommon among psychopaths. Something to ask Jenny about, anyway." He pointed to two thin, glossy leaflets on the dressing-table. "Were those there when the chambermaid came in?"

"No," said Loder. "Sorry. One of the crime-scene boys found them and forgot to put them back."

"Would you show us where?"

Loder opened one of the drawers, which was lined with plain paper, and slipped the brochures under. "Like this," he said. "I thought maybe he'd forgotten them, or they slipped under the lining by accident. The chambermaid said she cleans out the drawers thoroughly between guests, so they can't have been there before. They're ferry timetables, see. For Cherbourg and the Channel Islands. We reckon that's where he must have gone."

"What time do the ferries start?"

"Early enough."

"Did he have a car?"

"Yes, parked out back. A white Fiesta. See, he wouldn't need it to get to the ferry dock, and once he gets over to the Channel Islands or France, well . . . Anyway, our lads have taken it to the police garage."

"Is there anything else?" Gristhorpe asked.

Loder shook his head.

"All right, let's get out of here. Tell your boys they can get her to the mortuary. Will the pathologist be able to start the autopsy tonight?"

"I think so." Loder closed the door behind them. "As I said, he's been chomping at the bit all day as it is." The police guard resumed his post and Loder led the way downstairs.

"Good," said Gristhorpe. "I think we can leave it till morning to talk to the hotel staff. I trust your lads have already taken statements?"

Loder nodded.

"We'll see what a good night's sleep does for their memories then. Anything else you can think of, Alan?"

Banks shook his head, but couldn't prevent his stomach from rumbling.

"Oh, aye," said Gristhorpe. "I forgot we hadn't eaten all day. Better see what we can rustle up."

II

"Is this the place?" Susan Gay asked.

Richmond nodded. "Looks like it."

Rampart Street sounded as if it should have been situated near the castle, but instead, for reasons known only to town-planners, it was a nondescript cul-de-sac running south off Elmet Street in Eastvale's west end. One side consisted of pre-war terrace houses without gardens. Mostly they seemed in a state of neglect and disrepair, but some tenants had attempted to brighten things up with window-boxes and brass door-knockers.

The other side of the street, with a small Esso garage on the corner, consisted of several shops, including a greengrocer's with tables of fruit and vegetables out front; a betting shop; a newsagent-cum-video rental outlet; and the incongruously named Rampart Antiques. However one defines "antique," whether it be by some kind of intrinsic beauty or simply by age, Rampart Antiques failed on both counts.

In the grimy window, Susan spotted a heap of cracked Sony Walkmans without headphones, two stringless acoustic guitars and several dusty box-cameras, along with the occasional chipped souvenir plate with its "hand-painted" scene of Blackpool tower or London Bridge wedged among them. One corner was devoted to old LPs—Frank Sinatra, the Black Dyke Mills Band, Bobby Vinton, Connie Francis—covers faded and curled at the edges after too long in the sun. An old Remington office typewriter, which looked as if it weighed a ton, stood next to a cracked Coronation mug and a bulbous pink china lamp-stand.

Inside was no less messy, and the smell of dust, mildew and stale tobacco made Susan's nose itch.

"Can I help you?"

The man sat behind the counter, a copy of *Penthouse* open in front of him. It was hard to tell how tall he was, but he certainly had the short black hair, the squarish face and the broken nose that the woman in Johnson's building had mentioned.

"John Fairley?" Richmond asked.

"That's me."

Richmond and Susan showed their warrant cards, then Richmond said, in his formal voice, "We have received information which leads us to believe that there may be stolen property on these premises." He handed over a copy of the search warrant they had spent all afternoon arranging. Fairley stared at it, open-mouthed.

By then, both Richmond and Susan were rummaging through the junk. They would find nothing on display, of course, but the search had to be as thorough as possible. Susan flipped through the stacks of old 45s on wobbly tables—Ral Donner, B. Bumble and the Stingers, Karl Denver, Boots Randolph, the Surfaris, names she had never heard of. One table groaned under the whole of Verdi's *Rigoletto* on 78s. There were also several shelves of books along one wall: *Reader's Digest* condensed editions; old Enid Blytons with torn paper covers that said 2/6 on the front; books with stiff pages and covers warped and stained by water-damage, most by authors she had never heard of. She doubted whether even Banks or Gristhorpe would have heard of them, either. Who on earth would want to buy such useless and smelly junk?

When they were satisfied that there were no videos or stereos hidden among the cracked figurines and rusted treadle sewing-machines, they asked Fairley if he would show them the rest of the premises. At first he hesitated, then he shrugged, locked the front door, turned the sign to read CLOSED, and led them through the moth-eaten curtain behind the counter. Silent so far, he seemed resigned to his fate.

The curtain led into a corridor with a filthy sink piled with cups growing mould from old tea leaves. Next to the sink was a metal counter-top streaked with rust, on which stood, among the mouse-droppings, a bottle of Camp coffee, a quarter of Typhoo tea, some curdled milk and a bowl of sugar lumps.

The corridor ended in a toilet with a stained bowl and wash-basin, flaking plaster and spider-webs in the corners. It was almost impossible to open the door to the other room on the ground floor, but slim Richmond managed to slip in and discover that it was packed mostly with collapsed cardboard boxes. There were also some books, video cassettes and magazines of a slightly suspect eroticism, though perhaps not the more prosecutable variety of pornography.

After he had finished there, Richmond pointed to the other door off the corridor. "Where's that lead?" he asked.

Fairley tried to bluff his way out of opening it. He said it led nowhere, wasn't part of the premises, but Richmond persisted. They soon found themselves following Fairley down to a cellar with whitewashed walls. There, lit by a bare bulb, stood what looked like the remnants of the Fletcher's warehouse job. Two television sets, three videos and a compact-disc player.

"Bankrupt stock," said Fairley. "I was going to put them in the window when I've got room."

Richmond ignored him and asked Susan to check the serial numbers on the cartons with the list that the manager of Fletcher's had supplied. They matched.

"Right," said Richmond, leaning back against the stack of cartons. "Before we go down to the nick, I'd like to ask you a few questions, John."

"Aren't you going to charge me?"

"Later."

"I mean, shouldn't I have a solicitor present or something?"

"If you want. But let's just forget the stolen goods for the moment, shall we? Have you got any form, John?"

Fairley shook his head.

"That's good," Richmond said. "First offence. It'll go better for you if you help us. We want to know about Carl Johnson."

"Now look, I didn't have nothing to do with that. You can't pin that on me."

It was interesting to watch Richmond at work, Susan thought. Cool, relaxed and looking as elegant as ever in the dingy room, careful not to lean against the wall for fear of marking his suit, he

set Fairley at ease and led him gently through a series of preliminary questions about his relationship with Johnson and Poole
before he got to Chivers. At the mention of the name, Fairley
became obviously nervous.

"Carl brought him here," he said, squatting miserably on a box.
"I never liked him, or that girlfriend of his. They were both a bit
doolally, if you ask me."

"What do you mean?"

"Just that look he got in his eyes sometimes. Oh, he could be
pleasant enough on the surface, but when you saw what was underneath, it was scary. I couldn't look him in the eye without trembling."

"When did you see him last?"

"Couple of weeks ago."

"Did you ever think he might be concerned with Carl's death?"

"I . . . well, to be honest, it crossed my mind. I don't know why.
Just the kind of person he seemed."

"Yet you didn't come forward?"

"Do you think I'm crazy or something?"

"Did you know of any reason he might have had for killing
Johnson?"

Fairley shook his head. "No."

"There was no falling out over the loot?"

"What loot?"

Richmond kicked a box. "The alleged loot."

"No."

"What about the girl? Did Johnson make a play for her?"

"Not that I know of. She was sexy enough, and she knew it, but
she was Chivers's property, no mistaking that. NO ENTRY signs on
every orifice. Sorry, love." He looked at Susan, who simply gave
him a blank stare. "No," he went on, turning back to Richmond, "I
don't think Carl was daft enough to mess with her."

"What about Gemma Scupham?"

Fairley looked surprised. "The kid who was abducted?"

"That's her."

"What about her?"

"You tell me, John."

Fairley tensed. A vein throbbed at his temple. "You can't think I had anything to do with that? Oh, come on! I don't go in for little girls. No way."

"What about Chivers?"

"Nothing about him would surprise me."

"Did he ever mention her?"

"No. I mean, I *had* heard of her. Les complained about her some-times and Carl sympathized. Chivers just seemed to be standing back, sort of laughing at it all, as if such a problem could never happen to him. He always seemed above everything, arrogant like, as if we were all just petty people with petty concerns and he'd think no more about stepping on us if he had to than he would about swatting a fly. Look, why are you asking me about Gemma? I never even met the kid."

"She was never in this shop?"

"No. Why should she have been?"

"Where is Chivers now?"

"I don't know and I don't want to know. He's bad news."

Richmond sat down carefully on a box. "Has it never struck you," he said, "that if he did kill Johnson, then you and Les might be in danger, too?"

"No. Why? We didn't do nothing. We always played square."

"So did Carl, apparently. Unless there's something you're not telling me. It doesn't seem to matter with Chivers, does it? Why do you think he killed Carl, if he did?"

"I told you, I don't know. He's a nutter. He always seemed to me like he was on the edge, you know, ready to go off. People like him don't always need reasons. Maybe he did it for fun."

"Maybe. So why not kill you, too? Might that not be fun?"

Fairley licked his lips. "Look, if you're trying to scare me you're doing a damn good job. Are you trying to warn me I'm in danger or just trying to make me talk? I think it's about time I saw a solicitor."

Richmond stood up and brushed off the seat of his pants with his palm. "Are you sure you have no idea where Chivers went after he left Eastvale?"

"None."

"Did he say anything about his plans?"

"Not to me."

"Where did he come from?"

"Dunno. He never talked about himself. Honest. Look, are you winding me up about all this?" Fairley had started to sweat now.

"We need to find him, John," said Richmond quietly. "That's all. Then we'll all sleep a little easier in our beds." He turned to Susan. "Let's take him to station now and make it formal, shall we?" He rubbed the wall and held up his forefinger. "And we'd better get a SOCO team down here, too. Remember that whitewash on Gemma's clothing?"

Susan nodded. As they left, she noticed that John Fairley seemed far more willing to accompany them to the station than most villains they arrested.

"I'll tell you one thing for free," he said as they got in the car.

"What's that?" said Richmond.

"He had a gun, Chivers did. I saw it once when he was showing off with it in front of his girlfriend."

"What kind of gun?"

"How would I know? I don't know nothing about them."

"Big, small, medium?"

"It wasn't that big. Like those toy guns you play with when you're a kid. But it weren't no toy."

"A revolver?"

"What's the difference?"

"Never mind."

"Isn't it enough just to know the bastard's got a gun?"

"Yes," sighed Richmond, looking over at Susan. "Yes, it is."

III

Banks and Gristhorpe leaned on the railings above the beach and ate fish and chips out of cardboard cartons. The hotel didn't do evening meals, and, as in most seaside towns, all the cafés seemed to close at five or six.

"Not bad," said Gristhorpe, "but they do them better up north."

"If you like them greasy."

"Traitor. I keep forgetting you're still just a southerner underneath it all."

Banks tossed his empty carton into a rubbish-bin and looked out to sea. Close to shore, bright stars shone through gaps in the clouds and reflected in the dark water. Farther out, the cloud-covering thickened and dimmed the quarter moon. The breeze that was slowly driving the clouds inland carried a chill, and Banks was glad he had put on a pullover under his sports jacket. He sniffed the bracing air, sharp with ozone. A few cars droned along The Esplanade, and the sound of people talking or laughing in the night drifted on the air occasionally, but mostly it was quiet. Banks lit a cigarette and drew deep. Silly, he thought, but it tasted better out here in the sea air pervaded with the smells of saltwater and seaweed.

"Do you know," said Banks finally, "I think I'm developing a feel for Chivers. I *know* he's been here. I know he killed the girl."

Gristhorpe gave him a steady, appraising look. "Not turning psychic on me, are you, Alan?"

Banks laughed. "Not me. Look, there's the white Fiesta, the smile, the blonde, the neatness of the hotel room. You'll agree the incidents have those things in common?"

"Aye. And tomorrow morning we'll have a word with the hotel staff and look over Loder's reports, see if we can't amass enough evidence to be *sure*. Maybe then we'll know what the next move is. If that bastard's slipped away abroad . . ." Gristhorpe crumpled up his cardboard box and tossed it in the bin.

"We'll get him."

Gristhorpe raised an eyebrow. "More intuition?"

"No. Just sheer dogged determination."

Gristhorpe clapped Banks lightly on the shoulder. "That I can understand. I think I'll turn in now. Coming?"

Banks sniffed the night air. He felt too restless to go to bed so soon. "Think I'll take a walk on the prom," he said. "Just to clear out the cobwebs."

"Right. See you at breakfast."

Banks watched Gristhorpe, a tall, powerful man in a chunky Swaledale sweater, cross the road, then he started walking along the promenade. A few couples, arms around one another, strolled by, but Weymouth at ten-thirty that Friday evening in late September was as dead as any out-of-season seaside resort. Over the road stood the tall Georgian terrace houses, most of them converted into hotels. Lights shone behind some curtains, but most of the rooms were dark.

When he got to the Jubilee Clock, an ornate structure built to commemorate Queen Victoria's Diamond Jubilee, Banks took the steps down to the beach. The tide hadn't been out long and the glistening sand was wet like a hardening gel under his feet. The footprints he made disappeared as soon as he moved on.

As he walked, it was of John Cowper Powys he thought, not Thomas Hardy. Somebody had mentioned *Weymouth Sands* to him around Christmas time and, intrigued, he had bought a copy. Now, as he actually trod Weymouth sands himself for the first time since he was a child, he thought of the opening scene where Magnus Muir stood meditating on the relationship between the all-consuming unity of the sea and the peculiar and individual character of each wave. The Esplanade lights reflected in the wet sand, which sucked in the remaining moisture with a hissing sound every time a wave retreated.

Heady thoughts for a lowly chief inspector. He stood for a moment and let the waves lick at his shoes. Farther south, the lights of the car ferry terminal seemed to hang suspended over the water. Loder was right, he thought: Chivers would have been a fool to take his car. Much easier to mingle with the foot-passengers and rent one wherever he went. Or, even more anonymous, travel by train if he got to France.

Seeing the dead woman in the hotel had shaken Banks more than he realized. Wondering why, as he doubled back along the ribbed sand at the edge of the beach, he felt it was perhaps because of Sandra. There was only a superficial resemblance, of course, but it was enough to remind him of Sandra in her twenties. Though Sandra had ridiculed the idea, the photo of Gemma Scupham had also reminded him of a younger Tracy, albeit a less doleful-looking one. Tracy took after Sandra, whereas Brian, with his small, lean, dark-haired Celtic appearance, took after Banks. There were altogether too many resemblances for comfort in this case.

Banks thought about what he had said earlier, the *feel* he was developing for the way Chivers operated. Then he thought about what he *hadn't* told Gristhorpe. Standing in that room and looking down at the dead woman, Banks had known, as surely as he knew what happened at Johnson's murder, that Chivers had been making love to her, smiling down, and that as he was reaching his climax— that brief pause for a sigh that Les Poole had mentioned—he had taken the pillow and held it over her face. She had struggled, scratching and gouging his skin, but he had pushed it down and ejaculated as she died.

Was he really beginning to understand something of Chivers's psychopathic thought processes? It was a frightening notion, and for a moment he felt himself almost pull in his antennae and reject the insight. But he couldn't.

The blonde woman—he wished he knew her name—must somehow have started to become a liability. Perhaps she was having second thoughts about what they'd done to Gemma; maybe she was overcome by guilt and had threatened to go to the police. Perhaps Chivers had conned her into thinking they were taking the child for some other reason, and she had found out what really happened. She could have panicked when she saw the newspaper likenesses, and Chivers didn't feel he could trust her any longer. Or maybe he just grew tired of her. Whatever the reason, she ceased to be of use to him, and someone like Chivers would then start to think of an *interesting* way to get rid of her.

He must be easily bored, Banks thought, remembering what he and Jenny had talked about in the Queen's Arms. A creative intelligence, though clearly a warped one, he showed imagination and daring. For some years, he had been able to channel his urges into legitimate criminal activity—a contradiction in terms, Banks realized, but nonetheless true. Chivers had sought work from people who had logical, financial reasons for what they employed him to do, and however evil they were, whatever harm they did, there was no denying that at bottom they were essentially businessmen gone wrong, the other side of the coin, not much different from insider traders and the rest of the corporate crooks.

Now, though, perhaps because he was deteriorating, losing control, as Jenny had said, Chivers was starting to create his own opportunities for pleasure, financed by simple heists like the Fletcher's warehouse job. The money he got from such ventures would allow him the freedom to roam the country and follow his fancy wherever it led him. And by paying cash, he would leave no tell-tale credit-card traces.

Now, it seemed, Chivers was escalating, craving more dangerous thrills to satiate his needs. He was like a drug addict; he always needed more to keep him at the same level. Gemma Scupham, Carl Johnson, the blonde. How quickly was he losing control? Was he starting to get careless?

A wave soaked one foot and the bottom of his pant leg. He stepped back and did a little dance to shake the water off. Then he reached for a cigarette and, for some reason, thought of Brian, not more than seventy miles east of him, in Portsmouth. College had only just started, and he might be feeling lonely and alien in a strange city. It was so close, yet Banks wouldn't be able to visit.

He missed his son. Much as Tracy had always seemed the favourite, with her interests in history and literature, her curiosity and intelligence, and Brian always the outsider, the rebel, with his loud rock music and his lack of interest in school, Banks missed him. Certainly he felt the odd one out now that Tracy was only interested in boys and clothes.

Brian was eighteen, and Banks had turned forty in May. With a smile, he remembered the compact disc of Nigel Kennedy playing the Brahms violin concerto that Brian had bought him for his birthday. Well, at least the thought was there. And he also remembered his recent row with Tracy. In a way, she had been right: Brian *had* got away with a lot, especially that summer, before he had left for the polytechnic: late-night band practices; a week-long camping trip to Cornwall with his mates; coming in once or twice a little worse for drink. But of one thing Banks was certain: Brian wasn't taking drugs. As an experienced detective, he knew the signs, physical and psychological, and had never observed them in his son.

He turned from the beach and found a phonebox on The Esplanade. It was eleven o'clock. Would he be in? He put his phonecard in and punched in the number Brian shared with the other students in the house. It started to ring.

"Hello?"

A strange voice. He asked for Brian, said it was his father.

"Just a minute," the voice mumbled.

He waited, tapping his fingers against the glass, and after a few moments Brian came on the line.

"Dad! What is it? What's wrong?" he asked.

"Nothing. I'm just down the coast from you and I wanted to say hello. How are you doing?" Banks felt choked, hearing Brian's voice. He wasn't sure his words came out right.

"I'm fine," Brian answered.

"How's college?"

"Oh, you know. It's fine. Everything's fine. Look, are you sure there's nothing wrong? Mum's okay, isn't she?"

"I told you, everything's all right. It's just that I won't be able to make the time to drop by and I thought, well, being so close, I'd just give you a ring."

"Is it a case?"

"Yes."

Silence.

"Are you still there, Dad?"

"Of course I am. When are you coming up to visit us again?"

"I'll be up at Christmas. Hey, I've met some really great people down here. They play music and all. There's this one guy, we're going to form a band, and he's been playing some great blues for me. You ever heard of Robert Johnson? Muddy Waters?"

Banks smiled to himself and sighed. If Brian had ever taken the trouble to examine his collection—and of course, no teenager would be seen dead sharing his father's taste in music—he would have found not only the aforementioned, but Little Walter, Bessie Smith and Big Bill Broonzy, among several dozen others.

"Yes, I've heard of them," he said. "I'm glad you're having a good time. Look, keep in touch. Your mother says you don't write often enough."

"Sorry. There's really a lot of work to do. But I'll try to do better, promise."

"You do. Look—"

His time ran out and he didn't have another card. Just a few more seconds to say hurried goodbyes, then the electronic insect sound of a dead line. When he put the phone down and started walking back to the hotel, Banks felt empty. Why was it always like that? he wondered. You call someone you love on the phone, and when you've finished talking, all you feel is the bloody distance between you. Time to try sleep, perhaps, after a little music. Sleep that knits up the ravell'd sleave of care. Some hope.

THIRTEEN

I

Hotel or bed and breakfast, it didn't seem to make much difference with regard to the traditional English breakfast, thought Gristhorpe the following morning. Of course, there was more choice at the Mellstock Hotel than there would be in a typical B and B, but no one in his right mind would want to start the day with a "continental" breakfast—a stale croissant and a gob of strawberry jam in a plastic container. As it was, Banks sat struggling over a particularly bony kipper while Gristhorpe stuck to bacon and eggs and wished he hadn't. Between them, they shared a rack of cold toast and a pot of weak instant coffee.

Gristhorpe felt grumpy. He hadn't slept well; the mattress had been too soft, and his back was bothering him. The breakfast didn't help either, he realized, feeling the onset of heartburn.

"I dropped in at the hotel bar for a nightcap yesterday," he said, pushing the plate aside and pouring more coffee. "Thought I might be able to get something out of the regulars."

"And?" asked Banks, pulling a bone from the corner of his mouth.

"Nothing much. There's a couple from Wolverhampton staying the week, and they said the Barlows, as they called themselves, were in once or twice. Always pleasant. You know, nodded and said hello, but never got into any conversations. The missis thought they were a honeymoon couple."

"You know," said Banks, "he's really starting to get on my nerves, Chivers. He turns up somewhere, goes around smiling like Mr Clean, and people die."

"What do you expect?"

"It's just his bloody nerve. It's as if he's challenging us, playing catch-me-if-you-can."

"Aye, I know what you mean," said Gristhorpe, with a scowl. "And we won't catch him sitting here picking at this fine English cuisine. Come on." He pushed his plate away and stood up abruptly, leaving Banks to follow suit.

The hotel manager had provided a small room on the ground floor for them to conduct interviews. First, they read over the statements that DI Loder and his men had taken from the hotel staff, then asked to see Meg Wayne, the chambermaid.

She looked no older than fourteen or fifteen, a frightened schoolgirl with her uniform and starched cap that couldn't quite contain her abundant golden hair. She had a pale, clear complexion, and with a couple of red spots on her cheeks, Gristhorpe thought, she could probably pass herself off as one of Tess's milkmaid friends in Hardy's book. Her Dorset burr was even more pronounced than Loder's, her voice soft and surprisingly low.

"Mr Ballard, the manager, said I could take the day off," she said, "but I don't see the point, do you? I mean, the rooms need doing every day no matter what happens, and I could certainly do with the money."

"Still," said Gristhorpe, "it must have been a shock?"

"Oh yes. I've never seen a dead body before. Only on telly, like."

"Tell us what you saw yesterday, Meg."

"We-ell, I opens the door as usual, and as soon as I does I knows something's wrong."

"Were the curtains open?"

"Part way. Enough to see by."

"And the window?"

"Open a bit. It was chilly." She fiddled with a set of room keys on her lap as she spoke.

"Did you go into the room?"

"Not right in. I just stood in the doorway, like, and I could see her there on the bed, with her head all covered up."

"Tell me exactly what you saw," said Gristhorpe. He knew that people tend to embellish on what they have observed. He also wanted to be certain that Loder and his SOCO team had restored the room to the way it had been when Meg opened the door. He grimaced and rubbed his stomach; the heartburn was getting worse.

"It looked like just twisted sheets at first," she said, "but then, when my eyes grew more accustomed, I could tell it was someone under there. A shape." She blushed and looked down at her lap. "A woman's shape. And the pillow was over her head, so I knew she was . . . dead."

"It's all right, Meg," said Gristhorpe. "I know it's upsetting. We won't be much longer."

Meg nodded and took a deep breath.

"Did you see the woman's face?"

"No. No, I just knew it was a woman by the outline of the sheets."

"Did you disturb anything in the room?"

"Nothing. Like I told Mr Loder, I ran straight off to Mr Ballard and he sent for the police. That's God's honest truth, sir."

"I believe you," said Gristhorpe. "We just have to make certain. You must have been upset. Maybe there's something you forgot?"

"No, sir."

"All right. Did you ever see the people who were staying in that room?"

"Not as far as I know. I don't see many guests, sir. I have to do my job when they're out."

"Of course. Now think, Meg, try to remember, was there anything else about the scene that struck you at the time?"

Meg squeezed her eyes shut and fiddled with the keys. Finally, she looked at Gristhorpe again. "Just how tidy it was, sir. I mean, you wouldn't believe the mess some guests leave you to clean up. Not that I mind, like. I know they pay for the service and it's my job, but . . ."

"So this room was unusually tidy?"

"Yes."

"Did you see anything at all on the table or the dresser?"

She shook her head. "Nothing. They were empty."

"All right, Meg, we're just about finished now. Can you remember anything else at all?"

"Well, it's funny," she said, "but just now when I had my eyes closed I did remember something. I never really paid it any mind at the time, though I must have noticed, but it stuck."

"What is it?"

"I don't think it can be important, but it was the smell. I use Pledge Natural on the furniture. I'd know that smell anywhere. Very clean and. . . . But this was something else . . . a sort of pine-scented polish . . . I don't know. Why would anybody want to polish furniture in a hotel room?"

"Thank you, Meg," said Gristhorpe. "You can go now. You've been a great help."

"I have? Thank you." She went to the door and turned with her fingers touching the handle. "I'm not looking forward to this, sir," she said. "Between you and me, I'm not looking forward to opening any doors in this hotel this morning." And she left.

Gristhorpe reached into his side pocket, took out a pack of Rennies he carried for such emergencies as English breakfasts and southern fish and chips, and chewed two of them.

"All right?" Banks asked.

"Aye." Gristhorpe pulled a face. "Just ought to watch my diet, that's all."

Next they saw the receptionist, Maureen, rather prickly at being called away from her domain. Gristhorpe basked in antacid relief and left Banks to do most of the questioning. She had very little to tell them save that the Barlows had checked in the evening of Wednesday, September 24, at about six o'clock with just one tan suitcase between them. She had told them about parking and got their car licence number, then he had signed the register Mr and Mrs Barlow and given an address in Lichfield. Loder had already checked this and found it didn't exist. No, Maureen hadn't asked for any identification. Why should she? And yes, of course he had skipped out on his bill. If you'd just murdered your lover, you'd hardly stop at the front desk and pay your hotel bill, would you? No, nobody had seen him leave. It wasn't a prison camp or one of those Russian gulags, you know. What did she think of them? Just ordinary, no one you'd look twice at if you saw them in the street. Her, maybe, but he was just a nondescript bloke with a nice smile.

In fact, Maureen remembered wondering what an attractive, if rather stuck-up, girl like her was doing with the likes of him.

And that was it. They talked briefly with Mr Ballard, who didn't remember seeing the Barlows at all, and to the bellboy who had carried their suitcase to their room and remembered nothing but the pound tip the bloke had given him. Nobody knew what they did with their time. Went for walks, the cinema in the evening, or to a pub. Nothing unusual about them. Nothing much else to do in Weymouth.

By the time they had finished the interviews, it was eleven-thirty. DI Loder had said he would drop by that morning as soon as the autopsy results became available, and they met him walking into the lobby. He looked as if he had slept badly, too, Gristhorpe thought, with bags under his eyes and his long face pale and drawn. The three of them decided to take some fresh air on the prom while they discussed the results.

"Anything?" Gristhorpe asked as they leaned on the railings. A faint breeze ruffled his thick grey hair. The weather was overcast, but reasonably warm. Seagulls squawked overhead.

Loder shook his head slowly. "First, we've made enquiries at the ferry dock and no one remembers anyone of his description. We can't really make too much of that, though, as it's very busy down there. And the autopsy findings bear out what the doc suspected. She died of asphyxiation, and the pillow fibres in her lungs indicate that's how it happened. No sign of drugs or anything, though it'll be a while before all the test results come back. We've sent the tissue for DNA testing—it looks like our man's Group O, by the way—but that'll take some time. She did have sex prior to death, and there were no signs of sexual assault, so we assume it was by consent. Otherwise healthy. Poor woman, we don't even know her name yet. Only one surprise: she was eight weeks pregnant."

"Hmm," said Gristhorpe. "I wonder if Chivers knew that."

Loder shrugged. "Hardly a motive for murder."

"I don't think he needs much of a motive. It could have pushed him over the edge."

"Or maybe it made her a liability," Banks suggested. "Not so much just because she was pregnant but because it softened her, brought out the guilt over what they'd done? If she found out she was going to have a child of her own . . ."

"There's no point in speculating," said Gristhorpe. "It's something we might never know. Anything else?"

"Nothing from the car," Loder said. "A few partials . . . fibres and the like, but you know as well as I do most stuff's mass-produced these days. Could have come from almost any blue cotton shirt. There's not a lot else to say. We've got men asking around about him, if anyone saw him after he left the hotel. Nothing so far. Oh, and I informed Interpol and the authorities on the Channel Islands."

"Good," said Gristhorpe. "That seems to cover it all."

"What next?" asked Loder.

"We can only wait, can't we?"

"Looks like it. I'd better be off back to the station, keep on top of it."

"Thanks." Gristhorpe shook his hand. "Thanks a lot."

They watched Loder walk off towards his car. "He's got a point," said Gristhorpe. "What *do* we do next?"

Banks shrugged. "I can only speculate."

"Go ahead."

Banks watched a ferry steam out of the dock. The flock of gulls swooped on a dead fish on the beach. "I've been thinking about Chivers," he said, lighting a cigarette and looking out to sea. "Trying to fathom his thought processes."

"And?"

"And I'm not sure, but . . . look, he must know we're after him by now. Surely he's seen the stuff in the newspapers. What does he do? He kills the woman, too much extra baggage, and he takes off. Now a normal criminal would certainly head for the continent and disappear. But we know Chivers isn't normal."

"I think I follow your train, Alan. I've had the same thought myself. He's playing a game, isn't he? Laughing at us."

Banks nodded. "And he likes the attention. Jenny said he's likely to be egocentric, but he's also probably impulsive and irresponsible. I've thought about that a lot."

"So where would he head, given the way he thinks?"

"Back to where it started, I think," said Banks. "I'll bet you a pound to a penny the bastard's back in Eastvale."

II

It was late that Saturday evening when Banks and Gristhorpe arrived back in Eastvale. They were delayed by a six-car pile-up into a jackknifed lorry on the M1 just south of Leicester, and as they passed by Pontefract and Castleford on the A1, the rain fell in buckets, slowing traffic to a crawl.

So it was that on Sunday morning, as the bells rang in the church and people crossed the market square in their Sunday best for the morning service, the members of Eastvale CID sat in the conference room around the large circular table drinking coffee and pooling their findings.

Richmond and Susan brought the others up to date on John Fairley's information about Chivers and the fact that he owned a gun.

"Fairley seems the least involved of them all," said Richmond. "We had a good long chat when we brought him in. He's got no prior form. I'm sure he's dealt with stuff that fell off the back of a lorry before, but the Fletcher's warehouse job is his first big bit of fencing, we're sure of that. Susan?"

"I agree," said Susan Gay, looking up from the notes in front of her. "Seems it was Johnson's idea, and he recruited Les Poole easily. They were mates of Fairley's, genuinely helping out at the shop for a bit of under-the-counter pocket money. Chivers was the prime mover. Without him, I don't reckon the others would have had the guts to go through with it. It was Chivers drugged the guard dogs and cut through the chain-link fence. Poole drove the van, backed it up to the loading bay and away they went. The back of Fairley's shop is just a quiet backstreet, so they got unloaded without any trouble. It wasn't too hard to make a few sales through their pub mates, word of mouth, and they'd already got rid of most of the stuff by the time we called."

"Was there any falling out over the loot?" Banks asked.

"No," said Richmond. "Not as far as we could tell. Everyone seemed happy with his share. Poole took the television and stereo as part of his cut. Johnson got a thousand in cash. Fairley's got no idea why Johnson was killed, though he said he wouldn't be surprised to hear that Chivers had done him. Chivers scared him, seemed the type who'd do it for fun."

"And he's seen or heard nothing of him since?"

"No, sir. And doesn't want to."

"What about Gemma?" Banks asked. "Does Fairley know anything about what happened to her?"

"Just confirms what Poole told us, that's all," said Richmond. "After we spotted the whitewash in the cellar, we had the team do a thorough search last night, but they've turned up nothing to indicate Gemma was there."

"Right," said Gristhorpe, standing up and looking at his watch. "I've told you what Alan thinks about Chivers being in the area, and I agree with him. What I propose is that we start trying to flush him out. Phil, I'd like you to muster as many men as you can and start knocking on doors, asking questions. Somebody must have seen the bastard. The station and the bus station are obvious places to start. He left his car in Weymouth and unless he stole one, the odds are that he took some other form of transport. The lads down there are doing their bit, too. We're co-ordinating with a DI Loder. I'll get in touch with the media and we'll see if we can't get something on the local news tonight. I want it all in the open. If he is here, I want him to know we're closing in on him. I want him to panic and make a run for it.

"Susan, get in touch with as many of those concerned citizens who helped in the search for Gemma and get them to ask around. Tell them to make sure they don't take any risks, though. This one's dangerous. You know the kind of thing to ask about. Smoke from a cottage that's supposed to be empty, odd noises, suspicious strangers, that kind of thing. Especially anyone who insists on paying cash in large amounts. We'd better put a watch on Fairley's shop, Brenda Scupham's place and the holiday cottage, too, just in case. And we'll ask around the pubs. He's not the type to lie low. He'll be wanting to see the effect he's having. And remember, he may have altered his appearance a bit. He's done it before, so don't rely on hair colour. The one thing he can't change is that bloody smile. All right?"

Everyone nodded and dispersed. Banks returned to his office and looked out on the church-goers pouring into the market square: women in powder blue suits holding onto their broad brimmed hats in the wind, clutching handbags; husbands in dark suits at their sides, collars too tight, shifting from foot to foot as their wives chatted, thinking maybe now they'd done their duty they'd be able to sneak off to the Queen's Arms or the Crooked Billet for a quick one before dinner; restless children dreaming of an afternoon at Kinley Pond catching frogs, or climbing trees to collect birds' eggs in Brinely Woods—either that or sniffing glue under the railway bridge and planning a bit of recreational B and E. And somewhere, in the midst of all that quotidian human activity and aspiration, was Jeremy Chivers.

Banks didn't notice Susan in his doorway until she cleared her throat. He turned.

"Sorry, sir," she said, "it slipped my mind at the meeting, but you had a call from Piet Kuypers, Amsterdam police. Said to call him back, you'd know what it was about."

"Did he leave a message?"

"No. Just said he had a few interesting speculations for you." Susan handed him a piece of paper. "The top's his work number," she said, pointing, "and that one's home."

"Thank you." Banks took the paper and sat down. In the excitement of the chase for Chivers, he realized, he had quite forgotten asking Piet to check up on Adam Harkness. He hadn't liked the man much, but as soon as it became clear that Chivers had more than likely killed Carl Johnson, there had seemed no real reason to consider Harkness any longer.

Puzzled, he dialled Piet's home number. A child's voice answered. Banks couldn't speak Dutch, and the little girl didn't seem to understand English. The phone banged down on a hard surface and a moment later a man's voice came over the line, again in Dutch.

"Piet? It's me. Alan Banks in Eastvale?"

"Ah, Alan," said Piet. "That was my daughter, Eva. She only began to learn her English this year." He laughed. "How are you?"

"I'm fine, Piet. Hope I didn't disturb your lunch but I've been out of town and I got a message to call you."

"Yes. You have a moment?"

"Yes, of course."

Banks heard the receiver placed, more gently this time, on the hard surface, and he put his feet on the desk and lit a cigarette while he waited for Piet to come back. He realized he had been talking too loudly, as one does on the telephone to foreigners, and reminded himself that Piet's English was almost as good as his own.

"Sorry about that," said Piet. "Yes, I did a little snooping, as you call it, about that man Harkness." His voice bore only traces of a Dutch accent.

"Anything interesting?"

"Interesting, yes, I think so. But nothing but rumours, you understand. Hearsay. I found his wife. She has since remarried, and she didn't want to talk about her relationship with Harkness, but she hinted that part of the reason they separated was that he had what she called filthy habits."

"Filthy habits?"

"Yes. Like what, I thought? What do you English regard as a filthy habit? Picking his nose in bed? But I couldn't get her to say any more. She is very religious. She had a strict Dutch Protestant upbringing in a small town in Friesland. I'm sorry, Alan, but I couldn't force her to talk if she did not want to."

Banks sighed. "No, of course not. What happened next?"

"I talked to some of my colleagues on drugs and vice, but they don't know him. Mostly they're new. You don't last that long working on drugs and vice, and Harkness has been gone, how long did you say, two years?"

"Something like that," said Banks.

"So I had an idea," Piet went on. "I went to see Wim Kaspar. Now Wim is a strange man. Nobody really knows how far it all went, but he was, how do you English say, made to leave work early?"

"Fired?"

"No. I know that word. Not exactly fired."

"Made redundant?"

Piet laughed. "Yes, that's it. Such an odd phrase. Well, there was something of a cloud over Wim, you see. Nobody could prove anything, but it was suspected he took bribes and that he was involved with the drugs and girls in the Red Light district. But Wim worked many years in the Red Light district, ever since patrolman, and he knows more than anybody else what goes on there. And I don't care what people say—maybe it is true—but he is a good man in many ways. Do you understand?"

"I think so," said Banks, remembering now that Piet was a nice bloke but took ages getting to the bloody point.

"Wim heard and saw many things that went no further. It's give and take in that world. You scratch my back and I'll scratch yours. Especially if what they say about him is true. So I talked to him and he remembers something. Now you must understand, Alan, that there is no proof of this. It's just rumours. And Wim will never repeat officially what he told me."

"Tell me, Piet."

"According to Wim's contacts, your Mr Harkness visited the Red Light district on several occasions."

"Piet, who doesn't visit the Red Light district? It's one of your main tourist attractions."

"No, wait. There's more. There are some places, very bad places. Not just the pretty women in the windows, you understand?"

"Yes?"

"And Wim told me that your Mr Harkness visited one of these places."

"How did your source know who he was?"

"Alan, you must remember Mr Harkness is well known in Amsterdam, and not without influence. Do you want me to go on?"

"Yes, please."

"It was a very bad place," Piet continued. "You understand prostitution is not illegal here, that there are many brothels?"

"Yes."

"And the live sex shows and the whips and chains and all the rest. But this one brothel, Wim says, was a very special place. A place that caters for people who like little girls."

"Jesus Christ!"

"It happens, Alan. What can I say? Girls disappear from the big cities, they turn up in these places. Sometimes they are used for snuff films. You know what they are?"

"I know. Why wasn't he arrested?"

"Sometimes it is better to leave the little fish. Also, Harkness was an important man and, how shall I say, perhaps pressure could be brought to bear. He could have been useful."

Banks sighed. He knew the scenario. Get something on a man like Harkness and you've got him in your pocket: the police version of blackmail.

"Alan, in Amsterdam, just as, I suspect, in your London, you can get anything you want if you have the money to pay for it. Anything. If we can find these places and find evidence, we close them down and arrest the people responsible. But these men are very clever. And sometimes policemen can be bought, protection can be paid. Or blackmailed. We all have skeletons in our closets. Alan? Are you still there?"

"Yes. Yes, Piet, I know. I was thinking. Listen, I'd like you to do me a big favour. I assume places like this are still in existence?"

"There is one place now we are suspicious of. On the surface, it seems like an ordinary brothel, but rumour has it that young girls can be had there, for a price. Our undercover men are watching, but we have no proof yet."

"I'd like you to find out if there are any new girls." He gave Piet Gemma's description, praying he was wrong. At least it meant she might still be alive, if Harkness kept his connections in Amsterdam. He still couldn't work out the whys and the wherefores, how everything linked up, but he knew it would not have been so difficult for Harkness or someone else to smuggle Gemma out of the country, even during the search. The ferry from Immingham, for example, was always crowded; it would be easy enough to slip in among the other families with a sleeping child on the overnight journey, when everyone was tired. "I don't care whether you get enough proof to lock them up or not. Rumours will do fine for me. Use your contacts, informers. Maybe even your friend Wim might be able to help?"

"Yes," said Piet slowly. "I understand. I'll try. What more can I say?"

"And Piet."

"Yes?"

"Thanks. Thanks a lot. You did a great job." Then Banks slammed down the receiver and rushed to find Gristhorpe.

III

It was about time the place had a good cleaning, Brenda thought, wielding the Hoover like a lawnmower. She knew she wasn't good at housekeeping, but now she had so much time on her hands and nothing but bad thoughts and terrifying dreams, she had to do something or she would fall apart. The ground-in dirt and the food stains wouldn't come out, of course, they would need shampooing, but the dust would. At least it was a start.

The vacuum was so noisy that she didn't hear the bell. It was only the steady thumping on her door that broke through. She turned off the machine and listened again. Another knock. For a moment she just stood there, worried it might be Les. She wasn't frightened of him—she knew he was a coward at heart—but she didn't feel like another public row and she was damned if she was going to let him in. On the other hand, it might be the police with news of Gemma. She glanced out of the window but couldn't see a police car. That didn't matter, she realized. The plain-clothes men drove ordinary cars.

She sighed and stood the Hoover in the corner. Well, if it *was* Les, she'd just have to tell him to stay away and call the police if he insisted on pestering her. The blurred figure through the frosted glass wasn't Les, that was for certain, but she couldn't tell who it was until she opened the door and saw Lenora Carlyle standing there with her long black hair and penetrating eyes. She didn't want to let Lenora in. Somehow, she thought, that entire episode had been a weakness, a mistake. She had been grasping at straws. And look what she was left with: nothing but a video of herself, which was already beginning to feel like an embarrassment. But she stood aside politely. Lenora hung up her coat and followed her into the front room.

"Tea?" said Brenda, feeling like a cup herself.

"Yes, please, dear, if it's no trouble." Lenora sat on the sofa and brushed down her skirt. "Been cleaning, I see."

"Yes." Brenda shrugged and went to make the tea. When it was ready, she brought it in on a tray and poured, then lit a cigarette.

"I sense there's been some great change," Lenora said, frowning with concentration. "Some sort of upheaval."

"If you mean I chucked Les out, I suppose you're right."

Lenora looked disappointed at such a prosaic explanation. "Any news?"

Brenda shook her head.

"Well, that's why I'm here, really. You remember what I said before?"

"That Gemma's still alive?"

"That's right." Her eyes glittered. "More than ever I'm convinced of it, Brenda."

"I don't think so." Brenda shook her head. "Not after all this time."

"But you must have faith. She's frightened and weak. But she's alive, Brenda."

"Don't."

"You must listen." Lenora put her mug down and leaned forward, clasping her hands. "I saw animals. Jungle animals, Brenda. Lions, tigers, leopards. They're connected with Gemma somehow."

"What are you saying? She's been taken to Africa or something?"

Lenora flopped back on the sofa. "I don't know. The message is very weak. That's all I see. Gemma and animals."

"Look, I really don't—"

"They're not harming her, Brenda."

"I don't believe you."

"But you *must* believe!"

"Why must I believe? What good has it done me?"

"Don't you want to see your Gemma again?"

Brenda stood up. "Of course I want to see Gemma again. But I can't. She's dead. Can't you understand? She's dead. She must be. If she's not dead by now she must be suffering so much. It's best that she's dead." The tears and grief she had felt welling up for so long were breaking the dam.

"We must cling to the gift of life, Brenda."

"No. I don't want to listen to this. You're frightening me. Go away. Leave me alone."

"But Brenda, I—"

"Go on." Brenda pointed at the door, tears burning her eyes. "Go away. Get out!"

Lenora shook her head slowly, then, shoulders slumped, she got up and left the room. When Brenda heard the door close, she sank back into her chair. She was shaking now and tears burned down her cheeks. Dammit, why wouldn't they all leave her alone? And why couldn't she know for sure? Every day that Gemma stayed missing was more like hell. Why couldn't they find her body, then Brenda could get her grieving done with, organize the funeral, move on. But no. Just day after day of misery. And it was all her fault, all Brenda's fault for not loving her daughter enough, for losing control and shaking her so much she was terrified what she might do the next time.

She stared at the large TV screen and saw her own reflection distorted through her tears. She remembered the interview she had watched over and over again. Vanity. Madness. It had all been madness. In a sudden burst of rage, she drew back her arm and flung her mug as hard as she could at the screen.

IV

Just a few hours ago the wind had been cool, and there had been only enough blue sky to make baby a new bonnet. Now, as Banks and Susan drove to Harkness's, the wind had dropped, the sun had come out and the afternoon had turned out fine. Gristhorpe had been out when Banks went to find him, so he had left a message and found Susan, who happened to be in the corridor at the time.

Enjoying probably the last fine weekend of the season, families sat out on the green at Fortford eating picnics, even though it wasn't particularly warm and the grass must still be damp. Banks turned right on the Lyndgarth road, and as they approached the bridge, they saw even more people ambling along The Leas or sitting on the riverbank fishing.

Banks drove in silence, tense and angry over the forthcoming confrontation. They turned in the drive just before the old pack-horse bridge, and the car flung up gravel as they stopped. They had no evidence, he reminded himself, only supposition, and every-thing depended on bluffing and scaring Harkness into blabbing. It wouldn't be easy; it never was with those so used to having things their own way. Piet's information wasn't anywhere near enough to get him in court. But Harkness *had* known Johnson, and Johnson had known Chivers. Jenny said the paedophile was likely to be over forty, lived alone, and probably knew Gemma. Well, Harkness hadn't known Gemma, but he could have heard of her through Johnson and Chivers. It made sense.

After the conversation, Banks had checked the time and, finding they were only two hours ahead, tried the South African police again. They still had nothing to report, and he got the impression they were dragging their feet. He could only speculate on the nature of the crime there, and on the depth of the cover-up. He had tried Linda Fish from the Writers' Circle again, too, but she had heard no more from her writer friend. He had felt too edgy simply to wait around for more information to come in.

Harkness answered the door at the first ring. He seemed nervous to see them, Banks thought, fidgety and too talkative as he led them this time into the living-room and bade them sit.

"Have you found out who killed Carl?"

"We're looking for a man called Jeremy Chivers," Banks said. "Someone Johnson knew. Did he ever mention the name?"

"Let's not go through all that again." Harkness walked over to the mantelpiece. "Who is this Chivers?"

"A suspect."

"So why have you come to pester me again?"

Banks scratched the little scar by his right eye. It wasn't always reliable, but it did have a tendency to itch in warning when he hadn't quite realized that something was wrong. "Well, I'll tell you,

Mr Harkness. I've just had a chat with a friend of mine on the Amsterdam police, and he told me some very odd things."

"Oh?"

"Yes. You lived there for some time, didn't you?"

"Yes, you know I did. But I can assure you I never came into contact with the police."

"Clever there, sir, weren't you?" said Susan suddenly.

Harkness looked from one to the other, reddening. "Look, what is this?" he said. "You can't just come in here—"

Banks waved him to silence, ready to make his accusation. But just before he opened his mouth to speak, he paused. Something was definitely bothering him. Even now, he didn't know what it was: tension in the air, a feeling of *déjà vu*, or that little shiver when someone steps on your grave. It would come. He went on, "Everyone knows you can get anything you want in Amsterdam. If you know where to go. If you can pay for it."

"So what? It's hardly different from any other city in that way, I should think." Harkness paced, hands in his pockets.

"True," said Banks, "though it does have something of a reputation for sex in various forms, straight and other."

"What are you suggesting? Get to the point."

"That's just it. We have information leading us to believe that you frequented a brothel. A very special kind of brothel. One that made young children available to its customers."

"What! This is monstrous. I've already told you the Assistant Chief Commissioner is a good friend of mine, the Commissioner, too. If you don't take back your slanderous allegations, I'll make sure you're out of the force before bedtime tonight. Damn it, I think I'll do it anyway."

"I don't think so," said Banks. "The Commissioner is particularly upset about this case. He has grandchildren the same age as Gemma Scupham, so I don't think the fact that you belong to the same golf club will cut a lot of ice with him, sir."

"But this is preposterous! You can't possibly be suggesting that I had anything to do with that?"

"Well, I—" Banks stopped, suddenly aware of what was bothering him. He shot Susan a quick glance and stood up. Looking puzzled, she followed suit. "Probably not," he said, "but I had to find out. I'm sorry, Mr Harkness. I just wanted to test your reaction to the allegations."

"You've got a damned nasty way of going about your business, Banks. I most certainly will be talking to your superior."

"As you wish." Banks followed Susan to the door. "But please understand, we have to follow every lead, however incredible, however distasteful. I'm very sorry to have bothered you, sir. I think I can safely say we won't be troubling you again."

"Well . . ." Harkness looked confused. He opened his mouth as if to complain more, then seemed to think better of it, realizing they were leaving, and stood there gulping like a fish. "I should damn well think so," he muttered finally. "And don't think I don't mean it about talking to the Commissioner."

"What is it?" Susan asked as they drove back onto the road. "Sir? Why did you do that?"

Banks said nothing. When they were out of sight of the house, about half a mile down the road, hidden by the roadside trees, he pulled into a lay-by.

"What is it?" Susan asked again. "I picked up signal to get out, but why? You were rattling him. We could have had him."

"This is the third time I've visited Harkness," Banks said slowly, hands still gripping the wheel. "Both times before the place has been a bit of a mess—dusty, untidy, a typical bachelor dwelling."

"So?" said Susan. "He's had the cleaning lady in."

"I don't think so. He said he didn't employ one. Notice how clean the surfaces were, and that silver goblet on the coffee-table?"

"Yes. Polished so you could see your face."

"You weren't there," Banks said, "but it's the same polish smell as in the Weymouth hotel room, something with a strong scent of pine."

"You can't be thinking . . . surely?"

Banks nodded. "That's just what I am thinking, Susan. We've got to radio for help." He gestured with his thumb back towards the house. "I think Chivers is in there somewhere, and he's armed."

FOURTEEN

I

To the casual observer, nothing unusual occurred around The Leas and Devraulx Abbey that fine Sunday afternoon in late September. If one fisherman approached another, had a chat, then replaced him at the riverbank, or if a picnicking family, shortly after having a few words with a passing rambler complete with rucksack and stick, decided to pack up and leave because the wasps were bothering them, then what of it? The Abbey closed early, and there were a few more cars on the road than usual, but then, it was such a surprisingly beautiful afternoon that everyone wanted to enjoy a bit of it before the rain and wind returned.

Still in the same position, about half a mile down the road, out of sight of the Harkness house, Banks and Susan waited. Birds called, insects hummed, a light breeze hissed through the trees. At last, another car joined them, and Superintendent Gristhorpe got out, along with DS Richmond, and strode purposefully over to Banks's Cortina. There wasn't much to say; everything had been taken care of on the radio. The replacement fishermen were policemen in plain clothes; the picnicking families had all been cleared from the area, and a tight circle had been drawn around Harkness's house and grounds.

"If he's in there," Gristhorpe said. "He won't get away. Alan, let's you and I go back to the house, say we have a few more questions. Let's see if we can't defuse this mess before it blows up."

"But sir," said Susan. "I think I should go, too."

"No," said Gristhorpe. "Stay here with Phil."

"But—"

"Look. I'm not doubting your competence, Susan. But what we need here is experience. Alan?"

"I agree," said Banks.

Gristhorpe took a .38 Smith and Wesson from his pocket and handed it to Banks, who automatically checked it, though he knew Gristhorpe would have already done so. Susan's lips drew tight and Banks could feel the waves of humiliation flowing from her. He knew why—she had potential, but she was young, inexperienced, and she had made mistakes before—and he agreed completely with the superintendent's judgment. There was no room for error in dealing with someone like Chivers.

"Ready?" said Gristhorpe.

Banks nodded and joined him in the unmarked Rover, leaving Susan to fume and Richmond to console her in Banks's own Cortina.

"How do you read it?" Gristhorpe asked, as Banks drove slowly back towards the pack-horse bridge.

"Harkness is nervous, and I think he's shit-scared, too. And it's not just because of what I think he's done to Gemma Scupham. If I had to guess, I'd say Chivers is either in the house somewhere, or he's been there and he's hiding out nearby. And Harkness isn't harbouring him out of the kindness of his heart. He's damn close to being held hostage. There's nothing he can do, though, without incriminating himself."

"All right," said Gristhorpe. "Let me do the talking. Keep your eyes peeled. We'll try and get Harkness out of there if we can."

Banks nodded, turned into the driveway and crunched over the gravel. He felt a claw tighten at the pit of his stomach; the gun hung heavy in his pocket.

They rang the doorbell. Harkness flung the door open and growled, "You again? What the bloody hell do you want this time?"

Gristhorpe introduced himself. "I think it might be best if we did this at the station," he said to Harkness.

"Am I under arrest? You can't be serious. This is nothing but a tissue of unsubstantiated lies."

He was sweating.

"I think it would be best, sir," said Gristhorpe. "Of course, you have the right to consult your solicitor."

"I'll sue the both of you for wrongful arrest. I'll have you off the force. I'll—"

Banks thought he noticed a flash of movement behind Harkness on the staircase, but it was hard to see into the house clearly. What followed next was so sudden and so unexpected, he realized in retrospect that there was nothing he could have done to prevent it.

They heard a sound like a dull pop and Harkness's eyes seemed to fill with blood. His forehead opened like a rose in time-lapse photography. Both Banks and Gristhorpe flung themselves out of the way by instinct. As Banks flattened himself against the wall of the house, he became aware of the blood and tissue on his face and chest. Harkness's. He wanted to be sick.

Time seemed to hang like over-ripe fruit ready to fall at any moment. Harkness lay half in and half out the door, only a small hole showing in the back of his closely cropped skull and a pool of dark blood thickening under his face around his head. Gristhorpe stood back, flat against the wall on one side of the door, Banks on the other. From inside, they heard nothing but silence. Then, it could have been minutes or just seconds after the shooting, they heard a crash from the far side of the house, followed by a curse and the sound of someone running.

They glanced quickly at one another, then Gristhorpe nodded and swung himself into the doorway first, gun sweeping the hall and stairwell. Nothing. Banks followed, adopting the stance he had learned in training: gun extended in one hand, other hand gripping the wrist. They got to the front room and found no one. But there, beyond the french windows, one of which had been smashed by a careless elbow as he dashed by, they saw Chivers running down the lawn towards the riverbank.

"Get on the radio, Alan," said Gristhorpe. "Tell them to close in. And tell them to be bloody careful. Get an ambulance here, too."

Banks dashed to the car and gave the message to the plain-clothes watchers, all of whom carried police radios in their fishing boxes or picnic hampers. After he had radioed headquarters for an ambulance, he hurried through the house after Gristhorpe and Chivers.

Chivers was in the garden, heading for the river. As he ran, he turned around and fired several times. A window shattered, slate chips showered from the roof, then Gristhorpe went down. Banks took cover behind the copper beech and looked back at the superintendent's body sprawled on the lawn. He wanted to go to him, but he couldn't break cover. Carefully, he edged around the tree trunk and looked for Chivers.

There weren't many places Chivers could go. Fences and thick hedges blocked off the riverbank to the east and west, enclosing Harkness's property, and ahead lay the water. With a quick glance right and left and a wild shot, Chivers charged into the water. Soon it was up to his hips, then his waist. He aimed towards the tree and fired again. The bullet thudded into the bark. When Banks looked around the trunk again, he saw the other police in a line across the river, all with guns, closing fast. Gristhorpe must have commandeered the whole bloody dale, he thought. Glancing back towards the house, he saw Susan Gay and Phil Richmond framed by the french window staring at Gristhorpe. He waved to them to take cover.

Chivers stopped when the water came up to his armpits and fired again, but the hammer fell with an empty click. He tried a few more times, but it was empty. Banks shouted for Richmond and Susan to see to the superintendent, then he walked down the slope.

"Come on," he said. "Look around you. It's over."

Chivers looked and saw the men lining the opposite bank. They were in range now. He looked again at Banks. Then he shrugged, tossed the gun in the water, and smiled.

II

Everything had been done by the book, Banks saw to that. Thus, when they finally got to talk to Chivers, the custody record had been opened, he had been offered the right to legal advice, which he had repeatedly refused, offered the chance to inform a friend or relative of his arrest, at which he had laughed, and even offered a cup of tea, which he had accepted. The desk sergeant had managed to rustle up a disposable white boiler suit to replace his wet clothes, as according to the Police and Criminal Evidence Act, "a person may not be interviewed unless adequate clothing has been offered to him." And the interview room they s t in, while not especially large, was at least "adequately heated, lit and ventilated" according to the letter of the law. If questioning went on for a long time, Chivers would be brought meals and allowed periods of rest.

In addition, Jenny Fuller had turned up at the station and asked if she could be present during the questioning. It was an unusual request, and at first Banks refused. Jenny persisted, claiming her presence might even help, as Chivers seemed to like to show off to women. Finally, Banks asked Chivers's permission, which galled him, and Chivers said, "The more the merrier."

Back at Harkness's house, Banks knew, the SOCO team would be collecting evidence, Glendenning poring over Harkness's body, a group of constables digging up the garden that Carl Johnson had so lovingly tended, and police frogmen searching the river.

Sometimes, thought Banks, the creaking machinery of the law was a welcome prophylactic on his desire to reach out and throttle someone. Hampered as he had often felt by the Act, today, ironically enough, he was glad of it as he sat across the table looking at the man who had murdered at least three people, wounded Superintendent Gristhorpe and abducted Gemma Scupham.

As he looked, he certainly felt the impulse to kill Chivers, simply to swat him as one would a troublesome wasp. But it wasn't an impulse he was proud of. All his life, both in spite of and because of his job, Banks had tried to cultivate his own version of compassion. If crime really was part of what made us human, he thought, then it merited deep study. If we simply kill off the pests that bother us, we make no progress at all. He knew that he could, in some strange way, *learn* from Chivers. It was a knowledge he might deeply wish to reject, but spiritual and intellectual cowardice had never been among his failings.

Banks sat opposite Chivers, Richmond stood behind him, by the door, and Jenny sat by the window, diagonally across from him.

Close up, the monster didn't look like much at all, Banks noted. About Banks's height, and with the same kind of lean, wiry strength, he sat erect, hands placed palms down on the table in front of him, their backs covered with ginger down. His skin was pale, his hair an undistinguished shade of sandy brown, and his general look could only be described as boyish—the kind of boy who pulled pranks and was amused to see their effects on the victims.

If there was anything outstanding about him at all, it was his eyes. They were the kind of green the sea looks sometimes, and when he wasn't smiling they looked just as cold, as deep and as unpredictable as the ocean itself. When he did smile, though, they lit up with such a bright, honest light you felt you could trust him with anything. At least, it was *almost* like that, Banks thought, if it weren't for that glint of madness in them; not quite insanity, but close enough to the edge. Not everyone would notice, but then not everyone was looking at him as a murderer.

Banks turned on the tape-recorder, repeated the caution and reminded Chivers of his rights. "Before we get onto the other charges against you," he said, "I'd like to ask you a few questions about Gemma Scupham."

"Why not?" said Chivers. "It was just a lark really." His voice, a little more whiny and high-pitched than Banks had expected, bore no trace of regional accent; it was as bland and characterless as a BBC 2 announcer's.

"Whose idea was it?"

"Mr Harkness wanted a companion."

"How did he get in touch with you?"

"Through Carl Johnson. We'd known each other for a while. Carl was . . . well, between you and me he wasn't too bright. Like that other chap, what's his name?"

"Poole?"

"That's right. Small-time, the two of them. Low-lifes."

"How did you first meet Harkness?"

"Look, does any of this really matter? It's very dull stuff for me, you know." He shifted in his chair, and Banks noticed him look over at Jenny.

"Humour us."

Chivers sighed. "Oh, very well. Harkness knew Carl was a gutless oaf, of course, but he had contacts. Harkness needed someone taken care of a couple of months ago." He waved his hand dismissively. "Someone had been stealing from him in the London office, apparently, and Harkness wanted him taught a lesson. Carl got in touch with me."

"What happened?"

"I did the job, of course. Harkness paid well. I got an inkling from our little chats that this was a man with unusual tastes and plenty of money. I thought a nice little holiday in Yorkshire might turn out fruitful." He smiled.

"And did it?"

"Of course."

"How much?"

"Please. A gentleman never discusses money."

"How much?"

Chivers shrugged. "I asked for twenty thousand pounds. We compromised on seventeen-fifty."

"So you abducted Gemma Scupham just for money?"

"No, no. Of course not. Not just for the money." Chivers leaned forward. "You don't understand, do you? It sounded like fun, too. It had to be interesting."

"So you'd heard about Gemma through Les Poole and thought she would be the perfect candidate?"

"Oh, the fool was always moaning about her. Her mother sounded as thick as two short planks, and she clearly didn't care much about the child anyway. They didn't want her. Harkness did. It's a buyer's market. It was almost too easy. We picked her up, drove around for a while just to be on the safe side, then dropped her off at Harkness's after dark and returned the car." He smiled. "You should have seen his face light up. It was love at first sight."

"Did either Johnson or Poole know about this?"

"I'm not stupid. I wouldn't have trusted either of them."

"So what went wrong?"

"Nothing. It was the perfect crime," Chivers mused. "But Carl got foolish and greedy. Otherwise you'd never have gone anywhere near Harkness."

"But we did."

"Yes. Carl suspected something. Maybe he actually saw the child, I don't know. Or perhaps he caught Harkness drooling over his kiddie porn and put two and two together. That surprised me, that did. I never thought him capable of that. Putting two and two together and coming up with the right answer. I must admit I underestimated him."

"What happened?"

Chivers made a steeple with his hands and his eyes glazed over. He seemed lost in his own world. Banks repeated the question. Chivers seemed to come back from a great distance.

"What? Oh." He gave a dismissive wave of the hand. "He tried to put the touch on Harkness. Harkness got worried and called me again. I said I'd take care of it."

"For a fee?"

"Of course. I wouldn't say I'm in it for the money, but I need a fair bit to keep me in the style to which I'm accustomed. Harkness arranged to meet him at the old lead mine to pay him off and Chelsea and I gave him a lift there. Poor bastard, he never suspected a thing."

"Chelsea?"

He stared at a spot above Banks's left shoulder. "Yes. Silly name, isn't it? Fancy naming someone after a flower show, or a bun. Poor Chelsea. She just couldn't quite understand."

"Understand what?"

"The beauty of it all." Chivers's eyes turned suddenly back on Jenny. They looked like a dark green whirlpool, Banks thought, with blackness at its centre, evil with a sense of humour. "She liked it at the time, you know, the thrill. And she never liked poor Carl anyway. She said he was always undressing her with his eyes. You should have seen the look in *her* eyes when I killed him. She was standing right next to me and I could smell her sex. Needless to say, we had a *lot* of fun later that night. But she got jittery, read the newspapers, began to wonder, asked too many questions. . . . As I said, she didn't fully comprehend the beauty of it all."

"Did you know she was pregnant?"

He turned his eyes slowly back to Banks. "Yes. That was the last straw. It turned her all weepy, the sentimental fool. I had to kill her then."

"Why?"

"Wouldn't want another one like me in this universe, would we?" He winked. "Besides, it was what she wanted. I have a knack of knowing what people really *want.*"

"What did she want?"

"Death, of course. She enjoyed it. I know. I was there. It was glorious, the way she thrust and struggled." He looked over at Jenny again. "*You* understand, don't you?"

"And Harkness?" Banks said.

"Oh, it was very easy to see into his dirty soul. Little children. Little kiddies. He'd had it easy before. South Africa, Amsterdam. He found it a bit difficult here. He was getting desperate, that's all. It's simply a matter of knowing the right people."

Banks noticed that Chivers had dampened a part of his cuff and was rubbing at an old coffee ring on the desk. "What happened to Gemma?" he asked.

He shrugged. "No idea. I completed my side of the bargain. I suppose when the old pervert had finished with her he probably killed her and buried the body under the petunia patch or something. Isn't that what they do? Or maybe he sold her, tried to recoup what he'd spent. There's plenty in the market for that kind of thing, you know."

"What about the clothing we found?"

"You want me to do your job for you? I don't know. I suppose as soon as things got too hot for him he wanted to put you off the scent. Does that sound about right?"

"Why did you come back to Eastvale? You could probably have got away, you know."

Chivers's eyes dulled. "Fatal flaw, I suppose. I can't bear to miss anything. Besides, you only caught me because I wanted you to, you know. I've never been on trial, never been in jail. It might be interesting. And, remember, I'm not there yet." He shot Jenny a quick smile and began to rub harder at the coffee stain, still making no impression. He was clearly uncomfortable in the boiler suit they had found for him, too, scratching now and then where the rough material made his skin itch.

Banks walked over to the door and opened it to the two uniformed officers who stood outside and nodded for them to take Chivers down to the holding cells for the time being.

Chivers sat at the desk staring down at the stain he was rubbing and rubbing. Finally, he gave up and banged the table once, hard, with his fist.

III

Banks stood by his office window with the light off and looked down on the darkening market square again, a cigarette between his fingers. Like Phil and Jenny, he had felt as if he needed a long, hot bath after watching and listening to Chivers. It was odd how they had drifted away to try to scrub themselves free of the dirt: Jenny, pale and quiet, had gone home; Richmond had gone to the computer room. They all recognized one another's need for a little solitude, despite the work that remained.

Little people like Les Poole and others Banks had met in Eastvale sometimes made him despair of human intelligence; someone like Chivers made him wonder seriously about the human *soul*. Not that Banks was a religious man, but as he looked at the Norman church with its low square tower and the arched door with its carvings of the saints, he burned with unanswered questions.

They could wait, though. The hospital had called to tell him that Gristhorpe had a flesh wound in his thigh and was already proving to be a difficult patient. The SOCOs had called several times from The Leas area; no luck so far in finding Gemma's body, and it was getting dark. The frogmen had packed up and gone home. They had found Chivers's gun easily enough, but no trace of Gemma. They would be back tomorrow, though they didn't hold out much hope. The garden was in ruins, but so far the men had uncovered nothing but stones and roots.

Harkness's body lay in the mortuary now, and if anyone had to make him look presentable for the funeral, good luck to them. Banks shuddered at the memory. He had washed and washed his face, but he could still smell the blood, or so he thought. And he had tossed away his jacket and shirt, knowing he could never wear them again, and changed into the spares he always kept at the station.

And he thought of Chelsea. So that was her name, the poor twisted shape on the hotel bed in Weymouth. Why had she been so drawn to a monster like Chivers? Can't people *see* evil when it's staring them right in the face? Maybe not until it's too late, he thought. And the baby. Chivers knew his own evil, revelled in it. Chelsea. Who was she? Where did she come from? Who were her parents and what were they like? Bit by bit, he would find out.

He had been alone with his thoughts for about an hour, watching dusk fall slowly on the cobbled square and the people dribble into the church for the evening service. The glow from the coloured-glass windows of the Queen's Arms looked welcoming on the opposite corner. God, he could do with a drink to take the taste of blood out of his mouth, out of his soul.

The harsh ring of the telephone broke the silence. He picked it up and heard Gristhorpe say, "The buggers wouldn't let me out to question Chivers. Have you done it? Did it go all right?"

Banks smiled to himself and assured Gristhorpe that all was well.

"Come and see me, Alan. There's a couple of things I want to talk about."

Banks put on his coat and drove over to Eastvale General. He hated hospitals, the smell of disinfectant, the starched uniforms, the pale shadows with clear fluid dripping into them from plastic bags being pushed on trolleys down gloomy hallways. But Gristhorpe had a pleasant enough private room. Already, someone had sent flowers and Banks felt suddenly guilty that he had come empty-handed.

Gristhorpe looked a little pale and weak, mostly from shock and blood loss, but apart from that he seemed in fine enough fettle.

"Harkness never expected any trouble from the police over Gemma's abduction, did he?" he asked.

"No," said Banks. "As Chivers told us, why should he? It was almost the perfect crime. He'd managed to keep a very low profile in the area. Nobody knew how sick his tastes really were."

"Aye, but everything changed, didn't it, after Johnson's murder?"

"Yes."

"And you were a bit hard on Harkness, given that chip on your shoulder, weren't you?"

"I suppose so. What are you getting at?"

Gristhorpe tried to sit up in bed and grimaced. "So much so that he might think we'd get onto him?" he said.

"Probably." Banks rearranged the pillows. "I think he felt quite certain I'd be back." The superintendent was wearing striped pyjamas, he noticed.

"And he claimed harassment and threatened to call the Commissioner and probably the Prime Minister for all I know."

"Yes." Banks looked puzzled. What was Gristhorpe getting at? It wasn't like him to beat about the bush. Had delirium set in?

"Let's assume that Chivers is telling the truth," Gristhorpe went on, "and he delivered Gemma to Harkness on Tuesday evening and killed Johnson on Thursday evening. Now Harkness *could* have spirited Gemma out of the house, say to Amsterdam, before Johnson's murder, but why should he? And if he hadn't done it by then, he'd probably be too nervous to make such a move later."

"I suppose he would," Banks admitted. "And he could have taken her clothes up to the moors to put us off the scent on Thursday evening or Friday, whenever Chivers told him Johnson was dead and came to collect his fee. Harkness must have known we'd visit him then, given his connection with Johnson. But he could have buried her anywhere. It's a very isolated house, and pretty well sheltered by trees. I mean, even someone passing by on the road wouldn't notice him burying a body in the garden, would they?"

"But our men have found nothing so far."

"You know it can take time. It's a big garden. If she's there, they'll find her. Then there's the river."

"*If* she's there."

Banks watched the blood drip slowly into Gristhorpe's veins. "What do you mean?"

"This." Gristhorpe rolled over carefully and took something out of his bedside cabinet. "I got one of the lads to tag it as evidence and bring it here to me."

Banks stared at the polished silver. "The goblet?"

"Yes. It's a chalice actually, sixteenth-century, I think. Remember when Phil and Susan took me into Harkness's living-room and laid me on the couch till the ambulance came? That's when I noticed it. I could hardly miss it, it was right at eye-level."

"I still don't see what that's got to do with Gemma," said Banks, who was beginning to worry that Gristhorpe was more seriously injured than he let on.

"Don't you?" Gristhorpe passed him the chalice. "See those markings?"

Banks examined it. "Yes."

"It's the banner of the Pilgrimage of Grace. See where it shows the five wounds of Christ? I'll explain it, then you can go see if I'm right."

Puzzled, Banks crossed his legs and leaned back in his chair.

IV

It was late twilight as Banks drove: the time of evening when the greens of the hillsides and the grey of the limestone houses and walls are all just shades of darkness. But the river seemed to glow with a light of its own, hoarded from the day, as it snaked through the wooded river meadows known as The Leas.

As he drove, Banks remembered Gristhorpe's words: "In Yorkshire history, The Pilgrimage of Grace started as a religious uprising against Henry VIII, sparked by the closing of the monasteries in 1536. Harkness's house was built later, so this chalice would probably be a precious family heirloom and a powerful symbol to whoever owned it. In the seventeenth century, it was often dangerous to be a Roman Catholic in this part of the country, but they persisted. They didn't take unnecessary risks, though. So while they would invite some wandering incognito priest around to perform mass or take confession in their houses, they knew they might hear the soldiers hammering on the door at any moment, so they built priest holes, cavities in the walls where the priests could hide. Some were even more elaborate than that. They led to underground passages and escape routes.

"I grew up in Lyndgarth, just up the hill from Harkness's," Gristhorpe had continued, "and when we were kids there were always rumours about the old De Montfort house, as it was called then. We thought it was haunted, riddled with secret passages. You know how kids dream. We never went inside, of course, but we made up stories about it. I'd forgotten all about it until we went there tonight—and I must admit things happened quickly enough to put it right out of my mind again. Until I saw this chalice. It started me thinking. The date's right, the history, so it's worth a try, don't you think?"

Banks had agreed. He turned into the drive and stopped at the police tape. The man on duty came forward, and when he recognized Banks he let him through.

Banks nodded greetings as he passed the SOCO team at work in the garden, receiving shakes of the head to indicate that nothing new had been discovered. The grounds looked like a film set, with the bright arc-lights casting shadows of men digging, and it was loud with the sound of drills, the humming of the generator van and instructions shouted above the noise. Inside the house, men examined the corners of carpets and settees, sticking on pieces of Sellotape and lifting off fibres, or running over areas with compact hand-vacuums.

First, Banks checked the kitchen, behind the fridge and cooker, then the dining-room, getting help to move out the huge antique cabinet that held cutlery and crystal glasses. Nothing.

The library yielded nothing either, so he went next to the living-room, where he had first noticed the grimy, tarnished chalice on the coffee-table. It was partly seeing it again and noticing how clean it was that had first made him uneasy earlier that day, on his visit with Susan.

The bookcase opposite the fireplace looked promising, and Banks started pulling out the old *National Geographics*, looking for some kind of lever or button to press, and feeling, as he did so, more than a little foolish. It was like something out of Edgar Allan Poe, he thought.

Then he found it: a brass bolt sunk perfectly in the wood at the back of the central shelf, on the left. It slid back smoothly, as if recently oiled, and the whole bookcase swung away from the wall on hinges, just like a door. Before him loomed a dark opening with a flight of worn stone steps leading down.

Banks called for a torch, and when he had one, he stepped into the opening. On a hook to his left hung two keys on a ring. He plucked them off as he went by.

At the bottom of the stairs, a rough, dank passage led on, probably far away from the house to provide an escape for the itinerant priest. Banks shone his torch ahead and noticed that the passage was blocked by rubble after a few yards. But the two heavy wooden doors, one on either side of the passage, looked more interesting. Banks went to the one on his right and tried to open it. It was locked. Holding his breath, heart pounding, he tried the keys. The second one worked.

The hinges creaked a little as he slowly pushed the door open. Groping in the dark, he found a light switch, and a bare bulb came on, revealing a small, square room with whitewashed walls. At the centre of the room stood a leather armchair, the kind with a footrest that slides out as you sit in it, and in front of that stood a television set attached to a video. Banks doubted that priest holes had electricity, so Harkness must have gone to all the trouble of wiring his private den himself. In a rack beside the chair, Banks found a range of pornographic magazines, all of them featuring children being subjected to disgusting and degrading acts. In the cabinet under the video were a number of video cassettes of a similar nature.

Afraid of what he might find, Banks crossed the passage and fitted the other key in the lock. It opened easily. This time, he had no need to grope for a light switch. Beside the narrow bed stood a small orange-shaded table-lamp. Next to it sat a book of *Thomas the Tank Engine* stories and a bottle of pills. The walls were painted with the same whitewash as the other room, but a quilt decorated with stylized jungle animals—lions, tigers and leopards with friendly human expressions—covered the small, still shape on the bed.

It was Gemma Scupham, no doubt about it. From what Banks could see of her face between the dirty patches, it looked white, and she lay motionless on her back, her right arm raised above her head. The scar of a thin cut ran across the pale flesh of her inner arm.

Banks could sense no breath, no life. He bent over to look more closely. As he leaned over Gemma, he fancied he noticed one of her eyelids twitch. He froze. It happened again.

"My God," he muttered to himself, and gazed down in awe as a tear formed and rolled out of the corner of Gemma's eye, leaving a clean and shining path through the grime.